NOBODY'S PRINCESS

NOBODY'S
PRINCESS

ESTHER FRIESNER

RANDOM HOUSE NEW YORK

Text copyright © 2007 by Esther Friesner
Jacket art copyright © 2007 by Larry Rostant

Visit us on the Web! www.randomhouse.com/teens

Educators and librarians, for a variety of teaching tools, visit us at www.randomhouse.com/teachers

The Library of Congress has cataloged the hardcover edition
of this work as follows:
Friesner, Esther M.
Nobody's princess / Esther Friesner.
p. cm.
Summary: Determined to fend for herself in a world where only men have real freedom, headstrong Helen, who will be called queen of Sparta and Helen of Troy one day, learns to fight, hunt, and ride horses while disguised as a boy, and goes on an adventure throughout the Mediterranean world.
ISBN 978-0-375-87528-1 (trade) — ISBN 978-0-375-97528-8 (lib. bdg.) — ISBN 978-0-375-87529-8 (pbk.)
1. Helen of Troy (Greek mythology)—Juvenile fiction. [1. Helen of Troy (Greek mythology)—Fiction. 2. Sex role—Fiction. 3. Adventure and adventurers—Fiction. 4. Mythology, Greek—Fiction. 5. Mediterranean Region—History—To 476—Fiction.] I. Title.
PZ7.F91662Nob 2007
[Fic]—dc22
2006006515

Printed in the United States of America
10 9 8 7 6

First Trade Paperback Edition

*This book is dedicated to the memory of
Elissa Nicole Sullivan.
Through her life, she gave an eternal gift of love,
Through her art, an enduring legacy of beauty.*

ACKNOWLEDGMENTS

I owe thanks to many people for their part in
helping make this book a reality.

To Tamora Pierce and Josepha Sherman, whose
Young Warriors anthology gave Helen her start.

To Elizabeth Moon, whose knowledge of all
things equine gave Helen the reins.

To my editor, Mallory Loehr, and my agent,
Russell Galen, whose ongoing support and
assistance have been invaluable.

Thank you all so much!

CONTENTS

PART IV: DELPHI

PROLOGUE

When I was four years old, my father, King Tyndareus of Sparta, dedicated a shrine to his favorite goddess, Aphrodite. He ordered it built on one of the rooftops of our palace because he said the queen of love and beauty was worshipped best under the beauty of an open sky. You could reach the holy place only by climbing an outside stairway, each step covered with painted tiles that told stories from the life of the goddess.

Most of the gods were born in the usual way, but not Aphrodite. She was never a baby, never a child, and she never had to put up with any of the problems of growing up. The goddess was born full-grown from the waves of the Middle Sea when the god Kronos spilled the blood of his father, Uranus, over the sea foam. I never did understand why *bloodshed* would give birth to a goddess of love and beauty, but that's the way I was told it happened: Aphrodite sprang to life out of the waves, and as soon as the world saw her, every living thing fell in love with her beauty. The winds themselves fought for the honor of carrying her to shore.

Now *that* I could understand. It was the part of the story I liked best. Even as a very young child I thought it would be a wonderful thing to be able to fly over the waves, free as a seabird, seeing new lands and having grand adventures. I didn't care if I grew up to be as beautiful as the goddess, as long as I could be just as free.

The shrine itself was a simple thing: A wooden ark sheltered the painted clay image of the goddess, an image as big as a two-year-old child. I was playing in the shadow of my father's throne on the day he received it from the Cretan artist who also made the tiles to adorn the stairs. At first I thought it was a wonderful doll and that it would be mine. I ran forward, threw my arms around Aphrodite's neck, and gave her such an enthusiastic kiss that my lips marked the paint on her cheek.

I didn't think I was doing anything wrong, and so I was confused when I looked up and saw expressions of shock on the faces of almost every grown-up around me. Some of them were whispering to each other and scowling at me. I began to feel afraid, until I heard my father laugh and say, "The child is wiser than all of us. My little Helen has hit on the perfect tribute for Aphrodite! What better welcome for the goddess of love than a kiss?" And he ordered the servants to make me a new dress for the dedication ceremony in three days' time.

On the dedication day, my nurse, Ione, held me and my twin sister, Clytemnestra, by the hands as we watched our father and mother perform the welcoming rites for the goddess. Our brothers, the twins Castor and Polydeuces, were nine years old, so they were given the honor of holding the garlands of fragrant springtime flowers that the king and queen would place at Aphrodite's feet. The boys didn't seem to be enjoying the privilege. The two of them fidgeted as if they'd caught fleas from one of Father's hunting hounds.

Though my parents and we royal children were the only ones entitled to come before the goddess in her new home, the nearby rooftops were crowded with the nobles of Sparta, all of them eager to have a good view. How splendid the men looked with their long hair curled and oiled, the women in their finest gowns, their blue and scarlet tiered skirts jingling with gold charms! The sunlight was striped with the rising smoke of precious incense brought from across the Middle Sea. The melody of flutes and Egyptian harps over the beat of little hand drums filled the air.

The music made me want to dance, so I did, pulling my hand out of Ione's grasp. She smiled. "What a clever child, wanting to offer the goddess such a lovely dance as a gift! But not just yet, dear one. This isn't the right time; you're interrupting the dedication ceremony. Wait until it's finished, like a good girl."

As Ione gently took my hand again, my parents called out to welcome Aphrodite-of-the-Foam. They were dressed in their finest robes and their best jewels, all to pay reverence to the queen of love and beauty. The image of the goddess was a marvel, but that day I saw something that I thought was even more marvelous.

"Look, Ione!" I cried. "Isn't she beautiful?"

"Hush, child," Ione said. "Everyone knows that the goddess is—"

"*Not* the goddess—*her.*" I pointed at my mother, Leda, with my free hand. "Mama. She's *much* more beautiful than the goddess." My voice carried loud and clear across the rooftop.

I no sooner spoke my mind for all to hear than the air cracked with the sound of Ione slapping my face. I was stunned. She'd never raised her hand to me until that moment. I hadn't known that the same hand that stroked my hair or tenderly touched my brow when I was sick could hurt so much. Before I could cry out, she swept me off my feet and whisked me away from the ceremonies. Poor Clytemnestra was left behind.

Our nurse had been a farmer's wife, but the other servants whispered that ever since she'd been brought to the royal palace, she acted as if she'd been born there. Maybe so, but she didn't act at all regal or haughty as she raced down the tower steps, carrying me over one shoulder like a bundle of old clothes. She didn't slow down until we reached the deserted central courtyard of the palace, where flowers bloomed around a white stone well. Here she set me on my feet and shook me roughly by the shoulders.

"Are you crazy? To say such things where the goddess can hear you!" she hissed in my face. "You'll bring a curse down on all of us."

My cheek hurt, but that didn't bother me as much as the feeling of having the ground yanked out from under me. I was totally bewildered. Ione hadn't acted like this when my dancing interrupted the welcoming rites for Aphrodite. Why had a few words turned everything upside down? One moment she'd been praising me, smiling at me. Now her smile was gone, vanished behind a mask of anger and fear.

Ione's afraid because of something I said? I gazed at her, astonished. She looked even more terrified than when Zeus made the sky blaze and roar with wild thunderstorms. I'd never imagined that I had that kind of power over grown-ups. *They* were always the ones who could do whatever they wanted, make all the choices, all the decisions about their lives and mine. Up until that moment, if someone had asked me the difference between gods and grown-ups, I'd have said, *What difference?*

Suddenly, it wasn't so. *Something* I *said made a grown-up afraid?* I *can do that?* What a wonderful, terrible, dangerous thing for a little girl to learn!

"No one is more beautiful than a goddess!" Ione told me urgently. Her face was stiff with fear. "No one, man or woman, is the equal of the gods. If they hear anyone even *hinting* that an ordinary person outshines the immortals, dreadful things happen! Do you want your mother to *die* because you said something stupid?"

I stared Ione in the face and stood up tall, the way I'd just seen my mother do when she called on Aphrodite. "Aphrodite wouldn't do anything so mean," I said, very sure of myself. "Mama and Papa just gave the goddess lots and lots of beautiful presents and a nice, new place to stay here with us. *That* means they're her hosts, and you taught me that guests and hosts mustn't hurt each other, not *ever.* Do you think the goddess would do something so *wrong,* Ione?"

"Oh, child, what's going to become of you if you keep saying such things? The gods don't have to worry about what's right and wrong for mortals!" she exclaimed.

"Can't they do *anything* wrong?" I asked.

"I—I don't know—I don't think so." My nurse squirmed as if her own words were giving her a belly-ache.

"Why not?" I asked.

"Because—because they can do anything they like. They're the gods." She acted as if that explained everything.

"Then why should we give them presents if it won't make them nicer to us?" I wanted to know. "They're only going to do whatever they want anyway."

I waited patiently for my nurse's answer, but the poor woman just stood there with her mouth hanging open. At last I said, "I think you're wrong about the gods, Ione. They're *much* nicer than you say, especially Aphrodite. She has to be nice. She's the goddess of love! She'd never hurt Mama, no matter *what* I say, be-cause Mama's the queen and she gives the best pres-ents, and if anything happens to her, no more presents for Aphrodite, right? And the goddess doesn't want *that*. Now do you understand?"

Satisfied, I gave my still-bewildered nurse a big kiss on the cheek and marched straight back up the stairs to the shrine. I heard her come scrambling after me, but I didn't feel the need to turn around to be sure she was there. Even if I was still too young to have ex-plored every part of our big, rambling palace, I knew that I wouldn't get lost, because now Aphrodite was with me. I was convinced that I'd pleased her with my kiss, and my dance, and the way I'd defended her to Ione. I imagined that I could feel her hands on my shoulders, helping me up the stairs. Just believing that she was near, watching over me, lifted up my heart and filled it with happiness.

The sun beat brightly on the tiles when I came back out onto the rooftop, and the wind carried the scent of mountain pine. The musicians were playing something light and joyous, and everyone smiled when I stood in the presence of the goddess and once more began to dance.

PART 1
SPARTA

1

A SACRIFICE
TO ARTEMIS

I grew up with the gods all around me. When the dawn came, it was because the goddess Eos brought it. The sun was Apollo's chariot, and the crescent moon was the hunting bow of his sister, Artemis. Every river had its god, and so did each of the winds that blew from north, south, east, and west.

Ione was the first person to teach me about Zeus, king of all the gods; his queen, Hera, who blessed marriages; his brother Poseidon, who was master of the great ocean; and his other brother, Hades, who lived deep under the earth and ruled the dead. But most of her stories were about Demeter, the goddess who gave us bountiful harvests. That was understandable. Ione was a farmer's wife.

Even though we were supposed to revere all of

the gods equally, most people honored some gods more than others. Why would a fisherman bother making a sacrifice to Hephaestus the armorer, god of the forge, when he could be praying to Poseidon for smooth seas and full nets? Why would a metalworker waste time worshipping Poseidon when he could be asking for Hephaestus's blessing?

Everyone did it, including me. Ever since the dedication of the rooftop shrine, Aphrodite was my favorite. When I was five, I made a little clay image of her and set it on a table in the room I shared with my sister. When Clytemnestra saw it, she sniffed. "What's *that* supposed to be?"

"Aphrodite," I told her.

"It can't be Aphrodite. It's *ugly.*" She sounded pleased with herself. "Throw it away."

"It is *not* ugly!" I cried, reaching out protectively for my little goddess. Unfortunately, I moved too quickly. Instead of cupping the image safely between my palms, I knocked it off the table and sent it tumbling to the floor. The unbaked clay shattered to bits and I burst into tears.

"You're such a baby, Helen," Clytemnestra said. "Why are you crying over *that* ugly thing? If you want a real Aphrodite, just tell Papa. He'll get you a *good* one."

But I still cried, because I didn't want an image of the goddess that someone else had made. I wanted a statue that was *my* goddess. The next day, I made another Aphrodite and hid it in the bottom of my clothes chest, safe from my sister's sneers.

By the time I turned seven, I'd learned that Ione had been partly right about the gods. They weren't all as kind as Aphrodite. Just as some people liked one god more than another, some of us *didn't* like certain gods at all.

My father, Tyndareus, didn't like Artemis, goddess of the moon in heaven, the hunt on earth, and the dark powers of magic from the underworld. I first heard him speak against her during a great banquet that took place ten days before the feast of the huntress. This was a yearly festival when my mother, Queen Leda, led a procession of maidens to the temple of Artemis and offered up the sacrifice while they danced and sang for the goddess. It was the one shrine in all Sparta where the queen worshipped alone and the king never set foot.

The banquet was being given to honor a group of very important guests, envoys from the island kingdom of Ithaka. I sat beside my mother and heard her tell one of our guests about the coming celebration.

"No men? Really?" the guest replied. "Well, if that's what pleases Artemis, I suppose you don't have any choice."

Even I could tell that he was just making polite conversation. He didn't really care about the goddess.

My father *did* care, very much, in his own way. "Oh yes, we must give Artemis exactly what she wants," he said. He was smiling, acting as if he was joking, but there was something serious under the light words. "She'll show us no mercy if we don't. If you ask me, she doesn't know the meaning of forgiveness."

"What makes you say that, Lord Tyndareus?" one of the guests asked.

"Oh, the proof's there, in the stories. Take the tale of the nymph Callisto, for instance. Now, if a goddess chooses to remain a virgin, like Artemis and Athena, I can't complain about that. I have nothing against virgins." He paused and winked at the other grown-ups at the banquet. Most of them laughed, including my mother; I had no idea why. "And if Artemis wants the nymphs who hunt with her to be virgins as well, fine. That's her choice too. But nymphs are beautiful, and the gods love beauty. The gods are also used to taking what they want, even when what they want says *no.* What chance does a nymph have against a god? Artemis adored Callisto until Zeus forced her to be his lover and left her with child. It wasn't Callisto's fault, but did the goddess care? Did she accept the fact that the nymph was Zeus's helpless victim? No, she just punished her by turning her into a bear! And *that* is why I leave other people to make sacrifices to Artemis, because I have kinder goddesses to honor."

"Lord Tyndareus, be careful of what you say!" The icy words rang out through the great hall. The man who dared to admonish my father in his own palace was one of the Ithakan envoys, a terribly serious stick of a man, young in years but old and bitter in spirit. I'd never seen anyone with such a vinegary face. I thought that if he'd ever smile, he'd crack his jaw. I'd seen how his heavy brows drew into a scowl while my father was talking about Artemis, how his mouth became small as an olive pit until at last it burst open with angry words. "The lady Artemis will not be insulted, not even by kings! She demands payment for all offenses, and no one has the power to refuse her."

"You mean that she'll take revenge on me? That would only prove my point." My father chuckled. He made it clear that he was joking, teasing that pompous creature. Everyone else laughed with him.

"Wait," the man said ominously. "Wait and see what comes of your sacrilege. The huntress's arrows never miss their target. Remember Niobe!"

My father stopped laughing. He stood up suddenly, his face dark as a thunderhead, and jabbed one finger at the Ithakan. "You *dare* to talk to me of sacrilege? In my own house, at my own table? You speak Niobe's name in the presence of my *children*? The sacred bond between host and guest is all that's keeping me from snapping your neck right now! Get out of my sight."

The Ithakan opened his mouth, but one look at the king's face was enough for him to seal his lips and rush out of the hall. Even though the road from Sparta to Ithaka was long and dangerous, he didn't wait for his fellow envoys. He was gone by next morning.

The day after the rest of the Ithakan envoys left us, I asked my father why he'd been so angry. He wouldn't tell me, but when I went to my mother's room with the same question, she gave me my answer. "Niobe of Thebes was a great queen but a foolish woman. She mocked Leto, mother of Artemis and Apollo, because the goddess had only two children while she had seven sons and seven daughters." My mother picked me up and held me close, as if I were still a baby. "For her offense, the divine twins slaughtered all her children in a single day. Their arrows cut them down, every one, even when the queen threw herself across the body of her youngest child and begged Artemis and Apollo to take her life instead. There was no mercy, and when Niobe's children all lay dead, there was no end to her weeping. The gods finally took pity on her and turned her to stone, but her tears for her children still stream down the face of the rock."

I began to shake. My mother was shaking too. "Don't be afraid, dear one," she said, giving me a tight squeeze. "I know it's a terrible story, but you mustn't worry. Artemis won't touch you or Clytemnestra or the boys. Even though your father won't worship her, I do. You're safe." With that, she gave me a kiss and told me to go back to my nurse.

I refused. I faced my mother and declared, "That's not fair! Father's right, Artemis *is* cruel. It's bad enough that she and her brother punished Niobe for one mistake, but then they made it worse. They had to turn her into a *lesson*. It's not even a *good* lesson! If they really wanted Niobe to learn from what she'd done, they could have brought her children back to life and said, 'Now do you see what can happen if you're too proud?' I bet she'd never have been proud again after that, because she'd want her children to live."

"And I don't want to risk your life even once," Mother said, laying her fingers to my lips to hush me. "Don't anger the gods, Helen."

"You want me to be afraid of them," I said.

"I want you to *respect* them," Mother corrected me.

"I thought I was supposed to love them."

Mother gave me one of her gentle smiles. "Can't you do both, my darling? You know you're supposed to respect Papa and me, but you love us too, don't you?"

I admitted this was true. "But not because I'm scared of what you'll do to me if I *don't*," I pointed out. "And that's why I'm never going to love Artemis, *ever*. Just like Papa!"

Mother sighed. "I respect the moon goddess, but I must admit, I don't . . . feel as fond of her as I do of some of the other goddesses. Still, there are some things that we must do, whether we like them or not. That's true for queens as well as other women; remember that, Helen. I don't think Artemis cares if we love her, as long as we worship her in the proper way. I hope that you and Clytemnestra will be good girls when you come with me to the huntress's shrine for the festival."

I made a face. "I don't like Artemis and I'm not going."

"We'll see," said Mother.

I knew what *that* meant.

My mother dragged me to the festival along with Clytemnestra and the other girls. I sulked through the whole thing, unlike my twin.

Clytemnestra and I were born together, but everyone said we didn't look alike—aside from both of us having the same thick, long black hair as our mother—and we certainly didn't act alike. The more I turned my back on the rituals that Mother and the old temple priestess were performing for the goddess, the more Clytemnestra behaved like Artemis's most devoted worshipper. She copied our mother's every gesture at the altar, and when the priestess nodded approvingly and some of the women began to murmur words of praise for her piety, she began to invent worshipful gestures of her own. Pretty soon she was raising and lowering her arms to the image of Artemis so vigorously that Mother finally intervened.

"That's enough, dear," she said. "I know you want to honor Artemis, but you look like a goose trying to fly."

Clytemnestra stuck out her lower lip and glared. "You wouldn't say that to *Helen*," she whined. "*She* does everything *right*."

"Nonsense. She hasn't done anything at all," Mother replied briskly, returning her attention to the altar.

My sister gave me a nasty look and started to stick out her tongue but quickly thought better of it and clamped her mouth shut. She smirked for just an instant, then walked to the altar and tugged at Mother's skirt.

"Mama?" she asked in her sweetest voice. "Mama, can *I* make an offering to Artemis? All by myself, to show the goddess how much I love her? *Please?*"

Once again the other women witnessing the rites began to speak softly about what a *good* girl Clytemnestra was. My sister's gloating smile grew wider and wider with every compliment she overheard until I thought she was going to burst with glee.

But she didn't burst. She was squashed.

"What a wonderful idea, Clytemnestra!" Mother exclaimed. "I think that you *and* Helen should do it together." She meant well, but her words were like a dipper full of cold water flung in my sister's face.

"*Her?* Why her? It was *my* idea!" Clytemnestra objected strenuously.

"Me?" I was just as angry as she was. "Do I *have* to?"

Mother's suddenly stern face was all the answer either one of us received. Without speaking a word, she let us know that we would behave like Spartan princesses or we'd suffer the consequences at the hands of Sparta's queen.

Mother could make me sacrifice a few crumbs of incense to Artemis, but she couldn't make me do it *right*. After my sister dropped her pinch of incense onto the coals and stepped away from the altar, it was my turn. Expressionless, I held my chubby hand over the brazier, opened my clenched fingers, and then . . . I missed. I'd held the pinch of incense very carefully, and then at the last instant I threw it away. The old priestess gave a little gasp as the costly crumb of sweet-smelling tree gum fell to the ground and tumbled down the temple steps, but neither she nor my mother nor the dancing maidens made any move to fetch it back.

"Oh, Helen, you clumsy thing!" Clytemnestra shoved me aside and ran down the steps so fast that she tripped, fell, and scraped her nose. She yelped with pain.

I was down the steps in an instant. "You're bleed-ing!" I cried, helping her get back onto her feet. "Does it hurt a lot? Do you want some water or——?"

"Leave me alone." Clytemnestra jerked away from me. "I don't want anything from *you*." She swallowed her tears and dashed back up to the altar, my cast-off incense clenched in her fist. She dropped it into the smoldering flames quickly, then turned her scraped, triumphant face to Mother and the priestess and waited to be praised.

"What have you done?" The old priestess's squawk of outrage shocked my sister back to the brink of tears.

"I . . . I only . . . ," she began, trembling. "Helen dropped the offering, so I——"

"Clytemnestra, what were you thinking?" Mother stepped between my sister and the fuming priestess, her voice unnaturally shrill. "I taught you girls the *proper* way to serve Artemis! Weren't you listening? Didn't you know that if an offering touches the ground, it's no longer fit for the goddess?"

"I'm not the one who dropped it!" Clytemnestra protested, tears streaming down her face. "Helen did that! Why aren't you yelling at her?"

"Because Helen isn't behaving like an infant!" Mother was so rattled by the scene we were making in front of the priestess, the maidens, the other women, and Artemis herself that she continued to scold my sister even when her words made no sense.

"But she *did!*" Clytemnestra stamped her foot. "She threw the offering away on purpose! She—"

"Not another word out of you, Clytemnestra," Mother decreed. "Not *one.*" She called for Ione and commanded her to take my shamed and sobbing sister away. Sometimes even the best parents can be as closed-minded and unreasonable as the gods.

Afterward, as we were returning to the palace citadel, Clytemnestra turned her red-eyed, runny-nosed face to me and said, "It's not fair! *You* do something wrong and Mama yells at *me!* Just because you're pretty, you get away with *everything.* I hate you!" Then she tried to slap me, so I pulled her hair, and poor Ione had to get four other servants to pull us apart and cart us off to separate rooms.

They put me in a storeroom where my father's tallymen kept the bales of sheepskins that were part of the tax payments from our people. I climbed onto a thick pile of fleeces, lay down in comfort, and stared at the ceiling, thinking about what had happened. No matter what else I thought of my sister, she was right: I *had* done something bad at the temple, but I *hadn't* been punished for it. And even when I did earn punishment for fighting with Clytemnestra, how bad was it? I was more comfortable on those fleeces than in my own bed. Was I just lucky, or was Clytemnestra right? Did things go more easily for me because I was *pretty*?

I'd never thought about it before, even though I'd

heard many people say, *What a pretty girl!* when they saw me. It happened whenever guests came to the palace. As soon as our parents presented the four of us to their visitors, the newcomers would praise how big and strong and handsome my brothers were. That made me giggle. Couldn't they see that Castor was a little cross-eyed and that Polydeuces never took his finger out of his nose except to eat? As for my sister, our guests called her things like *charming*, or *sweet*, or *delightful*, but I—

I was *pretty*. It never failed. One man even said that I was *beautiful*, until his fellow envoy was very quick to say that no one could be beautiful in the palace of Tyndareus except his queen.

Pretty. What did that mean, really? And was I? I had no way of knowing. I'd caught sight of my reflection in pools of water from time to time, but the image was dark and unclear. I wanted better. My mother owned a mirror that had come all the way from Egypt, but up until that moment I'd never understood why she spent so much time looking into it. I decided that as soon as my punishment was over, I'd sneak into my parents' sleeping chamber and see what *pretty* looked like.

The sun was halfway down the western sky by the time one of our house slaves let me out of the storeroom. She was a grouchy old thing who didn't like to waste time talking. When I asked her where my nurse was, she snapped, "How would I know?" before gathering up an armful of fleeces and waddling off.

I was thrilled! If Ione was busy elsewhere, it meant I had the chance to run to my parents' room and satisfy my curiosity right away. I stole through the corridors of the palace as fast as I could go without drawing attention. Silently I prayed: *O Aphrodite, please let me find Mama's mirror, and see what I want to see, and get away before anyone catches me!* Who better than the goddess of beauty to help me find out exactly what *pretty* meant?

Aphrodite heard my prayers. I didn't run into anyone on my way to my parents' room, the room itself was deserted, and Mother's mirror was lying out in plain sight on a little table, just waiting for me to snatch it up and stare at my reflection. I was still muttering a hasty *thank you* to the goddess when I heard, "Helen! What do you think you're doing?" It was my mother. She'd come into the room and stolen up behind me so silently that the unexpected sound of her voice made me jump half out of my skin. I gave a little yip of shock and dropped the mirror. The loud *clang* it made when it hit the painted tiles shook my bones.

"Oh dear." Mother bent to pick up the mirror while I stood there shamefaced. "It's all scratched and dented. I'm going to look like I've caught the pox. I suppose it's partly my fault for creeping up on you like that. I was a skilled huntress when I was a girl back in Calydon. You have to walk like a shadow when you're tracking deer." She shook her head over the damaged mirror, but she was smiling. "Sweet one, why are you meddling with my things?"

I clasped my hands behind my back and looked away. "I—I wanted to see what I look like."

"*That* much I could figure out," she said dryly. "But why now? Seven is much too young to start worrying about if you're pretty enough to attract a good husband."

"A what?" My head came up sharply. I stared at my mother as if she'd lost her mind. "I don't care if I'm pretty *enough* to get a husband! I don't *want* a husband. When you get married, you have to go away from home. I don't want to leave you or Father, not *ever*."

My mother laughed. She laughed so hard that she had to sit down on a carved folding stool. How *could* she? Didn't she see how upset I was by the idea of having to marry and leave everything I really loved?

When my mother finally caught her breath, she swept me onto her lap and kissed me. "Oh, my precious little girl! Where *do* you get your ideas? First of all, you *will* want a husband one day; that I promise you. But you needn't be afraid of leaving Sparta. You will stay here. It's your sister who'll have to leave when she marries. The two of you shared one birth, but you were the first one to see the light. The midwife tied a red thread around your wrist the instant you were born so that there'd be no mistakes made about your claim to the throne later on. You're older than Clytemnestra by just enough to make you queen of your father's land when the time comes."

"Me?" It was the first I'd heard of *this*.

My mother kissed me again. "Yes, *you*. Why are you so surprised? Has no one told you? Not even Ione?"

I shook my head. "I thought—I thought that Castor and Polydeuces would be the kings of Sparta when they grew up."

"Ah!" My mother nodded. "Well, I can understand why you'd reach that conclusion. You're too young to know that this land has always been ruled by queens. The only time a king rules is when his mother has no daughters. That's why Tyndareus is king but why your brothers won't be."

"Oh." I looked down at my hands, clasped quietly in my lap. I had come stealing into my parents' bedchamber just to see my face, and all at once I was staring at my future. Queen of Sparta! "Will Castor and Polydeuces mind that they're not kings and I'm queen?" I asked, suddenly feeling very sorry for my brothers.

My mother brushed away my fears like summer flies. "Castor and Polydeuces will be fine. They might not be the next kings of Sparta, but they'll have no trouble making great names for themselves in this world. I have faith in my boys. And don't you worry, my dearest one: Whether or not you're their queen, they'll always love you. How could anyone not love you, little Helen? You're such a beautiful child."

So there we were again. I could claim a kingdom, cause a scene at a shrine, refuse to sacrifice to a goddess, and get away with it all. My life would always be easy and pleasant because no matter what I did, everything would be forgiven, forgotten, laughed away because I was pretty. No, I was better than pretty. I was *beautiful.*

I had no reason to doubt that this was true.

I got off my mother's lap and picked up the mirror again. The face that looked back was certainly different from Clytemnestra's. The cheeks were rosier, the chin more rounded, the lips fuller and more clearly shaped, the teeth brighter when I smiled. Our hair was the same color, but mine was shinier, and my eyes were the deep, striking blue of ripe grapes, while hers were ordinary brown. Did all of those small differences add up to beauty? I frowned at my reflection, puzzled. Though it was the first time I'd seen my face so clearly—even a dented mirror shows you a better image than a pool of water—I felt as if I'd seen such a face somewhere else.

Then it hit me—my brother Polydeuces! My face

was a younger, softer version of his. Even our hair was the same in style as well as color, since in Sparta the nobly born men as well as the women wore their hair in long curls as far down their backs as it would grow. Polydeuces and I looked remarkably similar, but no one ever called *him* beautiful.

It was all very confusing. I needed to think about it. Very solemnly, I gave the mirror back to my mother and went to my own room.

Ione was there, spreading a new blanket on my bed. It was dyed the color of ripe barley, and one of my mother's maids had embroidered the corners with bunches of red grapes. There was no fine new blanket for Clytemnestra's bed. The way I saw it, I'd received this new gift as one more reward for being beautiful. I wondered if Polydeuces would be getting a new blanket too.

"What have you been up to?" Ione said, frowning. "Your sister is in the courtyard, working with her spindle. She was starting on her third skein of yarn when I left her. Go get yours and—"

"Ione," I cut in. "Why am I so much prettier than Clytemnestra?"

My nurse gaped at me. "My poor little lamb, has the sun cooked your brains? What a thing to say!"

"I'm serious," I insisted. "I know I'm prettier than she is. I'm beautiful. The queen herself said so. And it's all right for me to say it too, because I'm going to be queen myself someday. I just want to know *why* I'm prettier than she is, that's all."

"*There's* a fine question," Ione snorted. "I thank the gods that I'll be dead long before you rule this land, if that's a sample of your wisdom, O Queen."

"Don't make fun of me!" I cried. My head was still full of the new, dizzying awareness of power, the power of being beautiful. Even my sister said I was treated better than she was because of it. Yet here was Ione—Ione who always gave me my favorite foods, who made me dolls, who adorned my new clothes with embroidery and mended my old ones with care, who watched over me when I was sick—here she was, defying me! Teasing me! Was she blind? Didn't she understand that I deserved to be treated better than anyone else because I was beautiful? It was infuriating.

"Ione, if you don't answer my question I'll— I'll—" I tried to think of something to say that would make this stubborn grown-up take me seriously. Then I remembered what Father's palace manager always said to bring contrary slaves and servants back into line. If it worked for him—

"—I'll have you whipped!"

"I live in mortal terror of your wrath," Ione said, her face unreadable. "Far be it from *me* to keep you from learning the truth. You're more beautiful than your sister or any woman alive because you're not the daughter of a mere mortal like Lord Tyndareus. You must be the child of a god, of Zeus himself, master of the thunderbolt. There, is *that* good enough for you?"

"You are still making fun of me!" I shouted. "I *will* have you punished for that!"

"By all means, *try*, O Queen," she said, with a wry smile. "But first I'm going to show you a great marvel, in honor of your true father." Without warning she grabbed me by the belt of my tunic, sat down on my bed, hauled me across her knees, and declared: "I'm going to make it rain."

2

A GIRL'S PLACE

She *spanked* me! It didn't hurt all that much, but the humiliation was horrible. Ione loved me, cared for me, looked after me when Mother was busy, and yet she'd done *that* to me? I loved her with all my heart, but after she finished my punishment and left me alone with my thoughts, those thoughts were murderous. How *dare* she? I cried out my indignation facedown on my bed.

"Helen? Are you all right?" My brother Polydeuces stuck his head around one side of the doorway and peered into my room. "Some of the slaves heard you howling, so they raised an alarm. By the time things quieted down again, Ione was explaining to Mother why she spanked you."

"What did Mama do to *her* when she found out?"

I asked eagerly. I was still smarting with embarrassment, and I wanted Ione to suffer for it too, just a little.

"Nothing," Polydeuces replied. "Mother was surprised when Ione told her she'd never spanked you before, that's all."

I groaned and buried my face in my arms. I felt the bed sag as my brother sat down beside me and patted me on the back in sympathy.

"Don't cry, Helen," he said. "It's happened to all of us. Well, not to Clytemnestra. She's *perfect*." I looked up in time to see his lips curl. "Perfect at not getting caught."

"I'm not crying," I said. "I'm mad. She spanked me for *no reason*. I didn't do anything wrong."

"That happens a lot," Polydeuces said. Was that a snicker? "So, what set her off?"

"Nothing," I maintained. And I told him exactly what had happened between Ione and me so he'd understand the vastness of the injustice I'd suffered.

When I was done, he was silent. Then he let out a long, slow whistle and said, "You threatened her with a *whipping*? Little sister, when Ione comes back, you'd better get down on your knees and thank her for not telling Mother about that."

"Why should I thank her for anything?" I grumped.

"Because if Mother ever hears that you showed Ione that much disrespect, she'll spank you herself."

"Oh." I propped myself up on my elbows and leaned my chin on my hands. Now that the first shock of my punishment had faded, I realized what a little monster I'd been to my devoted nurse. What was the point of being beautiful if my actions were ugly and mean?

I looked earnestly at my brother. "Am I pretty, Polydeuces?"

"Huh? Where did that come from?" he asked, taken by surprise.

"Lots of people say I am, even Mama. Clytemnestra says I get treated better because of it, but it didn't seem to make any difference to Ione. She spanked me anyway, and she's slapped me, and——"

"Ione changed your dirty diapers. How pretty were you then?" Polydeuces grinned. "She loves you, Helen, and she doesn't want you to grow up vain and spoiled, believing you can do or say whatever you like just because you're pretty. Even if you were as beautiful as Aphrodite, you still wouldn't get everything your own way."

"I don't *want* to get everything my own way," I told him. "I just want—I want—"

What *did* I want? I'd never thought about it before. I knew that I hadn't wanted to worship Artemis, but Mother made me go to the temple anyway. I'd told her that I wouldn't want a husband, not ever, but she'd acted like I couldn't decide such things for myself.

Polydeuces was gazing at me, waiting for me to finish my sentence. If I said, *I just want to be free*, would he know what I really meant? Or would he say, *You're already free, silly. You're not a slave, right?*

I wasn't a slave, but as much as I hated carding and spinning and weaving wool, Ione and Mother forced me to spend day after day learning how to do it. What they said was: "This is what all women do, even queens," but what I heard was: *This is all that women can do, and even queens have no choice about it.* Was that being free?

Clytemnestra wasn't a slave, but when she was old enough she'd be married off and sent away to live with her husband. Would she get to choose him, or would she simply be told, *This is the man you're going to marry*, the same way that Ione told us, *This is the dress you're going to wear today*? Was *that* being free?

I sat up. I knew what I wanted. "I just want to say yes or no about my own life," I said. "Always."

"You can *say* yes or no all you want right now, little sister. The trick is getting other people to pay attention." Polydeuces gave one of my curls a playful tug. "You're pretty . . . for a toad"—his smile said he was only joking—"but even Aphrodite herself has to obey Zeus's commands. Now, if she could get her hands on a bundle of his thunderbolts—well, if she *could*, not even Zeus would dare tell her what to do. Of course, that won't happen. Aphrodite's happy with the way things are. She'd rather sip nectar all day than have thunderbolt target practice make her hands rougher than mine."

Polydeuces held out his palms so that I could see the calluses. "That's from all the time I've spent learning to fight," he told me proudly. "Castor's hands aren't half as tough as mine—our teacher Glaucus said so. That reminds me—" He stood up. "I've got to go help Castor rewrap the hilts on our practice swords with rawhide. If we don't, Glaucus will knock them out of our hands tomorrow."

I grabbed his wrist as he started for the door. "If I help you rewrap your swords, will you let me hold one?" A new idea had taken fire in my mind, a fire kindled by my brother's light words about Aphrodite: *If she could get her hands on a bundle of his thunderbolts, not even Zeus would dare tell her what to do.* "Will you teach me how to use it too?" I persisted. "Please?"

Polydeuces stared at me as if I'd grown fins and scales. "Why would you want to do that? Swords are for warriors, not little girls."

"Why can't I be both?" I countered. "I'm just as old as you were when you and Castor first started learning how to fight."

"How hard *did* Ione spank you? I think she rattled your brains." Polydeuces shook his head and tried a second time to walk out of my room.

I ran after him, seized his arm with both hands, and refused to let him go. "Why *can't* I learn the same things you and Castor do?" I demanded. "Why can't you let me *try*?"

"I'll tell you what, little sister," Polydeuces replied, pulling his arm free. "You can learn from me just as soon as you can"—he took off like a rabbit, sprinting out of my room and down the hall, calling back over his shoulder—*"catch me!"*

I tried. I ran as fast as I could, even though I knew I'd be in a lot of fresh trouble if Ione came back to the room and found me gone. I didn't care. Suddenly I knew what I had to do if I was going to have the life I wanted for myself, a life in which *I* was the one who said yes or no, the one who made her own choices.

It was a useless race, one that I lost. Polydeuces had longer legs, and they weren't all tangled up in a dress. He'd also had a lot more practice running; it was part of his warrior's training, along with sword-play, spear-throwing, archery, horse-taming, and racing chariots over the worst terrain.

By the time I gave up trying to catch him and went trailing back to my room, I knew three things:

Even if I was pretty, it wasn't going to be enough to bring me the life I wanted: one where I was free to make choices that mattered, one where people listened to what I had to say.

Aphrodite had the beauty; Zeus had the thunderbolts. Everyone loved Aphrodite, but everyone *listened* to Zeus.

I'd never get my hands on a thunderbolt, so if I wanted to be free, I'd better find a way to get my hands on the next best thing: a sword.

Polydeuces said he'd teach me how to use a sword if I could run fast enough to catch him. I didn't really believe he meant that, but he did make me realize that one of the first things a warrior must know is how to *run*.

Not run *away*—a Spartan would sooner die—just run. Even I knew that a fighter needed strong legs as well as strong arms. When the poets performed in our great hall, I loved to hear them sing about how famous heroes outraced the wind to reach the thick of battle.

No one can run in a dress, so the first thing I did was "borrow" a short tunic from my brother Castor. If my brothers hadn't been too big for a nursemaid, Ione would have turned that shabby old thing into cleaning rags long ago. Castor didn't pay attention to how his clothes looked, or even to where his clothes were. I was thankful for that.

Once I had the tunic, I tied my hair back the way my brothers did when they had their lessons with Glaucus. They called it a "club," because that's what it looked like hanging down the nape of the neck after they'd twisted up the long, thick strands. I'd never had to do anything with my own hair—Ione always washed and combed it for me—so it took a lot of work until I managed to do it.

Then it was only a matter of waiting for a time when I knew Ione would be busy elsewhere in the palace long enough for me to slip away. I waited until one of our countless small household crises popped up—in a household the size of our palace, they always did—and I had my chance.

I pulled on the tunic, rubbed a little dirt on my face, then said a quick prayer to Aphrodite. *Great goddess, Ione says that love makes people see things that aren't really there. If anyone notices me today, please let them think they're seeing my brother Polydeuces.*

And then I ran. I ran without sandals, even though it hurt, because the songs said that was how real warriors ran. As I dashed out through the palace gates, I heard one of our guards call out behind me, "Good day to you, young prince! The gods bless you," and I thanked Aphrodite for having heard my prayer.

From that day on, I ran whenever I had the chance, and the years ran with me. The hardest part was getting away from Ione and from all the times I was supposed to be with my sister and the other women, turning fleece into thread, thread into cloth, cloth into clothing. Before, I'd only disliked those chores because they were so tedious. Now they were obstacles that kept me from doing what I really loved, and I hated them passionately. I ran my best whenever I imagined that every stride was putting more distance between me and the carding combs, the spindle, and the loom.

On my tenth birthday, I was running across a field not far from the palace when a hare broke from cover in front of me and took flight.

You can learn from me just as soon as you can catch me!

I don't know why I heard Polydeuces's long-ago taunt at that moment. I only knew that the gods themselves had thrown a challenge my way, and I meant to accept it. Without breaking stride, I veered sharply and ran after the hare. The wind tasted sweet as my shadow flew across the grass. The hare ran, he leaped, he zigzagged wildly, but I matched him every time, move for move, until at last he slowed his pace. That was when I paused, bent my knees, and with a mighty leap flung myself onto the creature.

A moment later the hare was racing off, unharmed, and I was standing in the middle of the field holding a tuft of fur from his tail and shouting triumphantly at the sun, "*Got* you, Polydeuces!" Then I toppled backward into the meadow and watched the sky spin crazily above me as I gasped for breath and grinned.

When I recovered from my mad race, I felt ready

to take every last *You can't!* that the world wanted to throw at me and turn it into *Oh yes I can!*

It was time for me to learn how to do more than run.

I got back on my feet and looked across the field to a grove of olive trees, their silver-green leaves fluttering in the breeze. The palace citadel lay in that direction, and so did the narrow strip of open ground where Glaucus gave my brothers their daily training lessons.

If Polydeuces was so dead set against girls learning the ways of sword and spear, I was certain that his teacher would be even more unreasonable about sharing his lessons. Well, the hare hadn't wanted to give me the little tuft of fur that was now my prized trophy, but I'd still managed to take it. Why couldn't I do the same with those lessons?

I ran to the olive grove but took care to say a prayer to Athena before entering the trees. The goddess of wisdom created the olive tree so that we mortals would enjoy its gifts—especially the oil we used for everything from cooking, to protecting skin and hair, to filling the lamps that brightened our homes. The trees that grew near the citadel were kept sacred to her, their fruits never harvested except by her priests when they wanted oil to light her temple. I was sure that Athena would bless my plan to spy on Glaucus and my brothers, because she was a warrior herself, her images always wearing a helmet, carrying shield and spear.

I overestimated the goddess's kindness and I underestimated Glaucus. I thought I was well hidden, crouched behind one of the sacred olive trees, watching him coach my brothers as they fought one another with wooden swords. How was I to know that the old soldier still had eyesight that a hawk would envy? I didn't suspect a thing when he casually announced that he had to go pee and for them to keep up the good work. I was still spying on Castor and Polydeuces when he circled around the far side of the olive grove and swept down on me before I knew what was going on.

"What are you doing here?" he demanded, holding me by the back of the neck as if I were a puppy and dragging me out onto the training ground. When I squirmed, he shook me until my teeth rattled. "Answer!"

"Put me down!" I shouted at him. "I'm Helen! I'm your princess! I'm going to be your queen!" My brothers had dropped their swords and stood by, snickering.

Glaucus never cracked a smile. "Are you," he said. He set me down, but he didn't let go of my neck. "Queens work with spindles and needles. They card wool and weave cloth. They make medicines and perfumes. Do you see any wool to be carded and spun out here? Do I smell like I use perfume?"

"You smell like you ought to!" I snapped back. He still didn't laugh, but I saw that grim mouth creep up just a bit at the corners.

"Why don't you go back to the citadel and make me some, then," he said. "Or would you rather tell me what's brought you here?"

"I want to learn how to fight!" I declared, staring him right in the eyes to show him I wasn't afraid. "Even if I never have to use a sword, I want to know *how.* When I'm queen, I've got to be strong enough to protect myself. If I can't do that, how can I protect anyone else? And if someone thinks he can control my life and my decisions just because he's got a sword and I don't—I want him to get a *surprise.*"

This time, Glaucus laughed. Laughed? He roared! I was positive he was mocking me, and that was so infuriating that, like a fool, I lost my temper. My arms were too short for my fists to reach him, but I flailed at him with my feet. I had to do *something* to show him that I wasn't going to take an insult meekly, not even from a man who could throw me halfway to the citadel walls.

At my first kick, he dropped his hold on my neck, grabbed my foot in mid-arc, and had me dangling upside down in the blink of an eye. I was so startled I couldn't even scream.

"That," said Glaucus, "was your first lesson— keep your temper under control or it's going to control you. Here's your second—pick your battles." Still holding me upside down, he turned toward my brothers. Castor and Polydeuces were now laughing so hard that they'd fallen over and were rolling on the ground. Quietly and gently, Glaucus set me on my feet and gave me one of the boys' discarded swords. His eyes flicked meaningfully from me to them.

I didn't need a second invitation. I thwacked my brothers' backsides so fast and so hard with one of their own practice swords that the bruises left them looking like a pair of leopards. By the time they scrambled to their feet and out of reach, I was breathing hard, but I'd never felt happier. My brothers filled the air with their protests until Glaucus silenced them both with a look.

Then they had no other choice but to stand by, pulling long faces, while their teacher gave his attention to evaluating my improvised performance: "Good energy, even if it's not focused. Bad technique, but that's understandable and it can be corrected. Too much enthusiasm. There's no shame in honorable combat, but there shouldn't be so much unnatural pleasure. The man with the greatest thirst for blood ends up drinking at Hades's table. *Men!*" At the word, my brothers tensed like hunting hounds. I giggled to hear him use that word to address a pair of boys still shy of their fifteenth birthday, but I bit off my laughter the instant Glaucus glared at me. "Men, we welcome your new comrade."

The startled looks on their faces were beyond description.

"Is this a joke?" Polydeuces demanded. "Are you saying it just to punish us because we didn't fight well today? We'll do better tomorrow, I swear it by Zeus!"

"She can't join us," Castor said, shaking his head. "It's—it's—it's just *wrong*."

Glaucus soon put a stop to their protests. "Your sister has explained why she wants to share your lessons, and she makes good points. She's younger than you, but already she knows the wisdom of being able to take care of herself *and* her people, once she's our queen. Good: A weak ruler means a weak land; a weak land means war. Now if *you* can give me any reason why I should not teach her along with you, say it. If it makes sense, I'll heed it, but remember this: It must be a reason that would apply if she'd been born a boy. If all you can say is *She's a girl!* then save your breath. You'll need it to outrun me, and the gods help you when I catch you."

"But—but she's a— She's too *young!*" It was lucky Castor caught himself before he could utter the words that would earn him a beating.

"She doesn't need to worry about protecting herself once she's queen," Polydeuces put in. "We'll do that. We'd do it even if it *weren't* our duty! Helen, don't you trust us to take care of you?"

Before I could reply, Castor plowed on, "And she's weak. Look at her arms! All scrawny. She'll get hurt, and she'll never be able to keep up with us."

Glaucus folded his arms across his chest. "If she can't keep up, she'll get no special treatment. She can give up and go back to the palace anytime she likes. Once she does that, I won't allow her to rejoin us. Understood? *All* of you?" He gave me a hard look. I said nothing, but I clenched my fists and made a private vow to Zeus himself that the only way I'd leave the training ground would be as a small, cold corpse.

I was still enjoying thoughts of *And I'll be dead and then they'll all be sorry!* when Glaucus added, "As for her age, she's older than you were when your father first turned you over to me."

"Father!" Castor cried, like a starving man discovering a loaf of bread. "He'd never risk anything happening to Helen. She *is* going to be queen one day."

"Castor's right," Polydeuces said eagerly, his head bobbing up and down. "He'll *never* hear of her training with us."

"Exactly," said Glaucus, and he smiled.

So we entered into a pact of the deepest secrecy, my brothers and Glaucus and I. It was agreed that I would train in the use of sword and shield and spear whenever I could slip away from the women's world of distaff and spindle and loom inside the palace walls. Glaucus made Castor and Polydeuces promise that they would not speak of my lessons to anyone, not a word, not a hint. They clung to their initial reluctance. Castor kept repeating, "But what if Father finds out *anyway*? What will he do to us *then*?" until Polydeuces pointed out that I'd soon get tired of doing a *man's* work; it would be only a matter of time before I quit on my own. Castor didn't look convinced, but he went where Polydeuces led. Glaucus had them take the gods' own oath, swearing by the dreadful powers of the river Styx, the black water that flows between the lands of the living and the realm of Hades, lord of the dead.

Of course, Glaucus laid down some exceptions to our pact for me. "If you're clumsy enough to make anyone suspicious—anyone to whom you owe honor and obedience, I mean—and you're asked a direct question about where you're going or what you're doing, tell the truth."

I nodded. I knew that lying was wrong, but I drew a broken line around the whole matter of concealing my sword-training from my parents. If I didn't tell them I *was* doing it, it wasn't the same thing as telling them I *wasn't*.

"If you're discovered, it won't be anyone's fault but your own," he went on. "I know how to keep secrets, and your brothers have sworn."

"I'll be careful," I promised. "I'll make sure no one follows me, and I'll always come in disguise. And if Clytemnestra asks me where I'm going, I'll beat her until she stays quiet."

"Do *that*, and we're through," Glaucus told me. "I'm not teaching you how to fight if it means you'll turn into a tyrant. The world's got enough of those. If you want to learn from me, you'll work for the privilege, and you'll know that not all of my lessons will take place on the training ground."

3

LESSONS

My next lesson came between the time Glaucus first agreed to show me how to fight and the time I was at last able to steal away from the palace and join my brothers on the training ground. Seven days! Gods, how could seven days seem like eternity?

On the first day, I leaped out of bed, eager to throw on my "borrowed" tunic and run to the training ground, only to find Ione standing in my doorway with a stack of newly woven fabric.

"You need new dresses," she said, and proceeded to fumble and fuss over how tall I was growing and whether or not to add an extra layer of flounces to my skirt, just in case I grew taller still. I didn't know you could waste a whole day over dressmaking.

The next morning I learned that you can waste

another day over the same stupid dresses. Ione decided it was time for me to learn how to sew my own clothes. I objected, saying, "I'm never going to have to do this for myself when I'm grown up!" Ione countered with, "Well, you're not grown up yet."

I did a terrible job. Ione sat me down with a group of the palace women, and they all took turns undoing my mistakes and trying to say something nice about my clumsy efforts. Ione couldn't deny that I had no talent for needlework, but that didn't stop her from putting me to work embroidering dress sleeves on the third day.

Once again I was working in the company of other palace women—servants and specially trained slaves and the daughters of high-ranking nobles who had the honor of attending the queen. As soon as she gave me my work, Ione went off on her own errand, which gave me an idea: If I could find a pretext for leaving the courtyard, I'd be able to escape the palace!

I jabbed myself with the needle deliberately; it was the first inspiration that hit me. "Ow! My finger!" I held up my hand so that everyone could see the blood. I dropped my embroidery and stood up, pretending to be desperate with pain. "I have to find my mother!" I wailed. It was the queen's duty to treat sickness and heal injuries. "Oh, it hurts *so* much!" I started out of the courtyard.

Three of the older servants, all friends of Ione,

flocked around me before I'd taken five steps. "You poor lamb, what a dreadful, dreadful wound," one of them said, shaking her head. "We can't allow you to go to your mother unescorted, not with such a terrible hurt."

"I can find her myself, really," I said, but they wouldn't hear of it.

"And what if you bleed so much that you collapse before you reach her, dear Lady Helen? No, no, we must bring you to the queen. It's our duty."

"But it's not that serious! It's only a small—" I began. Then I stopped, realizing I'd tripped over my own hasty tongue. The women smiled and escorted me back to my place in the courtyard.

The fourth, fifth, and sixth days nearly drove me barking mad. I kept getting up earlier and earlier, hoping to escape before Ione could catch me. That was how I learned that you *can't* get up earlier than a farmer's wife. She was always there, always with a new set of tasks for me. At least she'd given up on the needlework, but that didn't stop her from dumping a herd's worth of fleeces in my lap for carding, or dragging me off to spin thread with my sister, or, worst of all, turning me over to Clytemnestra with the words: "I give up. *You* teach her."

The only advantage to having Clytemnestra for a teacher was that she wasn't an early riser. I suffered through my lesson with her on the sixth day—and if

I had one olive for every time she sneered at my un-even, snapped, snarled thread, I could press a whole jug full of oil! Earlier that year, we'd each been given our own rooms, so on the seventh day I slipped out of my room and past hers while she was still snuffling in her bed.

I hurried down the hall, Castor's tunic wadded up tightly against my chest, wondering where I could find the safest place to change. I was just about to sneak into one of the palace storerooms when a hand fell on my shoulder and Ione's voice sounded in my ear. "Oh good, there you are. I need you for some *very important* work."

"But Clytemnestra has to teach me how to spin better," I said, hoping Ione would accept my excuse. No need to tell her that once she let me go, I had no intention of going anywhere near my spindle or my sister.

"That can wait. Your mother will soon be making our winter medicines. She needs us to gather ingredients." So that was how I lost yet another day, picking herbs and flowers instead of learning how to use a sword.

Glaucus laughed when I finally came limping out of the olive grove to where he had Castor and Poly-deuces doing target practice with the throwing spear. "There you are, princess!" he cried. "I thought you'd changed your mind and given up on our pact before it began."

"Do I look like I've changed my mind?" I grumbled. I rubbed my arms, sore and aching, and spat dust from my mouth. My legs were covered with bloody scrapes, and it would take me hours to work the tangles out of my hair.

"Then why so long coming out here?" I liked Glaucus better when he was being stern; he had the most aggravating grin of any man alive. "Forget the path? Lose your way?"

"I'm watched," I said. "Ever since the day you promised to teach me how to fight, it's been next to impossible to get away. Whenever I knew you were taking the boys down here, I'd try to follow, but Ione always seemed to come along with a task for me to do. I wouldn't be here now if I hadn't gotten up *long* before dawn, dressed, and hidden myself in one of the storerooms all morning. Even then, I had to drop from a window and climb down the eastern side of the palace hill to be sure that no one would see me."

"The eastern side . . ." Glaucus rubbed his chin. "That's where the briars grow thickest, isn't it?" And his grin got wider and wider, until suddenly I understood exactly what had been going on.

"You did this!" I shouted. "I don't know what you said to Ione, but you're the reason why she hasn't left me alone for a moment all these days!"

"You look mad enough to throw a rock at my head," Glaucus said calmly. "Did you think I was going to make this easy for you, princess? You say you want to learn a fighter's skills. Well, patience is one of them, cunning's another, and no one can give those to you but yourself. If you'd rather have gifts fall into your lap, go back to the palace and put on a skirt, but if you still want to learn from me, let's see you throw something besides a rock." Instead of giving me the sharpened wooden practice spears he gave my brothers, he handed me his own weapon, a beautiful, bronze-headed spear made to fly to the target with a hawk's clean grace.

It wasn't as massive as the great hunting spears the men used to kill wild boar, but it was heavy enough. I envied my brothers, armed with sharpened sticks. They had no trouble hitting the bales of barley straw at the far end of the training ground. Meanwhile, I spent more time struggling to lift the genuine spear than I did throwing it. *Hit* the target? I was happy when I finally managed to fling that cumbersome weapon more than five paces away from me.

I'd come to the training ground with sore arms. As that day wore on, they felt ready to drop off like dead vine leaves. Still I kept at it, hoisting the spear, throwing the spear, fetching the spear, until I wanted to howl from the pain. Part of my staying power came from fear that if I quit or even complained, Glaucus would decide that I wasn't worth teaching after all.

Then what? My brothers loved me, but they'd never agree to teach me the ways of weapons. They'd just point to my failure as proof that there really were some things boys could do that girls shouldn't even try.

I needed Glaucus. I needed to show him that Castor was wrong, that I *could* keep up with my brothers after all.

"Well," Glaucus said when at last he took the spear from my shaking hands. "That was awful. Next time you'll practice with the same equipment as your brothers do."

I was aching so badly that I could have kissed his hands for those words, but I didn't want to let him know that. I had to make him see that I was strong enough to hold my own on the training ground, so I put on a brave show. "This was only my first day. I want to go on using the real thing. I don't want to learn how to throw some stupid *stick*."

Glaucus's scowl was downright terrifying. "What you will learn, princess," he said grimly, "is *obedience*. Or you'll learn nothing more from me."

I was tired and sore and frustrated. My mouth was dry, and my head was beginning to ache along with my arms. Glaucus was a famous warrior, the one man Father thought worthy to teach princes, but he was also the man who'd agreed to teach me, then made it almost impossible for me to come to my lessons, and now, *now* he was scolding me about obedience! I was so exasperated that I forgot his very first lesson. *Keep your temper under control or it's going to control you.*

"I know all about obedience." I spat out the words as if they were sour pomegranate seeds. "Obey my nurse, obey my parents, obey the gods. If the gods love obedience so much, why didn't they fill the world with sheep?"

I stamped my foot for emphasis. The sharp-edged bit of stone on the training ground wouldn't have hurt my foot if I'd only trod on it, but stamping drove it into my flesh like a dagger. The sudden pain took me by surprise so that I gasped instead of yowling. When I picked up my foot to see what I'd done, there was a lot of blood.

I felt the tears rising, but I also felt Glaucus's eyes on me, and my brothers' as well. I clenched my hands and screwed my eyes tight shut, biting down hard on my lower lip, all in a mighty battle to hold back my tears. *Soldiers never cry,* I thought. *Soldiers never cry.*

I lost that battle. The pain was too great, and my breath tore out of my body in a bone-shaking sob. I expected to see Glaucus turn to my brothers and say, "There, now you see the real difference between men and women. No man would ever act like this over a little blood."

Instead, I was startled out of my tears by the sight of the broad-shouldered warrior kneeling beside me and taking my wounded foot in his hand as gently as if he were my mother.

"Let's see that," he said. "Mmm, this isn't going to be easy to hide from your nurse. That was a stupid thing to do, princess, but I've seen worse. We'll find a way around it. Men! Are you going to stand there like deadwood or have you got any brains to bring to this problem?"

I stopped sobbing as I watched my brothers scramble all over one another like a pair of big-pawed puppies in their haste to help me.

"It's not such a bad wound, Helen," Castor whispered, trying to give me comfort. "It'll heal quickly."

"You actually managed to lift that spear," Polydeuces murmured. "Amazing. Wasn't that something, Castor?"

Castor agreed, echoing Polydeuces's pleasure in my accomplishment. I would have hugged them for their kindness then and there, but I didn't know if that would have embarrassed them in front of their teacher. They did love me, even if they'd have to be convinced that a girl's place was beside them on the training ground.

In the time it took for my tears to dry, Castor and Polydeuces managed to wash my wound, ruin their clothing by tearing strips from the hems for bandages, and wrap my foot as thickly and tightly as if they were swaddling an infant in wintertime. Polydeuces had even been able to scrounge up some spiderwebs to help stop the bleeding. When they were done, they stood back and gazed at Glaucus with happy, expectant faces.

The old warrior examined their bulky handiwork, shook his head, and undid it all. He retied the bandages, discarding most of the tattered cloth, muttering that Sparta was doomed if we were its hope for the future.

If I couldn't thank Castor and Polydeuces for their care any other way, at least I could stand up to Glaucus in their defense. "Don't say that!" I exclaimed, my face hot. "They did a *good* job, better than you're doing now."

Glaucus sat back on his haunches. "Loyalty, princess? That's commendable, but they should earn your praise."

"They're going to be heroes, not healers," I snapped. "So what if they can't tie a bandage? They're going to be the pride of Sparta someday—you just wait!—and when that day comes, the only reason anyone will ever remember *your* name is because you were their teacher!"

"Not all of us care if our names are remembered, in life or after death," Glaucus replied, his face stony. "Better men than I have become food for battlefield crows defending your father's lands. They could have broken away from the Spartan army and rushed into single combat against the enemy, all for their own glory. Instead, they died fighting in the ranks, for the good of all instead of the glory of one. They lost their chance to be remembered, but they won wars. Those are *my* heroes, princess."

"Then I don't want my brothers to be your kind of heroes," I said. "Sheep go where they're led. Are *they* your heroes too?"

I must have looked ridiculous, a small, filthy, scratched, and bleeding child facing up to a seasoned warrior who could have snapped my spine like a dry reed. For a time the two of us sat glaring at one another while Castor and Polydeuces looked on, too nervous to make a sound. Even if my belligerence cost me all future lessons from Glaucus, I wasn't going to back down. He had no right to belittle my brothers. I remembered the second lesson he'd taught me: *Pick your battles.*

Then Glaucus broke the silence with a roar of laughter. "Sheep again!" he crowed. "You drag them into your arguments time after time, yet I'll wager that you've never been closer to them than the meat on your table or the wool on your spindle. You have no idea what they're really like. You've just heard other palace folk say that sheep are stupid, spiritless beasts, so you echo their ignorance. If you'd been raised like me, on an upland farm, you'd soon learn the truth. Sheep *don't* always go where they're led, not half so easily as palace folk do, anyway."

He slapped his knees and stood up. "You're a blunt girl, but praise Athena, you're not stupid. You're just young. You'll learn. The gods know, I'm old and I'm still learning. I only pray they'll let me live to teach you the difference between sheep and heroes, blind obedience and discipline."

"What?" I'd expected to be sent away for being so outspoken. I glanced at my brothers. They'd been with Glaucus for years and knew him better than I did. Was he truly willing to keep teaching me, or was it an ugly joke, punishment for my audacity? I hoped they'd give some sign to let me know whether it was safe to take him at his word.

They were smiling. They looked proud of me.

I looked back at Glaucus. "You—you'll still teach me?"

"That will depend on if you'll learn." He cast a casual glance back toward where the royal palace of Sparta stood high on its fortified hill. "It also seems that right now it's going to depend on luck. While you and I have been bickering, your father's sentries have been watching, wondering why I've stopped instructing the princes just to waste so much time and attention on *this* grubby little creature." He nodded at me. "I helped train those men, and unless I did a rotten job, they'll follow their suspicions down here to find out what's going on."

"I—I think I see two of them now," Castor said, shading his eyes with one hand. "You're right, Glaucus, they're coming this way. Helen, you can't go back to the palace; they're on the only path. They'll recognize you and tell Father, and that'll be the end of your training."

"You should be happy, then," I said. "You didn't want me to train with you."

"That was because I didn't think you were serious about it," Castor replied. "But after hearing what you said, seeing you keep trying to use that spear, not giving up, well . . ."

Polydeuces stooped to murmur in my ear. "What he's trying to say is, anyone who'd stand up to Glaucus like you did deserves a chance. You stood up for us, little sister; the least we can do is stand up for you."

I climbed to my feet with a hand up from both my brothers. I don't think that I ever loved them so much as I did then. My foot throbbed, but Glaucus had done a good job of binding it up. It could bear my weight, which was a good thing because I was about to ask it to bear more than that. I dug my feet— both hurt and whole—into the dirt and took off at a run. Pain shot through my body with every other step, and I heard the shouts of Father's sentries on my trail, ordering me to stop, but I ran on.

4

CLYTEMNESTRA'S SECRET

I outran the sentries in spite of my injured foot. I escaped them by dodging through the olive grove, then circling all around the royal citadel until I reached the path back to the great gate. The men on guard there didn't think twice about letting me in. To their eyes I was just another one of the young slaves who worked in the palace kitchens or stables or any of a hundred other places inside our walls. Why should they care about a slave? They waved me inside impatiently, without a second glance. I scrambled past them and vanished into the cool shadows of the palace before their comrades could catch up to me.

I managed to avoid Ione or anyone else who might recognize me in my disguise. I tore off my clothing, hid the ragged tunic in the wooden box that held my dolls, and crawled into my bed, breathing hard. I stayed there the rest of the day, wrapped up in a blazing sheet of agony, until Ione found me at suppertime. She didn't know what to think when she saw my wounded foot and heard me spin a story about treading on a piece of broken pottery in the palace.

"Why didn't you find me when this happened?" she demanded, examining the wound tenderly. In spite of all that my brothers and Glaucus had done, it was a mess. I watched in dismay as Ione plucked a sticky olive leaf out of my foot and held it up between us.

"I—I was—" I began.

Ione raised one hand, silencing me. "Don't bother lying to me. I can't make you tell me the truth, but I don't need to waste my time hearing lies." She turned her head toward the little heap of bandages she'd unwound from my foot and picked up one of the longer strips. "I know who you've been with, at least. I know this cloth. I wove it myself to make a tunic for your brother Castor. My needle made this little pattern of sea creatures along the hem. I knew that my work would be wasted on him—he doesn't care what his clothing looks like as long as it serves its purpose—but I wanted to do it for him anyway." She let the tattered strip drop back onto the small, bloody heap.

"I'm sorry, Ione," I said meekly. She was hurt, and it wasn't because Castor had ruined her embroidery. It was because she'd always trusted me and now I'd tried to deceive her. She loved me, and I'd repaid her with lies. I didn't know how to apologize for that, so instead I said, "I'm sorry Castor tore that. It was very pretty. All the work you—"

Again her hand went up, demanding my silence. "You don't need to apologize to me. You're growing up, all of you, shutting me out of your lives. The boys were taken away from me long ago, because they claim it's bad for future warriors to be raised by women. Soon I'll have no more authority over you and your sister either. I'll be no more than a piece of furniture to you then, something you can ignore unless you need to use me. Keep your secrets. But next time you want to persuade someone that you were hurt inside the palace, get rid of this sort of thing"—she held up the telltale olive leaf—"and *wash* yourself. You look as if you've been wrestling with pigs. As for your hair . . ."

She went on like this for a while, fetching water and salve and fresh bandages for my foot as she chattered on. She sat beside me on my bed and cleaned my face roughly, like a mother cat with a wayward kitten. When she turned her attention to my hair, she yanked the tangles out so hard that I thought she meant to take my scalp off with them. When she was done with me, I looked like a presentable daughter of Sparta again.

"There," she said, holding me at arm's length and

surveying her handiwork. "That will do. Look at you! It won't be long before you're a woman, and what a beautiful woman you'll be."

I felt the tips of my ears turn red. My nurse had never given me such a compliment before.

"Ione, I'm nowhere near being a woman," I told her. "I'm only ten."

"Not forever. One way or the other, you'll fly away." She shook her head and sighed. "That Glaucus is a wise man, even if he's too tight-lipped. He told me to keep an eye on you, but he wouldn't say why. I don't know what you're up to that should involve him, and I don't want to know. All that matters to me is that he asked me to keep you close and I failed. Now look what's happened to you."

I thought I saw tears in her eyes. I tried to throw my arms around her neck, but she was on her feet and beyond my reach before I could do that.

"Go and eat, little bird," she said from the doorway. Then she was gone.

I limped a little as I walked through the palace, following the smell of food. It wasn't coming from the hall where my parents held feasts to honor Spartan nobles or foreign ambassadors. Instead, the aroma led me to the kitchen, where I found my brothers gobbling bread and sheep's milk cheese, with the bony remains of a broiled fish between them.

"Where's Clytemnestra?" I asked as a kitchen

slave hurried to find me a stool. Another fetched my food and some triply-watered wine.

"Been and gone," Castor said cheerfully, through a mouthful of bread crust. "Something's up with her. Every bite she took, she was smiling. I know that sly look: She's got a secret."

Polydeuces agreed with his twin. "I'll bet it's about the guest, the one who came today while we were all on the training ground."

"What guest?" I asked eagerly. It was always exciting when visitors came to our father's court. Visitors meant gifts, thrilling tales of the perils they'd braved to reach Sparta, and news from other kingdoms.

"One of the maids said that her brother was the one summoned to bring bread and salt to the king's hall." All of Sparta's important visitors were welcomed with the ritual that created the sacred bond between host and guest by the sharing of bread and salt. The gods punished any man who violated that holy trust.

"Any idea where he's from?" I asked. My brothers shook their heads ruefully. "I'll bet Clytemnestra knows. That's got to be her secret."

"Good luck making her tell us anything," Castor said sarcastically.

"Why do we have to ask her what we can find out for ourselves?" I said.

My brothers smiled. The next instant my uneaten

dinner was abandoned as the three of us fled the kitchen, off to haunt the great hall for news, to put our ears to a few doors, to talk to the servants, to do whatever it took to discover the identity of Sparta's newest guest. I had a hard time keeping up with Castor and Polydeuces on account of my injured foot, until the two of them made a carry-chair of their linked hands, scooped me up, and carried me along before I could protest.

They might have helped me, but their good intentions hurt our mission. You can't gather secrets when you're making a spectacle of yourself in the palace passageways. They no sooner set me back on my feet beside a pillar in the great hall than we were discovered.

"Why are you three lurking here?" Mother's girlhood skills as a huntress were as sharp as ever.

We whirled around, my brothers already babbling flimsy excuses. I didn't bother. *Mother's no fool*, I thought. *She knows why we're here.*

Of course she did. She folded her arms, regarded us severely, and said, "He's from Mykenae."

"Who is?" Castor was still trying to keep up the illusion of innocence.

Mother just rolled her eyes. "Do you want to play games, Castor, or do you want to know about our guest?"

"I do if he doesn't," Polydeuces spoke up. "Mykenae! Mother, is it true what I've heard about their royal house? Did Lord Atreus really make his brother eat his own—?"

"*Silence*," Mother commanded sharply. Her eyes flashed. "I forbid you to mention any of those awful stories while we're entertaining Lord Thyestes's ambassador. I thought you had more sense, Polydeuces."

My brother lowered his head, ashamed. "I'm sorry, Mother," he said.

"What awful stories?" I whispered to Castor, but he refused to tell me anything as long as Mother might overhear.

Which she did. "None you'll hear while that man is our honored guest, Helen. Unless you want to ruin your sister's marriage plans."

"*Marriage!*" I cried. The word bounced wildly off the painted pillars of the great hall. "Clytemnestra? But she's only—"

"Lower your voice," Mother told me. "I won't let that Mykenaean go home and tell his king that Sparta's future queen has no manners."

"So that was Clytemnestra's big secret," Polydeuces mused. He patted my shoulder. "Don't worry, Helen: Father is only making the marriage *agreement* with Mykenae now. Clytemnestra won't leave us for a while yet."

"Long enough for her to lord it over us because *she's* going to be queen of Mykenae." Castor did a deadly accurate imitation of how our sister always sailed through the palace, spine stiff with pride, nose in the air, lips pursed as if she smelled a rotten fish. Even Mother had to laugh. As much as she loved us all, she couldn't deny that Clytemnestra did like to put on airs.

That night, I went to bed with my head spinning from the news. Married! My sister was going to be married. I wondered when she'd have to leave Sparta. I wondered what her husband would be like. I wanted to lean toward her bed and whisper a dozen questions to her, to find out if she was really pleased with the future that Father and the Mykenaean ambassador were giving her. It would have to wait for morning.

Alone in the shadows, I whispered a small prayer to my favorite goddess. "O Aphrodite, make my sister's husband love her as much as Father loves Mother." It was the first time I hadn't called my mother "Mama." My sister was going to be married. Neither one of us was a child anymore. "If he loves her, he'll want her to be happy."

The next morning I rose early, dressed, gobbled my breakfast in the kitchen, and went in search of Clytemnestra. She was carding wool on a courtyard bench when I found her. It was a tedious job, pulling the matted clumps of fleece through the carding combs. I wished her a good day, then sat beside her on the bench and began to pick out some of the knots in the fleece with my fingers. We worked together in silence. It was as if nothing had changed, as if there were no Mykenaean visitor under our roof.

At last I put my clump of wool back into the basket of washed fleece. "Mother told us," I said. "I hope you and Lord Thyestes will be happy together."

Clytemnestra rolled her eyes and gave me a condescending look. "Oh, Helen, Lord Thyestes is *ancient*. I'm marrying his son Prince Tantalus."

"Oh. So you won't be queen of Mykenae?"

"You'd like that, wouldn't you?" She gave the carding combs a hard tug. "Sorry to disappoint you, but my husband will be king of Mykenae after his father dies, so you won't be the only queen in this family. And Mykenae is richer than Sparta too!"

"That's not what I—" I began.

She didn't let me finish. "I can't *wait* to get away from this place. I'm tired of having to listen to Ione and Mother and Father and—and to everyone say how *pretty* you are all the time, as if that's an excuse for why you never do any *real* work."

"But I don't think they—"

It was no use trying to get a word in. My sister had made up her mind: "You never pick up a spindle unless someone makes you do it, and I've never seen you having a lesson at the big loom. As for learning how to make medicines from Mother—" She made a scornful sound. "I feel sorry for Sparta when you're queen. What are you going to do? Tell your husband and the rest of the court that they can wrap your *beauty* around them to keep warm and well all winter?

"*I* made Father a long tunic," she went on. "I made it *myself,* start to finish, from carding the wool to weaving the cloth to embroidering a pattern of waves on the sleeves. When I gave it to him, I told him I chose waves because Aphrodite was born from the sea and I knew how much he loved her. Do you know what he said to me then?" Clytemnestra's eyes narrowed. "He said, 'What a lucky man I am to have one daughter who's as clever as Athena and another who's as beautiful as Aphrodite!' Even when you did *nothing,* even when you weren't there, he praised *you!*"

She threw down her carding combs and swept into the shadows of the palace, leaving me standing like a statue in the courtyard, all my wishes for her future happiness unsaid.

The ambassador from Mykenae stayed with us for ten days. The night before he left, Father gave a great banquet to honor him and to celebrate Clytemnestra's betrothal. Ione helped me get ready for the feast, picking out my dress, fussing over my hair, and chattering away the whole time.

"Ah, look at how well you've healed in just ten days' time!" she exclaimed, examining my feet before slipping them into my best pair of sandals. It was true:

The gash on my foot was almost gone. I only needed one thin strip of cloth to cover it. "You must have made a good sacrifice to Aesculapius the Healer."

She straightened up and began to arrange my hair. As much as I wanted to dress and groom myself, Ione refused. As my nurse, she'd get the credit or blame for how I looked at the banquet.

"What lovely curls!" she said, working diligently with the ivory comb. "That Mykenaean will have to fill his mouth with gold when he describes you to his master, Lord Thyestes."

"Why would he need to do that?" I asked.

My nursemaid chuckled. "Do you imagine that your sister's marrying the only prince of Mykenae? Lord Thyestes has plenty of sons, and his royal brother, Atreus, has at least two that I know of. Those Mykenaeans breed like rabbits."

I giggled, then clapped my hands to my mouth. "Ione, what an awful thing to say!" I exclaimed, still laughing.

"Well, no one can deny it. I only pray that your sister's getting a good man. With a family that large, there's bound to be at least one rotten apple on the tree. If even half the stories I've heard about the kings of Mykenae are true—"

"What stories?" Mother had stopped Polydeuces before he could tell me anything.

"I really shouldn't say a word; nasty things." She

put down the comb and began to weave a strand of freshwater pearls through my hair.

I turned around quickly and grabbed her hands. "*Please* tell me, Ione. I promise I won't repeat anything. You won't get into trouble for telling me."

"Hmph! There's no chance of that unless you come right out and mention my name. *Everyone* knows about those Mykenaeans."

"I don't. And I think I should; my sister *is* going to be their queen." I gave her my most persuasive smile, the one I'd used since babyhood whenever I wanted to get her to bend the rules for me, just a little.

"Oh, all right." She gave in easily. I think she wanted to tell me all the tales. "But turn around and sit still or you'll never be ready for the feast tonight, and then I *will* be in trouble. Your sister is marrying Lord Thyestes's oldest son, but that man wasn't always king of Mykenae. At first his brother, Lord Atreus, ruled."

She made a small scornful sound. "*Brothers.* Not all brothers are like yours, my dear; I helped raise Castor and Polydeuces, so I know. They may quarrel and scuffle, but it's all quickly over and forgotten. There's true affection and loyalty binding those two. If they were stones in a wall, you couldn't fit a knife blade between them.

"But Atreus and Thyestes—! I've heard they hate one another as fiercely as if they came from separate sides of the earth instead of from the same mother's womb. They both want Mykenae, and so they've spent their lives fighting and scheming and betraying one another in order to seize the throne. Back and forth it's gone—first Atreus was king, then Thyestes, then Atreus again—and every time the crown changes hands, it's stained with fresh blood. I heard that Lord Atreus even killed his own wife, a Cretan princess, because she dared to smile at his brother!"

"Just for *smiling* at him?" I couldn't believe it.

Ione coughed nervously. "Well, perhaps she did more than smile. But that's nothing. The worst is this: *I* heard that Lord Atreus actually killed some of his brother's children, then ordered their flesh cooked and served it *to their own father*! Lord Thyestes didn't suspect a thing until after that abominable meal, when Atreus showed him their *heads*."

For someone who hadn't wanted to tell me one word about the Mykenaeans, Ione was taking unnatural glee in repeating one grisly horror after another.

"What kind of a family is my sister marrying into?" I cried, jerking my head out from under Ione's busy hands.

My nurse seemed unconcerned with Clytemnestra's future among such people. "Tsk. Now look what you've done, torn the pearls loose and mussed your curls. I'll have to start all over."

"But Clytemnestra can't marry a monster!" I protested.

"Oh, hush," Ione said calmly, taking up the comb again. "Prince Tantalus never harmed anyone, and as for the stories about his father and uncle—I'm sure they're only stories. Do you think your royal parents would give their darling girl to Mykenae if the tales were true?

"Of course, you won't have that problem, little bird," she went on. "As our queen-to-be, you'll pick yourself a good husband."

"Husband?" This time I jerked my head so suddenly that my hair got tangled in the comb and I gave a little yelp of pain before I added, "I don't want a husband!" *And after hearing you talk, I* definitely *don't want a Mykenaean,* I thought.

"*Don't* isn't the same as *won't.*" Ione chuckled knowingly as she picked up the pearls.

It was a splendid, lavish feast intended to impress Lord Thyestes's ambassador so that when he went home he'd tell his master all about Sparta's wealth and power. The tables creaked under the weight of platters filled with stewed rabbit and mutton, broiled fish, crackling loaves of barley bread, round white cheeses, fresh salads decorated with mint and parsley, even the special treat of roasted venison. Mounds of almonds and slabs of honeycomb were offered to our guest in dishes that had come all the way from Crete. I loved their beautifully painted patterns of fish, dolphins, and big-eyed octopi.

Midway through the feast, my father made the ceremonial announcement about my sister's betrothal. Because she was the center of attention, Clytemnestra sat in a place of honor, between our parents, and glowed with pleasure when the Spartan nobles raised their voices in congratulations so loud they made the oil lamps flicker.

If my sister truly wanted to leave Sparta right away, Lord Thyestes's ambassador shared her eagerness. I was seated at Mother's left, so I had no trouble hearing when he leaned forward from his place beside Father and said, "Great lady, when can I tell Lord Thyestes to expect your noble daughter's arrival?"

Mother offered him a sweet smile. "Not for two years, at the very least. She's still too much of a child for marriage. I know that a young princess is often raised in her future husband's house, so she can learn her new people's ways, but if she's *too* young, she might become so homesick that she won't be able to think of anything except her family."

"With all respect, great lady," the ambassador said, bowing to my mother just a little bit, "Prince Tantalus will be her family."

I saw Mother's face harden until she looked like

an image of the goddess Artemis just before she sends an arrow through some unlucky mortal's heart. Her voice was icy when she replied, "With all my *royal* respect to your master, we who rule Sparta never employ messengers who think they can instruct a queen."

The Mykenaean turned pale. His apology was coldly formal, and Mother accepted it just as coldly. It took my father's hearty laugh to break the awkward mood and restore the banquet's festivity.

I wondered how disappointed my sister would be when she found out she'd have to spend two more years with us. I hoped she wouldn't feel that this was my fault too.

MY MOTHER'S PAST

The day after the banquet, I decided that I'd lost enough training time. I didn't want Glaucus to think that I'd given up my desire to learn a warrior's skills, so I bound my foot with extra cloth and slipped out of the palace to join my brothers. The gods be thanked, there was a big uproar at the gates as the ambassador left us. No one in the crowd noticed me, and Ione had quit being my watchdog.

When I reached the training ground, Glaucus was alone. And he didn't look happy. "Someone had better teach your brothers that only fools and children believe it's a brave thing to drink unwatered wine," he said. He pressed his lips together and shot a poisonous look at the palace walls. "If their heads hurt today, just wait until I get my hands on them tomorrow. Meanwhile, you and I had better find another place to work on your warrior skills, princess."

"Why?" I asked.

"Because once that Mykenaean wine-bag leaves, the guards will go back to their regular duties. They expect to see me training your brothers. Even the sight of a third 'boy' down here doesn't faze them—they probably reckon you for one of the princes' playmates, a servant's kid. But if they saw me spending my time on you alone, they'd smell a dead mouse in the barley and come charging down here to investigate. Understand?"

I nodded. Glaucus smiled, then picked up the bundle of practice javelins as easily as if they were made of straw. He strode off toward the river with me scurrying after him. I tried not to let him know that my heart was about to burst from sheer joy. Glaucus and all that he could teach me were mine alone, at least for one day. He wouldn't have to split his attention between me and my brothers. I felt like singing.

He led me to a narrow part of the river, forested on both banks, out of sight of the palace walls. He dropped the practice javelins and dove into the water without bothering to remove a single piece of clothing, not even his sandals. Once across, he cut rings into the bark of three huge trees on the far bank, then came swimming back before I could wonder whether I was supposed to follow him or stay put. (Just as well. I'd never learned how to swim.)

"Here," he said, handing me one of the practice javelins and nodding at the targets he'd improvised.

"Which one do you want me to hit?" I asked.

That amused him. "I'll be happy if I don't have to spend the rest of the day racing downstream, trying to recapture all the shafts that'll wind up in the river. Just try to get it across the water, princess."

His words made my face go hot. *He's trying to make me mad*, I thought. *He thinks he can control me like that, but it's my life: I say yes or no.*

I calmly picked up the first shaft, held it at eye level, and sighted down the length of it.

"I suppose that's all I'll be able to do with this one," I said. "It's warped. It won't fly true."

I picked up each one of the other fake spears and examined them in the same way. They were all just crooked enough to veer away from the target, no matter how skilled the thrower, and I said so.

The old soldier gave me a strange look, then checked the spears for himself. "Well, I'll be Hades's dinner guest!" he exclaimed. "You're right! Good for you, princess."

"I can still throw them across the river," I said, trying not to let him see how much his praise pleased me. "But you carved those targets for nothing."

"I have a better idea," he said. "Wait here."

He was gone for a while. I passed the time by flinging stones over the water. None of them made it to the far bank. Silently I gave thanks that there'd be no spear-throwing practice that day. My arm wasn't strong enough yet; I would have been mortified.

Glaucus came back through the trees, carrying something wrapped up in his cloak. He unfurled it and a short sword fell at my feet. It was the real thing, a bronze blade with a cutting edge that glittered in the sunlight. He must have gone all the way back to the palace to fetch it.

"Pick it up," Glaucus told me, drawing his own sword from his belt. "Let's see how it suits you."

I gazed at the weapon but couldn't bring myself to touch it. To hold a *real* sword—! It was a privilege I longed for and feared. Why was Glaucus giving me this chance so soon? Did he mean it to be an honor or a test? I hesitated, longing and just a bit afraid.

"Go on and take it, princess," Glaucus said. His smile was encouraging. "I just want to see what you can do with that. Don't worry: I promise not to hurt you, and the gods know you won't hurt me."

My hand closed on the hilt and I picked up the sword. "In that case, I'm ready to learn," I said.

My first real sword fight was a worse disaster than my first time using a real spear. The heavy blade was made for a grown man and was beautifully balanced.

That was the only thing that kept me from dropping it more than I did. My first swings were wild. When I swatted a tree trunk, the vibrations made my hand tingle and smart. I didn't even manage to cut the bark. As for my efforts to imitate Glaucus's fighting style, they were clumsier than a pig trying to walk on its hind legs. I know he didn't expect much of me my first time, but I'd expected more of myself.

I don't care what he said about just wanting to see what I can do with this blade, I thought. *He must be judging me. I've got to show him I can do better than this or he might change his mind about letting me train.*

The fear of being dismissed made me redouble my efforts, but with the same lack of effect. Glaucus held me at bay effortlessly, while I panted and stumbled and kept wiping sweat out of my eyes. I finally got so frustrated, trying to break through his guard, that I lost my patience and charged him, holding the bronze sword high over my head and howling like a wolf. He sidestepped and tripped me as I went flying past. When I sprawled on my face in the dirt, he touched the back of my neck lightly with the tip of his own weapon.

"There's no shame in dying in battle, princess," he said. "But this would have been a very stupid death. The lesson's done." Then he picked up my sword and strode away. I was left to trail back into the palace, sore, exhausted, and convinced that I'd made such a fool of myself that Glaucus would never want me on the training ground again. I decided that I wouldn't give him the chance to banish me. Instead, I stayed in the palace the next day, joining my sister and the other women. I sat near Clytemnestra while she worked at the big loom, surrounded by servants, slaves, and ladies of the palace, all of us busy at the woman's work of making cloth. My hands were still sore from my wretched attempt at swordsmanship, my fingers clumsy as I held the distaff and tried to make the spindle obey me. I hated every moment, but I stuck to the tedious chore because I'd decided it was my only future.

The room where we worked was well lit by the sun, heavy with the fresh scent of washed fleece. The women chattered while they worked, hummed old songs, told stories, spoke gently or impatiently to the younger girls who were still learning their skills. It was a peaceful, safe place, but so is a grave.

I looked at my sister. Her face was serene, all her attention focused on the pattern she was creating on the great loom. In that instant, I realized that she no longer envied me anything—not my looks, or the way the grown-ups seemed to favor me, or even the fact that I'd be queen of Sparta someday. Our rivalry was over; she had what she'd always wanted. She, too, was going to be a queen.

I spent five days with the women, inside the

palace walls. Every time I considered stealing back to the training ground I remembered my failure. My face burned with fresh humiliation, and I abandoned the thought once more.

On the sixth day of my self-enforced captivity, something happened that changed everything. We were all working together, as usual. By now it was quite clear that each thread we spun or wove or embroidered was intended for my sister's bride goods. The older women murmured about how strange it was that the queen didn't come to help prepare her daughter's dowry.

"It's natural," one of them remarked, her needle making a pattern of lilies along the hem of a gown. "She doesn't want to face the fact that she's losing her babies."

"That's true," another added. "Didn't you hear about what she said to the ambassador? He wanted our princess to come to Mykenae before winter, but the queen refused."

"What does she think *that* will do?" a third snapped. "Children grow up and leave us. That's how it is, even for queens. Does she think she can stop time by—"

Her voice dropped abruptly into silence. A hush fell over the room. The women around me were laying down their work and rising like a flock of herons taking flight. Even my sister stood up from her bench at the great loom and turned, making a graceful gesture of respect. Queen Leda had come.

I scrambled to my feet and made a quick, clumsy bow, holding up my hands to greet her. In public, even when the only other people present were slaves, we royal children had to salute our parents with the same reverence we would pay to the gods.

Mother acknowledged all of us with a curt nod, then pointed at my discarded distaff and spindle. "Helen, pick those up and come with me." Her voice was almost as sharp as when she'd reprimanded the Mykenaean ambassador. My stomach turned sour. *What have I done?*

We walked down the hallways of the palace in silence. I was almost too frightened to breathe. She led the way up a blue-and-crimson-painted stairway and brought me to the bedroom she shared with my father. It had a window that looked out over a small thicket of bright flowers and sweet-smelling herbs.

Mother sat down on the bed and motioned for me to sit beside her. The air was still and warm. I could hear the bees buzzing as they drank nectar from the courtyard flowers. Without a word, Mother took the spindle and distaff away from me.

"Is this the way you're always going to handle troubles, Helen?" she asked, her voice soft and kind. "By running away?"

I blushed. "I don't know what you mean."

She patted my hand, then without warning grabbed it and turned it over so she could examine the palm. One of her fingers traced the signs that the sword hilt had left on top of the calluses I'd already earned from the wooden spears. Six days hadn't been long enough to erase them.

"Oh, but you do," she said. "Why do your hands look more like your brothers' than Clytemnestra's? Tell me the truth."

"You already know it, don't you," I said. There was no need to make it a question. My mother nodded. "Who told you?" I asked.

"No one had to tell me," Mother replied. "I saw you practicing with the sword on the day Lord Thyestes's ambassador went back to Mykenae. I'd had enough of him, so I left your father to handle the ceremony of farewell without me and went off to hunt rabbits."

"Hunting rabbits?" I stared at my mother as if she'd grown a pair of horns. *"You?"*

She laughed, and twined a lock of my hair around one finger. "Your father loves rabbit stewed with onions. He says the ones I catch just for him taste best."

I tried to picture my tall, elegant mother crouching in the underbrush to set a snare. "Who taught you how to make rabbit traps?" I asked.

"Traps?" she echoed. "I haven't got the patience

for traps." She got up and reached under the big chest at the foot of the bed. The long wooden box she dragged out was painted with curls of ivy, garlands of pine boughs, and a pattern of wild boars, tusked and bristling. When she opened it, I gaped at the black bronze-banded bow and the arrows fletched with pheasant feathers.

"This is what I use to hunt," Mother said, grinning as she strung the bow. She did it as naturally as breathing. "Not just rabbits. I bring home game birds too, and deer, and even foxes, when I can outsmart them. The first time I saw your father, I'd just come home from the hunt. The forests of Calydon are thick with game, but the deer are so clever that it was the first time I'd managed to bring one down. I was so proud of what I'd done that I insisted on carrying the buck into the throne room myself and dropped it at my father's feet before I noticed we had a guest." She smiled at the memory.

"I'll bet Father thought you were Artemis herself," I said.

That made my mother laugh. "Not Artemis. You know how he feels about her. But he did say he mistook me for one of her huntress nymphs. That was just before he told me he had to marry me or die."

I made a face. "Father said *that*?"

"Men say many things when they want to win a woman. Whether or not they mean what they say . . ."

She shrugged. "Your father meant it. Poor soul, it seemed like he *would* die, because none of my father's advisers thought I should marry him. Tyndareus came to Calydon as a landless exile; his brother had stolen his kingdom."

The story of Father's early trouble and final triumph was so well known that the palace stones could tell it. "Did you come to Sparta to marry him after he won back his crown?" I asked. "Or did he have to go back to Calydon for you?"

"Are you asking because you want to know, or because you want to distract me from what we *need* to talk about?" Mother asked, her fingers curled around the polished curve of her bow.

I looked away. She touched my chin and gently turned me back to face her.

"It's all right, Helen," she said. "When I was your age, I, too, believed that if you buried a problem, it would go away."

"There's no problem," I said. "I'm through."

"Why? Because of what Glaucus said to you? I was standing in the shelter of the trees. I saw and heard everything. He was right, you know. You *did* act stupidly, running headlong at him like that, and it was just the sort of thing that would've gotten you killed in a real fight."

"I know," I said, miserable. "That's why I quit!"

"Yes," she said. "But why did you start?"

"I don't know. It was silly."

"We both know that's a lie," my mother said. She set aside her bow and picked up the women's tools I'd brought with me. She studied the thread wound around the spindle and the clump of carded wool tied to the distaff. I knew I'd made a mess of both and waited for her to say so.

Instead, she said, "For once, your distaff doesn't look like you stuck it into a bird's nest. And look at this: It's the smoothest thread I've ever seen you spin."

"It ought to be," I muttered. "I worked on it for five days."

"And how many days did you work with the sword? One. Don't you think the sword deserves at least as much of a chance as the spindle?"

I gave her a startled look. "Are you saying that you *want* me to go back to training with my brothers?"

My mother held my hands in both of hers. "That would be easy, wouldn't it?" she said. "So easy to let someone else make your choices for you. That way, if you fail, it isn't your fault." She clasped my hands more tightly. "You deserve to live a better life than that."

"I—I don't understand." My mother's words confused me. I was only ten years old.

She let go of my hands and leaned back. "You will, if you think about it. Then, whichever choice you make—sword or spindle or both—will be truly yours."

As I stepped out of the bedroom doorway, one

last question made me pause. "Mother?" I rested one hand on the doorpost, with its carved pattern of palm branches. "Mother, will you teach me how to hunt?"

She gave me a strange look. "Gladly. But why?"

"Because if I do choose to go back to the training ground and Father finds out and wants me to stop, I want to bring him a whole *cauldron* of stewed rabbit so he'll change his mind."

When Mother stopped laughing, she took me outside, off into the olive grove, and gave me my first archery lesson. I didn't hit anything, but as Mother told me (with a perfectly straight face), I did manage to scare the olives off a couple of trees.

I went back to the training ground the next morning. Glaucus didn't say a word about my absence. He was busy working with my brothers, so the only welcome I got from him was a silent nod and the hint of a satisfied smile.

He had the boys practicing with wooden swords, fighting both of them at once and winning. He made it look so easy, even though they outnumbered him and were younger and faster on their feet. When he smacked Castor's sword aside with one blow and disarmed Polydeuces on the backstroke, I first thought: *There's no shame in losing a match to someone like that.*

While my brothers scrambled to pick up their swords, Glaucus turned to me. "Well, princess," he said. "Will you be staying, or is this just a visit?"

I let his sarcasm wash past me. "I'm staying," I said simply. "If you'll take me back."

This time his smile was wide. "*She* spoke with you, didn't she," he stated. "The queen. I thought I caught sight of her in the woods that day."

"What? *Mother* told you to come back?" Castor exchanged a bewildered look with his twin.

"She didn't *tell* me to do anything," I said.

"No," Glaucus said, looking at me thoughtfully. "I don't suppose anyone could do that." I didn't know whether to be pleased or insulted.

The first day of my return to training didn't go well. I was rusty, and my brothers each took full advantage of that when paired off against me. Wooden swords leave wide, purple bruises, but by the end of the day I'd given back one for every five I got, which was good enough for me.

I knew I wouldn't be able to outshine my brothers anytime soon. Even if I trained with them daily and sacrificed a whole herd of sheep to Ares, it couldn't happen: They were five years older than me, and they'd begun their training when I was still an infant. Worse for me, at fifteen my brothers were already tough and strong. How I envied them for the way their bodies had changed, and how I wished mine would do the same!

6

NEWS FROM MYKENAE

I got my wish for a changed body the year I turned twelve, though not the changes I'd been hoping for. Overnight, my legs and arms became so long that I couldn't govern them. That made me clumsy, both in the house and on the training ground. Clytemnestra hadn't been cursed by any such sudden growth. She was still small and graceful. I hoped no one else had noticed how awkward, how *different* I'd become.

I had to give up that hope once and for all on a late-winter day halfway through my twelfth year. While cold rain pelted down outdoors, I stayed in the palace, helping Mother, Clytemnestra, and Ione store some of my sister's bride goods. Father came in to see how we were doing. If he intended to inspect the piles of carefully folded cloth, he forgot all about it when he took a good look at me.

"By Ceres, Ione, what have you been feeding her?" Father exclaimed, resting his hands on my shoulders. "She's taller than a boar spear!"

"You needn't tell *me*." My nurse snorted. "I'm the one who's got to make her new clothes all the time, so she still looks like she's wearing a dress instead of a boy's tunic."

"Well, Helen, whatever you've been eating that's made you sprout up like this, you could use a little more," he told me. He held out one of my arms. "Tsk. It's a reed." His tone was fond, but his words stung me anyhow.

Clytemnestra chimed in, oh-so-sweetly. "Father, don't make fun of Helen. I'm sure she feels bad enough about her face without you teasing about what's happened to the rest of her."

"What's this nonsense?" Father demanded, giving her a severe look. "There's nothing wrong with Helen's face!"

"Of course not," Mother said calmly. "My looks changed in just the same way when I was her age—my face, my body, everything so bony and bumbling! But after a couple more years passed, it was quite a different story." She smiled.

How could she tell such obvious lies? She'd *never*

been as scrawny and clumsy as me. It wasn't possible! A stork didn't turn into a swan. I couldn't stand to hear any more. "Will you all stop talking about me as if I were a stone?" I exclaimed. "I'm right here!" And with that, I *wasn't* right there. I ran off, my cheeks flaming with embarrassment, leaving my family to pick apart my appearance to their hearts' content.

The awful thing was, Clytemnestra was right. My face had changed along with my body. When guests came to Sparta, all their compliments now seemed to be about my height. I learned that *regal* is just a polite way to say spindle-thin and sapling-tall. I didn't need Mother's mirror to tell me that I was no longer "the pretty one," but every year on my birthday I stole a peek at it anyway. It told me what I already knew: My face was thinner, the cheekbones and chin sharper, the nose more prominent, and the mouth wider-looking.

I didn't *need* to be "the pretty one," but I needed to be *something*. If I wasn't pretty anymore, what was I? Who was I now?

I was glad to have the training ground for my refuge. When I was there, I didn't have time to brood over my changed looks. I used Glaucus's lessons to get my gawky arms and legs back under control.

By the time I was thirteen, I not only looked like a younger version of Polydeuces, I was fighting like one too. Sometimes I was even able to give my brothers better than I got during our sparring matches, though by that time they were eighteen, full-grown young men, using real swords except when I challenged them to a bout. They complained that I won because they'd forgotten how to handle a wooden blade. Glaucus just told them to shut up and accept defeat like honorable men. As for me, I told them that as soon as Glaucus let me use a real sword all the time, they'd need to find some new excuse when I beat them.

That day finally came when I turned fourteen. There had been a great fuss in the palace that morning. Clytemnestra and I stood beside Father while he made a thanksgiving sacrifice to his favorite goddess, Aphrodite, in our honor. After that, we were given sweetened, watered wine and plate after plate of cake drenched with honey and sprinkled with chopped figs and almonds. After just a few bites it got too sweet for me, but Clytemnestra made a pig of herself, honey dribbling down her chin.

I couldn't wait to get away. Glaucus had been dropping hints for a whole month about how there'd be something special waiting for me when my fourteenth birthday came. As soon as I could manage it, I ducked away, changed my clothes, and raced to the training ground.

My brothers were already there, grinning, nudging each other, and whispering until Glaucus reminded them that even though they had beards and brawn, he could still put a sandal up their backsides. They dropped their clowning, and only then he gave me the sword.

It was more like a large hunter's knife than the warrior's blades my brothers used, but it was new. I could tell that Glaucus had had it made specially for me. I was so overjoyed, I felt ready to fly.

Two months after our fourteenth birthday, on the very day that Clytemnestra sewed the final stitch of crimson thread into the delicate, saffron-yellow wool of her last and finest of her bridal dresses, a courier from Mykenae came running up the steep, rocky path to the palace. It was a most wonderful coincidence; you could almost hear the gods laughing.

We royal sons and daughters all knew that something significant was happening. Father sent word for us to put on our most splendid clothes and come to the great hall. This was the room where all important visitors were greeted and where Father handed down his most vital decisions about the future of Sparta.

There was a small blaze burning in the large, circular hearth that lay in the middle of the room, in front of Father's throne. The thin thread of smoke wafted up and out past the second-floor balconies that ran all around the wide square opening above. The sun was still high enough to pour light into the hall, so no one had to light the stone oil lamps.

My brothers were at Father's right, sunlight and flame flickering over their tanned faces. My place was at Mother's left, and Clytemnestra was between our parents. We were all supposed to keep our eyes straight ahead, the picture of dignity, but even though I stood as if my feet had taken root among the brightly painted patterns on the floor, I couldn't help letting my eyes wander.

The messenger stood on the far side of the fire, on travel-weary legs. He'd been given wine and other refreshments the moment that he arrived (we Spartans knew how to be good hosts) and was even offered some time to rest after the long journey from the north, but apparently he'd refused.

What he's got to say must be urgent, I thought. *I wonder if he's brought us good news or bad?*

Father's throne was carved from stone, massive and immovable, but for certain occasions a smaller, wooden throne was brought in for Mother. When I saw her sitting beside him like that, tall and proud and beautiful as a goddess, I found it hard to believe that this was the same woman who'd gone hunting through the hills with me just the other day. The deer we'd shot was in the hands of the kitchen slaves. My arrow was the first to hit it, but hers was the one that brought it down.

I saw how the messenger stared at Queen Leda, drinking in her beauty. *He's probably thinking that it's all true, the story about how Zeus himself fell in love with Mother,* I thought. He was so distracted that Father had to ask him twice to speak. *Finally* he did. "Hail, Lord Tyndareus! Greetings and love from my noble master, Lord Thyestes of Mykenae. My king asks the gods to bless you and your house and bids me say that the day you have all prayed for has come. Prince Tantalus is ready to receive his bride. Lord Thyestes has made rich sacrifices in all the temples of Mykenae and even sent offerings to Apollo's shrine at Delphi, asking for blessings on your children's future. The omens are good; the gods approve."

"May the gods bless Lord Thyestes and all his royal house," Father replied, speaking as formally as the occasion demanded. "You will feast with us tonight to celebrate the happy news you've brought us. You will then return to Lord Thyestes tomorrow and tell him to prepare to receive my daughter, the princess Clytemnestra. She'll leave in five days' time, accompanied by her bridal goods and attendants, including her brothers, the princes Castor and Polydeuces, the royal sons of Sparta. Tell your master that my queen and I pray our daughter will be a wife worthy of Lord Thyestes's son."

I looked at my sister. She'd spent the past four years of her life preparing to become Prince Tantalus's bride, the future queen of Mykenae. Now the waiting was over. In only five days, she'd leave her land, her home, her family. What was she feeling? I tried to read her face. Her lips were pressed together tightly and I saw a little red rising to her cheeks, but that was all.

She always did say she was eager to leave us, I thought. *I know we're supposed to stand here like statues, but if I were the one getting my heart's desire, at least I'd smile, just a little.*

After the feast that night, I took the earliest possible opportunity to go back to my room. I didn't bother calling for Ione to fetch a little oil lamp—the moon was almost full, and the stars washed the sky with light. I could see well enough, and I wanted to be alone. I needed some time to myself, to think about what my life was going to be like after Clytemnestra left.

My sister and I might not have gotten along as well as Castor and Polydeuces, yet there was still a bond between us. I treasured the times that she'd treated me like a friend, not a rival. What would she say if I let her know that I envied her as much as she seemed to envy me? She had such a talent for making beautiful things! The blouse she'd embroidered as a gift for me was the finest thing I owned. When she helped me with my own dreadful needlework, she did it without making fun of my poor skills. I think that was the best way she had to let me know she cared about me. I wished I had a way to show how deeply I cared about her.

A cool breeze came in through the window,

bringing the green scent of cedars and pine from the hills. I stood there gazing out toward the mountains, wondering if my sister would believe me if I told her how much I'd miss her.

A strange sound from behind me made me turn quickly. The moonlight couldn't reach every corner of my room; the small, half-choked sound was coming from a deep pool of darkness in the corner nearest the doorway.

"Who's there?" I called. The sound came again, and now I recognized it: a sob.

Before I could say another word, the sob broke into a harsh bout of weeping as a shadow came rushing out of the corner and into my arms. Soft hands clung to me, a tear-streaked face pressed itself against my cheek, and in my ear my sister's anguished voice cried, "Oh, Helen, it's really *happening*. I just realized that it . . . I'm scared. I don't care if I'm never queen of anything, I don't want to marry a *stranger*! Sister, save me; you're our future queen, there must be *something* you can do. Talk to Father, to Mother, beg them to change their minds; they'll listen to *you*. Don't let them do this to me! Oh, Helen, please help me. I want to die!"

I let her cry in my arms until we heard the sound of footsteps and Ione came running into my room, carrying a lamp.

"There you are!" she exclaimed when the light

fell on Clytemnestra. "When you weren't in your room, I—"

My sister threw herself into our nurse's arms and wept louder while I told Ione what was wrong. She was sympathetic, but coldly practical. "A fine time to change your mind!" she told Clytemnestra. Then she turned to me. "Not that it would've mattered if she'd said no to this four years ago. It's Lord Tyndareus's decision. You can talk to your father all you like, child, but don't expect him to call off the marriage. Didn't you hear the messenger? The gods have spoken."

Ione had a point. The gods desired my sister's marriage. More important, the king of Mykenae desired it, and Mykenae was powerful and proud. If Father called off the wedding, the insult could bring war. One girl's unhappiness was nothing next to the safety of all Sparta. He'd never budge, but I couldn't just accept that without doing something for my sister. At least I had to *try*.

Lord Thyestes's messenger headed back north the next morning. As soon as he was out of the palace, I went to my parents and said I needed to speak with them about an urgent, private matter. The three of us went up to their sleeping chamber, where I told them that when Clytemnestra and my brothers set out for Mykenae, I wanted to go too.

"Out of the question," Father said almost before I'd finished speaking.

"Tyndareus, wait," Mother said, taking my hand. "Let her tell you her reasons before you say no."

"What reasons could she have that would be more important than her safety?" he countered. "The roads are full of dangers."

"But you're sending Clytemnestra over those same roads," I pointed out.

"She *has* to go," he said. "You don't."

"But I *want* to," I said. "My sister needs me. She's going to a strange land, a strange house, a total stranger for a husband. It's terrifying! If I travel with her, she'll have something familiar to hold on to, someone to talk to on the journey."

"She'll have the boys," Father replied.

"They'll be on horseback all the way to Mykenae," Mother told him. "And they won't have time to talk to her or even listen to her: They'll be too busy staying alert for any perils on the road."

"She'll be riding in a cart, all alone," I put in. "Father, *please*. She's so unhappy. Let me go!"

"Let you go?" he echoed. "Have you forgotten you're the heir to Sparta? Do you expect me to put all of my children into Thyestes's power? Why don't I just hand him my sword and let him cut my throat?"

"But Thyestes is our kinsman now," Mother maintained. "He'd never—"

"A lot that means to a Mykenaean!" Father countered. "You know the stories."

"So do you," Mother said bitterly. "You still gave him our daughter."

"What choice did I have?" Father's jaw tightened. "He wanted an alliance, guaranteed by marriage. Clytemnestra is the price of peace."

"Is that what you want me to do when I'm queen of Sparta?" I asked. "*Buy* peace?"

Father gave me a sad look. "I don't do this gladly, Helen. We Spartans are never afraid to fight, but even if we'd win a war with Mykenae, it would take so many years and cost us so many lives that Sparta would be defenseless afterward. Your enemies will always be watching for any signs of weakness. Remember *that* when you're queen."

"Then why not show Lord Thyestes just how strong we *really* are?" I asked. "Father, if you let me go to Mykenae with Clytemnestra, it will be like saying, *See the power of Sparta, Lord Thyestes! We're so mighty that we have no fear of letting all of our children travel beyond our borders at once, even our future queen! We have no fear of you at all.*"

"That," said Father, "is a bad idea." And he sent me away.

In the days that followed, my sister did nothing but weep quietly in her bed while the servants packed her things. I spent my days at her side, trying to cheer her, telling her how much I envied her the chance to travel, to see new places, new people. Who knew what adventures the road to Mykenae might hold? She only sobbed that she didn't *want* any adventures, she just wanted to stay home or die.

She refused to eat, making Ione so frantic that she fetched Mother. Mother took one look at Clytemnestra's haggard face and went to speak with Father. Soon the palace halls echoed with sharp words and loud arguments as Father's counselors and highest-ranking noblemen were drawn into the matter.

On the afternoon of the fourth day, Mother sat beside me on Clytemnestra's bed and told me to go to my room. Puzzled, I obeyed, and when I got there I found Ione busily packing my clothes. Father came in before I could question her.

"Your idea about going to Mykenae with Clytemnestra isn't so bad after all," he said wearily. "It's certainly the best I've heard, these past few days. Others have just said everything from 'Call off the marriage' to 'Just send her, weeping or not; she's Lord Thyestes's problem now.' It's bad enough that I must give her in marriage to Mykenae. I'll tear out my own heart before I cause her any further pain. Your brothers will look after you, and you'll ride with my best soldiers for guards. Do what you can to comfort your sister, and may the gods watch over all my children."

PART II
MYKENAE

THYESTES'S SNARE

The next dawn found me seated beside my sister as our ox-drawn cart began the tedious overland trek to Mykenae. Even though the hard wooden slats we sat on were thickly cushioned with folded cloaks and blankets, I still felt as though my spine was going to be jounced out of my body when the lumbering wheels rolled over the next rock in our path.

And the smell! The gods alone knew what the oxen had been eating, to give off such a stench. I tried breathing through my mouth, but it didn't help.

Clytemnestra dealt with the discomforts of the road by complaining, her voice crowding my ears so thoroughly that it often blotted out the creaking of the cart, the tramping of our guards' sandaled feet, and the clash, clatter, and jangle of the wagons behind us, all loaded with my sister's bridal goods. I let her grumble all she liked—it was better than her helpless tears. Sometimes I persuaded my brothers to ride their horses alongside our cart and let her gnaw on their ears, for a change.

It worked, but it was tiring for all of us. By the time we reached the outskirts of Mykenae, the four of us were heartily sick and tired of each other's company. As our train of wagons began the climb up to the great gates of the city, two colossal stone lions above the entrance to the citadel glared down at us in vain. We were all too worn out to be impressed.

We were welcomed with bread and salt by Lord Thyestes himself. The ruler of Mykenae looked like one of Zeus's own thunderclouds, his hair and beard a stormy gray, his eyes flashing like lightning. I didn't believe his words of friendship for a minute. He had a wolf's smile. It made my skin creep every time he looked at me, and he looked at me much too long and too often for comfort.

That night I couldn't sleep. Lord Thyestes had given me a queenly room all to myself. Though there were two loyal Spartan soldiers standing guard outside my door, I was too tense to close my eyes. I'd wanted to share a room with my sister, but the king wouldn't allow that. He claimed it would be an insult to all Sparta if I weren't given lodging worthy of my rank. Maybe he was telling the truth, but I still felt like the deer that the hunting hounds isolate from the herd before they bring her down.

I tossed and turned, then got up and looked for the long, narrow box that held my jewelry and ornaments. As the heir of Sparta I'd been sent to Mykenae with enough necklaces, pins, and earrings to show off our land's prosperity. The box holding them was Glaucus's gift to me, and only the two of us knew its secret: When I tilted back the lid, with its inlaid patterns of pomegranates, and touched a secret catch inside, the false bottom of the box came loose, revealing my sword.

It comforted me to hold the little blade and practice some of the fighting moves that Glaucus had taught me. Just knowing that I wasn't helpless was enough to push my fear of Lord Thyestes and his wolfish grin back into the shadows. Smiling, I hid the sword away again and went to sleep.

My sister was married on the third day of our visit. It was a grand event, with lavish sacrifices made to all the gods and two nights of feasting. Clytemnestra's husband, Tantalus, wasn't young or handsome, but he wasn't *too* old or ugly either, and his homely face was so kind that it was impossible to believe he was Lord Thyestes's son.

"When he saw how frightened I was, he made it a point to tell me that even though we're married, we won't live as husband and wife until I'm ready," Clytemnestra confided in me as we sat together at the table during the first banqueting night. Her fears had begun to fade and she looked like her old self again. "Look at the wedding gift he gave me!" She proudly showed off the gold diadem in her hair with its embossed design of ivy leaves.

"I helped him choose it!" The boy seated beside me blurted out the words as though he'd been saving them up all his life. I knew who he was, because he'd been presented to us along with all the rest of the Mykenaean nobility: Prince Aegisthus, Lord Thyestes's youngest living son. He was skinny, dark, about the same age as my sister and me, and had the first soft sprouting of whiskers on his upper lip.

"It's beautiful," I said. "You did a good job."

The simple compliment made him blush crimson. "I just told Tantalus that girls like plant patterns more than animals," he muttered. "That's right, isn't it? Or do you like animal patterns better?"

I smiled at him. "I like both."

"Because if you'll tell me what you *really* like, I'll make sure to get it for you."

My smile wavered. "You don't need to—"

"But I want to!" Suddenly, Aegisthus was gazing at me as if I were something he feared and wanted at the same time. "At first I didn't, but now that I've seen you"—he gulped for air—"I want you to like me."

"I *do* like you." I said it without thinking. "You don't need to give me an expensive gift for that."

"But you've got to have a bridal gift from me," he said. "One that's good enough for someone like you."

I don't know how the rest of the banquet went. I was too stunned by Aegisthus's declaration. Only the bride's husband could give her a gift as rich and gorgeous as a gold diadem. Suddenly it was clear: Without anyone bothering to ask or tell me *or* my father, it had been decided that I was going to marry Aegisthus. No need to wonder who'd made *that* decision. How convenient for Mykenae.

That night I sent one of my guards to fetch my brothers. I sat in the dark, clutching the hilt of my sword, until they came. When I told them what I'd learned, they wanted to scoop me up and race back to Sparta as fast as their horses could run. Polydeuces wanted to kick Thyestes over a cliff first.

"Stop it," Castor said. "You know we can't do any of that. If we run away, the Mykenaeans will use the insult as an excuse to start a war."

"Even if they don't do that, they'll take it out on Clytemnestra," I added. "This is all my fault for insisting on coming here. I'm going to have to deal with the consequences." I took a deep breath to slow my racing heart. "It'll be all right. As long as Thyestes doesn't do anything to *force* me into marrying his son, I'll just have to put up with the rest of it until it's time for us to go home."

"*I* say it's time to go home *now*," Polydeuces insisted. "Before Thyestes can come up with some scheme to keep you here until you agree to the marriage."

"He can keep me here until the sky shatters," I replied. "I won't marry Aegisthus or any other Mykenaean princeling, and he can't make me!"

My brothers just shook their heads.

Castor and Polydeuces tried to stay with me as much as possible the next day. They were waiting for me the instant I stepped out of my room.

"What are you doing here?" I asked.

"Protecting you," Castor said.

"I don't think you need to do that," I said. "I doubt he's going to abduct me. Where would he take me? I'm already inside his walls." I was trying to make a joke of a tense situation, but my brothers didn't see the humor. They also didn't see that Thyestes's strength wasn't in direct attack but in subtlety.

Though my brothers did their best to stay by my side all day, Thyestes found one excuse after another to separate us. In the morning he told my brothers that the young warriors of Mykenae wanted to test their skills against the princes of Sparta. How could Castor and Polydeuces refuse? And how could I be allowed to go with them when girls were forbidden to watch men's athletic contests? In the afternoon he told them that they had to speak for Sparta before the Mykenaean nobles. That was no place for a girl either, even the Spartan queen-to-be.

Keeping my brothers and me apart was only part of the old fox's plan. While Castor and Polydeuces were elsewhere, the king pushed Aegisthus and me together. I could have hidden myself away in my room until the banquet, but I was no coward. I was Helen of Sparta, and I wouldn't run away when I could fight.

The gods must have approved of my bravery, though poor Aegisthus suffered for his father's arrogance. It was sad. He tried his awkward best to entertain and impress me, while I pretended he wasn't there. My coldness confused and hurt him, I could tell, but I didn't want to give him any false encouragement and I didn't know what else to do.

That night, during the second wedding banquet, my brothers tried to introduce the subject of our return to Sparta. Predictably, Lord Thyestes refused to hear a word about it. "How can you go so soon? You'll break your sister's heart." He gave Clytemnestra a look of false fondness that quickly became a frown when she made no move to look appropriately heartbroken. He tried a different tactic. "Of course, if you haven't found our hospitality here to be good enough for you, I'll understand if you leave."

What could my brothers say to that without insulting the king of Mykenae? Castor and Polydeuces had to assure the king that they'd only offered to leave because they didn't want to burden Mykenae with the expense of lodging and feeding us and all our followers.

That was a mistake.

"I see." Lord Thyestes steepled his fingers. "How kind of you to consider the welfare of your sister's new home. By all means, then, send half your men back to Sparta tomorrow. I did wonder why you felt you had to come here surrounded by a small army. The roads between Sparta and Mykenae have bandits, not monsters."

Castor and Polydeuces exchanged a stricken look. They were not much of a match for the old king's wit. Now, if they refused to send home half our soldiers, they'd be liars. If they complied, we'd never have enough men on our side if Thyestes decided that the time had come to force me into marrying his youngest son.

So we discovered that words as well as swords could win battles.

My brothers yielded, telling the king that we were very grateful for his generosity and we'd stay as long as he liked. They made no mention of sending away any of our men, but Thyestes let that pass. As he sat there, stuffing his face with food, the chief steward of the palace approached and whispered something in his ear. Thyestes sat up straight, annoyed at being disturbed while he was eating.

"Yes, yes, I know he's been waiting all day; I've been busy," he said irritably, wiping the grease from his lips with the back of his hand. "Send him in."

The steward bowed and withdrew. He returned shortly, followed by a short, scowling man whose hair and clothes were still heavy with the dust of the road.

"Hail, Lord Thyestes of Mykenae," the man declaimed. "I bring greetings from my master, Lord Oeneus of Calydon."

Thyestes's eyebrows rose. Calydon, my mother's native land, lay far to the northwest, across the isthmus of Corinth. The messenger had a tale of wonders to tell us, a tale of the gods themselves. Old men at Lord Thyestes's table listened like spellbound children while the road-worn man told about how his master had made the worst mistake any mortal can. When he sacrificed to the gods in thanks for a good harvest, he forgot to include them all. Artemis, goddess of the moon and the hunt, received no sacrifice. It was an oversight, but the gods don't care about mortal excuses: They only know that the payment for any insult is revenge.

"Now a wild boar is ravaging Calydon," the messenger said. "A monstrous boar like a mountain, with hooves of bronze and tusks as big and sharp as scythes. The goddess Artemis sent him to punish my lord Oeneus. The beast destroys everything that crosses his path. His hooves and tusks tear up fields of grain; he breaks down the walls of houses and rampages through the streets of towns. He slaughters our herds and chases all the other game from our forests. The people starve. The hunters who've tried to kill him are gutted with a single slash of his tusks, their hounds trampled into bloody muck under the monster's hooves. And that is why, Lord Thyestes, my master has at last realized that this beast can't be killed by ordinary men. For this hunt, he wants heroes."

There was a great murmuring when the messenger fell silent. Many of the Mykenaeans rose to their feet, eager to start out for wild Calydon that very moment. Every young man there was ready to proclaim himself a hero. My brothers were no exception, but not because they wanted glory. "Lord Oeneus is our uncle!" Castor cried, leaping up from his place at the table. "His queen, Althea, is our mother's sister."

"Our kinsmen need us!" Polydeuces, too, leaped up. He gave our host a wicked grin as he added, "My lord Thyestes, we have no choice. We must go." I could have kissed him.

Before the king could open his mouth to offer a word of protest or argument, I rose from my place. "My brothers, the gods bless your bravery." I pictured myself as Mother at her most queenly as I announced, "I make a sacred vow, by Artemis the huntress, that on

the day you kill the boar, I'll make a thanksgiving sacrifice at her temple in Calydon with my own hands.
May the gods destroy me or any other who keeps me
from fulfilling this promise."

The Mykenaeans cheered my sisterly devotion as
I sat down. I stole a sideways look at our host. He
wasn't cheering. Instead, he looked ready to bite
through bronze. Between my brothers and me, the old
fox had been outfoxed. It was all I could do not to
crow in triumph.

PART III
CALYDON

THE HUNTRESS

The journey to Calydon was long and grueling, but I felt like singing all the way. Being free of Lord Thyestes was worth a thousand jolts in the oxcart.

During the trip north, I came to realize that my brothers really were all grown up, men in fact as well as name. As soon as we were out of sight of Mykenae, they began to take precautions for our protection, in case Thyestes decided to try to regain what he'd lost. It made me proud to see how Polydeuces organized our soldiers to stand double watches by night and how he commanded them to scout the land by day. A mouse couldn't have sneaked up on us.

As for Castor, he opened all the supplies that Thyestes had given us and called for volunteers to taste a mouthful of everything, down to the smallest clay jar of water. Even then, he insisted that half of our men eat first while the other half waited to see if the food and drink had any ill effects. (They didn't. Lord Thyestes wasn't *that* desperate to recapture me.)

All of this made it slow going for us until we reached Corinth, where we were able to get supplies we could trust. It was also in Corinth that my brothers suggested I go home.

"Go back?" I said. "You might as well have handed me over to Thyestes in the first place."

"You won't have to go through Mykenaean territory," Castor argued. "You can go home by ship; we'll send word to Mother and Father to have you met at the coast—"

"And break my vow to Artemis?" I asked sweetly. I had him there. A messenger was sent to Sparta to let our parents know that I would be traveling safely with my brothers, returning to Mother's homeland.

From Corinth, we were lucky enough to find a ship that was ready to sail for Calydon. My brothers and I had never traveled by sea, but Poseidon blessed us with a calm, swift, comfortable voyage, a real relief after that miserable, tooth-clattering oxcart. *I could get used to this*, I thought as I stood in the prow and watched sunlight glint across the water.

We arrived safely in Calydon and were welcomed by our aunt, Lady Althea, and her husband, Lord Oeneus. The king beamed when he saw how tall and strong my brothers were, worthy additions to his hunting party. He took them away at once to introduce them to the other warriors and to see what they could do on the training field.

My aunt took care of me, which meant she led me to my room, summoned a slave to attend me, told me that someone would come for me when it was time to eat, and left. I felt I'd been dropped like a bundle of old clothes.

"Tsk, poor Lady Althea," the slave muttered while she shook dust from my mattress. She was a fat, gray-haired woman, sweet-faced and motherly. "She has so much to do these days, I pity her."

A slave pitying a queen? This was new. "What's keeping her that busy?" I asked.

"Why, the great hunt, my lady; what else? So many guests, and more arriving every day! It's doubled and redoubled the work we've got to do inside these walls. And the queen must oversee it all constantly, to make sure that everything is worthy of her husband's hospitality."

I was eager to begin exploring the palace of Calydon, but I didn't get the chance to do it on my first day there. When the slave finished tidying my room and left, I stretched out on my bed just for a moment—so I told myself—and woke up to the last glow of the setting sun. I was still yawning and stretching when the motherly slave returned with a lamp and helped me prepare for dinner.

The palace hall was filled with tables, the tables packed with the great men of over twenty lands. My brothers and I were given places of honor, not because we'd done anything to earn them but because we were the queen's kin. I knew that where you sat at the king's table was the king's choice, so your seat told everyone exactly how much or how little he respected you.

Polydeuces must have impressed Lord Oeneus already. After just one day's display of his skill with sword and spear, he was seated between the king and the queen. Castor sat at Lord Oeneus's other side, and I was next to him. It was a good spot for observing the hall.

The place beside me was empty, which was odd. With so many heroes under Lord Oeneus's roof, a seat so near the king *had* to be filled. If not, it was as if Lord Oeneus were telling his guests, *None of you is worthy to sit this close to me.* It would be an unforgivable insult; all the warriors would leave, and the boar hunt would end before it began.

Castor saw me eyeing the empty seat and quickly put my puzzlement to rest. "That's for our cousin Prince Meleager," he whispered. "Polydeuces and I already met him, out on the training ground today. He's twenty-one, a couple of years older than us, but he looks much younger, and sickly in the bargain. Lady Althea was with him, asking him if he wouldn't rather go inside and rest, fussing over him as if he were a child. Thank the gods Mother would never embarrass *us* like that! Finally Lord Oeneus sent her on her way.

"Once she was gone, we saw the *real* Meleager. Helen, he's incredible. The instant he picked up a spear, you forgot how pale and thin and fragile he looks. Fast? He outran every one of us. Strong? I'm still aching from the wrestling match I lost to him." Castor chuckled.

"You didn't mind losing?" I asked.

He reached for a bowl of olives and dropped a handful on my plate. "Glaucus taught me better than to resent the man who beats you in a fair fight. Or the girl." He winked at me.

"Oh, *now* you admit I beat you fairly?" I teased.

"Who says I'm talking about you?" With that, my brother indicated a table that stood at the far end of the great hall. The men seated there were plainly dressed, young, and nowhere near as well muscled or imposing as Lord Oeneus's other guests.

"Who are they?" I asked.

"Servants," Castor replied. "Weapons bearers who came here with their masters. And one more. I'm surprised at you, Helen: Can't you recognize your own trick when someone else plays it?"

"What are you talking about, Castor?" I demanded.

"Open your eyes, little sister."

I did, and I saw something wonderful.

She wore an unadorned tunic, like most of the young men at that distant table, with her dark bronze hair pulled back and tied horse-tail style. The flickering light of the oil lamps made it easy to mistake her for a man, especially when I wasn't expecting to see a woman among the weapons bearers.

"Who is she?" I asked Castor. And then, in a whisper: "She doesn't *look* like a man; she's just dressed like one. If she's trying to disguise herself, it's not——"

"I was only teasing you about her having stolen your trick, Helen," Castor said fondly. "She's never tried to hide the fact that she's a woman from anyone; she's proud of it, if you ask me. Her name's Atalanta, and she's the daughter of Lord Iasius of Arcadia."

"A king's daughter? And our uncle sat her all the way down there?" I asked, nodding to the far end of the great hall. "With *servants*?" I was flabbergasted. The king had placed her so far away from him that she might as well have been in another room. The insult didn't seem to bother her or affect her appetite. She was eating heartily and had all of her dinner companions laughing at jokes I couldn't hear. "Does Lord Oeneus *want* war with Arcadia?"

"Oh, she's not here as a daughter of Arcadia," Castor replied, smiling. "She's here as one of us; she's come to hunt the boar."

"That's disgraceful," a new voice spoke in my other ear, making me turn sharply from Castor at the sound. While I'd been staring at Atalanta, our cousin Meleager had taken his place beside me at the table. He was just as frail-looking as Castor had described him, but there was nothing weak about the anger burning in his eyes.

"What's disgraceful, cousin, that a woman's a huntress?" I asked coolly. As a guest, I had to keep my own anger under control, but I didn't like my cousin's attitude toward Atalanta at all. "I'm surprised that something like that bothers you. I thought that in this land it's acceptable for royal women to know how to hunt. My own mother, your aunt, taught me the same tracking and archery skills she'd learned when she was still a Calydonian princess."

"That's not what I mean," Meleager replied. "The disgrace is how Father treats her. Maybe it's because he's only king of Calydon by marriage. If he'd been raised here, he might be more willing to accept her for what she is. Atalanta's at least as strong and brave as half the men here, and she can outrace us all. The day she came riding up to the gates, some oafish palace guard tried to send her away. When she dismounted and told him she refused to go until she'd seen the king, he tried to—what was that stupid thing he said?—to 'teach her she's a woman.' " My cousin had a wicked smile. "It was an unforgettable lesson . . .

for the teacher. She didn't even have to use a weapon to disarm him, knock him off his feet, and hold him helpless until the king arrived."

"I wish I'd seen that," I said.

"And I wish Father could remember that he did. He says that it's one thing for a girl to bring down a rabbit or two with her bow but that there's something unnatural about one who also knows how to use sword and spear, who can wrestle, ride, and race like a man. He acts as if each of her achievements is a fluke."

"True," Castor put in. "When she beat me at wrestling, Lord Oeneus took me aside and apologized for the poor condition of the ground. According to him, the only reason I lost was that my foot must've slipped on a stone. I know better than that. I have to admit it. She's not bad."

"You mean for a woman?" I asked, putting a little bite into the question.

"Don't put words in my mouth, little sister," Castor responded. "After just a short while on the training ground with her, I saw what she can do. I *felt* it. I don't know about the rest of the hunters, but Polydeuces agrees with me: She's a worthy companion. A pity that our uncle won't see that."

Meleager shook his head over his father's obstinacy. "How many times can he blame her wins on luck? He can't stand to see a mere girl outdo men time after time. Hasn't he heard of her exploits? The singers already know at least half a dozen stories about her triumphs as an athlete and a hunter."

"Maybe he thinks they're just stories," I said. "That's why he won't believe them."

Meleager snorted with disgust. "Then why is he so eager to believe the high-flown tales the singers recite about all of *them*?" He made a sweeping gesture that included every man feasting in his father's hall. Two red spots flared on his pasty cheeks as he spoke with even more indignation. "They don't even need the singers' tales. They do their own boasting well enough. *Too* well. They come here with stories about how they've slain giants and monsters, but where's the proof?"

I smiled, liking my cousin more and more. "What do you want them to do? Haul a dragon's head around with them everywhere they go?"

I was teasing, but he took me seriously. "A dragon's tooth would be enough. The hunter who kills the boar will be given its hide as a trophy—Father said so. The tusks go with the hide. I'll bet that whoever wins that prize will always carry one tusk with him from then on and show it proudly. That's because *this* beast is real. Anyone can destroy a thousand imaginary monsters."

He took a long drink of wine and fell silent. His eyes never left Atalanta for the rest of the meal.

As the feast went on, I saw what Meleager meant

about the other hunters' love of boasting. It didn't take much to get them started. Mention the weather and someone would claim to be the son of Zeus, master of the thunderbolt; say that you couldn't eat another bite and someone would start telling the tale of how he'd slain a giant who could eat a whole ox in one mouthful. As soon as one of them would finish, another would start.

I leaned toward Castor and whispered, "Want to play a game? If we hear ten stories about dead monsters before we hear ten about who's a god's son, I win. Otherwise, you do."

"Not fair! We've already heard at least six men speak." He lined up six olive pits on the table in front of him. "*All* of them claimed their fathers were gods. If I can't count them—"

"No, the game starts now, but you can count four of those, because I'm generous," I teased, snagging away two of the six pits. "I'm still going to win."

I had seven olive pits to Castor's nine when Pirithous of Thessaly stood up. He must have been a famous man, because he was seated just three places away from Lord Oeneus. He began by letting all of us know that he was the son of Zeus. Castor ate another olive, spat the pit into his hand, set it down with the others, and mouthed *I win* at me. I was just about to ask him for a rematch when Pirithous finished his brag with the words: "But my lone adventures are only half of it. For the rest, Lord Oeneus, we must hear my dearest friend, my heart's brother, Lord Theseus, king of Athens!"

At the sound of his name, Theseus rose from the seat next to Pirithous, a seat even closer to the king. I gaped at the sight of the handsomest man I'd ever seen, tanned and strong, with a ready smile. We were close enough for me to see his sea-green eyes and the streaks of gold running through his long, chestnut-colored hair. I didn't know why the sight of him made my blood pound in my ears and my breath grow short. Even though he was much older than I, I couldn't help feeling drawn to him. I even found myself thinking, *My sister's husband is much older than she is too.* When he caught me gazing at him and flashed me a grin, I blushed from neck to hair.

Then he opened his mouth to speak.

To hear him talk about his adventures, you'd think he and Pirithous had fought their way to the throne of Hades and back. Not only was he Poseidon's son, but he claimed a human father as well, the previous king of Athens. The monsters he'd slaughtered as a young man were the human sort—bandits who murdered innocent travelers—and then came his greatest victory: the minotaur! He'd sailed to Crete to face that terrible creature, half bull and half man. It feasted on human flesh, and Athens was compelled to send Crete seven youths and seven maidens every nine years to feed the beast. He slew it single-handedly, of course, freed the Athenian captives, and carried off heaps of Cretan gold, but not before he'd won the ardent love of the king's own daughter, Princess Ariadne.

"*I* put an end to the minotaur," Theseus declared. "Just as I'll put an end to the Calydonian boar!" No one challenged his story—or even thought to ask what had become of that devoted Cretan princess—partly because the scars crisscrossing his chest and arms proved he wasn't afraid of a real fight, but mostly because the other men soon went on to tell equally far-fetched tales of their own exploits.

So much for finding *that* attractive. I sighed. Theseus was handsome, but he was loud and arrogant. I remembered how Clytemnestra used to claim that my looks earned me unfair privileges, back when I was still a pretty child instead of the gangly girl I'd become. If someone would say the same of Theseus's appearance, I bet he'd simply reply, *Why, yes, of course I get special treatment, I'm entitled to it.* Ariadne could keep him, if she even existed in the first place.

While the hunters took turns praising themselves, I nudged Castor and whispered, "Where's the training ground?"

He thought he knew my reason for asking. "Oh

no you don't," he said. "This isn't Sparta. You heard what Lord Oeneus thinks of women who act like men. You'll offend him."

"What offends him is women who do *better* than men," I said. "Don't worry, I don't want to do sword practice with any of them." I indicated the still-swaggering hunters. "If one of them beats me, he'll claim I had twelve arms, six heads, and spat poison. I just want to watch how you're all preparing for the hunt."

"Well, well, so you want to watch *men* exercising?" Castor snickered. "My little sister's growing up!"

I gave him a hard look. "The boar isn't the *only* pig around here."

That made him laugh outright. "Ah, Helen, I'm only joking. But never mind where the training ground is. You can't go. Lord Oeneus has forbidden any woman from lingering there, distracting us. He wants us to concentrate on getting ready to hunt the boar."

I didn't say another word on the subject. My brother was wrong. I didn't want to go to the training ground to see the men; I wanted to watch Atalanta. I wanted to see for myself what a woman could achieve and how she did it.

I knew there was no question of sneaking there in my old disguise. My brothers would recognize me at once and send me away. They were honor-bound to respect the rules that our uncle had laid down.

That was all right. The training ground wasn't the only place where I might be able to observe that astonishing woman. I'd find a way to get what I wanted: I was a huntress too.

It took me three days before I was able to find Atalanta away from the training ground, even though my aunt's hectic life as hostess to all the hunters left me completely free. Each morning I disguised myself as a boy again and explored. No one bothered me. The coming boar hunt had filled the court of Calydon with dozens of new faces. I passed for just another one of the hunters' servants.

My plan was simple. Meleager said that Atalanta had come riding up to the gates of Calydon. I didn't know how to ride or much about horses, but I'd heard my brothers talk about the beasts often enough to know they needed to be exercised. I'd wait until Atalanta came to the stables to exercise her horse and follow her from there. I might not get to watch her practicing with weapons, but just being able to *see* her would be enough for me.

I went to the stables, made friends with one of the workers, and got a good look at Atalanta's horse. He was a fine animal, short and sturdy, with a broad back the color of autumn oak leaves and a sooty muzzle, mane, and tail. *She'd never let anyone else take care of him,* I thought.

I'd guessed right: Atalanta did exercise her own horse daily. The problem was *when* she did it: She didn't devote one set time for that activity. The first day I came to the stables, I learned she'd already been and gone. The second day, I loitered so long that one of the stablehands grew suspicious of a "servant" with no work to do. He chased me away before she got there. The third day, I thought my luck had changed: Atalanta arrived and mounted her horse while I was waiting.

That was when I learned that my simple plan to follow Atalanta from the stables had a simple flaw: No matter how fast I could run, a horse could run faster. She and her steed were away from the palace and lost in a cloud of dust, heading for the woodlands, before I even managed to pass through the citadel gates.

Running after her wasn't the answer. I looked down at the trail the horse had left and began to track it. The fresh hoofprints showed how horse and rider left the road and took a hunter's path into the foothills. Once or twice I lost the trail and prayed to keen-eyed Hermes to help me find it again. The trickster god answered my prayers with a fresh pile of horse dung right in the middle of my path.

I marched on without any sight of them until I began to worry whether I'd gone so deeply into the forest that I risked finding the boar before I found

Atalanta. Plus I hadn't thought to bring my sword, so I was defenseless.

Stop that! I told myself severely. *Have you seen or heard the beast nearby? Or do you think that a gigantic boar's like a forest nymph, able to slip through the trees and brush silently? You know he'd make enough noise to give you lots of warning. By the time he crossed your path, you'd be safe. Can he climb trees?*

That was when I heard hooves pounding through the undergrowth. I ducked behind a big beech tree just in time to see Atalanta come riding back down the path. I stayed hidden until she was well out of sight, then continued up the trail. If she had a favorite spot for exercising her horse, I intended to find it. On the other hand, if she only rode him into the hills and back to the palace, I needed to know that too.

I continued uphill, eyes on the horse's path, until I came to a clearing. It was ringed with ancient oak trees, and a little freshwater spring bubbled out of mossy rocks that cropped out of the earth at the northern end. The grass was torn up, and there were too many hoofprints for it to be a place she'd come to only once.

I crouched beside the spring and said a prayer of thanks to the unknown god who dwelled there, letting him know that he had my sincere gratitude for permitting me to find what I'd been seeking. Tomorrow I wouldn't try to follow Atalanta. I'd wait for her to come to me.

9

ATALANTA'S STORY

The following day, I was up and out of the gates with the sunrise. In my hurry to reach the clearing, I forgot to bring any food or drink along with me, so by the time Atalanta appeared, my stomach was grumbling. I didn't care. I was convinced that any sacrifice of comfort was worth it, just to watch her. I found a venerable oak tree whose branches made for an easy climb and scaled it high enough for the foliage to conceal me. Then I waited.

I had no way of knowing how long I'd have to wait or even if this might be the one day that Atalanta decided to take her horse elsewhere for his exercise. My stomach kept up a long recitation of complaints until at last I decided it might be wise to ask the gods' help.

But which god? The answer was obvious, even though I didn't like it. Atalanta was a huntress; therefore, Artemis the huntress was the only one who could answer my prayer.

I muttered my petition quickly, not really expecting the goddess to hear me. Like Father, I disliked Artemis for her heartlessness, her readiness to punish the smallest insult, even if it happened only by oversight. I'd sworn an oath in her name, and though I fully intended to fulfill it once the hunt was over— I knew better than to cheat the gods—wouldn't she know I'd only used her as an excuse to escape Mykenae? Couldn't she tell how little I cared for her? Why should she do anything for me?

As I sat straddling the branch, alone with my thoughts and a very unhappy stomach, I heard the sound of hoofbeats approaching from farther down the hill. The next moment, Atalanta's horse burst into the clearing. I whispered my thanks to Artemis, though the part of me that didn't like that goddess still wondered whether I could trust her gift.

It was a joy to watch Atalanta ride. She moved smoothly and naturally with her horse, making it look as though together they were one miraculous creature. I forgot all about my empty stomach as I watched her put the little stallion through his paces. Sometimes, while riding him around the clearing at a gallop, she'd drop lightly to the ground and race beside him. She had no trouble matching his stride, and there were moments when I believed she could have outdistanced him, if she'd wanted to do it. When she grabbed the dangling reins and leaped back onto him as easily as if she had wings, I had to bite my tongue to keep from cheering her name and giving myself away.

I might as well have cheered, because she caught me.

"What are you staring at, boy?" Atalanta drove her horse straight at the tree where I was sitting and shouted up into the branches. Until that moment, I'd thought my shelter was impenetrable.

"Nothing," I muttered, clinging to a leafy limb of the ancient oak.

"Oh?" She raised one eyebrow. "Then what are you doing up there? Building a nest?"

"I'm picking acorns," I replied with as much dignity as I could manage. It was a stupid thing to say, but it made her laugh.

"Get down, little squirrel," she commanded me. "I won't hurt you."

I hung by my hands from the branch for a moment, then dropped to the ground in front of her, landing on an oak root and sprawling into last autumn's fallen leaves. My tumble startled her horse, but she controlled the huge creature with just a touch of her knees to his barrel.

When I stumbled back to my feet, brushing crushed leaves from my clothes, the horsewoman studied me closely. "Ah," she said at last. "I was wrong. You're no boy. You're the twins' sister Helen, the Spartan princess. I've seen you at dinner, always sitting next to Prince Meleager. Hasn't anyone ever told you that queens-to-be don't belong in trees?"

"And you're Atalanta the huntress, the one all the men are talking about. Hasn't anyone ever told you that women don't belong on horseback?" I shot back deliberately.

That made her laugh even more. "You tell *me* where we belong," she said, and before I could catch a breath, she leaned down, hooked one arm around me, and swept me up in front of her on the horse. With a shout and a light flick of her heels, she set the stallion into a gallop through the forest.

We left the little clearing far behind. The horse laid back his ears and ran flat out, threading a break-neck path around the trees. Atalanta shoved me forward just in time to dodge low-hanging branches and kept me from slipping off sideways whenever her steed made a sharp turn. I felt the wind whip across my face and thought, *So this is what it's like to fly!* I knotted my hands into the horse's mane and felt all my fears blow away behind us like so many dead leaves. I let out a whoop of joy and didn't want our wild ride to end until we'd ridden across the world.

Atalanta finally reined the horse back to a canter, then a trot, and finally a slow walk. We were on a rise just above the royal palace of Calydon. She dismounted gracefully and offered me a hand down, but I decided I'd show her I could do that for myself.

I swung one leg up and back, lost my balance for the second time that day, and hit the ground, splayed out like a starfish on a rock. I took the sheepskin pad with me. Atalanta's horse looked down at me, snorted, and walked away, flicking his tail disdainfully.

"Did he just laugh at me?" I asked, slowly sitting up. Every bone in my body felt like it'd been beaten with sticks.

"I hope so," she replied, grinning. "You earned it." She picked up the sheepskin, sat down on a large boulder, and rested one arm across her updrawn knees. "Now, care to tell me why you're wandering through the woods, dressed like that?" She indicated the sleeveless tunic I'd filched from Castor. It was much too big for me, even belted tightly. "Is it some Spartan custom, raising daughters to be sons?"

"My father's got sons," I said, standing up and shaking the dirt from my "borrowed" clothes.

"Mine didn't." Atalanta's mouth turned up at one corner, but it wasn't a smile. "When I was born, he was so disappointed that he ordered one of his servants to take me out to the mountains and leave me there to die." She gave me a sudden, penetrating stare. "I guess you've heard the stories?"

"The men say that you were fed and protected by

a she-bear until a party of hunters found you." I looked her in the eye. "I don't believe it."

"Good for you, girl," she said. "The part about the she-bear makes a good story, but it's not the truth. The rest is." She shrugged, then spoke matter-of-factly about what came of her father's coldhearted decision. "I was abandoned to die but found by the sort of people my father wouldn't understand. To them, a child was a child. To him, children were . . . tools. He only wanted a certain number and a specific kind; the rest were disposable. It was probably good that he didn't need a daughter; otherwise, I'd have spent my life being forced to fit the mold of what *he* decided I should be."

Her face was grim, and I saw her hands tighten into fists as she told me her story. I didn't want to make her dwell on so much ugliness, but I had to ask. "How do you know all this? About your father, I mean."

She relaxed a little and even smiled. "Oh, I like you! You can think. Yes, how *would* I know anything about either of my parents if I was abandoned as a baby? Well, the person my father sent off to do his dirty work was a slave, a man with no choice except to obey. The king might have owned his body, but his heart was his own. He wrapped me in a good, warm blanket before he followed my father's orders to abandon me in the wilderness, and he didn't lay me on the ground until he caught sight of a hunting party coming through the trees. Even then, he hid until he saw they'd found me." She looked into the forest, as if hoping to catch sight of that good man's spirit. "Then he came forward and told them who I was and why I'd been thrown away like an old rag. The only thing of any value that he owned was a single carnelian bead with a bear carved on it, but he offered the huntsmen that if they'd agree to help me."

"So that's where the she-bear in the story comes from," I said.

"Probably." Atalanta reached into her tunic and drew up a loop of leather cord. The brilliant burnt orange of carnelian glittered in the sunlight. "The man who became my foster father accepted this from the slave who saved my life. He didn't need it, but he took it because it was the only way he could make that good man believe he'd keep his promise to raise me. When he was dying, he gave it to me and told me the whole story." She cupped the carnelian bead in her palm and gazed at it as if it held her soul. "He never thought to ask the slave's name, but the gods know it, and I pray to them all to reward him."

She shook off the somber memories and tucked the necklace back out of sight. "Maybe I ought to thank my father for throwing me away. He'll never know it, but he gave me my freedom. I intend to keep it, and thanks to my foster father, I've got the means to do it."

"Is he the one who taught you to hunt?" I asked. Atalanta's reputation as a master of spear and arrow was already legendary.

"Yes, and how to ride a horse too." She whistled softly, and her stallion came trotting up, as obedient as a well-trained hound. She stroked his muzzle fondly. "There aren't enough men like him."

Something puzzled me. "The first time I saw you, my brother Castor told me you're the daughter of Lord Iasius of Arcadia. If your father abandoned you—"

"Why am I burdened with his name?" Atalanta finished the question for me. "Simple. Because men, even slaves, reveal many secrets on their deathbeds, and so when that good man died, my father found out what really had become of me. By then he'd changed his mind about needing a daughter, so he ordered my return, as if I were a borrowed cloak." She blew softly into the stallion's nostrils, a strange action that seemed to please the animal. "You can guess how well *that* worked. But he did acknowledge our blood tie so that now all the world knows it. I can't evade or deny it, much as I'd like to."

She took the bit out of the stallion's mouth, then looked back to me and said, "You still haven't answered my question: Why are you dressed like that?"

"It was the easiest way to get out of the palace and follow you," I replied. "No one stops a boy."

"That's clever," Atalanta admitted. "Though I wouldn't say you *followed* me. And why would you want to do that, anyway? Am I so fascinating because I'm a curiosity, the woman who hunts and rides like a man?"

"Is that what you think you are?" I said stiffly. "Back home, the warrior who taught my brothers how to fight with sword and spear taught me too. My mother taught me how to hunt. I hoped that you'd have something new to teach me; that's why I've been watching you. But if you say you're just a curiosity—" I turned away and started down the hillside.

Her hand fell on my shoulder before I'd gone ten paces. "The way to learn is face to face, not hiding in the treetops, little squirrel," she said. "Especially if I'm going to teach you how to ride."

"You'll do it?" I was her devoted worshipper once more. "You'll really teach me how to ri—?"

Just then, my belly gave a growl worthy of an earthquake, loud enough to silence me in mid-word. I lowered my eyes, embarrassed, but the huntress patted me on the back, and when I looked up again, I saw that she was smiling.

"I will, Helen. And the first thing I'll teach you is

this: Don't come to your riding lessons on an empty stomach!"

We sat down together on a nearby rock while the stallion grazed. Atalanta had some sheep's milk cheese wrapped in oak leaves stowed in the pouch at her belt, also a bit of bread and an apple. She was happy to give me the bread and cheese, but when I eyed the apple too she said, "No, greedy squirrel. This is for Aristos." She whistled, and the horse came trotting up to claim his treat.

While he gobbled the fruit, she stroked his neck and told me, "Aristos *is* the best. Why should I give him any other name? When you're on his back, see to it that you respect him or he'll have you off again before you can blink."

"I will, I promise, but . . . how could he tell if I didn't?" I asked.

"Trust me, horses *know* things." Atalanta offered me a drink of water from the leather flask she carried.

"I can believe that," I said, gazing at the stallion's dark, intelligent eyes.

"Now, the important thing for you to know before we begin is not to be afraid of him," Atalanta went on. "Aristos is very patient with children."

"I'm no child!"

"To him, you're an infant, which is good and bad at the same time. The bad part is that you know absolutely nothing about horses. The good part is that infants learn fast. Well, infant, are you ready?" She replaced Aristos's bit.

I stood up and wiped crumbs of bread and cheese from my hands and tunic. "Try me."

I had grand visions of mastering Aristos that very day, before the sun reached noon, and racing him all the way back to the palace. I was so taken by that image, I didn't bother including a place in it for Atalanta. It was just me and Aristos and a chorus of admiring gasps from everyone who saw us come galloping through the citadel gates.

Instead, I spent what was left of that morning just learning to get on the horse. Better to say *trying* to get on the horse. As Atalanta said, it didn't count as *on* if I just went toppling *off* the stallion's back as soon as I mounted him.

We began with Atalanta positioned by the horse's head, with me facing his left side. She offered her linked hands and told me, "Take hold of the reins, then put your left foot here and I'll give you a boost up."

"But I want to do this the same way you do," I objected. "No one helps *you* mount."

"Humor me." She bent forward a little so that her linked hands were lower. "You can try it without my help next time. For now, just do as I say and, whatever you do, *don't* let go of the reins."

I wanted to say, *You told me that already*, but decided to

hold my tongue. I was sure that once Atalanta saw how well I sat that horse, she'd realize I was ready for more-advanced lessons. I grabbed the reins in my left hand, rested my right on the sheepskin pad covering Aristos's back, placed my left foot in the huntress's hands, and bounded upward just as she gave me the promised boost.

I went over the top and off the far side, dropping the reins in mid-flight. Luckily for me, I rolled when I hit the ground and only got a light bruising. Aristos gave me a disdainful look over one shoulder, then ambled away.

Atalanta stood over me, arms folded. "Would you like to try that again?" she asked, doing her best not to smile.

I got up, trudged over to Aristos, took his bridle, and led him back to his mistress. "As many times as it takes."

It took many, *many* times. My second attempt at mounting ended when I dropped the reins just as I landed on the fleecy pad and Aristos bolted, sending me tumbling. My third failed when I knocked the sheepskin off on my way up and found nothing between me and the stallion's back. That was when I learned just how slippery horsehair is. By good fortune, Atalanta managed to catch me when I slid off.

On the fourth try, I held tight to the reins, landed on the sheepskin, and straddled the horse proudly. Atalanta looked pleased, or perhaps just relieved.

And then I looked down. Sweet Aphrodite, was the ground *that* far away? Aristos's back hadn't seemed so high up when I'd ridden under Atalanta's protection, but now I was all by myself atop a horse who was suddenly tall as an oak tree! I yelped and leaned forward, clutching for his mane and neck, trying to hold on to his body the way I'd held on to that branch.

The branch was narrower. The branch didn't *breathe*, shifting shape constantly, making itself wider and narrower by turns and far more difficult for my legs to grasp. The branch didn't decide to start moving without warning. I made the mistake of leaning even farther forward, lost my balance, and fell off once more.

Aristos took about ten steps, then came back to give me a long look that as good as asked, *What are you doing down there?*

By the time Atalanta announced that the lesson was over, I'd managed to mount Aristos and stay mounted, but just barely. Dismounting—deliberately and with some style, not merely falling off the horse—was another story. I begged her to give me more time.

"I'd like to, little squirrel, but I need to go back to the citadel, to join the others. If I don't show up on the training ground, they'll all say it's because I'm just another undependable woman."

"Not *all* of them," I said. "My brothers respect you, and Prince Meleager thinks you're skilled *and* beautiful."

The moment the words left my lips, I regretted blurting them out. Atalanta gave me a quizzical look. "Did he *say* that? That I'm beautiful?"

I shrugged, hoping she'd let the matter drop. No matter how my cousin had praised Atalanta, it wasn't my right to repeat it.

"Mmm. I see. Well, Helen, if you ever find your tongue again, feel free to tell your cousin that I thank him for thinking highly of my abilities but to save his opinion of my looks. I didn't choose my face. It's a random gift from the gods. But I am pleased to know that he appreciates my *true* accomplishments. That compliment's worth even more to me, coming from a man whose own athletic skills are so impressive."

"Do you—do you *like* my cousin?" I asked.

A strange, thoughtful expression crossed the huntress's face before she replied. "I do like him, but not the way I think *you* mean it. And I respect him. You can tell him that too."

I'd seen the longing in Meleager's eyes when he looked at Atalanta at dinner. I had the feeling that he wanted more than her *respect*.

Holding the reins herself, Atalanta gave me a lift onto Aristos, then jumped up in back of me. We rode most of the way back to the citadel together. I asked her to stop and let me down in the shade of some pine trees beside the road at a point from which the stronghold gates still looked as small as the first joint of my thumb. I could see the citadel, but as long as I stayed behind the trees, no one there, however hawkeyed, could see me.

"I'll walk from here," I told her as I stood stroking Aristos's neck. "I don't want anyone paying too much attention to me when I go back inside, and if I come riding in with you, it'd be too conspicuous. One of the guards might take a *good* look at me and realize I'm not a boy. Then he might start asking questions."

"I think you give those men too much credit," Atalanta replied. "If you don't look like a threat or an oddity, they won't give you a second glance. But be as cautious as you like."

"I'd rather do that than risk discovery," I said. "Especially when that might mean I'd be forbidden to leave the citadel again *and* be watched." I remembered how Glaucus's way of testing my dedication and Ione's vigilance kept me from the training ground for so many days. I refused to have to deal with a nuisance like *that* again. "Nothing's going to interfere with my riding lessons."

"Well said." The huntress was pleased, and my heart rejoiced to have her approval. "Tomorrow I'll leave the palace at sunrise. You'll be safe enough from discovery if you meet me here, then we'll ride on together. Oh, and make sure you wear something that protects your legs a little more than that tunic."

"Like what?" I asked. "You're wearing a man's tunic too."

"I wear more than this when I ride Aristos over longer distances," she told me. "Mykenaean horsemen have a reputation for endurance because they wear short breeches when they need to make long journeys; so do I. Even now I'm wearing a loinwrap that covers my upper thighs. If you don't wear something that gives you at least that much protection tomorrow morning, you'll regret it by tomorrow night, believe me." She pressed her heels to the stallion's sides and was gone.

She was wrong. I didn't regret wearing inadequate leg covering the next day. I regretted it that very night. I was sore from all the bruises I'd gathered in one fall after another, and my legs were badly chafed and aching after straddling Aristos's wide body.

I also had more problems to deal with than my aches and pains. After that morning in the hills, I was filthy and reeked of horse. Though I'd tied up my hair, my repeated tumbles had left it snarled. How I missed Ione! My long strands of black curls fell well below my waist, and the tedious work of washing and unsnarling them had always been her job.

Though Ione was still in Sparta, I *did* have someone to help me with this sort of thing here in Calydon—in theory, anyway. My aunt had ordered the motherly slave woman I'd met on my first night in Calydon to attend me, but after she'd neaten my room in the morning for the day, she'd vanish until it was time to help me get ready for dinner. I had no idea of how to summon her if I needed her between those times, and I didn't dare go searching for her while I was still dressed as a boy.

I had to do what I could for myself before I could even begin to seek her out. There was some water in a large jug by my bedside, so I used that to wash off the worst of the grime on my face, arms, and feet. Next I put on a dress and wrestled a comb through my tangles. I had to remove any telltale bits of twig or leaf before I got the slave woman to help me wash my hair thoroughly. I didn't want her to start asking questions, or even thinking of them.

As I passed through the palace halls looking for her, I came across the large room where my aunt and her women sat working. It was like a glimpse of home. The great loom stood in the best light, with the queen herself making the shuttle fly back and forth between the up-and-down threads. Three nobly born ladies of Calydon sat nearby on low stools, one spinning thread, two doing needlework while they gossiped. The gold ornaments in their hair and decorating their brightly patterned gowns proclaimed their rank. The remaining five women at work were plainly dressed—slaves or servants, by the look of them—two using spindles, three toiling through a huge basket of raw fleece with their carding combs.

As I watched them from the doorway, unnoticed, I caught sight of the shallow basket standing next to the loom. It was filled with newly made cloth. Atalanta wanted me to protect my legs better for tomorrow's lesson, and this looked like my chance to get something for the purpose.

I'll tell the queen that I've lost my mantle and I need some cloth for a new one, I thought. I wasn't sure of exactly *how* I'd alter the simple length of woven wool to shield my legs, but I decided Atalanta could help me with that. My task was to get the cloth in the first place.

Without pausing to think things through any further, I stepped into the room and greeted my aunt with reverence. She was pleased to see me and insisted that I sit beside her at the loom.

"Helen, my dear, you've found me! I've been so busy, I hope you haven't been *too* bored? Have you found enough to do?" Abruptly, her affectionate expression froze. She wrinkled her nose grotesquely, then leaned a little closer, sniffed, and asked, "What *have* you been doing? Er, I mean, what have you been doing to entertain yourself so—*strenuously?*"

One of the noblewomen sniffed as well, then

smiled. "I'd say she's found the stables." She squeezed my hand gently. "I loved horses when I was your age too. My nurse had to drag me away from them almost every day. When she caught me helping the grooms brush my father's stallion, she was scandalized." She mimicked her long-gone nurse's gruff, scolding voice: " '*What* do you think you're doing, my lady? What evil spirit told you that *this* is fit work for any woman? What would your mother say if she could see you now?' "

When we all finished laughing, I lowered my head and said, "You're right; I was with the horses. I'm sorry if I . . . brought some of the stables along with me." I looked up and grinned. That brought fresh laughter.

My aunt patted my cheek. "You're Leda's daughter, right enough. She was just the same, when we were girls together. If it weren't for the stables, you'd never find her inside the palace at all."

"Did she know how to ride?" I asked eagerly.

Lady Althea shook her head. "She got into enough mischief without that. She just thought they were beautiful, fascinating animals. Besides, she was such a formidable runner that I think being on horseback would've only slowed her down. Did you know that she was quite the huntress?"

"Just like Atalanta." I was proud to compare my mother to my new friend and teacher.

My aunt didn't share my enthusiasm or my opinion. Her face darkened. "Don't liken my sister to that unnatural creature. Leda might have known how to run and hunt, but she also knew how to do a woman's *rightful* work. As soon as she married your father, she was glad to give up all those silly girlhood pastimes."

I thought of my mother's pleasure when she'd taught me archery, her joy when my arrow brought down my first quarry. *And when did she learn that "rightful" woman's work if you say she was never in the palace?* I wondered. But I decided not to voice my thoughts to the queen. What would it accomplish except to irritate her even more?

"All that Atalanta needs is a good husband and a house full of babies," the second noblewoman spoke up. "*That* will cure her quickly enough."

"Cure her of what?" I asked. I couldn't help it. "She's not *sick*, she's just not like you."

"I should hope not!" The lady looked smug about it. "And I thank Hera for it. If I were anything like that—that—that want-to-be man, I'd throw myself into the sea!"

I decided that if I didn't leave then and there, I'd say something to my aunt's self-righteous companion that would cause unnecessary trouble for everyone. A guest who broke the peace of her host's home wasn't worthy of the sacred bread and salt. I mumbled my tale about the lost mantle, Lady Althea cheerfully gave me a suitable piece of cloth from the basket beside her, and I ran from the room.

As I fled down the corridor, I heard the smug noblewoman tell my aunt, "Such a sweet child. What a pity she's such a sharp-faced, skinny thing."

"*Exactly* like her mother," my aunt's voice trailed after me. "And you *know* what a beauty she grew up to be."

10

THE BOAR COMES

The cloth I'd been given by my aunt turned out to be useless. I tried several ways of wearing it under my tunic, wrapped and tucked this way and that, but it kept slipping off or bunching up when I walked. I had enough trouble getting up on Aristos without a wad of wool snaring my legs and getting in the way. I wound up leaving it behind in my room before I ran out to meet Atalanta by the pines.

We rode into the hills before the early-morning mist was completely gone from between the trees. The silvery haze held secrets. Once I thought I saw the slim, swift shape of a dryad slipping back into the bark of her tree, but it might have been nothing more than an ordinary shadow. The sun burned the mist away by the time we reached the clearing.

My second morning of riding lessons went only a little better than the first. As soon as I mastered mounting Aristos with a boost from Atalanta, she decreed I was ready to try getting up on the horse without her helping hands.

"Like this," she said, demonstrating the proper way to do it. It was much the same business as the assisted mount—reins in the left hand, a little jump, a little push upward with the right hand, the right leg swung over the horse's back, and there she was.

There *she* was; not me.

The best thing you could say about my attempts was that at least I'd stopped dropping the reins. At first my jump up wasn't high enough, and I slammed my chest into Aristos's side. When I jumped harder, I still couldn't manage to swing my leg over the horse and ended up hanging over his back on my stomach before sliding back down.

Atalanta let me have half a dozen tries before she stepped in and showed me how to use both hands to help me make the midair turn without losing my grip on the reins. That was the only reason I was finally able to mount Aristos, though not without a lot of squirming myself into a proper seat once I was on the stallion's back.

Then the *real* lessons began.

By the time Atalanta had to return to the citadel,

she seemed pleased with my progress. "Not bad, little squirrel; not bad at all," she said as she watched me guide Aristos around the clearing at a walk. "You're still sitting too far forward—that's why you fell off both times today—but you have the right instinct for balancing control between your hands and your legs. Tomorrow we'll see if you can stay on him when he picks up his pace. Here's a taste."

She gave the horse a light swat on the rump and he went into a lively trot. My teeth clattered together as I bounced along, but I pulled back firmly on the reins, and brought him to a stop before every bone in my back shook loose. I turned Aristos's head toward Atalanta, touched his side with my heels, and walked him back to her.

"I think I'll be ready," I said, smiling feebly through the fresh pains of that day's lesson.

I wasn't smiling when she dropped me off at the little roadside pine grove. The insides of my legs were hurting too much. I was used to dealing with aches and bruises from all the time I'd spent learning weaponry with Glaucus and my brothers, but having my skin rubbed raw by a horse's flanks was something new. My flesh stung as if I'd landed on my behind in a beehive. The simple act of putting one foot in front of the other to walk back to the citadel became a bizarre, agonizing dance.

I was lucky that Atalanta didn't simply go galloping off as soon as she let me off Aristos. She saw my pain and she knew the reason.

"Didn't I tell you to protect your thighs?" she asked.

"I tried," I replied. "I tried, and I *really* wish I'd succeeded, believe me." I went on to explain my failed attempts at turning that length of cloth from my aunt into a usable undergarment.

"Hmm. Where's that cloth now?" Atalanta asked.

"I left it on my bed this morning."

"Good; easy enough to find. If there's enough material to make myself a new pair of Mykenaean riding breeches, I'll swap it for my old ones. They won't fit you perfectly, but they'll do, and I could use a new pair."

"You know how to sew?" I was unwilling to believe it.

Atalanta was amused by my incredulity. "Don't gape at me like that, girl. It's not as if I knew how to *fly.*" And with that, she rode off.

It took me a long, painful time to walk back to the citadel. As I limped through the gates, one of the guards jeered, "Next time work harder, boy, and your master won't beat you so badly!" I gritted my teeth and ignored him as I made my way back to my room.

Pain or no pain, I had to move much more

quickly once I was inside the palace, in order to avoid being seen and questioned. A scruffy, ragged "boy" could have a dozen excuses for passing through those parts of the Calydonian citadel where people did real labor, but next to none for being caught on the upper floor where the highborn had rooms.

I was climbing the stairs to the upper level when I ran into one of the hunters coming down. He took one look at me and his eyes widened. "By Zeus, boy, what happened to *you*?"

"I fell off a horse." There was no harm in telling the truth, as far as I could tell. I tried to move past him before anyone else might happen to come along.

He stayed where he was, blocking the narrow stairway. "A horse?" he echoed. "Are you all right? Did you get hurt?"

I shrugged. "It's nothing." Again I tried to move past him, adding, "Please excuse me, sir; I have to see if my master needs me."

I only wanted an excuse to get away from him, back to my own room. In my haste, I'd picked a poor one, because the next thing the man asked, quite reasonably, was, "Who is your master? I doubt you'll find him in his room at this time of day. Why don't you come along with me to the training ground? I'll help you look for him."

He sounded genuinely concerned, as if he really

cared about helping a grubby, unimportant "boy" like me. He seemed to be only slightly older than my brothers, with nothing remarkable about his looks— he was shorter than most of the other hunters, had dull black hair, brown eyes, pockmarked skin, and a body as solid and ordinary as a bullock's—yet it was clear he had a good heart. Even though his concern was bringing him dreadfully close to undoing my disguise, I found myself drawn to him.

"Thank you, sir, but I still have to go back to my master's room," I replied, evading his question. "I'm responsible for carrying his weapons. If he's not still there, he'll be waiting for me at the training ground, and he's not a patient man. *Please* let me pass!"

"Ah, so you're one of the weapons bearers?" (Under other circumstances I might have appreciated his friendliness, but not when it was delaying me, no matter *how* attractive I found him.) "It's a thankless job, isn't it? I remember my days serving my uncle on his adventures. Talk about a man with no patience! But a celebrated hero, then as now. The places he took me, the exploits we shared, the marvels I saw him perform, sometimes with his bare hands! It was an honor to serve—" He stopped, suddenly self-conscious. "I'm sorry, lad—you're in a hurry and I'm keeping you from your duties." He stepped to one side on the stairs.

But I made no move to go on my way. All at once I recognized the face I'd only glimpsed at my uncle's table. "Sir, are you—are you Iolaus, great Herakles's nephew?"

He gave an uncomfortable laugh and scratched his head. "I can't deny it. How did you know me?"

"I saw you at dinner." That was the truth, even if he'd believe I'd done so from a place at the servants' table, not the king's. "I've heard the poets sing of your exploits. It's an honor to meet you."

His mouth curved into a charming smile. "The real honor would be to meet Herakles. Surely you've heard what some of the other hunters say about me? That Lord Oeneus allowed me to join the hunt only because of my uncle's deeds, not mine."

"If you ask me, some of the men who scoff at you wouldn't fare so well if anyone looked closely at *their* claims to fame," I replied hotly. "Everyone knows that you were the one who helped Herakles slay the nine-headed Hydra!"

"Yes, well . . ." He took a deep breath. "Lad, did you ever *see* a nine-headed beast of any sort, mouse or monster?"

"No, but—"

"No one has, including me *and* my uncle. But the poets who sing for their living know they won't earn a full belly from spinning tales about how Herakles and his nephew slew an ordinary swamp snake; a monstrously *big* swamp snake, as thick around the body as a pillar, but with just one head, after all."

"Oh." I was deeply disappointed.

"Now, now, cheer up." Iolaus put on a jolly face. "No need to lose heart just because *my* adventures are such trivial things. All the more reason for you to grow up strong and brave and perform *truly* heroic deeds. Show the rest of us how it's done, eh? Now run along. Your master's waiting and I'll feel awful if he punishes you because I kept you chatting here." He turned and bounded down the stairs. I was sorry to see him go.

I made it to my chamber without further incident and saw that Atalanta had been there. The length of cloth was gone, replaced by an unfamiliar piece of clothing. My bedside water jug had been refilled to the brim, and there was a small, sealed clay pot next to it. I broke the seal, removed the lid, and dipped one finger into the thick yellow salve inside. It felt cool, smelled like honey, and brought me sweet relief as soon as I smoothed it over my suffering skin. I blessed Atalanta's name.

My third day of riding lessons slipped by in a dance of walk, trot, and canter. My style when mounting and dismounting the horse still left a lot to be desired, but Atalanta was satisfied with how much better I sat once I was on the stallion. When Aristos moved, I straightened my spine without making it rigid and leaned back a bit, instead of bending forward to steady myself. The Mykenaean breeches helped, giving my legs a more secure grip on his sides.

Trotting still jounced me almost as much as an oxcart ride, but I didn't fall off. The canter was a smoother gait—I loved it!—but what I really wanted to do was recapture the amazing sensation I'd experienced when Atalanta first swept me up onto horseback and gave Aristos his wings.

"Can I run him?" I asked. "*Really* run him?"

"Don't let me stop you," Atalanta replied. "If you think you can—"

I was off before she could finish her sentence. A kick of my heels to Aristos's flanks and we were off. The first burst of speed stole my breath. I was ecstatic, feeling the wind, skimming across the ground—

—sliding too far forward to control the horse properly, sheepskin or no sheepskin beneath my seat, breeches or no breeches on my legs. I wasn't ready to deal with how slippery a horse's back could become once he worked up a sweat. As if horsehair needed something to make it even more slippery than it already was! The stallion wasn't just running, he was running away with me, heading for the trees. If I hit a low branch head-on—

I panicked and pulled back on the reins, trying to turn him, but I used too heavy a hand and Aristos wouldn't stand for it. He jerked his head up sharply, tearing the reins from my hand, then down, humping his back and flinging out his heels.

I'd wanted to fly *on* horseback, not *from* it. The gods were merciful and let me plunge well clear of the stallion's flashing hooves and all of the larger rocks in the area.

I was still lying on my stomach, getting a close view of mud and grass roots, when I heard Atalanta's shrill whistle and Aristos's footsteps, deceptively dainty for such a powerful creature. The two of them walked over to where I lay so that I got a good look at the huntress's bare feet and the horse's mucky hooves before I pushed myself up to sit.

"Do you know what you did wrong?" Atalanta asked me.

"Everything?"

It wasn't as bad as that, according to her, but bad enough. Aristos had to be sweet-talked for a while before he'd allow me to approach him again. I found myself apologizing to a horse for having acted heedlessly. At first I felt silly doing it, but the longer I spoke to him, quietly asking him for another chance, the more his attitude toward me seemed to soften. When I finished begging his pardon, I swear by Zeus himself that Aristos turned sideways as if to offer me his back once more!

We finished the morning with a few more attempts at galloping, though nowhere near as headlong as the first try. Atalanta told me to sit back, and I was so eager not to repeat my initial mistakes that I made a bunch of new ones, toppling backward over the stallion's rump two times out of three. I was lucky I didn't break my neck.

"Well, one good thing about today's work," Atalanta said when it was time for us to return to the citadel. "You've spent so little time actually *on* the horse that you might not be quite as sore as yesterday."

As if he understood and agreed with his mistress, Aristos let loose a long, scornful whinny in my face.

"Just you wait until tomorrow," I told him.

The next morning, long before the sun was up, I was jolted awake by the sound of running feet, voices shouting curses and commands, and the clash and jangle of weapons. My room on the second floor of Lord Oeneus's palace opened onto a pillared gallery that ringed a courtyard. I threw my blanket around me, stepped out of my room, and gazed down. The huge space below was mobbed—the gathered heroes, their weapons bearers, palace servants, and Lord Oeneus himself—all of them milling around, weaving between the pillars, everyone trying to find someone else, all of them blundering in a dozen directions at once.

Then I heard the sound of my brothers' voices

sweeping along the gallery, racing toward me. I turned to greet them and was bowled off my feet.

"Agh! Who'd I just knock down?" The sky above the courtyard was still dark and the moon was already set; Castor never did have good night vision. "Are you all right?"

"I'm fine, stupid," I replied, holding on to the gallery railing and hauling myself back to my feet.

"Helen?" Polydeuces peered at me. "Go back to sleep; there's still plenty of time before you have to get up."

"*You're* up," I pointed out. "What's going on?"

"The boar," he replied shortly. "Once Lord Oeneus decided there were enough of us for a successful hunt, he sent out teams of men to search for it. They've been scouting the countryside for days. One of them spotted it and sent a runner back with word. It's been living on the great mountain to the west of the palace, the one with the big slash of trees burned off by lightning."

"The gods are on our side," Castor added. "I heard that mountain's got plenty of places we can corner the beast for the kill. I hope I'm the one who brings it down. Wouldn't Father be proud to see me come home wrapped in a monstrous wild boar's hide!"

"It'd go well with your manners," I said, but both of my brothers hustled past me and were already gone.

I hurried to dress, putting on the same tunic I'd

worn every time I went to meet Atalanta. I threaded the scabbard of my small sword through the belt, then secured my dark curls into a club even more carefully than usual. It took me longer than I liked. By the time I'd tied the last knot in the thin strip of cloth, the courtyard was empty. The hunt was on the move.

The guard must have thought I was some hero's servant who'd overslept. He shouted good-natured threats after me as I ran through the gate. "Run faster, boy! You'll get a whipping from your master when he sees you lagging behind!"

The night sky was paling to smoky blue, and the rising sun was just beginning to show a few thin strands of pink and gold over the eastern hills. It was simple enough for me to track the hunters. They'd all set out on foot because there was no way of knowing when the boar would turn to a mountain path too steep or thickly grown to let horses pass. They left a clear trail to follow, and the dogs—let's just say that dogs have a way of making it easy for you to know where they've been. I heard the hounds baying in the distance, their voices echoing among the trees above when I reached the base of the mountain. Following the tracks of so many feet and the cry of the hunting pack, I plunged into the forests of Calydon.

The sun was well over the horizon before I caught up to them. By that time, they'd scattered through the woods. I said a quiet prayer to Hermes, patron of thieves and tricksters, asking him to see to it that I didn't run into my brothers. Dressed as I was, only Castor and Polydeuces would recognize me at a glance. No one else could imagine the princess of Sparta to be here, with a sword at her hip.

My brothers would be livid if they caught me. Though they might have accepted my presence on the training ground back home, they'd never stand for my being a part of the boar hunt, with all its thrills and perils. They'd force me to go back to the citadel, even if it meant one of them would have to drop out of this grand adventure in order to enforce their decision. The unlucky twin would never forgive me for stealing his first chance at fame.

O Hermes, be with me! Let me find the hunt, but not my brothers!

The trickster heard, and being a trickster he answered my prayer in his own special way. The first hunters I found weren't my brothers. They were that handsome braggart Theseus of Athens and his friend Pirithous.

"Well, what's this?" Theseus boomed when he saw me loping through the underbrush. He was leaning on a huge boar spear, the shaft as thick as a young tree, the bronze point bigger than my hand. "Lost your way, boy? Don't be afraid, we'll protect you." He and Pirithous roared with laughter.

"I can protect myself," I told them calmly, drawing my blade.

It only made them laugh harder. "Who told you we were hunting bunnies?" Pirithous sneered. He was carrying a bundle of lighter spears and had a weighted net slung over one shoulder. "Ever *seen* a wild boar, puppy? Even a young one can open a man's belly with one stroke of his tusks."

"I've seen wild boars," I lied. "This is at least as long as any boar's tusk." I held up my sword proudly. "When I meet the Calydonian boar today, we'll see whose belly gets torn open."

It was a silly, empty boast, like those they spouted about themselves, but it seemed to win me some friends. The two men traded a look of amusement, then Theseus said, "I like your nerve, boy. What's your name?"

"Glaucus."

He didn't ask me where I was from; he must've assumed I was a Calydonian. "Well, Glaucus, Theseus and I travel light, so we didn't come to Calydon with a whole crew of servants like some of these other so-called heroes. Why don't you give us a hand with our gear?" Pirithous held out the bundle of spears. "When I kill the boar, I'll give you one of his teeth to wear 'round your neck as a reward."

I shook my head. "I only work for one person."

"A servant with a sword?" Theseus's eyebrows rose. "Who'd allow that?"

I looked him steadily in the eye. "Atalanta."

"Her?" Pirithous spat. "This is the first I've heard that she kept servants. Theseus, didn't we see her arrive at the palace gates alone?"

"I'm not hers," I said quickly. "I serve Prince Meleager. He ordered me to attend her on the hunt, but she outran me. He's the one who gave me this." I made a great show of brandishing my sword.

"That explains it." Theseus's mouth twisted into a mocking smile. "Meleager's in love with that monstrosity, the gods alone know why. The way he looks at her makes me want to puke."

"He'd better watch himself," Pirithous put in. "A woman like that devours men. I heard that when he was born, the Fates told his mother that he'd live only as long as the log burning on the hearth. She poured water on it, wrapped it up, and put it away somewhere safe, but I don't think it worked. Call me a liar, but I swear there are times he looks like he's burning to ashes from the inside out."

"He's still a good warrior," Theseus said. "*And* a fine hunter, who'll beat us to the boar if we don't stop jabbering with this brat and get going." He shouldered his massive spear and started off.

Pirithous followed, though he did spare me one backward glance. "Go back to the palace, Glaucus;

this isn't for you," he told me. "You're almost as weak and soft-looking as a girl. Your hands should hold a lyre, not a sword." Then he, too, was gone.

I went after them, but only because the whole hunting party was heading in the same direction, higher up the mountain. As I made my way through the trees, I heard a new note in the music of the hunt. The howls and wails of injured dogs, the shrieks of men in pain, and, over all, the bone-chilling bellow of the Calydonian boar.

Then the trees ended. I stepped out onto a spear-head-shaped swath of open ground, the old forest all burned away by a lightning strike, just as Polydeuces had said. There were only a few brave sprouts of new green beginning to poke up from the charred earth, among the blackened stumps of trees. About halfway up that bleak terrain was a small, narrow ravine, like the bite of an ax. That was where the sounds were coming from.

Other stragglers were running toward it, men sweating and shouting, brandishing their weapons and cheering for the kill. I ran with them. I recognized my brothers from the back, already moving toward the front rank of the hunters, but I no longer cared if they saw me. The hunt was almost over; let them send me back to the palace now and it wouldn't matter. In fact, I *wanted* them to see me. I'd enjoy their look of surprise when I tapped them on the shoulder and—

My hand was already outstretched to touch them when my sandal slipped and I fell on my face. I pushed myself up on my forearms and stared at the ground.

No wonder I'd fallen. The earth was slick with blood.

11

THE GREAT HUNT

I was still sprawled on the blood-soaked ground when a strong hand hauled me upright and a familiar voice commanded: "Get up or get trampled, lad."

I regained my feet and found myself again face to face with Iolaus. "Thank you, sir," I said. "I got separated from my master in the woods. What's happening? Do we have the boar?"

He grimaced. "That depends on if you ask the boar or the hunters. He's got his back to the wall and there's no way he can fight his way through so many of us. He's got no choice but to surrender." Another heartrending howl tore through the air. A hound as big as me went flying up and over the hunters' heads, its body streaked with red. The cornered boar had tossed the poor creature as easily as if it were a wisp of straw. "Too bad he disagrees."

"Where's Atalanta?" I cried, clutching Iolaus's arm. The blood underfoot, the unlucky dog's fate, the uproar from the ravine all suddenly combined to strike my heart with terror. But I wasn't afraid for my own life. I feared for my friend. Without thinking, I grabbed Iolaus's shoulders and sprang up, desperate to see over the heads of the hunters in front of me. I would have clambered all the way up his back to gain a better view if he hadn't shaken me off like water.

"Calm yourself, lad. You'll see her if it's the gods' will. She's the one who found the beast. The way that woman can run, no wonder! With the hounds, she drove him into that narrow spot, and her spear drew first blood." Iolaus looked grave. "That was when he turned and attacked."

"No!" In my head I could see the boar turning, charging, and who would be his nearest target? I threw myself forward, into the mob, and shoved my way through.

I struggled past men holding a whole forest of heavy boar spears—unwieldy weapons that were made to be braced against the earth, to meet the infuriated beast's charge and let his own strength impale him. As I squirmed my way through, I encountered someone whose luck had run out. The body lay face to the sun, arms and legs flung out at strange angles, one hand still curled around a spear's splintered shaft. His face looked like a smashed piece of fruit. The boar had trampled him, then ripped his side open. I saw the white slivers of exposed ribs just before I vomited.

Someone grabbed my shoulder and shook me. "Help or get out of the way, pup." It was Theseus and he was unarmed. "The monster broke my spear," he said tersely. "Get me another!"

"Get it yourself," I growled, wiping my mouth on the back of my hand before lunging away from him.

Atalanta was standing at the entrance to the ravine, behind Meleager and about four other men. She had her boar spear in hand and was trying to elbow her way ahead of them. I was so happy to see her alive that my voice broke when I called out her name.

"What are you doing here, you idiot?" she shouted. She broke away from Meleager and the others to confront me. "Do you *want* to die?" She slapped my face so hard it made echoes.

Then she looked at her hand, smeared with blood, mud, and ashes from my face. Her anger turned to alarm. "What's this? Are you wounded? Show me!"

I began babbling out a rapid explanation of what had happened, but she stopped me as soon as she saw

I wasn't hurt. "Never mind. I have to finish what I started. I'd have had that beast on my spear by now, except for Prince Meleager. He saw me wound it and thought I was in danger. The gods protect me from men who mean well! Those others with him got between me and my prize because they want to steal the honor of the kill. They're too stupid to know what they're up against. I don't think half these men ever faced a boar on their own."

"But there are so many hunters here—" I began.

She raised her hand to silence me: "No matter how many hunters set out together, we each face the boar alone."

As if the gods heard her words, there was a fresh chorus of screams as the boar broke through the mob of armed men. He was a moving mountain of flesh, blood, and bristle, draped in shredded hunting nets. Foam streamed from his mouth, and a wake of blood sprayed out behind him from the dozen shallow wounds on his flanks. Hounds held on to his ears, throat, and haunches, their jaws locked. Only death would make them lose their grip. Their ferocious loyalty to their masters' orders was a gallant, tragic thing to see.

"He's heading up the mountain!" Atalanta shouldered her spear and took off, her feet flying fast as dragonfly wings. But instead of rushing up the steep, naked slope after the boar, she raced back into the trees and down through the forest.

"What are you doing?" I gasped as I tried to keep up with her.

She paused. "Trust me. He's gone up the mountain, but he's got to come down again. I know where to meet him when he does." And she was off.

I don't remember the path we took. I was too anxious about keeping up with Atalanta to notice much. Twigs scratched my face, and brambles clawed my legs. I panted for breath as I ran and inhaled a spiderweb. While I stopped for a moment to spit out the sticky strands, I heard the sound of the hunt up the mountain, dogs and men making an uproar loud enough to shake boulders from their beds.

"Not much farther!" Atalanta called over one shoulder. I wanted to shout back that I didn't care how much farther we went, I could do it, I wasn't tired at all, except . . . I was too tired. By the time she stopped and wedged her spear into the earth, I was ready to collapse.

I didn't dare. Atalanta's eyes were fixed on the trail, a steep, twisting, narrow path marked by the prints of cloven hooves and the smell of boar droppings. The clamor was getting louder.

This is real, I thought, staring at Atalanta. My mind filled with images of the dogs, of the dead man I'd seen. I stood frozen, feeling danger rolling down on me like a flood and unable to do anything but wait for it to wash me away.

"Here!" Atalanta's shout shattered my trance. "Get behind me. Hold the spear straight and steady. The slope will give him speed and power. Hold him until the spear point reaches his heart!"

I obeyed, imitating her grip on the spear, the way she braced her feet in the earth. There was a thin, slippery covering of fallen pine needles underfoot, making it hard to stand firmly. My nose filled with the pungent scent of the pines around us, the musky, spicy smell of mushrooms and ferns from the forest floor, the reek of my own sweat. The dazzle of sunlight through the boughs and the kiss of a breeze on my cheek were unbearably sweet. Even through the din of the oncoming hunt, I could hear the beauty of a bird's song.

I could die here. I was surprised that the thought didn't frighten me. I was sad, but for my parents, my brothers, even for Clytemnestra. *I could die here,* I thought. *But not without a fight.*

I closed my eyes, tightened my grip on the spear, dug in my feet even more deeply, wedged my left shoulder against Atalanta's back, and waited for the boar.

His roar crashed over me the instant that he hit our spear. The impact threw us down the path like a rockslide. Baying dogs came rushing past us, unable to stop their mad chase of the boar and overshooting their prey. I fell to one knee, scraping it raw, but I never let go of the spear.

As swiftly as it happened, it ended. There was a deafening crack as Atalanta's spearhead broke off in the boar's shoulder. We were swept to one side as the beast took off down the trail.

Atalanta was still cursing his escape when we both heard the twang of a bowstring, the whiz of an arrow, the hit, and the boar's last squeal of rage and pain. The beast toppled like a tower into the dust, the hounds swarming over him in bloody triumph.

The men were cheering. Their exultant cries soon changed to one word, one name, a name they roared over and over again: "Me-lea-*ger*! Me-lea-*ger*! Me-lea-*ger*!"

As the hunters forced the dogs to retreat from the dead boar, my cousin stepped forward and laid one hand on the monstrous body: The kill was his.

Tears joined the sweat streaming down my face as he claimed the quarry. *It isn't fair!* My thoughts blazed with frustration. *This should be Atalanta's glory! They should be shouting* her *name!*

But as the servants struggled to hoist the dead boar onto their shoulders and the still-cheering hunters began the trek down the mountain, back to the citadel of Calydon, I heard Atalanta's voice ringing out, chanting, "Me-lea-*ger*! Me-lea-*ger*!" as heartily as them all.

I let the jubilant procession pass well ahead of me before I started back to the palace. Even though it was all over, I still didn't want to run into my brothers; I was too bone-weary to be bothered with their reactions if they discovered my presence.

I returned to find the citadel transformed into a storm of wild rejoicing and headlong preparations for the victory banquet. No one noticed me as I trailed back to my room, stripped, scrubbed away the day's dirt and blood, crawled under my blanket, and collapsed into a dreamless sleep.

My brothers woke me when the sun was beginning to set. "What's the matter with you, Helen?" Castor cried, shaking me by the shoulder. "How can you sleep at a time like this?"

"Are you all right?" Polydeuces put in. "You're not ill, are you?" He touched my forehead to check for fever.

I brushed his hand away gently. "I'm *fine*, 'Ione.' You don't need to fuss over me just because I'm smart enough to catch some sleep before the feast. I'll still be awake when the two of you are snoring with your heads on the table."

"Ha! If not for us, you'd've slept right *through* the feast," Castor countered.

"I'll build a temple in your honor to show my thanks," I said, straight-faced. "Now if you really want to lend a hand, go find a servant to help me get ready. This is a special occasion and I want to look my best."

"Ooooooh, our little sister wants to look *nice*, does she?" Polydeuces crooned. "I wonder why?" I saw him wink at Castor and knew I was doomed to be teased to death.

"Don't you mean, 'I wonder *who*?'" Castor replied. He tried to look sly and all-knowing, but his tendency to go cross-eyed ruined the effect. "Do you think it's Meleager himself?"

"He's the hero of the day, but I think she'd rather have a *brawnier* man," Polydeuces said. "I'll bet I can guess who. I saw how you looked at him the first night we were here." He flung his arms around his twin, pitched his voice high, and cried, "Oh, Theseus, you're *soooooooo* strong! Make me queen of Athens too!"

"*Out!*" I shouted, snatching up my nearly empty water jug. My brothers retreated at a run, laughing.

I was doing my best to arrange my hair and dress for the banquet when the slave woman showed up, carrying a small oil lamp. She also brought me gifts from the queen: a new dress in all the colors of a springtime sunrise and a necklace of rock crystal and gold beads.

"The lady Althea asks you to accept and wear these, to celebrate the prince's triumph," she explained. Then she picked up a comb and set to work on my hair.

When I was finally ready, I went downstairs to the

great hall. My brothers were already waiting for me at the king's table. We were seated together, close enough to the king to satisfy the pride of Sparta, but nowhere near the place of greatest honor, between Lord Oeneus and his queen.

I knew for whom that seat was reserved, but I didn't know why it was still empty.

The hide of the Calydonian boar was spread out on the floor in front of the royal table, the heavy head propped up on a chair so that everyone could see Meleager's arrow still sticking out of the beast's left eye socket.

Every table in the hall was laden with a token piece of meat from the great kill. Even the slaves and servants would have the privilege of tasting broth made from the monster's bones, but the meatiest ones went to the surviving hounds. While we all shared a taste of Meleager's victory, Lord Oeneus added so much more food to the banquet that even the mice under his table would be waddling back to their nests that night.

And yet we ate with ghosts. The boar had killed four of the hunters. Two more were gravely wounded. The king swore that they were all heroes whose names would live through the songs of the hunt. No one bothered to count or name the servants who'd died that day, even though they'd lost their lives for venturing closer to the boar than many of the "heroes."

Only the master of the royal hunting pack mourned for the slaughtered dogs.

My brothers couldn't be bothered by phantoms. Tomorrow the dead would be burned, their ashes entombed with honor, the survivors would compete in athletic contests to please their spirits. Tonight Castor and Polydeuces sat near the king and basked in the congratulations of their fellow hunters. Apparently they'd done great deeds during the hunt—there were witnesses!—and had earned the right to be called heroes. If they'd noticed my presence on the mountainside that day, they washed the memory from their minds with cup after cup of wine.

And still the place between the king and queen of Calydon stayed empty.

"Where is he?" I whispered to Polydeuces. "Where's Meleager? Is something wrong?"

"Nothing, nothing." The wine slurred his speech just a bit. "This is all the king's idea, keeping us waiting for Meleager just to make us cheer him even louder when he finally shows up." He hiccuped.

As if in response to Polydeuces's words, Lord Oeneus rose up from his chair, bawled for silence, then spread his arms wide and called out, "Come forward, Meleager, my son!" If there hadn't been enough oil lamps to light the great hall that night, his face was radiant enough to do the job. "Come and claim your prize!"

Cheers shook the pillars of the hall as Meleager entered, but my cousin seemed indifferent to the praises thundering in his ears. His face was clouded as he approached his father and the boar. Something dark rode his shoulders, something that touched my heart with foreboding. I wasn't the only one who felt it: I was seated near enough to his mother, the queen, to see how anxiously she leaned forward.

Meleager ran one hand down the boar's bristly crest. He touched the bloodstained tusks, closed his eyes, and sighed, then opened them and said, "I can't accept what isn't mine. This beast would still be alive, ravaging our land, if not for the hero who truly deserves this trophy. My arrow never would have been enough to kill the monster if her spear hadn't weakened it. Atalanta! Take your rightful prize!"

He seized the hide, head and all, and slung it over his shoulder. He strode down the hall to where Atalanta still sat among the weapons bearers. He dropped it at her feet and gazed at her with all the worship in his heart.

I don't know who sprang up first, crying out against him, calling her a hundred vicious names. Several men leaped over the tables like deer in order to grab the skin.

"If you don't want it, Meleager, it's mine!" someone shouted. "*My* spear made the boar bleed; *I* deserve the prize. You insult us all."

Atalanta was too wise to try to stop them. I couldn't hear whether she flung their insults back in their faces, but I could see her laughing at them just as if they were a bunch of rowdy little boys who needed a good spanking. My cousin didn't share her wisdom. His white face was streaked with feverish color as he drew his sword and attacked the men who tried to take the boar's hide from Atalanta.

"This is bad," Polydeuces muttered, suddenly sober. Before I knew what he was going to do, he and Castor grabbed me. As we ran from the hall I heard weapons clashing, Lord Oeneus bawling for his guards, and the queen screaming. My brothers whisked me up the stairs, down the gallery, and into my room, where they barricaded the door with one of my travel chests and spent the night with their swords in hand.

I don't know whether or not my brothers were able to keep watch all night or whether, like me, they fell into a light doze. I only know that I was startled awake by a loud pounding. As I blinked in the morning sunlight, I saw Polydeuces on guard at the door, demanding to know who was there.

"It's me, Iolaus! Let me in; it's safe. I've got news."

Polydeuces admitted him. Iolaus looked terrible: his face haggard, his eyes red with dark circles under them. He moved unsteadily across the floor and sat down heavily at the foot of my bed, head bowed.

"Well, it's over," he said. "Artemis has her revenge.

Even after death, the boar she sent still had the power to kill. Ah, what a waste! Once the king gave Meleager the hide, it was his property; he could do whatever he liked with it. So what if he gave it to that girl? It was his choice, not an insult to anyone's honor. Where's their precious honor now that they're dead?"

"Who's dead?" Polydeuces asked.

I bit my lip and prayed that Iolaus wouldn't say *Atalanta.*

"Five men that I know of, though I couldn't tell you who four of them were. You know how many of us were here, and I don't pretend to have a praise singer's memory for names. I can't even figure out who they were by seeing who's missing this morning. After what happened last night, a lot of the hunters left Calydon at dawn. Some of the ones who stayed are saying that the dead men were Meleager's uncles." Iolaus made a disgusted face. "That's the way to heap filth on a man, calling him a kin-slayer when he can't defend himself anymore."

"What are you saying?" Castor asked. "Our cousin's dead?"

Iolaus nodded. "Those four men . . . well, Meleager killed them. He slashed the neck of the first man to lay hands on that stinking trophy. That was when the whole room erupted. Half the lamps were knocked over; it's a marvel that the palace didn't catch fire and burn to the ground. By the time Lord Oeneus's braver servants brought fresh light, the floor was red with blood and five bodies lay over the boar. Your cousin was the fifth. He had a few minor wounds, nothing that should have killed him. His skin was scarred with fire too—someone must have flung one of the lamps at him—but again, nothing serious enough to take his life."

"Then how *did* he die?" Polydeuces demanded.

Iolaus shrugged. "Depends whose story you hear. They say that when Lady Althea saw that her son had killed his uncles, she ran back to her room and—"

"The log." I hardly spoke above a whisper, remembering what Pirithous had told me, but Iolaus had good hearing.

"That's right, the one from the tale about the Fates coming to his mother when he was a baby." He stood up again and sighed. "They say she was so blinded by grief for her brothers' deaths that she threw that log back into the flames. It burned to ashes and Meleager died."

"But it's not *true*," Castor protested. "Althea is our mother's sister. We *know* that none of their brothers is still alive!"

"The truth steps aside for a good story," Iolaus said dryly.

"Let people entertain themselves some other

way," Castor snarled. "To say that the queen killed her own son! If I catch any man spreading that slime about Lady Althea, I'll—"

"Save your anger," Iolaus said, resting one hand on my brother's shoulder. And as kindly as he could, he told us my mother's sister was dead too.

The best lies hold a small, withered seed of truth. The queen *had* rushed back to her room after the slaughter in the feasting hall, but not to throw some nonexistent piece of wood into the fire. As soon as she saw her son's dead body, her heart broke, her mind shattered. She hanged herself with her own sash from one of the beams in her room before any of her maid-servants could reach her.

My brothers and I remained in Calydon for ten days after that cursed feast. We attended too many funeral pyres—for my cousin, my aunt, the victims of the boar, and the victims of stupidity. Castor and Poly-deuces won enough prizes at the funeral games after-ward to confirm their budding reputation as heroes. I sat on the sidelines like an ordinary girl, feeling the sting of the hidden, slowly healing scrapes and scratches I'd gotten during the hunt. I didn't see Ata-lanta anywhere.

The palace of Calydon was a house of mourning. Meleager's father moved through the corridors like an avenging wraith. The slaves and servants walked softly, afraid of the king's sudden, senseless outbursts of rage. Once I saw him beat a boy black-and-blue with his own fists for whispering the queen's name to one of his fellow slaves. When I tried to stop him, he gave me a crazed, red-eyed look that reminded me of the maddened boar. I fled, terrified and ashamed.

Many times during those ten endless days, I wished that my brothers and I could have left Calydon as soon as the other boar hunters did. Once the funeral games were over, my uncle's former guests couldn't wait to put plenty of distance between themselves and Lord Oeneus. Castor and Polydeuces and I were among the last to go. Our family ties forced us to linger. Meleager was my cousin, and the lady Althea was my aunt. I dreaded having to tell Mother that both of them were dead.

As I watched my uncle perform the daily sacrifice for his dead wife and son, I wondered whether anyone but my brothers and I would ever tell the truth about what happened that night. As Iolaus said, *The truth steps aside for a good story.*

At least Iolaus had the kindness to remain in Calydon a little longer. Men like Theseus and Pirithous might have sneered at him behind his back, calling him a poor substitute for his uncle Herakles, but they were the cowards who ran away as soon as possible. Iolaus stayed. I saw how he took pains to approach Lord Oeneus at meals, even when the king was sunk deep in despair, and spoke words of comfort to him. It wasn't his fault that my uncle's grief had left him too numb to respond. I loved Iolaus for trying. I wanted to tell him so, but the thought of saying something like that to a man was more daunting than facing the boar all over again. By the time I found the courage to do so, he'd traveled on.

At last it was our turn to leave. My brothers agreed that we'd done our family duty to our uncle and to the spirits of our dead kin. Polydeuces came bearing the good news to me as I sat alone in the room where my aunt's loom stood untouched and abandoned. None of the palace women had found the backbone to return to that place just yet; Lady Althea's last weaving still waited unfinished in the tall wooden frame.

"We'll leave tomorrow," Polydeuces said, sitting beside me on the bench before the loom. "Can you be ready?"

"Of course." I spoke listlessly, even though he'd brought me the news I'd been hoping to hear for days.

He got up to go, then looked back at me. "You don't sound like yourself. What's troubling you, little sister? Are you still mourning Lady Althea and Meleager?"

"Yes," I whispered, because it was easier than telling him the truth. But then I set aside the easy answer and told him, "No. No, that's not it. I'm sad because . . . because . . . Oh, Polydeuces, do you know what happened to her, to Atalanta? I haven't seen her since that night when——"

"No one has," he replied, his face stern. "Vanishing like that, avoiding the funeral games for the man who *died* because of her, running away——"

"She didn't *want* him to die!" I shouted, springing to my feet. "You were there! You *know* she didn't ask for the boar's hide! And you know she'd never run away."

"Then where is she, little sister?" he asked softly.

I shook my head. "I don't know." I sank back onto the bench, tears rolling down my cheeks. "I don't know."

He sat beside me and hugged me. "I'm sorry, Helen," he said. "You're right. She's gone, but she didn't run away like a coward. I can't blame her for leaving, not with Lord Oeneus out of his mind over what happened. If he'd seen her at the funeral games, the gods know what he'd have done to her. May the gods protect her, wherever she is. It was an honor to be her companion in the hunt."

It was a greater honor to be her friend, I thought as I clung to my brother.

The morning of our departure was glorious, with fat white clouds gliding across a brilliant sky. Our soldiers were gathering by twos and threes, chatting with one another or just standing around patiently until they were given the word to go. Some of them were awkwardly saying good-bye to teary maidservants, while their comrades looked on and laughed.

I was standing beside the oxcart, waiting for my brothers to finish the official ceremony of farewell inside the palace, when someone called my name. It was the same slave boy who'd earned my uncle's mindless wrath for whispering my aunt's name. He clung to the shadow of the palace's outermost defensive wall, gazing at me through a thatch of dirty brown hair with owl eyes, huge and golden. He looked about my age and even skinnier than I was, if that was possible. Even at that distance I could see the fading marks of my uncle's fists on his scrawny arms and chest, the purple and red bruises dappling his pinched cheeks. He clutched a cloth-wrapped bundle under one arm and beckoned me.

As soon as I came near, he bowed his head and held the bundle out for me to take. "She left this for you," he said.

I didn't need to ask who *she* was. I opened the bundle and found the bronze head of Atalanta's broken spear. It was still flecked with the boar's blood.

"I wanted to clean it, lady," the boy said. "She said no. She said that even if the blood ate up the blade, you'd earned it all, blood and bronze together."

"When was this?" I asked, my eyes never moving from the trophy in my hands. "When did she give this to you?"

"The day she left," the boy replied. "The day before I—the day before I angered the king." He lowered his eyes.

So she hadn't disappeared right away. She'd stayed to honor the dead, even if from a distance. A hunter knows how to hide.

I held the spearhead to my heart. "What's your name?" I asked the boy.

"Milo."

"Milo," I repeated. "How did she come to choose you to bring me this?"

His smile was hesitant. "The cook sent me out to gather mushrooms in the hills. I found her there, camped high up on a slope that had a view of the citadel. She asked me if I was going to tell Lord Oeneus where she was. She wasn't *afraid* I'd tell; she just wanted to know. I said no. I was the one who fetched fresh water to the hunters' rooms. She always thanked me, and sometimes she'd even give me extra food. While she was still up there"—he gestured out the open gate, toward the mountains—"I did the same for her, when I could."

"But she's gone now?" I asked. "You're sure?"

"When I could go back to her camp again—when it didn't hurt to walk—it was deserted." He bowed his head. "I'm sorry."

I took his hand. "Come with me, Milo."

He cringed. "Have I done something wrong,

lady? Have I displeased you? Please don't tell the king that I saw her! He'll have me killed!"

"We're not going to see the king, Milo," I told him, pulling him firmly after me as if he were a small child. "You'll never have to see the king again."

In the palace, I questioned one servant after another until I found the person I sought, my uncle's chief steward. That big-bellied, easygoing man was in one of the storerooms, checking the supply of olive oil, but as soon as he recognized me, he left his work and raised both hands in deferential greeting.

"Lady Helen, what a joy to see you still here!" His voice dripped honey. "I thought that you and your noble brothers were leaving us?"

"We are," I told him. "But there's something I want before we can go."

"What might that be, Lady Helen?" He pressed his palms together. "If one as humble as myself can be of any help to you at all, you only need to ask."

"The gods will bless you for your kindness," I said, smiling as I reached up and removed my gold earrings. They glittered even in the dim, dusty light. "There's something I wish to take away with me when I leave Calydon. I don't want to trouble my royal uncle with the details."

The steward's bright eyes darted from me to Milo and back again. He gave me a questioning look. I nodded and placed the earrings in his plump, soft palm. His fingers closed around them and he beamed.

"Great Lady Helen, you're as wise as you're beautiful." False flattery came easily to him. "There will be no need to burden Lord Oeneus with such a trivial matter at all."

Later that morning, when we were finally free to leave the citadel, my brothers asked the obvious questions about Milo's presence beside me in the oxcart.

"I bought him and freed him," I said casually, as if it were something I did every day. "You know I promised to make a sacrifice of thanksgiving to Artemis if you did well in the boar hunt. I've chosen to sacrifice this boy's former life as a slave. Artemis should approve. A huntress values freedom." I patted Milo's shoulder and added, "He's going to stay with us, though, at least until he finds a way to feed himself."

Polydeuces reached out and grabbed Milo's chin, turning his head from side to side. He frowned as he surveyed the boy's battered face, then glanced down at the bruises on his body. "A fitting sacrifice, then," was all he said.

We rode away from Calydon, down the citadel road, past the little pine grove, into the hills where I'd learned how to ride a horse—a little—and where Milo said Atalanta had made her now-abandoned camp.

Is she really gone? I wondered. *We couldn't say good-bye, but wouldn't she wait somewhere out there in the forests of Calydon to watch me leave?*

As I stared with longing into the trees, trying to read their secrets, I thought I heard the sound of a horse whinnying. *Aristos . . . Atalanta . . .* I raised my hand in a gesture of farewell.

"Lady, what do you see?" Milo asked.

"Nothing," I said, lowering my hand. "Nothing at all."

PART IV
DELPHI

AN UNEXPECTED HARBOR

Our trip home from Calydon was to be the reverse of the route we'd taken to go there, sailing east as far as the isthmus of Corinth and then going by land south and west to Sparta.

The voyage was uneventful, with fair skies above and calm waters under our keel. The only bad thing was that we weren't blessed with favorable winds to speed us along. The crewmen complained loudly as they bent their brown backs over the oars, but I was happy. I loved to feel the gentle roll and swell of the sea, to see gulls and pelicans swooping and soaring overhead, to lean out over the rail and wave to the folk on other ships, and to watch the ever-changing coast-line slipping past. As long as I was on the water, I was surrounded by beauty and peace, but once I reached home, I had dreadful news to give to my parents. I'd gladly delay it. I wished the voyage could go on forever.

My brothers, too, were at home on the water. They passed the time talking to the crewmen, asking countless questions about the workings of a ship. How do you steer? What are all the ropes for? Which prayers and sacrifices did Poseidon like best? How do you keep the ship from running aground or going too far from the safety of the coastline and becoming lost? They even insisted on taking a daily turn at the oars. This left some of our Spartan guardsmen ill at ease, not knowing whether my brothers expected them to join them on the rowing benches or just stand by and watch. The ship's master turned down the few who volunteered. On our third day out, I overheard him remark to one of his crew: "Bad enough trying to sail a ship with no wind and *two* inexperienced newcomers tangling up the oars!" I was so intent on smothering my giggles that I didn't bother pointing out that my brothers had become very good very fast at the work of sailing.

If the ship's master didn't know what to make of two princes who wanted to be sailors, he would have been even more perplexed if he'd known how much I wanted to do the same. As it was, I managed to share a little of their lessons on seamanship by listening and lingering nearby. That was easy. It was a small ship.

After each day's voyage, once the ship had been

beached for the night, we all lay out on the shore, under the frosty swirl of stars. My brothers and Milo were soon snoring, but I thought that the night sky was far more interesting and enchanting than any painted palace ceiling. I'd have time enough for sleep when we got home.

One of the ship's crew noticed my wakefulness and my fascination with the stars. He was a friendly, talkative old man with leathery brown skin and the only hair on his head a short white beard that traced his jawline. He delighted in filling my ears with tales of the beings—human and animal, beast and hero— whom the gods had placed among the stars as reward or punishment. I knew most of those stories already, but I enjoyed hearing him retell them.

"Who knows, my lady?" he said. "Maybe one day when you're a grown woman, your beauty will make Zeus himself fall in love with you and put your image up there as well, for us ordinary men to see and envy."

"I can think of better reasons to end up among the stars," I said, smiling at such harmless flattery.

Milo didn't share any of my brothers' or my plea- sure aboard the little ship. Sailing didn't agree with him, except when he took shelter in sleep. My new friend, the seasoned sailor, took pity on Milo and of- fered one infallible cure for seasickness after another. None worked.

"I can't understand it," he said as the two of us

watched Milo giving the latest potion back to the sea. It was our fourth day on the water, and the poor boy was limp and green as seaweed. "I even put in *three* extra anchovies, just to make sure it would take effect."

"Well, it did," I pointed out. "Just not the effect we were hoping for."

The old man shook his head over this latest defeat. "That last tonic saved my stomach back when I was just a lad aboard a trading ship bound for the tin mountains of Hyperborea! Here we've got easy sailing across a gulf that cradles our ship and steals the teeth of serious gales, but may Poseidon never send you beyond the Middle Sea, my lady. The waves out to the west are ferocious things that'll devour your ship out from under you. And before that happens, you'll be so miserably sick that you'll pray for the mercy of shipwreck and drowning!"

I did my best to look suitably terrified at the very thought of those western storms—the old man took such joy in seeing his tales have their intended effect!—but secretly I was thrilled at the possibility of riding wild waves.

"What's going on, Helen?" Polydeuces came up behind us, followed closely by Castor. They'd been working hard down among the oarsmen again, and it was no pleasure to stand too near them on that windless day.

"The usual, from the look of things," Castor said,

glancing at Milo's sagging body at the rail. He gave the boy an encouraging pat on the back. "Try to drink something, even if you can't keep your food down, lad," he said. "Shall I bring you a little watered wine?"

Milo lifted his sallow, haggard face and tried to thank my brother for his kindness but had to turn away quickly and spew over the side again.

Polydeuces sighed. "How can he still do that? I haven't seen him eat a bite of food since we boarded. You'd think his gut would be empty by now."

"Maybe it's a sacred mystery and only the gods know the answer," Castor said, smiling. "Like the horn of the she-goat who suckled the infant Zeus, the horn he broke off and blessed as soon as he was king of the gods so that it poured out a never-ending stream of food and drink."

"I always thought it was a strange way to thank the poor beast, breaking off one of her horns," Polydeuces said. "But it's not my place to question the gods." He, too, patted Milo's shivering back and added, "So, boy, how does it feel to be pouring out a never-ending stream of—?"

"*Stop that!*" I scowled at my brothers as I shooed them away from Milo. "How can you make such jokes in front of him?"

"To be honest, the only thing in front of him right now is the sea and the supper he ate three days ago." Castor's grin got wider.

Polydeuces was contrite. "We mean well, Helen. We're only trying to make him laugh. A good laugh might take his mind off being so ill."

"It's a shame we're bound straight for Corinth," the old sailor said, rubbing the back of his neck. "Since nothing else seems to be working for this lad, could be that a short rest on dry land would steady his stomach."

"You think we'd ever be able to get him back on board afterward?" Castor asked.

The sailor shrugged. "What would he have to say about it? He's your slave, isn't he?"

"He's our sister's slave, or was," Castor replied. "She freed him as soon as she bought him."

"And still he came onto this ship with you, sick as seafaring makes him?"

"This is his first voyage," I said, stooping beside Milo to place one arm protectively around him. "He didn't *know* he'd get sick."

"Oh, he'd have come along even if he'd known that a sea monster was waiting to gobble him up," Castor said, with another of those annoying, conspiratorial winks to his twin. "Anything rather than be separated from *you*, little sister."

Polydeuces eagerly took up his brother's game. "That's true," he hastened to tell the old sailor. "If you could have seen the way he's been gazing at her, all the way from Calydon!"

"Can we blame him, Polydeuces?" Castor asked with mock sincerity. "Our little sister is the most beautiful woman in the world." They collapsed laughing into each other's arms.

Milo made a great effort and pushed himself away from the rail, away from me. He took two staggering steps, fists clenched. "She *is*." Then he spun around and lurched for the ship's side once more.

My brothers exchanged a look of pure astonishment. The old sailor chuckled. "He may have been a slave, Lady Helen, but he's braver than many a free man, to talk back to princes that way! But it wouldn't be the first time a man found courage he never knew he had until he met the right woman."

My face flamed. I wanted to thank Milo for putting an end to my brothers' teasing—whether or not it was all in fun, I still found it annoying—but I was strangely tongue-tied.

Fortunately for me, the old sailor chose that moment to say, "That's not something you see every day, a mouse trying to take a bite from a lion's tail. Mark my words, this lad has the makings of a great hero. Why, if I had it my way, I'd put in at the next port and carry him all the way to Apollo's temple at Delphi, just to see what marvels the Pythia would have to predict about his future."

"*Delphi?*" my brothers echoed as one.

We all knew the name of Delphi, we just hadn't realized it was so near. The town was a famous place of prophecy where Apollo's chief priestess, the Pythia, foretold the future. The poets who'd sung of Delphi in our father's hall told how she answered questions and made her predictions in a small room under the sun god's temple, a cave where a crack in the rocky floor released strangely scented vapors from the earth's core. Seated in a giant tripod set above that crevice, holding a twig from Apollo's holy laurel tree, she inhaled the rising mist, then spouted a jumble of weird gibberish. Only the priests of Apollo could interpret it for you.

Now my brothers felt the inescapable need to hear what the Pythia might have to say to them. So that was why, after a short conversation with the old sailor and a shorter one with the ship's master, we all came to be put ashore at the port just south of Apollo's sacred city.

The old sailor who'd become my friend insisted on carrying me from the ship to the land, so I wouldn't wet my feet. As we said our good-byes, he gave me a leave-taking present, a little carving he'd made out of a smooth, creamy white nub of material too hard to be wood, too soft to be stone. When I asked what it was, he told me, "That's the tip of a genuine monster's tooth, a beast that was a gray, five-legged mountain! I saw it with my own eyes in the lands south of the Middle Sea."

"*Five* legs?"

His head bobbed emphatically. "Four where you'd expect 'em to be and the fifth not so much a leg as a long, boneless arm growing right out of the middle of its face."

I smiled at him. "Now you're teasing me as badly as my brothers."

He held both hands out, palms upward, as if to show me he was hiding nothing, not even the truth. "Lady, if I'm lying, may Poseidon the earth shaker, ruler of the seas, make this my last voyage! The world is full of marvels, if you're willing to travel far enough to see them."

I looked at the carving he'd given me. It was the image of a goddess, her feet resting on the back of a dolphin.

"Do you like it?" he asked eagerly. "That's Aphrodite."

"I know," I whispered. My goddess had found me. I wondered if this meant that someday she'd bring me luck enough to see even one of the world's marvels.

Once we were ashore, it didn't take long for our escort of Spartan guardsmen to attract the attention of one of Apollo's priests. The sun god's shrine kept several of them on daily watch down by the waterside solely to deal with the arrival of unexpected, important guests. The man who hurried forward to place himself in our service was overjoyed to learn that Delphi was about to be honored by a visit from the royal house of Sparta. He wasn't much older than my brothers, fresh-faced, and struggling gamely to grow a beard that was only coming out in tufts and patches. He took a slender branch of sweet-scented laurel leaves from his belt and used it to direct the three temple servants attending him. One wave of that branch and our travel chests were hoisted onto their backs, one word of command and they were heading up the road to Apollo's shrine.

"Lady Helen?" Milo spoke my name timidly as we fell into line behind the priest's entourage. Even though his health and appearance had improved miraculously the instant he'd stepped onto dry land, now his large eyes were filled with distress. "There's nothing left for me to carry." He pointed at the servants' slowly retreating backs.

"Don't worry about it," I told him. "You wouldn't have been able to lift those things anyway."

He stared at me as if I'd slapped his face. I was only telling the truth. He was too small and skinny to budge a packed wooden chest, besides which he was drained by his recent unfortunate voyage. I never meant to hurt his feelings.

"I'm *not* useless!" he protested. "There *has* to be something I can do to serve you!" He looked all around him desperately at every step we took and finally dashed into the trees along the roadside. He emerged proudly carrying a newly broken branch of pine needles. He waved it diligently back and forth near my head as we trudged along. It stirred up a nice little breeze, kept off the flies, and made him happy.

To reach Delphi, all roads led up, up, up. The sun god's shrine was set high amid looming crags and deep fissures in the earth, and as steep and sun-baked as the road was, it was thick with pilgrims. Some had come to Delphi the same way we had, by water, but others were so covered with dust that it was obvious they'd come solely by land.

Our priestly guide kept up a pleasant, nonstop stream of chatter all the way from the seaside to the gates of Apollo's temple, though most of it was directed at my brothers.

"Noble princes, surely Apollo himself brought you to us," he said. "This place calls out to heroes. It was here, in the depths of a lightless cavern, that the young sun god performed his first and best heroic feat, killing Python, a hideous, man-eating monster. That's why his chosen priestess here, his all-knowing oracle, is always known as the Pythia, to commemorate Apollo's greatest foe."

"How soon will we be able to see her?" Castor asked.

The priest rubbed his hands together. "Oh, soon, soon! I'm certain she'll have wonderful things to tell you about the splendid futures awaiting you when you rule Sparta someday."

Castor stopped dead in his tracks. *"May the gods forbid it!"*

Polydeuces spoke more quietly, but with just as much heat. "What sort of oracle doesn't know that our *sister* is the heir of Sparta? If you think ill-wishing her will make us favor you, you're a jackass."

Oh, that unhappy priest! If he could have squirmed out of his skin and slithered off into the bushes, he'd have done it in a heartbeat. As it was, he fidgeted and stammered and nervously plucked laurel leaves from the branch that was his badge of office, crushing them one by one until their fragrance was overwhelming.

I couldn't stand to watch his ever-growing embarrassment. "Weren't you two listening?" I said, nudging my brothers. *"He's* not the oracle. You can't blame him for not knowing everything." When they continued to glower at the priest, I turned to him also. "But you *can* tell us what we'll have to do in order to understand what the Pythia says to us, can't you?" I asked lightly. "I've heard that her words are sometimes confusing." I already knew the answer, but I wanted to divert attention from his blunder.

"Yes, yes, surely!" The priest was almost quivering with relief. "In his wisdom, the sun god makes the Pythia speak in his divine voice to those who bring him worthy offerings. Just so Apollo gives us, his humble servants, the power to interpret whatever he inspires her to say—"

"We know that," Castor remarked.

"—for a small additional offering," the priest concluded. Then he was off chattering again, telling us all about the glories of Delphi, assuring us that we'd have no need to find an inn, that it would be an honor to provide us with the best lodgings on the temple grounds.

The higher we climbed, the thicker the crowds grew, until by the time we entered Delphi itself we were surrounded. So many people! The streets teemed with them. Delphi was an ever-growing weed of a town that sprang up to serve the visitors to Apollo's shrine. People came from all over Greece to lay their questions at the Pythia's feet. I was dazzled by the sight of such crowds, rich and poor from every corner of the mainland and even from the islands scattered over the Middle Sea.

But soon the excitement of being part of that hubbub faded. The brightly colored clothes, the flash of gold ornaments, the sudden appearance of a chariot rolling by, all of the initial glamour shrank down into a clogged mass of hot, aggravated, pushy, impatient savages. All of them seemed to have been born with at least six knobby elbows, and each person acted like he owned the street. Milo's ever-waving pine branch was knocked aside and trampled. Even with our guardsmen at our sides, we were lucky that the same thing didn't happen to us.

"Are all of these people dying to know how they're going to die?" I muttered.

The priest mistook my grumble for a real question. "That's not the only reason that brings people to Delphi. Heroes seek to learn which road will take them to their next triumph. Kings ask the oracle's guidance when they wish to know whether or not to make war. Those who are fortunate enough to be granted an audience with the Pythia come away with the blessing of knowing their destiny."

"But what good does it do to know your *destiny*?" I argued. "You can't escape it. The three Fates spin, measure, and cut the life thread of every human being. Their decisions are final. Even Zeus can't change them."

"But Lady Helen, surely you're skilled enough with the spindle to know that every length of thread is made of many smaller fibers twisted tightly together?" the priest said smoothly. "The Fates themselves grant us one or two places in our lives where the thread untwists and we can follow either one strand or the other. Better to know when and where those choices will come to us instead of being taken by surprise."

"Why only one or two?" I asked, thinking of all the moments my life had already accumulated in which I'd chosen to follow a different path than the one most people would expect of me. "Why not say that every day lets me choose my own future?"

The priest chuckled. "What a gift you have for joking, Lady Helen! You *know* your future. You'll be Sparta's queen, living a life blessed by the gods. Your only surprises will be the name of your husband and whether your babies will be sons or daughters. You don't need to visit the Pythia. But your noble brothers will be heroes, making their own futures; heroes should know what awaits them."

"He's right, Helen," Castor said. "Polydeuces and I should know our fate."

Castor's fate? He didn't need an oracle to discover that; I could tell him exactly what it would be. The young priest's glib words were better than underground fumes for giving me a vision of what lay in store for both of my brothers: They were going to have their ears filled with flattery, then be persuaded to leave a rich gift at Apollo's shrine just to hear some poor girl babble riddles while she choked half to death on smoke. Then they'd make *another* offering just to have Apollo's priests translate the Pythia's wild words. If their gifts to the sun god were too extravagant, I could also predict what Father would have to say about it when we got home.

As soon as our party came through the shrine gates, we were greeted by one of the senior priests. He directed the servants to take our baggage to the finest room the temple could offer.

"Unfortunately, noble guests, it is only *one* room," he said. "My apologies, it's all we can provide. Perhaps as you passed through the town, you saw how busy things are at the moment. Your attendants will have to find other lodgings. There are many fine inns at Delphi."

Polydeuces frowned. "Our sister is the heir of Sparta and it's our duty to protect her. Separating her from her guards . . . I don't like it."

The priest gave him a reassuring smile. "Noble prince, if you doubt that your strength alone will be enough to safeguard her, are you also unwilling to trust your sister to Apollo's own protection? Do you believe that a few armed men can shield her better than the sun god himself? The temple grounds are sacred and secure. Of course, if you insist . . ."

"No, no." Polydeuces turned a little pale at the thought of insulting Apollo, even accidentally. "I was only worried about what might happen if she left the shrine."

"Why would she want to do that?" the priest asked. He had begun to talk about me as if I weren't there, or worse, as if I were just another traveler's chest to be stowed in one room or another. "If you tell her to stay on the temple grounds, you have no problem."

Castor's mouth twisted into a wry smile. "That's our sister, all right—just as tame and obedient as every other girl." I jabbed him with my elbow.

"Perhaps you could help us find lodgings for our men at the inn that's *closest* to the shrine?" Polydeuces asked the priest.

"A fine idea, noble prince." He was all smiles. "It's the best in Delphi. I know it well: It belongs to my cousin. Your men are lucky to have such a generous master."

As he spoke, I became aware that Milo was edging closer to me. He looked fearful and unhappy. "Lady Helen, must I go away too?" he whispered. "You need me, don't you?"

"Of course I do," I whispered back to reassure him. "Go follow the men who carried our traveling chests and see what the room we've been given is like."

He brightened immediately. "I'll do better than that for you, Lady Helen! I'll make sure that it's clean, and that you have the best bed, and that—"

Either we'd been incautious and not whispered softly enough or the senior priest had the ears of a greyhound. Suddenly he was standing between us, and though he was still smiling, his words had a hard edge to them. "My deepest regrets, Lady Helen, but your slave cannot be lodged here with you."

"Milo is *free*," I said sternly, standing very tall. "He serves us very well, and my brothers and I need him with us. It's not going to insult Apollo's ability to protect me if he stays. He's no guard."

"So I see." The priest gave Milo a patronizing look. "Gracious Lady Helen, how kind of you to tell me what will or won't insult the god I've served since childhood. Alas, how deeply I regret to tell you that you are . . . mistaken. Do you believe that great Apollo would allow his noble guests to enjoy his hospitality unattended? You might as well say that you'll need to provide your own food and drink because the sun god is too poor or too ungenerous to do so in his own house! Or perhaps you think that those who are good enough to serve Apollo *aren't* good enough to serve you?"

"That isn't why I—" I began, but Polydeuces cut my protest short.

"Our sister would *never* offend Apollo, would you, Helen?" I saw real fear in his eyes when he looked at me. It was clear that the sun god's wrath had the power to terrify my bold, strong brother even when nothing else could.

I couldn't let him be so afraid. I bowed my head to Apollo's priest and said, "We'll do as you tell us. Our guards and servants will all sleep elsewhere."

"Oh, I'd never dare to *tell* you what to do, Lady Helen," the priest replied. I didn't have to look at his face. His voice alone told me that he was wearing a smug, victorious smile.

13

ENCOUNTER
IN DELPHI

The senior priest did tell the truth about our lodgings. We were given a fine, comfortable room and spent a restful night. Early the next morning, one of the temple servants arrived with bread, wine, cheese, and news: "Noble guests, you will be permitted to see the holy Pythia today, as soon as you feel you are prepared to hear her voice."

Castor and Polydeuces almost danced for joy. They talked together intensely, debating whether they'd do better to give Apollo two identical offerings or a single, truly impressive one. I stood by the doorway, arms folded, and said nothing.

At last they noticed my silence. "What about you, Helen?" Polydeuces asked. "What will you give to Apollo?"

"Nothing."

"Helen, you can't—" Polydeuces began to object. I stopped him cold. "I'm giving the god nothing because I'm not coming with you to the temple. Why should I? You heard that priest. *My* future's set."

"We all know you don't believe that," Castor said, smirking. "Or is this your way of telling us that you've decided to put down the sword?"

"Oh, but I do believe it," I replied. And I did. My future *was* set: The choices it held belonged to no one but me. I didn't need or want the Pythia's prophecies to guide me through them.

"This is about those two priests, isn't it?" Polydeuces said. "You can't fool me, little sister. I saw the look on your face, especially when you were listening to the young one. You were as skilled and gracious as Mother at changing the subject to save him from his own foolish remarks. He repaid your help by dismissing you as just another little girl."

"You know, they were only *two* men," Castor put in. "I doubt that all of Apollo's priests here are like them."

"And what if they are?" I countered. "Is Delphi about prophecy or greed?"

"So you think Apollo's oracle is a fake?" Polydeuces asked quietly. He genuinely revered the gods.

"I didn't say that and I don't believe it," I replied

truthfully. "I'd gladly see Apollo's oracle if it didn't mean I'd have to see his priests."

My brothers exchanged a look of resignation. "No use trying to talk her out of it, is there?" Castor asked.

"We know better than that," Polydeuces replied. "Much better." He turned to me. "Are you sure you won't be too bored here, waiting for us to come back? We don't know how long our time with the Pythia will last; I hope you'll find something to do."

"Of course I will," I told him. "I'll be exploring Delphi."

"No you won't," my brothers responded in perfect unison. Then they took turns telling me exactly why I couldn't do what I wanted.

"You wouldn't be safe," Castor said.

"You'd get lost if you went wandering around the city on your own," Polydeuces added.

"It's too big."

"Too noisy."

"Too confusing."

"Too busy."

"You could run into the wrong sort of people."

"Dangerous types."

"But sneaky enough so you couldn't tell they're dangerous until it's too late."

"We're responsible for your safety."

"We have to know where you are at all times."

"It's not that we don't trust *you*, Helen."

"It's *them*."

"It's for your own good."

I flopped down on my bed. "Fine. Go. I'll stay here," I told the ceiling.

Castor and Polydeuces each grabbed one of my wrists and pulled me back to my feet. "I don't think so," Castor said, chuckling. "You'd stay here, all right. You'd stay here just until you saw us go into Apollo's temple, and then you'd be a little cloud of dust sailing out through the gates."

"You don't have to come with us," Polydeuces said. "But if you want to tour this city, you'll have to do it on *our* terms."

With that, he left me in Castor's company.

"Where's he going?" I asked.

"Probably to see if the priests of Apollo have an oil jar big enough to stuff you inside for safekeeping." He winked at me.

No matter how much I loved my brothers, I wasn't in the mood for more teasing. "Aren't you afraid you'll insult the Pythia if you don't go to see her right now? You *were* summoned. She could foretell terrible fates for the two of you if you keep her waiting."

Castor didn't seem worried. "If she's truly blessed with the gift of prophecy, she already knows we're going to be delayed. And if she can't foretell that, she's as much of an oracle as I am, so why should I care *what* she predicts?" He laughed out loud, then added, "But don't tell Polydeuces I said that. He's the devout one."

Polydeuces returned only a little while later, accompanied by two of our Spartan soldiers. "I sent a messenger to the inn where they're staying," he told us. "They'll look after you while Castor and I are with the Pythia. Have a good time in Delphi." He acted as though he'd just solved every problem in the world.

I didn't see it that way.

As we crossed the temple grounds together, I asked Polydeuces, "Is there a *good* reason you're treating me like a silly sheep?" I indicated the two soldiers behind me. "Or are you embarrassing me like this just because you *can*?"

Castor spoke up before his twin could answer. "Stop making a fuss over nothing, Helen. These men will protect you, not steer you."

"That's right, Lady Helen," the taller of the two said. "We're your shadows, not your sheepdogs. Go anywhere you want."

I gave him a sweet, innocent smile. Then I barked at him.

The soldiers and I watched my brothers enter Apollo's temple. Then the taller one asked me where I'd like to go.

"I want to see Milo," I replied. "He's going to come with me while I look around Delphi."

"Milo?" the other soldier echoed as we left the sanctuary grounds.

"You know, the little Calydonian," his comrade said. "How stupid are you? It's not like he blends in with the rest of us. A good lad, but fretful. He was up half the night worrying about how he'd ever know whether Lady Helen would need him to run errands for her while we're at Delphi."

"Is that right?" I asked.

The soldier nodded. "Yes, Lady Helen. It was a great kindness you did, freeing him from slavery, but now gratitude's made him enslave himself to you. You've got a fine servant in that boy."

"Not forever," I said. "Right now there's no choice about it—he's got no family, no way to feed himself—but once we get home I'll apprentice him to one of the palace craftsmen. Then he can live his own life."

"A jug of wine says he'll only be happy if he can live it close to *her*," the first soldier muttered to the other, but when I demanded he repeat his words to my face, he claimed he'd said nothing at all.

My sheepdogs took me to the place where Milo was staying along with some of their companions. Even if the senior priest wanted his cousin's inn alone to get our business, it wasn't big enough to accommodate all of our Spartan guards together, so they'd split up into smaller groups staying at a handful of different lodgings.

As soon as Milo heard I had come for him, he ran out of the inn, overjoyed. "Lady Helen, are you well? What do you need me to do for you? How can I serve you?"

The soldiers escorting me snickered over his eagerness, until I silenced them both with a look colder than the snows of Mount Olympus. "Well, Milo, are you ready to get that cloak I promised you?" I asked.

"Cloak?" Of course he didn't know what I was talking about, but he didn't have to. After only a moment's hesitation, he raised both hands to me, bowed his head, and said, "Whatever pleases you, Lady Helen."

I walked through the streets of Delphi with one soldier ahead of me, one behind me, and Milo at my side. The day was new, but the city was already bustling. The crowded streets with all their noise and commotion were still annoying, but now that I'd had a good night's sleep they were also exciting and challenging. I felt as if Delphi herself were calling out to me: *Come and know me if you can! It takes a special kind of person to learn my secrets. Are you strong or nimble enough to fight through my crowds? Are you smart enough to find your way through my streets? Are you wise enough to deal with any peril or adventure I might choose to throw across your path? I am Delphi, and I dare you to conquer me!*

And I *am Helen of Sparta,* I thought. *I'm your match, just wait and see. But first . . .*

First I'd have to slip away from my sheepdogs.

The two Spartan soldiers escorting Milo and me were puzzled by my intention to get him a cloak, and they didn't hesitate to say what they thought of the matter.

"A cloak?" the taller one remarked from behind me. "In *this* weather? That poor lad's going to sweat away to nothing!"

"You know how cold the nights can get back home," I said. "He doesn't have to wear it *now.*"

"Then I can't say it makes sense for him to *get* it now, Lady Helen," the soldier ahead of us put in. "The palace women make better cloth than any of this foreign stuff. A Spartan cloak for Spartan weather, that's what *I* say."

"The palace women aren't here, and who knows what the weather's going to be like on the road home?" I pointed out. "I want Milo to be prepared." I paused at a place where two streets crossed and tapped my chin. "I wonder where the marketplace could be?"

"Everywhere, from the look of things," the shorter guardsman said.

He was right. The whole city of Delphi teemed with buyers and sellers. It didn't take us long before we found a house with piles of cloth displayed on a long bench just outside the door. The instant that I touched the first one, a fat, gap-toothed woman swooped down on me.

"Little girl, who gave you permission to— Oh!" She bit off her words the moment that she noticed how well I was dressed, to say nothing of the two guards attending me. Her expression transformed from sour to sweet with stunning speed.

"Ah, noble lady, I see that you have a keen eye for quality," she cried. You won't find better cloth anywhere in Delphi—warm in winter, light in summer, tightly woven, and proof against wind and rain. And just *look* at those colors!"

I did. They were all drab grays and browns. I held the first cloth up to the sunlight. If that was what she called a tight weave, so was a fishing net.

"I want a cloak," I told her, tossing the cloth aside. "Something long and *heavy*. It's for him." I nodded at Milo.

"Of course, just as you wish, I have exactly what you want, wait right here," she chattered. "I'll bring out the best I have, something worthy of the noble lord." She raised her hands to Milo in a gesture of reverence before ducking back into her house.

" 'The noble lord'?" the tall guard repeated, incredulous. He and his companion snickered. Milo looked miserable.

"Ignore them," I told him, speaking low. "I promise you, before today is over, you'll be the one laughing at them."

The weaver came out of her house carrying a fresh pile of cloths. These were better work, solidly woven. They were all still the color of the dusty streets, but that was what I was after. She tossed them over Milo's shoulders one after the other, to demonstrate the different lengths.

"What would the noble lord prefer?" she cooed at Milo, embarrassing him terribly. "If you're most concerned about keeping out the cold, this one's long enough to cover you from neck to heels and provide enough material to pull up over your head. But if you'd rather have something shorter . . ."

"That one will do," I declared. It was perfect, but I knew better than to let her know that. "It's not very well made, and there are snarls in the wool the size of locusts, but I have better things to do with my time than look at every scrap of cloth in Delphi." So the bargaining began.

Milo's cloak cost me the taller soldier's small bronze knife. I promised him I'd give him a new spearhead in exchange, once we returned to Sparta.

"It's an honor to serve you, Lady Helen," he said as we continued to walk through Delphi. "I don't require anything in exchange."

We both know you don't mean that, I thought. Aloud, I

said, "Then honor me by accepting it as a gift. I only wish there were something I could do for you now to show my thanks." I coughed as if my throat had gone dry suddenly. "Ugh, what a hard time I had, getting that woman to agree to a decent bargain! I'm ready to die of thirst. Let's find a wineshop."

"That shouldn't be too hard," the taller soldier said, sniffing the air. He was right. We came across one before we'd gone thirty steps. It was very small, little more than a storeroom with a serving table full of cups inside and a bench out on the street. I rejected it.

"I don't want to drink out in the sun," I said. "I'll only get thirsty again. Keep looking."

The next wineshop we found had a shady arbor covered with grapevines next to it, a very comfortable place for customers to take refuge from the sun. I peeked into the shop itself and then rejected this one too.

"Too few amphoras," I said. "They haven't got enough wine to sell. I want to drink wine thinned with water, not water flavored with wine!" I caught my guards exchanging a look and demanded, *"What?"*

"Oh, nothing, Lady Helen, nothing," the shorter man said, rubbing his chin. "It's just that we never expected you to be so . . . knowledgeable about wineshops."

"I want us all to share a cup of wine together," I told him. "It's to thank you for looking after me so well. I could settle for just *any* wineshop, but you deserve better than that."

"I thought you didn't want us to—" the taller man began. He was the one I'd barked at earlier.

"I was being foolish," I said sweetly. "Now that I've seen what Delphi's like, I know that I'd have been lost if I'd left the temple grounds without you. I want to apologize."

What could they say after that? They let me have my way, and soon I did find exactly the sort of wineshop I'd been seeking: dark, cavernous, crowded, and noisy. As soon as we were seated at a table, I snapped a little silver ornament off my belt and held it out to Milo.

"Bring us wine, boy," I said grandly, but instead of placing the silver into his hand, I deliberately missed and let it drop to the floor.

"I'll get it, Lady Helen!" he exclaimed, falling to his hands and knees.

I uttered a short, exasperated sound. "You'll *never* find it by yourself." With that, I ducked beneath the table as well, while my guards laughed.

Safely out of my sheepdogs' sight and hearing, I grabbed Milo's hand just as it closed over the silver ornament. "Milo, do you want to help me?" I whispered urgently.

"Yes, always," he whispered back. "Anything."

I told him my plan as quickly and quietly as I

could, then said, "I just need you to drop the cloak where I can get it and create a distraction so I can slip out. Do you think you can do it? Find some way to distract them?"

Milo smiled more happily than I'd ever seen him do before. "You'll see," he said.

I pulled myself back onto my bench while Milo scurried off to fetch the wine. The silver ornament bought more than enough for what I had in mind. Even though he drank with us, as my servant it was Milo's job to add water to each helping of wine. I drank only one cupful, which was mostly water, but he made sure that the guards drank almost pure wine.

After a while, the tall one exclaimed, "Hey, look at that! Isn't that his fourth cup?" He pointed unsteadily at Milo.

"So what?" his comrade said. "It's our fourth too."

"But he's—he's just a boy. He can't drink like that," the first man objected.

"Who says I can't?" Milo thumped his cup down loudly on the table. He sounded ferociously drunk, though he wasn't. He *had* emptied four cups, but the soldiers couldn't know that there wasn't enough wine in all of them together to equal the wine in one of theirs. "I'm from Calydon, an' in Calydon we know how to drink. Dionysus, god o' wine himself, taught us how to make the bes' wine. Song about it. Listen."

He climbed onto the bench, flung his new cloak to the floor, then leaped onto the table and began a frantic dance while singing a loud, vulgar, hilarious song that soon had my guards and every other customer in the wineshop roaring the chorus and pounding out the rhythm on the tables.

While Milo kept them all distracted, I grabbed his discarded cloak, threw it over my head so that my face was well hidden, and slipped out into the streets of Delphi.

I wanted to explore the city on my own terms, but the city decided otherwise. The crowds carried me along like a tuft of feathers caught in a gale. I was jostled up one street, down a second, straight through a third, and from one side of the road to the other. When I pulled myself out of the human current to look at the buildings, it was always in some dull little side street where there was nothing worth looking at. I had no choice but to rejoin the endless rush of people, hoping I'd be able to see something interesting the next time I got away from the crowds.

I finally got my wish when I managed to put myself behind an oxcart. It was so bulky that it cleared a wide path through the mob, and the oxen walked slowly enough for me to stroll after the cart at a pleasantly unhurried pace, looking around at my leisure. I just had to look *down* from time to time to watch where I was putting my feet, oxen being oxen.

That was how I happened to stumble across the image maker's house. It stood at the intersection of two paths near the place where the street widened into a market square. This open space was filled with even more merchants than the ordinary city streets, some selling their wares from the doors of the houses, some camped in ramshackle wooden booths, some with their merchandise spread out on a blanket, and some simply squatting in the dust with a basket full of goods.

I let the helpful oxcart go on without me as I wandered up to have a closer look at the house selling the clay images. They stood in rows on a narrow table beside the door, watched over by a dull-eyed girl who yawned with every breath she took.

"What are *you* looking at, you little grub?" she lashed out when she noticed me. "Touch any of my dad's stuff and I'll snap your dirty fingers like bean pods."

I stood as tall as I could and shrugged back my plain-looking, dusty cloak. My brothers had told me to wear my best dress that morning, hoping until the last instant that I'd change my mind and come into the temple with them. Now the gorgeous colors of the tiered skirt, the intricate embroidery patterns on the short-sleeved jacket, the gold and silver charms sewn over everything, all hit the girl with the force of a tooth-rattling slap in the face. Her jaw dropped and she stared at me.

At that moment, a bald, beaming, potbellied man came out of the house to see what was going on. When he saw me, his smile stretched so wide it seemed like the corners would meet at the back of his head. He clutched the stunned girl by the shoulders, shoved her back into the house, and gave me his full attention, apologizing for his daughter and begging me to handle as many of the figurines as I liked. He didn't need to ask twice.

Oh, they were wonderful! There were images of leaping bulls and placid sheep, goats and doves and donkeys, and many different sorts of men and women. All of them were painted with extraordinary skill and detail. I'd seen plenty of such things before—everyone took clay images to the temples as offerings for the gods—but these were works of art. I picked up one figurine shaped like a priestess of Gaia, the great mother goddess of the earth. She was holding up two snakes, creatures sacred to Gaia because their whole bodies were always pressed against the ground. The potter had painted in every detail, from the serpents' eyes to the scales covering their backs.

"I'll buy this one," I said. "What will you take for it?" I got ready for the haggling to begin.

He was about to reply when a hand slammed down on the boards between us and a brash voice proclaimed: "*There's* your price, old man!" It was a voice I knew. I looked up as Theseus of Athens lifted his hand from the table. He'd slapped down a strand of silver beads worth enough to buy every image in the shop. Rings of gold and crystal glittered on his fingers, and an enameled silver belt clasping his embroidered tunic gleamed in the sunlight. He looked so splendid that for a moment I forgot just how much I disliked him.

"Well?" he demanded. "Is it a bargain?"

The potter was overwhelmed. His hands trembled as he reached for the silver, as if he were afraid that this would all turn out to be a dream. He jabbered nonstop thanks and blessings at Theseus. Then he picked up one after another of his best figurines, offering them to his new benefactor as humbly and reverently as if he were offering them to a god.

"Give them to the lady Helen, if they please her," Theseus said. If he was trying to impress me by playing the part of the grand, noble, open-handed king, he failed. All *I* could see was a loudmouthed show-off.

"This one is enough for me, thank you," I said. "Now I have to bring it to the temple. Good-bye." I started down the street, trying to melt into the crowd.

"Not so fast, little lady." Theseus pushed and shoved his way to my side as if the other people were bales of hay. When one man protested, Theseus casually backhanded him so hard that he staggered into a wall. The great hero of Athens planted one hand on the small of my back and forced me to walk beside him. "It's a good thing I happened to find you," he said, leering like an ape. "If you want to go to the temple, you're heading the wrong way."

I gave him a haughty look. "I'm not taking this to the temple of Apollo," I said. "I'm going to a little shrine to Gaia. You wouldn't know where it is; only women can worship there." I was rattling off one lie after another, hoping Theseus wouldn't catch on, since he was also a visitor to Delphi.

"But I *do* know the place you mean," he replied so smoothly that I was willing to bet he was lying too. "And you're still heading in the wrong direction. At least let me take you there safely, even if I can't go in."

As I walked along in his unwanted company, he tried to keep up a conversation. I let him yap away, hoping he'd give up and shut up. No such luck. He was one of those people who adored the sound of his own voice.

"Ah, Lady Helen, look at you today, dressed the way you should be. It suits you. A far cry from the rags you wore when you were that insolent boy Pirithous and I met during the hunt, eh? I knew it was you. I figured it out not long after you ran away from us, waving that silly little splinter you called a sword. Where'd you get that toy, anyway? Filched it, I'll bet. No man in his right mind would give something that dangerous to a girl.

"You've got spirit, and that's all right. I like a

woman with spirit, in moderation. But what were you thinking, tagging along on a boar hunt? You could've been killed or, worse, the boar could've ruined that pretty face of yours. You'll be a beauty someday, Lady Helen, even if you are still a wild little thing. Well, a few more years and a good husband will make you settle down."

That did it. I didn't know which was worse, his lies about my looks or his gall about dictating what my future *had* to be. I stopped dead, digging in my heels the same as when I'd helped Atalanta spear the boar. Theseus tried to push me forward, but I held firm, lifted my chin, and said, "I don't know why you're blabbering silly flattery about how *pretty* I am, but you can stop now, before you make an even bigger fool of yourself. I didn't ask for your company and I don't want it. Go away and leave me alone."

He smirked and nodded at the priestess figurine cupped in my hands. "Is that any way to talk to me after I gave you such an expensive gift?"

"You bought this, not me," I said. "Take it." I thrust it at him, and if I just *happened* to drive my fist into his belly while I did it—

That was stupid. No matter how well I could handle a sword or a spear, I was still just a fourteen-year-old girl, and a blow from my fist against a grown man's well-muscled gut hurt him about as much as the flick of a hound's tail. He grabbed my wrist and twisted it until I dropped the figurine into the dirt. I cried out in pain.

"Maybe you shouldn't have to wait a few more years for a husband," he said. "Someone needs to teach you how a *good* woman behaves."

I screamed and thrashed and kicked, but he wouldn't let go of my wrist, and no one in the street made any move to help me. Who'd dare interfere with a man who was so obviously rich and strong, especially when the victim was just a girl, even if she was well dressed herself? How I wished I had my Spartan sheepdogs with me now!

"What are you doing to her? Stop at once!" The words cut through the air like the crack of a whip. Theseus's grip went slack, though he still held me. I saw the astonishment in his eyes: The voice that had just commanded him to let me go was the voice of a young woman.

VISIONS FROM THE GODS

The young woman was standing in the street before us, flanked by two frail, white-haired men. One held a blue-fringed red sunshade over her head, the other waved an oxtail whisk to shoo away flies. She was half a head taller than I, with waist-length curls of hair so black it gleamed with blue highlights. She had the whitest skin I'd ever seen, as if it never saw the sun. Her almond-shaped face was as carefully painted as any of the old potter's images, lips and cheeks reddened with dots of carmine, emerald-green eyes outlined with a heavy black border of kohl. The flounced layers of her skirt were so elaborately decorated with gold, silver, pearls, and precious stones that walking must have been like wading through muddy water. The laurel wreath on her head was made of gold.

When Theseus didn't obey, she strode forward, eyes blazing. I know it was impossible, but I could have sworn that they grew larger, changing from green to midnight black laced with a sudden flash of crimson fire. "Son of Aegeas," she intoned. "Your father is dead, the princess who loved you is gone. How many more will you lose? Son of Poseidon, free the daughter of Zeus or lose more! Friend, mother, son, city—"

"Hear the voice of Apollo!" one of the old men cried out in his shaky voice. "Hear the Pythia!"

But Theseus didn't stay to hear any more. He dropped my wrist, held up his hands as he babbled an apology, then wheeled around and ran. The young priestess solemnly watched him go and stooped to pick up the clay figurine he'd forced out of my hand. "Oh, good, it's not broken," she said as she handed it back to me. "It's very pretty." Then she burst into giggles.

The priest who carried the fly whisk approached us. "You are the lady Helen of Sparta, yes?" he asked me politely while his companion hastened to shadow the Pythia with the fringed sunshade.

"Yes, I am," I replied. "How did you know? I'm afraid I don't remember meeting you."

He had a kind smile. "You didn't. I saw you and your brothers arrive at Apollo's shrine yesterday, that's all. I don't pretend to have *her* blessed powers." He nodded at the young woman who'd rescued me.

I drew the priest a little aside and murmured for his ears alone, "Is that *really* the Pythia?" He nodded, still smiling indulgently. "But why is she *here*, walking through the streets just like anyone else?"

"Because she has already spoken this morning to those who sought Apollo's words, including your brothers, Lady Helen. After she has prophesied, she always enjoys breathing fresh air."

I remembered what I'd heard about the Pythia's vapor-filled lair; I couldn't blame her for wanting to escape it. "I'm just surprised that she *walks*," I said. "She's the Pythia; shouldn't she be carried wherever she wants to go?"

"You can't see anything when you're being carried along in a litter," the Pythia said, coming up behind me. "I *like* walking, Lady Helen, and now I'd like to walk with *you*."

I couldn't have asked for a safer escort back to the temple precinct. When the Pythia went by, people drew back, raised their hands to their foreheads in prayer, fell silent, or spoke in whispers. I kept silent too.

"Lady Helen, what's the matter? Why won't you talk to me? Have I offended you?" The Pythia linked her arm through mine as if we were sisters.

"I—I didn't know if I should," I answered. "You're the god's voice." I hadn't believed it that morning, but after seeing firsthand evidence of her abilities, I was ready to change my mind.

She tossed her hair, making the gold leaves tinkle. "My *name* is Eunike."

"You saw my brothers today," I said.

She nodded. "They talked about lots of things while they were waiting to hear me, including you and how you were growing up to be the most stubborn woman in the world. Lord Castor told the man waiting next to him that you were lucky to be so pretty or you'd *never* find a husband."

"*Now* Castor claims I'm pretty?" I shook my head. I couldn't believe he'd said that. I knew it wasn't true. I still remembered what that Calydonian noblewoman had said about my looks. *That* I believed. "Everyone else at home *used* to say I was pretty, but when I was five he'd call me Frog-face, and even Polydeuces once called me a toad."

"What brothers say to tease their sisters has nothing to do with what they really think of them," Eunike said.

"I don't care about Castor's opinion of my chances at marriage or my looks. I'm just surprised that he chose to talk about me when he was in your presence. It's disrespectful to you and Apollo. Polydeuces must have been ready to kill him!"

"Oh, he didn't tell me himself," Eunike said. "First the priests bring the pilgrims into the sacred underground chamber and let them wait there, while they kindle the brazier and make sure that my tripod is properly positioned above the crack in the earth where the god's breath rises. I wait in another room, well aboveground, until they come to fetch me."

"Then how did you hear what Castor said about me?" I asked.

"Sound travels very well inside Apollo's house. Even when people think no one else can hear them, my priests always do, and they always make sure to tell me what they've overheard."

"Is that where your prophecies come from? From whispers and spies?" I'd really wanted to believe that there was something truly divine at the heart of Delphi, in spite of my encounters with those first two greedy priests. I narrowed my eyes at Eunike. "Why are you telling me this, about how you and the priests fool everyone?"

"I didn't say that." The Pythia's lighthearted expression became more serious. "Now *you're* interpreting my words to suit yourself, just like some of the priests do. I'm telling you about what happens in Apollo's shrine because you'd figure it out for yourself, sooner or later. You never simply accept what you're told, Lady Helen. You ask questions. You challenge things as they are."

My mouth twisted into a mocking smile. "Is that something you saw in a vision or something else your priests overheard my brother Castor say?"

"I won't lie to you: It didn't come from any vision.

The priests insist on telling me everything they hear, whether I want to know it or not," she replied.

"Well then, I hope both of my brothers paid your priests enough to buy themselves a lucky prophe—"

The words died on my lips. Eunike was staring at me. I swear I'd never met another human being with such intense eyes. They went from emerald to onyx in an instant and held an inner glow that was unnerving to see. Their vision penetrated straight to the secret places of my heart, to the dreams where I wasn't tied to a skirt or a loom or a throne or any future but the one I'd make for myself.

"What I learn from spies and whispers isn't what I prophesy," the Pythia said gravely. "The priests don't need to translate my words for the people. Some of them do try to persuade our visitors that if I say, 'It's going to rain,' it really means, 'Your wife will give you five sons,' but only the most foolish pay to hear such nonsense.

"It wasn't always like this. Some of the women who served Apollo before me needed to know as much as possible about each visitor so that, when they spoke, it would seem as though the all-seeing sun shared his infinite sight with them. But some of the Pythias were like me: I *see* things, Helen. I don't know why or how, but I do. It doesn't only happen when I breathe the god's breath. My visions come when and where they will."

"What about the things you said to Theseus?" I asked, curious to learn more. "It's no secret that his father's dead. Everyone in Lord Oeneus's palace knew that. But what about the rest? The lost princess . . . ?"

"Lady Ariadne, King Minos's daughter," Eunike said. "Visitors from Crete said she and Theseus fell in love when he made a raid on their island. They ran off together, yet when he finally came home to Athens, there was no Cretan princess on his ship."

"Do you think he—?" I didn't want to finish the awful thought. Theseus had shown me that he had no qualms about hurting people, but I couldn't imagine him as a murderer.

"His eyes fill with tears when he remembers her," Eunike said. "Whatever became of her, he mourns her memory. His hands are clean."

"Ah." Much as I despised Theseus, I felt relieved to know that. "And I'll bet Poseidon's *his* father the same way Zeus is mine," I said sarcastically.

"He's not the only man to pretend he was fathered by a god. They think it adds to their reputation as heroes. But the other things I said to him . . ." The Pythia sighed like someone carrying a heavy burden. "Those were what I *saw* waiting for him, whether or not he let you go. His mother, his son, his city, he'll lose them all." And she began to cry.

The priest with the fly whisk hurried forward to take her into his arms and murmur words of comfort in her ears. I was afraid he'd blame me for her tears, but when he looked at me it was only with kindness.

"This happens to her all the time," he murmured. "Sometimes the god's breath lingers on her lips after she leaves the temple. When she sees a truly dark future for anyone, it breaks her heart. Let's walk on. She'll be herself again soon. Won't you, child?" He gave the all-seeing Pythia a hug. I wanted to hug him myself, for his goodness to her.

Eunike recovered her cheerful manner before we reached the temple. Just as we were entering the grounds, she clutched my arm, dragged me aside, and whispered, "Do you want to know what's going to happen to *you*?"

I hesitated. It was tempting, in spite of all my protests that morning. *Maybe I* ought *to ask her for my fate*, I thought.

"Tell me," I said softly.

The Pythia clasped my hands in hers. Her eyes were shining, but they stayed green. "You're going to grow up rich and beautiful, you're going to meet a handsome man who'll change your life, and you're going to go on a long voyage with him." Then she burst out laughing. "Isn't that what every girl wants to hear?"

"Very funny." I gave her a hard look.

"If you can't take a joke, say so," she said lightly. "But really, Lady Helen, I haven't had any visions about you, so all I can tell you about your future is this: You're going to have to get back to Sparta with no one's help but your own."

"What?" The Pythia had tossed her ominous words at me as if they were a trifle. "How can you say—?"

"Helen! Thank Apollo, there you are!" Castor came sprinting out of the temple precinct gate, lifted me off my feet, and swung me around. He was so ecstatic to see me that it was as if the Pythia and her attendant priests were invisible to him. As I whirled in Castor's arms, I saw Eunike smile and move silently back through the gateway with her escorts, heading for Apollo's temple. My brother was so focused on me that he was never aware of their presence.

"What kind of a trick was that to play on Hippomenes and Arctos?" Castor demanded when he set me down again. I held his arm to steady myself. My brother's enthusiastic welcome had left me dizzy. "They went crazy when you gave them the slip. You wouldn't have been so quick to pull that stunt if you'd seen their faces when they came back here, dragging poor Milo between them. All three of them smelled like the bottom of a grape vat! None of them had any notion of where you were, but the men were convinced Milo did know and wasn't telling. I had to stop them from kicking an answer out of him."

"If they laid one finger on him—" I growled.

"Milo is fine," Castor said. "Forget Milo. Helen, listen, I've got something fantastic to tell you. Today, after Polydeuces and I saw the Pythia, we met Prince Jason of Iolkos. He's calling together a crew, even more men than Lord Oeneus summoned for the boar hunt, to make the greatest voyage anyone ever heard of, from Iolkos all the way through the Hellespont to Colchis, on the shores of the Euxine Sea, a voyage of *heroes!* Jason had gone to see the Pythia too, and she told him the names of the men he must bring if he wants his quest to succeed. Oh, Helen, you'll never guess what she said!"

"She told him he should bring you and Castor," I said dully. "I'll have to return to Sparta with no one's help but my own."

I looked toward the temple, seeking Eunike, but as I suspected, she was long gone.

That evening, my brothers took me with them to the inn where most of our guards were staying, to confer with them about the arrangements that had to be made before they could depart for Iolkos. They ordered the innkeeper to provide a lavish meal, everything from freshly caught fish, to roasted lamb, to raisin cakes laced with honey. They also sent messengers to the other inns, carrying word that similar delicacies were to be served to all of our loyal men. They were in the mood to celebrate.

"I *knew* it was a good idea to come to Delphi," Castor declared, splashing more wine into his cup. "The gods themselves wanted us to meet Jason, so they saw to it that our paths crossed. When I return from this voyage, I'll thank them with such a splendid sacrifice that all Sparta will talk about it for years after!"

"We should make an offering before we leave Delphi as well," Polydeuces said. "We can use the gods' favor on the road north to Iolkos. And it's only right that we also give something more to Apollo. The Pythia herself told us that this would happen." He was always the prudent one.

The seniormost soldier at the table spoke up. "Lord Polydeuces, before you leave Delphi, do you want to send word to Sparta, to let your royal parents know why you won't be coming back with the lady Helen?"

Before Polydeuces could say a word, Castor barged in. He'd been drinking two cups of wine to his twin's one all through the meal. "No need for that. This wonderful news should reach them only from our lovely little sister's lips. You'll tell them, won't you, Helen? Tell Father and Mother all about how we first earned glory on the hunt in Calydon and how now we're off to secure our names as heroes by bringing the Golden Fleece!"

I looked up from my plate. My brothers had

heaped it with all the finest pieces of meat, the whitest cheeses, the plumpest olives, and the best-baked breads. I'd taken two bites before I lost my appetite. "Bringing back the Golden Fleece," I repeated, mocking him. "As if it exists."

Castor frowned. "What's biting *you*? Of course it exists! We told you what Jason said. It belonged to a marvelous ram sent by the gods to rescue two royal children, Phrixus and Helle, from their murderous stepmother. A pity it wasn't a perfect rescue. Phrixus reached Colchis safely, but his sister, Helle, fell off in mid-flight and drowned. Jason says that's why the place where she plunged into the sea's called the Hellespont. If that doesn't prove the story's true, what *will* satisfy you?"

"Anyone can give a place a name," I said, rolling my eyes. "When I get home, I'll name that olive grove near our training ground Wolf Forest and see what happens. A ram with a fleece of real gold, a *flying* ram that could carry the children through the skies to Colchis, where there are dragons, oh yes, *that's* believable! *That's* worth risking your lives for on a voyage across the world! I'll bet you don't care if that story's true or not. You just want an excuse to go off chasing fame!"

Polydeuces set a honey cake on my already brimming plate. "There must be something waiting for us in Colchis, little sister," he said gently. "Maybe not the gold fleece of a flying ram, but *something*. Why would Jason go to the trouble and expense of outfitting a ship for such a long, dangerous voyage otherwise?" He smiled wistfully and added, "You mustn't worry about us. We'll come back; we'll be fine."

He was right: I was worried about what would become of my brothers on that great adventure. But more than that, I envied them with all my heart. So what if the goal of their expedition was the phantom fleece of a ram that never existed? The fascinating lands my brothers would see and the exploits they'd share would be real enough. And I'd be left behind.

They'll see marvels I can't begin to imagine, I thought. *Maybe they'll even see that old sailor's five-legged monster! Meanwhile, I'm going to be trundled home in an oxcart so thickly hedged around by Spartan soldiers that all I'll see during my journey will be spears. It's not fair! I can handle a sword almost as well as either of them, and I know I'm better with a bow and arrow!*

My brothers left Delphi early the next morning. They left their traveling chests behind, to be carted back to Sparta along with me. Each carried only his weapons, a waterskin, a cloak, and a small leather sack of personal possessions. We said farewell at the temple gateway, with just one of our soldiers there to witness it and attend me. Prince Jason and the other heroes he'd already recruited weren't there; Castor told me that they were waiting for my brothers to join them on the road that led north out of the city.

"This trip would be a lot easier if we had weapons bearers coming with us," he grumbled, toeing his waiting pile of belongings. He looked rumpled, red-eyed, and hurting, not much of a surprise after all he'd had to drink the previous night. "You'd think every lad in Delphi would jump at the chance to join us on a fabulous quest like this."

"We'll have weapons bearers when we reach our quest's start at Iolkos," Polydeuces told him. "Maybe before. We'll pass through many cities before we reach Iolkos. Jason hasn't completed his crew yet."

"I still don't see why we can't find any *now*," Castor persisted. "It's a fine opportunity for any boy who hopes to be a warrior someday. They can't *all* have kinsmen to teach them about the warrior's life and how to fight. We'd see to it that they learn how to use the sword and spear and shield they carry for us."

"You don't have shields," I pointed out.

"We'll get them in Iolkos!" Castor snapped, then winced and cradled his head tenderly in one hand. "Just as well I don't have a shield yet: If that scrawny boy'd had the sense to become my weapons bearer, the weight of it would've crushed him."

"*What* scrawny boy?" I asked.

"Someone with no stomach for adventure, that's

all," Polydeuces said, resting one hand on my shoulder. "Not like us, eh, Helen?"

I'd meant to be cool and dignified about our leave-taking, wanting my brothers to remember me as a young woman, not a silly little girl. My intentions shattered the instant Polydeuces touched me and I realized that this might be the last time I'd ever see him or Castor alive. I burst into tears and held on to him fiercely.

"Don't go," I whispered.

"Shhh, Helen, shhh." He stroked my back. "We'll be fine, you'll see. When we come home, I'll bring back a tuft of gold from the fleece, just for you."

"Tell the truth, little sister," Castor said, tugging a lock of my hair lightly. "You're upset not because we're going but because you're returning home." He laughed as he swept me away from Polydeuces into his own strong embrace.

I gave him a hug and a kiss before pushing him away and declaring, "If I *did* want to go running off after an imaginary dead sheep, do you think you could stop me? You remember how well *that* worked when you didn't want Glaucus to teach me how to use weapons."

"Oh, I learned my lesson there," Castor replied, feigning humility. "I know better now. If you wanted to win the Golden Fleece, I'm sure you'd find a way to reach Colchis long before we do. No one can stand in *your* way; no one would dare. Now that *that's* settled, how about one last hug to see us off? Come on, let's see if you can crack a rib or two for me, Frog-face!"

I thought I'd smother when both my brothers threw their arms around me. When they let me go and started down the street, I stood stone-faced until they were out of sight. Then, without bothering to see if my guard followed, I raced back to my room on the temple grounds and crumpled to the floor at the foot of my bed, sobbing.

I was still crying when a shadow fell across my bed. I looked up to see the Pythia, her moon-white face serene and comforting. She sat down beside me on the tiles and took my hand. "They'll be fine."

"That's what *they* said," I responded, trying to smile as I wiped away tears with my free hand. "When you say it, is it a prophecy or are you just trying to make me feel better?"

Her lips curved up. "If it were a prophecy, you'd have to make an offering to Apollo first. You know the rules." She was pleased when her joke cheered me up a little. Then she added, "When do you leave, Helen?"

"The day after tomorrow. I'm surprised you didn't know. I'm being hauled down to the port, loaded onto a ship, carried to Corinth, then piled into an oxcart and sent home."

"You make it sound like you're cargo."

"That's what I feel like." I clasped my arms around my updrawn knees and rested my chin there. "I wish you could stay with me until then, Eunike. I miss my brothers already, teasing and all, but it hurts less when I can talk to someone."

The Pythia's green eyes filled with regret. "I'd be happy to stay, Helen, but I'd be poor company. I have to be ready to answer at any time that the god calls to me. My life's not my own."

"I know what that feels like," I said.

My friend stood up and stretched. "Maybe I can't help you, but someone else can. I have to go." And, that simply, she was gone. *Everyone leaves me behind,* I thought.

Not long after, as I sat sunk in lonely misery, I heard soft footsteps behind me and a voice I knew well. "Lady Helen?" Milo stood in the doorway of my room, looking unsure of his welcome. The old priest who'd carried the fly whisk was with him.

"Go on, boy, it's all right," he said, giving Milo a gentle push forward. To me he said, "Your servant will be permitted to stay within the temple grounds, to escort and attend you wherever you choose to go during your remaining time in Delphi. Your guards and my fellow priests here have been informed of this."

"And they didn't object?" I asked. I didn't want to get my hopes up and then find out that Eunike's decision could be overruled by someone else. "No one objected, not even the other priests?"

The old man shrugged. "What would be the use of their objections? The Pythia has spoken."

I raised my hands in reverence. "Bless the Pythia," I said solemnly, holding back my joyful smile.

15

THE PLOTTERS
AND THE PLAN

The following day, my last full day in Delphi, I woke up at dawn, determined to take advantage of the precious gift that Eunike had given me. Apollo's shrine was already busy. The sun god's servants always rose to greet their divine master's first appearance in the east. Milo was up with the rest of them, having been given sleeping space with the shrine's other male servants.

"What can I do for you, Lady Helen?" he said happily. "Bring you something to eat? Clean your room? Get your things ready for tomorrow?"

"Come with me somewhere that isn't inside city walls, Milo," I said. "Delphi's amazing, but I miss seeing trees."

Milo flew to fulfill my wishes, and soon, with some helpful information from the old priest, the two

of us were sitting under an oak tree not too far beyond the gates of Delphi. A pair of our Spartan soldiers loitered in the shadow of the city walls, keeping
watch over me at a distance, but if I turned away I
could pretend they weren't there. For a time I just sat,
feeling the warm breeze on my face and listening to
the song of the leaves overhead. I'd once heard a visitor to Sparta tell about his trip to Zeus's oracle at
Dodona, where the god spoke to mortals through the
rustling branches of his sacred oak trees.

*If I really were Zeus's daughter, would he speak to me that
way?* I mused. *Would he even listen?*

It was good to be there with Milo. When had I
stopped thinking of him as merely the slave boy I'd
freed and started thinking of him as a friend? The
question was, did he think about me in the same way?
I didn't know how to tell. I'd never had many friends,
not even back home in Sparta. When I wasn't spending time with my brothers and sister, I preferred to
keep to myself or to practice the lessons Glaucus gave
me rather than share the company of the nobles'
daughters. Those girls and I had nothing to talk
about.

It was different with Atalanta and Eunike. I could
talk to them, but with Atalanta gone and Eunike so
busy, I'd have to look elsewhere for friendship. That
left Milo. He'd proved his devotion to me that day
in the wineshop, but did he distract the soldiers just

because I'd told him to or because he really wanted to help me? I glanced his way, watching the dappled shadows of the oak leaves play across his face. He saw me looking at him and smiled.

"Do you need anything, Lady Helen?" he asked. (Would he laugh if I said, "A friend"?)

"No thanks, Milo. It's just nice to be out here, lazing in the shade. There'll be no more time for it once we get on the road tomorrow. It's a long, long way back to Sparta." I sighed loudly.

Milo sat up attentively at the sound. "Why are you troubled, Lady Helen?" he asked. "Aren't you happy to be going home?"

"I am," I replied. "And I'm not. I'm sorry if that sounds like nonsense."

"Not to me," Milo said. "When Calydon was my home, I was happy to be there with my mother, but even then I wished I had the freedom to go elsewhere. The palace kept me safe, but it also kept me imprisoned." He peeled a bit of bark from the oak's root. "After my mother died, it became a cage."

"Things will be different for you when we reach Sparta," I said. "I promise."

He looked at me closely. "Except you don't want to go back there. You want to go to Iolkos and sail on to Colchis with your brothers."

"Who are you, the Pythia?" I said. "How do you know where I want to go?"

"It's where I'd go, if I could." He twirled the strip of bark idly between his fingers. "When I used to sneak away from the palace in order to bring things to the lady Atalanta, she'd thank me with tales about her travels, her exploits, all the places she'd seen. I'd repeat those stories to myself all the way back to the citadel gates, pretending I was the one who'd done those deeds and seen those sights. She talked about you too. Whenever she finished telling one of her stories, she'd always say, 'I wish Helen could have been there with me. She'd have enjoyed it! That girl's as hungry for adventure as I am.'"

"She said that about me?" I leaned toward him, eager to hear more.

Milo nodded. "She said that until she met you, she thought she was the only woman alive who'd ever wanted something more than a husband, a family, and a hearth fire. Was she wrong?"

I shook my head. "I hate it that my brothers are sending me home like a bundle of old clothes. I've had the same training from the same weapons master they did, even if they had a few extra years of lessons. I know how to handle a sword, how to use a bow, how to hunt and ride. I never used a boar spear before we went to Calydon, but I learned how. *I* should be on the road to Iolkos with them!"

"Yes, you should," Milo said in his sensible, soft-spoken way. "Lady Helen, I know what you did on the boar hunt. You were wonderful. But if you went to Prince Jason and told him how you were trained to fight just like your brothers, how you were taught to hunt and ride, if you found people to tell the prince about all your deeds during the boar hunt and showed him the trophy Atalanta gave you with the boar's blood still on it"—he took a deep breath and looked at me steadily before concluding—"what do you think he'd say?"

We both knew the answer to that, but I had to say it. "That I shouldn't bother about any fleece, golden or not, unless I was going to spin it into thread for weaving." I hit the tree trunk with my fist. "It's not fair, and there's nothing I can do about it."

"It's probably better this way," Milo said, gazing up into the tree's leafy crown. "Maybe if you were older—"

"Most of the men are taking weapons bearers with them. You can't expect *heroes* to fetch and carry and clean up after themselves. I saw those boys in my uncle's palace, before the great boar hunt. Some of them were younger than me!" I slumped against the oak and sighed again. "I could have gone with my brothers and done that kind of work for them from here to Colchis! They didn't have to leave here without even *one* weapons bearer to serve them while they chased after the fleece. Castor said that no one in Delphi wanted the opportunity that you or I would die to have."

"Why didn't they ask two of the guards to go with them?" Milo asked.

"A soldier's not a servant," I told him. "The most loyal Spartan warrior would be insulted if he was asked to be a weapons bearer, even for a prince. It looks like Castor and Polydeuces will have to take care of themselves."

Milo looked away from me. I was puzzled by this sudden shyness and tried to catch his eye, but he deliberately avoided my gaze. He reeked of guilty secrets.

"You're the one," I said. "You're the scrawn—the boy Castor asked to go with him." His silence was the same as shouting *Yes!* I knew it. "You just told me you *wanted* to join the quest for the fleece. You could have done it: Why didn't you?"

"I couldn't," he mumbled.

"Why not? Because it's safer to talk about dreams than to try making them real? What are you so afraid of?"

"Nothing!" He yelled so fiercely that a pair of oxen grazing in a nearby field snorted and moved farther away from us. It was the first time I ever saw fire in Milo's eyes. "I'm no coward. That's not why I wouldn't go with your brothers. I have to go with *you*."

"Who said so? You're *free* now, Milo. Don't you know what that means? You can come and go anywhere you like. You ought to appreciate it."

"I appreciate *you*, Lady Helen!" Once Milo raised his voice, he couldn't stop. He shouted so loudly that the two oxen trotted to the far side of the pasture as fast as they could move their massive bodies. "You're the one who gave me my freedom. If I live to be fifty, I'll never be able to repay you!"

Milo's uproar attracted the attention of the two guards, but I waved them back when I saw them coming toward us. "Do you think you could be grateful *quietly*?" I asked. "This is between us, not us and all Delphi. You owe me nothing. Listen, if you leave now, you might still be able to catch up to my brothers. I'll ask the Pythia for help. There must be at least *one* of Apollo's pilgrims heading north today, one who's going on horseback. If she tells him to carry you with him, you'll overtake Prince Jason's party in no time! I'll give you whatever you'll need for the road and—"

"Then I *will* be in your debt," Milo countered. "If you say I'm free, why aren't I free to stay with you, if that's what I want?"

"Because it's *stupid*!" I forgot my own caution about keeping our voices low. I'd decided that if I couldn't win our argument with facts, I'd do it with volume. "Don't you see, Milo? This is a better opportunity than anything that's waiting for you in Sparta! What could you become if you went there? A potter, a tanner, a metalsmith, maybe a farmer's boy or a shepherd. But if you sail to Colchis with my brothers, you could be—"

"Seasick," Milo finished for me.

I raised my eyebrows. "Is *that* why you won't go? Not even if it means passing up a once-in-a-lifetime chance for adventure? For a *real* future? I'm disappointed."

Milo folded his arms. "Why don't you just *command* me not to be seasick? *Command* me to go away and leave you, while you're at it. *Command* me to join your brothers. It's not what I want, but I guess that doesn't matter after all."

I was about to launch into another list of reasons why he should rush after my brothers when his words stopped me. *Lord Oeneus was open-handed with commands,* I thought. *And it was worse for Milo when his hand closed into a fist. I shouldn't bully Milo into joining the quest for the fleece just because I wish I could do it myself.*

In that instant, a happy inspiration struck me with the force of one of Zeus's own thunderbolts: *Why can't I?* I found an unripe acorn lying on the ground beside me and flicked it at Milo.

"All right," I told him. "You win. You can stay with me." A look of utter relief spread across his face until I added, "But I win too. You're going to go with my brothers."

"But how can I do that if—?"

"And so am I."

Milo and I went back to Delphi, back to Apollo's shrine. While Milo waited in the portico outside my room, I dove into the baggage my brothers had left behind. It didn't take me long to find enough clothing for the trip ahead. Castor and Polydeuces were traveling light and had taken their newer garments and their best sandals, but I was still able to scrounge up a couple of tunics, a spare loinwrap, and the much-used pair of sandals that Castor had abandoned. Leaving the sandals aside, I spread a spare blanket from my own chest on the floor and on top of it laid out all the things I'd taken plus the riding garment Atalanta had given me. When the clothes were in place, I fetched the spearhead from the great boar hunt from my own chest. I placed it at one edge of the blanket, then rolled the whole thing up and tied it with leather lacings.

Before I hid this package back in my chest, on top of my sword, I had to dig out the tunic I'd worn on the boar hunt. I'd kept it at the very bottom of my traveling chest, folded inside a cloak. It still stank of blood and sweat. When would I have had the chance to get it cleaned? I was lucky that the smell hadn't gotten into the rest of my clothes. But it didn't matter now. In fact, it was a good thing, adding to the illusion I was building. I exchanged my dress for that reeking garment, clubbed back my hair, smeared my face with a dab of olive oil from the clay lamp on my table with a little dirt from the floor mixed in, then decided to add an extra touch of soot from the lamp's blackened wick. I had a passing worry that I might have overdone the whole business of hiding my face with a mask of grime, but I shrugged it off. *More's better than less*, I thought. *And safer.*

I stuck my head around the doorpost and softly whistled to get Milo's attention. "Well, what do you think?" I asked. "Am I ready to go see the Pythia?"

"Lady Helen, why did you have to change yourself like that?" Milo asked. "Why couldn't you just go to see the Pythia as you really are? It would be easier. No one would stop you."

"I don't care if I'm stopped, just if I'm recognized. I need to test this." I indicated my filthy new appearance. "If I can't reach the Pythia without someone saying, *Look at the crazy Spartan girl, running around Apollo's shrine dressed like that!* then I might as well go home."

"But if they think you're a grubby *boy* it'll be all right?" Milo asked dubiously.

I grinned at him. "Now you've got it."

He still wasn't convinced that I'd made a good plan. "Maybe I should try to bring the Pythia here to see you, Lady Helen," he said. "Even if you can pass for a boy, you look *too* grubby for anyone to believe you've got an audience with her. What if one of the priests thinks you're a beggar and throws you off the temple grounds before you find her? You might not be able to get back in, looking like that."

"You worry too much, Milo," I told him.

"Lady Helen, wait!" he called out as I turned to go. He thrust the water jug into my hands. When I gave him a questioning look, he said, "If you look like you're running an errand for your master, no one stops you. They look at you, but they don't *see*."

His inventiveness left me openmouthed with admiration. "Milo, that's *brilliant*."

He blushed at the compliment. "It's no great skill to be invisible in a palace." He folded the blanket from my bed so that he'd have something to carry as well, and we left.

Between my new appearance and Milo's ruse, we found Eunike without any of Apollo's priests or servants challenging us. She was just coming out of a room at the very back of the temple when we spied her. Milo was right, it *would* have looked suspicious if someone as dirty as I dared to approach the holy Pythia. That was why he scampered up to her and fell to his knees, holding out the blanket as if it were something she'd sent for. Eunike had a quick and clever mind. She recognized him immediately and pretended to inspect the folded cloth, giving the two of them the opportunity to exchange a few swiftly whispered words.

Abruptly, she straightened up. "You useless thing, I asked for a *brown* blanket. Bring it to my room at once and don't you *dare* to dawdle!" She turned on her heel and strode off, leaving Milo to scurry back to me.

Milo knew where Eunike's room was, thanks to the short time he'd spent among the temple servants. They didn't want to have him wandering lost, so they'd taught him how to find his way everywhere within the shrine walls. He had no trouble bringing me there. It was a small, neat chamber tucked away in an obscure corner of the temple precincts. The kitchen herb beds were within sight of her door. When we entered, the pungent fragrance of rosemary, basil, and bay leaf followed us.

I couldn't help looking around doubtfully at the undecorated walls and floor, the plain red-clay water jug and cup on the table, the patternless blanket on the bed where the Pythia now sat regarding us. Four large, painted wooden chests lined up against the walls provided just a touch of fading color. The only luxuries were a splendid bronze mirror and the alabaster pots holding the kohl and carmine to paint her lips and eyes, all sharing space with the homely cup and jug on the table. I'd expected something more extravagant, a setting worthy of the Pythia's divine gift.

Eunike seemed able to read my thoughts as well as the future. "It doesn't have to be fancy here," she said. "This is the way I like it. Now come sit down and tell me why you're dressed like that."

Milo sank to the floor at her feet, cross-legged, while I sat on the bed beside her. She caught one whiff of my clothes, wrinkled her nose, and slid as far away from me as possible. "I'm sorry about the smell, but it's part of my plan," I told her. Suddenly I was embarrassed by how badly my tunic reeked, and I had to say something to save face.

"What plan? To empty Delphi? By Apollo, Helen, I spend the best part of my life surrounded by the smoke of braziers, inhaling harsh fumes from the heart of the earth, and even *I* can barely stand to smell you!"

"And that means no one else will want to linger near me for too long either," I said. "It's all I want, at least until Milo and I are well away from this city." And I began to tell her what I had in mind.

"A weapons bearer?" Eyes wide with incredulity, the Pythia interrupted me before I was done. "You're going to try passing yourself off as a *weapons bearer* in order to reach Iolkos?"

"We *both* are," I said, indicating Milo. "Every hero

needs one, so it makes sense that my brothers would need two." I sprang up and struck a pleading pose, speaking to an imaginary traveler. "May the gods favor you, good sir, can you help us get to Iolkos? My friend and I are following our masters, Castor and Polydeuces, the Spartan princes. We were separated on the road when Milo here fell ill." Milo coughed dutifully from the floor, then looked to me for approval.

"And what if you happen to meet your brothers *before* any of you reach Iolkos?" Eunike asked. "Would you like me to breathe the god's breath and tell you how pleased they'll be, or can you guess?"

"Oh, I already thought of that," I replied breezily. "We'll be careful enough to let Castor and Polydeuces stay well ahead of us on the road. My brothers can't be the only heroes who've joined the fleece quest without weapons bearers of their own. Once we get to Iolkos, we'll surely be able to find at least two men looking to hire servants. They'll be glad to have us."

"Probably gladder than you know."

"What do you mean?" I asked.

The Pythia pressed her palms together and tapped her fingertips to her lips in thought. "Helen, what if your disguise fails? What if someone finds out you're a girl?"

I went over to her table and picked up the bronze mirror. It was smaller than the one Mother owned but in better condition. I could see my reflection perfectly.

In spite of what Theseus had said about "that pretty face of yours," all that met *my* eyes was angles and awkwardness. My over-eager application of olive oil and dirt was already making the skin erupt into angry red bumps. I couldn't see anything feminine about me at all.

I set the mirror back down. "Unless someone demands that I grow a beard on command, I'll be safe enough, Eunike. And I do have a sword and know how to use it."

"That's not what I mean," she said. "I'm talking about women's matters."

"Women's—"

"And the moon. What I mean is the time each month when—"

"I know, I know!" I exclaimed, stopping her before she could say any more. My cheeks burned. "My nurse, Ione, told my sister and me all about that when we were ten years old. Mother repeated all of it right before my sister left Sparta to marry. They both told us that this *isn't* something for men to hear." I nodded at Milo. He looked disappointed.

"Men know more about women than you think," Eunike said. "But since you're already so knowledgeable, how *are* you going to manage to hide it when you're on the road and you—"

"I won't," I said sharply. "It hasn't happened to me yet. I don't know why. My sister, my *twin*, she's been a woman for at least two years. I'm still a girl." I hated recalling how Clytemnestra had lorded it over me when she'd changed and I'd stayed the same. Worse, every month after that she made it a point to ask me whether "it" had happened to me yet, and every month I had to say no. Ione told me not to fret, that every woman walked the same path eventually, that it would come to me before I knew it. I was still waiting.

"Hmmm." The Pythia was silent for a time, then said, "This may be a blessing for you, Helen. It might even be an omen, a sign from the gods to let you know they want you to succeed."

"Do you really think so?" I asked eagerly. *About time my monthly humiliation did me some good!* I thought.

"It's a shame I can't tell you if it's a blessing that will last," Eunike continued. "The gods might whisk away their favor at any time if you offend them. Even if you don't, they might simply change their minds one day. You'd better give some thought to what you'll do then."

"Don't worry. I'll come up with something." I spoke with a nonchalance I didn't really feel. *I'll come up with something* was what I'd told myself when I first began to lay my plans for joining the quest for the Golden Fleece. I'd only thought matters through as far as getting Milo and me to Iolkos and on board Prince Jason's ship. But how big would that ship be? Would

Milo and I be able to keep ourselves out of my brothers' sight and still manage to serve our new masters? What would happen if our luck ran dry and Castor and Polydeuces recognized us when we were too far out to sea for turning back? I hadn't thought that far ahead. I didn't want to. No matter. *I'll come up with something.*

"Well, at least you're confident," Eunike said. "Even if you are insane." She giggled.

"This is a perfectly reasonable plan of action," I told her, sitting back down on the bed. "We're going to have a magnificent adventure, and I'll pledge a fine sacrifice to all-seeing Apollo when I return."

"But before you go, you want something *from* him, don't you?" Eunike smiled knowingly.

"How did you guess?" I mirrored her smile.

"I never guess," Eunike said with mock seriousness. "*I'm* the Pythia." She squeezed my hand. "And I like you. You've set your heart on this exploit. I doubt I can persuade you to change your mind. I think it would be an insult for me to even try. So instead, I promise to help you. What do you need?"

"Nothing much," I said. "Just Apollo's blessing. What can the all-seeing sun do to give us a successful departure from Delphi?"

"Isn't that the whole purpose of your disguise?" Eunike waved her hand at my overall shabbiness.

"This is to hide my identity once we're on the

road," I replied. "I could escape the temple precincts and the city in my own clothes, if that were all I wanted to do. Simply getting out of Delphi doesn't have me worried half as much as what might happen here *after* I go. I don't want anyone who's left behind to suffer on account of what I've done."

"Who'd suffer?"

"My guards, first of all," I said. "Castor and Polydeuces gave them their orders in detail before they went off with Prince Jason. They're supposed to bring me back to Sparta tomorrow morning, shielding me by sea and land. They'll come here at dawn and send the gatekeeper to fetch Milo and me. What do you think will happen when he comes back to tell them that we're gone? They'll pull this place apart stone by stone, searching."

"You're exaggerating. They wouldn't dare touch Apollo's shrine," Eunike said.

"Maybe not the buildings, but they'll have no qualms about touching the people. If no one can tell them where I've gone, they'll keep knocking innocent people's heads together until they find out or run out of heads! Panic makes people go mad."

"Panic? That's not a word I've heard applied to trained, experienced Spartan soldiers," Eunike remarked. "Are they guards or geese in a thunderstorm?"

"Guards; the guards who'll be punished for my

sake," I replied. "If Father doesn't have them fined or beaten or banished for losing me, they'll still have to live with the shame of having failed him. They're good, loyal men, and I can't ask them to bring my parents word of the tragedy in Calydon *and* that my brothers have gone off to the world's end *and* that I vanished while in their care! I need to *know* they won't be blamed. Please, Eunike, can Apollo let you *see* that future for them?"

"My prophecies come to me according to Apollo's will." The Pythia sighed. "I'm sorry, Helen, but no matter how rich an offering you bring, it's not like ordering a potter to make you a jar that's just the size and shape you want it to be."

"I know." My shoulders slumped. "I was only hoping that just this once . . . Oh, Eunike, I have to find a way around this! I don't want my men to harm your servants or be punished for my disappearance, and above all, I don't want my parents to suffer for one moment on my account."

"You're asking for a lot, Helen," Eunike said gently. "Are you begging me for a prophecy because you're worried about all of those people, or is it something else? Are you having second thoughts about this quest of yours?"

"I *want* to go to Iolkos," I repeated with passion. "To Iolkos, and from there to Colchis, and wherever Prince Jason's ship sails! I want it more than I've ever wanted anything. This may be the last time in my life that I'll have the chance to see the world, to decide to take this road and not that one, to choose whether I walk, or go lumbering along in an oxcart, or ride, or even *fly*! I know it's going to be dangerous, but so is having babies, and everyone expects me to do *that* someday. But if there's no way for me to reach Iolkos except by hurting my parents and the rest, then I—I won't go."

Before Eunike could respond, Milo sprang up, eyes wide with apprehension. "Someone's coming! Lady Helen, quickly!" He grabbed my hand and pulled me down to kneel beside him at the Pythia's feet. "Keep your head bowed," he muttered. "Whoever comes, don't look him in the eye."

I did what Milo told me, fixing my eyes on the tiles. I heard footsteps come shuffling closer and a piping, aged voice calling to the Pythia, asking for permission to enter. She gave it, and the footsteps grew louder. I glimpsed the embroidered hem of a priest's robe out of the corner of my eye.

"Holy Pythia, an embassy from the king of Thebes is here to see you," the priest said. I recognized his voice: He was the good-natured old man who'd carried Eunike's fly whisk. "Will it please you to greet them now?"

"Have them wait for me at the main altar," Eunike said. "I'll see them as soon as I've finished with these two." I saw her point one foot at Milo and me. "They'll be fetching me some things from the town, and you know how it is with boys: They don't pay attention. I have to repeat everything at least four times before it sticks to the straw between their ears."

The old priest chuckled. "Ah, just like I was at their age. The world was filled with so many captivating things, each one *much* more interesting than my responsibilities. Isn't that so, lad?"

I watched in horror as his brown wrinkled hand reached down and cupped my chin, forcing me to meet his gaze. His eyes were bright and clear, with none of the clouding that sometimes blurs the vision of the old. I had nowhere to hide. I could only look up and shiver as I saw how drastically his expression changed the longer he looked at me. The friendly smile dwindled, rapidly replaced by a look of shock and disbelief. *He's recognized me,* I thought. *Farewell, Iolkos! I'm doomed.*

"By Zeus, that *face!*" He gasped and jerked his hand away, wiping it briskly on his robe. "Don't you boys *ever* wash? I swear by the all-seeing sun, if I catch you looking half this filthy the next time you serve the holy Pythia, I'll drag you down to the shore, throw you in the sea, and scrub your skin off with my own two hands."

I ducked my head, muttering a breakneck string of apologies, but he left before I was done. Even the nicest of Apollo's priests had more important things to do than listen to a servant. I heard his steps retreat and fade to silence while I was still speaking.

I raised my head, elated. "Did you see *that*?" I crowed at Milo and Eunike. "He looked right at me, and all he saw was a servant—a servant *boy*!" My heart danced with glee.

"That was all he expected to see," Eunike said. "Haven't you noticed that people don't really *look* at ordinary things? If I told you, 'Look at this apple,' I doubt you'd even *think* of biting it to make sure it wasn't painted clay. Most folk are too busy looking after themselves to ask too many questions; they accept what they're told, as long as it's not something that will make their own lives harder to bear."

I grew thoughtful. "And if they're told something that they believe will make their lives *easier*?"

"Oh, they'll swallow *that* whole and swear it was soaked in honey," Eunike replied. She raised one eyebrow. "Helen, why are you smiling like that? You look even happier than when you were mistaken for a boy. What are you thinking?"

"I'm thinking that the road to Iolkos just laid itself down at my feet."

THE PYTHIA HAS SPOKEN

That night, with a fat, nearly full moon dying in the western sky, I stole across the temple grounds to the Pythia's room. I crept along barefoot, my dress tucked up high, my ears alert for the smallest sound. Once, I thought I heard a dog bark. I threw myself into the shadow of a building and held my breath, wildly wondering if the servants who patrolled the temple grounds at night kept dogs with them on their rounds. A good hound would smell me out in an instant. Then the bark came a second time, too weak to have come from nearby, and I could breathe again.

The herb garden outside Eunike's room was thick with fragrance. I stepped on a mint plant and released a fresh burst of scent into the night. Peering through the open doorway, I saw a small oil lamp burning on the table and two figures waiting for me inside. Milo and the Pythia were standing together, deep in urgent discussion, when I joined them. Eunike glanced my way, then went back to arguing with Milo.

"Why *won't* you take this?" she said, holding out her hands. The flickering light of the oil lamp danced over a dagger almost as long as my sword. A pattern of golden leopards and grapevines glimmered down the center of the blackened blade. "You'll need it for the road ahead. You can't go defenseless."

Milo stared at the wonderful weapon. I could see how he longed to accept it, but what he said was: "I told you, I *can't* take it. It's too fine for me to have, even for a little while. If my masters ever found me with something as costly as this, I'd be beaten for stealing."

"Milo, you *have* no masters anymore," I said softly. "And it's a gift, freely given. Do you know how to use it?" He nodded. "Well then, take it. Who ever heard of weapons bearers who didn't have at least one weapon of their own?"

Eunike put the dagger into Milo's hands. He gazed at the blade, fascinated and a little apprehensive. "Holy Pythia, this blade isn't—it isn't an offering someone made? It doesn't belong to the god, does it?"

"It belonged to my father," Eunike replied. "He was a cousin of the king of Corinth and the first to recognize my visions for what they were. He brought me here, to serve Apollo, and left this with me."

"To remember him by?" Milo asked. "Holy Pythia, if that's so, you should keep it."

"I was ten when he left me. If he wanted me to remember him, he could have come back to visit or sent a message in the six years since then." She shrugged, though her eyes were sad. "I know my visions can make people fear me, but I thought my father was braver than that. The dagger's mine to give, Milo. You *will* be glad to have it."

"This is a noble's dagger," Milo said. "It's not for me." He turned his face to me. "But I'll carry it if it will please you, Lady Helen."

Milo's declaration made Eunike cover her mouth and do a bad job of smothering a snicker. I didn't mind so much. I was glad to see her cheerful again.

"Instead of wasting time making fun of me, why don't we get started?" I said. "It'll be dawn before you know it."

"Not before *I* know it," said Eunike. We all laughed at that. Then she went to one of the four large chests and motioned for me to help her lift the lid. Milo dashed ahead of me, removed the heavy lid, and set it silently on the floor all by himself. He might look scrawny, but his life of slavery had given his skinny arms and legs hidden strength. I was impressed.

Eunike rummaged around in the chest and finally pulled out the most splendid, colorful, magnificent gown I'd ever seen, even among all of my parents' royal finery. The flounced skirt must have had at least fifteen tiers, each one vibrant with patterns of red, blue, orange, white, and green, all of them decorated with twinkling gold and silver charms. The tight green bodice was so thickly embroidered with wild roses that it could have fooled a swarm of honeybees.

"Wait outside, Milo," Eunike said before helping me take off my own dress and put on that fantastic garment. The weight was staggering, but she cinched in my waist so tightly with a wide enameled belt that I *had* to stand straight as a spear shaft or I'd snap in two. Once the gown was on, she began adding to my burden with earrings, necklaces, and finally a diadem of beaten gold for my hair.

"Am I ready?" I asked. I yearned to pick up Eunike's mirror and see what I looked like, but she wasn't yet satisfied with what she'd done to me.

"I'll let you know when you're ready," she said, reaching for the pot of kohl on her table. I had to stand perfectly still, not even daring to sneeze and *definitely* not daring to blink while she painted my eyes, then traded kohl for carmine and painted my lips. Last of all, she dug a third jar out of the open chest and told me to put out my hands, palms up. "Henna," she said, tinting my fingertips a deep, rich red, then working the colorful dust through my hair.

She stepped back and considered the results for a while, then nodded. "Yes, that will do; that will do *very* well, I think." She glanced out the open doorway. "And just in time too. Dawn is almost here."

I never did get to see what I looked like in my borrowed glory. Eunike insisted that there wasn't enough time for that. She herded Milo and me out of her room and across the grounds to Apollo's temple. We were climbing the steps when a young priest came out to bar our way.

"Halt! Where do you think you're going?" he demanded. Then he realized whom he was confronting. "Holy Pythia, forgive me, I didn't know you were—" His words froze. He'd seen me. His hands seemed to rise on their own in a gesture of reverence. "Lady, how may I serve you?" he asked in a voice so worshipful it frightened me.

"Summon the others," Eunike snapped at him, yanking his attention away from me. "The god has spoken concerning the lady Helen of Sparta. Tell the gatekeeper to let no visitors enter the sacred ground until I have revealed what I know to you all. The only exception will be the lady Helen's guards, when they come for her. Bring them into the temple the instant that they're here. Go!"

The priest bolted down the temple stairs, and the three of us went up as fast as we could. Eunike hurried

Milo and me into the same small room at the back of the temple where we'd found her yesterday and shut the door behind us. The room had a window set high on one wall. It let in enough of the predawn light for us to be able to see one another's faces dimly.

"I'd ask you to sit down and rest until it's time," Eunike said, waving at the lone chair that was the only piece of furniture in that room. "But I've worn that dress and I know you *can't* sit down in it. You can't even have a sip of water; you'll smear your lip paint."

"I can wait to rest and drink," I said. "How soon do you think everyone will arrive?"

"Soon enough. You know what you're supposed to do?"

"Stand there and look pretty," I said archly. "I ought to know: It's my plan, after all. What about you? Do you know what *you've* got to do?"

"Stand there and speak for the god," Eunike replied just as playfully. Her expression turned suddenly earnest. "But I won't lie, Helen. Remember that. I like you and I want to help you, but I won't, I *can't* dishonor Apollo with lies."

"I wouldn't want you to," I replied.

"Holy Pythia?" Milo ventured. "You would never lie, I know it, but . . . well, just now, when you told the priest you'd had a vision about the lady Helen—"

"I never said I'd had a vision about her," Eunike replied. "I said that the god has spoken concerning her. I didn't say which god or what form his words took or that he'd spoken to *me*. The gods are always speaking to us. Some people are just better listeners."

"It sounds to me as if you've been listening to Hermes the trickster as well as Apollo," I told her fondly.

"And why not? Hermes was an infant when he stole Apollo's cattle and forced them to walk backward into a cave. The backward hoofprints fooled Apollo into thinking that they'd come *out* of that cave and gone who knows where. He finally did catch Hermes at his tricks, but the new god bought Apollo's pardon with the gift of a lyre, an instrument Hermes had created himself from a tortoise's shell. All this on the very day that he was born! Apollo will pardon me too, as long as I don't lie outright."

"May Apollo and Hermes both help you, Lady Helen, and bring you everything you want today," Milo said gravely.

I felt someone give my hand a brief, reassuring touch in the small, dark room. *Milo? No, impossible.* I wouldn't mind if it were him, but I couldn't imagine him finding the courage to do that. *It must have been Eunike*, I thought.

A faint clamor sounded from outside. The Pythia cocked her head, listening as the sound got louder. "They're coming," she said. "We must be waiting for them." She opened the door, directed Milo to take a hiding place behind a pillar in the darkest corner of the temple, and led me forward to stand beside her before Apollo's altar.

The god received his sacrifices on a painted stone slab at the top of three shallow steps. Standing there, I had a wonderful view looking east out of the temple door. The dawn sky was streaked with peach and pink, purple and gold, as the priests brought my Spartan guardsmen into the temple. My men looked extraordinarily ill at ease, as if they were being led into a mountain pass where an enemy army lurked in ambush. They murmured among themselves and darted suspicious glances into every angle, every shadow, every face, including mine.

I met their wary, unhappy looks calmly. In my mind, I pictured the statue of Aphrodite that stood in the rooftop shrine at home, the one I'd loved from childhood. I also thought of the smaller figure of the goddess, the one that the old sailor had carved from a monster's tooth and given to me. I tried to hold myself as coolly and elegantly as those images.

Eunike stepped forward and raised her arms to the dawn. "Hear me, servants of Apollo, men of Sparta!" she cried.

"Silence for Apollo's chosen!" one of the priests called out. "Hear the Pythia!" The murmurs stopped. Somewhere in Delphi, a rooster crowed.

"It has been revealed to me that the lady Helen will not leave Delphi this day," Eunike declared. "She will not go back to Sparta until it pleases Apollo to bless her return. This is how it must be." She lowered her arms. "Men of Sparta, who is your leader?"

The same soldier who'd witnessed my brothers' leave-taking stepped forward. "I am, holy Pythia."

"Hear me, then. You will lead your men home and tell the lady Helen's royal parents what I have told you, that she will not come back to them until it is the will of the gods."

The man bowed his head. "Yes, holy Pythia, I'll do as you say, except . . ." He took a deep breath. "Great lady, *when* will they see the lady Helen's return?"

One of the priests glared at the man. "You question the Pythia?"

My guard returned the priest's scowl redoubled. "I have a daughter, and I know how I'd feel if she were taken from me. I've served Lord Tyndareus and his queen long enough to have seen how dearly they love their children. I ask this for their sake. If that's an offense, let me be the only one to suffer for it."

"Spartan, you are a faithful man; you commit no offense in questioning me," Eunike said. "Tell the lady Helen's parents this as well: that although it will be a year or more before they can hope to see their daughter, they will have frequent word from Delphi to comfort them. Let them be content with that."

With that, Eunike turned her back on the crowd and faced me, holding her hands above my head. "May the all-seeing sun bless you in all your paths, Lady Helen, and bring you safely home."

Later that morning, Eunike, Milo, and I stood in the gateway of Apollo's shrine, watching my guards march away. They raised their spears to me in one last salute as they passed, and though some still looked a little dubious about the whole matter of leaving me behind, most of them were smiling. They believed that the gods had spoken. I was not supposed to be going with them, and that was that. They accepted this unconditionally.

When the last of the Spartans were out of sight, Milo murmured a few words to Eunike and darted back into the temple grounds. "Who lit a fire under him?" I asked.

"He has things to do." She linked her arm in mine and drew me aside far enough to keep our conversation private from the gatekeeper. "He's got to be ready for when you leave tomorrow."

"Thanks to you," I said, squeezing her arm. "Eunike, you were wonderful. Now there's no way that my parents can blame those men for coming home without me. The Pythia foretold it."

"I never foretold a thing," Eunike reminded me. "Can I help it if people expect everything I say to be a prophecy?"

"Not even when you said it was *revealed* to you that I wouldn't be leaving Delphi today?"

"So it was, just not by the gods. *You* told me you'd need one more day to prepare for your journey." She winked at me. She was right. There wasn't a single thing she'd said in the temple that morning that couldn't be interpreted two ways. I *wouldn't* be going home until at least a year had passed. My parents *would* have frequent news from Delphi; it just wasn't going to come from me. And as for *why* I wasn't going back to Sparta with my men, when the Pythia said, *This is how it must be,* no one demanded a more specific reason, because those words came from her lips. My friend controlled an awesome power. She'd used it to help me, but I thanked all the gods that she was too honorable to abuse it for herself.

"Eunike, you should serve Apollo *and* Hermes," I told her. "How can I ever thank you for—?" I clapped my hands to my mouth: A sudden flash of revelation struck me. "The priests!" I exclaimed. "What about the priests? How can I leave for Iolkos tomorrow if they're expecting to see me here, in Apollo's temple, for at least a year to come?"

"Helen, I doubt your father has the power to

punish Apollo's priests for misplacing you," Eunike said calmly.

"And who'll have the power to comfort him and my mother once they find out that *no one* knows where I am?" I countered.

"Well, you can't change your mind about going to Iolkos now—"

"I'm not doing that!" I cried.

"—even if you wanted to," Eunike concluded. "It would make me look like a liar, even when both of us know I'm not. Apollo would *not* be pleased." She planted her hands on my shoulders and steered me back through the temple gates. "Don't worry about it. Prepare for your journey and leave the priests and their expectations to me."

I'd seen how clever Eunike was; I decided to put my confidence in her. She *would* come up with a way for me to leave for Iolkos and stay in Delphi at the same time. I simply couldn't imagine *how* she'd manage it.

That night, I dreamed I was standing beside her at the sun god's altar once more. The temple filled with sparkling golden light, and Apollo himself appeared to us. *I have heard your prayers, my Pythia,* he said to Eunike. His divine voice shook me down to my bones. *I will answer them.*

He touched my head with a branch of laurel, and suddenly there were two Helens standing before the altar. My other self turned to face me, but before I could say anything she grabbed my arms and shook me violently, shouting in my face, *You're not Lady Helen! You never wanted to be Lady Helen! I'm Lady Helen! Say it! Say my name! Lady Helen! Lady Helen!* I tried to ask her, *Then who am I?* but my tongue wouldn't move. And still my other self shook me, crying out, *Lady Helen! Lady Helen!* until I realized that I was awake and Milo was standing over my bed, calling my name.

"Lady Helen, hurry, it's almost dawn, it's time!"

I sent him out of my room while I put on one of my brothers' tunics. It wasn't the foul-smelling one from the hunt; I'd decided to keep that in reserve for only the most dire emergency. I didn't want to draw anyone's attention on the road to Iolkos, and I'd realized that being *too* filthy might have just the opposite effect. I bound back my hair, tied on my sword, draped Castor's old sandals around my neck, picked up my bundle of belongings, and was out the door.

We didn't leave the temple precinct by the front gateway. Because Milo knew the grounds, I let him lead me to a place where the wall was low and a broken gardener's wagon gave us just the bit of extra help we needed to scale it. Once over the wall, Milo guided me carefully through the dark, silent streets until we were clear of the city.

The road we took away from Delphi was easier than the road we'd scaled to reach Apollo's sacred city. Our feet picked up speed on that downward slope. I smelled pine needles, which was nothing remarkable, but I also breathed in the scent of the sea. The longer we walked, the stronger it grew. That shouldn't be: The sea lay *south* of Delphi, and to march to Iolkos I knew we had to take the northern road.

"Milo, are you sure we're going in the right direction?" I asked.

"This is the way we need to go, Lady Helen," he replied, looking back over one shoulder. "She's waiting for us by the shore. She sent for me last night, after the two of you said your good-byes, and told me to bring you to her here this morning."

I didn't have to ask who *she* was. "Why?"

Milo shrugged. "I don't know. I've told you what she told me, Lady Helen."

"Milo, we're going to be traveling together," I said. "Don't call me Lady Helen anymore."

"It would be disrespectful if I only called you Helen, my lady," he said.

"It would be *ridiculous* if you called me Helen. I'm supposed to be a boy, remember? Call me Glaucus."

"Yes, Lady—*Glaucus*," he muttered. I could tell he wasn't happy about it.

Happy or not, you'd better get used to it, Milo, I thought. *We've got a long way to go, and this isn't the road that's going to take us there. What's Eunike up to, I wonder?*

She was waiting for us by the sea, standing beside

the smoking embers of a driftwood fire. She was wrapped in a rumpled cape that looked like she'd slept in it. She must have sneaked out of the temple as soon as Milo left her and spent the night on the beach in order to meet us here at this hour. While we'd made the downhill trek from Delphi, the new day had come.

Eunike wasn't waiting alone. A stocky, middle-aged man wearing only a loincloth stood on her left, his skin the same deep brown as his hair. On her right stood—

"Lady Helen," Milo breathed, staring at the girl with Eunike.

At first glance, she did look like me as far as height, weight, and the color of her eyes and hair. She was dressed in the same elaborate gown I'd worn to Apollo's temple, adorned with the same jewelry, her face painted with the same carmine and kohl. But if you didn't allow yourself to be distracted by details, if you really *looked* at her, studied her closely, you could tell she wasn't me.

"Who are these people, Eunike?" I asked, bewildered.

The Pythia beamed. "This good fisherman came to Apollo's shrine years ago, to hear if his daughter here would recover from a fever. The god allowed me to give him good news. Since then, he's felt that he's in my debt, no matter what I say. He and his daughter come to honor Apollo every day, when he's not out at sea, and never empty-handed. While you were in your room yesterday morning, preparing for your journey, I saw them in the temple and realized how closely this girl resembles you. It was as if Apollo himself was giving you the way to stay in Delphi and still seek a *hundred* Golden Fleeces!"

The fisherman stepped forward and raised his hands to me. "The holy Pythia told us what you need, great lady. I've sworn to keep your secret safe, and so has my girl. May Apollo destroy us both if we betray you."

"You can't do this," I told him earnestly. "You can't let your daughter masquerade as me. Think of what could happen to her if she's discovered!"

The fisherman smiled awkwardly, avoiding my eyes. "Great lady, my girl's all I've got, since her mother died birthing her. I don't know what I'd've done if I'd lost her too, when that fever hit. When I serve the Pythia, I serve the god who gave her back to me, and the Pythia says she wants us to help you. Let us."

"I won't let anything happen to this girl, Helen," Eunike said, stepping between the fisherman and me. "Not even if she's found out."

"What do you mean, *if*?" I said. "She might fool someone for a moment, but to pass as me for a year or more? One good look at her——"

"Who'll bother doing that?" Eunike replied smoothly. "How often did Apollo's priests pay any attention to you when you passed them on the temple grounds, let alone *look* at you? Even the servants never really *saw* you. You could be any girl at all to them, as long as that girl dressed like a princess."

"And what if one of them has to *speak* with me?" I demanded. I turned to the fisherman. "Do you think your daughter can *talk* like a princess too?"

"Oh yes, great lady, yes, certainly." He bobbed his head eagerly. "My Alkyone's *very* bossy, when she wants to be."

I saw that I wouldn't be able to talk anyone out of this scheme. The fisherman saw it as the best opportunity he'd ever get to repay Apollo for his daughter's life. His daughter saw it as a dream come true, the chance to live like a princess. They trusted Eunike to save them in case the plan failed, but you could tell by looking at their faces, radiant with confidence, that they refused to believe anything *could* go wrong.

If I wanted to go to Iolkos and then on to Colchis and the Golden Fleece, I'd have to borrow some of that wholehearted faith. I bowed my head and raised my hands to the fisherman's daughter. "Lady Helen, do I have your permission to go?" I asked.

She stood tall and looked down her nose at me, but her lips curved up in a graceful smile. "Go with the blessing of the gods," she said. Her voice was only a little lower than mine. "And with Poseidon's blessing above all." She gestured at the little boat rocking on the waves not far from where we stood on shore.

"No road for you, Helen," Eunike said gaily. "Not yet. This man has promised me to take you as far as Corinth." She patted the fisherman's shoulder. He looked ready to die of joy at receiving such a sign of favor from Apollo's chosen one.

"I'll do better than that!" he declared. "I'll take you all the way to Iolkos, if the gods let me."

We said our farewells and the three of us waded out to his boat. Milo looked as if he were going to his own funeral. Considering what a sorry sailor he was, he might have been right. Once we climbed aboard, he sank down on the deck and buried his head in his hands.

"What's wrong with him?" the fisherman asked me as he prepared to set sail.

"He gets seasick," I told him. "*Badly* seasick."

Our new friend pursed his lips, then went toward the back of the boat and returned carrying a small, sealed clay flask. "Have a swig of this," he said, forcing it into Milo's hands. "It's mostly mint and ginger; settles the stomach. Back that up with a proper sacrifice to Poseidon, and I guarantee you'll think we're sailing over glass."

While Milo sniffed the neck of the flask warily,

then drank, a favorable wind sprang up. The fisherman made haste to set the sail. The painted cloth belled out and we were under way. I waved good-bye to Eunike until a curve of the coast hid her from my sight, then I went to see if there was anything I could do to help the fisherman.

"Help? Bless your kind heart, no," he told me. "I'm used to sailing this sweet girl on my own. You look after your friend and see to it that you don't forget to make that offering to Poseidon, like I said. The gods are watching."

I went back to Milo, but he'd stretched himself out on the boards and had fallen asleep. Maybe there was something stronger than ginger and mint in that little flask, but as long as he wasn't being sick again, I was happy. I left him in peace and walked forward, to the small vessel's prow.

With Milo napping and the fisherman busy, I'd have to come up with an offering to Poseidon on my own. I opened the soft leather pouch at my belt and fished around inside. It was packed with beads of gold, silver, and precious stones. As part of my preparations for this trip, I'd taken apart several of my necklaces, intending to trade them, bead by bead, for supplies on the road.

"Lord Poseidon of the seas, earth shaker, horse tamer, guide my hand," I prayed. "Choose your sacrifice." My fingers closed on what I thought was just another bead, but when I pulled it out into the light, I saw that it was the monster's tooth that the old sailor had carved into the shape of Aphrodite riding a dolphin. Poseidon had made his choice.

I held the little image to my heart. Out of so many possibilities, why had the god chosen this for his sacrifice? Did it mean something? I wished that Eunike were still with me. She was used to understanding divine messages. Aphrodite was born from the ocean's foam and I was giving her back to the sea. Was that a sign that I'd return safely to the place where I'd been born or a warning that the ocean would swallow me up too?

If I'd never left home, I wouldn't have to tangle my brain over omens, I thought. *I wouldn't need to worry about my fate, or Milo's, or what will happen if I—if I don't come home at all.* I filled my lungs with briny air and let out my breath slowly. *A rock at the bottom of a well is safe from worries too.*

We were sailing east, into the sun. I raised my arms and called out, "Lord Zeus, ruler of gods and men, even though I'm not your daughter, give me a father's blessing. All-seeing Apollo, give me your light; Athena, lend me your wisdom. Beloved Aphrodite, let Milo and me find only kindness on this journey. Lord Poseidon, grant us a safe voyage and accept this sacrifice!"

I threw the carving of my goddess as high and far

as I could, into the sky above the waves, and watched its arcing path through the air. As it fell, I saw a golden shape come diving toward the plummeting image, a huge eagle that seized the monster's tooth in his talons. The feathers on his breast skimmed the sea before he soared back into the sky and flew away.

"Did you see that, La—Glaucus?" Milo's voice sounded in my ear. He'd woken from his nap and come up behind me unexpectedly. I almost jumped overboard with surprise. "It's a good sign, isn't it? Or is it predicting that something's waiting to snatch *us* away? If that's so, I swear I won't let it touch you. But *is* it a good sign after all? Ah, what does it mean?"

"You worry too much, Milo," I said as if I had no such worries of my own. "If every hero stopped to think about all the what-ifs in his path, none of us would ever take one step beyond our own doorways."

"But you saw what it did," Milo protested. "The eagle is Lord Zeus's bird. We can't just ignore it. Ah, what does it *mean*?"

"What it *means*," I said, smiling, "is that you and I have just seen either the world's most unmistakable omen or the world's most nearsighted eagle." *May the gods stand by us,* I thought as I laughed and Milo stared at me in dismay. *May they favor and guide us, but may they never hold us hostage through our fears.*

"Don't look at me like that," I told him, wiping

sea spray from my eyes. "I haven't said anything wrong. I love the gods and honor them, but I'm not their slave. Neither are you. From now on we're going to make our own omens." I took his hand, and when he pulled it away, I took it again. This time he let me.

We were free.

SOMETHING ABOUT HELEN

People have always loved stories. We love them, and when we find one about the adventures of a truly fascinating character, we hate to see it end. For every storyteller who concludes his tale with "And they lived happily ever after," there's always someone in the audience who says, "Great, and *then* what happened?"

Sometimes there *is* nothing more to tell. The dragon is slain, the war is won, the world has been saved from Evil, the main character has fallen off a cliff and *died*, for heaven's sake! After all that, how can there possibly be a "*then* what happened?"

Never underestimate the power of an eager audience, or the desire of a storyteller to keep that audience happy. There can always be another dragon to slay, another war to fight, another world to save, and as for those characters who died at the end of the first story . . . well, it was all a dream, or a trick, or a case of mistaken identity. The sequel will go on!

But what about when the climax of the original story is so awesome that the sequel falls flat because "and *then* what happened?" is a letdown by comparison? Sometimes it's better to have no sequel instead of a lame one. (Though you can always try telling the story of one of the original tale's supporting characters. Spin-offs have been around since long before TV sitcoms, but I don't know if Homer would have liked to think of the *Odyssey* as a spin-off of the *Iliad*.)

Never mind, all's not lost. When a favorite character reaches the unmistakable end of his or her adventures and there's honestly zero chance for coming up with further exploits that are believable and interesting, there's something left to tell: "Well then, what happened *before* that?" Which is just what I asked myself before I began to write about Helen of Troy.

I wanted to tell more of Helen's story than the best-known version, the one that's come down to us in the *Iliad*. Did she *know* that everyone agreed that she was the most beautiful woman in the world? Did knowing that make her feel proud, or smug, or embarrassed, or bored with all the never-ending compliments? ("Yes, yes, I know I'm gorgeous, but what I *asked* you to do was please pass the olives!") Did she *like* being thought of as nothing more than The Beautiful

One? Did she worry about who she'd be when she got old and her beauty faded away? Was she just another (spectacularly) pretty face, or was there more to her than that? Who *was* Helen?

Daughter of the king of Sparta, she was so beautiful that it was said she couldn't possibly be an ordinary woman and that her *real* father was Zeus, king of the Greek gods. What did a story like that imply about her father *or* her mother? Did Helen mind hearing her real parents whispered about in that way?

The Trojan prince Paris fell in love with her at first sight, stole her from her husband, Menelaus, and carried her off to his father's walled city. Was it true love, or was it the work of the gods? Did she go with him willingly, or was she kidnapped? If she didn't want to leave Sparta, did she ever try to get away from her kidnapper? Did she even believe she had the chance of succeeding if she tried to rescue herself?

Menelaus's brother, King Agamemnon of Mykenae, rallied an army led by the greatest kings and heroes in Greece and fought for ten years to reclaim her. Countless men died in battle, the great city of Troy was destroyed and its people slaughtered or enslaved, all because of one beautiful woman. When it was over, Paris was dead and Helen was given back to her husband. The end of her story makes her sound like nothing more than a pretty prize to be awarded to the winner of the Trojan War. Was she heartbroken, furious, frightened, relieved, or did she feel anything at all?

And so she went home to Sparta with Menelaus, which is more or less where Helen's story ends, as far as the Greek writers were concerned. ("Hey, Helen! You just caused a ten-year war and the destruction of one of the world's mightiest cities! What are you going to do *now*?" "I'm going to Disney World!")

Helen's "and *then* what happened?" was pretty well sewn up, but her "well, what happened *before* that?" was wide open. Plenty of her story remained untold, and I wanted to tell it. The only traditional tales about young Helen concern her birth as Zeus's daughter and her abduction by the Athenian hero Theseus when she was still just a girl but already incredibly beautiful. There's no mention of her being at the Calydonian boar hunt, though her brothers, Castor and Polydeuces, were. There's certainly nothing in the old tales about her knowing how to use weapons or hunt or ride. Exploits like these make a good story, but did I have any sound reason for letting her do them?

Oddly enough, though Helen herself is mythological, much of what I've written about her in this book is based on ancient Greek history. Many people used to believe that myth and history had nothing to do with each other. They thought that Troy itself was an imaginary place, like the lost city of Atlantis. Then in 1876, the German amateur archaeologist Heinrich Schliemann was so deeply inspired by the *Iliad* that he decided to search for Troy. He was only a merchant, but a merchant with vision, passion, and an abiding love for a good story. He, too, must have believed that there was more to the tale of the Trojan War than what the *Iliad* had to tell—maybe not "and *then* what happened?" or "what happened *before* that?" but "did it really happen at all?" Using information from that ancient epic, he astonished the world when he uncovered the ruins of a great city on the very spot Homer's poem described. There was even evidence that the city had been destroyed by violence and been burned, just like Helen's Troy.

Since Schliemann's success, we no longer look at myths and legends in the same way. Fantastic stories may contain hidden grains of truth that archaeologists and historians can use to guide them in putting together a more complete picture of the past. Even the sinking of Atlantis might be based on a real event, the volcanic explosion that destroyed most of the Mediterranean island of Thera.

Myths take place in the past, but some of them can be assigned to a *specific* part of the past rather than a vague "once upon a time." Helen's story takes place during the Bronze Age, almost 2,500 years ago. We know this for various reasons, including the fact that the great kingdom of Mykenae, where Agamemnon ruled, flourished during this era. Therefore, the weapons, clothing, food, transportation, royal palaces, and such that appear in this book belong to Bronze Age Greece. Most of what is known about this time comes from archaeological finds, including jewelry, statues, wall paintings, pottery, and sites of major ruins. In addition, some of Homer's descriptions of life in Helen's day make the archaeological evidence come alive.

Helen's era was quite different from what most people think of when they hear the words *ancient Greece*. The Parthenon, the graceful statues, the works of Sophocles, Euripides, Socrates, Aristotle, and Plato, all came nearly a thousand years after Helen's time, during the classical era. In the Bronze Age, no one yet knew how to make brittle iron flexible enough to use for tools and weapons. Art, especially sculpture of the human form, was stiffer and more stylized. Few people could read or write. Instead of signing important papers, you would use a stone seal to leave an impression on clay tablets. The design on the seal would be as unique as a signature. There *was* a kind of writing in Bronze Age Greece, but it was mostly used to keep track of financial matters, such as royal tax records. Messages, poems, songs, and stories were not written down but were memorized and passed along by word of mouth. Inevitably, they'd change when someone with a poor memory or a rich imagination retold them. Money hadn't been invented yet. The first coins were centuries in the future, so Helen lived in a barter economy, with lots of haggling, negotiating, and trading goods for goods instead of paying for them outright.

Though markedly different from Helen's time, there were some aspects of life in classical Greece that influenced me while writing this book. Chiefly, these things concerned the Spartans, who lived a thousand years after Helen. Today we use *Spartan* as an adjective meaning "plain," "austere," "strict," even "harsh." Spartans of classical times were famous for being all of these, as well as being known for their warcraft. At birth, all infants were brought before the elders, who decided whether a child would be allowed to live or be left in the mountains to die from exposure. This decision was based entirely on whether the child looked strong enough to survive. It's hard to think of anything harsher than that. The Spartans' whole way of life seemed to center on physical perfection, endurance, and skill in handling weapons. Most significant was the fact that, unlike other Greeks, they trained their daughters as well as their sons in athletics. The girls ran, wrestled, practiced throwing the javelin or spear, and, like the boys, they exercised unclothed, to strengthen their bodies. Spartan men were frequently away from home for long periods of time, fighting wars. This left Spartan women in charge on the home front. As a result, they were much more independent than other Greek women.

In spite of the centuries separating them, I like to think that the classical Spartans' attitude toward women might have had its roots in Helen's time. There is archaeological evidence that Bronze Age women were powerful and respected, holding important positions in their society. One image, taken from a seal, shows a huntress armed with bow and arrows.

No doubt Greek females could also be independent. Mythology is full of stories about such women, but unfortunately they usually end with some great disaster caused by the woman's independent behavior. Was this the original ending of the story, or was it changed over the course of the centuries and turned into a "lesson" against women's freedom by those who feared it?

I like to think that the part of Helen's story I've told is about not fearing freedom. Freedom wasn't something to take for granted in Helen's time, nor is it now. Slavery was very much a reality of the Bronze Age, classical Greece, and even some parts of the world today. Other kinds of oppression are even more widespread. Little by little, we're challenging and overcoming the attitude that people are *things*. It's not easy work, and accomplishing it means that sometimes we have to become warriors, even when we're told that it's not the path we're expected to follow in life. We do it anyway, because it's the right path.

Helen would approve.

ABOUT THE AUTHOR

Nebula Award winner Esther Friesner is the author of 31 novels and over 150 short stories, including "Thunderbolt" in Random House's *Young Warriors* anthology, which led to the creation of *Nobody's Princess.* She is also the editor of seven popular anthologies. Her works have been published in the United States, the United Kingdom, Japan, Germany, Russia, France, Poland, and Italy. She is also a published poet, a produced playwright, and a onetime advice columnist. Her articles on fiction writing have appeared in *Writer's Market* and Writer's Digest Books.

Besides winning two Nebula Awards in succession for Best Short Story (1995 and 1996), she was a Nebula finalist three times and a Hugo finalist once.

She received the Skylark Award from NESFA and the award for Most Promising New Fantasy Writer of 1986 from *Romantic Times.*

Ms. Friesner's latest publications include *Temping Fate;* a short story collection, *Death and the Librarian and Other Stories;* and *Turn the Other Chick,* fifth in the popular Chicks in Chainmail series that she created and edits. She is currently working on the sequel to *Nobody's Princess,* titled *Nobody's Prize.*

Educated at Vassar College, receiving a B.A. degree in both Spanish and drama, she went on to receive her M.A. and Ph.D. in Spanish from Yale University, where she taught for a number of years. She is married, the mother of two, harbors cats, and lives in Connecticut.

Ms. Friesner's proudest public-appearance moment came while serving as toastmaster for the 2001 World Science Fiction Convention in Philadelphia, when she took the stage as Rapmaster Toast and, yes, *rapped* before an audience of thousands. And at her age, too. She has promised her children not to do that again.

Maybe.

THE ADVENTURES CONTINUE IN

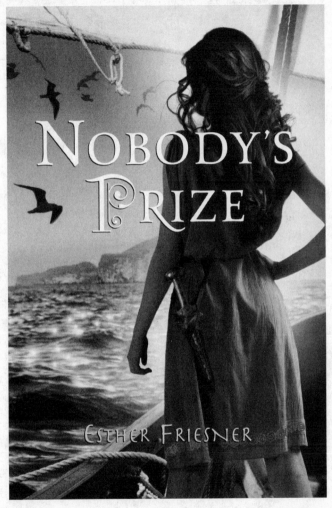

NOBODY'S PRIZE

ESTHER FRIESNER

Read on for a sneak preview of Helen's journey on the high seas—available now!

PART I
IOLKOS

I stood in the bow of the little fishing boat and gazed at the glittering city high on the bluff ahead. Even so late in the day, with the sun setting and the early summer light fading from the sky, I could see how tall the palace walls stood. I marveled at how many buildings clustered at their feet. Only the richest cities were so crowded with houses and shops and temples.

Iolkos! I thought happily. *It* must *be Iolkos. After so many days' sail from Delphi, the gods grant it's no place else.* My heart beat faster as I scanned the harbor that lay in the shadow of the citadel, seeking one special ship among all the rest. Where was it? Where was the vessel that would carry me off to adventure? Was it that one, with the almond-shaped eye painted in red just above the prow? Or that one, with a swarm of men busily at work, taking down its blue-bordered sail? Where was *my* ship, the ship Prince Jason was going to sail to the farthest shores of the Unfriendly Sea, the ship of heroes who would dare anything to fulfill the quest for the Golden Fleece? Where was the *Argo*?

"There she stands, lads, Iolkos!" the fisherman called out to Milo and me from his place at the steering oar, confirming my hopes. "And less than a day's sail away." He winked at me when he said "lads," and I grinned back. Though I wore a boy's tunic and my skin was deeply tanned from our voyage, I was no more a lad than that man's daughter.

The fisherman knew my true name and rank—Helen, princess of Sparta, Lord Tyndareus's heir, Queen Leda's daughter—but I'd spent so much of our voyage from Delphi teaching him to call me "Glaucus," the boy's name I'd chosen for myself, that it came to his tongue naturally. He'd keep my secret. The real question was whether I could do the same. My brothers, Castor and Polydeuces, waited behind the walls of Iolkos, waited to sail with Prince Jason on his quest for the Golden Fleece. I intended to join them on that quest, but for that to happen they must not recognize me as their sister or my adventure would be over before it began.

I leaned as far forward from the prow as I could

without toppling out into the waves. Sea spray was cool and salty on my lips. There was a fine breeze filling our sail, and the sky swirled with squawking gulls. Soon we'd land, and I'd put the next step of my plan into action.

I wasn't the only one in a hurry. "Is it true?" Milo exclaimed eagerly, scrambling to stand beside me. "Are we there at last?" My friend was *not* the world's happiest sailor.

"Soon enough," the fisherman said. "Tomorrow morning." He leaned against the steering oar and turned our boat's nose toward the shore.

" 'Tomorrow'?" I echoed. "Why not today?"

The fisherman chuckled. "You know the answer to that."

So I did. "Always keep the shore in sight," I recited dutifully. While I'd spent our voyage from Delphi teaching the fisherman to call me by a boy's name, he'd spent it teaching me the basics of sailing. "A strayed boat's a doomed boat."

"And—?" he prompted.

"And only owls and foxes can see in the dark," I went on. "The wise sailor beaches his boat by dusk."

"Good. Now come here and show me what else you've learned." He stood to one side and patted the steering oar that guided our little vessel.

"You want *me* to beach us?" I could hardly believe

it. I'd never expected such a privilege. My father could buy a dozen great ships with the oil from just one season's olive harvest, but for the fisherman this lone little boat was his entire existence, his livelihood, his only way back home.

"Are you *sure*?" I asked.

"I know this shore. It's friendly enough. Go on, steer us. I'll mind the sail, but I'll step in if I see you doing something wrong."

I said a prayer to Poseidon as I took the steering oar with both hands and braced my bare feet against the boat's sun-warmed hull. I leaned against the long wooden oar and felt the power of the waves pushing back against me. There wasn't much resistance, just enough for me to feel the message of the sea: *I am immortal, endless, stronger and wilder than a thousand bulls. If you think that you've tamed me because you've made me carry you where you want to go, you're a fool. Respect me, or pay for your pride.*

Yes, Lord Poseidon, I thought as I turned the boat toward shore. *I hear. I know. I ask your blessing.*

The god answered in his own way, by letting me beach the boat without much trouble. When I felt the bottom grate along the sand and pebbles, I took a deep breath of relief.

Milo was the first to leap from the boat. "I'll make the fire!" he called out, racing away to gather bits of wood.

"Helpful, isn't he?" the fisherman remarked as we dragged the boat a safe distance onto the beach.

"He'd volunteer to kill a dragon if it meant he'd have solid ground under his feet," I replied.

After Milo got the fire started, we cooked some red mullet we'd caught and ate them along with the last of the bread and cheese we'd bartered for at a small village two days' voyage south. I was convinced that I'd be too excited to eat or sleep that night. My mind rang with *Iolkos! Iolkos! Iolkos!* My body had other ideas. I gobbled up every bit of food in front of me and my eyes closed as soon as my head touched the ground.

That night, my dreams were strange and terrifying. I was back in the forests of Calydon, once more running with the hunt for the monstrous boar that was ravaging the land. The beast rushed out of the darkness the same way that he'd come when I'd helped the great huntress Atalanta meet his attack.

In my dream I stood alone.

Stop! I shouted at the charging beast, holding the great boar spear steady. *Stop! I order you, as Sparta's future queen!*

The boar kept coming. I jammed the spear's butt against the earth and dug in my feet to meet his attack, but when I glanced down, I saw a blood-chilling change. Instead of wearing a boy's tunic, I was weighed down by a heavily flounced dress. Instead of a spear,

I held a spindle tangled with gleaming gold thread. A strand leaped out and lashed itself around my wrists.

Then the boar struck. One moment I was standing, the next I was sprawled across the beast's back. The boar tore on down the mountain, through the trees. My thoughts were thunder. With one win-all/lose-all motion I jerked my bound hands down and slashed the thread apart on the boar's own tusk. I gave a shout of triumph as I grabbed the creature's shaggy pelt and threw one leg over his spine, ready to ride him to the edge of the world.

"Wake up! Lady Helen, wake up! You're having a bad dream." A strong hand on my shoulder shook me. I bolted upright. The sky was just beginning to turn light, the horizon shimmering with a pearly glow soft and rosy as the smile of Aphrodite. As I rubbed grit from my eyes, I felt my hair stir in the dawn breeze. My nostrils filled with the clean, briny smell of the sea, my ears with the cries of gulls and other seabirds.

"You've *got* to stop calling me 'Lady Helen,'" I said drowsily.

"I'm sorry, Lady Hel—" Milo squatted beside me on the beach, biting his lower lip.

"Never mind, it's all right." I wanted to take that look off his face. Milo was my friend, but he always took anything I said to him much too seriously. It was as if I were already queen of Sparta instead of just fourteen, probably not much older than he was himself. Of course, it was impossible to say exactly how old he was: No one kept track of a slave boy's age.

Milo was no slave now. I had bought his freedom from my uncle, the king of Calydon. I had bought my own freedom as well, freedom from skirts and spindles and the life everyone said a royal daughter *must* lead, but I hadn't made that bargain using gold. I'd bought my liberty with a decision, choosing to turn away from the safe road home to Sparta to go on the quest for the Golden Fleece.

I got up and stretched, then patted Milo's shoulder. "There's no harm in you calling me by my real name when there's only the two of us. I'm just worried about what could happen if you slipped up in front of other people."

"You can trust me," Milo replied. "I'd die to protect your secret."

"You won't have to." I spoke quickly. "Just watch how you speak to me. The moment we set foot in Iolkos, there is no Lady Helen of Sparta, understood?"

He ventured a small smile. "I'll guard my tongue, but who's going to guard yours?"

"What do you mean?"

"When you were asleep, you kept yelling about who you are, how you're Sparta's next queen—" He spread his hands, letting go of any blame. "It woke me up."

It was my turn to feel embarrassed.

"People say all sorts of things in their dreams," he reassured me. "Once we're aboard the *Argo*, I'll look out for you, awake or asleep."

"And what happens when you topple overboard and drown because you've spent your nights standing guard over my dreams?" I teased.

"If it was for your sake, I'd be glad to—"

"What are you two jabbering about?" The fisherman appeared from behind the far side of his beached boat, a wooden spear in one hand, a string of fat fish in the other. "Not bad for a little wading in the shallows, eh?" He held up his catch proudly. "Now build up the fire or we'll have to eat these beauties raw."

Later, as we picked the last of the fishes' meat from their bones, our host looked at me and said, "Today we part ways. You've brought me good fortune and safe seas on this journey . . . Glaucus. Is there any favor I can do for you when I return to Delphi?"

I didn't have to think twice to answer that. "Tell Eunike I send her my love and thanks for everything she's done for me," I replied. "Tell her that you left Milo and me well, safe, and happy at Iolkos."

The fisherman made a face. "As if it's that simple for a man like me to get an audience with the holy Pythia."

I gave him a knowing smile. "You'll be able to do it easily enough if Lady Helen of Sparta puts in a good word for you."

Then we both laughed, for we shared a secret: The only reason I'd been able to steal away to Iolkos was because people have eyes and ears, yet most don't use them. My friend Eunike was the Pythia, priestess and prophet of Apollo's shrine at Delphi. When she spoke, people heard the all-seeing sun god's own words, predicting the future. When she declared that Lady Helen would not leave Delphi when her guardsmen headed home, everyone assumed it was Apollo's will. (She didn't lie: My guards marched off to Sparta one day before Milo and I sailed for Iolkos.) After that, whenever any of the priests who kept Apollo's shrine saw a royally dressed girl walking through the temple grounds, who else could she be but Lady Helen? In reality she was the daughter of the same fisherman who'd brought me this far in my journey.

I hoped that the same trick that let a fisherman's daughter pass for a Spartan princess would also fool my brothers on the *Argo*. Even the largest ship is a small, enclosed world. We *would* run into one another, unless I spent the whole voyage hiding in a chest, and what would be the point of that? When my brothers saw me, I wanted them to look right at me and say to each other:

Is that our sister?

What, here? Did you get too much sun? That's just one of the other men's weapons bearers.

I was very confident that was exactly how things would work out. I was so eager to see it all unscroll smoothly that after breakfast I danced around our smothered fire, urging the fisherman to launch his boat. I wanted to be in Iolkos *now*.

The winds were with us. The sun wasn't even a hand-span above the horizon by the time we beached on the strand at the foot of the great city on the Wavy Sea. I reached into the leather belt-pouch I carried and pulled out a little golden disk as big as my thumbnail. My best skirts from home were trimmed with a fortune in such charms, dresses fit for a princess. Before we left Delphi, I'd harvested the gold, silver, and gemmed ornaments to trade for necessities. I tried to give this one to the fisherman, but he refused it.

"Pay me back by coming back," he said. "My daughter's life is in your hands. That's worth more to me than a fistful of gold." He threw his wiry arms around Milo and me in a quick hug, and walked away.

Milo turned to me with a *Now what?* look in his eyes.

"Now we go up there," I said, pointing to where the citadel walls of Iolkos shone in the early morning sunshine. "We'll find a pair of warriors who've come to Iolkos to sail with Prince Jason but who haven't got weapons bearers to serve them. This quest may fetch more men than the Calydonian hunt. We'll get to pick and choose from a whole mob of masters."

Milo and I had to hike a fair distance along the shore before we reached that part of the waterfront where the great ships and their crews waited. Once again I felt my heart beat faster as I looked from one grand vessel to the next.

"Glaucus, put on your shoes," Milo said. I ignored him. Men scurried here and there on a hundred unknown errands, or grunted under the burden of massive clay amphorae and wooden chests. Some sat mending nets, others untangling lengths of rope. The reeks of fresh pine pitch, salt, and sweat fought each other, no one winning.

"*Glaucus . . .*" Milo's hand fell on my shoulder and gave me a little shake.

"Oh! Sorry. Were you talking to me?"

"Were you listening?" he countered. "If you won't answer to 'Glaucus,' why insist I call you by that name? I said, put on your shoes." He gestured at the pair of sandals I was carrying slung around my neck. On the fisherman's boat, I'd gone shoeless for better footing.

Now I was ashore, and it was pure luck that I hadn't stepped in something disgusting or rammed a chunk of broken wood or baked clay into my foot. I knew from painful past experience how long such wounds took to heal. What warrior would hire a lame weapons bearer? I leaned against a building and put on my sandals, then announced, "Let's get started. If the gods are with us, we'll be serving good masters before the sun's overhead."

"The gods grant it," Milo said. "How do we find *good* masters?"

"First, by finding the *Argo*," I replied.

"And how are we going to do that?"

I waved away his question. "Easily." I set off with a light step, arms swinging, heart full of confidence.

It didn't last. I can't tell you how many ships, great and small, we passed. The longer we walked along the water, the less certain I felt. I began to stare at every vessel, struggling to find a clue that would tell me beyond any doubt that it was the one we sought. All I knew was that the *Argo* would have to be *big*. Before my brothers went off with Prince Jason, all they'd talked about was how their ship would sail crewed by *fifty* heroes. I thought it would be easy to find a single vessel large enough to carry so many.

There were many big ships at Iolkos, all pulled up onto the shore to keep them safe. Their sails and masts were down to keep any sudden strong winds from carrying them away.

Then Milo said the unthinkable: "What if the *Argo*'s already sailed?"

My heart went cold. Could he be right? It was

possible. It could've happened the day before we arrived, for all I knew.

Lord Poseidon, help me, I prayed, fighting back the ghost of bitter disappointment. *Grant that the Argo hasn't sailed without us. Master of the seas, send me a sign and I'll make a rich thanksgiving sacrifice to you as soon as I have something worthy to offer.*

Suddenly Milo tapped my arm and pointed farther down the strand. "Look there, Glaucus," he said. My false name no longer sounded forced on his lips. I shaded my eyes and let out a yelp of joy when I spotted what he'd already seen: the ram.

It was painted in mid-leap on a green sail edged with blue. Its fleece wasn't golden, but the next best thing, a crocus yellow brilliant enough to dazzle the eyes. You could tell that sail was still waiting to see its first voyage. When the wind blew toward me, I swear that I could smell the newness of the cloth, the tang of the dyes.

The ship itself was the largest craft in the harbor. The only reason I'd missed seeing it before was that it lay beached between other vessels, around a curve in the shoreline that disguised its length. The shallow black hull was as newly made as the sail unfurled from the single mast, the gleaming prow freshly painted with a long blue-and-red-rimmed eye for luck, to watch over the waves ahead. The prow itself curved up like a beckoning arm, and was decorated with carvings from base to tip. I was standing too far away to see whether they meant anything or were just for decoration, but I was positive that I'd get a close enough look at them soon.

"That's it, Milo," I said as we walked a little closer. "That's got to be the *Argo*. I thought those other ships harbored here were big, but this . . ." I couldn't help counting the short wooden poles sticking up in pairs along the side rails. I'd overheard enough sailors' talk on the few voyages I'd made to learn those were called thole pins, and that they were used to hold the oars steady when the crew rowed. "Enough of them on this side to hold twenty-five oars steady, so there must be the same on the other. Fifty oars, fifty men, just as my brothers said. And the picture on the sail—"

"Why have they got it unfurled?" Milo asked. "The ship's not going anywhere."

"It must be Poseidon's doing, a sign that he *wanted* us to find this ship," I said. "We couldn't ask for a better omen! Now let's see whether the god will also help us find our new masters." I started toward the ship, only to have Milo's hand close on my shoulder yet again and hold me back. "What's wrong?" I asked.

"Let me go first."

"Why should I—?"

"In case your brothers are there."

I could see he was right. The ship wasn't deserted.

My brothers very well might be there among the men who were swarming everywhere, bringing aboard and stowing supplies. I grabbed the side of another beached ship and pulled myself up to get a better view of what was happening aboard the *Argo*. Craning my neck, I caught sight of wooden storage chests being set down alongside the oars so the crew would have places to sit while they rowed. One man was examining the ropes that controlled the single sail. Another was stowing clay amphorae under the small wooden shelves at either end of the ship, as well as in the bottom of the shallow hull, taking care to distribute the weight evenly.

I let go of the other ship's side and dropped back to the beach. "All right," I told Milo. "You go ahead. I'll be waiting for you over there." I nodded toward the row of buildings along the seaside. "Bring me good news."

It was a hard thing to have to let Milo approach the great ship without me. I loitered well out of sight, between a stone building and a shed that smelled of fish and sour wine. I didn't like being left behind, waiting. I wanted to meet my fate head-on. I also wanted to examine every hand-span of the ship's body to see where I'd best be able to lie low once we set sail and my brothers were on board. A smart rabbit doesn't wait until the hounds are on her trail before she digs her burrow.

"A warm, satisfying tale about the love that binds even the most dysfunctional of families."
                                                                    —*People*

"With clear prose and a straightforward plot, Green spins a breezy story."
                                                    —The Associated Press

"No one understands complicated families like Jane Green. In *The Sunshine Sisters*, she uses her trademark warmth and wit to bring us a deeply engaging story of parents, siblings, and lovers alike. She is the undisputed queen of the beach read."
     —Emma Straub, *New York Times* bestselling author of *Modern Lovers*

"An absolutely fabulous read . . . A superbly entertaining story about sisters that will make you laugh and cry, of course, but also ponder a dead-serious issue of what to do about mom. It's perfect for book clubs. I adored it!"
          —Dorothea Benton Frank, *New York Times* bestselling author of
                                                    Same Beach, Next Year

"*The Sunshine Sisters* glitters . . . Intuitive and wise, this is Jane Green at her masterful best. You will love this story and share with your sister or your best friend, or both. I know I did."
               —Adriana Trigiani, *New York Times* bestselling author of
                                                  All the Stars in the Heavens

"Whether you have a sister or not, *The Sunshine Sisters* is my definition of the perfect beach read."
               —Lauren Weisberger, *New York Times* bestselling author of
                                                     The Devil Wears Prada

continued . . .

"Shocking and dramatic, but always heartfelt and genuine in its multi-layered portrayal of betrayal, redemption, and healing. Jane Green's writing is impossible to resist."

—Susan Wiggs, *New York Times* bestselling author of *Map of the Heart*

"Of all Jane Green's wonderful books, this is my clear favorite. Utterly compelling, relatable, and page-turning, it is a triumph."

—Sarah Pekkanen, international bestselling author of
The Perfect Neighbors

"Jane Green always takes us through the complexities of personal problems and family turmoil with writing that is as delicious as the food her characters enjoy. *The Sunshine Sisters* is a brilliant book, her best book, warm, wise, and delightful."

—Nancy Thayer, *New York Times* bestselling author of
Secrets in Summer

"*The Sunshine Sisters* is a poignant story of love, loss, and the power of forgiveness."

—Liz Fenton and Lisa Steinke, authors of *The Year We Turned Forty*

"Another warm and winning family tale."   —*Booklist*

"Green does a wonderful job of creating realistic and lovable (despite themselves) characters. Fans of the author and readers who enjoy Elin Hilderbrand and Kristin Hannah will love this book."

—*Library Journal*

"Another perfect beach read."   —*Kirkus Reviews*

the
Sunshine
Sisters

....
....

JANE GREEN

BERKLEY
New York

BERKLEY
An imprint of Penguin Random House LLC
375 Hudson Street, New York, New York 10014

Berkley trade paperback ISBN: 9780399583339

The Library of Congress has cataloged the Berkley hardcover edition as follows:

Names: Green, Jane, 1968– author.
Title: The sunshine sisters / Jane Green.
Description: First edition. | New York : Berkley, 2017.
Identifiers: LCCN 2017002238 (print) | LCCN 2017009626 (ebook) | ISBN 9780399583315
(hardcover) | ISBN 9780399583322 (ebook)
Subjects: LCSH: Mothers and daughters—Fiction. | Sisters—Fiction. | Domestic fiction. |
BISAC: FICTION / Family Life. | FICTION / Contemporary Women. |
FICTION / Literary.
Classification: LCC PR6057.R3443 S87 2017 (print) | LCC PR6057.R3443 (ebook) |
DDC 823/.914—dc23
LC record available at https://lccn.loc.gov/2017002238

Berkley hardcover edition / June 2017
Berkley trade paperback edition / May 2018

Printed in the United States of America
3 5 7 9 10 8 6 4 2

Cover photograph by Claudio Marinesco
Cover design by Rita Frangie
Book design by Laura K. Corless

For Ian Warburg
Always

acknowledgments

This is the first book in a while that has felt like I am back to myself, and I have many people to thank, but primarily Jackie Cantor, Claire Zion at Berkley, and my US agent, Christy Fletcher. We brainstormed the idea over lunches, and then all three trusted me enough to let me take the story in the direction it chose. I am eternally grateful.

The entire team at Berkley is owed a huge thank-you for their hard work and brilliance: Ivan Held, Christine Ball, Jeanne-Marie Hudson, Jin Yu, Craig Burke, Heather Connor, Diana Franco, Caitlin Valenziano, Lily Choi, and everyone else who has helped bring this book to life.

Crystal Ellefson and Daisy Melo, who ease the burden and make my life easier.

Dr. Amiram Katz for his guidance, kindness, and for being a prince among neurologists and a prince among men.

To Nanci Ross-Weaver, Janice DeRosa, Kara Feifer, Kim Raver, and Emily Jillette; I can't wait to see what the future holds.

The lovely people who surround me and make it all possible, particularly Fiona Garland and Andrew Bentley, David Dreyfoos, Jerri Graham, Sharon Gitelle and John French, Kat Gloor, Russ and Jodi Hardin, Beth Huisking, Annie Keefe, Lisa Lampanelli, Steve March, Billy Nistico, Ian and Debbie O'Malley, Stefan and Sophie Pollman, Michael Ross, Dani

Shapiro and Michael Maren, Kirk and Nicole Straight, Julian Vogel, Lauren Weisberger, and all my rowing moms. A huge thank-you to all of you for your friendship and love.

To my amazing readers, and the incredible book community out there, especially Robin Kall Homonoff, Brenda Janowitz, Andrea Katz, and Jennifer O'Regan.

And to my family. Our children, Max, Henri, Harry, Tabitha, Nate, Jasper, and to Ian, who brings the sunshine into all of our lives every day.

A FEW WEEKS AGO

prologue

All those years when Ronni thought she was sick, all those years convinced that every mole was melanoma, every cough was lung cancer, every case of heartburn was an oncoming heart attack, after all those years, when the gods finally stopped taking care of her she wasn't scared.

What a pity, she thought after the doctor first diagnosed her. Then, when she refused to believe it, after the second, and the third, agreed, she thought again, what a pity I wasted all those years worrying about the worst. Somehow now that the worst was upon her, it was peaceful, calming, as if this was what she had always been waiting for. Now that it was here, it wasn't scary at all.

She had gotten her life in order. There were many, many amends she wasn't able to make, would never be able to make. If she hadn't completely healed her relationship with her daughters, at least she had brought them back together; at least they would now have each other.

Ronni stirs in bed and blinks at the sunlight pouring in through

the window, dust circling in the glow. There is a thick layer of dust on the top of the chest of drawers at the bottom of her bed. A few months ago she would have been furious, calling for Lily, the housekeeper, to come and clean. It no longer matters.

Her legs don't work anymore, and it's getting increasingly hard to hold her head up. The choking when she ate made it simpler not to eat, and she no longer has the energy for the liquid smoothies Lizzy has been making. She turns her head slightly to see a full smoothie Lizzy brought up earlier today, packed with spinach for iron, almond butter for protein, coconut milk because Lizzy swears coconut is the ultimate cure-all for everything these days.

Not for Ronni. There is no cure for Ronni, no anti-inflammatory that will stop the fatigue or muscle jumping, not enough iron, minerals, or vitamins in the world that will bring sensation back to her body, allow her to lead a life comparable to the one she has led all these years.

It has been a good life, she thinks. Sixty-five years. She would have wanted longer, and before this disease took hold of her body, she passed for much younger, presumed she would go on forever. She reaches for the handheld mirror she keeps on the bedcovers, aware that she is slowly losing this hand as well. Slowly she holds it up, just for a few seconds, to examine her face. She hasn't had Botox for over a year. Nor fillers, nor any of the treatments that kept her looking young and firm. She had her eyes done in her forties, but now they are sunken in what is left of her face, her cheeks gaunt, her skin graying. She stares, fascinated at how different she looks, at what she has become.

It is not the way she would have chosen to go, but nor would Ronni ever have wanted to grow old. The makeup, the treatments, the wigs, the working out, the gracious, charming persona she was known for, all kept her looking young, even if she didn't get the acting parts she once got.

Three years ago she was offered the part of a grandmother in an edgy new series on HBO. She turned it down, horrified. They told her she would be a "glamorous granny"; they wanted to portray aging in a sexy, vibrant way. Ronni flounced out of the office, not saying a word, her displeasure clear. The show went on to win numerous awards. The grandmother was played by Betty White. Ronni refused to watch until last year, when season two won every award it was possible to win, then she binge-watched it. Everyone else who had seen it raved, saw instantly why it was such a hit—the clever dialogue; the edgy, astute observations; the horrible, self-absorbed, selfish characters you wanted to hate but couldn't help but love because they were so vulnerable, their hearts so needy, and bleeding, and real. Ronni did not see any of that. What Ronni saw was a woman much older than her playing a role they had offered to her. Which meant they saw her as the same age, the same type. And she was devastated.

She booked a Thermage treatment for the next day, and a chemical peel. She made an appointment with her plastic surgeon in New York to discuss a face-lift. How dare they see her as perfect for the part of the old lady. How dare they see her as an old lady. Wasn't sixty the new forty? She would reverse time, would ensure she continued to play evil mothers-in-law rather than eccentric elderly ladies.

The day of the appointment, she had a bad dizzy spell and spent the day in bed. She never got around to another appointment. None of which matters, she thinks now. All those years of beauty, of a wonderful figure, and all I could think was that I was never pretty enough, never slim enough, never quite good enough. What I would give to have those years back, to appreciate them more, to appreciate the life I had while I was living it.

All those years when I could have been a better wife, a better mother, a better friend. She sighs. It's too late now. She did the best she could. And now she is ready. It isn't quite how she wanted to do it. She had a

vision of looking beautiful again, of being dressed, made-up, of falling back against the pillow with a mane of hair from one of her famous wigs.

She had envisaged her daughters sitting around the bed, perhaps clasping her hands, smiling beatifically as Bach played on the iPhone speaker, as she quietly swallowed the pills she has been stockpiling before drifting seamlessly into a sleep that would last forever.

Gathering the pills was challenging. Her housekeeper removed the bottles of OxyContin and kept them downstairs. She learned to ask visitors to bring her the pills, pretending to take them, or announcing she would take them later, before hiding them away with her growing mound.

She had hoped there would be a camera in the corner, capturing this final scene in a documentary that would be made about her life, as she drifted from this one into the next.

She has left plans for her funeral, which will also be filmed. The biggest stars of stage and screen will be speaking, certainly. She has left instructions as to who she wants to eulogize her and what poems they might read. She has imagined the obituaries, the retrospectives, the huge picture of her on the screen at the Oscars, the sadness and tears from all who have known her, or loved her, or admired her movies for years.

The first part of the plan has not come together. None of her daughters will cooperate. Nell won't speak about it, other than to say there is absolutely no way she will help her mother take her own life, then have to live with that on her conscience for the rest of hers. It is unconscionable that she would ask, says Nell. Meredith keeps bursting into tears. And Lizzy, Lizzy who is most like her, Lizzy, her darling baby girl, has refused to believe that there isn't something that can be done. How typical of Lizzy, to believe that sheer force of will can make anything happen, including miracles.

Lizzy, who has been making her liquid smoothies packed with

nutrition, who is researching cutting-edge stem cell treatments, certain that there will soon be a cure. Her daughters have demanded more time. Give them six months, they say, to try to find something that will help. They will not let her go now.

But Ronni has reached the end. With her one good hand she reaches under the pillow where she has been quietly storing the pills.

She has enough now, to ensure she won't wake up, throw up, swim back to consciousness. There is a small wave of regret that she isn't going the way she had planned, surrounded by family, drifting off in a wave of forgiveness and love, but they will not let her go.

And it is time to go.

1981

one

The director jumps out of his chair and strides over to Ronni Sunshine, clasping her arms as he gives her an extravagantly European air kiss, his lips pursing on either side of her perfectly made-up face as he kisses once, twice, three times.

"Darling! You look more beautiful than ever!" Andras Marko's Eastern European accent now has an American twang, picked up in Hollywood over the last ten years. He steps back, admiring her short, tight skirt and beautifully fitted red jacket with large shoulder pads. Her hair is immaculately flicked, the black eyeliner on her striking green eyes slanting up ever so slightly at the corners, her lips full, glistening with red lip gloss, and pouty, a small smile playing on them, as her face fills with a flush of pleasure at the compliment.

"Darling! It's good to see you!" Once upon a time, he had a crush on her. She knew this, used it to her advantage, even though nothing had ever happened, for she was so young, barely out of her teens; he couldn't have taken advantage of her in that way. Instead, he was sweet

to her, took her under his wing. If anyone dared to flirt with her, or try to take advantage, he was the first to jump in and set them straight.

"It's better to see *you*." He smiles. "You have grown into your beauty."

"Thank you, Pappy."

The people who loved Andras called him Pappy. Ronni made sure she called him that from the beginning. It made him feel loved, helped him take even better care of her.

Her voice is still the throaty purr that she developed for her first film role, at eighteen, a voice that has subsequently become her trademark. That first film role, as Michael Caine's fifth love interest, led to a series of B-movie roles, which led to her moving to Hollywood two years later.

Andras Marko directed the first movie she made after landing in her little studio bungalow in Silver Lake. He was relatively new to the game back then, but over the years produced a number of huge hits. Now he is a hot Hollywood director, with a penchant for dark, exotic actresses in their twenties.

"It's been a long time," says Andras, admiring her from head to toe. "What is it, ten years? Twelve, since we made that movie?"

Ronni tips her head back with a peal of laughter. "No, darling! It's only been six or seven years. Time in Hollywood just feels longer."

She has to say that. She is thirty now, but her résumé says twenty-six. Andras would know she is not twenty-six, knew her age when they made that movie together all those years ago, but he is willing to play the game they both know they are expected to play.

"And you're married now! With babies! I can't believe how things change in such a short time."

There is a quick flicker of discontent in Ronni's eyes. It's not that she doesn't like being married, doesn't appreciate her children, but reminding Andras of her role outside of the movie set is not something she wants to do.

"Come, come." He takes her hand, dipping his head with a smile as he leads her through the people who have been watching her screen test, all of whom applaud as she passes. A warm glow seeps through her. This film could be huge. The rumor is that Robert Redford is up for the lead. Winning this role would catapult her onto the A-list in a way she has always dreamed. "Tell me," he says. "Tell me about the babies."

"The babies are adorable," she says, even though Nell is seven and Meredith is three. "How are your children? How old are they now? And Diana? Is she well?"

"Pfft." He waves with his free hand, as they leave the room and head across the lot to his office. "They are all well. All driving me crazy! Come! Come! There is much we have to talk about!"

He turns to her, his eyes crinkling as he laughs, Ronni laughing with him, her excitement threatening to bubble up and spill out. It looks like she's done it! She's really, really done it! This time it looks like she's landed the role of her dreams.

They walk into his office, Andras gesturing her to sit down. "Your test was wonderful," he says then, smiling a beneficent smile at her. "You have grown and matured as an actress, but you still have the glow of youth. I think you would be perfect for the role of Jacqueline. What do you think? Are you ready to take on something like this?"

"Really?" Ronni can hardly sit still, wriggling with delight as she looks into his eyes. "Are you saying I've got the part?"

"Do you want the part?"

"Oh, Pappy! This is the part I've been dreaming of all my life! This is wonderful!"

"So you do want the part?" He is smiling at her with a smile she doesn't recognize from all those years ago, a smile she wouldn't have been able to read, even if she weren't wriggling with an excitement that failed to prepare her for what was about to happen.

"I do."

"If you really want the part," he says, leaning back on the sofa, his voice low as he moves his legs apart, "all you have to do is be nice to me. Be very nice to me."

Usually, a massage is enough to calm Ronni down. The studio sends a masseuse once a week to the house. Usually it's on a Thursday, but Ronni calls her agent as soon as she gets home, and requests—no, *demands*—the masseuse come today. She drove home gritting her teeth, replaying her audition over and over.

Be nice to me. She knows, as every young actress in Hollywood knows, what that particular euphemism means. She has never done it, and she will never do it. Andras Marko can go fuck himself.

Oh, but she would have been perfect for the role. And she was certain she had gotten it. The screen test went as well as any screen test in her career. She could see the people in the room rapt as they watched her. She was naïve, and innocent, and inhabiting the character so well, she forgot that she was Ronni Sunshine, actress and B-movie star, and thought she was a young mother whose daughter had been kidnapped. She had them. When it ended, there was that split second where she blinked, had to come back to herself, and she looked around that room, at the faces of all those people sitting in there, and she knew she had them. They believed her too.

That sleazeball Andras. When had he become a sleazeball? How had that sweet, nurturing man she worked with all those years ago become the gross, presumptuous, sleazy director who spread his legs for her today and expected her to acquiesce? Had fame and fortune corrupted him that much? Well. Clearly, it had. Ronni could name ten actresses in ten seconds who'd built their careers on the casting couch. She had never been one of them. She had never needed to be one of them.

She wasn't about to start now. No matter how badly she wanted the part.

As she drove home, she could feel the tension building in her neck and shoulders, a headache already starting to pound. Stress. Disappointment. Fury. *How dare he.*

A wave of nausea hit her as she walked into the house. She ran to the bathroom, disgusted with herself for throwing up, at having such an extreme reaction to what had just happened. But she was more disgusted with him. That was when she picked up the phone and called her agent.

The massage table is set up, as it always is, in her bedroom. As soon as she lies down, she's hopeful she will get some relief. But as the masseuse kneads her back in the darkened room, all Ronni can think about is Andras, with a fury and an upset that no amount of stroking or kneading can dissolve.

Long, exasperated sighs keep coming from her mouth. She hears the front door close downstairs and the voice of the German nanny as she shepherds Nell and Meredith in from their afternoon activities.

A thump of small footsteps comes racing up the stairs. She hears "Mommy? Mommy? *Mommy!*" in ever-escalating shrieks until the door to her bedroom, her quiet, peaceful sanctuary, bursts open, and her two daughters tumble in and clatter over to the table.

"Not *now*, girls," she snaps, her words harsher than intended, her head turned to the side as the masseuse pauses. "Mommy is busy. Go and find Iris."

"But I want to show you what I made in school today." Nell, the eldest, stands her ground, proffering artwork, as Ronni feels a surge of fury. This is her time, for God's sake. After the day she's had, doesn't she deserve some time to try to feel better?

"Not now!" she says, even more harshly than before. Meredith, who has been standing by the door, lets out a small whimper, and both the girls run out, to the safety of their nanny, who is patiently waiting for

them outside their mother's bedroom. Ronni hears the woman reminding the children she told them not to disturb their mother. But they still
have to learn that when the door is closed and the massage is under way,
it is never a good time.

Things are not much better at breakfast the next morning. Ronni
wakes slowly. The room is still ghostly quiet and pitch-black, thanks
to her satin eye mask and wax ear plugs. Robert is traveling in the
Midwest until later today, which is both liberating and irritating.
She likes him home, likes him being by her side, likes him taking care
of her.

The girls have gone to school. The only audible noise is the faint
sound of the vacuum downstairs, which means Rosa is here.

Ronni lies for a while in bed, thinking about her audition. She can't
stop thinking about it. She woke up in the early hours, still angry, only
managing to fall back to sleep at around four. And now it's past nine,
and quiet, and all she can think about is the audition. The disgust has
abated, leaving her second-guessing herself. This is a huge part, after
all. Having it would propel her to superstar status. Marilyn Monroe
did it all the time, was renowned for sleeping with those on high to
get a part. And that was Marilyn Monroe! Who does Ronni Sunshine
think she is, not doing the same thing?

But I'm married, she tells herself. I am a mother. It's inconceivable
that I would do such a thing.

She lies in bed, staring into space, the pink satin eye mask pushed
up to the top of her head. This part! This movie! They could undoubtedly push her up there to the one thing she has always craved, proper
movie star status. This role could change her life.

And all she had to do was . . . what? She isn't sure. A blow job might
have sufficed. Wasn't that what his spread legs meant? And a blow job

isn't exactly infidelity, is it? If she were to give Andras a blow job—she shudders in disgust at the thought—but if she were to do it, just once, just to get the job, she could still claim to be faithful. It wouldn't be the lowest of the low, surely.

But she can't. Surely she can't. *Can she?* She always knew she was his type, but back then he wasn't famous enough to have dared make the move. Or perhaps she was too young. Either way, he has always cast women in his movies who look just like her: blond, petite, exotic.

Ronni reaches over to her nightstand for a handheld pearl mirror and brings it a few inches in front of her face, staring at herself.

The product of a Swedish mother and an Anglo-Jewish father, even first thing in the morning (for her), Ronni is exotic. She is exactly Andras's type. Dark skinned like her father, petite, with her mother's large green eyes that have the tiniest of slants, and thick blond hair, she has been destined for stardom from the moment she was born. Not the B-movie stardom she has enjoyed for the last twelve years—the kind of stardom where she will sometimes get better tables in restaurants and asked for autographs should she encounter people who may have seen her movies—but the real Hollywood superstar stardom. The kind of stardom that can generate the parting of the Red Sea.

Adoring parents, grandparents, aunts, and uncles watched as she performed for them as a child, her green eyes sparkling as she sang, dipped, and twirled on a wooden box her father had made for her as an impromptu stage. They kept it behind the sofa in the living room of their pretty stucco Georgian house just off Downshire Hill in London's leafy Hampstead.

At eighteen she got her first film part. At twenty she moved to Hollywood. At twenty-one she had an affair with Warren Beatty, which, although not entirely unusual for a beautiful young actress in Hollywood at that time, nevertheless resulted in her being featured in all the gossip columns. At twenty-two she landed the first in a

number of leading roles in B movies. At twenty-three, she unexpectedly discovered she was pregnant, courtesy of a passionate but relatively new relationship with Robert Sunshine, who was beginning to make a name for himself in New York with commercial real estate deals.

He was developing a shopping mall in Los Angeles and traveled there frequently. Ronni, still climbing her way up the movie ladder, had accepted a booking to be a hostess at one of Robert's cocktail parties. Her role was to greet and charm.

By the end of the night, it was clear that Robert was the most charmed of all. The affair went from there, and what with the pregnancy, she married him and took his name, as the gossip columnists went wild. Ronni Sunshine! Didn't it sound like she was heading for the top? They moved into a rambling wooden contemporary nestled in Laurel Canyon that felt like a magical tree house.

Ronni hated being pregnant, felt like a giant moose. Her figure, which she had always worked so hard to maintain as a young actress embarking on a career in which looks were paramount, was transformed into something unrecognizable.

She snapped back within three months of her daughter's birth, and soon won the part of a young housewife in a gothic horror movie that was set to be a huge hit, but didn't do as well as anyone hoped. Most of all, Ronni.

She continued working. She was one of the lucky ones, she supposed, although it didn't feel like it. Being a steadily working actress, occasionally being recognized, wasn't enough. It was never enough.

The stardom she craved was always just out of her reach. Her pregnancies weren't planned, either of them. But she believed having a successful husband, a good-looking, glamorous husband, would surely help propel her further.

Now, finally, she has a real shot at something big. A role that will

put her in the major leagues. And all it will take to get it is a blow job. Perhaps she could call Andras today and ask to meet with him again, apologize for storming out in disgust. She could tell him it was her time of the month. She'll think of something.

She thinks about him sitting on the sofa, his legs spread, an eyebrow raised, and a wave of nausea hits her just as there is a knock on the door and Rosa comes in without waiting for her to answer. Rosa does this all the time, oversteps her boundaries. If she wasn't such a good housekeeper, Ronni always says she would have got rid of her years ago, but the house is sparkling, the children love her, and the truth is, Ronni loves her too.

"You wanna get up?" Rosa stands in the doorway. "The man is here to fix the pool and I don't know what to tell him. Mr. Robert says to talk to me, but I don't know nothing. You wanna talk to him?" Rosa peers at Ronni and seems to suddenly notice she is a frightening shade of gray. "You okay?" she says.

Ronni jumps out of bed with her hand clapped over her mouth and races to the bathroom. She just about makes it to the toilet, where she heaves into the bowl, her stomach clenching in tight cramps, her body heaving and retching, even though nothing comes out except the tiniest bit of stomach bile.

She splashes her face with cold water, relieved the nausea has passed, then swishes water around her mouth. When she comes back into the bedroom, Rosa is still standing in the doorway, this time with her arms crossed and one eyebrow raised.

"I'm absolutely fine," says Ronni. "Can you make sure my black dress is pressed? The one with the deep neckline? I'll be going out in two hours."

two

"Mommy! You look pretty!"

Ronni sails into the kitchen, twirling around her daughter in her long eggplant Halston dress, feeling feminine and beautiful as the little girl lets out a peal of laughter. Meredith laughs in delight as her mother circles around her, leaning down to flutter butterfly kisses along her little pudgy cheek.

"Where are you going?" asks Meredith.

"Just to school for Nell's little poetry performance," she says, shaking out the chiffon scarf and wrapping it around her shoulders. "Do I look alright?"

"You look like the movie star you are," says Iris, a nanny who has lasted beyond six months, long enough to know what flattery will get her with her employer.

"What about the stomach?" Ronni turns to the side, showing the tiniest of swells. "Don't I look enormous? Aren't I huge?"

Iris blanches in horror. "You don't look pregnant at all. But even

if you did, pregnant women are beautiful. It's what our bodies are made for. You must be proud to be pregnant, not ashamed."

"I am not ashamed." Ronni sinks into a chair at the table, unconsciously reaching out for a French fry from Meredith's plate, only realizing the sin she is about to commit when the food is almost touching her lips. She puts it back on Meredith's plate, wiping her fingers on the tablecloth. "I just don't want people to know unless they have to know. There is still work I can do as long as I'm not showing."

"What about the part in that movie? With the kidnapped child? Is that your next project?"

Ronni frowns. "It was offered to me," she says, as the memory of Andras in his office flashes into her mind, "but I turned it down once I realized I was pregnant. The filming schedule didn't work."

The whole debacle was something she prefers not to think about. She went back to speak to Andras. She did what she needed to do to get the part, determined to forever put it out of her mind as soon as it was over, determined that no one would ever find out, no one would ever need to know how low she had sunk for the sake of her career. She told Andras that she was married, and happy, that this was a one-off, and he agreed, even as he was unzipping his pants for the blow job she reluctantly gave him.

She had no idea she was pregnant at the time. They were due to start filming in six months. She would be eight months pregnant. She hadn't even signed the contract yet when she realized her condition. She met with the studio and asked for filming to be pushed back by three months. They said they would consider it, but that afternoon a messenger showed up on the doorstep with a letter. Their offer had been rescinded. They wished her lots of luck with her pregnancy and her career.

"There will be lots more, yes?" says Iris. Ronni says nothing. The last thing she needs is to be comforted by the nanny.

"Ronni?" Robert comes into the kitchen, going straight over to Meredith and covering her with kisses as she squeals and laughs. He reaches over her shoulder to take a handful of French fries and pop them in his mouth before looking over at Ronni.

"You look very dressed. Are you sure that's the appropriate attire for a second grade class party?"

Ronni stares at him. She chose well, she thinks. He is the perfect complement to her, with his towering height and long legs, his dark hair and handsome, preppy looks. She chose well even though they seem to be drifting apart, even though there are times she feels they are speaking to each other from different planets, have lost what little they had in common in the first place. "Do you even know me? How do you think I'm supposed to dress? In Jordache jeans and Bass Weejuns? Or clogs? I'm not a suburban housewife. I'm an actress. And most of the parents at the school are in the industry, which means this isn't about a class party, it's about work."

"You know they'll all be in jeans and sneakers, and it's a new school for us. Are you sure you don't want to just blend in?" He looks at her face before backtracking. "If you feel good in that, who am I to tell you differently."

Ronni stares at him before turning on her heel and walking out of the kitchen. All she needed to hear was that she looks beautiful. It doesn't seem so much to ask. He is traveling, and distracted, and things are so different from when they first got together, when Robert treated her like his precious jewel, when he couldn't get over how lucky he was that she had chosen him.

three

There is a murmur around the room of parents when Ronni walks in. She has made sure they are late; she always makes sure they are late. Not too much, just enough to be able to create a bit of a stir.

There are a couple of major stars who have their children in this elementary school, but none in Nell's grade. She is the biggest celebrity here, even though her star does not appear to be rising just now.

Still, she has a face that is familiar to the people in the room. Even if you didn't know her name, you would recognize her from a late-night movie you accidentally stumbled upon and paused to watch before flicking over until you hit *The Tonight Show*. She has a face you may have registered while driving past a giant poster on Sunset Boulevard. Not right in the front, but to the right. Not the lead, but in the picture.

The parents who aren't sure murmur to the people they are standing with. Who *is* that? She must surely be *someone*, in that fabulously over-the-top dress for a classroom party. She looks like a movie star,

so beautiful, with those gorgeous eyes. She's definitely familiar, but they can't quite place her.

"That's Ronni Sunshine, the actress," their friends murmur back. "You know, she was in . . . oh, what was she in? She's been in so much. You've definitely seen her. Those gothic horror movies. What are they called? Oh, why can't I think. *Mommy brain!* I can't remember anything anymore."

Ronni swishes through the crowd, casting gracious beatific smiles on the parents. Those she knows she stops to air kiss, always European-style, one on each side.

"You look beautiful!" everyone says, for indeed she does, pregnancy always suiting her, giving her a glow that radiates around the room. But the glow is real, quite aside from the pregnancy; she has always blossomed in the face of an effusive compliment.

The children are all huddled in a corner, excitedly whispering among themselves as the parents take their seats. Nell stands slightly off to the side, noticeable for her height—she is the tallest in the class, towering over everyone by at least four inches—and her stillness. The other children jig from side to side, unable to be still, waving to their parents, whirling around to catch the attention of a child on the other side of the group. Not Nell. Nell stands, staring into space, the only movement her lips, which, if you look very closely, are ever so slightly mouthing the words of her poem as she ensures she knows it by heart, reciting it over and over again.

The teacher gets up. Ronni and Robert settle in the front row. From there Ronni bestows her most radiant smile on the young Miss Ellison, who confessed, the first time they met at the beginning of the year, that she was an enormous fan and had seen all her movies. She even asked if she—could she—if she might—would it be possible, and please don't think this inappropriate, but might Ronni autograph a

black-and-white photograph of herself that Miss Ellison had bought some time ago?

Miss Ellison keeps looking at Ronni, who smiles encouragingly as she steps up to the small riser.

"Welcome, all my second grade parents. We're very excited to have you here to listen to our poetry readings. The children have all worked very hard and spent a huge amount of time practicing their poems." She pauses for the parents to applaud, which they do, complete with a small amount of whooping from a couple of fathers in the back.

"First up, we have Nell Sunshine." She turns to welcome Nell up onto the stage before leaning into the microphone again. "I just have to say that we are all incredibly blessed to have Nell's mother here today, the wonderful actress Ronni Sunshine." She extends an arm to Ronni, before clapping and casting a glance around the room to encourage the other parents to clap too. Which they do, although it is slightly more muted than before. This is Hollywood, after all. As Ronni rightly said to her husband, half of this room are directors or soundmen or caterers for the studios. It isn't such a big deal for them, even though it seems to be for their child's teacher.

Miss Ellison pauses, an idea striking her at that moment. "Ms. Sunshine, I wonder if we might ask you . . . I hope this isn't too presumptuous, but I once heard you do the most wonderful recital of a poem on a radio show. I think it might have been by Roald Dahl? I'm just wondering whether you might still know it? Whether you might give us all an enormous treat by introducing today's performance with that poem? If you remember it . . ."

She trails off, stepping back with a big smile, for Ronni has already stood up, gliding to the riser, lifting her long skirts to step up, taking the microphone with assumed humility and a smile that seems embarrassed, as the room applauds again.

"I'm so embarrassed," Ronni starts, with a laugh and her signature throaty purr, and everyone sits up. They recognize that voice! That deep English accent! Now they know who she is!

"I didn't expect to be performing today, and I haven't rehearsed at all. Goodness, I'm not even sure I can remember that poem. It was Spike Milligan, I believe. Does this sound familiar?" She turns to Miss Ellison and recites the first line.

Miss Ellison nods dreamily, enthusiastically, as Ronni turns back to the microphone, playing up to the crowd, flinging her scarf off, delighting in performing in front of a live audience, delighting in the laughter she hears, in the rapt attention of a room full of people who all love her! They all seem to love her!

All eyes are on her. She is mesmerizing. No one notices the tall blond child standing next to the riser. They do not see her lips stop moving, nor the way she looks at the floor. Even if they had noticed before how nervous she was, they do not now realize that she no longer cares about stepping up to perform. No one, least of all Ronni, notices what is so clear on her face: that she knows she could never be as good as her mother, and that her day is now destroyed.

1991

four

The bell rings as a sea of bodies emerges from classrooms, teenagers swarming through the wide corridors and shouting to each
other as the tide moves toward the exit doors.

Outside they go, great big football-playing boys throwing balled-up
papers to friends and cheering when their misses are caught; studious
kids keeping their heads down, making their way to the line of yellow
buses waiting to drop them all off at the ends of their streets.

When Nell is with Emily, they sit together, near the back. On days
like today, when Emily has an appointment with the orthodontist and
was an early pickup, Nell sits by herself, toward the front of the bus,
plugging in her father's old Sony Walkman so she doesn't have to engage with the rest of the kids.

The irony is, despite her expectations—and fears—there is much
she loves about her new school and living in Connecticut. When her
father's real estate company merged with another, bigger, company,

in New York, and he announced they were moving to the East Coast, she was the only one who didn't want to leave Los Angeles. Leaving meant starting a new school for her senior year of high school. Not that she had a fantastic social life or tons of friends—Nell has always been something of a loner. But it was her life; it was the only life she knew.

Meredith, who always seems to go with the flow, seemed perfectly happy to make the move, although even if she wasn't, she wasn't likely to complain. If her parents were happy, Meredith was happy.

And Lizzy was positively thrilled! A whole new school to charm! New friends! An entire new coast to conquer! She is only ten, but she is a natural charmer, and change has always been exciting for her.

The only one who struggled with the decision was Nell.

They settled on the town of Westport, Connecticut. It was an easy commute into the city for her father, and the town had the famous Westport Country Playhouse, not to mention Paul Newman and Jo-anne Woodward. As soon as her mother heard that, her mind was made up. They stopped trawling around the towns in Westchester and Dutchess Counties in New York. If it was good enough for Paul and Joanne, it was good enough for Ronni Sunshine. She refused even to think about looking anywhere else after that.

Her parents found a majestic Colonial on a private street opposite Longshore, the town's country club. The neighborhood was near the beach and filled with kids on bikes and skateboards. Apparently they were all going to be blissfully happy.

Before the move, Nell had looked at all the pictures of the house, pictures of the room that was going to be hers, the description of the town, but she hadn't been able to get excited. She was leaving be-hind her best friend, Sandy, and she wasn't good at making new friends. She had been so lonely before she and Sandy had found each other,

and she couldn't bear the thought of going back to that loneliness again.

Thank God for Emily Sussman. Small, petite, and interesting looking, Emily walked up to Nell on her first day, curious about the new girl she had spotted on the bus that morning. She introduced herself, and invited Nell back to her house after school to do homework.

Emily lived a few streets down from Nell, in an old yellow house on a little island that you could access only by foot, walking over a small wooden bridge. There were no cars on the island, but a parking lot just before. Residents pulled their groceries to the houses on small wooden wagons.

"This is so cool!" breathed Nell, walking along the pretty path, feeling like she was back in California, water everywhere she looked.

Emily's mom was in the kitchen when they arrived. She had a platter of chocolate chip cookies on the counter that were warm and chewy, just out of the oven. They ate them while they drank tall glasses of ice-cold milk, and it struck Nell, that day, looking out the window at the sun glinting off the waters of Long Island Sound, that this might be the best day of her life.

Emily was so relaxed and curious and at ease in her own skin, it helped Nell feel at ease in hers. Her house was funky and cozy and cool, sitting right on the sand, with magnificent views of the water, and little beach cottages sitting in the distance.

And her mom! Her mom who was a real mom! Who'd baked fresh chocolate chip cookies even though she didn't know Emily was bringing a friend over, who poured them milk and came to sit with them at the table and talked to them, really talked to them, about their day, and how they felt about life, and did Nell find it overwhelming to be new here, in such a big school, surrounded by people she didn't know.

After that, the joke was that Nell had moved in with Emily, in the

little yellow house that was only supposed to be a summer rental, until Mr. and Mrs. Sussman got divorced and Mrs. Sussman had ended up staying, so delighted by the sun rising over the water outside her window every morning that she knew she'd found her new home.

Emily and Nell became inseparable almost overnight. Emily helped Nell fall in love with Westport. Growing up in Los Angeles with a father who traveled so much and an actress mother who lived for the adoration of her fans, Nell had no idea what a normal suburban childhood was like.

Discovering Westport, and Emily Sussman, was a revelatory experience for Nell. Not only did she learn what a normal childhood could be but she could experience one at Emily's side. In Nell's eyes, Mrs. Sussman was a perfect mother, with her giant wooden-sided station wagon parked in the parking lot at the end of Compo Mill Cove; and the way she cooked for her daughter and whatever other friends might be around (usually just Nell, but sometimes Claire and Jennifer D., and even Jennifer R. and Jennifer S.); and the way she stopped what she was doing to give Emily a ride, or pick her up, or both. You could talk to Mrs. Sussman about anything, unlike her own mother, who was far too busy going to auditions, or getting her beauty sleep, or rehearsing for another role, to talk to her daughters about anything ever. This was the *Leave It to Beaver* mother, and Nell had always believed she'd only been imagined by Hollywood writers. Now Nell knew such a mother existed in the real world, and she knew this was the kind of mother she wished she had.

Indeed, Nell trusted Mrs. Sussman and Emily so much that she had told them—and no one else—about how she felt when she had first seen Lewis Calder. He was the tallest boy in the school, towering above everyone at six foot five. She had seen him gliding through the corridors with his distinctively short hairdo, and thought he was so

handsome he looked like he belonged in the pages of *Seventeen* magazine. He was, she confessed, probably the most handsome boy in the world.

Mrs. Sussman worked on Fieldstone Farm over in Easton. It was part-time, so she could be home every day by the time Emily got out of school. She ran the barn, which incorporated a farm stand where they sold fresh produce and pies made by local cooks using that same produce. Everyone within a ten-mile radius came to them for their apple and rhubarb pie, pear caramel pie, and cinnamon peach tart.

Nell and Emily would go up to Fieldstone after school sometimes and help out. Nell fell in love with the farm the first time she went. It was only twenty minutes away from Westport, but it felt like another world. It was peaceful and quiet, and when she was there Nell felt as if she had stepped into the deepest, darkest countryside.

She loved working there, whether it was helping Mrs. Sussman out at the farm stand and ringing up the cash register, or cleaning out the chicken coop. This is what I want, she would think to herself as chickens were pecking at her red-painted toenails in flip-flops. This is what I'm going to have when I'm an adult.

Now Nell sits on the bus without Emily, her headphones on, the Rolling Stones, Neil Young, and the Grateful Dead playing on the cassette that sits inside her Walkman, when she finds herself looking at a giant pair of legs. She looks up to see Lewis Calder, who slides in next to her, giving her the faintest of nods.

And she is so thrilled she thinks she might throw up.

"Hey," he says. "Aren't we in math together?"

"I think so," she says, although there is no doubt they are in math together. She lives for math class, the highlight of her day, knowing that Lewis Calder always sits in front of her, slightly to the right, where

she can gaze upon him throughout the class, with no one seeing, no one knowing. At least she thought no one had noticed her.

Nell's hair is blond, long, and straight. It falls on either side of her face from a perfect center parting. If she pulls it forward, it acts like a curtain. She can gaze out from behind the waterfall of hair, with no one seeing what she is gazing at, namely, Lewis Calder.

Every day for the past seven months has been highlighted by a glimpse of Lewis Calder in math. But it's never enough. Each time she leaves a class, she unconsciously scans the corridor for his head, high above the sea of people beneath him. He doesn't notice her, doesn't seem to look at anyone as he walks from class to class, lost in some other world.

Emily has known Lewis all her life. She has told Nell that he is quiet, not particularly sociable. He rows, she says, at the new rowing club by the railway station. He's the only kid in school she knows who is rowing there, but has heard he's good, good enough that he goes to the rowing association every day after school, good enough that even though they don't yet have a proper junior program, there is already talk that the University of Washington has been in touch and talked about recruiting him for crew.

He was in a pack of boys through elementary and middle school, Emily says. Was popular and well liked. But his friends have gone on to be football and lacrosse players, and they're loud, boisterous, and rowdy. They like to party. Lewis Calder is fixated on rowing, on being the best at his sport that he can possibly be, so those friendships have drifted away over the years.

"You're Nell, right?" says Lewis Calder, pulling his own Walkman out of his backpack. "What are you listening to?"

He looks her over as she hands him her headphones, her heart pounding. She can't believe he's sitting next to her, can't believe he's so casually chatting with her. She wishes she could find the words to

answer him, but in lieu of finding the words, silently offering her headphones to him will have to do.

He puts the headphones on, a slow smile spreading over his face as he nods his head along with the music. He looks at Nell, still smiling. "Nice." He takes the headphones off and hands them back. "You don't look like a Deadhead."

"I'm definitely not a Deadhead," says Nell. "Just someone who appreciates great music."

"What else is on that tape?"

"The Rolling Stones. Neil Young. It's just a mix. What are you listening to?"

Lewis Calder reaches out and puts his own headphones on Nell's head as she flushes a bright red, not looking at him until he presses play and she hears the sounds of Neil Young's "Cinnamon Girl." She looks at him, delighted.

"Nice. I expected Nirvana."

"Oh yeah? Well, I expected Janet Jackson on yours."

Nell grimaces. "You don't even know me. What would make you think I like Janet Jackson?"

"An assumption. That I'm very relieved to find out is wrong. So what's your story, Nell Sunshine?"

Nell just stares at him. How does he know her last name? When did he notice her? What does this mean? If he knows her last name, surely he has noticed her, even though she has never seen him so much as glance at her, even though she has never seen him so much as glance at anyone.

"How do you know my name?"

"You just told me you were Nell. I guess I've been paying attention."

Nell laughs. "You're not paying attention. I've seen you walking through the corridors. You're always staring straight ahead."

"That's because I'm freakishly tall, which means everyone's always

staring at me, and I don't know what to do with my face when I make eye contact. It's easier to look straight ahead."

"Do you actually feel freakishly tall?"

Lewis Calder shrugs and nods.

"I kind of feel freakishly tall too. Although people don't stare."

"What are you, five-ten?"

"And a half. It's pretty freakishly tall in this town. Most of the girls in school are tiny."

"You hang out with Emily Sussman, right? She is tiny."

"She is. So how's crew?"

He smiles. "You know I row?"

"I hear things," she says, astonished to find she is relaxed, and chatting, and it is easy, and nice. *He's* nice. For the past few months she has had a huge, mad crush on him and has built him into some sort of demigod, with otherworldly qualities that would mean he would never have a normal, human conversation with someone like her.

In her fantasies, and there had been many, she dreamed of something exactly like this happening, except in her dreams the conversation wouldn't be as prosaic as this one, and he wouldn't be looking at her now with an amused twinkle in his eyes. But she did always imagine him with a large smile on his face, like he has now, and she dreamed their conversation would be this easy, and there would be maybe . . . maybe . . . maybe . . . just a hint of flirtation, like there is now. Is there? This is all so far and beyond her wildest hopes she can't quite believe it is actually happening.

"You should try it," he says. "They're starting a women's team, and you'd be good. You're tall and strong. You have the perfect physique for a rower."

He's noticed my physique, thinks Nell. He has noticed me!

"Maybe I'll come along and try it."

"What are you doing today?" he says. "I'm going to the boathouse

now. You could come too. I'll show you around. Maybe you could try it out."

Nell turns to look out the window, making sure he can't see that she is so happy there are tears in her eyes. "Sure," she says nonchalantly.

"We could get off the bus before it turns down Compo and walk. How does that sound? You okay with that?"

"That sounds great," she says, grinning like a lunatic as she looks out the window and issues a silent prayer of thanks for Emily having her orthodontist appointment today.

Nell stands on the banks of the Saugatuck River and watches Lewis Calder glide past her in his boat, eight boys sweeping the oars on water so smooth it is a pane of glass. Her breath catches in her throat. She has never seen anything so beautiful. She sits on the bank of the river, feeling the same sense of peace she feels at the farm in Easton.

When Lewis gets off the boat, he comes straight over to her with a grin. He gives her a tour of the boathouse, introduces her to Coach Mangan. The coach asks about her interest in rowing and takes her to an ergometer and demonstrates how to row. He explains that she should keep her arms loose and relaxed, that all the strength comes from her legs. Lewis stands silently by, watching her as she tries it on the machine.

"We could use more young people here," says one of the other coaches. "You should come back. You're the perfect build for a rower."

"Maybe I will," she says, her legs slightly shaky.

"Do you want to get an ice cream at the market?" Lewis says. "You can call your mom and have her pick you up from there."

Nell hesitates. Her mom is not the kind of mom who will drop everything, indeed drop anything, to come pick her up. The likelihood is her mom isn't even home. She's now starring in the new summer play

at the Westport Country Playhouse, which means she's probably in rehearsals all day.

"I can walk home," she says. "It's not far."

"Okay. I'll walk you home," says Lewis, picking up his backpack and slinging it over a shoulder. "How's that?"

five

Nell walks in the house, high as a kite, with plans to give rowing a try tomorrow. Which means more Lewis Calder. She's practically dizzy with the turn her life has taken. It doesn't even feel real yet.

She pauses just inside the front door, trying to gauge the temperature of the house. She does this a lot; they all do this a lot, pause just inside the front door to try to sniff out their mother's mood, try to figure out who they need to be.

Lizzy is the only one who seems not to care, but perhaps it is because she is so young. No. Nell cared, even at ten. Nell always cared. She always knew to remove herself when her mother was in a bad mood. Meredith, on the other hand, would always try to make her mother feel better at such times.

Sometimes Nell can smell her mother's state of mind as soon as she walks in. Other times she has to tiptoe around, waiting to see the expression on her mother's face. Meredith has described it as a veil.

Nell agrees that when her mother is in one of her moods, it is as if a veil of darkness has fallen over her.

Today Nell can't tell what's going on. The house seems unusually quiet. She puts down her backpack and goes into the kitchen. Neither of the other girls are there, which is always a bad sign. When their mother is in a good mood, they are all in the kitchen, doing homework at the table. Sometimes their mother is even there, cooking one of the few dishes she is able to make. Or she is with them, perched on a stool at the island as they all split a packet of Jaffa Cakes, which their grandmother sends over on a regular basis.

There is a tiny office off the kitchen. Now Nell can hear noises from the room, knows her mother is in there, and in a bad mood. She turns to leave, but it's too late. She has been heard.

"Nell?"

"Hi, Mom." Nell affects nonchalance. "I have a ton of homework. I'm going to go up to my room."

Her mother appears in the doorway, invisibly veiled. "Where have you been?" Her voice is flat, as it always is when she is in a fragile state.

Nell freezes. She just wants to get away as quickly as possible, but she knows if she leaves too abruptly even that might trigger her mother.

"The new rowing club. I just went to check it out."

"Oh. How was it?" Her mother comes in the kitchen now. "Do you want something to eat?"

"I'm fine," Nell says. "It was great. I might try it."

"How do you have the time? Between school and working on the farm, how on earth are you going to fit in rowing?"

"I don't have to do it competitively," Nell says. "I just thought it would be fun."

"How much is it?"

"I don't know anything about it. I just went to see it with a friend

from school. Mom, I really have a lot of work . . ." She stops as a loud crash comes from upstairs.

"What the—?" Her mother runs up the stairs, Nell following behind.

As they reach the master bedroom, an overwhelming stench of Calvin Klein's Obsession engulfs them. Her mother's perfume. And on the floor, on hands and knees gathering up broken glass, a stricken look on her face, is Meredith.

"What the hell are you doing?" demands their mother.

"I'm really sorry." Meredith is so frantically trying to pick up the mess that she hasn't noticed she has already cut her fingers on the glass and blood is now dripping on the floor, mixing with the pools of musky perfume.

"Stop touching the glass!" shouts their mother. "What happened?"

Meredith looks down at the floor. Her cheeks are a glittery bronze, her eyes lined in black.

"Have you been using my makeup?" Their mother has expressly forbidden them to use her makeup, to touch her things, even to come into her bedroom unless they are invited. The only one who gets away with creeping into this bedroom is Lizzy, but here is Meredith, a chubby thirteen-year-old who has never been interested in clothes, hair, or makeup, standing before them all, made-up and bleeding.

"What have I told you about using my things?" says their mother, fury rising.

Nell wants to say something, to tell her mother to leave Meredith alone, that it was an accident. But experience has taught her that her mother is unable to hear when she is in this space, that she can feel nothing but her own rising tide of fury.

"How dare you," she spits out, as Meredith stands still, looking down at the floor, her face bright red.

Nell knows how this will go. Her mother needs to get a reaction,

needs to see Meredith cry. She knows she *can* make Meredith cry, and sometimes Nell thinks her mother somehow thrives on controlling that reaction. She's often thought that is perhaps why Lizzy is never the victim of their mother's worst furies. Lizzy won't cry; Lizzy doesn't care when her mother is upset. She just ignores her. As a result, nine times out of ten if Lizzy does something wrong, their mother will turn and start taking it out on Meredith or Nell.

"How dare you use my new bronzer! You look ridiculous, Meredith. Get it off. Who do you think you are? You look like a cheap hooker. You think the boys will start noticing you if you wear makeup? You'll need to do a lot more than put on makeup. Losing thirty pounds would help for starters. Look at you. You're enormous."

Nell inhales sharply, willing Meredith to cry, for crying will end it. She is relieved when she hears Meredith take a great inhale of breath and then dissolve into loud, gasping sobs. It is exactly what their mother needed.

"Get out and get Estella to clean this up. Just get out."

Meredith runs out in tears, and Nell follows her to her room.

"I hate her!" Meredith says as soon as they get in the bedroom, bumping her desk as she tears into the room, knocking a pile of pen and ink sketches to the floor. She throws herself on the bed, crying into the pillow. "I hate her, I hate her, I hate her!"

The door opens and they both look up, terrified their mother has followed them for some reason. But it is Lizzy.

"Get out!" screams Meredith, throwing the pillow at her. "Get out of here."

"What did *I* do?" says Lizzy. "It's not my fault you got caught and she's in one of her moods."

"How would you know? You're never, ever the target," says Nell. "You get away with everything. We're left to deal with her craziness."

"It's not my fault I'm the baby." Lizzy shrugs. "Plus, if you didn't let it bother you, she wouldn't do it."

"Just fuck off," Nell says, staring down Lizzy until she backs out of the room and closes the door. Nell knows Lizzy might be able to ignore her mother's rants, but she won't stand up to her big sister's anger. She turns to Meredith. "I'm sorry," she says. "I knew she was in a mood when I saw her in the kitchen. I'm sorry I didn't have a chance to warn you."

"I really do hate her," says Meredith, her pillow now streaked with shimmery bronze. "I'm so jealous you're a senior. I can't wait to leave home and get away."

"Me too." Nell climbs on the bed and sits with her back against the wall. And she realizes that as much as she likes this town, and her new school, and Emily and Mrs. Sussman, and Lewis, it is true. She can't wait to get out of this house. "A few more months and I will never live in this house again. I wish it was tomorrow."

Meredith nods, reaching down and opening the door of her nightstand, burrowing around until she pulls out a huge bag of York Peppermint Patties.

"Want some?" she says to Nell, who shakes her head.

Meredith unwraps four at a time and swallows them quickly, barely tasting them, then four more, and four more. She keeps going until she starts not to feel better, but to feel nothing at all.

1997

six

Lizzy uses her toes to push the bedspread up, stretching out her arms with a happy sigh. Next to her on a cot bed is her best friend, Jackie, who is already awake, propped up against a stack of pillows, reading *The Thorn Birds*, which she grabbed from the bookshelf downstairs.

"Morning!" She yawns, rolling onto her side. "How's the book?"

"Great," says Jackie without looking up. "What are we doing for breakfast?"

"Want to bike ride over to Grubb's?" says Lizzy. "Maybe the gang will be there. What time is it?"

Jackie looks up. "The clock on your nightstand tells us it's nine forty-three." She closes the book. "And I'm starving. Let's go get some food."

Lizzy gets up, examining herself in the small oval mirror on the wall. Her dirty-blond hair is kind of ratty, so she tips her head upside down and shakes it out before gathering it in a loose bun on the top of her head. She pouts at her reflection approvingly.

"Can I wear my pj's?" she muses, looking down at the pink-and-blue-striped pants.

"You definitely can." Jackie looks over at her. "You look insanely cool in everything."

Lizzy examines herself in the mirror. It is true, she does seem to be able to pull off anything. She's lucky. She looks just like her mother, with the same dirty-blond hair, green eyes, dark skin, and tiny body. Everything looks good on her. Everything works. It always has. Thank God, she now thinks, she wasn't born an amazon like Nell or heavy like Meredith. Thank God she was born Lizzy.

The girls put on identical pairs of Converse shoes. Jackie pulls on a sweatshirt and then runs to the bathroom to straighten her bangs with the hair dryer and big round brush in there. They thunder down the stairs, whooping, for the house is empty and the girls are free to do whatever they want for the weekend.

The house is often empty these days. This weekend Lizzy is supposed to be with her dad, but she told him she had rehearsals for the school play and had to stay in town.

Just as they are running out, the phone starts to ring. "Damn," Lizzy says with a twang, turning around to get the phone.

"Hello, darling, it's Daddy. I'm just checking up on you, making sure you have everything you need."

"Hi, Daddy." Her voice is instantly little-girlish. "I miss you."

"I miss you too, peanut. I'm sorry you're not with me this weekend. I was thinking maybe I could come up tonight and take you out for a special daddy-daughter dinner. We could go to Zanghi's as a treat."

Lizzy makes big fearful eyes at Jackie, who stifles a giggle. "Oh, Daddy, that would have been amazing. But we have a cast dinner for the school play after rehearsal tonight, and we all have to attend."

"Of course. What about brunch on Sunday? I could come pick you up at eleven. I do want to see you soon. I have to be honest, I'm not

real comfortable with you being in the house by yourself and your mother not being there."

"Daddy! I'm sixteen! I'm not a baby. Also, Jackie's staying with me and you know she's very responsible."

Her father laughs. "I know you're both responsible. I'm not worried about that. I would just feel better if you had a parent around this weekend. What about brunch, then? How does that sound?"

"That sounds awesome," she says, rolling her eyes at Jackie. "I'll call you Sunday morning, okay? And don't worry about me, I'll be fine, and I'll call you if I need you. I love you, Daddy."

"Love you too, peanut."

Lizzy is smiling as she hangs up the phone. She loves her dad, but it is increasingly difficult to love him, given that her mother has hated him ever since the divorce (even though her mother was the one who was unfaithful, causing the divorce in the first place) and wants nothing more than for her daughters to hate him too. Ronni won't forgive him for leaving her, and anytime the girls mention their father, their mother follows it with a snarky remark. They are learning to keep quiet about loving their father, needing him. These times, when their mother is away, are the only times Lizzy can feel unreservedly good about seeing her father.

She hangs up the phone and the two girls walk out the front door, leaning against each other, as Lizzy shakes her head. "I really don't know why he would care. Like, what's the worst that could happen? I throw a party and my mom's house gets trashed? He hates her. He'd probably be happy." Her parents don't actually say they hate each other, but when her father has to ask about anything that involves her mother, she sees his jaw clench with a slight tick.

Not that she can blame him exactly. Lizzy loves and hates her mother in equal measure. She loves her more than her sisters do, she is sure, because she has never been in her mother's crosshairs. She

doesn't quite understand why her mother's moods bother her sisters so much. Or why they react to her the way they do. It just makes things worse. Lizzy figured out early on that the thing to do when her mother lost it was to laugh. Lizzy laughs, and her laughter invariably seems to diffuse her mother's rage. Meredith tried the same approach, but when she laughed, it only served to make her mother angrier.

The people who set her off have always been Nell and Meredith, and their father. Not when they were all young, but as they got older, he ended up being a target too. None of them knew about her affairs. Once the marriage broke up, all three girls learned everyone else knew that their mother had been having affairs for years.

The affair that broke up the marriage was different. He was a guest director, brought in to direct a performance of *A Doll's House* at the Playhouse. Ronni played Nora. Naturally. And fell in love with the director. Naturally. Except this one wasn't just an affair. This one, Ronni announced, was her *soul mate*.

Her soul mate was her soul mate for two years. Ronni managed to be charming, and her best self, for a year and a half of those two years. Even Lizzy knew that the last six months were hell. She saw how her mother, once she felt the director distancing himself, became more and more needy, more and more stressed. She would explode at the girls, her now ex-husband, and eventually, the director. Who ended it by having another affair with a well-known actress in New York.

Ronni then tried to make her way back to Robert, realizing, perhaps, what she had given up when she had left him, but it had been too long. Lizzy's father told her that the two years away from her mother had been the most peaceful of his adult life. He explained that the end of the marriage was painful only in that he saw his three daughters far less than he would have liked, but—he told them—at least he no longer had a fourth daughter to look after in the form of an emotionally volatile

wife. He was sorry he couldn't protect his daughters from her, he told the girls, but he thought that if he went back to her he might die.

Lizzy knew her mother hated her father after that. She would roll her eyes anytime one of the girls would talk about their father, and fill them with stories about how boring he was, what a terrible father he'd been—traveling for work so much instead of having a relationship with them. She would get in one of her moods and rage in front of the audience that was her daughters that no one would make him happy again and he would never, ever find a woman like Ronni.

As it happens, Robert did find someone. None of the girls particularly like her. But Lizzy thinks that has less to do with her mother than it has to do with her and her sisters, who, despite recognizing how difficult their mother is, still feel an obligation to protect her.

Their father now lives in Greenwich with his new wife, which is, in itself, a major pain in the ass. If he still lived in Westport, Lizzy would definitely see him more. Going to his house for the weekend means having to miss out on her friends, and hangouts and parties in Westport. And that's just no fun at all.

He will drive Lizzy back and forth, but she doesn't want to be so far away; she doesn't want to miss out on anything, not when being a sophomore is so much fun. It's the perfect grade, she and Jackie have decided. You're over the newness and *overwhelmingness* of being a freshman in high school, where the school is huge and you feel like the baby all over again, and going to the cafeteria at lunchtime fills you with dread because you're terrified you're not going to be able to sit with your friends, or anyone nice, and eating on your own means you'll be designated a loser for the rest of your school days.

Then in junior year you have to spend all your time worrying about college, and the pressure is really on the first part of senior year, so sophomore year is perfect.

Not that Lizzy ever had to worry about who to sit with in the cafeteria. Not that, in fact, Lizzy has ever had a moment of insecurity in her life. She has always been popular, pretty, and perfectly well accepted wherever she goes.

"You lead a charmed life," Jackie would say, as she bemoaned the fact that her thighs rub together, that she always has a roll of fat over the top of the waistband of her jeans, that her naturally frizzy hair always looks terrible unless she manages to tame it into straight submission with a very powerful hair dryer. All of this adds up to her lamenting the fact that the boys she likes only ever like her as a friend. "It's not fair."

"Your life is charmed too," says Lizzy, who does not point out that even though Lizzy's life seems wonderful, she secretly covets what Jackie has: parents who love each other, a mom who is available and present, two cute little brothers, an even cuter golden retriever, and a bunny rabbit called Stanley who lives on the porch.

Lizzy has none of that. She has divorced parents who hate each other. She has a mother whose fame has waned on a national scale but who is still considered a local celebrity here in Westport, where she hardly ever *is* these days, thanks to touring with a regional production of *A Chorus Line*. Her sister Meredith lives in London, and Nell, who discovered she was pregnant after she had split up with her boyfriend, decided to be a teen mom and have the baby. Nell and her son, River, both now live on a farm in Easton. It's only about twenty minutes away, and River is exceptionally cute, but Nell is busy with her life as caretaker of the farm. Lizzy is busy with being a sophomore with a social life. And Ronni? Well, Ronni just isn't around very much.

Most of the time, Lizzy feels like an only child. Most of the time, Lizzy loves being an only child. She was always the baby of the family, always knew she was special. Being left on her own so much these days means she can do whatever she wants, which is perfectly fine with her.

Most of the time.

She and Jackie have breakfast at one of the little picnic tables outside Grubb's (the little café by the beach isn't actually called Grubb's, but that's what some of her friends say their parents used to call it, and she likes the name so much she refuses to call it anything else), and by the time they are finished there is a pack of kids sitting with them.

"We should do something tonight at your house," says a boy named Ryan, who Lizzy is starting to think might be quite cute. She's known him forever, but they haven't been friendly until just this year when he started making her laugh on the school bus. Now they're in the same crowd, and Lizzy is pretty sure he might like her too.

"Like what? I can't have a party. My mom would kill me."

"Not a party," says Ryan. "Something small. Like, a little party. For just us. And maybe a few more."

"Your mom's not home?" says another kid, Craig. Lizzy doesn't really know Craig. He was at Greens Farms Academy through middle school, apparently with some issues. But he's back at Staples now and seems fine, if a little hyperactive.

"She's touring. We have a housekeeper during the week, but it's just me and Jackie for the weekend."

Craig's eyes light up. "Oh, it is *so* party time, it's not even funny."

"Don't be a douche." Ryan shakes his head. "We can't do anything big. But we should do something. You cook, right?"

Lizzy nods. "Yeah. I can cook. I love cooking."

He shrugs. "Why don't we come to your house to hang out. We can throw something on the grill, chill out. Swim. Hot tub. It will be awesome."

"I'll bring the beers," says Craig, as they all grin.

"Okay." Lizzy nods approvingly. "Done. I'll get food. Come over at seven. And bring your bathing suits."

"What?" Craig leers. "No skinny-dipping?"

"Seeing your teeny wiener will send everyone home," Ryan says, and the rest of the gang all laugh.

Lizzy happens to love cooking. Her mom rarely goes near a stove, so it was always up to the girls, and the housekeeper, to cook if they wanted to eat something other than takeout every night.

Nell is vegetarian, and not, unfortunately as far as Lizzy can tell, the kind of vegetarian who lives off cheese, bread, and yummy pasta, but the kind of vegetarian who eats vegetables. When Nell lived at home and used to cook, it meant vegetable soups, and lots of salads, nuts, and seeds. Which was okay once in a while, but not every night.

Meredith only ever cooked from a cookbook, and it wasn't dinners to which she gravitated, but baking. She loved baking, would read baking cookbooks as if they were novels, trying out different recipes for hours. And eating them, which drove their mother, who wants all her daughters to be slim and beautiful, insane.

Lizzy is a terrible baker. It is much too precise. She likes being creative in the kitchen, which means throwing in a little of this, a little of that, trying out different things. Often the food is inedible, but that is okay. It just means she'll try something else next time.

She looks at recipes to use as a jumping-off point. Once she has read them, she doesn't tend to look at them again. Her mother describes Lizzy's cooking, frequently and to anyone who will listen, as being a bit like Russian roulette: you never know what the outcome will be. She will also say that when it's good, it's very, very good, but when it's bad, it's horrid.

The one thing she is very good at is pesto. She started with a basic traditional basil pesto, adding lemon on a whim, which transformed it into something her family asks for all the time. Even Nell. Lizzy also

makes a spinach and nutmeg pesto and a great mushroom and walnut pesto, livened up occasionally with truffle oil.

Jackie says she's addicted to the mushroom and walnut; she thinks Lizzy should be selling all of them at the farmers' market, as well as at Nell's farm in Easton. Sometimes she will make a big batch for Nell to sell, and they sell out immediately. Nell asks Lizzy for them all the time, but she can't be bothered to do it regularly. She's sixteen! This is the time when she should be going out and having fun and living the life of a sixteen-year-old, not a mini mogul in the making.

Today she's going to make pesto to go with the burgers they'll throw on the grill. Almost all her friends subsist exclusively on a diet of burgers, pizza, hot dogs, and cheese, but she's going to make the pesto anyway.

Lizzy has her driver's permit but not her license, so Jackie's mom is enlisted to take them to Hay Day for groceries. Once there, Lizzy blows through most of the money her mom left her for emergencies to buy mushrooms, walnuts, basil, garlic, Parmesan, pine nuts, lemons, truffle oil, ground beef, chicken, buns, chips, dips. And candy, because why would you not have candy if there were no adults around to cast a disapproving eye?

Jackie's mom doesn't know that Lizzy's mom is away. There is no way in hell she would let Jackie stay if she knew they were unsupervised. Not that she doesn't trust Jackie, but she recently told them about a friend's daughter in another town who had a crazy party that almost burned down the house, and what kind of a parent would leave her sixteen-year-old daughter unattended?

On the way back from the grocery story, Lizzy and Jackie both keep very quiet in the back of the car. When Jackie's mom turns around and says, "I should come in and say hi to your mom," Lizzy says, smoothly and without a trace of guile, "Oh, she's in New York for the day for rehearsal. I'll tell her you said hi."

Jackie's mom winks. "No surprise you bought all that candy, then! Don't worry, I won't tell!"

As soon as the girls close the front door behind them, they collapse in giggles.

"Oh, my God!" heaves Jackie. "I can't believe you're such a good actress."

"But of course," says Lizzy with an immaculate English accent, gliding down the corridor holding an imaginary cigarette, "you know I'm the daughter of the *mahvellous* Ronni Sunshine. It runs in the genes, don't you know."

The girls have everything prepared by early evening. They have brought up all the candles from the basement and placed them on all the tables outside. The beautiful day is coming to an end, but it will give way to a warm, apricot glow from the candles and the string of Christmas lights also brought up from the basement. They've twisted the lights through the lower branches of the old cherry tree that sits on the lawn over the rattan sofas on the other side of the yard from the swimming pool.

Jackie, who doesn't really cook but wants to keep up with her friend, has sort of followed a recipe in *The Silver Palate Cookbook* for Chicken Marbella. But she's calling it Chicken *Bella* because it's missing the prunes, the capers, the oregano, and the parsley. In any case, it's cooking slowly in the oven.

They put a CD of En Vogue in, then run upstairs to get dressed. Jackie squeezes into a short, tight black dress. Lizzy grabs a gold sequined minidress from her mother's closet and steps into her mother's high, gold, strappy Manolo Blahniks.

"Won't your mom kill you?"

"Nah. She doesn't care if I wear her stuff. She loves that we look so similar. The way to get my mom to really love you is to tell her we look like sisters. It gets her every time."

"O-kaaaay. Except your mom is old and you're young . . . and you don't really look that much alike."

"I know. But she likes to think we do. Of course she thinks she looks like me, as in, sixteen." Lizzy rolls her eyes.

"You look amazing." Jackie stares at her friend, and Lizzy can see the hint of envy in her friend's eyes. But that's why she loves Jackie—it's just a hint.

"So do you," says Lizzy, smiling at her friend. "Let's go downstairs. They'll be here any minute."

This is what it feels like to be an adult, thinks Lizzy, proud of herself for being such a good host. She made everyone have some pesto with their burgers, and they all declared it awesome.

They sit around on the outdoor lounge furniture, drinking the beers Craig brought, watching the sun set over the water, reflecting a golden glow over everyone there. Each time she looks at Ryan, he is looking at her, and each time their eyes meet, it takes them longer to look away. He's usually the one who breaks the gaze first, as Lizzy's heart does the tiniest of flips. He really is cute, she thinks to herself, and he likes me! The knowledge is potent, makes her more aware of her beauty, her power, more aware of the fact that she is on the brink of womanhood. She swigs the last of her bottle of beer, not drunk, but happily tipsy, enough to give her the confidence to stand up and announce she is going swimming.

"Do you have any more beer?" Johnny, an old friend of Ryan's, slides his empty bottle to the center of the table.

"We're all out," says Craig. "I lost my fake ID last week, so this is stuff I took from my parents' garage. Lizzy? Isn't there alcohol here?"

"Yes, but no way are we touching it. My mom notices nothing, except for missing alcohol. Sorry, dude, but you're shit out of luck."

"I can get someone to replace it tomorrow," says Craig. "Go on. It will be there before she comes back."

Lizzy shakes her head. "Nope. Can't do it."

"How about we ask someone who has a fake ID to bring some over?" Johnny nods enthusiastically at Craig's suggestion.

"Kevin always gets it for his friends. Why don't we ask him?"

"Great idea! Is that okay, Lizzy? We'll call Kevin and see if we can get him to do it."

"Just Kevin?" says Lizzy. "You can't tell him we're in the house by ourselves, okay? Just tell him, I don't know, tell him it's a small party, okay? I don't want word getting out."

Craig shakes his head forcefully. "Word's *not* going to get out. I'll go inside and call him. What do we want? More beer?"

"And vodka!" shouts Johnny, as Lizzy rolls her eyes.

"I'm going for a swim." Lizzy kicks off her heels and stands up, peeling her dress down unself-consciously as if every boy's eyes aren't glued to her body, as if she is in a room by herself. She reveals a red bikini, a flat, golden stomach, and strong, slim thighs. "Who's coming with?"

"I'm in," says Ryan, unbuttoning his jeans and hopping on one foot to pull them off. Lizzy watches, swaying by the edge of the pool, knowing how good she looks in a bikini, hoping he won't be able to take his eyes off her. She stands for a second, shaking out her hair, before executing a perfect dive. She swims to the bottom of the pool, getting used to the brisk chill of the water, kicking her way back up as she emerges, pushing the water off her face with her hands, to see Ryan diving in after her.

Everything suddenly seems far away. She is vaguely aware of Craig disappearing into the house to call Kevin; she can see Jackie, Johnny, Chuck, and Isabel still sitting under the cherry tree, a burst of laughter coming from them all as the boys pick up each beer bottle on the table and tip it back, just in case there's anything left.

She can see the lights twinkling in the cherry tree, can hear Puff Daddy from the boom box they have outside, but it all seems far away from the velvet blackness of the swimming pool. The pool lights are off, and everything is dark, but for the reflected glow from the lights over on the other side of the yard.

She yelps as she feels Ryan grab her legs and pull her under the water. She comes back up, sputtering, leaping on top of him to try to push his head underwater. Both of them are grinning. He is standing and she can't do it, no matter how much she wrestles, her skin slip-sliding against his as she clasps her legs around his body to try to wrest him off balance.

"You won't be able to." He grins.

Lizzy slides off him and pauses behind him, slipping underwater like a fish, grabbing his ankles and yanking them behind him as he finally goes under.

They both emerge, breathing heavily, looking at each other and grinning.

Ryan shakes his head. "Oh man," he says softly. "You've got super-powers."

"I do?" She moves ever so slightly closer to him in the blackness.

"You do," he answers, moving ever so slightly closer to her.

"You know I'm completely unlike any other girl you've ever met."

"I do know that," he says softly, and this time he is not smiling.

"You do?"

"You're more beautiful than any other girl I've ever met," he says, moving closer still.

Lizzy's heart skips. She can see the light glinting in his eyes. They are both submerged in the water but for their heads. As he slips his hands around her waist she reaches her arms around his neck and raises her legs around his waist. She grins.

"Because I have magic powers," she whispers, "I can make boys do whatever I want them to."

"What do you want me to do?" he whispers back, his head now inches from hers.

"I want you to kiss me," she whispers.

And he does.

The mood is broken by a slamming screen door as Craig shouts out from the house, "Success! Kevin's on his way. He's bringing a few people with him. That's okay, right?"

"Whatever." Lizzy shrugs, not paying attention, twining her arms around Ryan's neck again. She has far more important things to focus on.

It had started out for most people as a quiet Saturday night in Westport. Nothing much was going on. A few groups of kids were hanging out at the beach, others were at home, talking on the phone with their friends.

A rumor started that there was something going on at Lizzy Sunshine's house, and the game of telephone began. "Something going on" became no parents, became a crazy party, a buzz of excitement fizzing across the phone lines and through the houses on Compo Beach, stretching over to Greens Farms, down to Saugatuck, to Coleytown, the Hunt Club, and Old Hill.

Before long, kids all over town were jumping into cars, grabbing liquor from their parents' cupboards, basements, and garages. They all made their way to Minuteman Hill, none of them knowing exactly which house it was, but driving up the hill, winding around the road until they saw the cars. The giveaway was always the cars.

Some were dropped off at the bottom of the hill by unsuspecting parents. "Lizzy Sunshine is having a small party," they told their parents, wide-eyed and innocent. "There are only about fifteen of us. Can you drop me off?" They converged with friends as they walked up the hill.

First there were five, including Kevin with the beers, vodka, and

tequila. Next came three more. Then fifteen. Then twenty-five. Then they lost track.

Everyone had alcohol with them. Bottles of wine swiped from the rack in the kitchen and hidden in their backpacks, flasks of Jack Daniel's tucked into jacket pockets, water bottles that innocently hid the fact that they had been swiftly emptied and filled with vodka.

They followed the cars, sniffed out the party, let themselves into the back garden via the gate on the side. They turned the music up and shouted across to people they knew from school. Someone brought weed—joints started to be passed around from hand to hand as they talked and smoked, and drank and laughed, high on weed, high on life, high on having a spectacular house with no adults in sight.

Lizzy was loving it. This was what high school was all about! This, surely, would be her crowning glory through her high school years! She was now, officially, Queen of the Sophomores. Everyone kept telling her how cool this was, how great, how this was the best party they had ever been to.

She and Ryan couldn't keep their hands off each other. They were now official, given that practically the whole high school was there and watching them. Even seniors were there; even they were declaring it the coolest night of the year.

Ryan pulled her into the house and up the stairs. The house was smoky and loud and filled with people lounging around on furniture, smoking in the kitchen, dancing in the family room. She was vaguely aware of something being spilled, but what the hell, she had had far too much to drink herself, too much to worry about anything tonight, and she could clean up in the morning.

She giggled as Ryan led her to the wrong bedroom, correcting him by taking him to hers. They shut the door and fell on the bed, making out furiously as he undid the ties of her bikini top and she sighed with anticipation.

But just as it was getting good, the bedroom door burst open. Lizzy shrieked and grabbed the sheet to cover herself, and Ryan rolled off her and looked blearily at Jackie, who stood in the doorway white as a sheet and panting like she'd just run a marathon.

"What is it?" Lizzy said, a frisson of alarm racing down her spine.

"The police are at the door. Everyone's freaking out. Neighbors complained. They want to see you. The police!"

"Oh, shit," said Lizzy, knowing there was weed and alcohol and underage teenagers everywhere. "Oh, shit," she said again as she stumbled off the bed and went to the front door.

It turned out it wasn't such a big deal. The police just sent everyone home. When they realized Lizzy was Ronni Sunshine's daughter, they said they wouldn't take it any further. They pretended they couldn't smell the weed, hadn't tripped over empty beer bottles on the front lawn. If everyone left, they said they would forget about it. If they could come back and get an autograph for his grandma, said one, they would let this one slide. And they smiled as drunken teenagers slipped out past them in the foyer.

After one last lingering kiss, Ryan left. Everyone left except for Jackie and Lizzy, who stumbled up to bed as soon as the house was empty, both falling into a deep, drunken sleep.

seven

Lizzy is swimming back to consciousness, vaguely aware of someone shaking her. Her head is pounding, a wave of nausea washing over her even before she opens her eyes. Slowly she realizes the sound she is hearing is her sister's voice.

"What the heck? What the heck, Lizzy? Wake up! Get up! Mom's going to kill you. Get out of bed now!"

Lizzy opens her eyes to see Meredith standing over her with a stricken face. Nothing makes sense. Why is Meredith here? She's supposed to be in England, living with their grandparents while she does her year at the University College London. Unless this is still a dream . . . Lizzy closes her eyes again, sinking back into the pillow. This must be a dream.

"Get the hell out of bed, Lizzy!" Meredith shouts in her ear.

Lizzy groans and opens her eyes properly this time. "Okay, okay, I get it. This isn't a dream." She sits up. "Meri? What the fuck are you doing here?"

"Never mind that. What the hell happened? The house is ruined."

"What do you mean, ruined? I just had a few people over last night."

"A few?" Meredith is almost hysterical. "The house is totally trashed. What the hell, Lizzy?"

Lizzy perches on the edge of her bed, holding her head and groaning. "Do you have any painkillers?"

"No, I don't have any painkillers," snaps Meredith, who disappears for a couple of minutes, returning with a glass of water and two pills. "Take these."

"I think I need three." Lizzy groans as she stumbles out of bed, takes the pills, and starts making her way downstairs.

"Start with those. You need to get up and help me clean this house. I already woke your friend and she's dealing with the kitchen. How many people did you have here? I presume Mom has no idea. Where is she anyway?"

But Lizzy doesn't answer. By now she has seen the living room. Even Lizzy is shocked at the state of the house. There is broken glass all over, tipped-over bottles of wine on the sofa, and red wine on the carpet. There are cigarette burns on the rug and floor, kitchen cupboard doors are hanging off the hinges, and all over the counters, on every visible surface, all over the garden, even in the pool, are empty cans and bottles and cigarette butts.

"You have got to be kidding me," Meredith mutters over and over. "You have got to be *kidding* me."

"Why don't you just say, 'You have got to be *fucking* kidding me,'" says Lizzy. "Why don't you actually swear, because I know you want to. I know that you're judging me. Just get it all out."

Meredith ignores her. She goes into the kitchen and gets a bucket, fills it with soapy water, grabs a big scrubbing brush, and gets on her

hands and knees to work on the wine stains in the carpet. Jackie is wiping every surface in the kitchen with Clorox, her face ablaze with shame at being caught by Lizzy's older sister.

Lizzy starts doing a half-assed job of pretending to clean up. She moves slowly around the house and yard, her head still pounding, gingerly holding a trash bag into which she is throwing all the empties. She's telling herself it really doesn't look so bad, the cleanup really isn't so much. She fills the bag, ties it, and puts it outside to take to recycling, before coming back inside to stand in front of Meredith.

"So what are you doing here? Actually?"

Meredith pauses, sits back on her haunches. "I was homesick," she says. "I wanted to come back and see everyone."

"You were homesick for Mom?" Lizzy is astonished.

"Not Mom, exactly."

"Right, because you escaped! You managed to get free of her, and not just free, but all the way over to England. Lucky you."

"You're a sophomore. Two more years and then you can leave too. Anyway, she's not that bad with you. You're the only one who has ever been able to handle her."

"You mean I stand up to her?"

"Whatever it is you do, it makes her less horrific. Where is she, anyway?"

Lizzy shrugs. "Busy as ever. She's touring for *A Chorus Line*. Didn't she tell you?"

"I haven't spoken to her in a while. When will she be back?"

"Probably when the director of the show realizes what a nightmare she is." Lizzy grins at Meredith, and for the first time since she walked in the house, Meredith grins back.

"Poor, poor director," she says. "You know he won't be the one to dump her."

"I know. She'll dump him once she realizes how *desperately dull and boring he is*." Lizzy parrots her mother as Meredith shakes her head.

"It's awful how well you do her."

"That's because I'm stuck with her all the time. Actually, that's not true, because she's hardly ever here, but when she is, I'm the one with her." Her face grows serious. "I wish you weren't living in London, Meri. I wish you were still here."

"But I wouldn't be living at home even if I were here," Meredith reminds her. "I'd be living in New York at Columbia, remember? I probably wouldn't ever see you."

"I would be taking a train in to see you, though," says Lizzy. "It would be fun."

Meredith peers at her sister. "Does it actually bother you, being on your own here? You never needed help from Nell or me. You always had both Mom and Dad wrapped around your little finger. All Nell and I did was get in your way."

"True," says Lizzy, and they both laugh. "But I do miss you. I'm totally fine with Mom being away as much as she is, but it was more fun when I was little and I had my sisters with me. That's all."

"I'll be home in six months," Meredith reminds her.

"Home, home?"

"Well, not here. Obviously. I wouldn't move back in with Mom for a billion dollars."

"Christ, I can't wait to leave home."

The doorbell chimes, making them both jump. They stare at each other, eyes wide. Lizzy is in an old T-shirt, her hair ratty and tangled, mascara smudged around her eyes, her skin tinged gray. And the house is far from cleaned.

"Whoever it is, let's just ignore it. They'll go away," she says.

"We can't," Meredith says, standing up. "It might be important."

"If it's important, they'll come back," Lizzy argues, as the doorbell rings again. But when she sees her sister heading for the door, she mutters, "I'll go. Please, God, let it not be Ryan." When she gets to the front door, she peers out through the sidelights.

"Urgh," she says. "It's the next-door neighbor. At least it's not Mom."

eight

Meredith doesn't mind that Lizzy has left to meet Ryan and she is left to clean up the house. It's what she does, after all: takes care of things and cleans up other people's messes. Other things she does? Not complain when she is living in London and comes home to be with her family, only to find her mother is not there. She's learned not to complain about her mother. She learned from Nell not to flinch at her mother's raging but to slip quietly out of the room as quickly as she could. Then she figured out on her own that, sometimes, bringing her mother a big glass of wine would calm her down. In the end, that was the difference between the three sisters. Nell would disappear. Meredith would try to please. And Lizzy would ignore it.

When the house is finally back in order, including the cabinets in the kitchen fixed, Meredith sits on the side porch with a beer, one of the few left after Lizzy's party. She puts her feet up on the ottoman, smiling as she sips and looks out at the treetops, enjoying this reunion with the peaceful view.

You can't see the water from the house, but you know it's there; you can smell it. The light is different too. Whatever bad memories this house contains, it is still, it will always be, home.

In the corner of the yard, hidden by the darkening sky, is the trampoline. Lizzy was the one who loved the trampoline the most, but Meredith would lie on it for hours with her friend Rachel, the two of them talking about everything under the sun. Every now and then Meredith's mother would rap on the window to get them to jump, to exercise, but as soon as she disappeared they would flop back down on their bellies again.

At the bottom of the hill is Longshore, where she learned to play tennis, badly. Where she went every day during summer in the hope that one of the pool lifeguards would notice her, that she might finally have a summer romance.

She never did. They never noticed the chubby girl with the mousy hair and sweet smile, but that's okay. She found her solace, her romance, the life she should have been living, in the pages of books. And now, at nineteen, she finally has a boyfriend. A fellow student at University College London, he is studying PPE (philosophy, politics, and economics) and she switched her major to study the same.

She had originally thought about Goldsmiths or Central Saint Martins, wanting to do a degree in fine art, but her father hadn't understood. "How will you make money from art?" he had asked, bemused. And so she had applied to a number of universities in the UK, choosing English as a general degree.

She soon found she was doing less and less of the art she had always loved. There wasn't the time. She was involved in the student union and had joined the bridge club. Which was where she met Gavin. They formed a team, and a friendship, which grew into a romance after he stammered that he wanted to take her to a film one night and perhaps for a bite to eat afterward.

They went to the Everyman in Hampstead to see *Good Will Hunting*, and then to Maxwell's for a burger and terrible fat, soggy French fries that were nothing like the French fries she was used to in America.

She found Gavin very nice, if a little odd. He had a mop of black curly hair, and tortoiseshell glasses, plus a nervous tic of clearing his throat, which she found endearing and sweet. His trousers were always a little short, and his socks a glistening white. He wasn't exactly the romantic hero she had pictured herself with, after all those years of losing herself in the pages of hundreds of novels, and she wasn't exactly attracted to him, but he really, really liked her, and she liked him enough to give it a go.

What she really liked, though, was having a boyfriend. She would insert it into every conversation. At the corner shop she would say, "Oh, and can I have some Polos for my boyfriend?" At the sandwich shop she would say, "I'll have an egg salad with lettuce, tomato, and cucumber, and my boyfriend will have Coronation Chicken on a bap, please." When strangers struck up conversations with her, she would casually insert "my boyfriend" as soon as she could, just in case the encounter ended quickly and she'd lose the chance to mention to the universe that someone loved her, that she was finally, *finally* enough.

Being able to say she had a boyfriend, being able to insert the fact into conversation, transformed her in the eyes of the world. Or so she thought. No longer would they see her as a shy, overweight American girl who had never fit in. Now she was one of them! Whoever "them" might be.

And it was very nice being adored. Gavin did adore her. He didn't show he adored her with flowers and chocolates, but he did buy her a fancy set of cards for bridge, and he always paid when they went out for dinner, and he kissed her when she went back to his flat one night to watch a video.

Meredith had been kissed by three boys before, but never as

enthusiastically as Gavin. After that first kiss their relationship progressed and now they are sleeping together, but it isn't quite what she expected either. She has yet to experience the elusive orgasm, and sex always seems to be over quickly, after a little bit of awkward thrusting in and out. But she does love the cuddling afterward, and Gavin is very good at cuddling.

The problem is it's hard to find a place to cuddle. He can't come back to her place because she's living with her grandparents in Hampstead. As a result, she and Gavin are spending more and more time at his slightly grungy flat off Goodge Street. Now that they are officially an item, her grandparents seem to be fine with her spending the night. Judging from their stories about her mother, whatever Meredith did was tame by comparison.

Moving to London for university was the best thing she ever did. Moving away from her mother was the best thing she ever did. She misses her father and her sisters . . . well, Nell . . . but the strain of having to look after her mother and keep the peace was too much. However lovely it is to be home, she thinks, it is even lovelier to know that it's temporary.

Not that things are easy with her father. He has remarried, to a woman named Selena, who was initially very nice to all the girls, taking them for pedicures and manicures when they came to stay, taking them out for "girls' lunches," insisting they be flower girls at the wedding.

And then Robert and Selena had a daughter, and the girls were swiftly sidelined, no longer welcomed, no longer part of this new family. They all tried, staying with their father's new family for the holidays. But they couldn't help noticing that Arianna, their half sister, received armfuls of gifts for Christmas, while they each got a small, single gift. Arianna's bedroom was like a perfect fairy-princess palace, while they had to share the attic when they visited, sleeping in mismatched beds and stuffing their clothes in old drawers that didn't quite close.

Nell and Lizzy eventually stopped going. Meredith tried to go by herself, but Selena was so unwelcoming, so passive-aggressive in her sideways comments about "weight issues," that Meredith realized her sisters were right: they were now unwelcome visitors in their father's home. It wasn't a position she enjoyed or wanted to repeat. So now, she talks to her father on the phone from time to time, and wishes he would be the father he was before Selena came along.

Meredith sits up as a car growls into the driveway. An old Ford pickup truck from the 1950s, cherry red, with polished wood on the sides of the flatbed. There is only one person she knows who would drive a truck like that.

Meredith gets up, smiling, as Nell emerges from the driver's side, walking over to the passenger side to let out a towheaded boy.

"Nell!" Meredith hustles over and hugs her sister, as the little boy stands by with a wide grin. Shyly he allows himself to be picked up and squeezed by his aunt.

"Do you know who I am?" Meredith asks, surprised at the wave of love and affection that is sweeping over her as she holds this little boy she has only met a handful of times.

"Aunt Meri," he says, and she laughs in delight.

"I am! Oh, it's good to see you! You got so big! How old are you? Twelve? Thirteen?"

He shakes his head solemnly, holding up four fingers of one hand.

"Four? Well, my goodness. I thought you were much older. You are so grown-up!" She puts him down and looks at Nell, marveling at how little Nell has changed, how comforting it is to see her. Nell has always been comforting. Her solidity, her quiet confidence, her sense of purpose in the world have always been Meredith's port in the storm of her mother's volatility. Tears spring into her eyes as she looks at her sister, wishing she saw her more.

"How's the farm? How's life? I can't believe River!" The boy runs

up the steps and lets himself into the house. "Look at him! He's so grown-up."

"And independent," Nell says. "Life on a farm. He's mucking out stables and feeding chickens. I have taught him well."

The two women walk inside their mother's home, now almost spotless thanks to Meredith's day of cleaning. There are some things she couldn't fix: the shattered glass of the coffee table, the red wine poured on the sofa, the broken chair leg. But there is a throw covering the wine stain, the glass has been removed, and the chair is now in the garage. There are only so many miracles Meredith was able to conjure up in the space of a day. She is in any case relieved that Nell doesn't seem to notice anything amiss.

"Do you hear from Lewis?" It is a sensitive subject, Meredith knows, and not one that has ever been easy for Nell to speak about.

Nell and Lewis dated for a long time, all through senior year and then after he went to the University of Washington on a rowing scholarship and she went to the University of Vermont. In her sophomore year of college, she discovered she was pregnant. Six months pregnant. She had forgotten about her periods, had assumed the weight she was gaining was due to the amount of chocolate she had started eating. When the baby started kicking, she thought it was a muscle spasm.

Lewis was devastated. The parents met to discuss what would happen, but Lewis's parents were adamant: a baby was not going to ruin his rowing future. Lewis seemed overwhelmed. He loved Nell, he said, but things had been hard for a while—a long-distance relationship wasn't what he wanted, he had realized, and a baby definitely wasn't what he wanted. He did not want to keep the baby and said he thought adoption was clearly the only right solution to this dilemma.

Not for Nell. She couldn't, wouldn't give her baby up. She dropped out of college, but she didn't go back to her mother's house. Rather, she found a home at the farm where she had worked with Mrs. Sussman.

Lewis stayed in touch until River was six months old. Meredith knows Nell hasn't heard from him since then, although his parents send a large check every Christmas.

The farm saved her sister. The caretaker had recently left when Nell got in touch to ask if there might be a live-in position she could take.

"I promise I won't let the baby get in the way of my job," she knew Nell said to Theodora Dorchester, the lovely old patrician owner, who was the third generation of her family on the farm.

She knew Theodora told her sister that she had known her for years, that no one had a stronger work ethic than her and few knew the farm as well as her. She told Nell she had raised six boys there, each of whom turned out okay. "Except for Peter," she muttered, shaking her head, refusing to talk about Peter. Nell could move in whenever she liked, she said. They were all used to babies around the place, even though it had been a while. Nell was already "part of the family."

Nell told Meredith that the old woman had been businesslike as she said it, but there had been a glimmer of a tear in her eye as she looked away. Meredith knew that Theodora had once told Nell that she had always wanted a daughter, and that Nell was just the kind of girl she would want her daughter to be. Meredith understood now that her moving in was as good for Theodora as it was for Nell, and for River.

Seeing her now, Meredith knows for certain that her sister has found a place to belong. Nell is happy. Nell once told her that being a single mother is hard, but farm work is harder, and she loves doing both. Plus, there is a team of workers on the place who all love River, who take turns looking after him; plus, now that River has started preschool, it's easier. Kindergarten is only a year away, and then Nell will have hours every day when she won't have to worry about him at all.

Nell opens the fridge and helps herself to a bottle of cranberry juice. "Want some?"

Meredith nods as Nell gets the glasses, moving around the kitchen they both know so well. However much they both wanted to leave, it's still home. "What about you? I heard you have a serious boyfriend!" Nell has always been the expert at diverting the conversation away from herself, thinks Meredith wryly. But she bites at the opportunity to talk about Gavin.

"I don't know how serious it is, but it's nice. And I love being in London."

"So far away, you mean?" Nell smiles. "I get it."

"How is Mom at being a grandparent? Does River see her?"

"Actually, she's pretty good. She's a much better grandparent than parent. He gets to see all the good stuff with none of the bad, or mad."

"Wow. I always hear people talk about how the worst parents can still make wonderful grandparents, but I never believed it."

Nell nods. "I know. I wouldn't have believed it either. She's still impossible, but not with River. She adores him unreservedly, and he adores her."

"It's so weird to think of Mom as a grandmother. She doesn't seem old enough."

"She isn't, really," says Nell. "I'm the one who screwed her up with a pregnancy at nineteen. Still, she won't be called Grandma. She's Ronron."

"As in 'Da doo'?" Meredith starts to laugh.

"Exactly!" Nell starts to laugh too as she sings the well-known chorus. "I suggested Gigi, but she says she knows far too many reluctant grandmothers called Gigi. Where is she anyway? Isn't she supposed to be here?"

"I thought so too. Especially since I haven't seen her in months," says Meredith, turning as they hear yet another car, then a car door. "Speak of the devil," says Meredith as they both turn to see their

mother swoop through the front door, scooping River up and covering him with kisses.

"What a lovely surprise!" she declares. "My darling boy is here to welcome me home!" She walks into the kitchen and sees Meredith. "Oh, my goodness!" Her hands fly to her mouth. "Meredith! I completely forgot you were coming! Oh, my Lord! Two surprises in one day!" She gathers Meredith in her arms for a hug, then releases her, holding her at arm's length. "You look like you've been eating well," she says, in the same delighted tone, as Meredith feels her heart sink. She glances at Nell, who shakes her head and rolls her eyes. "London food clearly agrees with you."

Meredith says nothing. All she can hear in her head is her mother saying, *You are still not good enough. You are not slim enough, pretty enough. I do not approve of the way you look, and I cannot love you looking the way you do.* It is the same message Meredith has always gotten from her mother: *You are not lovable.*

"Can one of you take my bags upstairs?" says Ronni, unaware of the impact of her words as she moves to the fridge for a bottle of wine. "Nell? Be a dear and open this wine for me."

"I'll take the bags," says Meredith, whose heart has plummeted, who is on the brink of tears. And once again, she wishes she had never come home.

2007

nine

For years and years River was the earliest of risers. When he was tiny, he would pad into her bedroom and stare at her, his nose inches from her face, until Nell opened her eyes, grinning always at the little face so close to hers. She would jump out of bed to make him breakfast before setting him in front of a cartoon so she could get the farm organized, go through the daily routine of waking up the animals.

Today she wakes up at her usual time of 5:15 a.m., the sun almost up outside her window, and she listens. Nothing. No footsteps on the stairs, no chinking of china as River pours cereal into a bowl, no faint cartoon fighting coming from the little room next to the kitchen where he watches TV.

A teenager, she thinks. We are finally there. At fourteen he is now a morning sleeper, sometimes not rousing until she goes in to physically shake him. He is up all night, playing computer games, watching television, and then he sleeps the day away. It seems absurd for a boy

brought up on a farm, brought up in an environment where everyone is up as soon as the roosters start crowing, but there it is. A teenager.

Padding along the whitewashed bedroom floor she smells the fresh coffee from downstairs, throws open the curtains, and squints at the brightness, even though she can't see much beyond the old stacked stone wall thanks to a slight morning fog. It happens from time to time in the summer, this gray chilly haze in the morning. But it almost always burns off to a bright, clear, hot day, revealing acres of lush green fields and trees.

This farm is still the most beautiful place she has seen. The fact that she is able to live here still gives her a shiver of pleasure as she looks out the window every morning. Even on the days she can't see much, she knows the old stacked stone wall is there, the split-rail fence beyond, meadows stretching farther back, the old red barns breaking up the landscape, lines of trees ending the view.

Often she pauses to consider how peaceful her life is. There is no chaos, no drama. No one who works here has even the slightest whiff of volatility or emotional instability.

Theodora Dorchester is old now, in her eighties. While other workers on the farm talk about her in the same terms as a loving and beneficent grandmother, Nell has always thought of her as more of a mother. Theodora is the mother Nell would have chosen, if she had ever been given a choice. She is wise, calm, loving, and consistent. These are qualities Nell has tried to embody for River, but first she has had to learn from Theodora.

Nell is no longer simply the caretaker; she is the manager. She is the person to whom everyone turns for any decision. She is Theodora's right-hand man, as the old woman is now too infirm to walk the farm in the way she once did.

Even a year ago the two of them would walk the farm together in the afternoons, Nell pointing out any problems she saw, asking Theo-

dora for advice. But Theodora is suddenly frail, and not recovering well from a fall that resulted in a broken hip a few months ago. Nell worries about her all the time, about how much longer she'll be with them. Theodora is still sunny, though, always smiling, always delighted to welcome Nell into her bedroom in the main house to fill her in on all the details of the farm.

Nell jumps into a quick, hot shower before pulling on jeans, clogs, and a T-shirt. She has never bothered with makeup or fancy hairstyles, instead pulling her long, sun-bleached hair into a tight ponytail, slipping her arms into a sweatshirt to ward off the cold.

She doesn't see what she looks like, her appearance never having been important to her. She is what would once have been called a classic beauty, although she has never thought so. Now thirty-three, Nell has slowly grown into her looks. Her features are strong and lovely. Her skin is dark from the sun, and tough, making her look older than her years, but her body is lean and strong.

She is what you would call statuesque, although she is not yet fully comfortable in her skin, not yet completely at ease with who she is. The mystery to everyone who visits the farm is that she is still single.

She must be lonely, they think. Surely a lovely young woman such as herself would want to meet someone. Every now and then someone will try to set her up, but Nell is too busy with the farm, too busy as the mother of a teenage boy, to go on any dates. On the rare occasions she has allowed herself to be introduced to someone, it is out of politeness rather than desire.

And now, after all these years, Nell is used to being on her own, just her and River, the pair of them entirely self-sufficient. Granted, she was a child when she met Lewis Calder, but she was not a child when he left her, not a child when she realized that being in a relationship ran too great a risk of getting hurt. She didn't need to go through that again. Her priority is River. And the farm.

Nell downs the coffee before going outside to feed the chickens the vegetable scraps from yesterday and refresh their water. This was River's job for years, before he morphed into the sleeping teenager, but she doesn't mind. She likes the routine of going out there herself, hearing the chickens cluck with excitement as they hear her approach, all of them racing to the edge of their run to greet her, see what treats she might have for them today.

On the way back to the house, she stops to wave to Theodora's caregiver, who beckons her toward the porch.

"You're up so early!" says Nell, with a wave. "Did you catch the sunrise?" Carly shakes her head as Nell notices how tired she looks. "Are you okay?" She walks up the steps. "Is everything okay?"

"It's . . . I think we may be beginning the journey." Carly's voice is low. "She's barely eating. I have made all her favorites, but she turns her head. She won't have anything. She said if I saw you she wants to talk to you. Can you go and see her?"

Nell nods, a lump in her throat. "I can't go now, too many things to take care of, but I'll come by late afternoon when I've got everything done. Thank you." She walks off, whispering a prayer that when the time is right, Theodora's journey will be peaceful and pain free.

ten

The smell of the studio is enough to calm Meredith down. It's why she keeps coming back, she tells herself. She loves the meditative quality of the quiet room that smells faintly of turpentine and linseed oil. There are old wooden easels placed around the studio and a naked model lying on a large wooden box in the middle of the room. She is perfectly still, staring vacantly into space, a pillow under her head, the soles of her feet dark with shaved pencil and charcoal dust.

Meredith comes back because an art studio has always been the place she's turned to for a sense of peace and calm. Growing up, she always had an art desk in her room, busied herself for hours, losing herself in shapes, colors, and swirls. Later, she took courses at the Silvermine School of Art, until she moved to London, when she put it aside for a few years. Now she has rediscovered her early love. She comes back because art has always been her escape. She is coming back here, to the Frognal Arts Center, because of that. Nothing to do with

Nicholas, the art teacher, who may be the most perfect man Meredith has ever laid eyes on.

She has been coming for two years. Her painting skills have improved dramatically, as has her appearance, both of which are largely due to Nicholas. For the first year, Meredith was invisible. She'd arrived at college pudgy, and the freshman fifteen she gained at university soon became thirty, then forty, and her own veil of shame, her mother's voice echoing in her ears, would keep her quietly at the back of the class, hiding behind her easel. Very occasionally Nicholas would lay a hand on her shoulder or say something to her, direct her pencil, and she would flush scarlet, her heart pounding as she stared straight ahead, wanting his hand to rest there forever, wanting him to move away so she could regain her equilibrium and pretend it had never happened. Pretend she wasn't unable to breathe, let alone speak. She would sit and nod, hope that no one noticed.

She would watch as Nicholas leaned down to whisper in the ears of the prettiest girls, the slimmest of girls, the girls who breathed confidence and coolness, who perched on stools with ease and moved through the studio as if they owned it. They were the ones who flirted with Nicholas and joined him after class for a boisterous, noisy night in the pub.

It was rumored that sometimes they went home with him. Meredith never knew the details. She wasn't invited to the pub. Whatever she knew was from watching silently, picking up snippets of conversation from disgruntled girls who were not on their teacher's radar, or perhaps, no longer on their teacher's radar.

Meredith had never been on Nicholas's radar. She left her flat every Wednesday evening and took the number 13 bus along the Finchley Road, crossing over to the arts center and making her way up the stone steps. Every week she chose her outfit carefully, put the tiniest bit of makeup on, blew out her hair, as her mother's voice echoed in her head: *You have such a pretty face; if only you'd lose some weight.*

She finally listened. After a year of being ignored and watching Nicholas flirt with the skinny, confident women in the tiny tight jeans with ripped knees and cool sneakers, Meredith decided that she wanted to change herself.

She started a diet that didn't call itself a diet, but instead a food *program*. Diets don't work, they said; the only way to change your body is to change the way you eat. That's the reality of life, they said.

Three weighed and measured meals a day, they said. No carbs, no sugar, no alcohol. Teams of two, with weekly support meetings for the group, and daily chats with your team member. It was the easiest thing Meredith had ever done.

Every week she would sit and listen to questions about how other people could possibly measure food in restaurants, how embarrassed they were, how difficult it was to eat out, and Meredith would look at them and think: *Don't go to restaurants.* For her it was easy; she never went out anyway. Her idea of a good night had most often been a video from Blockbuster and Chinese takeaway. And perhaps a few chocolate bars picked up from the newsagent on the way home, because—English chocolate! Who could resist? Now it was just a video from Blockbuster and a huge bowl of salad with some oil-free grilled chicken breast, or salmon. And no chocolate.

For a while she didn't feel very different, aware only that her skirts were a little looser and her shirts stopped gaping between the buttons. Eventually, though, at her CPA firm, people started noticing her, and occasionally asking what she was doing, because she looked so good.

Yesterday, she went shopping. All her clothes were swimming on her. It was time. She went to Warehouse, Top Shop, and Miss Selfridge. She spent very little, but emerged with an entirely new closet. She had work suits and shirts and floral skirts and pretty, summery tops. There were a couple of things she bought that she didn't particularly like. A

purple dress and a blue skirt. The sales assistant happened to show up when she was trying both of those, and was so effusive in her praise, Meredith didn't want to offend her by not buying them.

She came home and threw out the five pairs of leggings she has lived in for years, the Lycra stretched so tight it was shiny and worn. She put the purple dress and blue skirt aside. She will go back another day to return them and hope the sales assistant isn't there.

Today, for art class, she is wearing the jeans she bought, the first pair of jeans she has owned in years. She channeled Cecilia as she dressed, one of the skinny, beautiful girls from last year, a girl who drew all of Nicholas's attention, a girl who, thankfully, has now moved to Norfolk.

Faded jeans with artful rips up and down the legs. Meredith sat and looked at her legs, unable to believe they fit her. A white tank top with a large baggy shirt over it. The chunky gold handwrought pendant she has always worn, but removed from the fine gold chain and put on leather. She tried on the heels, but they looked ridiculous with the outfit. Cecilia could carry off towering heels, strappy sandals, and platforms for the Frognal Arts Center, but Meredith cannot. The suede espadrilles she bought would get ruined. Her old Adidas sneakers are fine. They never looked particularly good, or particularly cool, with her stretched, shiny leggings, but now, with the faded jeans and white shirt, they are the epitome of trendiness, the height of casual chic.

Meredith spent hours that afternoon contemplating what to do with her hair. It is much like her mother's, much to her despair. Ronni Sunshine is famous for her thick mane of blond hair, but the girls know it is really as fine and wispy as a baby's. As a young woman she used weaves and falls and trickery, until the stress and strain of the weight of the added hair caused huge and permanent bald patches. Now, half of Ronni's closet is filled with wigs.

Meredith has the same lank hair, darker than her mother's, more

of a mouse brown, and not half as thick as she would like. She usually wears it in a somewhat pathetic ponytail, but on Saturday she went to the hairdresser for a trim and ended up with highlights. The hairdresser explained that bleach would give her hair a texture and body that it needed. The hairdresser was right.

It looked breathtaking when the hairdresser was done. It looked full. And blond. And sexy. And completely unlike Meredith. She actually gasped when she looked in the mirror.

"You know who you look just like?" said the hairdresser. "That actress. Ronni Sunshine. I swear, you could be her daughter."

"Really?" said Meredith, astounded and thrilled. She had never seen it before. No one had ever seen it before.

For art class today, she wears her hair back in a ponytail, not scraped back, as she so often wears it, but loose, with white blond tendrils that fall around her face. She has come in late—the class has already started—and everyone is staring at the model, a girl named Rosie who is one of the regulars.

Sally, who always takes the easel just in front of Meredith, looks up with a smile of greeting as she passes, freezing as she sees Meredith, her mouth falling open. "You look amazing," she whispers. "I almost didn't recognize you!"

Meredith shrugs with a small smile as she takes her seat, opening her art box and taking out her pencils.

She loses herself, as she always has, in the drawing. It is the stillest thing she has ever done. There are no thoughts, no concerns, no worries, just an intense focus on the naked body in front of her. Although the truth is her focus isn't even on the naked body, but rather on the lines and shapes, the areas of light and dark that appear on her page.

Her body relaxes as she draws, first mapping out the proportions: an oval for the head, a line across to indicate the shoulders, the concave curve of Rosie's body, her legs extending across the block. She draws,

and redraws. The left leg isn't quite right. Look at the space between, she reminds herself; the negative space will help you get the body right.

She shades and crosshatches, before reaching for her paintbrushes and ink. She has become more and more comfortable with mixed mediums. Pencil, charcoal, watercolor, and ink, together in one piece.

This one will be monochromatic, she decides, diluting the black ink into a pale wash of gray as she sweeps it down the body. The sketching is quick, but this takes time, building the layers of ink just as she would with watercolor. It is good, she thinks, pausing to sit back slightly and really look. She doesn't always think her work is good, and often she is too close to tell, but this, she knows, is good.

A hand on her shoulder makes her jump. It has been so long since Nicholas has paid attention to her, she has quite forgotten this is what he does. But there he is, smiling down at her.

He leans down so his head is level with hers, both of them looking at her picture. "This is lovely," he murmurs, turning his head to look at her but not standing up, so his eyes, his lovely, soft, warm brown eyes, are only inches from her own.

Meredith feels herself coloring. She doesn't know whether to lean back, to clear her throat, or to look away, but she does none of those things. She merely turns scarlet, as she so often does, as she watches his eyes roam her face, her hair, her body.

"You should come to the pub with us after class." His voice is as quiet as a feather, brushing her cheek as he stands up and pads off, leaving Meredith's cheeks finally able to go back to their pale, pale pink.

eleven

There is nothing in the world that Lizzy thinks she would not be able to achieve, should she set her mind to it. It is that fierce confidence that helps her to ignore the overgrown weeds and crumpled-up pieces of garbage that have blown to the edges of the yard as she grabs a can of beer from the fridge and takes it out to the back porch.

Tom won't come here, but that's okay. His loft apartment in Soho is way nicer than here and she's quite happy to stay there most of the time. She has no desire to be in Queens when she could be in Soho. She only rented this place because it was cheap, and available, and she knew she would barely be here. She's come today because Tom is busy looking for a new refrigerator on Restaurant Row, giving Lizzy an opportunity to grab some more clothes from her own place.

She and Tom are both waiters at a crappy café downtown. His apartment is nicer only because his parents, who live in a duplex on the Upper East Side, believe their son should continue to live in the

style to which he is accustomed. Lizzy is quite sure her father would happily pay for her to live in a loft—he would be horrified if she ever allowed him to see the squalor of the apartment she rents—but Lizzy wanted to have the New York experience, and part of that experience meant leaving the comfort of suburbia for grit and dirt and toughness. Also, her father's wife, Selena, would probably stop him from giving her any money. She has stopped him from giving her anything else.

She loves being a true New Yorker. It is irrelevant that she is now spending almost every night with Tom; she still gets to say she rents a shithole in Queens, should anyone ask.

Her relationship with Tom is one born of shared circumstance rather than a great, enduring love. They bonded over the awfulness of everything at their job: the chef who didn't really know how to cook, the frozen foods that were delivered on a regular basis. They grimaced together over the fact that they couldn't accommodate any special requests—no dairy in the sauce, no bread crumbs on the chicken—because all the food was prepared in a factory far, far away. They commiserated over their shared horror that this was where they had landed, when they were both so passionate about food.

Tom taught himself to cook by experimenting and watching the Food Channel. He isn't quite as good as he thinks, and Lizzy sometimes winces when she sees his bizarre combinations. But he is very good at giving the appearance of someone who knows what he is doing. He can chiffonade herbs like a pro and knows all the little tricks, like not salting potatoes when you boil them, and crisping up soggy lettuce in iced water with lemon.

Lizzy is a good cook. She is probably even better than she thinks she is, with a natural instinct for what works and what doesn't—hence her wincing at Tom's introduction of too many anchovies and sun-dried tomatoes to what should be a simple country meat loaf.

She has the tiniest bit of training. Not enough to qualify her to

work as even the lowliest of line cooks in New York City, but enough to know what she is doing. She managed three months at the Culinary Institute of America before getting bored, itching to get into the real world and make her mark.

Now she is at the café with Tom, both of them dreaming of one day starting their own restaurant, working together, being the hot new chefs that everyone would be talking about. They don't always have the same shifts, but the nights are always long and finish with barhopping: too much drink, too little sleep.

Her phone rings. Tom.

"Hey, you. Did you get your refrigerator?" She puts her feet on the railing and reaches for a Marlboro Red, inhaling deeply.

"I did. And I met this really cool guy. Sean. He left New York a few years ago for San Francisco, and he's just moved back. He's got this great idea for some kind of pop-up supper club. I'm gonna meet him for a drink before my shift. Do you wanna come?"

Lizzy pauses. She is supposed to be working, but talking about a pop-up supper club sounds far more exciting. They warned her that if she called in sick again they would let her go, but . . . fuck it. She inhales again, letting the smoke out in a long, steady stream. She is young and gorgeous. And honestly, she could probably get a waitress job anywhere she chose. If she chose. But helping run a pop-up supper club sounds like a much better option.

Lizzy's hair is never down these days. It's too hot, too sticky, too humid, and it's easiest just to scrape it back in a bun. She has to wear it in a bun for work, but given the temperature in the city, it's how she has worn it now for months anyway.

Not tonight, though. Why not make an effort for Tom and Supper Club Sean? She decides to wash it and let it dry with its natural wave,

spraying some product on to give it some body. Seeing herself in the mirror, she realizes she had forgotten how sexy it looks like this. She decides to add some peachy blush to her cheekbones, and shimmery gloss on her lips. She puts on the shortest of denim shorts, the skimpiest of white linen tops, and the chunkiest of sneakers—this is New York City after all. She's certainly not going to wear heels.

She looks good. Great. She knows this from the admiring glances of the men who pass her on the crowded street. Good. It's nice to have made an effort, to have appreciative looks, to feel like a woman again. The grind and grit of restaurant life does not beautiful make. Tom will be surprised, pleasantly so, she thinks, lighting up another cigarette as she strides down the street.

She sees Tom first, head down with the man who must be Sean, talking intently, the pair of them smoking as they sit at an outdoor table at the café where they're meeting. His eyes light up when he sees her, and he waves, pulling a chair over and kissing her hello.

"This is Lizzy," he says to Sean, who stands up to take her hand.

Whoa, she thinks, speechless for just a second. *Those might be the bluest eyes I've ever seen.* It isn't just that they are blue, but that they are sparkling and alive and fun. And completely compelling.

"Nice to meet you." She regains her composure, sitting down and twining an arm through Tom's for reassurance, to steady herself.

"Lovely to meet you," says Sean. "Tom has been telling me so many great things about you."

"Did he tell you I was gorgeous and talented?" Lizzy doesn't mean to sound arrogant, just trying to make a joke, but Sean doesn't smile.

"He did. But he didn't do you justice, clearly."

Tom frowns before letting out a laugh. "Hello? This is my girlfriend?"

Sean breaks into an easy smile. "No need to worry. I'm married! I'm just messing with you. It's great to meet you. What will you have to drink?"

They skip over the small talk and are soon animatedly discussing the concept of the pop-up supper club. Tom is in paroxysms of delight, the prospect of cooking for people, of bypassing the ranks that would lead him to chef (if he were talented enough to become chef, which he doesn't yet realize he is not), filling him with waves of enthusiasm.

"I like it outside," says Sean. "I think there is magic in a summer night, in strings of twinkling lights and lanterns hanging from trees."

"Outside like where? Central Park?"

"No. Like rooftops. It's a private supper club and we do it gonzo-style. We find a rooftop and show up with everything we need. Someone needs to be in the building so we have access to a kitchen, but we can bring tables, chairs, lights, and candles and set it up, almost like theater—create the night."

"I love it." Lizzy is excited. "It is theater. One-night theater. We're not just cooking for people, we're giving them an experience."

"Yes!" Sean's eyes are shining. "She gets it." He turns to Tom. "She gets it."

"I get it too," says Tom, even though his eyes aren't shining. "So where do we start?"

"We find the rooftop, then we price it out, then we find the people. We tell our friends, and they tell their friends. We start word of mouth. If the food is great, they'll tell more people and it will grow."

"We could use my parents' rooftop!" says Tom suddenly, excited by his own idea. "It's perfect. It has trees, and it already has tables and chairs. We wouldn't have to do anything."

"It already has everything?" Sean looks skeptical. "Where is it?"

"Sixty-eighth and Park."

Sean suppresses a smile. "That's not quite the vibe we're looking for. It should be downtown, or the Village . . . not Upper East Side. Remember, gonzo-style. We're creating crazy magic out of nothing rather than accessorizing what's already there."

Tom is quiet. Embarrassed.

"Does it have to be in the city?" asks Lizzy, slowly.

Sean turns to her, interested. "Why? What are you thinking?"

"My sister works on a farm in Easton, Connecticut. It's about an hour and a half away, but it's beautiful. We could do something in the apple orchard, and string your famous lights," she says, pausing as Sean grins, "between the apple trees. We could cook with food from the farm. Not all of it, maybe, but fresh eggs, tomatoes—a simple summer menu that reflects what's grown on the farm."

Sean sits back, gazing at Lizzy. "Oh, my fucking God," he says. "I love it. It's not what I was thinking at all—I was thinking of an urban experience—but if your sister has a farm, and we three could put a menu together and test it, see how we cook together, that would be the perfect test lab. And it sounds beautiful."

"It is beautiful." Lizzy is almost wriggling with excitement. "Shall I call her now?"

"Would you?"

Lizzy picks up her Palm and scrolls the wheel to find Nell's contact. Early evening means she is almost undoubtedly home, having dinner with River, or so Lizzy assumes. She doesn't know because she barely sees her. The seven years between them has always felt like more. They weren't close as children, and since then, she has come to think of Nell as more of an aunt than a sister, at least not a sister who has any understanding of, or interest in, Lizzy's life.

They do speak from time to time, and do get together for occasional family celebrations like their mother's birthday (celebrated at the Four Seasons in New York, and a very lovely, if completely stiff and somewhat uncomfortable affair), Thanksgiving (although Lizzy got out of it last time by going to Tom's family), and Christmas.

Still. Nell is her big sister, and she does live on the farm, and she will see, immediately, what a wonderful idea this would be for everyone.

"Nell? It's Lizzy!" Lizzy pushes her chair back and walks away from the table. She has never been good at conducting phone conversations with other people around. She leans down and kisses Tom lightly on the lips, then waves at Sean as she mouths that she'll be back in a few minutes.

"Lizzy! This is a surprise. Is everything okay?" This is so like Nell, to skip all the niceties to get straight to the point.

"It's great. How's River?"

"Lounging around in a slightly hairy, smelly, grunting teenager kind of way." They both laugh. "How's life in New York?"

"Smelly, grunting, not very hairy." Lizzy leans against the building and gets out a cigarette. "And home. How's Mom? I haven't spoken to her for a while."

"She's okay. The usual. Being dramatic about these dizzy spells she's been having. I saw her last week and she was in bed."

"God, she's still such a drama queen."

"I know. She says she's getting these spells regularly."

"I suppose she's diagnosed herself with something awful rather than go to a doctor?"

Nell chuckles. "Not awful enough. She's decided she has vertigo. Dr. Internet advised. Are you smoking?" There is disapproval in Nell's voice as Lizzy inhales sharply then turns her head away from the phone to exhale.

"Nah. Only heroin," says Lizzy, which elicits only silence. "I'm *kidding*," she says in a voice that comes out as surprisingly childish. She corrects herself mentally, determined not to regress like that just because she is talking to her oldest sister. "Listen, I wanted to ask you something. I've just met this amazing guy, Sean, who was a chef in San Francisco, and they've been doing pop-up private supper clubs over there, which he's looking to do here."

Nell says nothing as Lizzy talks, explaining what it means, what

their vision is, how she suddenly realized the farm would be the perfect place to try the idea out. She finishes, waiting for Nell to exclaim her shared delight, but there is only silence.

"Well?" Lizzy has to prompt her. "What do you think?"

"I don't know," says Nell. "I think in theory it's an interesting idea, but it's not something we can do on the farm right at the moment. I'm sorry, Lizzy. I can hear you're excited, but everything's upside down here. There are a lot of changes, and it's just not the right time."

"But you wouldn't have to do anything," Lizzy bursts out. "We would take care of everything. We don't even need to use food from the farm. If it's easier, we can just borrow an orchard. Nell, we could even rent it from you if you wanted. We can set up a catering kitchen somewhere as long as we have power. I realize it might sound complicated, but I promise, you wouldn't even know we were there."

There is a sigh on the other end of the phone. "Lizzy, I'm sorry, but no. I already told you. It's not the right time. I'm not changing my mind."

Lizzy pauses, knowing she should hold herself in check, shouldn't say the words that are filling her head, her mouth, her tongue, but she can't. "You really are a bitch, aren't you? What fucking difference would it make to you to let us use an orchard for a night? You've always fucking resented me, haven't you . . . ?" And she stops. "Hello? Hello? Are you there? Are you fucking kidding me?" This last one is a shriek as Lizzy stomps around the corner and back to the table. "She hung up on me. Can you believe it? My own fucking sister."

twelve

The bedroom was dark and hot. Nell had been saying for years that she ought to get the farmhouse air-conditioned, but Theodora always said the heat didn't bother her. This wasn't just heat, though; it was stifling, airless, and it smelled of old people, and sickness. It smelled of a life coming to an end.

Theodora was lying back, propped against pillows, not wide awake, as Carly had told her downstairs, but fast asleep. Her chest heaved up and down, her breathing labored. Nell watched her sadly, marveling again at how frail Theodora had become, how tiny she now was, how pale.

She sat in the old Windsor chair that was next to the bed and slipped her strong hand underneath Theodora's frail one, as her eyes filled with tears.

This happened sometimes, explained the doctor. At this age, a fall and a broken hip sometimes meant the beginning of a demise. There wasn't anything to be done, other than to make Theodora as comfortable as possible. As long as she was eating and drinking, she would carry on.

How long will it take, thought Nell, if she is no longer eating or drinking? Days? A week? She stroked Theodora's hand, thinking about how much she loved her. This was the mother Nell should have had, but it didn't matter, for Theodora was always more of a mother to her anyway. Nell wasn't the kind of woman who needed motherly advice, who needed cossetting or coddling. But Theodora loved her in exactly the way Nell needed to be loved.

Theodora had always looked at Nell as an equal. Even when she was seventeen. Theodora respected her, asked her advice, and listened when Nell gave it. She was always available when Nell sought her out. Theodora wasn't a big talker, much like Nell. Their walks were often conducted in companionable silence, the two of them striding across the fields side by side, or riding the Cushman through the orchards.

Theodora was always the same. Her moods were never changing; she was always cheerful, and she was direct. If she didn't like how you were doing a job, she would tell you, in a matter-of-fact way that never caused offense. You knew where you were with Theodora. How unlike my mother, Nell had always thought. In many ways, Theodora was almost masculine. She ran the farm by herself and had to make tough decisions without worrying about what other people might think of it, of her. In doing so, of course, she was adored by everyone who worked there.

None more so than Nell. One of the workers once joked that Nell had imprinted herself on Theodora, like an orphaned duckling. Nell had flushed bright red, although later she realized it was true. In the absence of a consistent, present, emotionally stable, unconditionally loving mother, she had chosen Theodora, without even realizing it.

River, too, looked upon Theodora as a grandmother. She had raised him alongside Nell, with her no-nonsense approach and insistence that he be taught responsibility as soon as he was able to sit up. Theodora was the one who gave River jobs around the farm as soon as he

could walk and talk; she was the one who taught him to read with flash cards, just as she had taught her own sons. Her boys were now all grown-up and far away, none of them with an interest in the farm.

Nell blinked away the tears that were pooling. It's life, she tried to tell herself. Theodora has had a good run, and she is old, and this is what happens. *I cannot sit here and cry.*

She looked up and realized that Theodora was awake, and watching her. Nell squeezed her hand, then drew her own away, unused to intimacy. She's embarrassed that she could not continue holding the hand of this woman she loves, this woman who would not be around much longer.

Theodora smiled at her. "I have never said this to you, Nell, but you know I love you. You have been my daughter all these years." The tears were back in Nell's eyes, this time trickling down her cheeks. "You've been a better daughter to me than I could ever have wished for, and a better farmer than I have ever been."

"That's not true," said Nell.

"It is true. You have the build of a farmer. You're tall and strong. More than that, your instincts are perfect." She smiles warmly, gazing at Nell. "I want you to know I'm ready to go. Not today"—she reached up, slowly, and patted Nell's arm reassuringly—"but soon. And, Nell, I want you to know I'm leaving the farm to you."

Nell froze. She stared at Theodora, thinking she must have misheard.

"None of the boys have ever been interested in the farm. They're too busy making money, and the last time Jeffrey came up, all he kept talking about was the value of the land and how many subdividable plots there might be. I want this farm to stay a farm, and I want it to be yours."

"But . . . your children . . . Theodora. I can't. It's so kind of you, but . . ." She thought how shocked Theodora's boys would be, how they would threaten lawsuits.

"I told them long ago. They've all got insurance policies on me that will see them each right. It's in my will, and everything has been drawn up. They've acquiesced to all of it. I meant to talk about it with you before, but then I had the fall, and . . ." She didn't say anything else, just shrugged and closed her eyes.

"I don't know what to say." Nell shook her head, then realized that without another word Theodora had once again fallen asleep.

She walked downstairs in a daze. Carly was standing in the kitchen on the phone. Nell waved a good-bye to her that she may or may not have seen, then she walked down the porch steps. She stood for a minute staring out at the familiar and comforting landscape, breathing deeply and trying to still the ache in her heart. She looked around at this farm she had loved for the last sixteen years, this farm that had become her home. This farm that was about to be hers. She was in shock. Those meadows, with their cornflowers waving in the breeze, would be hers. The orchards, at the other end of the track, would be hers. The huge barns, used to store feed and equipment, hers. The cattle? Hers. The sheep? Hers. The chickens, hers. The farmhouse? All hers.

Her phone started buzzing. She paused, at first not recognizing what it was. But then she took the phone from her pocket and saw that the call was from Lizzy. She hadn't spoken to her sister in months. Something must be wrong. She answered and put the phone to her ear.

Lizzy's words came spilling out in a jumble, Nell hardly understanding any of what she was saying. Something about wanting the farm, pop-up dinners, cooking. She couldn't do this right now. Whatever it was Lizzy wanted, she couldn't do this at all, not with Theodora dying, not with having just begun to realize the weight of responsibility that was about to settle on her shoulders.

She tried to say no gently, kindly, but Lizzy threw a shit fit, shouting and cursing. Not now, thought Nell, ending the call in her sister's midshout.

The phone buzzes again and Nell shakes her head in tired disbelief. Her sister is the last person she wants to talk to right now, particularly her sister when angry. She looks at the screen and sees it isn't her sister calling back but her mother. Her mother whom she rarely hears from unless she needs something. She presses accept.

"Darling!" Her mother's voice is jarring, the clipped English accent that has never softened despite spending her whole adult life in America, still as English as if she stepped off the *Queen Mary* yesterday. "I'm so glad I got you! I'm in New York but they're holding a dress for me at Mitchells. Can you dash into Westport for me and pick it up?"

Nell breathes a sigh of relief. "You're not calling about Lizzy?"

"Lizzy? Why would I be calling about Lizzy?"

"I thought she may have called you just now. She just phoned to ask me something about the farm, and ended up screaming at me when I said no."

"The farm? What can Lizzy possibly want with the farm?"

"I wasn't really listening. I just had some . . . big news."

Nell waits for her mother to ask if she is okay, perhaps what the news is, to express some concern.

"So can you?"

"Can I what?"

"Pick up the dress at Mitchells?"

She knows she shouldn't have expected anything else. "I don't know, Mom. I'm in the middle of my working day at the farm. I don't know if I can get away. Isn't there someone else who can do it?"

"The housekeeper's gone home and she's not returning my calls, and I've been feeling a bit nauseated so I'm going to lie down for a while. Please, Nellie. Try and do something for me. It's not much to ask. You know I've been having these terrible dizzy spells lately, or I'd hop in a car and get it myself."

Nell refuses to take the bait. Her mother has a history of dizzy spells, or headaches, or backaches, a series of mystery ailments when she feels she isn't getting quite enough attention.

"It's nothing to worry about, but I do think it's getting worse. I just haven't been quite myself. Dizzy and now nauseated, and a little weak in my feet. It's very odd."

Nell frowns, now alert. "Weakness? I think it's time you went to see a doctor."

"If it doesn't go away in a couple of weeks, I will. I'm quite sure it's because I'm dehydrated and it's been so hot. I'm sure I'll be fine, but, darling, would you get the dress?"

"I'll try. I just saw Theodora . . ." She doesn't know why these words are coming out of her mouth, nor the ones that come after. Later that night she thinks she must have still been in shock. What other explanation can there be for her wanting to share news, good, bad, or otherwise, with her mother?

"How is the old goat?" Theodora and Ronni have never liked each other. Neither has ever said it out loud, but on the rare occasions her mother has been to the farm, Theodora has been formal, and reserved. She knows Theodora does not approve of frippery, of drama, of manipulation—all qualities her mother personifies.

"Dying," says Nell.

"I'm sorry." Ronni has the grace to seem embarrassed. "I wouldn't have been so flip about her if I'd known."

"She has had a wonderful life, but it looks like it will be over soon. And . . ." She pauses. "She has left the farm to me."

There is a long pause. "She what?"

"She has left the farm to me. In her will. The farm is mine."

"How do you feel about that?"

Nell tries to think. "I don't know," she says eventually. "I have no

idea how I feel. I only found out a few minutes ago. I think I'm in shock."

"Well, that's nice of her. I thought she had all those children. At least River won't have to worry about his education now. What do you think the farm is worth? There are plenty of developers looking for land. I can talk to that lovely Jim. He's a Realtor and he can give you a valuation."

Nell frowns as she holds the phone to her ear. "I'm not selling it. She's leaving me the farm precisely because she wants it maintained as a farm. I just have to figure out how to have it make more money. I'm the farmer here. There's no point being a farmer with no farm." Nell resists the derisive laugh that threatens to punctuate her point. "Even if it isn't yet making the money it needs to."

"But that's ridiculous," says her mother. "You're thirty . . . thirty-five? Thirty . . . What are you?"

"Thirty-three." Nell again fights the urge to laugh in disbelief.

"Thirty-three and a single mother of a teenage son. The last thing you need is to single-handedly shoulder the responsibility of a huge farm that's in financial trouble. If you want to farm, sell it and buy yourself a small gentleman's farm somewhere in Litchfield County. Not an ugly working farm with cattle and sheep and equipment and hundreds of workers. That's far too much for someone like you."

Nell feels her jaw tense. "What does that mean? Someone like me?"

"Nell, you're a single mother. What hope can you possibly have of finding someone, of having a relationship, of finding happiness, when all you do is farm work? It's bad enough that you've devoted your life to this farm, have given it the best years of your life, and now you want to take on even more? You can have your cake and eat it, but this farm is too much. Even for you."

Nell holds the phone away from her ear and shakes her head as she

stares at it, with absolutely no idea what to say next. There is nothing to say. She walks over to a bucket of feed next to the driveway and drops the phone into it.

Feeling better, she sets off, forgetting her mother, forgetting the dress at Mitchells, forgetting everything other than Theodora, and the farm.

thirteen

It was Tom who found the space for their pop-up supper club. Not his parents' rooftop, but one belonging to a friend who had an apartment in Gramercy Park, with a rooftop no one used. They could do it there.

The three of them met at the apartment and jumped in excitement at the rooftop—it was perfect. The fact that it had nothing whatsoever on it, no greenery, nothing, didn't seem to phase Sean in the slightest. "We'll bring it all in," he said. "We'll turn this place into a rooftop fairyland." They immediately got busy organizing their opening night.

Earlier this morning, the day of the first show, they arrived with borrowed tables and chairs. They hauled everything up in the service elevator, then carried it by hand up the last staircase to the roof.

They brought poles to string lights on, and sandbags to hold the poles, but, looking at it now, Lizzy can see it isn't really working. All the poles lean in different directions, the lights extremely precariously taped to each, all of it swaying with the wind.

"We'll just tell everyone to stay away from the poles," says Tom, who, Lizzy knows, has never been more excited than he is now at the prospect of debuting his cooking skills to a paying public, and whose idea the poles and sandbags were in the first place. "It will be fine. Relax. It's going to be great."

Lizzy doesn't see how it is going to be fine, but Sean seems okay. He just shrugs as they go back downstairs to the apartment to cook.

This supper club will be small. Sixteen people. Sean is doing a starter of burrata, peaches, and a basil-infused oil. Lizzy is making dessert, a caramel apple tart with vanilla thyme crème fraiche. Tom insisted on cooking the main course, curried braised lamb with a parsley, apricot, and pignoli stuffing; a wild mushroom and truffle quinoa; and anchovy cream.

Friends have offered to be servers, and they've helped set up the long table that will seat all the guests. It isn't quite the wonderland they had hoped. Lizzy thinks the table is pretty enough, with its checkered tablecloth and Mason jars of wildflowers, but it just sits in the middle of a big square gray concrete rooftop, surrounded by air-conditioning units. Maybe it will be better at night, she thinks. Hopes. Maybe the lights will stay up and the candles will cast a warm glow, and our guests will be transported.

The kitchen in the apartment is tiny. Tom is in the narrow galley trying to dry rub his lamb and finely chop the pignoli and parsley for the stuffing. Lizzy is in the living room rolling out pastry on a marble slab that sits on top of a rickety old wooden table. Sean has gone out to grab the burrata fresh from the market.

It is awkward, and exciting, and nerve-racking and squashed, to have to keep sliding past Tom to reach ingredients in the fridge, to figure out how to cook all the pies in the one tiny oven that also has to handle Tom's lamb.

Tom is confident. Lizzy stays in the living room, but every time

she asks if she can help him in any way, he waves her away with an "I got this." Every now and then Lizzy thinks about how they could have been on the farm in Easton, and she gnashes her teeth with fury remembering how Nell dismissed her so quickly.

She hasn't spoken to Nell since that fight. To make things worse, her mother then texted her that Nell was inheriting the farm. Even more of a fucking bitch, she decided. Screw her, and her stupid farm. But oh, my God, she kept saying to Tom, who does that? What kind of a sister actively hinders her younger sister's career?

Tom's take on it is that Nell is jealous. "Look at her and look at you," he said, insisting Lizzy bring up a family picture on her phone. "She looks like a guy with long blond hair. You're gorgeous and fun and vibrant. She looks serious and dull."

Lizzy feels a pang of wanting to protect Nell. She is her sister, after all. And she isn't like a guy with long hair; she is . . . gorgeous. Handsome, actually, if more masculine than Lizzy. And she isn't really serious and dull. Maybe just quiet and a little detached.

And not for a second does she believe Nell could be jealous of Lizzy. Nell isn't jealous of anyone. Nell doesn't really care about anyone, other than River, and certainly doesn't care enough to compare herself to someone else and find herself wanting. That isn't her style at all. The only things she cares about are River and the farm. And once upon a time Lewis Calder, but look how that turned out.

Fuck her. Really, fuck her. Arranging some apple slices carefully, if a bit energetically, Lizzy vociferously agrees with everything Tom said, and piles on some more.

"It wasn't a complete fucking disaster," says Sean, lighting up two cigarettes and handing one to Lizzy, who takes a deep drag before knocking back the vodka and pouring them all another glass.

Tom is sitting on the ledge, elbows balanced on his knees, head down and swaying slightly as he looks at the floor.

"Just a partial fucking disaster," Lizzy says. "Did we have to refund more than the two who created a stink?"

"Only one more. Everyone else was very understanding. I didn't bother asking them if they wanted to join our mailing list, though. Didn't want to push it." Sean meets Lizzy's eye and grins. "Oh, come on"—he looks at Tom—"you have to laugh, Tom. Shit happens. We fucked up. You'll get over it."

Tom sways, lifting his head to take the vodka and down it in one.

"My food was shit," he slurs. "It tasted like shit."

"It didn't really taste like shit," says Sean. "It was . . . interesting. The anchovies were just a little . . ."

Tom groans. "I know anchovy brings out the taste in lamb. I didn't know it was going to be so overpowering."

"And it wasn't your fault the wind picked up."

"It was our fault for trying to have the lights," Sean says. "If there had been no wind they definitely wouldn't have smashed to the ground in a million pieces."

Lizzy tries, and fails, to suppress a smile.

"Oh, fuck off," says Tom. "You smug fuckers. Just because your food was good. I know, I know: everything that was wrong about this evening was my fault. I get it. You don't have to rub it in. Jesus. I'm going." He swigs back the refilled vodka and walks out.

"Were we mean?" says Lizzy, who has a few seconds of thinking she probably should go after Tom, but decides not to. His food was terrible. Dreadful. It was an instant, glaring reminder that watching hours of the Food Network does not a talented chef make.

"Are you kidding?" Sean snorts. "Neither of you have ever worked in a professional kitchen. I know Tom hasn't. Not just because the food was shit, but the first thing you do is develop a skin as tough as

leather. That lamb would have been thrown in the trash and he would have been fired. He's lucky that people were polite enough to just move the food around the plate and not say anything."

"Other than the people who demanded their money back?"

"The shit food combined with the wobbly poles and smashing lights was a bit too much for them. But it was a learning experience. Do you know what I learned tonight?"

Lizzy winces. "That working with amateurs is a really bad idea?"

"Only when they have no talent. But you, for one, are a great cook. That apple tart was fantastic. You saved the day. I think you and I should talk about doing this again. Properly. We'll find a much better location than this. How about it?"

"What do I say to Tom?"

"I have no idea. But I'm not interested in Tom. I'm interested in you. And I think you and I could do something really cool together. What do you think?"

Lizzy sighs. She knows he's right, but it feels like a betrayal already. Tom is sweet and loving, and he doesn't deserve the humiliation of tonight. He definitely doesn't deserve to be further humiliated by being pushed out of the trio. "I don't know. Maybe. I see what you're saying, but I have to think about it. I better go and find Tom."

"Don't wait too long." Sean looks up at her. "Talented chefs are easy to find."

Oh, fuck off, she thinks, giving him a tight smile and a brief hug before walking out the door to find Tom and apologize, and try to help him feel a little bit better.

fourteen

It has been a couple of weeks since Meredith first joined her classmates and teacher at the pub. Tonight she is with them again, starting to feel as if she belongs in this busy, noisy pub. The regulars crowd around the bar, shouting to each other, to their friends who arrive. The art class has a regular table in the corner. Nicholas is well-known to the bartenders, as he walks in and waves before gathering his favored students around the table.

He buys the first round. Meredith does not drink, but everyone is drinking, and a Diet Coke is so uncool. She will not order a Diet Coke. Sally orders a gin and tonic, so Meredith does the same.

By the beginning of the third round, Meredith is pleasantly, delightfully, tipsy. In fact, she may have crossed the line from tipsy to being ever so slightly drunk, but she is having a glorious time.

Nicholas is sitting opposite her, and although he is embroiled in a conversation with a couple of students on that side of the table, his eyes keep sliding back to Meredith.

Three gin and tonics make her daring. She catches his gaze and stares back, for just a second or two longer than is altogether comfortable. A small smile plays upon his lips as he looks away. Meredith blushes at her daring, at how his attention, or perhaps the alcohol, gives her a confidence she would never otherwise have.

Meredith is louder, funnier, brighter with his gaze on her. Come to my side of the table, she thinks. Come and sit next to me. If you like me you will come and sit next to me.

It is not until the end of the night, when they have rung the bell and announced last call, that Nicholas answers her silent call. He sits on the bench next to her, so close she can feel his leg squeezed up against hers, feel the heat of his body through his jeans. She thinks about moving her leg, but there is a tremor running through her body, a tremor so delicious, she just wants to freeze this moment and enjoy it forever.

He reaches forward to grab his pint. She looks at his arm. How old is he? she wonders. His skin is tanned, his arm slim, with pronounced veins, and hairs bleached by the sun. Now his hair is gray, but what must it have been when he was young? Light brown perhaps, or mouse brown.

She can't look at him. Flirting across the tabletop was safe. She didn't have to talk to him, didn't have to look at him. She knows those brown eyes very well, has watched them from afar for two years now. She knows the deep creases around his eyes when he smiles, the teeth that are ever so slightly crooked. To her shame, she knows his bottom very well, has watched him stride across the room more times than she can count. She knows his boots in winter, and his Birkenstocks in summer. Meredith hated Birkenstocks for more years than she can remember, until Nicholas turned up in them. Overnight they became the height of cool, and now, every time she sees a pair, she thinks of him.

He looks like a rock star or a movie star, she has often thought. Like Keith Richards crossed with Sam Shepard or Bryan Adams. With the kind of lazy upper-class drawl she has always loved. She has no idea how old he is. Old. Older than her. In his forties, certainly, maybe fifty. No. Not fifty. But it doesn't matter. He has a vibrance, an energy, a curiosity that allows you to see past the lines and crags on his face to his youthful core.

"Someone told me you are American." Meredith hears his voice and turns with a start. He is talking to her, clearly, for there is no one else on their side of the table, but he is not looking at her.

"I am," she says.

"You don't sound American."

"Ah. Well, I'm actually a hybrid. My mother is English and I came here for university."

"What happened to your accent?"

"It seemed to fade once I was here. I lived with my grandparents and . . . I suppose I'm one of those people who picks up accents, wherever they are. I know when I go home I start to sound more American again."

"I'm so glad you don't have a mid-Atlantic drawl," says Nicholas, draining his glass and turning to look at her. "Are you ready?"

"What for?"

"We're leaving."

"Oh." She turns to see the three others who are still there, still sitting on the other side, deep in conversation, something about Klimt versus Schiele and who inspired them more. "We, as in . . . ?" She doesn't finish the question, can't quite believe two years of fantasies may be coming true tonight, in this way, quite so easily. Real life didn't happen like this. *Her* life didn't happen like this.

Nicholas stands, says good-bye to the others, then takes her elbow as he leads her out of the pub. Again, when he touches her, Meredith

feels a deep tingling through her body, and she's light-headed as she follows him.

"Where are we going?" she asks.

"A bar in Chalk Farm. We can carry on drinking there. And talking. You are enormously talented, Meredith. I have no idea why you have kept your light hidden under a bushel. Your work today was unutterably beautiful. I am now"—he stops and turns to her, with eyebrow raised—"officially intrigued. I want to know who you are. I want to know"—he leans toward her, his head now inches from hers as his voice drops—"your stories." He gives a wolfish grin before hailing a black cab. He turns to her as he opens the door. "Tonight seems as good a night as any to start."

Meredith flushes in pleasure, and a hint of fear. Her stories? Goodness! Her stories aren't very interesting. Once a week she comes to an art class, which is probably the most interesting thing about her. Otherwise she works at a CPA firm, which is not something Nicholas would be interested in. Her stories? What the hell are her stories?

"So, Meredith," he says as he turns to her in the cab. "Start at the beginning." His teeth glint as they pass the neon-lit shops, as Meredith relaxes. She may not have stories, but look who she is! Look at her family! There are enough stories about that to last for weeks. Meredith never discusses her family. No one at work knows who her mother is. No one knows she was raised in Los Angeles, then Connecticut. They don't know, because knowing would change everything. She wouldn't be allowed to continue living under the radar. They would see her differently, as if her mother's fame had somehow brushed off on her.

She could tell Nicholas, though. Perhaps he would find her more interesting if she did. She studies his face. Perhaps now.

"I was born at Cedars-Sinai Hospital and spent the first few years of my life in Los Angeles with an actress mother and a businessman

father, both busy working, being raised mostly by nannies . . ." As she speaks, Nicholas reaches an arm back and rests it on the seat behind her, casually playing with the loose tendrils of her hair.

"What kind of nannies?" he asks, and Meredith smiles. What kind of an actress, is what she thought he would ask, leading to the inevitable.

"The nice kind," she says. "Some were from England, very strict, and others were Mexican, very loving and kind. We just didn't have a lot of discipline." She pauses, catching her breath as his fingers start to lightly trace the back of her neck, up and down, his touch so faint as to be almost imperceptible, were it not for her body quivering so in response.

"Go on," he says.

"I have two sisters. Nell is older, and Lizzy is the baby."

"Are you close?" His fingers have moved to the front, lightly tracing her clavicle as she catches her breath.

"We were when we were young, although we have drifted apart. My mother is very dramatic, very self-absorbed, and we all dealt with it differently. My older sister, Nell, withdrew. She is very quiet and introverted and serious. She has detached from all of us. Lizzy is the baby. She's twenty-six and wild, and working as a waitress in New York. She's an incredibly talented chef, but she's not very focused. She's never had to work very hard for anything, and I'm not sure she knows how."

"Does she want to be a chef?" His voice is as soft as his fingers tracing down her arm as if they are painting her in his mind.

"What I think she really wants is recognition. She wants to be seen. Like our mother. She was drinking and drugging as a teen, but I think she has cleaned up. Lizzy is definitely the one most likely to get what she wants."

"What about you?" Now he traces the underside of a breast as she

inhales sharply, her body on fire. "What is it that *you* want?" His voice is now a whisper as she turns to him in the back of the darkened cab.

She doesn't say anything, just looks at him, watches as his face moves closer, this face she has dreamed of for so long, as his lips finally brush against hers, so soft. He takes her top lip in his, as her head tilts and her tongue meets his, and her body threatens to melt into the seat.

Meredith cannot wipe the disbelieving smile off her face. Nicholas has fallen into a deep sleep, snoring lightly, rolled over to the side of the bed. Meredith lies back, smiling, the covers pulled up to cover her breasts (just in case he wakes up; she may have lost weight, but she is still self-conscious).

She turns her head to look at Nicholas's sleeping form in the dark, reaching out a hand and lightly brushing his hair. She gets to do this! She gets to touch him! To kiss him! To hold him!

She got to do it earlier tonight, when they kissed their way up the stairs to his flat, when he turned the light on to a tiny room with empty wine bottles on the coffee table and newspapers and sketch papers strewn everywhere. He kicked a path to the unmade bed, threw her down, and unbuttoned her shirt, her jeans, pulled them off, pausing only to take off his own clothes.

It wasn't quite as romantic as Meredith's dreams, nor quite as soft, teasing, anticipatory as the light tracing in the taxi. Nicholas was all business, grabbing her legs and thrusting them high in the air as he entered her, thrusting as he smiled through her legs, as if he ought to be congratulated for such prowess, for being able to thrust as well as he did, and for so long.

Meredith, still enthralled by being able to actually touch Nicholas, to have him interested in her, to be having sex with him, doesn't stop to consider what she has just gotten out of their encounter. But really

she just feels the fact of it is enough! Why should it matter that she didn't orgasm, that he wasn't concerned with whether she did or not, that as soon as he had come, he gave her a peck on the lips then rolled off and went to sleep?

She is lying in bed with Nicholas! She strokes his shoulder, his back, as he grunts and moves his arm to flick her off. Feeling sated, full, and completely happy, she snuggles down in the duvet, pushing it down only when she buries her nose in it and finds it doesn't smell of lavender, like her own meticulously laundered sheets, but of unwashed bodies, and time. Still. Nicholas! She closes her eyes and drifts off to a happy, tipsy sleep.

"Darling? Darling!" Meredith is aware of a faraway voice. She opens her eyes to see Nicholas's face inches from hers. Nicholas! Last night! It all comes flooding back as she sits up in shock.

"You have to go," he says. "I'm leaving for work and I have to lock up."

"Oh. Right. Of course." Meredith clutches the duvet to her chest as she leans over the side of the bed to look for her underwear. No way in hell is she getting out from under these covers naked while he's in the room.

"I'll get you some coffee in the kitchen," he says, walking out as a wave of disappointment hits her. Where was his morning kiss? Where was the affection of last night's cab ride home? They made love!

Well, in the cold light of day, perhaps it's fair to say it wasn't quite making love, but they had sex, which is the most intimate thing you can do with someone. It's certainly the most intimate thing Meredith can think of to do with someone, and not something she does on a regular basis. Nicholas is the fourth person she has slept with. At almost thirty years old. It's not a fact of which she is particularly proud, but nor is she someone comfortable having sex unless it is meaningful.

And serious. With someone with whom she is preferably in a committed relationship.

Obviously, she isn't in a committed relationship with Nicholas, but this is just the beginning. He's a man of the world, so much older, this is clearly how things are done with someone like him, getting the sex out of the way on the first date, getting to know each other afterward.

It wasn't really a date, she thinks, as she scrambles into her underwear and yesterday's clothes. More of a slightly drunken fuck after a night in the pub, but that's okay. There is plenty of time for dates. He did want to take her to a bar last night, after all, before the kissing in the back of the cab got them so hot and heavy that when he suggested they go straight back to his place, it would have felt childish and churlish to refuse.

She gets dressed and walks into the kitchen, recoiling ever so slightly at the flat. In the morning light, sober, she sees just how messy, and grimy, it is. What she can see of the wooden coffee table is marked by rings and stains. As is the carpet.

Still. Nicholas! She walks into the kitchen, to find a mug of coffee there, Nicholas swigging his back.

"Great!" He is clearly relieved that she is dressed. She waits to see if he will kiss her, put his arms around her, give her some indication that this is the beginning of something special, that it wasn't just—oh, please no—a one-night stand.

"Did you sleep well?" Meredith attempts small talk, hoping, still hoping, for a hand snaked around her waist, a nose buried in her hair, some affection, any kind of affection to help her push away the dawning realization that last night was a terrible mistake.

"Yup. Not bad. Little too much alcohol last night." He barely looks at her while he talks. "Ready?"

"Sure." Meredith puts the cup down and follows him out. She waits for him to lock the door, before clomping miserably down the stairs in front of him.

"Right." He stops once they get back outside and finally looks at her, standing directly in front of her and holding her arms. "Thank you for a lovely night, Meredith. We both clearly had much too much to drink."

He laughs and Meredith attempts a smile but finds her face merely twists into an odd kind of grimace.

"See you in class," he says, leaning over and pecking her on the cheek while squeezing her arms, before releasing her and walking off down the street without a backward glance.

Meredith stands still as humiliation floods her. She has never had a one-night stand before, has never offered her body to anyone other than men with whom she felt completely safe, men who she knew loved her, or at least cared about her. A tear threatens to trickle out of her eye. Furiously blinking it away, she gets out her phone to check the time. Shit. On top of everything else she's going to be late for work.

She gets through the day, escaping every now and then to the loo for a quiet cry. It isn't that Nicholas is so fantastic. If she really stops to think about last night, his flat was filthy, and the sex was pretty awful. It felt like hours of thrusting, there was no foreplay, and indeed he showed no concern for her at all. The duvet stank. He made really awful instant coffee this morning.

But still. She would have liked to reach those conclusions on her own, and not be marched there because he had so clearly rejected her.

And he did reject her. He didn't even pretend he might be interested in seeing her again. He didn't ask for her number, didn't give any indication that this meant any more to him than a drunken mistake.

Meredith has never been more humiliated in her life. Clearly she can't go back to the class again. How could she ever face him? Not to mention the classmates who saw her leave with him. How could she watch him flirt with whatever new girl might strike his fancy, knowing

what would happen, dreading that maybe she would be one who he would want to stick around. Unlike Meredith.

Deciding that there is no way in hell she will set foot in the Frognal Arts Center again, for the rest of her life, makes her feel ever so slightly better. She'll miss the classes, though; they were the one bright spot in her week. But she can find another class. She has no idea where, but she'll travel farther afield and find somewhere fabulous. Maybe with a female teacher. Or at least one who is married. And faithful, not given to flirtations with the students.

At lunch she goes to the sandwich shop around the corner from her office. She hasn't been there for a long time, instead bringing her salads and protein in for lunch, or grabbing a salad from Pret on her way in. Today she waits in line at the sandwich shop that used to be her favorite, looking at the boards, trying to decide what she wants.

What she wants is *everything*. She wants to stuff the loneliness, the humiliation, the disappointment, the shame, the sadness until she can't feel it anymore. What can she stuff it with?

She steps up to the counter and orders a turkey and Swiss with tomato, cucumber, and extra mayonnaise on a whole wheat roll. Without pausing she also asks for a bacon, lettuce, and tomato on a baguette with melted cheese. She adds some chips and four brownies too.

Meredith eats the turkey and Swiss, chips, and a brownie in the park. On the bench outside the Gap she eats the bacon, lettuce, and tomato baguette, chips, and another brownie. On the way back to the office she buys a Double Decker and a Bounty and eats those in the loo. With another brownie.

The rest of the day is spent in a sugar coma. She is so tired, she can barely keep her eyes open. Her boss comes out at three and gently asks if she's feeling okay.

"I think I'm coming down with something," she lies. She may not

be exhibiting flu symptoms, but emotionally, physically, and spiritually, she is definitely sick.

She is sent home, where she crawls into bed and thinks about what else she can eat to stop her feeling anything. She watches old black-and-white films and sleeps. At six o'clock she wakes up hungry again. She can't face going out, so phones the Chinese and orders spare ribs, seaweed, prawn crackers, and noodles. And four Diet Cokes. So they will think they are feeding four people.

Meredith eats in bed, tasting nothing. The food is devoured as if she is starving, swallowed without being chewed, wolfed down as she tries to feel better, and if not better, numb. She drinks two of the Diet Cokes before running to the bathroom and throwing up. Seeing some of the food in the toilet bowl is the only relief she has had today. At least it wasn't as bad as it could have been; at least some of the calories do not count.

She hasn't eaten like this for years. Since she lived in Westport, since she was a teenager and came downstairs ready to go out, only to see her mother shake her head sadly, almost imperceptibly, as she tried not to look at her daughter's thighs. She hasn't eaten like this since her mother slid the bread basket away from her and over to her sisters, with wide warning eyes to not let Meredith have any more bread.

And what did Meredith always do when she felt alone, or unloved? Go to her room and pull out the Oreos from under the bed, the chip packets from the bottom drawer, the Peppermint Patties from her closet. Sugary, salty, crunchy, sweet, it was the only thing that made her feel better; the only thing that made her feel loved.

When Meredith is finished, she brushes her teeth then gets rid of all the evidence. She buries the foil containers underneath the rest of the rubbish in the bin, sprays her sheets with lavender spray, changes into a clean T-shirt that doesn't have noodles on it.

She gets back into bed feeling bloated and ashamed. All these

months her eating has been so good. All these months she has felt, and looked, so great. And now she has blown it in an epic way. I will start again tomorrow, she thinks, looking down at her bloated stomach, self-disgust roiling through her.

Her phone rings, making her jump. She looks and sees it's Nell. How strange. She never hears from Nell.

"Hello?"

"Hi, Meredith."

"How are you, Nell?"

"I'm okay. How are you?"

Meredith is about to say she's okay, but she's really not okay. She has spent the entire day awash in shame and making self-destructive choices.

"I'm pretty shit, actually," Meredith says, which in itself is unusual, for she does not swear. "I had a one-night stand last night with my art teacher, which was stupid not only because I was naïve enough to think he liked me and wanted to get involved with me, but also because I have now fucked myself as far as going back to art class, one of the only things in my life that makes me happy. I have spent the day eating enough food for ten people, and I've just thrown up. And I feel humiliated and stupid. I can't believe I fell for this sleazy guy." She stops, remembering that it is Nell on the other end of the phone, Nell who has never had any patience with painful relationships, her own or anyone else's.

There is silence on the other end of the phone.

"Nell? Are you there?"

"I'm here. I'm just listening."

"Do you have anything to say?"

"What do you want me to say?"

Meredith shakes her head in disgust. "It would be really nice to hear that you're sorry, or that you feel my pain, or just a hint of sympathy. That's what I want you to say."

"I am sorry," says Nell. "Obviously, you're my sister and I don't want to hear you're in pain. And the food thing isn't the solution, as you know."

"Of course I fucking know!" Meredith bursts out. "Do you think it feels good to have eaten so much I just threw up?"

"How much have you had to drink?"

"Not enough."

"You know, why don't we just talk tomorrow when you're feeling better."

"You called me, Nell. I never hear from you. You must have something you want to talk to me about."

"It's okay. It can wait until tomorrow."

"Just tell me. It's fine."

"I was going to ask you if you'd look at some financial papers I've just received. It's the farm. I haven't got the money for a CPA and I thought maybe you could take a look and explain it to me."

Meredith pauses. It's so like her sister, to brush over emotions, to not want to engage in anything uncomfortable, in any show of emotion, then to move on to business, anything else.

Today is the first day she won't play. She has suddenly had it with how much her whole family has always taken her for granted.

"Nell?" she says. "Fuck off." And she puts down the phone.

2016

fifteen

Derek reaches over and places a hand on her hand. She knows what this means. This is to stop her talking, stop her doing whatever she is about to do, so he can insert himself and choose for her.

"My *fiancée* will have the steak, medium rare, with no potatoes and extra spinach, please. I'll have the shepherd's pie. And we'll all have another bottle. Thank you."

He looks approvingly around the table, as Meredith sits back. She wouldn't have ordered the steak. She quite fancied the chicken tonight, even though it did have a mushroom cream sauce, but really, how much harm would a mushroom cream sauce do?

"We do have a wedding dress to get into," Derek explains to the couple sitting opposite them. "I'm trying to help Meredith be as perfect as she can for the big day."

The wife, Tilly, looks at Meredith for a reaction. Meredith merely smiles and picks up her glass of wine.

"You're allowed to drink wine?" says Tilly, archly. Clearly she disapproves of Derek.

"Do you know, I hadn't checked." Meredith realizes she is ever so slightly drunk. She is ever so slightly drunk quite a lot of the time these days, especially when she is forced to play wife at a client dinner like tonight. "Am I?" She turns to Derek. "Am I allowed to drink wine?" She stares at him as she takes a long, drawn-out sip, watching Derek arranging his features into a smile.

"Of course you are," he says, turning to his clients. "One has to have a little fun, after all."

Tilly doesn't like Derek. Meredith can tell. The people who do like Derek are very much like him. Conservative. Stuffy. Overeducated and pompous. They are always pompous. His client, Richard, is pompous. Tilly, on the other hand, Richard's wife, is suddenly seeming quite nice. Most people don't realize quite how awful Derek is, thinks Meredith occasionally, swayed, as she once was, by his good looks. For he is good-looking, and those looks have opened doors, paved pathways, secured relationships. When Meredith is filled with doubt, she finds herself looking at his aquiline nose, his perfect teeth, reminding herself how lucky she is that someone who looks like Derek should even be interested in her.

"Where are you getting married?" asks Tilly, as the men start chatting about Richard's next tax return.

"We're getting married in a country church in Somerset that's incredibly beautiful. Derek chose it."

"Lovely," says Tilly. "And do I hear the faintest of American accents?" Meredith nods. "I thought so. Will your family be coming over?"

"No." She smiles. "My mother hasn't been very well so it's hard for her to travel right now, and I haven't been close to my crazy sisters for years."

"Is your mother okay?"

"I don't speak to her that much. My mother is very dramatic, so it's always hard to tell what's real and what's a cry for attention."

"So you don't think she's sick?"

"I think a normal person would go to the doctor and get a prescription. My mother just has symptoms that send her to bed, so everyone can gather round and make a fuss of her."

"So she's like the boy who cried wolf?"

"Exactly." Meredith rolls her eyes. "My mother is the quintessential boy who cried wolf."

"What about your sisters? I always wanted sisters. I can't imagine having sisters and not speaking to them all day every day."

"You definitely wouldn't if you had my sisters. You'd be diverting the phone calls at every opportunity. Not that either of them ever calls," she adds, with a hint of sadness.

"How many do you have?"

"I am the middle of three."

"Ah." Tilly sits back. "The people pleaser."

"Is that an observation or a classic middle-child trait?"

Tilly pauses as Meredith sips more wine. "Both?" She lowers her voice. "So, marriage to Derek is the fulfillment of all your fantasies?"

Meredith lets out a bark of laughter. "I wouldn't say that." She looks fondly at Derek. "He's a good man. He loves me. He will make a wonderful husband."

"Do you love him?"

Meredith turns to stare at Tilly. "Of course! I wouldn't be marrying him if I didn't. Do you love Richard?"

Both of their voices are low, the women leaning close to each other across the table. They both turn their heads to be sure their men are deep in conversation.

"No," mouths Tilly. "I mostly hate him."

Meredith sits back, shocked.

"I shouldn't have said that. I'm just exhausted, and we've got six-month-old twins, and I feel like I'm doing everything. I'm sorry. I didn't mean that. I hate him right now because I've been waking up all night long for what feels like months. The twins are horrible sleepers. I'm just tired." She shakes her head and attempts to laugh it off. "What about you? Will you have children?"

It was only a matter of time before this question was asked. It's only a matter of time before this question is ever asked. As soon as people know the details of the wedding, and the dress, they ask about children. There is usually a slight reticence in their voices, for Meredith, at thirty-eight, is well past her prime, but when she tries telling them those days are over, everyone assures her they have a friend who had a baby at forty-five, forty-six, forty-seven. She has plenty of time, they say.

It doesn't occur to anyone that Meredith might be relieved the baby factory is almost closed, that there is a reason she smiles and changes the subject whenever it comes up.

Long, long ago, well before Derek, before anyone, when Meredith was only a child, she remembers telling her best friend that she was never going to have children. She told anyone who would listen she would never have children. While her friends nodded solemnly when they were young, as she got older people started telling her that she'd change her mind, that she just wasn't ready, that she should wait until she got older, *then* she'd want children. She learned to keep quiet and not say anything at all.

Now she shakes her head with a light laugh.

"The only baby I have time for is my fur baby. Butch. He's a mini schnauzer and the true love of my life. Don't tell Derek."

"Butch will be a perfect space saver for the real thing," says Tilly, as Meredith smiles and says nothing. She is still in baby mode, this

younger woman. As much as her twins are exhausting her, she would never be able to understand someone saying they were absolutely clear that they didn't want children.

The last time she remembers telling someone she didn't want to have children, it was during one of her early dates with Derek.

She admired Derek very much by the time he asked her out on a date. Certainly she found him spectacularly handsome. Everybody did. At least that's what she now tells herself on a fairly regular basis. She didn't truly like him when she joined the CPA firm where he worked. But then he made a concerted play for her, and the simple fact that he liked her as much as he appeared to was like catnip for a people pleaser like Meredith, a people pleaser with a low sense of self-worth, who couldn't believe someone that handsome would notice her.

He would knock on the door to her office on some inane pretext, then come and sit by her desk and chat away about all kinds of things. Meredith sat and listened, flattered that a junior partner would take so much interest in her.

Meredith hadn't had a proper relationship in years. She once thought that one day she might have made enough money as a CPA to give it up and do something creative. But she never went to another art class after her one-night stand with the art teacher, and that dream slowly faded to a vague thought once every couple of years.

She stopped fighting the dullness of accounting. She followed the rules of what the women in her office wore: twinsets and pearls, sensible heels, pastel dresses in summer with nipped-in waists and white tights. She forgot she had once expressed horror at white tights and began to wear them, with closed-toe pumps (even Meredith wasn't silly enough to wear white tights with open-toed sandals, although plenty of women at her office did).

Mostly, she is happy with her life. She still wishes she were prettier,

thinner, more, somehow, but she is okay. When Derek asked her out to dinner, she said yes, flattered beyond measure that he had asked. And when the doubts set in, she reminds herself to remain flattered. If this was the life she was going to live, even if it wasn't the life she once wanted, then Derek was surely exactly the sort of husband she should have.

She is thirty-eight years old, after all. She was supposed to have been married and having children long ago. And so, when Derek flew her to New York for her birthday and got down on one knee in the Rainbow Room, how could she possibly say no?

Derek's looks hide the fact that he is, or can be, patronizing and superior. She feels guilty even thinking that. Far easier for her to focus on his good qualities, even if sometimes it is quite hard to think what they are. He is . . . affable . . . and kind, surely? At least, he isn't *unkind*. He is turning fifty, and treats her like a princess, at least he did in the beginning, before they got engaged. He seemed unable to believe someone like Meredith would go out with him, let alone marry him. Attention and adoration were not something Meredith was used to.

The experience with Nicholas, being treated as disposable, had put her off men for years. She hadn't trusted anyone until Derek appeared, like a knight in shining armor, to restore her faith.

If he is a little dull, surely that is a good thing. Where has excitement gotten her? It seems far safer to give her heart over to someone like Derek. Although there are times when she isn't entirely sure she has given her heart to him, but perhaps it is safer this way. This is pragmatic, sensible. This is the stuff of which the strongest marriages are made, surely. *Choosing* your mate is so very much wiser than falling in love with someone who will undoubtedly break your heart.

Everyone at work gets on with Derek. Everyone seems to laugh at his jokes and clamor for his attention, although he *is* partner. There *is* that. Would they find him quite so amusing if he didn't sign off on

their paychecks every week? Certainly she doesn't always find him amusing. Or even likable.

Her family doesn't like him, which partly explains why their relationship has become so strained. Lizzy has never been known to hide her feelings. He met them all when they went to New York and their mother insisted they meet up for a family dinner.

Lizzy got them into Jean-Georges, last minute. No one can get a reservation, but Lizzy has become quite the supper club maven. People travel from all over for her pop-up supper clubs; her name is well-known in the tri-state area. Restaurants that are booked for months magically find a table for Lizzy at a reasonable time.

Lizzy was there when they arrived, Nell sailing in late with their mother. Lizzy was as manic as ever, ordering wine, chattering away with the waiters, some of whom she seemed to know. Nell was watching quietly from the sidelines. Ronni attempted to charm Derek, but Meredith could see instantly that they came from different worlds, that her dramatic, overbearing mother saw her boyfriend from the suburbs and disapproved.

Thankfully, Ronni wasn't her usual biting self. She looked ill and she was walking with a cane after a fall at home. And there was something wrong with her left hand, which must have been bruised in the fall. It was the first time Meredith thought there may have been something in her complaining. Meredith was starting to worry, was about to ask her mother what was really going on, when Derek excused himself to go to the bathroom.

"You are joking, Meri, right?" Lizzy said, leaning over.

"What are you talking about?" Meredith stared at her sister.

"He's just . . . I don't even know how to say this. But really? For *real*? You're planning on spending the rest of your life with that man?"

Meredith instantly regretted having told her mother she thought this might be serious. Her mother had clearly passed on the news.

Lizzy had put on an English accent when she asked her question, and did something with her mouth, with her teeth, that was very English, and very Derek, and shockingly accurate.

Meredith stiffened. "Derek and I are serious, and we're very happy together. I didn't ask your opinion, Lizzy. If I wanted it, I would have asked, but I didn't."

"Ouch!" said Lizzy. "You're right. I'm sorry, Meri. It's just . . . he's such an . . . accountant."

"I'm an accountant," said Meredith, the color rising in her cheeks, turning them the precise shade of raspberry she had always hated. "Why don't you just learn to keep your mouth shut, Lizzy? You only ever open it to offend someone."

Lizzy's eyes widened. "Oh, God, Meri, I'm sorry. I totally forgot! I swear. I just meant I thought maybe he was a bit . . . straight for you."

"When you say 'straight,' you mean boring?" Meredith happened to glance over at her mother then and saw she was trying not to laugh. "Forget this," she said. "I'm not staying for this."

She started to walk out, only for Nell to come after her and apologize, remind her that Derek was still in the bathroom, and lead her back to the table so her mother and Lizzy could apologize as well. So she sat down even before Derek came back from the men's room. She didn't talk to her sister or her mother for the rest of the meal.

The thing is, Derek probably is too straight for her, whatever that means. And he is boring. But not everyone can be interesting and he has so many other wonderful qualities. She is quite sure she will never find anyone as nice as Derek again, nor someone who loves her in the way he does. He cares enough about her to even order her dinner, stop her from making choices they both know she'll regret in the morning.

As for being boring, she has learned to nod in all the right places and look interested in what he's saying even as she is thinking about how to redecorate the living room or what she should be making for dinner.

Perhaps a bigger problem—although really, is it a problem or is it something that she actually prefers?—is the fact that Derek doesn't really seem to see Meredith. Or hear her. Or listen to her. He has very clear views about who Meredith is and how she should dress (note the white tights) and what she wants (steak) and what she likes (spinach), and he refuses to consider the possibility that he might be wrong. If Meredith tries contradicting him, he laughs indulgently and pets her, stroking her arm or cheek as if she is a mischievous cat.

Meredith has told him she feels she is too old for children, and that she has never wanted them anyway. She hasn't told him the reason why. She hasn't told him that she has always been terrified of being a mother, terrified of being the kind of mother her own mother was. She told him she just didn't feel she had a maternal bone in her body.

Derek surprised her with the mini schnauzer, partly, she suspected, to disprove her theory, to show her how capable she is of loving a small creature who is utterly dependent on her. But Meredith knows that dogs and babies are very different propositions, even if Derek doesn't.

The last time she mentioned she didn't want to be a mother, he laughed and patronizingly said many women feel that way until their babies are placed in their arms. His eyes were all twinkly as he beamed at her, nodding, as if he understood something she did not, and it was the very first time she actually wanted to smack him. She doesn't want children, and she knows she will not change her mind. She just isn't sure how to help Derek hear her.

She has wanted to smack him a few times since then. She is quite sure that isn't a good thing. But Meredith, the good girl, the people pleaser, is on a path, and she has absolutely no idea how to get off. So she just keeps telling herself that Derek will surely make a wonderful husband—and he wants to marry her! He thinks she is special enough to marry her. No one else had even thought she was special enough to have a relationship with in years.

Who is she to say no?

Her phone vibrates suddenly, which is strange. She pulls it out of her bag to see who it is, and her mother's name is on the screen. How odd. She hasn't spoken to her mother, or in fact either of her sisters, since that disastrous trip when Lizzy called Derek boring.

Her calling can't be a good thing. She would only be calling if something were wrong. Meredith excuses herself from the table and walks quickly outside the restaurant to take the call, astonished that however detached she thinks she is, there is a sliver of anxiety in her heart.

sixteen

The sun is beating down as Lizzy stands with her clipboard, directing the men hauling hydrangea trees in huge square wooden pots onto the roof.

"No, no!" she barks, rushing over. "Not there. I said five feet apart. And it's not straight. See that? They need to be straight." She sighs as the men bring back the dolly and slide it under the pot, move it as they keep looking at her, checking that it's okay, nervous of her disapproval.

"Okay. Good. Thank you. How many more do you have? Three?" The men nod as they shuffle back along the rooftop. "Great. I'll stay until they're all here to make sure they're placed properly." She slides a loose tendril of hair back and tucks it into her bun. At least today her hair is clean. These days she tends to wash it only once a week, if she is lucky, scraping it back and out of the way when she cooks and when, like tonight, she is running a supper club.

The rooftop has been transformed from a blank slate with simple wooden decking to a lush, elegant wonderland. Huge Balinese daybeds

now occupy one side of the terrace, with white cushions and piles of pillows that invite you to sit and lounge. Groupings of white furniture sit around low Indian coffee tables covered with lanterns and tea lights. Everywhere there is greenery, trees and shrubs that have been brought in for the occasion; afterward they will go back to the farm they have found just outside Tarrytown that rents them out.

Tonight they are seating the guests at one huge table that snakes around the edges of the living room on the rooftop they have created with the furniture and accessories. They have covered the table in burlap, with Lizzy's signature candles, all different heights and sizes, running down the middle. The chairs are bamboo, the linens a mixture of natural and white. On each person's plate will go a small galvanized steel pot containing a starter salad, with white ramekins of ingredients the guest can add if he or she chooses: maple-chipotle-glazed pecans, cubes of golden fried halloumi cheese, caramelized onions, crispy lardons from a farm in Ridgefield. Everything served at Lizzy's dinners is organic, grass fed, and as local as she can find.

Some of the produce comes from her sister Nell's farm. Not that Nell is involved, beyond giving Lizzy a good price. Lizzy invited her, frequently in the beginning, when she finally got the supper clubs right and knew she was onto something big. But Nell was always busy, always sent texts saying so sorry, maybe next time. Lizzy has stopped asking, but hasn't stopped buying her lettuce, collard greens, tomatoes, and strawberries, not least because she has yet to find better.

The men bring the rest of the plants up as Lizzy checks everything is in place. They always string fairy lights across the rooftops; it is part of her signature style. But now they have large poles with concrete bases and hooks at the top to hold the lights. Now the lights never come crashing down, instead creating a magical arbor over people's heads and making them forget they are in New York City, imagining

they are, perhaps, on a country farm. But now she notices the job hasn't been finished properly.

"Can someone secure these lights, please?" she shouts over her shoulder, to no one in particular, for there are plenty of workers milling around, each of whom really should have already done this. "Christ." She shakes her head and mutters to herself as she tries to loop the string of lights over the hook, but it is too high and she can't reach.

A young man appears, takes the string of lights from her hand, and does it effortlessly, smiling at her. His eyes twinkle in his suntanned face, his thick, bushy, hipsterish beard setting off his blue eyes.

"I hope this is okay to ask, but may I have your autograph for my girlfriend? She's a huge fan. I mean, I am too. We're both huge fans. She went to the Culinary Institute of America because of you, and she watches your show all the time."

"Thank you," says Lizzy, who is still unused to dealing with people who treat her like a celebrity. "Of course. Do you have a pen? What's her name?"

She will never get used to this. She's not a celebrity, she's a chef, who happens to have made a huge success of the supper clubs and of creating gorgeous rooftop scenes for New Yorkers willing to pay almost five hundred dollars per person for a unique experience, and possibly one of the best meals they will ever eat.

It helps that she was approached by the Food Network three years ago and offered a weekly show on garden parties. Initially she said no, it seemed like too much work, but they persisted, offering her a producer and team of researchers to put together the ideas for the shows. All she has to do, other than show up for filming, is approve, or veto. The first season were all her ideas, and the show was a huge hit. Her golden looks, her easy charm, the fact that she is Ronni Sunshine's daughter made her an instant star.

Now she is in discussion with one of the large chain stores about a line of Lizzy Sunshine products, all to do with entertaining. Her candles in their woven holders, signature linens with the frayed edges, uneven ceramic bowls and plates, her huge Dutch ovens, dark gray with copper handles, her bread boards and cheese domes and marble pastry slabs, will soon be coming to stores near you.

She has a cookbook coming out next year. Never has she been busier, but she can't forget the thing that made her, can't stop cooking for the supper clubs, because now she's as big a draw as the event; now people travel from all over the country to try her food and maybe, maybe, get a glimpse of Lizzy herself.

Her assistant, Candy, taps her on the shoulder. "Sean is downstairs; he wants you to come and sample the main course."

"Thanks, Candy." Lizzy smiles and squeezes Candy's arm, no longer seeing the tattooed sleeves, the dyed jet-black hair, the piercings in her ears, her nose, her lips, and God only knows where else. Candy is the best assistant she has ever had.

The elevator rumbles downstairs to the apartment where she and Sean are cooking, or, at least, overseeing the cooking. Every time she does this, she remembers their very first one, the tiny galley kitchen, three of them working their asses off to get the food ready with no help.

Now they consider rooftops only if a large apartment with a professional-quality kitchen is part of the deal. There has to be room for the sous-chefs to cook, for them to plate, for the staff to get a family meal before the event.

She walks into the apartment, into the kitchen, marveling at how amazing these kitchens are. Who said New York City apartments were small, she often thinks. This particular kitchen is ten times bigger than her own at home in Brooklyn. The equipment is always top of the line— La Cornue ranges, or Ilve, or Wolf. This one has Sub-Zero refrigerators

that line an entire wall, a Nantucket farmhouse sink, and marble countertops that are as thick as an encyclopedia.

Sean is stirring something by the stove. He's in his chef pants, an apron tied around his waist, a thin, worn, white T-shirt showing off his dark tanned arms. He turns to see Lizzy approaching and goes back to stirring.

"How's the taste?" She checks there is no one around before snaking her arms around his waist and pressing her body into his, burying her nose in his T-shirt and inhaling his smell, amazed that the simple aroma of a man can drive her so wild.

"It's gorgeous. Here." He takes a spoon and turns to face her, dipping it into her mouth, never taking his eyes from hers.

"Mm-mm. That's wonderful. That's the perfect amount of butter. Well done."

"Speaking of wonderful," he says, putting the spoon down, "you know it's just you and me in the apartment right now. Everyone else is up on the roof."

Lizzy leans back against the island as Sean keeps advancing. "It is? How nice."

"You know what I'm thinking?"

"I couldn't possibly begin to imagine what you're thinking."

"I'm thinking there's a pantry around the corner that is bigger than my whole house, and I'm almost certain it hasn't been . . . *christened*."

"Why, whatever do you mean? What are you suggesting?"

Sean steps forward until his body is pressed to hers. He looks down at her, taking her hands and entwining his fingers with hers as her breathing deepens and her pupils dilate. He dips his head to meet her lips, but as soon as they brush hers, she pushes him back.

"Not here," she says quietly, her eyes glazed with lust. "Pantry."

He leads her to the room, which is ridiculously big, and moves her

back against the spice jars, closing the door and taking her face in his hands as his tongue sweeps her lips. He pulls the hair band out of her hair and moves his fingers through it, gathering it up as he pulls her close.

He pulls her T-shirt up, impatient, cups her breasts out of her bra, tonguing her nipples as she writhes against him and slides her hand under the waistband of his trousers. She pulls them down and opens her legs, pulling her panties off, kicking them out of the way as he pushes inside her, banging her back against the spice jars, but she doesn't care. All she feels is him thrusting quickly, hard, inside her, his mouth seeking hers, his tongue, his cock, his fingers rubbing her, the excitement, the smell of him, his feel, his taste, and—oh! oh! I'm there! I'm there! And the wave of her orgasm crests and washes over her.

She inhales sharply, quickly, repeatedly, moaning in a high-pitched quiver, as quiet as she can be, her legs trembling as Sean explodes inside her, as he collapses against her, pulling his head back to kiss her on the lips and smile into her eyes, just as her phone starts buzzing.

"Who the fuck is that?" he whispers. "Talk about inopportune timing."

Lizzy reaches down for the phone and bites her lip. "Oh, shit," she says. "It's my husband." She pushes him away, frowning at the screen as she reads the text. "Connor has a fever and he's coming home from day camp. I have to get home. Shit, shit, shit." She pulls down her T-shirt, finds her underpants on the other side of the pantry, and tucks herself in, makes herself neat again, scrapes her hair back into the tidy bun.

"We're not doing this again," she says to Sean. "I mean it this time. I can't do this again. I can't stand the lying."

"Whatever you want," says Sean, who has heard her say this many, many times before.

"Shit," says Lizzy again, grabbing her purse from the apartment. "Do I even have time to get to Brooklyn and back? What time is it?"

"You're good," Sean says. "It's noon. We've got it all covered. Everyone should be arriving any second, so as long as you're here by four, we're good."

"Thank you." She looks at him, drinks him in, turns to go, then turns back and walks toward him. "Oh, fuck," she says, as she drops her bag and puts her arms around his neck. "What the hell do you do to me?"

"I don't know," he murmurs into her neck, "but whatever it is, it's the same thing you do to me."

seventeen

For months now Stephen has been dropping in to the Coffee Barn at Fieldstone Farm, pretending to be getting his daily coffee and having a quick read of the papers, when everyone in town knows he is there to admire Nell.

Nell knows. She always knows when men are looking her up and down appreciatively, and she knows why—they admire her strength, her fearlessness, the fact that she runs the farm and has built it into a real business all by herself. She has turned the big barn by the road into the Coffee Barn, bringing in gourmet coffee from a small-batch roaster in northern Connecticut, with freshly baked goods and sandwiches every day. She doesn't do full cooked breakfasts—they have the Olde Blue Bird Inn for that—but her scones and muffins are the best for miles, and her coffee is untouchable.

The Coffee Barn quickly became the local hub to catch up on news, gossip, read the papers, and run into everyone you've ever met in town. The men would come early, on the way to their jobs, with young moth-

ers and children dropping in before school. The men thought she was a "handsome woman." She knew this because they would tell her so, ask her whether they could introduce her to a friend, in some cases invited her out themselves. She always said no. Raising her son and running the farm were full-time jobs; there was no time for a relationship.

Stephen is a little different. He is, for starters, exceptionally tall. Nell is no slouch at five foot ten and a half, and while she's certainly more comfortable with her height now than when she was in high school, the fact of Stephen's height alone—he towers over her at six foot four—makes her feel little, and vulnerable. His height reminds her of Lewis Calder. Much about Stephen reminds her of Lewis Calder. He is big and brawny, with an easy smile and low expectations.

She liked him the very first time he came in, felt him watching her as she moved about the room, collecting empty coffee cups, stopping to chat with the locals, grabbing a mop to clean up some spills on the floor.

Nell had not had a date in years. She tried not to think about it too often; when she did she'd sometimes start to worry there might be something wrong with her because she just never missed having a man in her life. For years she buried herself in single-mom-dom, raising River, consumed by the work involved in having to be the mother, father, babysitter, farmer, coffee-shop owner, *everything*.

People would often ask her where her parents lived, and when she said her father had moved to California a few years back, but her mother was in Westport, they would exclaim how lucky she was—what a help she must be!

While she was a better grandmother than mother, *Ronron* could never be relied upon to pick up any slack. She was more a good-time grandmother: huge fun if she was in the mood and didn't have any other plans, but she would never stop and cancel something she wanted to do for anyone else.

Ronni is still shockingly self-absorbed. That is what Nell would say about her mother, if she was ever inclined to talk about her at all. But what would be the point? Nell isn't the type of woman to moan and groan about her terrible childhood, the deficiencies of her own parents that have led to her leading a life alone.

Nor does she need to punish her mother for it, unlike Lizzy, who tells everyone who will listen about what a narcissist her mother is, and Meredith, who is over the pond and far away, and never, almost never, comes home.

Neither of her sisters is able to accept their mother with all her self-absorbed, dramatic flaws. They resent her for not being warm, interested, concerned—for not being maternal. Whereas Nell learned never to really expect anything from anyone, not since Lewis Calder left her high and dry with a baby in her belly. She finds life is generally easier when you operate this way. And as a result, she feels less angry at her mother than her sisters seem to be.

Nell doesn't really accept Ronni, but her proximity means she is the one to whom her mother turns when she needs something. Nell does a basic job of looking after her. She was the one who insisted, finally, on her mother going to a doctor. The falls were happening more and more, and the last time she had visited, she watched as a cup of hot tea fell out of her mother's hand.

Her mother has always, for years and years, complained steadily but then insisted that she was fine. Nell has long been in the habit of believing her, because of her mother's legendary hypochondria and bids for attention. If there truly were something wrong, surely she would be milking it for everything she could get.

And yet. So she insisted her mother go see a doctor. Afterward, Ronni did not report back immediately, as she normally would have done. When Nell did eventually see her, she had a limp and a cane. She said she was suffering from some motor neuron issues, which could

be managed. She said she was changing her diet, cutting out all carbohydrates and sugar, trying to reduce inflammation. Hopefully, she said, she would be walking without a cane again soon.

"Maybe River can come and spend some time with me," her mother said. "When he has a break from grad school."

Nell stared at her. Her mother had always swooped in for the occasional visit with her grandson. She'd never suggested he come and stay with her.

"Maybe the three of us could go on a vacation somewhere," her mother went on, as Nell resisted the urge to gape at her with open mouth.

Nell hasn't had a vacation in years. She's much too controlling to leave the farm in the hands of anyone else. Why on earth would her mother want to have a vacation with the three of them? Frankly, Nell can't think of anything worse. Not to mention, what would she do on a vacation? Lie on a beach and deepen her already dark farmer's tan? She shudders in horror. She has always been happiest working.

She works hard. Raising her son, running the farm, ignoring vacations. She has been perfectly happy with her life, although as River grew older she would occasionally think of what it might be like to have someone around. But whenever that thought arose, she'd remind herself that she lived in a relatively small town, a town in which she pretty much knew everyone, and if she spent the rest of her life on her own, that would also be absolutely fine. There was more than enough to keep her busy.

And then Stephen walked into the barn. Easy to be around, he hung out longer than the others, long after people had left the café otherwise empty. For some weeks now, she has been pouring herself a cup of coffee after the morning rush and sitting with him out on the porch, chatting easily.

He ran a farm in Montana when he was young, and knows just what

it is like to be a farmer, to grow crops, to raise animals. Nell has no livestock to speak of anymore, other than the kind of animals that would qualify as a petting zoo. Still. He knew what her life was like without her having to explain it, a fact that made her instantly comfortable with him.

He is a single dad of two grown-up daughters. These past few weeks, Nell has found herself looking forward to her chats with him, happy every time he walks in. When they talk, she feels understood.

She knew he would eventually ask her out, and determined, long before he did so, that she would say yes. They have now had three dinner dates, each of them lovely. He is old-fashioned and courteous, holding the door open, standing when she has to leave the table and when she comes back, walking around to her side of the car to open the door.

And Nell, who is so self-sufficient, who has never seen much of a difference between men and women, who has more than proven herself in a man's world, found herself first shocked by his politeness, then pleased. It made her feel like she had been transported into an old Cary Grant movie. Not that Stephen is anything like Cary Grant.

She likes him very much, likes the way he thinks, the way he talks, likes how she feels around him. The only thing she isn't sure about is her attraction to him. It should be there, but somehow it isn't. At least, she doesn't think it is.

She doesn't have too much experience, but she once knew passion, of course, many moons ago with Lewis Calder, when all he had to do was brush the back of her hand with his fingers and a surge of electricity would run through her body, leaving her breathless and gasping. It was so long ago. Perhaps that doesn't happen to a woman in her forties, she thinks. Perhaps it is just me. Perhaps it is that there is no chemistry with Stephen.

Everything else about Stephen is perfect. Tall, smart, funny, kind,

and handsome enough. Not head turning, but neither, Nell has to admit, is she. Nor has she ever been the kind of woman who is particularly interested in what people look like.

At their last dinner, when Stephen drove her back to the farm, she didn't know whether or not to ask him in, worried that she would be leading him on, feeling stupid that she was worrying about such a thing at the ripe old age of forty-two.

She didn't invite him in, but he did get out of the car and walk her up the path to the front door, and he did, rather awkwardly, pull her to him on the porch. She laughed in an embarrassed fashion as his lips were suddenly planted on hers, and there she was kissing him, reaching around to feel the sheer breadth of his back as he bent his head. Curiously, when he pulled away, she felt nothing other than a vague embarrassment at making out on the porch.

It wasn't unpleasant, it just . . . was. It was fine. She quite liked being held; that she did have to admit. It had been a long time since she had been held in a man's arms, which was really rather lovely. But the kiss itself? It didn't really do anything for her, which started the old worry up again. Was it her? Was it *him*? Was she—and this was the thing she had always, always worried about—was she . . . frigid? Was it possible that Lewis Calder was the only man who had found—*would* find—the key to making her gasp in pleasure, tingle to her toes, shake with lust? And if she never found that feeling again, would that be bearable? Could she settle down with a lovely man like Stephen, who took her in his arms and made her feel safe? Could she sleep with him, lie beside him in bed every night, even if she didn't feel anything at all when they touched?

She mentally shakes herself every time these thoughts flutter in her mind. They have been out for dinner a few times, that is all. How ridiculous for her to be thinking long term, worrying about their life together, their future.

And yet, there is something so compelling about him. Can you have one without the other? Can you have tremendous friendship, companionship, partnership, without passion? For years Nell has watched passion in other people's relationships dissolve over time. Sometimes it dissolves to nothing, but sometimes it is worse. It becomes resentment and rage, loneliness and fear.

But it does always seem to dissolve, and if that is necessarily the case, how important is it in the first place? She knows what other people would say. Lizzy would say that passion is compulsory in the beginning because even though it goes, as it has gone with her and James (and Lizzy is the first to admit this, even with James in the room; James just shrugs, knowing that trying to stop his wife from saying anything that's on her mind would be an entirely futile exercise), there are still moments when you look at your spouse, or you smell him, or you see him walk into a room unexpectedly, looking handsome as hell, and your heart lifts and does a small flip, and you know it is still there, even if it's mostly hidden. This, she would say, is the foundation on which every strong relationship is built.

Meredith would not say that. Meredith would likely say absolutely nothing on the subject of passion, but Nell's pretty certain that's because there's no passion whatsoever with Derek. Once you got past his pretty-boy looks, who could possibly feel passionate about *Derek*?

At the dinner when they met, Nell found him humorless and patronizing and arrogant. And what on earth does he have to be arrogant about, other than the genetic blessing of his features, which, frankly, have nothing to do with him? She could add that he is also deeply petty and narrow-minded, but what would be the point. She is almost certain Meredith feels exactly the same way about him as she does. She can't imagine what her sister is thinking, getting engaged to such a man, other than that Meredith must not see past his looks, or more likely, must think he is the best she can do.

If Nell were closer to her, she would talk to her about it. But Meredith hasn't really spoken to her or Lizzy since that awful last time they saw her, and Nell doesn't want to risk alienating her altogether. Not that they could be further apart right now, a fact of which Nell is increasingly regretful. She wishes they were closer, she and her sisters. She understands that their lack of relationship is more to do with their family background, with none of them having a healthy notion of what family means. Nevertheless, she wishes they could all let the past go, forgive each other for whatever transgressions they might have made over the years, and be there for each other.

Tonight Stephen has invited her to his house for dinner. She is worried it might be smart, fancy. Nell has no idea what to wear, but knows that following the kiss from the other night, tonight is almost certainly going to be the night that he invites her up to his bed. Maybe her feelings about that kiss will prove to be entirely wrong. Maybe she was just in the wrong headspace. Maybe tonight she will have a couple of glasses of wine, and that tingling will happen again, the tingling that used to happen all those years ago with Lewis Calder.

eighteen

Every time Lizzy approaches the small brownstone in their leafy
Brooklyn neighborhood, she pauses as the waves of delight and
disbelief wash over her. It's not like she wasn't brought up with everything she ever wanted—she is well aware her childhood was charmed,
at least in terms of material possessions, the houses they lived in, the
vacations they took. But none of it was hers.

This charming little house is all hers, bought with a combination
of savings, the TV deal, and the advances from both her cookbook and
the line of products. She saw this house alone, while James was still
working at his job in Manhattan and unable to get away to come see
it. She tiptoed around the rooms, practically holding her breath, as the
smile on her face grew wider and wider. It was unfathomable to her
that they could afford a whole house, in a pretty neighborhood, with
great restaurants and coffee shops on every corner and, even better,
great schools.

She walked through, noting that each floor had two square rooms

that opened into each other. All the windows had old paneled shutters that could be closed, although the Realtor explained that she had sold many houses with similar shutters and no one ever used them. They were easy to remove, she said, which was what everyone did.

Not me, thought Lizzy. I will strip the layers and layers of old, thick paint off, find the lovely warm wood underneath, and admire them every day as I curl up on the old sofa we stumble upon at a thrift shop, covered with a suzani rug and Indian hand-blocked pillows, as I extend my toes into the soft bamboo throw on the sofa. Not me, she thought, as she walked downstairs to the basement kitchen and family room, both small and dark, knowing that the burgundy walls could be painted a sunny yellow or a cornflower blue and lights could be added and surely, surely those windows could be made larger, that back wall could maybe become glass . . .

Upstairs there was a library, every wall filled with floor-to-ceiling bookshelves with many more books than the shelves could handle, and as she walked in, she saw that all the books were about food.

"Whose house is this?" she whispered to herself, walking over to the desk and studying the papers that were lying on it, the piles on every surface. She gasped when she saw the name, a food writer she had obsessively followed for years. This is where she writes? Lizzy turned around reverentially to look at the house with fresh eyes. This is where she entertains? On this rickety table with mismatched chairs in the dark burgundy kitchen?

It is meant to be, she announced to James, after she said good-bye to the Realtor and practically skipped to her car, clutching her phone with excitement as she called him. It is *bashert*, she said, invoking a Yiddish word she hadn't thought of in years, not since she would sit on the knee of her lovely Jewish grandfather when they visited their grandparents in London when she was a young girl.

"It's what?" James was laughing at her ebullience.

"It means it's fate. This is *supposed* to be our house."

He went to see it that evening. And agreed. And still, every day when she comes home, a year later, she pauses and hugs herself. She still can't believe it is theirs.

James is standing in the living room with a huge pair of goggles on and a wand in each hand, earphones on his head. He is moving slowly, gingerly, every now and then shooting the trigger on a wand. Lizzy's heart plummets. At least, she thinks to herself, with more than a small amount of derision, he isn't watching porn. At least it's the zombie game.

"James!" she barks, knowing the only thing he can see right now is groups of zombies lurching toward him and his guns, probably the machine guns, at the ends of his virtual hands. She pulls the headphones off his ears as he turns, startled. "Where's Connor? And what have we said about you not doing the virtual gaming when Connor is in the house?"

"He's sleeping." He takes the headphones and goggles off and drops the wands, guiltily. "He's fine. I just put him down."

"What do you mean, he's fine? You texted me that he has a fever. Does he or does he not have a fever?"

"He does, but it's only ninety-nine point one. I thought I'd let him sleep it off."

"Does that even count as a fever?" She stares at him, but he shrugs. "Did you give him anything to bring it down?"

"No. Should I?"

"How else did he seem? Was he tired or lethargic, or complaining of anything else?"

"He's definitely tired." James doesn't meet her eyes.

"What time did he go to bed last night?" She was out, the keynote speaker at a charity dinner in Midtown to raise money to help feed homeless children. It was a late night, although she is used to late

nights. Once upon a time, before Connor, James would come with her everywhere. They were a couple. Lately they have been feeling like ... colleagues. Colleagues that don't particularly get on very well, who are forced together in the shared project of raising their son. And last night James was home with him.

"Later than we thought."

She inwardly rolls her eyes at his euphemistic use of "we." "What time? Nine? Ten?"

James grimaces. "I think it was closer to eleven."

"Jesus, James. He's five years old, and he had camp today. Of course he's exhausted. How did you let him stay up so late? What were you thinking?"

She is standing in the doorway, her purse still over her shoulder, her hands on her hips as she glares at him. James continues to shuffle around the room, putting the virtual reality stuff away, but ignoring, Lizzy now sees, the many empty bowls and cups that litter every surface.

"Oh. My. God. Seriously? You haven't put any of this stuff in the dishwasher? I can't stand this, James. I am working my ass off to support you, and Connor, and I really don't ask for much. I ask that you are a responsible parent to him, and that you keep the house clean and tidy when I can't. And you don't even do that. I don't know what to say."

"I was busy. I know I was gaming when you came in, but earlier today I was working on a freelance project," he mutters as he gathers the empty bowls.

Lizzy knows, without taking a step closer, that all of them are from today, and all of them contain the last drops of Cap'n Crunch, Coco Pops, and Lucky Charms. If he has to feed himself, it's all James eats. How ironic that his wife is a chef.

"What freelance project? You're always saying you're working on a freelance project, but you never get anything commissioned. I don't even believe you anymore." Lizzy hates the accusatory tone coming

out of her mouth, so reminiscent of her mother as to make her feel she stepped into a time warp, but she can't stop. "It's all bullshit. You're full of nothing but bullshit."

James stops in his tracks and stares at her. "If you feel like that," he says, "why are you even here? Why do we even carry on? What's the point? You are the one who had an affair, so you don't get to act so high and mighty. You want to leave? Leave. Why are we continuing with this farce of a marriage?"

"It's a very good question," she spits out, turning on her heel and making her way upstairs. "I've been asking myself the same thing for months."

I should leave, she thinks, sitting on the end of Connor's bed and stroking his back softly as he sleeps, the blackout blinds in his room down, his stuffed elephant trapped under his little arm.

No, *he* should leave, is her next thought. I should have kicked him out years ago. It isn't enough that we have a child together. Surely it does more harm to Connor than good to have two parents living in the same house who can't stand each other. *I don't want Connor to grow up in a house filled with shouting and resentment and anger . . . like I did.*

What kind of a house would I want him to be raised in, she wonders, as Sean's face moves into her mind. God, no. He's not husband material. Look at his poor wife, at home with their four small children, with him gallivanting all over New York with . . . me.

She shudders. She can't think about Sean now. She did promise it was over, when James found out. That was a nightmare! She and Sean had gone downtown to buy some equipment, and afterward they went to a Starbucks to grab some coffee. They were sitting at the counter in the window, far away from everyone and everything they knew, safe, with their heads together, talking, murmuring, occasionally kissing. Sean had her fingers in his, both their elbows on the counter, when something made Lizzy turn her head. She still remembers she was

smiling as she turned, as she saw her stricken husband outside. The smile wiped off her face as she jumped up and ran after him.

There were tears that night, and in the days afterward. He moved into the spare room, although by that point his leaving the marital bed wasn't so strange. They have had sex maybe a handful of times in the last four years, and none at all for the last two, each blaming parenthood, work, the stresses and strains of modern life.

A few days later, with shaky voice, James said he recognized there had been problems in the relationship, but never thought she would have an affair. He would go into couples counseling with her if she promised to end it. He wanted her to promise she would never see Sean again.

"I can't do that," said Lizzy, who was so racked with guilt she would have agreed to almost anything. "He's my business partner. But I promise I will end our affair. It isn't really an affair," she then lied. "We just slept together a couple of times."

"How many?"

"What?" She couldn't believe James wanted to know.

"How many times did you sleep with him?"

"Seven," she lied. It seemed like a credible number, not too few and not too many, and certainly nowhere near the hundreds of times they had snuck into bedrooms, closets, even toilets, for two years.

Two years. Even she couldn't believe it. She promised James it would stop and she believed she would keep her promise. She went to couples counseling, for a while, and told Sean it was over. And it was. For a while.

Three months ago, she and Sean found themselves the last two left at the end of an event. They walked outside and, standing on a street corner, waiting for an Uber ride, he put a hand on her back and left it there, as a shiver ran through her whole body.

Fuck it, she thought. I deserve to be appreciated, she thought. I deserve to know what it is to feel this again.

She turned to him and kissed him, and they both forgot the Uber ride and ended up getting a hotel room.

What do I do about James, she thinks, still sitting in the darkness, still stroking Connor's back. She loved him so much in the beginning, all those years ago. She met him only a year after she and Sean went into business together. Those days her job was all consuming, and she felt like she worked twenty-four/seven without ever getting a break. James was an up-and-comer at an ad agency and came to one of their events, which his company was hosting for a client. He caught her eye immediately and then stayed after everyone else had left, after cleanup, and they ended up chatting all night. From the very first, he was so calm, like an oasis in the sea of her chaotic life. His calm calmed Lizzy down. He slowed her down. And he loved her. She would sometimes catch him gazing at her when she wasn't looking, his eyes awash with love. Lizzy, impulsive, wild, mercurial Lizzy, felt her heart physically slow down when she was with him. And that made her feel grounded, safer with him than she had ever felt before.

When did it all change? Not when Connor was born. James was amazing, left his full-time creative director job at an ad agency to freelance so he could be there with Connor while Lizzy built her career. James instinctively knew how to parent in a way Lizzy did not; he changed the diapers, got out of bed in the middle of the night when the baby cried, allowed Lizzy to sleep because the supper clubs were taking off.

And now? He is still the present parent, but only just. She thinks of him playing his virtual reality games downstairs and clenches her jaw, just as her phone buzzes. It's her mother. *Oh, for God's sake,* she thinks. *What now?*

nineteen

Nell pulls out a plum-colored lipstick from her purse on the passenger seat and quickly slides it over her lips. She gazes at her reflection in the mirror, at how unlike herself she looks with lipstick, and with a sigh grabs a tissue, immediately wiping everything off. Makeup doesn't suit her. Stephen has always known her natural and makeup free. Why she thought she had to look different tonight is beyond her. Nerves, she thinks, looking at his house and wondering if he knows she is sitting in the driveway, too jittery to come in.

She has already done two drive-bys of Compo Beach, past the groups of people enjoying sunset cocktails with beach chairs and blankets and coolers filled with wine and snacks. So little has changed, she thinks. Her mother's house is around the corner, but her mother is in bed with one of her dizzy spells. And she's not here tonight to see her mother.

Stephen told her he inherited his house from his parents when they died. For years he rented out the pretty 1930s cottage on a small private street right on the water, but last year he moved in himself. He says

he doesn't think he will stay. Developers have been leaving notes in his mailbox, desperate for his land, desperate to build a big new beach house, and there is only so long he can stave them off.

He prefers the country, he told Nell. He recognizes how lovely living by the beach can be, but it is greenery, trees and fields, that stir his soul, not the sound of the ocean waves and the smell of the sea.

Nell reties her hair in an elastic band, the smooth ponytail hanging down her back, and takes a deep breath. He must know she's here. She has to go in. She pauses outside the car, smelling the salty air, jolted back to her childhood with the smell of seaweed and possibility.

She is wearing old, comfortable boots with a low stacked heel, a long floral skirt, and a T-shirt. Nell, who lives in jeans, and old clothes and clogs and fleeces, feels alternately odd and pretty. And completely unlike herself.

The air is different down here. Everything is different. She comes to the beach so rarely, each time she does she sees the changes. The houses she grew up in, Emily Sussman's house out on Compo Mill Cove, the houses of their other high school friends, most are now gone, so many torn down for larger houses that spill onto the edges of their small lots, their yards protected by high fences.

She and Emily spent their teenage years pool-jumping, sneaking into people's yards for a late-night dip, running off screaming with laughter and adrenaline if the owner of the house happened to wake up and catch them. There were no fences. She knew everyone in this beach neighborhood. It was her home until she discovered Fieldstone Farm.

Easton, less than twenty minutes away on a very good day, has always felt like living in the country to Nell. She knew what Stephen was talking about when he rhapsodized the fields and trees. Stephen's house is clearly waiting for a developer to tear it down, she thinks. There is a huge maple tree in the front yard and dandelions sprinkled

through the overgrown grass. The house is yellow, and charming, although Nell knows this kind of charm is no longer desirable. It is also tired, with its sagging roof and sloping windows.

Clasping a bottle of wine, she finally goes up onto the porch, her skirt swishing around her legs as she strides. She opens the screen door and calls hello, walking in when there is no response. She is in a large room, sectioned off. There is a dining table and chairs on one side, sofas and a couple of chairs on the other, and a small kitchen at the front.

But the view! She sets the bottle of wine down on the kitchen table and walks to the bank of windows at the back, her face alight with the glow of the setting sun, casting a vibrant orange and red light over everything in the room.

"Just in time!" The sound of footsteps come down the stairs, and Stephen appears, leaning down and giving her a hug. "I was worried you'd miss it. I kept thinking I should have told you to come earlier."

"I'm glad I got here when I did. The view is incredible." Nell looks around. "I had forgotten about the sunsets here. Actually, I'd forgotten about the beach. I so rarely come back to this neighborhood anymore, and it is lovely. This"—she gestures at the sunset—"is absolutely beautiful."

"I ordered it especially for you," he says, smiling. "But the view is why the developers want it. And the land. They can squeeze at least six thousand square feet here, and have a pool."

"How can you think of selling it? It's really something special."

"Thank you. Although as you know I do prefer being in the country, I do appreciate how special this place is. But it's falling down, and I haven't really got the funds to fix it up. It isn't that I want to sell it, but that I may have to. There's too much that needs doing. It hasn't been touched since the fifties, and it's now showing."

"Such a shame. I think it's perfect," says Nell, accepting the glass

of wine he offers. "It reminds me of the Westport I grew up in. What work do you think you need to do?"

"The windows are all completely rotten, as is the roof. The whole house needs shoring up. That's the problem; it isn't really worth putting any money into it because it's only seen as a teardown. Any money I put into it, I would never see again. And I don't mind so much. It's perfect for me, but it's not what anyone wants today. Formica worktops and avocado green bathroom suite? It's getting to the point where I'm not even sure I could rent it."

"But you don't want to rent it. You live here now."

"True. And I'm perfectly happy for the time being, and right now I can afford to live here. Everything works." He chinks glasses as Nell follows him into the kitchen, where something delicious is simmering on an old electric stove.

"You cook?"

"Only on very special occasions." He grins, taking off the lid so Nell can bend down and smell. "Corn chowder."

"My favorite!"

"Who doesn't love corn chowder? I'm throwing lobsters on the grill. I have coleslaw and rolls. Is that okay?" He looks worried, but Nell nods.

What did she expect? That Stephen, Stephen who looks like he still belongs on a dude ranch in Montana, would serve up some fine, fancy French cuisine? Of course this is what he would make—good, solid home cooking, involving a barbecue and chowder. Exactly the kind of unpretentious food Nell loves.

They take the wine outside to sit in Adirondack chairs on the small, pebbled beach and watch the sun slipping down past the edge of the water, the sky glowing pink and purple and orange, the rocks along the coast seeming to be on fire.

"How could you ever have left?" Nell sinks back in the chair as the

warmth of the wine spreads through her body. She thinks how utterly content she is in this moment, the water lapping at the rocks, the wine in her hand, a good man at her side.

Yes, she thinks. I could get used to this.

Stephen smiles over at her, clearly content to see her so peaceful. He has only ever seen her at the farm, where she is always busy, slightly distracted, or at dinner, where she is charming, but formal. Here, dressed in the skirt that shows the odd flash of a strong leg, she can see his admiration, and the pleasure he takes in her obvious pleasure.

She closes her eyes before turning to him, questioningly.

"I left because I wanted to explore the world."

"And did you?"

"No." He laughs. "I explored a few states. Had a few loves. Then decided to come home."

Nell heard about the loves before, over dinner. How he had been a serial monogamist, never marrying, but moving from one long-term relationship to another. He had often found himself with women he reluctantly described as "high maintenance," which was why, he said, he liked Nell so much. She could take care of herself. She was independent. Not a needy bone in her body, he said.

It was true, thought Nell. But sometimes she wished she needed more. Perhaps if she needed more she wouldn't be quite so alone. She had River, of course, but he did exactly what he was supposed to do: he grew up and left for college, then grad school. Now it was just her.

Unless someone should come along. Someone perhaps much like Stephen. He is different here, she realizes. More at ease in his skin than she has ever seen him.

She finishes the glass of wine, then stands up, moves over to him, sinks slowly onto his lap as she slides her arms around his neck.

That kiss the other night? The one that didn't do anything for her? Surely now is the perfect opportunity to prove herself wrong.

. . .

The bedroom is dark, Stephen softly snoring beside her as Nell disentangles herself from his arms, careful not to wake him.

She gathers her clothes noiselessly and pads downstairs, then quietly slips them on before gliding out the door, pulling the screen door softly behind her, and getting in the car. She drives slowly through the deserted streets, onto the Merritt Parkway, and on until she reaches the farm, lurching over the uneven gravel driveway and pulling up in the courtyard in front of the house.

Even though it's the middle of the night, the rooster wakes up and crows as she makes her way inside, and she croons to him as she often does, hearing some of the hens wake up and softly cluck before shifting and settling their way back to sleep on their perch. The air smells like hot summer nights, cicadas buzzing in the background, as Nell lets herself into her house, heavy with disappointment.

She grabs a bottle of single malt and pours herself a glass, sinking onto the sofa with a deep sigh as she takes a large gulp.

She liked Stephen so much. She wanted so much for him to be right, for them to have, if not something serious, at least some fun. But when she kissed him, out there on the grass overlooking the water, she felt nothing other than a little curiosity.

And later, when she pulled him by the hand and led him upstairs to his own bedroom as he beamed with delight, she thought—hoped—that it was just the kissing that maybe didn't work, and that everything would be fine once they slept together.

And so they slept together. It was . . . fine. But fine was not what she wanted. She didn't expect to feel what she felt all those years ago with Lewis Calder, that much she knew, but *something*. Was that too much to ask? That she should feel something?

She worried that it was her, that there was something wrong with

her, and now, after tonight, after this sweet, handsome, charming man elicited no response from her whatsoever, she knows it's true. She's frigid. That has to be it. What other explanation is there?

The phone buzzes as she sits, and she pulls it out of her back pocket, dreading it will be Stephen, wondering where she went, so she grins delightedly when she sees it is River.

"Prodigal son!" she says, a warmth in her voice that only ever emerges when talking to, or about, River.

"Mother," he says formally. "Did I wake you? Is it too late?"

"Never too late to call your mother. And no. You didn't wake me. I'm sitting downstairs drinking scotch."

"Alone? Should I be worried? Calling AA perhaps? Do we need to stage an intervention?"

"Hardly." Nell laughs. "This bottle has been here for about two years. It's a rare treat and I am enjoying every sip."

"Sip, not gulp? Okay. I can relax. Anyway, I'm calling because we were thinking about coming home, Daisy and I."

Nell sits up, puts down her glass, a large smile on her face. "Really? When? I'd love to see you!"

"We thought maybe next week? Daisy was supposed to be interning in a garden center for the summer, but there's nothing to do—the woman gave her the job as a favor to her mom, so now we're thinking we might do a road trip in August. We thought maybe we'd come and help out on the farm for July?"

"Perfect! We always need extra hands during the summer and Cheryl wanted to take off, but I haven't said yes because I didn't think I could manage by myself. Oh, River! You have completely made my night!"

"Also, would it be okay if Daisy's mom came too? Daisy promised to spend at least part of the summer with her, so now that we're not staying here, we thought maybe she could come with us. You'd really

like her. And she bakes amazingly so she could totally help out with that too."

Nell doesn't know what to say. She doesn't particularly want someone she doesn't know staying with her for the summer. She doesn't really know Daisy, has only met her a couple of times, let alone her mother. But the girl seems sweet, and she adores River, and Nell will put up with pretty much anything if it means she can have River back home for a while.

"If Cheryl's not there maybe Daisy's mom could stay in the caretaker's cottage? I know you don't want strangers in the house, although is it okay if Daisy and I stay with you?"

"Of course," says Nell, relaxing. It is true, she is a creature of habit and does not like sharing her space with strangers. Last year a woman in town tried to convince Nell to go on a meditation retreat with her. Nell was enthusiastic until she discovered she would be required to share a bedroom and bathroom with two other women. She politely declined. She is too old to share her space with people she does not know, too set in her ways to share her space even with people she does. Apart from River, who doesn't count. And Daisy, who counts a little but gets away with it by association.

"Does Daisy's mom have a name?"

"Greta."

"And does Greta know about this plan? Is she on board? Should I be calling her and introducing myself?"

"We haven't talked to her yet. We wanted to clear it with you first. But she'll be fine with it. She's very laid-back. I think you'll really get along."

"Well, let's hope so," says Nell, instructing River to call his grandmother in the morning, as her screen suddenly lets her know her mother is on the other line. She has been avoiding her calls for days.

Shaking her head, she realizes she's going to have to take this one, if for nothing else but to get it out of the way, and she wonders why her mother might be calling so late. "I have to go," she tells River. "Your grandmother is on the other line and it might be important. I love you, sweetie," she says.

"I love you too."

twenty

Billy Hart shuffles on the doorstep as he waits, mentally going over his checklist. He definitely packed his tape recorder and notebook, his video camera, but did he pack spare batteries? He didn't, but he's pretty sure there are spare ones already in there. He has only ever once had a tape recorder break in midinterview, and resolved to always travel with a spare, but he never has.

He looks around as he sniffs the fresh salty air, nervous suddenly at meeting an actress he has seen in countless movies, an actress he once saw in a play in New York, an actress he has admired his entire life. He waited at the stage door afterward for her autograph, when he was young and had just moved to New York, before he became jaded, before he decided he had to leave.

Not being able to take the pace of New York City is what Billy tells everyone who wants to know why he left for Litchfield, Connecticut. A lifelong passion for living in the country, is what he says, and every-

one who has been to Litchfield nods with understanding. "What a beautiful town," they say. "I would love to live there too."

Some express surprise that someone who seems like such a city kid would leave for bucolic bliss. People assume that all documentary filmmakers/journalists need to be based in New York to make a living. His friends were astonished when he announced he was leaving. What would someone like him *do* in Litchfield? What stories could he possibly cover? What literary soirees did he think he would find up there?

As it happens, there have been plenty of literary soirees. Not so much in the town of Litchfield, but the surrounding towns—Washington Depot, Roxbury, New Preston—are filled to bursting with refugees from the New York scene: writers, actors, movie directors. He isn't nearly as stranded as people imagine. And the lovely thing about it is that he can dip in and out. He met someone at the library who introduced him to a major movie director in Washington, who invited him to a cocktail party, where everyone was interesting, and friendly, and he found himself inundated with invitations to what felt like a roving dinner party held at different people's houses that went on for months.

Sometimes he went, sometimes he didn't. He loved being surrounded by interesting people, then waking up and looking out the window to the view of fields and a few cows. He loved that there was nothing in his town that ever reminded him of New York, where every step held memories of his ex-wife.

It was painful enough that he had discovered Veronica had been having an affair with George Salisbury, the incredibly dashing literary agent and king of New York's literary scene. But worse that it wasn't, as he thought at the time, a flash in the pan. Veronica and Salisbury had just gotten married, a full page in the *New York Times* devoted to the joyful nuptials.

Billy had tried very hard to avoid the *Times* that day, but, like

picking a painful scab, in the end he just couldn't resist. A huge photograph of Veronica and George kissing, with a lavish description of their country wedding. Billy read about the hay bales placed amusingly around the grounds of their farm in Millbrook on which the great and the good sat to watch them join hands in matrimony. He learned that tomato and goat cheese tarts were served, tomatoes from their large organic vegetable garden, walled in traditional English style so, laughed George, the goats couldn't get in and eat everything. The goat cheese, naturally, was from their own goats.

Billy examined the photographs with a keen eye. There were so many people at the wedding that he had once thought were his friends. The people who had phoned him up when they heard he and Veronica had split up, to tell him that they didn't believe in taking sides, that they had very clear boundaries and would never talk about one with the other. None of them realized all Billy wanted to hear about was Veronica, however painful it might be to do so.

He had believed them, had naïvely thought it would be possible to continue friendships, until he would hear that they had been to Veronica and George's party. Or he would spy them in the corner of a gallery opening in Soho, laughing with Veronica and George (he left immediately). Or he would see them in the pages of the *New York Times*, clutching Tiffany crystal flutes of champagne while sitting on hay bales, beaming as Veronica and George faced each other with adoring looks as they clasped hands, about to be wed. And Billy would know he just wasn't mature enough, or advanced enough, to ever see them again.

He really had tried to be a grown-up about all of this. He tried to avoid the parties, make new friends. But he had only found himself growing more and more lonely in his new, somewhat sterile apartment in the East Village, an apartment he hadn't ever wanted in the first place.

Veronica had kept the apartment that had been theirs, the rent-stabilized apartment she had lived in for almost twenty years, an apartment Billy had lived in with her for the last seven, until he discovered her affair and had flounced out, imagining she would come running back within the month. She hadn't. Instead, as things with George grew more serious, Veronica let the apartment go, moving into George's famously beautiful brownstone in Chelsea.

That fact alone made Billy angrier than he had even been when he found out about the affair. She let an eight-room classic prewar apartment, in a gorgeous, sought-after building, with a rent that was next to nothing *go*? *He* could have had the apartment. Well, he could have. She had in fact offered him the apartment out of guilt, but he didn't want to allow that guilt to be assuaged, so he said no. But of course he had just been biting off his nose to spite his face.

One weekend in January, he ended up in Litchfield, Connecticut, quite by chance. It was bitterly cold, and beautiful. He went up to stay with his old friend from school, Henry, who was living in an old barn on the outskirts of the village with his wife, Georgia, and their two kids. Everything about the weekend was idyllic. They wandered around town and stopped for hot chocolate at the Village, had dinner at the West Street Grill, where enough New Yorkers from surrounding towns were eating that Billy took one look around and thought, I could do this. I could live here. I have found my people. This is where I can finally get that book written.

Billy had been making documentaries for years, and writing features for various magazines. He had long thought of writing the novel he had outlined numerous times in his head. He had made copious notes over the years, but had always seen himself living in the country to do it. The New York apartments, both the one in which he lived with Veronica and the one he rented afterward, never fit his fantasy, so the book never got written.

But there he was, in the idyllic village of Litchfield, which was quiet enough but cultured enough to satisfy everything Billy needed in order to be able to write his book. It was, in short, the perfect fit.

Henry and Georgia were of course delighted. Every time anyone came to stay they attempted to convince them of the charms of Litchfield, but they had never actually succeeded in tempting someone to move out before. And here they were with Billy, not just wandering around with a Realtor, but looking at houses!

Billy fell in love with a house on North Street, but it was completely out of his price range. As someone who had rented in New York for years, he had presumed he was going to rent, but he couldn't find anything he loved, until he was shown an old Dutch Gambrel on a pond, close to the village. It was both for sale and for rent, so he took a year-long lease, with a view to buying it once the year was up.

He moved in this past March, and thus far he is still floating on the pink cloud of joy at his country fantasy being even better than the reality. No more squeezing into smart parties trying to butter up the various editors and writers from the *New Yorker*. No more nervous laughter with the people at *Vanity Fair*, hoping they'll commission another piece! No more hobnobbing with the *New York Times Magazine* editors, seeing them at restaurants and pitching them on the fly because it might be the only opportunity he'll ever get. Well, that's not actually true, because he does run into many of the same people up here, but it's less competitive. Everything about his life now is more relaxed.

Billy isn't making nearly as much money since he left these opportunities behind, but he doesn't seem to need as much money up here. He has stepped away from the filmmaking to write more, although he still does some pieces for the magazines, with a column in one of the trendier gentlemen's ones. They call it "A Broken Hart." In the first several months he bravely wrote about the breakdown of his marriage, the

pain and desolation of betrayal; of his wife leaving her iPhone behind when she went to a yoga class and the terrible push-pull of picking it up, knowing he wasn't supposed to be looking at her texts, knowing that he had to, that even before he started reading he knew exactly what he would find, but that seeing it in black and white, glowing ominously from a small, heavy screen (it was small—they hadn't yet brought out the iPhone 6 Plus), was still enough to make him throw up. He wrote about how he expected to have the huge fight they had, which led to him stomping out, and how his equal expectation that her guilt would send her after him, pleading, had been disappointed. He wrote about his first forays back into single life once he realized she was not going to come back, even though he had forgiven her, would have done anything to get her back. He wrote about how in New York he had decided the best way to get over an ex is to treat it like a hangover, and go for the hair-of-the-dog method. How finding someone with whom to practice was as easy as leaving the apartment, and within a month (after the first two months of lying around crying), he had slept with eight women, and all it had done was to make him feel emptier and lonelier and entirely hopeless about ever finding happiness again.

He wrote about going to visit Henry and Georgia and finding a peace in Litchfield that had always eluded him in the city. He had been raised in Redding, Connecticut, which, while not the wilds of the countryside, was still rural enough that being in Litchfield made him feel at home, at peace, in ways he hadn't even realized he missed.

Every now and then he would get an e-mail or a phone call from one of his so-called friends, who he knew was no longer truly a friend because the person would ask him to stop writing about Veronica. The basic line was that Veronica was increasingly embarrassed by him, by his exposure of her, their life together, and did he realize he wasn't hurting anyone as much as he was hurting himself.

The first couple of times people called, or e-mailed, he went to great lengths to explain that hurting Veronica was the last thing on his mind, which was true. He wasn't writing about Veronica to try to hurt her; he was writing about her because writing about things was the only way he knew to make the pain go away. He had never been good at expressing himself unless it was through his fingers or a video camera, where his rigorous honesty had earned him a loyal following and regular work. Even once he left New York.

He had to write about what he had gone through in order to make sense of it, to understand it, and, finally, to move on. He started his novel then. It was vaguely autobiographical in the way so many first novels are. It featured a protagonist who had thought he was going to spend the rest of his life with the woman he considered his soul mate, until he came home early from his job as a publicist for a large publishing house to find his colleague—his boss, if we are to be specific— in bed with her.

It was going well, this novel. He found that everything that had ever happened to him mixed together in his head as he wrote, flowing out through his fingers in ways that made his heart sing. His protagonist, Julius, was of course entirely based on Billy for the first three pages, but very quickly became his own man, a character who dictated to Billy just what he would do next.

And Sophia, the soon-to-be ex-wife, was cold and heartless in a way Veronica never had been. She had red hair, as opposed to Veronica's blond, and was altogether more calculating and cruel than the Veronica who had inspired her.

I wonder what she will make of this, thought Billy from time to time, wondering if he ought to rewrite parts to make her less recognizable as Veronica to people they knew. But this was fiction, if drawn from a single circumstance in his life, and it was clear to him that Sophia, like Julius, was very much her own person.

And quite frankly he no longer cared what Veronica thought. Not much.

He continued freelancing, his filming equipment now safely stored in the basement. Everything was going along pretty well, and he was happier than he had once thought he ever would be again, when he found himself unable to sleep the other night, switched on the television, and was quickly riveted by a movie starring a young Ronni Sunshine. What had happened to Ronni Sunshine? he found himself wondering. He went online and found pictures of her at various galas, but nothing for the past year or so. And then he found a small item announcing they had recolored one of her earliest movies and would be reissuing it in the new year.

Wasn't it time, he thought to himself, for a big feature to be done on her? The rerelease of one of her classic movies would be a perfect hook, not to mention that one of her daughters was now a celebrity chef. Surely there was a story there. Maybe even a documentary.

He found her agency's website and sent an e-mail to her agent, introducing himself, saying that he was a huge fan of her work, wondering if she might be interested in a feature, possibly even a documentary. Why not?

Billy hadn't thought about making another film, but perhaps he could interview her—perhaps some combination of the two. With all the publications going online, it was entirely possible that he could write a feature and perhaps film some of it, interspersed with old clips from some of her classic movies. There might be a good audience for that, a good bit of money in it for him.

Two days later, her agent e-mailed him back. She was interested, and would he go for lunch to her home so they might chat. Billy was stunned and delighted. He hadn't expected such a quick response, and certainly not one inviting him to lunch at her home.

And here he is, on the doorstep of her lovely home set back from

a private road, high on a hill near the beach in Westport. Now he hears something behind the door, and then the door is opened by a small Filipina woman.

"Hello, sir," she says. "You must be Mr. Hart. Ms. Sunshine is on the porch waiting for you. I'll take you there. Can I get you something to drink? Iced tea? A glass of wine?"

"Iced tea would be lovely," he says as he follows her through the foyer, eyeing everything as they walk, all of it potential fodder for an article, a film.

Down steps into a living room, and then through onto the porch, where Ronni Sunshine sits on a sofa, glasses perched on the end of her nose as she stares at the screen of an iPhone. The Filipina woman gently takes the phone out of her hand and puts it on the table next to her, as Billy walks over, shocked at how different she looks in the flesh.

He knows she is sixty-five, but she is still glamorous, exquisitely made-up with her thick, wonderful trademark blond hair. Her ankles are still slim and exquisite, her fingers loaded with large, chunky stones. But her face underneath the makeup is drawn, and she seems to be having problems with her left hand, for it lies limply in her lap as she uses her right to shake Billy's. And the Filipina had seemed to take her iPhone—an odd thing in itself—with the kind of care and consideration that is used only with people who are not well.

Billy sits in the armchair next to her, complimenting her on her lovely home, on this beautiful room, on how well she looks.

"I don't look as well as I used to," she says, matter-of-factly.

"None of us do."

"True." She smiles. "Where did you travel from?"

"Litchfield. Do you know it?"

"I once had an affair with a movie director who had a weekend home there. We snuck up when his wife was away. What terrible

things I got up to in my youth. It's a beautiful town. I would have liked to live there, only it was so far away from New York City. Westport seemed a more sensible compromise."

"You've been here a long time?"

"Forever and a day. I loved your film about the greyhounds."

"Thank you." Ten years ago, Billy made a documentary about greyhound racing and what happened to the greyhounds once they were retired. It won awards, was the talk of the town for just a very short while, and every now and then, like today, people will bring it up, praise him for the work.

"I thought you showed tremendous compassion, and it was beautifully shot."

"Coming from you, that's a tremendous compliment."

"It's true. I filed you away, thinking that one day I would like to work with you. What a delightful surprise to have my agent pass on your e-mail."

"I had no idea this would happen so quickly. Thank you for being so open, and for this invitation. You haven't done any big interviews in a very long time, and I'd love to do something. I'm seeing perhaps a feature in the *New York Times Magazine* or *Vanity Fair*. We could shoot some film too, add some digital content for online readers."

"So you're thinking of doing something a little more than a vanity piece?" She smiles and looks at her hand, before looking back up to Billy, who notices, for the first time, the cane leaning against her chair to one side.

"I think you have a fascinating story that hasn't been told. Your start in England, and those early Hollywood days when you took the town by storm. I think it's time to tell your stories."

"Maybe you're right. How enormously flattering at this stage of my life for you to want to do something like this." She smiles. "But, as

you can see, I'm not well." She gestures to the cane. "I ignored it for a very long time, thinking I would wake up one day and be back to myself, but that hasn't happened. The doctors tell me I have ALS. Do you know what ALS is?"

Billy nods, shocked.

"So you will know it's amyotrophic lateral sclerosis, also known as Lou Gehrig's disease. You will know that it is a progressive deterioration for which there is no cure."

"I'm so sorry." Billy is shocked to find he has tears in his eyes. She seems so stoic, so resigned, so brave. This is the very last thing he could have imagined. "I don't know what to say."

"You don't need to say anything. I have done plenty of research and it seems my fate is sealed. My doctors keep raising Stephen Hawking and the fact that he has lived such a full, important, relevant life, and for so long. But he seems to be an anomaly." She sighs. "And I wouldn't want that life. The question is not if, but when. I hadn't anticipated dying in my sixties, but—what's that saying? Life is what happens when you are busy making other plans."

"What can I do? How can I help?"

"Let me tell you a little about ALS. It starts for most people just as it did with me, with dizzy spells and fatigue. From there, I started tripping, and sometimes falling. As the nerves die, they twitch and jump under the skin, together with muscle cramps. As we get weaker, we get clumsy. I have lost most of the use of my left side and am only able to walk with a cane. It won't be long before I'm in a wheelchair. As the disease progresses, the paralysis will spread until it is one hundred percent. In the end, I won't be able to eat, drink, or speak. I will be fed by a tube until my organs are ready to pack it up. Then I die. It's not a pretty way to go."

Billy shakes his head, still swallowing the lump.

"And it's not a way I choose to go. Nobody knows other than Lily,

who you met when you got here. My daughters don't know. My friends don't know. My agent doesn't know. My manager doesn't know. My publicist doesn't know. Other than Lily, you are the only person who knows. I cannot die this way, Mr. Hart. I will not die this way. And I am sorry that I brought you over here to explain why I won't be featured in a story, other than my obituary."

She pauses then and sighs. "I'm sorry. I'm talking too much. I haven't seen anyone other than my housekeeper in much too long. I have been very private about this, but it is in fact something of a relief to be able to talk about it. My daughters and I are more or less estranged, although Nell is up the road in Easton. She does the occasional errand for me, but I barely see her. Lizzy is in New York, and Meredith is in London. I speak to each of them once in a blue moon, and they speak to each other even less. I was not a good mother, Mr. Hart. I was too focused on my career." She sighs again. "I was too focused on myself. I was self-absorbed and selfish and disinterested in my children. By the time they were old enough for me to want to get to know them, none of them were interested. Who can blame them? I would have been the same. But now I have called my daughters home, and I plan on apologizing for the mother I was. I want them with me when I die."

Billy's eyes widen.

"Do you know how long you have?"

"Oh, I'm not going to wait for the disease to take me. I'm going to do it myself. I want my daughters with me when I do."

Billy sits forward, alert, in the way he always is when he inadvertently stumbles upon the hidden story, the one he never realized was there. "Ms. Sunshine," he says.

"Please. Call me Ronni."

"Ronni, I am so sorry for all of this, and this may be entirely inappropriate for me to even ask, but if you would consider it, I would still want to write a piece. Maybe I write a piece about this, your

extraordinary bravery, your choice to take your own life. You would be helping so many people, not just by telling your story, but by showing them. It would be your legacy, together with your movies, obviously, but this is so important, that people see you, and what you are choosing to do. If you would consider it, it would be my honor to be here and to capture it, in words and pictures and film."

She stares at him. "I'm flattered. At any other time in my life I would have been thrilled, but I have much work to do. I have been a terrible mother. Typical actress," she says with a wry smile. "Selfish, self-absorbed. And not there for my children. And it took this diagnosis to make me realize the damage I have done, and the things I have to do to fix it so they have each other to lean on when I'm gone. I think being filmed, or having you here, may be a huge distraction."

"But that's exactly what the story is." Billy can't hide the excitement in his eyes. "Your redemption. That you and your family come together in your final days."

Ronni looks at him. "Forgive me. I'm dying, but I'm not dead yet, and if we were to do this, and I'm not saying yes, but if we were, there are certain things that would be important to me. Would you show what it is like to have a debilitating disease, and why euthanasia is the only option for a vain old actress like myself? Would you be kind when you explain that this is as far as I want to progress? I want to die still being able to walk. I want to die still beautiful. I want to leave with the same passion I have lived my life. And I want my children to forgive me. Can you capture all that? Are you up to the challenge?"

She pauses, but he is patient and waits for her to go on. "Maybe you could interview me, alone. Maybe I could talk to you about my daughters, leave them something to remember me by. Something that will help them remember me in a different light."

She trails off, as Billy nods, trying to take it all in. He wasn't plan-

ning on this kind of story, this kind of film, but Ronni Sunshine choosing to take her own life is—as grim as it sounds—exactly the sort of story he would have jumped at when living in New York. The sort of story that might make his name important again.

The whole project is bigger than he expected when he sent that e-mail. It would mean uprooting his life, living here for a while, getting to know the family, being part of everything. It wasn't what he imagined for himself these next few months, but what a story. What a privilege. What choice does he have?

"So you will allow me to interview you, and to film you?"

"Yes."

"And you know I would need to be here all the time? You know that's how I work? The fly-on-the-wall documentary. I would fade into the background, but I would have to be here always."

She smiles. "Don't think I don't know exactly what this entails. My daughters are all on their way home. They know nothing, and I'm almost ready to tell them. I have been hoping for some change, some cure, but it is clear there is nothing to be done. I need the girls to try and find a relationship with one another again. Once they have settled back in here, I will tell them. And you should probably be here, yes?"

Billy nods. "I should. And thank you. It is an honor that you are allowing me to do this. Do you think your daughters will be okay with it?"

"I imagine they will be. My whole life has been about me, and all my self-centered mess has done is push the girls away from me, and away from each other. I have three daughters I barely see, barely speak to; and worse, they barely speak to each other. If I can do one last thing for them, it will be to try and bring them back together. As soon as they know I'm dying, it will be all about me again. So I am going to try and wait." She meets his gaze. "What do you say?"

Billy thinks. "You said I could interview you about your daughters, leave a legacy. I have a camera in the car. Would you be willing to talk to me this afternoon? Allow me to film you a little as you talk about your daughters?"

"Yes," says Ronni. "But first let's have Lily bring us some lunch."

twenty-one

There are many things Meredith feels she is not allowed to do since she has been with Derek, and some of them are things she really, really used to enjoy.

Meredith used to smoke. Derek was appalled when he found a packet of cigarettes in her nightstand, even though she explained she really didn't smoke regularly, only when she'd had a drink, and only late at night on her own.

Derek's mouth squeezed into a tight little knot as he shook his head. "You won't be doing that again," he said, taking her cigarettes and crunching them in his hand into a ball as tiny flecks of tobacco floated down onto the carpet. Meredith vacuumed them up later.

She doesn't eat shellfish anymore, because Derek doesn't eat shellfish, and every time she mentions thinking about ordering it in a restaurant, he sneers and asks how she can eat such filthy creatures, bottom-feeders, disgusting things that aren't fit for human consumption. Meredith doesn't point out that there is growth hormone injected

into the spare ribs he gnaws on, and thick brown sauce smeared all over his face, every time they go out to his favorite restaurant for dinner. He would just tell her she was being overdramatic and ridiculous.

Meredith has learned to keep very quiet about her politics. Derek describes himself as a true Tory, with a fascination for American politics. When Derek rails on about the left-wing media collaboration, Meredith says nothing. She tries to leave the room. She doesn't engage in the slightest.

Meredith used to love watching what she always thought of as popcorn TV. Mindless, delicious, and easy to digest without even thinking about it. She could sit for hours watching the American shows she downloads: *The Voice*, *Real Housewives*, *Catfish*.

Now she watches the news with Derek. Or *Poldark* or *Downton Abbey*. The only thing they vaguely agree on is *Law & Order: SVU* on cable, but within the first five minutes of every show it always dawns on her that she has seen this one before. As has Derek, except he never remembers until the very end, when he will frown and say, "You know? This is very familiar. Have we seen this before?"

When her mother phoned and said she needed Meredith to come on Friday with her sisters, Meredith knew, immediately, she had to go. Almost as quickly she thought, why not take a day off on Thursday and have a day to herself with no one making demands on her? Hell, why not even leave Wednesday? Why not turn it into a mini vacation? God knows she hadn't had a mini vacation by herself in years. Just the thought of being alone in a hotel room filled her with joy.

But where to go? Not Westport, not until the weekend. Before that, she would go somewhere she didn't know anyone. Somewhere with a spa, perhaps, that was quiet and peaceful. She Googled "best spas in Connecticut" and lingered over one in Washington. She had been to Washington Depot, years before, and remembered it being beautiful and quiet. It was perfect. It was also a small fortune, but ...

why not, she thought. How often did she do this? This would be a night to remember. Or nights.

She told Derek her mother had summoned her (he was starstruck enough by the fact of Ronni Sunshine being Meredith's mother that she knew he would never question her being called back to Connecticut) and she had to leave early afternoon Wednesday. With a combination of excitement and guilt, she booked herself into the spa for two nights, with a massage each day. Why the hell not? What she really wanted was to stretch out on crisp white hotel sheets all by herself. She wanted to pick up a phone and order room service breakfasts, price be damned. She wanted giant American omelettes oozing with cheese, bread rolls and Danish pastries she could slather with butter if she felt like it, platters of fruit arranged so artfully they resembled abstract paintings.

She wanted to stay in her pajamas all day and watch hours and hours of television. She wanted to catch up on her favorite shows in real time; to find out what Ramona and Bethenny were up to this season, and what work Brandi had done to her face.

She wanted to leave the hotel only if she felt like it, and only if she felt like going to a gas station and buying armfuls of peanut M&M's, Reese's Pieces, and Almond Joys. She hadn't indulged her eating, her stuffing of feelings, for years. Not until she met Derek. Then she began to find, once again, her solace in food. Derek noticed, disapprovingly. The more he disapproved, the more she wanted to buy the food she felt like eating and she wanted to eat it all, without anyone frowning at her or criticizing or telling her, like a naughty little girl, that she wasn't allowed.

And if she felt like it, she wanted to wander the town. Maybe find an art gallery.

She wanted to be on her own.

She wanted to be able to breathe.

Here she is, luxuriating in the crisp white sheets she imagined, waking up again after the second sleep, after the big breakfast she gleefully ate in bed. Derek does not allow breakfast in bed, heaven forbid a lone crumb may jump off the tray and into the sheets. Now there are toast crumbs everywhere, which she brushes off the bed with a nonchalant sweep of the hand.

She has a massage later, and hours to kill. Too many hours to spend watching television, she thinks. It is sunny, but there is a cool wind. I'll go shopping, find a wrap, she decides. One of those boutiques on the green is bound to have something pretty. Maybe I'll wander. It has been so long since I have been back in the States.

And so she gets up and dressed and walks out to the green. She does not find a wrap but a crocheted cardigan. She happily bundles herself into it and continues walking around the town, nosing along, remembering there is a bookstore close by, a bookstore she has been into, a bookstore she loved.

And there it is. The Hickory Stick. She smiles as soon as she walks in. It makes her happy, shuffling among the shelves, pulling out whatever strikes her as interesting, standing and leisurely reading a few pages, adding it to the pile in her arms, or placing it carefully back. She had forgotten how happy this made her, for the only bookstores she has easy access to in London are large and impersonal, and it's impossible to just browse. She doesn't want to. They don't make her happy in the way this small bookstore does.

"That's great."

She looks up to see a youngish man with glasses looking at her. She closes the book she's holding to see the cover, not even sure what it is she's reading.

"I read it a couple of months ago," he says. "You should buy it."

"Okay. Thanks. Anything else you recommend?"

"Depends. What do you like?"

"I don't really know. I have a couple of days off and plan to spend them watching crappy TV shows and reading. Maybe my reading fare ought to be a little more substantial than the crappy TV."

He smiles. "Have you read this?" He turns and pulls a thick book off the shelves, one that got rave reviews from everyone. But Meredith worries it is too serious, that she will not be able to finish it.

"I haven't. I'm worried . . ."

". . . it's too heavy?" He finishes her sentence off for her and they both laugh. "I thought that, too, and the first three chapters are a bit slow, but after that you won't be able to put it down. Cross my heart, this is the best thing you'll read all year."

He hands it to her, with a slight bow, then gives her a squinched-up sort of smile and a wave as he wanders over to the other side of the store. He looks nice, thinks Meredith. Cute. Probably her age, maybe a little younger. He has the sort of baby face that makes his precise age hard to guess.

He's dressed like a typical bookstore clerk in an old, faded, pinkish T-shirt and blue jeans, leather sneakers on his feet. Nice sneakers, actually. Trendier than she would have expected.

He has cool Elvis Costello–ish black glasses, and hair that sticks up. And crow's-feet when he smiles. Not handsome. But boyishly charming, she thinks, casting another glance his way.

Maybe she should ask him advice on something else. But what for? she sharply reprimands herself. To continue the conversation? With what end in sight? Stop it. You are engaged to be married to a wonderful man. This is what she often tells herself when she finds herself talking to a man her age who seems to be reasonably attractive, when she finds her mind wandering into all kinds of directions it shouldn't be wandering.

Meredith knows her tendency to match. Half, no, three-quarters

of the people she has ever dated she didn't even like that much. She only dated them because they liked her. Meredith, the ultimate people pleaser, felt she had to say yes, even when she wasn't the slightest bit interested.

Just as she feels she ought to carry on this conversation with the cute bookstore clerk, just because he instigated it. Not that he's interested in her. Absolutely not. Still. She casts a surreptitious glance and sees him walking to the other end of the store.

I wonder what's at the other end of the store, she thinks. Maybe I should just go in there and find out. Stop it! Go and get a coffee instead. There was a coffee shop just around the corner. And there were some delicious-looking coconut pastries in a case near the window.

In the coffee shop, she finds a quiet table in the corner. A couple of women sit two tables over, one with a voice that is particularly loud and piercing. Meredith fishes in her bag for her headphones, plugs them in, and pulls up a classical music playlist, grabbing the first book from the top of her pile and opening it to the first page.

She doesn't hear anything, isn't aware of anything, until she feels a tap on her arm and looks up to see the cute bookseller, now squeezing in next to her, a coffee and sandwich in front of him.

"I didn't mean to disturb you," he says. "How's the book?"

"Heavy. And slow. But I'm trusting you. Is this your coffee break?"

"What?"

"They let you leave and take breaks here. That's so nice."

He laughs. "Oh, I don't work there. I was just browsing, same as you."

A deep flush colors Meredith's cheeks. "I'm so sorry."

"Why? If I didn't do what I did, I'd kill to work in a place like that. It's exactly where I would be happiest."

The flush fades, to Meredith's gratitude. "Go on, then. Now you have to tell me what you do."

"I'm a writer," he says, with an embarrassed laugh. "Unsurprising that I love a good bookstore."

"Me too," she says, hoping there is no stray desiccated coconut from her pastry on her lips as she smiles. "I mean, I'm not a writer, but there's nothing I love more than a good bookstore."

twenty-two

Lizzy is not happy. Today they were supposed to be filming at an organic orchard in upstate New York, owned by an eccentric former banker. She was supposed to taste the apples, interview him, then make an apple coconut chutney and a spiced-apple-stuffed pork loin in his kitchen, before sitting down with a selection of his friends around a table set up in the orchard, with all the plates, china, candles, and natural linens from her upcoming line.

She had to cancel everything, which will cost a fortune, not to mention God only knows when they will be able to organize all the people again. Her mother called and demanded she come out with her sisters to hear some kind of news. Normally Lizzy would have ignored it, or insisted her mother tell her over the phone, but apparently Meredith was flying over from London, so whatever it was it had to be big enough that it warranted Lizzy being there.

Lizzy sits on a Metro-North train as it shoots through Westchester and into Connecticut. Staring out the window at the coastline, at

the boats bobbing in Greenwich Harbor, she wishes she felt more attached to the place where she grew up, that she felt a sense of homecoming. But she has no feeling of roots in this place, any more than she does anywhere else.

She was the daughter who stayed the longest, who seemed to have the easiest time of it, who was allowed to get away with the most. But once she left, she left. She stayed in touch with no one from home, never gave them a second thought. When people asked her where she was from, she said she was a New Yorker. It didn't seem untrue; she felt like a New Yorker, and surely that was what mattered.

"I hope this is something big," she mutters to herself as she looks out the window. But the truth is, there is a part of her that is relieved to have canceled today. Sean was booked to be the head chef, which normally would have filled her with excitement, but it's all getting too much—the secrecy, the lies, the roller coaster of highs and lows. She needs a break from all of it, needs to figure out just what she's going to do.

And so while she was never one to give in to her mother's demands, on some level she realized this summons could be just what the doctor ordered. She packed a bag and told James her mother needed her and she would be gone for a few days. Maybe just the weekend, maybe slightly longer.

They were barely talking, the resentment an invisible force field between them, their smiles and laughter, their conversation, forced and false, for the benefit of their son. Before leaving, she held Connor close and told him to be good for Daddy. Then she made her way to Grand Central Station to catch the train. She hadn't touched James. Just stood in the doorway before she left, with a small shrug and a good-bye, saying that she would be in touch. He glanced up from his laptop and said okay. And she had left.

She leans her head on the glass and watches the changing scenery,

aware that a couple of people on the train have recognized her. She can feel their eyes constantly coming back to rest on her. Her celebrity—and, oh, how she has come to hate being a celebrity—pulling their attention back over and over, even when all she is doing is resting her head on a window and losing herself in thoughts.

At the Westport train station, she pulls her bag off the shelf and moves through the compartment. Sometimes she flashes a big smile at the people who clearly recognize her, but today she ignores them. Fuck it. They are used to seeing her lose her shit on TV—she is, in fact, famous for losing her shit on TV, but only when things aren't as perfect as she needs them to be, when people aren't pulling their weight, when the sous-chefs fuck up, all of which happens on a regular basis. Usually in the real world she tries to be polite and charming, the perfect celebrity. Today she just can't be bothered.

With a scowl on her face she steps off onto the train platform and makes her way down the stairs to the cabs. In the old days, there was a man who would gruffly direct you into the cars, she remembers. He would stand with a cigarette drooping out of the corner of his mouth and a clipboard in hand as he pointed you to a cab that smelled overpoweringly of cigarette smoke and the odor from the fake pine cardboard Christmas tree hanging from the rearview mirror. The cabs are still the same, but the man is gone. She puts the window down to breathe the fresh air as the driver heads out of the parking lot.

It hasn't changed, she thinks, as they drive down Bridge Street, the old Italianate Victorians on the right still exactly the same. She resists a small smile as she remembers nights of drunken beer pong in one of the garages of one of those houses, many, many years ago.

They turn onto Compo, and she's surprised at how many new houses there are, large and impressive, spilling onto the edges of their lots, their yards shielded from prying eyes by large, dense fencing. How long has it been since I was here? she thinks. A year? Two? With shock

she realizes it has been almost four. She sees her mother a handful of times a year, but in the city, and usually when her mother brings someone she's trying to impress to one of Lizzy's supper clubs. That is her concession to their relationship, to always find room for her mother no matter how sold out the supper club may be.

Her mother does come in occasionally to spend time with Connor, but James organizes that now that Lizzy's schedule is so busy. She has little reason to come back to Westport, as evidenced by the fact that it has been so long since she was here.

The driver turns and drives up the hill, stopping outside the house and turning to Lizzy.

"I thought this was you. You're Lizzy Sunshine. I wasn't sure, but I've driven your mom. I know the house. You home for a while?"

"I don't know," says Lizzy. "Hopefully not too long. Too much going on in New York, you know?"

"Nah. I hate New York," he says, grinning to reveal a couple of missing teeth. "Too much for me. I like the water out here, and look at this neighborhood. Best in town."

"Keep the change," she says, handing him a twenty as she gets out, pausing for a minute to look at her mother's unchanged house, smell the familiar air, as she resists the urge to be swept back to her teenage years. She is not nervous exactly, but things haven't been good with her sisters for ages, and she isn't sure how to feel about seeing them. The last time they were all together was for that dinner in New York when Meredith practically stormed out. They haven't spoken since. Lizzy can forgive and forget, but she isn't sure about Meredith. Oh, well, she thinks, opening the front door. It's now or never.

"Hello?" She hears Nell's voice from the kitchen, drops her bag, and heads in.

twenty-three

It doesn't matter how many years go by, how grown-up we think we are, how much we presume we have changed or evolved, when we are back in our childhood homes, we become exactly who we have always been, thinks Meredith. I bet we will all just slip back into the roles we have always played, whether we were ever comfortable with them or not. Meredith smooths her dress, tucking her hair behind her ear, inhaling sharply as she prepares to walk up the garden path and into her mother's house.

They are about to be back together again; the Sunshine girls. And even though they have barely spoken in years, even though they may be married, or getting married, when the three of them are together, they will always be the Sunshine girls, the three daughters of the famous movie star.

Nell is here. There's her beat-up vintage pickup truck, the same truck she has driven for ten years, taking up the last available parking

space. Meredith had to park on the street, two houses away to make sure she wasn't blocking anyone's driveway.

But there you see it. She's always been the Good Girl. Careful not to, heaven forbid, park in what little was left of the driveway with the trunk of her car sticking into the road, getting in someone's way. Meredith has always looked at people who cut lines, simultaneously hating and envying them. She wants to be the sort of person who cuts lines, rather than the person who waits patiently at the end, silently cursing those who march confidently to the front and board the plane well before her, their bags tucked comfortably in the overhead compartments as Meredith has to shove past all the people to the very back of the plane to find a space for hers, squeezing all the way back again to her seat, often on the verge of tears.

Sometimes she wants to be that selfish. But most of the time Meredith feels affronted when people break the rules, push into lines, are rude to waitstaff. She has broken up with boyfriends because they were demanding or offhand to a waiter in a restaurant. And she would do it again. It is one of the things she really likes about Derek; he is polite to everyone. Except perhaps her, but that doesn't count. He never cuts in front of lines. He follows the rules as assiduously as she. Perhaps even more so.

Here she is, about to enter the bosom of her family, parking up the street, putting herself out so as not to disturb anyone else. She would never go inside and ask Nell to pull the car up just a little bit so she could squeeze in behind. Meredith will just find a way to make it work and say nothing, ignoring any vestiges of resentment that might be lurking inside her.

After a lifetime of this, she holds so much resentment at her sisters, particularly Lizzy, that she has been relieved not to see them for so long and is not especially eager to do so now. Lizzy once said Meredith

hated her from the moment she was born, resented her for being the baby, an unwelcome addition, the child who stole her mother's attention away. It wasn't true. Partly true, perhaps. But it was much more the fact that Lizzy was born going to the front of the line, and has never even glanced back.

Nell wasn't ever around much during their childhood. She remembers in the distant past, Nell sometimes being an ally to her against the storm of their mother's moods. But she also remembers a kind of desperate sense of survival of the fittest between them. In the worst moments, they had each looked out for themselves. So Nell and she are not close now as adults either.

And the last time they were all together was the last straw, as far as Meredith is concerned. Meredith became fed up with their snide remarks about Derek. She didn't want them to point out his deficiencies, sarcastically or otherwise, because it was rude. And because, she could at least admit to herself, then she might have to face them. And what would the point of that be? It's not as if she can get off this path she is so clearly traveling down at great speed.

Everything is booked now for fall. Which, given that it is now early July, is only three months away. The country church in Somerset is arranged and the village hall has their deposit. Jane Packer is doing the flowers: apricots and peaches, russet reds and creams, perfect for a fall wedding. They tried a tasting menu and decided on shot glasses of creamed parsnip soup, delicate beet crisps balanced on top, and French onion soup, also in a shot glass, with a tiny bite-sized baguette covered in melted cheese. The entrée will be a choice of roasted pork with caramelized apple slices and potatoes dauphinoise or roasted salmon with a crème fraiche ratatouille of winter vegetables. For dessert, lemon curd tarts, with salted chocolate caramel truffles placed on each table. Afterward there will be trays of glasses filled with warm

milk, each with a huge homemade chocolate chip cookie balanced on top. Just in case people are still hungry.

The gift registry is under way at Harrods. Not only have gifts already been bought, but they have received some. A distant aunt of Derek's sent a set of brown china serving platters that apparently was given to her on her own wedding day; she has been waiting for a special occasion to pass them down to another member of the family.

"Because God forbid anyone should ever actually use them," muttered Meredith on opening the box and physically recoiling at quite the ugliest platters she had ever seen.

"It's very kind," said Derek, unpacking them and placing them on the dresser so they could be admired publicly.

After he was asleep Meredith went back downstairs, packed them up again, and put the box in the garage.

"We can't ruin them," said Meredith days later when Derek remembered and asked where they were. "We need to preserve them for our own nieces and nephews . . . or children," she added quickly, seeing his face. "And we need to ensure they are in perfect condition. They're very delicate," she pointed out, although they weren't. The china was as thick as bricks.

She bought a dress, for heaven's sake, and it is being tailored. She is supposed to be losing weight for her wedding but seems to be gaining instead. It must be the stress. Instead of taking the dress in they have been letting it out, centimeter by centimeter, every time she shows up for a fitting.

Derek's mother—and was it Meredith's imagination or was there some reluctance in this gesture?—handed over the pearl and diamond earrings she wore for her own wedding. The pearls were large, the diamonds small. They were quite beautiful, but Meredith felt greedy, somehow, in taking them from her when she so clearly didn't want to give them up.

Everything is steaming ahead—the wedding, the conversations, the chatter, their future life together, the children they are going to have (even though Meredith has not changed her mind one iota about having children) and all she wants to do is escape, run away, disappear into the night.

When Derek senses her hesitation, he thinks it is because Meredith's father moved to California years ago, and in doing so, seemed to renounce all parental responsibility. None of the girls have visited or even spoken with him much in recent years—his new wife made sure the girls knew they were unwelcome visitors in his life. Out of a sense of duty, Meredith asked if he wanted to walk her down the aisle. He explained that unfortunately he couldn't as the date coincided with a vacation he'd been planning with his wife and daughter. She wasn't surprised. And while Meredith has been pretending that this must be the source of her sadness, it is not. Of course she is sad that her father will not be there, and sadder still that she and her sisters barely had a relationship with him once he remarried and had the dreaded Arianna, but it is not the reason she has been increasingly so depressed by the thought of her wedding that she can't entirely hide her reluctance from Derek.

Last night, after a lovely day, a *perfect* day by herself, the cute man in the bookstore, the massage back at the hotel, Meredith ordered room service—a burger *and* fries—ate both chocolates left on her pillow, and lay on her bed afterward, perfectly content. She watched no television and read no books, although the stack was on the nightstand. But she wore a huge smile on her face. She had no idea she was smiling, and when she did realize it, and wondered why, the only thing she could think was that she was happy to be in a hotel, on lovely sheets, eating lovely food.

She couldn't possibly admit it was because she was so relieved to be on her own.

"Meri!" Lizzy comes barreling out of the dining room, flinging her arms around Meredith, who stands rather stiffly, accepting the hug, before her arms automatically creep up and find their way around her sister's back.

"Big sister!" croons Lizzy, rocking Meredith back and forth until Meredith has no choice but to allow herself to be squeezed, and to rock back and forth in rhythm with Lizzy, until Lizzy decides to release her. But when she does so it is only to pull her back in for another hug, and Meredith knows Lizzy is only doing this because she can tell Meredith is uncomfortable—she recognizes that impish look in her sister's eye.

Lizzy does feel impish. And happy. Happier than she has been in months, now that she is away from James, away from Sean, away from the terrible stress and strain of keeping secrets, of leading two lives.

"I'm gonna make you love me again," she sings in Meredith's ear before she lets her go. "I am. I'm gonna make it happen. You're going to want to be my best friend by the end of tonight."

And despite herself, Meredith laughs.

"Where's Mom?"

"Upstairs." The smile leaves Lizzy's face. "Nell's in the kitchen. Come and say hi."

"Do you have any idea why we've all been called home?"

"Maybe she's going to tell us she's dying or something." Lizzy is matter-of-fact.

Meredith turns ashen. "Do you actually think that?" And she realizes she hasn't given it a second thought, why her mother would call them all to her house when they barely speak.

"No. I mean, I didn't think that. Up until now. Or maybe I was thinking it. I just didn't realize it. Fuck." Lizzy whistles through her teeth. "Do you think that's it?"

"I guess we'll find out soon. Maybe Nell knows something."

They go and find Nell standing at the kitchen counter squeezing lemons, a small pan on the stove starting to bubble. She turns the heat down and wipes her hands on a dishcloth tucked into the waistband of her jeans.

"Hey, Meri," she says, turning to greet her.

Meredith never knows quite how to greet her sister. She worshipped Nell when she was younger, but now finds her cold and reserved. Frankly she's surprised Nell comes over, more so when Nell gives her an awkward hug.

Lizzy watches them, feeling an odd pang of nostalgia. Wasn't there a time when the three of them were close? She feels like when they were teeny tiny, they must have all sheltered from their mother's rages in Nell's bedroom, or let their big sister whisk them outside, where they would run down to Longshore and sit under the shade of a huge maple tree, all of them staying together so they could stay away from home. She feels like that must have happened. But the truth is she can't really quite remember when it did.

How did they all grow so far apart? thinks Lizzy sadly, a flash of resentment rising as she remembers Nell's refusal to let her host dinners at the farm. She shrugs it off by telling herself it's irrelevant. It doesn't matter now, she thinks, given that people all over Connecticut, New York, and New Jersey offer up their own farms on a daily basis, all desperate for Lizzy to host one of her supper clubs there. What a pity that the only farm she really wants is the one her sister refuses to give her.

Not now, she thinks. Don't think about it now.

"Where's Mom?" says Meredith.

"Upstairs lying down. Lily's gone to wake her up. I haven't seen her yet." Nell turns the heat off under the pan and stirs it with a wooden spoon as Lizzy walks over.

"I thought I was the one who's supposed to be the great chef," Lizzy comments as she peers into the pan. "What are you making? Simple syrup? Lemonade?"

"Yes. Lily says Mom has a craving. I make it at the farm fresh daily. Usually lemon and blackberry, or mint, but I only found lemons here." Nell looks at Lizzy. "You look tired. How's work?"

Lizzy lets out a bark of laughter. "Thanks, Nell! You always did know how to make me feel good."

"Oh, come on, Lizzy. Don't start already. You're gorgeous. You've always been gorgeous. Saying you look tired doesn't mean you look terrible. You just look like you've been overdoing it. How's Connor?"

"You're right. I'm sorry. I get oversensitive when I'm tired." She grins. "Connor is delicious, and work is fantastic and nonstop. I keep thinking I'm just going to get over this hump and then it will be calm for a while, but it's never calm." She takes a breath. "Why are we here, Nell? What's going on?"

"I have no idea. I haven't seen her in a while. I know she's still getting those dizzy spells and there's something wrong with her left side. I don't know. I'm guessing she's been diagnosed with something. I can't imagine why else she'd call us all here."

"I thought it was vertigo."

"Who knows. You know Mom. It could be total attention-seeking hypochondria, or cancer."

"Oh, my God, don't say that." Lizzy recoils, alarmed, before dropping her voice. "Do you think it's cancer?"

"I don't know what it is. But the last time I saw her it was clear there's something not right."

"Cancer would be awful," says Lizzy. "Can you imagine? I mean, cancer would be awful, period, but Mom with cancer? She'd milk it for everything."

"Don't say that. You'll feel terrible if it is. Lemonade's ready." Nell slides a pitcher over, half-filled with ice cubes. "Give it a few minutes to cool down."

"So why *do* you think we're here?" Meredith asks. "Do you think it might be nothing?"

"I don't think it's nothing," says Nell. "She's been having tests for the pins and needles."

"Pins and needles?" Meredith knows nothing about any of this.

"Yes. And cramping in her legs. Some kind of nerve damage, it would seem, although the last time we talked she said they haven't been able to find any definite diagnosis."

"Well, that's good, isn't it?"

"Better to have a diagnosis, I think," says Nell. "So you know how to treat it."

"Are you sure there's something wrong?" Lizzy rolls her eyes. "This sounds like her wanting us to gather around and make a fuss of her."

"I guess we'll find out soon," says Meredith, as they hear noises. "Lily must be bringing her downstairs. Let's bring the lemonade into the sunporch."

"Just remember, be careful in there," says Lizzy, as the three of them gather their things and walk into the hall. "You never know what mood she'll be in," she adds in a mutter.

When their mother joins them a few minutes later in the sunroom, even Lizzy, who has been so determined to start this visit on an upbeat note, is stilled at the sight of her. She looks tiny, old, and impossibly frail. Lily is helping her, she is using a cane, and it is quite clear to all of them that she is having tremendous problems walking. Ronni sinks into a chair as Lily props pillows behind her back, then places a small pillow on the arm of the chair, lifting her left arm onto the pillow.

Meredith and Lizzy swap alarmed glances. They know their mother is not the woman the rest of the world sees. They know the makeup is artfully applied for every public appearance, the thick blond hair one of myriad wigs, the Chanel bouclé jackets and tailored skirts selected only for chat shows, opening nights, premieres, and parties. They know what she really looks like, when she comes down first thing in the morning, after Lily has brought her breakfast in bed. She will have shadows under her eyes and skin that sags ever so slightly when she is due for her shots of Botox and Sculptra, her Thermage. Her hair is completely white, as fine as a baby's, scraped back into the wispiest of ponytails, an inch long, held in place by a tiny blue elastic band that she gets from the orthodontist—nothing bigger will hold her thin hair in place.

At home she is always nicely but simply dressed. She will opt for comfort, with just a few ounces of style, completely unlike her over-the-top, glamorous, overly made-up, overstyled public persona. She will wear old, soft T-shirts and cashmere sweatpants. Her chunky antique Victorian belcher chain is always around her neck, and she wears one heavy gold ring on her left hand, but no other jewelry. She will wear sneakers and flip-flops. She will never leave the house like this, just in case photographers are lurking, but this is how her daughters know her; this is what they all expected to see.

But today, they don't. Instead, their mother seems to have aged twenty years. She has lost weight she cannot afford to lose, her frame almost birdlike as she sits in the chair, beckoning them over with her good hand. She kisses them one by one, a hand on each of their backs as she keeps her lips pressed to each of their cheeks, reluctant to let each of them go, in what feels like an expression of the kind of love, affection, gratitude that none of them have ever before seen.

Because it doesn't feel like a show, it feels genuine. It feels like she

loves them. And none of them know quite what to do in the face of love from a woman who is so rarely able to show it. In the past, whenever she has, they didn't trust it. But today each of them is surprised to find this expression of love feels genuine.

None of them know what to say.

twenty-four

I don't understand," Lizzy says a few minutes later. "So they have a name but nothing else, no idea what's causing it? This small fiber . . . what is it again?"

"Small fiber neuropathy," says Nell, looking at her mother, who nods. "And they don't know what's causing it, whether it's an indicator of something bigger going on."

"What kind of bigger?" asks Meredith, fearfully.

"Could be thyroid, diabetes, celiac disease . . ." Lizzy is reading from her phone, having Googled it as soon as Nell repeated more clearly the words her mother had spoken. "Could be idiopathic, which I think means they don't know. Oh, God." She looks up at her mother. "It could be something really awful like HIV."

"It's not HIV," says Nell with disdain. "I'm sure the chances of that are infinitesimal. Even if it were, the cocktail of drugs now means it's entirely manageable." She turns back to their mother. "So what tests are they doing now?"

"I don't remember," says Ronni. "But I'm going for a series of them, and I want you all to stay here until we know what's going on. I haven't seen any of you properly for years, and you haven't seen each other. Until we know more about my health, I want you to stay here."

"I'm twenty minutes away," says Nell. "You don't mean actually stay in this house, because I have a farm to run, so . . ."

"Yeah. I already canceled a day of filming today, which cost me a fortune, and I can't just stay here indefinitely," Lizzy adds in a rush. "It's not that I don't want to, but, Mom, I have a really busy life and a lot of commitments."

Meredith is trying to suppress her tears, sitting next to her mother and clutching her good hand. "I'm staying," she says. "I'll stay as long as it takes."

"Right. Any excuse to get away from Derek," Lizzy says.

"And I'm sure you're rushing to get home to jobless James," Meredith bites back.

"Are you fucking kidding me?" Lizzy, who has forgotten what it is like to be spoken to like this, rises like a snake. "You have no idea what my life is like. How dare you call my husband that."

Meredith backs down immediately. "I'm sorry. I didn't mean that. I really am sorry. I know he's the mom figure while you work."

Lizzy glares at her.

"Please," says Ronni quietly. "Girls. Please don't. Not today."

The two of them actually look abashed. Lizzy settles down, albeit with a final glare at Meredith.

"I do want you to stay here until these test results come back." Ronni looks at each of them, seeing that Lizzy sees no reason to stay. "There is a small chance it might be something serious."

"Serious like what?"

Ronni thinks about whether to throw ALS in the ring, prepare them for the news she isn't yet ready to impart, but it's too early. "They don't

know yet. And there is another reason why I want you here. There is a filmmaker who is planning a documentary about my life, and he'll be around to get some footage. I want him to be able to speak to each of you."

Nell stares at her mother, anger rising. What if this is all just a ruse to get them back to take part in some film? What if she's not sick at all? She looks at her mother, her limp hand, her dropping foot, and swallows. Her mother is sick. There's no doubt about that. "Speak to him about what?" she asks.

"Your childhood, probably. Memories."

Nell laughs. "I don't have any memories. I barely remember anything about my childhood."

"Me either," says Meredith. "I'd be hopeless. Also, there's no way I want to be on camera."

"Why?" says Lizzy, and Meredith glares at her. She knows Lizzy knows why. Because the camera adds . . . she can never remember if it's ten pounds or ten percent of your body weight. Either way, she has spent her entire life avoiding being on camera.

"You're really photogenic," Lizzy says, surprising her. "I have wonderful pictures of you. You shouldn't worry about being on camera. You always look gorgeous in pictures."

Meredith is so shocked, she can't think of anything to say.

"Meanwhile, I don't mind speaking on camera," Lizzy adds, turning to Ronni. "But I really don't know how long I can stay. Do you have a time frame in mind?"

"They should have some results back in a week," Ronni lies. "And the rest in two. I understand that two may be too much to ask, but I would like to ask the three of you to stay for a week."

"Here?" says Lizzy, and Ronni smiles. She realizes the very fact that she is asking where tells her mother she will stay.

"I would love that, but in the area is fine. I know you girls like your space."

"You could stay at the farm as well," says Nell, clearly reluctantly. "River's coming next week with his girlfriend, and the girlfriend's mother, but I can find more space this week. If I have to."

Lizzy laughs. "Nell, you always have space. You live by yourself in an old farmhouse with, what, five bedrooms? Six? River could have brought his whole fraternity and there would still be room."

"First of all, he's in grad school now, and River was never in a fraternity."

"Of course he wasn't in a fraternity," Lizzy says. "This is River we're talking about. Did his old school even *have* fraternities? That's not my point. My point is that you rattle around in a big old farmhouse by yourself, so don't pretend you don't have room."

"Don't start," says Ronni with a sigh, before looking at all of her children, one by one. I created them, she thinks. I grew them inside my stomach, and yet they are all so different, so unlike me. She recognizes that Lizzy perhaps is the most similar; she is her baby, her sparky, driven, gorgeous girl who needs to be seen in just the way Ronni herself always has. But when she looks at all three women here all together, she almost wonders where they came from.

Nell is so strong and self-sufficient, so terrified of appearing vulnerable, of letting down her guard. Who is so alone because of those fears.

And sweet Meredith. Who would be so pretty if only she lost some weight. Who is getting married to a handsome but awful man because she doesn't think she can do any better.

None of them know that she is dying. None of them will until the last possible minute because Ronni needs them to focus on getting to know each other again. For the first time in her life, there is something that's more important to her than her own drama, her own needs. Dying has brought everything into focus. It's no longer all about her anymore, because in a very short time, there will no longer be a her.

Perhaps more than anything, she has come to know a new emotion these past few months, which is fear. And in allowing herself to accept, and feel, that fear, she has also come to recognize how lonely she is. The only people she wants around her are her children, the very people she was never interested in when they were young. It's not too late, she thinks. Surely it's not too late.

A smile plays on her lips as she realizes how new this kind of thinking is for her. This may be the first truly selfless act she has ever performed.

She knows how this particular production will end, but she needs unity among her daughters to get there. Ronni is determined to go out her way: surrounded by her girls, who will assist her.

Probably with pills. She can't unscrew the caps on her pain pills anymore. Lily has been doing it, but Ronni has only pretended to take them, palming them in her hand as she swigs water and makes a show of swallowing them. Good God. She's a Tony Award–winning actress; this is the easiest thing in the world. She is collecting them in a tin at the back of the drawer of her nightstand, claiming great pain and renewing her prescription of oxycodone every month. The spasms and twitching, the terrible cramps are getting worse, but she would rather save the pills for the final hurrah, for when she will really need them. In the meantime, she goes through the topical lidocaine, tube after tube after tube.

There are people who can help her, and she hasn't yet decided whether or not to ask. She would rather just have her family around. And the filmmaker. But she has found a right-to-die advocate who travels the country helping people "cross to the other side." She has been e-mailing him for some weeks, and although he is keen to meet her, to help her figure it out, she isn't sure she needs him. She has her growing stash of pills. But it was a relief to be able to share her feelings

with someone who understands, and the right-to-die advocate did seem to understand. She wrote to him last night:

> I don't want to disappear. I want to be remembered exactly as I am right now, sitting here today, so this has to be sooner rather than later. I have three daughters, and I plan to tell them imminently, just as soon as I can be certain they will lean on each other, find a family in each other, a support and the unconditional love that, much to my shame, I wasn't able to give them. I have no idea what they will think about my decision to end my life on my own terms. We are not close, which I have always accepted, but now that my life is unequivocally and presently finite, I find that I wish it were different. I have been scared, but mostly numb, although as I write this to you I'm aware that I feel stronger. I am hopeful that I will gently and quietly expire, having put my affairs in order and said my good-byes.

He wrote back, as he always did, expressing understanding and support. Now she looks again at her daughters and wonders if she will find the same when she decides to tell them. Meredith will understand, she thinks. But not Lizzy. And she isn't sure about Nell.

"Tell me about your lives," she says now, turning to Lizzy. "Lizzy, how is the new house? Is Connor loving his new room? Nell, would you mind lifting my leg onto the ottoman? Oh, girls, it is so nice to have you home."

twenty-five

I need a fucking drink." Lizzy sinks her head into her hands.

"There's white wine in the fridge," Nell offers.

Meredith walks into the kitchen.

"What's going on?" Lizzy asks, looking up at her.

"She says she's just tired. I sat with her until she fell asleep."

"That's really nice of you," says Lizzy, and Meredith flushes with pleasure. Usually Lizzy accuses her of sucking up. "Does she still have three thousand skanky old white pillows on her bed?"

Nell shakes her head. "Lizzy, don't be cruel. She's sick. There's definitely something very wrong. The very fact that we're all home and she managed about an hour before claiming a dizzy spell and having to lie down tells us this isn't just for show. I don't think this is one of her usual plays for attention. If it had been, she would have stayed in the living room and had all of us run around getting her things. She went upstairs to bed. Alone."

"She isn't alone," mutters Lizzy. "She has three thousand skanky pillows to keep her company."

"They're not skanky anymore," says Meredith. "The three thousand pillows have been bleached by Lily so they are now sparkling white."

"Does she still have four million dusty old tchotchkes next to the three thousand sparkling pillows?" Lizzy doesn't miss a beat, and the other two laugh, all of them picturing their mother's nightstands, toppling over with pillboxes, and not the medicinal kind but the English, Victorian, porcelain decorative kind, as well as with papers, vases, teacups and saucers, figurines, books, scripts.

"She now has *five* million," says Meredith, laughing in spite of herself.

"Seriously, though, can we have a drink? Not wine here, but can we go somewhere?" Lizzy is now uncharacteristically serious. "I need to just go somewhere other than my childhood home and have a few martinis."

"A few?" says Meredith. "Didn't Dad always say martinis are like a woman's breasts . . ."

Lizzy laughs. "Yeah, but he was wrong. Three isn't too many. It isn't nearly enough when you're back in your childhood home with your very estranged"—she shoots a dark look at Nell—"sisters and your narcissistic mother, who for the first time isn't playing at being sick for attention, but actually seems to be sick."

The others are quiet, because they know this is true. All those claims of headaches (which were never headaches but *migraines*, despite no aura, no throwing up), backaches (which were always surely a slipped disc), Epstein-Barr virus or Lyme disease, and broken ankles that were only a strain, all those years of lying on sofas, they were just demands for attention. Now that she is visibly not herself, possibly

seriously ill, Ronni is muted and quiet. Not the mother they all know at all.

"We could go to the beach," says Nell. "Take the beach chairs from the garage and go down to Compo."

Lizzy considers it for a moment. "I would love to go to the beach, but right now I would prefer to be in a bar, with an excellent bartender making me very stiff drinks. I'm sorry," she says, seeing Nell's face, which is aghast at the thought of being in a noisy bar. "I know it's not your thing, but I need people and noise. It's my comfort zone. I promise that tomorrow we can do whatever you want to do."

"That means you're going to be sitting at my kitchen table at the farm," Nell says. "I'm a total hermit."

"Perfect." Lizzy rests her chin on her hand with a smile. "I finally get to stay at the farm."

"You're going to stay at the farm?" Nell is shocked.

"You did offer. I'll even help you make the space for me." Lizzy flashes a grin. "In one of your numerous empty bedrooms. Where shall we go for a drink?"

"Black Duck?" says Nell. "Dunville's?"

"Too old-school," says Lizzy. "I want to see what's new in town. Let me Yelp." Seconds later she looks up. "We're going to Bartaco. Nell? You're the oldest so you can be designated driver. Let's go."

"Oh, my God," Lizzy keeps exclaiming as they drive to the bar, passing through the town. "Remember when that was a movie theater? What happened to Max's? It's gone? No! That's awful! Christ, what's going on with the Y? It's going to be stores and condos? That's so *weird*. Oh, my God, come on, just drive me down Main Street once. No? Tomorrow, then. What's that? Vespa? Cool looking. Has anyone been? We

should try it. The Inn at National Hall *closed*? But that was my favorite hotel. Urgh. I hate change."

They park the truck and thread their way through the buildings to Bartaco, a few people already sitting on the sofas outside.

"It's nice and quiet here," says Nell, pausing at an empty group of seats. "And it's a lovely view of the river. Shall we stay here?"

"Absolutely not," Lizzy says as she keeps marching to the door. "I need music and a bar. Come on. Follow me." She doesn't see Meredith and Nell exchange a look, nor Meredith roll her eyes. She also doesn't hear Nell whisper to Meredith, "It's one night," with a small shrug.

"We're heading to the bar," Lizzy tells the hostess, whose mouth hangs open as she recognizes who has just walked in; the woman nods in excitement and rushes off to whisper to a coworker that Lizzy Sunshine is in the bar.

Lizzy pauses as she looks around, at the woven willow lamps hanging from the ceiling, the huge framed vintage photographs on the walls, the whitewashed wood booths, and the huge, busy, buzzing bar in the middle. "Love this place," she says. "Bartender better make a mean martini." She heads over and sits on a stool, as her sisters sit on either side. She may be the youngest, but her personality made her the star long before she was a star.

The bartender walks over and does a mock bow. "Ms. Sunshine," he says, a twinkle in his eye. "What an honor to have you here."

"Thanks," she says. "I'm Lizzy. These are my sisters, Nell and Meredith. What are your specialties?"

"I make a great Red Sonja."

"Great. We'll have two of those, whatever the hell they are, and one dirty martini, on the rocks."

"I'm actually fine with a Diet Coke," says Meredith.

"Meri, no. This is the first night of what is probably going to be a very long two weeks. I have no idea whether I can even get out of my

commitments for two weeks, but either way, however long I stay, it's going to feel longer, and we all need some proper sustenance. It's one drink." She turns then and really looks at her sister. "You shouldn't be drinking Diet Coke anyway. Not only is it poison, it helps people gain weight. You're better off with water if it must be nonalcoholic, but unless you're sober and can't risk falling off the wagon, tonight you are going to be joining me in a drink."

"In that case I'll have a Red Sonja," Meredith says, her shoulders slumped in resignation.

"I didn't know you liked dirty martinis," Nell says to Lizzy.

"Dad's legacy."

"Have you heard from him?" Lizzy asks as Nell shakes her head, then Meredith.

"No. I haven't spoken to him in years."

"Me neither," says Nell.

"God, what a fucking shame that he managed to be such a cliché. Married a bitch who refused to allow him to have a relationship with his children from his first marriage, and then he fucks off to California never to be heard from again." She sighs. "Ah, well. Every cloud has a silver lining." She grimaces. "At least we never have to see Arianna the Grotesque again."

"Come on, Lizzy. She is our half sister."

"Yeah. Not going to claim that one, I'm afraid."

They all picture Arianna, who was a horribly spoiled, indulged child, and who, despite being twenty-one, continues to throw a tantrum when she doesn't get her way and continues to be supported entirely by her parents. It doesn't help that Selena, who appeared quite beautiful when their father met her, was beautiful only thanks to copious amounts of plastic surgery. Arianna has unfortunately inherited not only her mother's horrible personality but her somewhat unfortunate natural looks—a weak chin, bulging eyes, a large beaky nose.

The nose has been slimmed and bobbed to a nose just like her mother's, but no amount of plastic surgery can change the fact that she is ugly inside and out.

"I did ask him if he would walk me down the aisle," says Meredith. "Unsurprisingly he had a prior commitment."

Lizzy snorts. "Was he putting the garden hose away?"

"Too busy making money to buy Arianna a Ferrari?" says Nell in disgust.

"Here's to fatherless daughters." Lizzy raises the glass that has just been placed in front of her.

"And motherless daughters," says Nell.

"Fuck! Don't say that!" Lizzy says. "I know she hasn't exactly been the greatest of mothers, but still. I don't want her to die. Here's to long, healthy lives." And they all chink glasses and drink.

"I can't believe how much this town has changed." Lizzy looks around. "It's so weird being back."

"How is it you don't come back more? You're an hour away," says Meredith. "It's weirder for me, being in London."

"I'm crazy busy," says Lizzy, as two waiters appear, bearing trays of food.

"We didn't order anything," says Meredith.

"These are compliments of the chef," say the waiter. "He has made you a selection of tacos—Baja fish, portobello mushroom, and sesame rib eye—and some of our guacamole. Please, enjoy."

"This is free?" Meredith says when they have gone.

"Perks of the job." Lizzy shrugs, taking a corn chip and scooping a large amount of guacamole.

"Nice work if you can get it," says Meredith.

"Speaking of work," says Lizzy, "how's your job?"

"It's fine."

"How's London?"

"Good."

"How's Derek?"

Meredith fixes her a level stare. "I knew it would come to that."

"Jesus, Meri. Seriously. Don't be so oversensitive. He's the man you're going to marry. Of course I'm going to ask how he is."

"I just feel that you're always going to follow it up with an eye roll or some kind of snide comment about how awful he is."

Lizzy takes another deep swig of her drink. "Meri, I love you. I know we're not close, but you two are the only big sisters I have. If Nell and I have ever made fun of Derek . . ."

"I have never made fun of Derek," Nell says.

"Okay, me, then. But if we've ever said anything that felt like it was negative, it's only because we want you to be happy, and I just wasn't sure that Derek was the real love of your life."

"He is the love of my life," Meredith says, although even as she says it, she is wondering if that's true. No, she admits, she *knows* it's not true. But he's the man who has chosen her, she thinks. And he will make a very good husband. Everyone says so.

"Great," says Lizzy. "Speaking as an old married woman, albeit the youngest here, you need to be crazily in love and think he's fantastic when you get married. Because God knows married life is hard enough without you looking at him every day and wondering why the fuck you married him in the first place." She calls the bartender over and orders another round, even though hers is the only empty glass. She doesn't see Meredith and Nell exchange worried glances.

"How's James?" Meredith ventures, and Lizzy shakes her head with a deep sigh.

"Don't even ask," she says. "I need at least two more drinks before I venture down that particular road. Just take it from me, marriage is

hard enough when you go into it thinking he's the greatest thing that ever happened to you. God only knows what it would be like if you went into it because you thought it was the best you could get."

Meredith says nothing. She won't think about that now. "How about you, Nell?" she says, to change the subject. "How's the farm?"

"Same as always." Nell shrugs.

"Did you ever get anyone to help you with the financial stuff? I'm really sorry I . . ." She trails off, not wanting to remind anyone of the difficult conversation they once had. "I'm happy to look at anything while I'm here."

Nell looks into her glass thoughtfully. The truth is, she buries her head in the sand when it comes to finances. She inherited the farm and realized very quickly she had to make big changes to make it a viable concern. She and her staff supply many of the local restaurants, and some in New York and New Jersey. They have the coffee shop, which has morphed and grown into more of a restaurant. They have the petting zoo and now ask for voluntary donations from parents bringing their young children there. So she has made innovations. But always, always, they could do with just a little bit more. And she's never had anyone she could talk to about it.

The good news is there is no mortgage. The bad news is that the workers have to be paid. Every few months it seems like a struggle. Every time, Nell is not entirely sure why.

Nell believes that Meredith wouldn't be able to tell her anything other than what she already knows, that they are struggling, that there is no safety net, that her ability to pay her workers depends on the weather, the yield, and a huge amount of luck. She doesn't need anyone to tell her that no matter how hard she works—and she really doesn't know how she can work much harder than she is right now—she can't see a way to make any more changes.

"Thanks," she says to Meredith. "I appreciate your offer."

Lizzy's phone buzzes, and she quickly pulls it out of her pocket and looks at the screen, excusing herself as she walks off.

"Hey, you," her sisters hear her say, her voice suddenly low and sultry. "I was wondering when I'd hear from you." She disappears outside to take the call, leaving Nell and Meredith to polish off the guacamole.

"I didn't realize how hungry I was," says Meredith. "I think it might be tiredness and jet lag. I always get more hungry when I'm tired."

"So it's only another, what, three months until the wedding? How are you feeling?"

"I'm excited," says Meredith, her voice flat. "It's just there's so much to do."

"I can imagine."

"What about you? Any prospective men in your life?" Meredith asks, again to change the subject. "Any hot young farmers making your heart beat faster?"

"Ha!" Nell smiles. "Hardly."

"Now that River is launched, you can't claim you're putting all your energies into motherhood. You need to get out there and start dating."

"Who says I haven't been dating?"

"Really? Good for you! Anyone nice?"

Nell shrugs. "I was seeing this guy, but . . . I don't know. The chemistry wasn't there."

Meredith stares into her glass for a moment. "Do you think chemistry is all that important? I totally get it when you're younger, but I think chemistry just gets you into trouble. There's a large part of me that thinks it's better to have stability, and kindness, and friendship. Those are the things that make a relationship last, I think. Not chemistry."

Nell watches her sister, who does not look at her when she says that. "So . . . what do you do about sex?"

"Close my eyes and think of England?" Meredith laughs, as if she is joking, but she and Nell both know she isn't.

"I don't know. Maybe you're right," Nell replies, trying to match Meredith's honesty. "I tried closing my eyes and thinking of America, but it didn't work for me. I wanted it to—he's a great guy—but my life is really full, and really good. There would need to be something extra, something big, in order for me to open up and let someone into my life. And this guy wasn't it."

"Yeah. I know what you mean," says Meredith, thinking that her life is really small, and kind of dull, and maybe she set her sights too low. Maybe the problem isn't Derek, but rather that she isn't leading the life she should be leading. Too late now, she thinks. She's thirty-eight. Lucky that anyone wants to marry her, let alone a partner in a CPA firm, someone who can love her and support her, and prevent her from going into middle age all by herself. She shudders with what feels like horror at the prospect of her life stretching out ahead of her with no one by her side. At least, that's what she tells herself is making her shudder.

"Do you know what I mean?"

"I do. I just don't think sex is that important."

"Maybe you're right," says Nell, who also thinks sex is not that important, but nor are relationships, and life on her own is perfectly fine.

Lizzy walks back in and climbs on the stool.

"How's James?" says Meredith.

"What?"

"How is he? Wasn't that him?"

Lizzy stares at her for a second. "Oh! No! That was my business partner, Sean. We just had to iron out some stuff about the pop-up supper club on Sunday. Obviously I won't be there, so he's in charge."

"Wow. You have a very . . . intimate . . . relationship."

"It's just what happens when you work together closely," says Lizzy. But no one misses that her face has flushed a bright scarlet. "Another round?" she says, changing the subject as she waits for the color to fade.

"So what's going on with your partner?" asks Nell later that night, as she and Lizzy pull onto the Merritt Parkway on their way back to the farm. They have dropped Meredith at their mother's, but have promised to return to the house the next day for lunch.

"What do you mean?"

"'Hey, you,'" Nell says, doing a credible imitation of Lizzy's sexy voice when she picked up the call from Sean. "That kind of greeting means there's something going on."

"Because you're the expert in relationships?" Lizzy lets out a bark of laughter.

"C'mon, Lizzy. I'm concerned."

"Don't be. I know what I'm doing."

"You have a husband who loves you and a small child who loves his parents and wants them to be together. I know this because I know what it's like when parents divorce." She turns her head to look at Lizzy in the darkness.

"Well, I certainly know what that's like too," she snaps. But then she turns to look out the window. "I don't think James loves me anymore," Lizzy says quietly. "I don't think I love him. Mostly when I look at him I think that I hate him."

"Jesus, Lizzy. That's awful. What about Connor?"

"Why do you think we're still together? That's exactly it. What about Connor? I don't want to do to him what was done to us."

"You mean, have an affair, then have your husband find out about it and leave you, then basically check out of mothering because you're too focused on your career to be there for your kid—or kids?"

"Fuck. You don't have to put it like that."

"I was talking about Mom."

"Oh." There is a long silence. "Jesus." Lizzy lets out a long sigh. "I have no idea what I'm going to do."

"Maybe it starts with ending the affair."

"I've done that. Multiple times."

"You have to end it for good. It puts too much in jeopardy. Not just your marriage and your relationship with your child, but your business. He's your partner. I don't see any version of this that's good for you. You cannot focus on what you need to focus on when you're romantically linked."

"You're right. You're right. I know you're right. It's just so hard."

"No, it's not. It's just sex. It's not that hard at all."

They are silent as they turn off the Merritt and go along Sport Hill Road, then turn, turn again, and again, until they reach an old wooden gate. Lizzy jumps out to open it and then pull it shut behind the truck. She pauses before climbing in to smell the sweet country air.

"I haven't been here since I was a teenager," she says, rolling down the window so she can keep smelling the air. "I had forgotten how lovely it is. Twenty minutes away from Mom's house, but it feels like it's the middle of nowhere."

"It is the middle of nowhere." Nell slows down as she steers the truck around the large pothole caused by a delivery truck the week before. "That's why I love it."

"It looks completely different." Lizzy squints out the window, making out the new barn and outbuildings, noting that it is manicured in a way it wasn't back then. They pull into a cobblestone courtyard, with large square wooden planters filled with hydrangea trees.

"This is gorgeous," Lizzy says, stepping out of the truck and stretching. "We use planters just like that for our supper clubs."

"Yeah? Nice. Can you manage your bag? I'm going to put you in the room next to mine, if that's okay."

"I can manage." Lizzy pulls her bag out, well used to hauling heavy things around. "God, this is lovely," she says, walking up the steps to the porch of the farmhouse. "If I lived here I'd never leave."

"I never do," says Nell, pushing open the front door.

twenty-six

There is some kind of clattering in the kitchen, which starts off as clattering in her dream, and it's only as Nell starts to swim up into consciousness that she realizes it is actually in her house. She has overslept. Hugely. It is 7:23 a.m., and there is so much she already hasn't done, her heart starts palpitating. She never sleeps this late! And what is all that noise coming from downstairs?

Lizzy, she thinks, remembering that she brought her sister home last night. Lizzy must be looking for coffee. Shit. Why has she overslept? Pulling on yesterday's jeans and grabbing a clean T-shirt from the closet, she rushes downstairs and into the kitchen, expecting to see Lizzy.

Except it isn't Lizzy in her kitchen, but a woman she doesn't recognize, in denim cutoffs and a white T-shirt, with an apron tied around her waist. She is pouring milk from a measuring cup into a white bowl.

Who on earth is this? Nell's first thought is that it must be an intruder, but what kind of an intruder breaks in, ties a floral apron

around her waist, and proceeds to whip up a batch of muffins? Pancakes? Scones? Whatever it is, it looks like she knows what she's doing.

The woman must be around her own age, Nell thinks, watching her. She's so focused on what she's doing she apparently doesn't realize the owner of the house is now standing in the doorway. She has strawberry blond hair, caught up in a clip, and unusually wide-set eyes. She frowns as she pours, biting her lower lip in concentration, before taking the milk back to the fridge and opening cabinets, looking for, Nell presumes, a pan.

"A skillet? They're in the cabinet next to the stove," Nell says eventually. "Or muffin pans? If that's what you need they're in that thin space on the other side."

The woman looks up at Nell, startled, then smiles. Nell is instantly disarmed by her smile. No, it's more than that. She's kind of mesmerized by the radiance of the woman's smile.

"You must be Nell," she says, putting down the bowl and wiping her hands on her apron.

"I am, but I have absolutely no idea who you are." Nell walks into the kitchen, taking a large ceramic coffee cup from the shelf as she turns to the woman.

"Oh no!" The woman's hand flies to her chest as she laughs. "You didn't know we were coming early?"

"We?"

"The kids. River said he'd call you."

Nell puts down the coffee cup, her face lighting up. "River's here?"

"They're asleep upstairs." She shakes her head. "I told him to call you and let you know we were coming early. He wanted to surprise you, but I said it wasn't a good idea. If I'd known he hadn't told you, I would never have started baking in your kitchen."

"You're Daisy's mom!" Nell finally understands.

"Greta Whitstable." She extends a hand for Nell to shake. Greta's

eyes are too wide apart, her cheekbones too rounded, and her chin too pointed, but put together there is something compelling about her. She is not beautiful, but arresting, with her strawberry blond hair pulled back, a few tendrils around her face. It is an interesting face. Nell stares, trying to place her. There is something familiar about her, but she can't figure out what.

"Have we . . . met before?" she says finally.

"I doubt it," Greta says. "Unless you've made your way to St. Louis?" She turns to grab the coffeepot. "Why don't you sit down and I'll make you some breakfast. I'm just putting these muffins in. They'll be ready in a few, now that I know where the muffin pans are." She laughs. "Sit. How do you take your coffee?"

"Black. Nothing in it."

"You're easy," says Greta Whitstable with a smile, as Nell unexpectedly finds herself flushing.

She is suddenly very aware of sitting at her own kitchen table, in front of a stranger, with bedhead hair and unbrushed teeth. She doesn't mind treating her sister to terrible hair and morning breath, but she's suddenly uncomfortable appearing this way in front of this woman. Her chores are forgotten. "I'm just going upstairs for a couple of minutes," she says, clearing her throat.

Greta just smiles and nods, seeming completely at home in Nell's kitchen, as if she has been there many times before.

"I'll be right back," says Nell, moving toward the door.

Greta Whitstable, she thinks, walking up the stairs. What an interesting name. What an interesting woman. Alone in her bathroom, brushing her teeth, washing her face, and making sure there is no sleep left in her eyes, Nell whispers it to herself, just once, surprised. What is it that is so familiar about her?

"Greta Whitstable," she mouths. "What kind of a name is that?"

She smiles as she brushes her hair and pulls it back in its customary ponytail.

She pauses outside River's door, wondering whether to wake him, but decides to let him sleep before walking back down the stairs to the stranger who feels like she belongs.

"River!"

It is an hour later when River finally emerges from his bedroom, sleepily walking into the kitchen to wrap his arms around his mother.

Nell has been sitting at the kitchen table as Greta Whitstable buzzed around, baking muffins, then scones, explaining that River had told her Cheryl the caretaker was away and that anything she baked would be needed and appreciated.

She refilled Nell's coffee cup several times and brought over a muffin, then a scone, before wordlessly cutting up an orange and laying it out on a plate like a small sun and placing it in front of Nell without asking if she'd like it. Nell ate it, thinking it might have been the most delicious orange she had ever tasted.

Greta Whitstable is completely at home in this kitchen, thinks Nell, wishing she were a better cook, more of a homemaker. I wonder if I would look as good in denim cutoffs and a floral apron. Maybe I should clip my hair up like that, with tendrils falling around my face instead of pulling it back into such a severe ponytail all the time.

Greta Whitstable catches Nell staring at her and blows a strand of hair out of her eyes, then laughs. Nell is so charmed by the attention of Greta Whitstable, so distracted by this feminine energy that has blown in out of nowhere seemingly to take care of Nell (who didn't, up until an hour ago, know she needed taking care of), that she has completely forgotten about her mother, and her sisters, and why she

slept right through her alarm and was only woken up by the clattering of Greta Whitstable downstairs.

"Well, good morning!" Lizzy wanders in, her eyes half closed, yawning and stretching. "Nephew!" She spies River at the table and leaps over, snaking her arms around him and squeezing as he laughs.

"Hello," she says, turning to Greta. "I'm Lizzy. Errant younger sister. Are you the chef?"

Greta laughs. "Hardly. I'm the mother of the girlfriend. Daisy, that is. River's girlfriend. I'm Greta." She shakes Lizzy's hand.

"And you made all these?" Lizzy looks at the trays of muffins and scones.

"She made far more. The rest have already been sent over to the coffee shop," Nell explains.

Lizzy turns to look at Nell, noting how smiley she is this morning, an unfamiliar sparkle in her eye.

"May I?" She picks up a muffin, feeling how light it is, noting the poppy seeds evenly sprinkled throughout, then tearing off a piece and holding it in her mouth before chewing slowly. Her mouth fills with an intense lemon flavor. "Jesus, these are good." She sighs. "These are actually insanely good."

"Thank you." Greta pours her some coffee and hands it over. "My mother's recipe."

"What are the scones? They're an interesting color."

"Coffee chocolate chip."

Nell raises an eyebrow. "Mom's recipe too?"

Greta smiles. "This one is mine. Here." She breaks one in pieces and hands them around the table.

"I told you Daisy's mom is an amazing baker," River says, his mouth full of scone as Lizzy chews thoughtfully.

"I didn't remember," says Nell.

"Do you cook professionally?" Lizzy turns her focus to Greta, who shakes her head. "*Would* you cook professionally?"

"I don't think so. I love doing it for fun, but there are too many other things I have going on."

"I would love you to bake some of these for one of my supper clubs. You could be the guest baker."

Greta frowns. "Supper club? What is that?"

Lizzy smiles. Since her television show, it feels like everyone knows who she is. Even when they don't mention anything, even if they pretend she is a stranger, at a certain point in the conversation they reveal their awareness of her. Sometimes it's with a throwaway comment, but they always know. Usually.

"Do you watch the show?" River grins.

"I don't watch television really," says Greta. "What show?"

"My aunt has a big food show. *The Supper Club*. And she hosts supper clubs, like, pop-up restaurants on rooftops in New York that people pay a fortune to come to."

"You're a chef?"

Lizzy bows her head in false modesty. "I am."

Greta blushes slightly. "I didn't know. I'm so sorry."

"Don't be," Lizzy says, surprisingly delighted at this unexpected anonymity. "Be happy. I'm not sure I've ever tasted a scone quite like this."

"It's all in the ingredients," Greta says modestly. "Nothing to do with me."

"You and I both know that's not true. If you won't bake for me, you know I'm going to have to try and figure out this recipe."

"Be my guest," says Greta. "But I'll give it to you. I'm not precious."

"I like this woman," Lizzy says, turning to River and grinning, then sitting down and reaching for another scone. "I approve."

Nell frowns. What does Lizzy mean?

The doorbell rings as they all jump. Who on earth is ringing the doorbell so early in the morning? Nell goes to the back door and sticks her head out. "In here," she calls. Turning to the others, she says, "It's Meredith."

"What's she doing here?" asks Lizzy, as Meredith walks in with a sigh, lighting up temporarily when she sees River and is introduced to Greta.

"Bad night?" asks Lizzy, once Meredith is settled with a cup of coffee.

"The night was fine, but the veil is on today. I had to get out of there."

"Oh, God," groans Nell, suppressing a small smile. "I'd forgotten about the veil. I see her so rarely she's usually on her best behavior. The veil!" She buries her head in her hands for a second. "We're supposed to be going there for lunch. I can't deal with her when the veil is on."

Greta leans forward. "I hope this isn't presumptuous, but what does that mean, the veil is on?"

"Our mother can be enormously fun and charming and sweet," says Lizzy.

"And when the veil is on, it is as if she is possessed by the devil," says Meredith. "She is angry and vicious and punitive."

"When we were children we used to be able to tell, as soon as she came into the room, what kind of mood she was in," Nell explains. "Her eyes would be different when she was in one of the moods. It was as if there was a veil covering them, and if the veil was on, we would get out of the way."

"When we were old enough," Meredith clarifies. "There were plenty of times as children when we didn't have a choice but to take it."

"God, she could be awful," says Lizzy. "Remember when she used

to scream at you that you were fat and would never have a boyfriend?" She turns to Nell. "And she used to say you looked like a lesbian."

"Thanks, Lizzy," says Nell, coolly. "As I recall, you were the only one who escaped it."

"Baby of the family," says Lizzy. "What can I do? I didn't escape it entirely, but she could never think of suitable insults because I'm perfect."

They all laugh and shake their heads.

"That doesn't sound like a lot of fun," says Greta. "How could any of you have felt safe?"

Meredith smiles. "We didn't. Hence my moving to London to get away. God, I hope it passes."

"I'll tell you this much," Nell says, getting up to clear the plates, "I'm not going over there for lunch if she's like that."

"Me neither," says Meredith. "I may move my stuff in here. I can't believe I haven't even been here twenty-four hours and she's like this already. It makes me want to get straight back on a plane and go back to London. I told Lily I'd check in later."

"It's so typical." Nell sighs. "Look at how lovely it was just yesterday, how happy she seemed to have us all back together again at home. And then she has to sabotage it. She always has to sabotage it."

Nell stands at the sink as Lizzy brings over the rest of the plates and then rubs her back gently. Nell startles, unused to being touched unexpectedly, unused to affection from . . . anyone. She abruptly excuses herself for the bathroom and quickly leaves, and Lizzy quietly washes up.

Nell's phone buzzes as she stands in the bathroom looking at herself in the mirror, unsettled, and unsure why. It is her mother, but she ignores the call. A text comes in, then another.

Urgent, says the third text. Call. Nell sinks onto the edge of the bath and makes the call, promising herself she will hang up at the slightest provocation.

"What is it, Mom?"

"I need to see you," says her mom. "Now."

"Mom, I have stuff to do on the farm. I don't know that I can make it this morning."

"It's an emergency," says her mother imperiously. "Don't tell your sisters. Be at my house in half an hour."

Nell goes back into the kitchen. "I have been summoned," she says drily. "And told not to tell you."

"You're going?" Lizzy is impressed.

"She says it's an emergency. Lily isn't picking up the phone. Let me just go and get it over with. If she's a bitch, I'll leave."

"Want me to come with you, Mom?" River pushes his chair back.

"No, sweetie. If you can open up the farm and make sure everyone has what they need, that would be great."

"I'll help," says Greta.

"Me too," says Lizzy.

"Me three," volunteers Meredith, who has no idea what to do on a farm.

twenty-seven

Nell parks the truck and lets herself into Ronni's house, bracing herself for her mother's anger. But Lily, in the kitchen, bestows a beaming smile on Nell as she walks in.

"Ma'am is not so happy today," she says calmly.

Nell apologizes for her mother. She has watched her take it out on her staff for years, amazed that anyone has ever stayed with her for long. Lily has been here for years, her smiling, sunny disposition a tonic for Ronni's moods. When Ronni gets vicious, Lily just laughs at her, and, oddly, Ronni usually stops. It's strangely not unlike the dynamic between Ronni and Lizzy as a little girl.

"Where is she?"

"In bed. Her legs are bothering her today," Lily says. "I'm making a hot water bottle for her to help the cramps, but they are bad. She's not really able to walk."

"What do you mean, she's not able to walk?"

Lily frowns. "It has been much worse recently. She has a cane, but she can't really walk much. Her legs don't work."

"You don't think she just wants you running after her?"

"No. This is different. She is very tired and breathing is sometimes hard for her."

"Have you called the doctor?"

"She saw him last week. She says there's nothing they can do."

"Well, that's just my mother being overly dramatic. I can speak to him, if that makes it easier. There's always something they can do. Here. Give me the hot water bottle. I'll take it up to her."

Nell walks up the stairs clutching the cashmere hot water bottle to her chest, smiling at the fact that it is a hot water bottle with a cashmere cover. Only my mother, she thinks.

She knocks on the door and pushes it open to find her mother lying in bed, no wig, no makeup, her hair thin and wispy, her skin pale, almost gray. Her eyes are closed and she is breathing raspily.

"Mom?" Nell whispers, shocked at how different her mother looks since yesterday. Without the effort to look normal, Ronni looks shockingly old and frail. Unwell.

For the first time, Nell understands that this is truly not yet another of their mother's claims for attention. Something is clearly very wrong.

Ronni opens her eyes, seemingly discombobulated for a few seconds. "Nell," she says eventually, regaining her composure. "Can you help me sit up?"

Nell leans her mother forward gently and reaches behind and fluffs the pillows, before helping her mother lean back. She tries not to think of how unready she is to be nursing her mother, for this does feel like that is what she is doing.

Ronni reaches over with her good hand and clasps Nell's. "Sit," she

says, and Nell reluctantly perches on the bed, unused to affection from anyone, let alone her mother. She clasps her mother's hand awkwardly, wondering how quickly she can extract her own at the same time that she is relieved that the veil is apparently gone.

"What happened with Meredith?" she asks.

"I woke up on the wrong side of the bed," says her mother, wryly.

"I think she might want to stay with me instead . . ." says Nell. "She can't deal with you when you're . . . when you've woken up on the wrong side of the bed."

"I know. She never could. Which always made it worse. She would get so upset it always made me angrier. You just shut down."

Nell shrugs, impassively, not really surprised to learn that their mother is fully aware of their various coping strategies.

The sight of her expressionless face, such a perfect example of one of the ways Nell used to escape, makes Ronni smile. "And Lizzy didn't give a shit."

"About anyone or anything."

"No, that's not quite right." She meets Nell's gaze. "I understand Lizzy because . . . she's the most like me."

Nell's not sure she's ready for this talk. She's certainly not used to heart-to-hearts with her mother. She changes the subject. "So what's the emergency, Mom? I have so much to do, I can't stay."

"First you have to promise not to tell your sisters."

"Fine."

"You don't mean that. Swear on . . . River's life."

"No. I won't do that. I can only promise. I don't break promises. You know that about me."

Ronni nods. "This small fiber neuropathy. I do know what else is going on."

"You do? Why didn't you tell us?"

"Because I'm not ready for everyone to know. I need your sisters to figure things out with each other first. I need you all to find each other again."

"What are you talking about? What's going on?"

Ronni sighs. "I've got amyotrophic lateral sclerosis."

Nell remembers how her mother has always loved Latin names, the longer and more complicated the better, particularly when it comes to describing her various ailments that are never as serious as they sound.

"ALS," her mother then adds, with no emotion whatsoever. "Also known as Lou Gehrig's disease."

That Nell understands. "What?" She just can't take it in. She shakes her head. "What are you saying?" She was prepared for histrionics, for weeping, for hushed breath and drama, not for news like this. But her mother is quiet, calm.

"I have a terminal disease. I have probably had it for years. Remember those dizzy spells that started all those years ago? When I had to keep lying down because the nausea was so bad? And my hair breaking off and the tingling in my scalp? All of it was early signs of ALS."

"But they tested you for everything and couldn't find anything."

"No. Isn't it ironic that all the tests came back normal? And yet, it isn't. It's often hard to diagnose. They found it when I started falling, and then they noticed my muscles twitching."

"So . . . when you say terminal . . ." Ronni's words are finally sinking in and Nell finds a lump in her throat. She pauses and swallows, takes a deep breath. "How long does that . . . ?"

"Most people have a life span of three to five years after diagnosis. But since mine came late, it seems I have already had more than my fair share. I am well on my way to ending up one hundred percent paralyzed, unable to breathe or eat unaided."

She pauses, and Nell feels her breath catch. If you were to ask her

if she loves her mother, she might say yes, of course. But the truth is, she has never felt love for her mother. If her mother has been anything in her life, she is more a source of annoyance or unhappiness, an obligation to be met, a duty that Nell fulfills in the most minimal of ways. And yet, here she is, forgetting that she and her mother are holding hands in an unprecedented display of affection, forgetting that five minutes ago she was desperate to get out of here as quickly as possible. Her eyes are filled with tears as she opens and closes her mouth, not knowing what to say, but knowing this is real. This is not her mother's histrionics. This is happening. Her voice is a whisper. "How long?"

Her mother levels a cool gaze at her, squeezing her hand. "I refuse to let this disease take me," she says quietly. "I refuse to become paralyzed. I refuse to become a vegetable, knowing exactly what's happening to me but being unable to do anything."

Nell stares at her.

"I am going to take my life, Nell," her mother says. "And I want you to help me. I want to go peacefully, surrounded by my family. My legs are now essentially paralyzed. I can drag myself around sometimes, but I'm losing strength in my arms, particularly the left side. I don't want the hospital visits and the doctors and the nurses and the caregivers. I have had months to think about this, and I am ready. I want you all with me, and I want to do it soon."

Nell stares at her.

"Nell? Say something. I'm telling you, because you're the one I'm closest to." She gives a sad smile. "I know. We're not actually *close*, but you are the one I see the most. You're the one I rely on. I don't know how to tell your sisters."

Finally, Nell blinks. "You managed to tell me perfectly well."

"Because you can handle it. You've always been the strong one. I'm sorry I've always been so tough on you."

Nell tries to find the words.

"I want you to be prepared for when I tell your sisters," continues her mother.

"So when are you planning on telling them? Because this isn't fair, for me to carry this burden by myself." Nell's voice comes out sounding like a child's.

"I can tell them tonight," says Ronni. "If you think I should."

"I don't know," Nell snaps. "I have no idea. I have no idea what to tell you. Jesus. When are you planning to do this?"

"I'm ready," says her mother. "I want to do it while you're all here, before it gets worse. And I want to know that you'll all look after each other after I'm gone."

Nell lets out a long sigh. "Mom? I don't know that we can do this. I don't know that we can sit here and watch you die."

"You're going to be watching me die." Ronni smiles sadly. "It's just a question of when."

twenty-eight

Nell drives home feeling numb. There are no tears, just a feeling that she is submerged underwater. The landscape passes by out the window, unfamiliar, everything blurry and strange.

How can this be happening, she thinks. How does she not tell her sisters when she sees them in a few minutes? They will see, surely, there is something wrong as soon as she walks in the door.

Nell is not close to her mother, has never been close to her mother, but Ronni *is* her mother, the only one she has ever known, and she is not ready for her to die. She is certainly not ready to assist in any way.

And yet, her mother is the vainest creature she knows. Nell understands her mother not wanting to be paralyzed, not wanting to lose control, to relinquish everything to caregivers and nurses. No. That would not be what Ronni Sunshine would ever choose for herself.

Isn't this the bravest thing of all, for her to take her own life? But she doesn't want to take her own life exactly; she wants her daughters to do it. The thought is inconceivable.

Why did she tell me, she thinks, but she already knows the answer: *Because I can handle it. Because I am the strong one.*

The house is quiet, the kitchen cleaned up and tidy, the sound of water upstairs indicating that someone is in the shower. On the counter is a note in handwriting she recognizes as Lizzy's.

Gone to Westport shopping with Meri! Text if you need anything. Obsessed with this farm!

L xxx

How does she tell them? *Does* she tell them? Does she wait for her mother to tell them tonight? She did promise, after all.

Why me? she thinks. Why this? Why now?

She goes into her little office and sits behind her desk, staring into space, her mind a blank. She is used to sitting in here and avoiding thinking about her problems. On her desk is a pile of financial papers she hasn't had the heart to look at for days. To avoid it, earlier in the week she picked up a magazine and put it on top of the papers to hide them completely. Since, she has been able to pretend she doesn't have financial challenges facing the farm. The papers have been waiting patiently for her to deal with them.

But her mother's illness cannot so easily be avoided. It is real, and it is happening now. If she pretends it's not, it will just happen anyway.

Taking a deep breath, she turns to her computer and slides the mouse to look up ALS, jumping from website to website, stopping every few minutes to scribble thoughts and questions into a notebook on her desk.

She lingers as she reads about Stephen Hawking. He has this, has had it for years. Maybe her mother could live a full life, she thinks,

looking at a picture of Stephen Hawking. No, she realizes. Her mother would never want a life like this, even if the disease might allow it.

There is a faint knock on the door as Greta pops her head in. "I hope I'm not intruding," she says, looking around as her eyes light up with pleasure. "Oh, look how lovely it is in here. What a beautiful room!"

"Come in," Nell says, closing down the screen, welcoming the distraction, unaccountably delighted it is Greta disturbing her.

She is surprised at herself. Usually she allows no one to come in here. This is the space that Nell thinks of as truly hers. Her sanctuary. She put a lot of effort into making it so. It had been a dark, oppressive, wood-paneled office in Theodora's day. When she took over, she told her mother her plan to paint the wood and Ronni gasped.

"You can't paint mahogany!" she protested, but Nell could. And did. She painted the paneling on the walls a cornflower blue and the floorboards the palest of grays, almost white. And she put a soft blue and white woven rug over the top.

She pulled out the built-ins and painted an old desk the same gray as the floor. A white ceramic vase, its sides fat and bulging, sits on one corner, stuffed with bright pink cosmos from the garden.

On one side of the room is a slip-covered sofa, white with a tiny hint of a hand-blocked Indian print in a pale coffee color, almost undetectable. Large, soft blue and white pillows are scattered along the back of the sofa.

Nell has covered the walls with framed paintings that River did in elementary school, not that you would ever know. Abstracts, she has always thought, that could cost thousands of dollars in an art gallery. Swishes of paint, spatters of ink, scribbles of pencil. They are surprisingly sophisticated, and every time she looks at them she is reminded of River's chubby hands and sweet smile, how he would pad into her room and wake her up by whispering loudly, "Mommy? Are you

awake?" And she would keep her eyes closed and smile, whispering back, "No," before grabbing him and smothering him with kisses as he giggled and squirmed.

How happy they were.

"Can I sit?" Greta sits without waiting for Nell to say yes. Nell wonders whether she makes herself this much at home wherever she goes.

"I just wanted to check in on you." Greta fixes her cool gaze on Nell, who moves to the other end of the sofa. "I know we've only just met, but I was curled up on the window seat upstairs when you came back and I saw you come in here, and you looked like you have a lot on your mind. I just wanted to see if you were okay."

Nell doesn't know what to say. "That's very perceptive of you." *I promised,* she thinks.

"It sounds like your mother is a challenging woman," Greta says.

"She is, but that wasn't the issue today. It's . . . something else. I don't think I can talk about it yet. I'm sorry. I hope you understand."

"Of course. I would hate to intrude. Can I get you anything? I thought maybe I could make lunch for everyone. I have no idea how things work here, but I noticed you have an overabundance of vegetables growing. If I'm allowed to harvest, I can make a big salad, and there are some chicken breasts in the fridge. I can make a little go a long way."

"You don't have to cook. It's incredibly kind of you to offer, but after all your work this morning, it's really not necessary. Lizzy is here, and if anyone should be cooking, it should be her."

"I feel awful that I had no idea who she is. Daisy filled me in. Do you think I offended her?"

Nell laughs. "It takes a lot more than that to offend Lizzy."

"I like her. And Meredith. You have a wonderful family. And I really would be happy to cook."

"Do you always take care of people like this?" Nell asks, feeling an inexplicable sense of gratitude, an inexplicable desire to reach out and place her hand on Greta's cheek. She has no idea why, only that sitting here, on this sofa, with this woman so close, she wants her to be closer.

Nell blinks. What on earth is happening to her? *It is the upset,* she tells herself. *I am not myself.*

"Yes." Greta smiles. "Taking care of people is what I do. Now that Daisy has left home I find myself pulling in stray ducks from all over the place."

"Is that what you think of me?" says Nell. "A stray duck?"

Greta thinks for a while. "No," she says finally. "You strike me as enormously strong and self-sufficient. A lone lion, perhaps, rather than a stray duck. Strong. But alone."

"God." Nell exhales, the first hint of a smile since she got home playing around her lips. "That sounds awful. I think I'd much rather be a stray duck."

"It was a compliment. Lioness, then. Regal. Beautiful. Powerful."

"I don't feel powerful," says Nell, thinking, *Regal? Beautiful? Am I?*

"Many of us don't recognize our best qualities, even when women as wise as me are pointing them out. River was telling me that you and your mother, your sisters, haven't ever gotten along that well. That the three of you being together in this house is unusual. So that means it also must be hard for you, having this . . . reunion. How do you feel about everyone being here? I would never have guessed that you aren't close from this morning. Maybe this will be healing for all of you, this trip?"

Healing? thinks Nell. That's what her mother said she wanted. But how could this be healing, when they are all about to discover news that will change them forever, news that will change the rest of their lives?

Nell looks at Greta, then looks away, feeling an overwhelming impulse to tell this woman everything. She promised her mother she

wouldn't tell her sisters, but Greta is someone else. And she seems gentle and wise, and like a good listener, someone who wouldn't judge.

Nell does not talk about her mother with anyone. She doesn't talk about much of anything with anyone. She has a convivial, friendly, warm relationship with everyone who works on the farm, but none of them are friends, exactly. She talks to Cheryl, the caretaker, every day and considers her as close to a friend as anyone else.

But this knowledge is too weighty for her to carry alone. Greta is sitting there, so serene, so understanding, so warm. Why would she not tell her? Why would she not tell her that she knows this is real? That her mother has spent her entire life craving attention, but now that she has a terminal illness and could command everyone's attention for quite some time, she is planning something else? She wants her children to help her end her life and seems to think she's doing some great altruistic final act by bringing her estranged daughters together to reestablish some strong familial bond that never existed in the first place.

Meanwhile, Nell is the only one who knows. She agreed to pretend everything is normal, not to share the secret, just as her mother wants, but the shock and sadness are welling inside her, a bubble that is threatening to burst in the face of Greta's sympathy and concern. She doesn't speak. She can't speak. She closes her eyes, just for a few seconds, and shakes her head. She feels Greta lay a cool hand on her hand.

"It's okay," Greta croons softly. "It's going to be okay."

And much to her surprise, Nell finds tears trickling down her cheeks. The thing is, it isn't going to be okay. Or, not the kind of okay where life carries on as it has been before. It isn't going to be Nell's mother phoning her and demanding Nell do something for her. It isn't going to be Nell's obligatory visits, filled with not so much resentment as weariness.

Why does it always come down to Nell? Why doesn't her mother ask anything of anyone else?

Because Meredith is too far away, and Lizzy doesn't give a shit. Lizzy is far too busy with her successful supper clubs and her successful TV show and her perfect son to ever take the time to do anything for their mother. So it falls to Nell. Lizzy and Meredith do absolutely nothing. They show up for holidays, spend two or three days with their mother, and sail off into their lives, as if that's all that is ever required of them.

And that is all that is ever required of them, because Nell is there, has always been there, to pick up the slack. And because their mother does not want to alienate Lizzy and Meredith further than she already has, when she is upset, with them, or about life in general, the person to whom she complains is Nell.

And when she is angry, as she so often is, the person on whom she takes it out is Nell.

And when she is dying, and doing so in her own time frame, on her own terms, the person she chooses to help her with her pain, fear, and sadness is Nell. She's the strong one. Her sisters can't deal with it. She needs Nell.

Usually Nell doesn't care. Sometimes she is resentful that she has to handle her mother effectively on her own, but mostly she just does it. But today, with the weight of all that she knows, it is too much. As she sits on her office sofa, a kindly hand on her hand, a look of grave concern on the face of the woman sitting beside her, it is unexpectedly too much for Nell to carry on her own. Much to her shame and embarrassment, her body is suddenly racked with sobs, and she is taken into Greta's arms and held tightly.

Like a mother would hold a child, she thinks, later, when she is calm again. Like I have held River so many times, when he was small and frail and scared.

Like I have wanted to be held for years.

She tells Greta everything, astonished at how easy it is, how freely the words flow from her lips. She describes her childhood, her relationship with her sisters, the struggle she has with what she alone now knows, given how hard her mother has always been on her.

As she talks, it feels less painful. As she talks, and cries, encouraged from time to time by Greta, she is astonished to feel the burden easing. Not disappearing, but she had never realized that the saying was true; a burden shared is truly a burden halved. She had never thought to share her burdens with anyone before. How much easier, she suddenly thinks, my life might have been if I had.

"I'm so sorry," she says eventually, embarrassed, blushing at how much she has revealed, at the extraordinary intimacy these walls now contain. "I didn't mean to say all of that. I don't even know you. I don't know where all that came from."

"Haven't you ever heard that it's almost always easier to reveal your innermost secrets to a stranger? I'm not a stranger, anyway. At least, you don't feel like a stranger to me."

"Not now. Certainly. After the last half hour you probably know me better than just about anyone else in the world."

"I'm sure that's not true." Greta dismisses the idea, but Nell knows it is so. She has never spoken to anyone like this before.

Greta looks at Nell again, curiously. "Is that true?"

"Would you think less of me if I said it was?" Nell asks, reluctantly.

"It wouldn't change my opinion at all. You clearly needed to let some of this out. I'm only glad I was here."

"I'm so sorry. I feel . . . embarrassed. I've never been good at talking about emotions."

"Why not? How does it make you feel?"

Nell thinks for a moment. "Vulnerable."

Greta laughs. "And that's a bad thing?"

"Isn't it?"

Greta shakes her head. "Allowing ourselves to show our vulnerability is how we make human connections. If we're not showing other people our true selves, our weaknesses and flaws, how can we ever allow ourselves to be known?"

"I'm not sure I've ever wanted to be known."

"Then you're missing out on ninety percent of what this life has to offer." Greta shrugs lightly. "Being known is about connecting with people. I believe we're put on this earth to connect. Without it, life would be terribly lonely."

Yes, thinks Nell. It is terribly lonely. And she is shocked that she is finally able to admit that.

"At times like this we're supposed to be at our most vulnerable, and we are not supposed to be lonely. Your mother is dying," she says gently. "And choosing to do so on her own terms. I think she must be an incredibly brave woman. But it is always hardest on the ones the dying leave behind."

"But it shouldn't be hardest on me," Nell finds herself saying. "On any of us. We've all had such a difficult relationship with her. And with each other. We've never been a close family. I don't understand why I'm finding this so painful."

"That's why," Greta says simply with a smile. "It's harder when love isn't easy. Which doesn't mean the love isn't there. And it doesn't mean you can't now say the things that were never said long ago. It's not too late, Nell. Not yet."

"How do you know so much?" Nell says quickly, trying to change the subject because otherwise she might cry again. "Are you a therapist? I don't know anything about you."

"I have a degree in social work," says Greta. "Now I work with an

organization that sponsors therapeutic retreats. I'm not practicing as a therapist, but I'm well versed in talking to people who are going through major issues in their life. I'm a good listener."

"And a good cook," says Nell. "Kind of the perfect woman! Is there anything you can't do?"

"Tons!" Greta says with a laugh. "I'm not even going to get started or you'll never look at me in the same light again. But since you don't want me making lunch for everyone, maybe we could do something else. I wanted to find some time to visit Westport. Do you want to go there for lunch? It would be nice to get to know each other away from everyone."

"I would love to," says Nell. "I have some work stuff to do, but lunch sounds great."

"Meet you in the kitchen at quarter to one?"

"It's a date," says Nell, flushing. That's not what she meant.

After her talk with Greta, Nell feels much better. The cloud is still in her head, but it's not quite so dense. She realizes she can avoid her sisters this afternoon, surely, and then her mother can tell them tonight. Nell doesn't want to carry this burden alone. What she hasn't yet said to Greta, what she might not say to her, or indeed anyone else, is that mixed in with the sadness is relief.

Nell sits at her desk and turns back to her computer. Sighing, she finds herself typing "Greta Whitstable" into Google. She doesn't find much. A Facebook page, limited profile. A laughing picture. Freckles. Nell didn't notice before and unconsciously traces the bridge of her own nose. I always wanted freckles, she thinks, as there is a loud knock on the door and, startled, feeling guilty, she clicks the window closed.

It's River. "Daisy and I are going to Ronron's. Shall we take her some muffins?"

"She'd love that," says Nell, although she has no idea what her mother is eating these days, whether any of her rules about food persist now that she is ill. She thinks of everything her mother has done over the years to stay skinny enough to look good on camera: the Scarsdale diet, the grapefruit diet, the cabbage soup diet, Weight Watchers, Jenny Craig, Nutrisystem, the Atkins diet, paleo, vegetarian, vegan, juice fasts, the Master Cleanse. Urgh. The Master Cleanse. That one was the worst. Her mother persuaded Meredith to try it and Meredith threw up after the first salt flush. Carbohydrates haven't crossed the threshold of her mother's house in years. None of it matters now. River should take her muffins.

River hesitates, then walks in, reaches down, and puts his arms around his mother, enveloping her in a hug, in a way he hasn't done in years. Her little boy, now so big, so grown-up. Sometimes she looks at him and is amazed that he is hers, that she held him as a baby, that she managed to produce a boy as handsome and kind and clever and perfect as he. Nell lights up in his arms.

"I love you, Mom," he says, and Nell smiles, losing herself in love for her son. He is the only person she has ever been able to love completely, wholly, and unconditionally.

It has always been easy, because she is his mother. She has never had to be vulnerable with him. She hasn't been vulnerable with anyone since Lewis let her down, since she realized her mother would never put her first. The whole idea of vulnerability feels new to her. Could she love someone as completely as River, but on a more equal level? The idea intrigues her, surprises her. What surprises her more is that for the first time, she is thinking she might like to try.

"Hello?"

Nell has been counting down the minutes to meet Greta in the

kitchen, when she hears Lizzy's voice. She wasn't expecting her back so soon and walks reluctantly to the kitchen from the office to see Lizzy standing by the counter, helping herself to the grapes in the fruit bowl, as if she lived there. Nell smiles. It's a blessing and a curse, this ability of her sister's to make herself at home anywhere. Nell wishes she were more comfortable in the world, even though nothing would make her want to swap lives with Lizzy.

"Hi. Where's Meredith?" Nell asks.

"I dropped her back at Mom's. She was feeling guilty."

Nell laughs and shakes her head. "Poor Meredith. I can't believe she's almost forty and still bound by what other people think of her."

"I know." Lizzy rolls her eyes. "I still can't believe she's planning on marrying the Dreadful Derek. Do you think she'll go through with it?"

"I don't know, but you can't say anything. She'll just resent you if you do, and it won't help her at all. We all have to make our own mistakes."

"You don't have to remind me. I plan on saying nothing." Lizzy pulls out a chair and sits down, putting her feet up on another chair as she munches through the grapes, looking around the kitchen.

"I never thought I'd say this, but it is really nice to be out here. I feel peaceful here in a way I haven't for a really long time."

Nell smiles. "You're finally coming back to your suburban roots?"

"This is hardly suburban. This is country. Except it's close to everything. You really lucked out, getting this farm as a gift."

Nell is cautious. "I did, but it wasn't exactly a gift. It was an inheritance. It's also a lot of hard work. It's not like I can sit back and let it take care of itself."

"I know that. I can see the work you put in. And all the employees you have to manage." She pauses. "I know I shouldn't bring this up, but it's really a shame you don't think about doing farm dinners."

"Your supper club, you mean."

"My supper clubs, yes. And dinners on the farm. People pay a fortune now to sit in a meadow at an old trestle table. You could make proper money."

Nell looks at her sister closely, feigning disinterest, although "making proper money" is what she needs right now. "Making proper money" would mean she could stop hiding the pile of financial papers on her desk under a magazine.

"How much money, do you think?" Nell tries to sound as if she doesn't much care, as if the farm's future isn't reliant on making, somehow, proper money.

"Look, I don't really take care of the business end; Sean does that. But I can tell you that we run two to three supper clubs a week that range in size from a minimum of fifty, to three hundred if we're doing it on a farm. People pay up to five hundred dollars a head in the city, usually two hundred fifty elsewhere . . ."

"Two hundred and fifty dollars a head? Are they crazy?" Nell isn't aware that she is shrieking, even as she does the math. "You get seventy-five thousand dollars for one night?"

"No. All of our costs come out of that. The food, the staff, the rentals. But we do make a nice profit. We could make more"—she stares at her sister—"if we partnered with a farm, thereby cutting our costs significantly. If we had a supplier who would give us food at wholesale, we could probably split the profits with them." She shrugs as she pops another grape into her mouth.

"I'd have to see the numbers."

Lizzy sits up straight. "I can show them to you."

"How often would you do it?"

Lizzy shakes her head. "I have no idea. I haven't thought about this since you said you definitely wouldn't do it. I'd have to talk to Sean, but my dream would be to actually have a base on a farm, maybe even

a restaurant of our own . . . We could continue doing outside dinners as special events during the summer."

"We don't have a restaurant space," says Nell. "Nor do we have the funds to build one. We have the coffee shop, but that isn't big enough . . ."

"No, but there is the big hay barn." Lizzy has spent the past hour walking the farm, looking at all the outbuildings, the cogs in her brain turning and turning as she thought it through. "That could be repurposed. We could put a kitchen in the back space, eventually. We're used to setting up catering kitchens for the farm dinners . . . That would work temporarily."

Nell pictures the barn. It is enormous, too big for the amount of hay they harvest. They do a hay bale maze every fall for the local children to try to make use of it, but it wouldn't be the end of the world to move the hay to a smaller barn. A smaller barn would be much cheaper to build than a restaurant space. And she gets how her old barn would help keep the rustic feel of Lizzy's pop-up dinners.

She focuses her attention back to Lizzy, who is looking at her expectantly. "You actually think people would come to Easton, Connecticut, for dinner in a barn?"

"They travel all over New Jersey, Dutchess County, and Westchester for them."

Nell continues to look skeptical. "And you would commute in from Brooklyn?"

"Yes. I guess so. I don't know. I have no idea how it would work. But if you're serious, we can really talk about it. Maybe . . ." She pauses. "Maybe I would sell the place in Brooklyn and move out here permanently."

"You don't mean live on the farm!" A look of visible horror crosses Nell's face. "Because I don't see how that would work."

Lizzy laughs. "No, don't worry. The farm is clearly yours. But maybe I could buy something in Easton. Or Redding. Somewhere like

that. Maybe Connor could grow up surrounded by nature and animals. He could ride bikes with friends and pick apples fresh out of the orchard."

"You know you're completely romanticizing life out here."

"Yeah, but it's more fun that way. I could get a car and driver for when I'm filming." She laughs. "Seriously, though, that hay barn could be repurposed, couldn't it? You see it, don't you? We could even do a trial run this summer and see how it goes. People could sit on the hay bales as seats! They would love that."

"People would pay two hundred and fifty dollars to sit on hay bales and eat in a dirty barn?" Nell starts to laugh.

"Oh, Nell. You have no idea. We're giving them an *experience*. We could even eventually have a small shop here, selling my product line. Remember when you used to work here as a teenager and sell my pestos? We could do it again, only bigger! Nell, we could be partners. I have to figure it out with Sean, but I bet he'd go for it. Everyone in the suburbs wants the New York rooftop, but everyone in the city wants the orchards and barns."

"Well, the one thing we can give them is orchards and barns. And hay bales." Nell smiles. Seventy-five thousand dollars in one night, she keeps thinking. Even if they kept a quarter of that, it might get her out of the hole. Even if she didn't do it permanently, but let Lizzy hold the dinners this summer, with her catering kitchen, and tables in the orchard, just a handful of them, then maybe Nell could wake up in the morning able to breathe, without the albatross of financial fear hanging around her neck.

"Shall we go out for lunch and talk about this more?" Lizzy's eyes are bright with excitement. Nell had forgotten this about her, how she loves a project, how part of the reason she is as successful as she is now is not just that she's a talented cook, that she's photogenic, or that she's easy and relaxed on camera, but also because she is a *doer*—she makes

shit happen. Probably the best thing Nell can say about her sister Lizzy is that she has never been afraid of hard work.

"I can't today," says Nell. "I'm having lunch with Greta."

"Oh." Lizzy pouts. "Can't you rearrange? I'm on a high and, you know me, I need to keep talking about this."

Nell laughs. "I know, but you'll have to find someone else to talk about it with. I said I'd take her into town."

"Don't take her into town," says Lizzy. "I mean, you can if you want, but where are you going to eat? All the old faithfuls have gone." She grimaces. "Poor Acqua."

"Never mind Acqua, what about Oscar's?"

"Ugh!" Lizzy shakes her head. "It's awful that Oscar's has gone. Take her to Southport Harbor. It's so gorgeous. Get lunch at Spic and Span and take it down to the harbor so you can watch the boats bobbing while you eat. It's very romantic," she says nonchalantly, her back turned as Nell feels her cheeks fire up. What does she mean? She wants to ask, but doesn't want to ask. She can't defend herself when her cheeks are flaming red. "That's where I'd go for lunch," Lizzy adds, as if she had never mentioned romance at all.

"I'll just go and get changed," Nell says as an excuse to leave. She goes pounding up the stairs and examines her bright eyes in the mirror. What did Lizzy mean? Why did she say that? Is Daisy's mom a lesbian? Has Lizzy picked up on something Nell has not? It makes her uncomfortable and . . . What is that flutter in her stomach? It feels like excitement, but that can't be it. It must be discomfort. Even though Nell doesn't remember the last time she felt this comfortable with anyone, let alone someone she has just met.

She smiles as she thinks how easy Greta is to talk with. Nell has never found it particularly easy to talk to people on anything other than a superficial basis. Years ago someone once suggested, after Lewis had left and she was raising River on her own, that she might want to

think about going into therapy. Nell laughed out loud. She was the last person on earth who would ever choose to go and sit in a stranger's office and tell all her secrets.

Not that she has any secrets. Of that she is certain. Not ones she's conscious of, anyway.

twenty-nine

Derek discovered FaceTime about six months ago, and ever since, he's seemed to have lost the ability to make a phone call, at least when it comes to Meredith. Wherever she is, whatever time of day or night, if Derek wants to get hold of her, he FaceTimes her.

Meredith is lying on her childhood bed in her mother's house, having just woken up from a nap, feeling jet-lagged and sad. Nothing much has changed in here. The bookshelves under the window still contain the Laura Ingalls Wilder books she loved as a girl, the immaculate dolls lining one shelf, her bedspread a sunny yellow. Nell's room was instantly turned into a craft room once she moved out as a teenager, which was only odd given that her mother was the least crafty person she knew. To this day she's not sure Ronni ever set foot in that room. But her mother preserved Meredith's room, and Lizzy's, as they were.

Her mother was so horrible this morning, in just the way she used to be when Meredith was young, and defenseless, with no ability to answer back. And here she is, at thirty-eight years old, not so young

but still defenseless, with no ability to answer back. How can she, when her mother seems so old, so frail? She's sure Ronni doesn't mean all the cruel things she says. She never does. This morning, after Meredith came back, her mother apologized profusely, told her she loves her, asked for forgiveness, demanded Meredith come home and stay. So here Meredith is, back in her teenage bedroom, resenting everyone.

Her phone starts to ping and she picks it up, seeing it is Derek FaceTiming her. Propping the phone on the pillow, she turns on her side to see him. There he is, as handsome as ever, beaming at her.

"Darling!" he says. "Look at you! You look like you just woke up. What time is it there? Isn't it almost lunchtime?"

"It is, but I'm jet-lagged. I didn't sleep well last night so I just had a nap." She is aware that this is an unflattering angle, that she looks puffy and double-chinned, but it's Derek. Who loves her whatever she looks like.

"You can't nap, sweetness. That's the worst thing for jet lag. You have to get straight into the new time zone and plow through until bedtime. No more naps!"

"I couldn't keep my eyes open."

"How's your mother? What's the big news?"

"She's not well, some kind of neuropathy, and they're testing to see if it could be anything else."

"What kind of neuropathy?" Derek fancies himself an amateur doctor, priding himself on Latin medical terminology. "Diabetes perhaps? That's a common cause of peripheral neuropathy. What are the symptoms?"

"Who the fuck knows." Meredith is tired, and annoyed by Derek. She didn't mean to swear, and instantly regrets it.

"Meredith!" Derek barks. "I have people in the room. Good God! I'm so sorry," she hears him say in apology to whoever is with him. "She didn't mean that. Meredith!" He chastises again, the jolly expression on his face now gone.

You idiot, she thinks. He does this all the time. FaceTimes her without telling her there are people seeing her, or hearing her, no idea of the etiquette of warning someone on loudspeaker that others can hear. It serves him right. Who the hell cares, anyway.

"Why didn't you tell me there were people in the room?"

"They can't see you. I thought you just get upset when people can see you."

Meredith closes her eyes. "You know what? Let's just talk later. I have to go."

"Okay, fine." He is still clearly unhappy. "I love you," he says, without much feeling.

Meredith says nothing, just presses end.

She is still holding the phone when the doorbell rings.

"Meredith!" calls her mother from her own bedroom. "Lily has gone out shopping. Can you get the door?"

"Sure," Meredith yells back. Going downstairs, she pauses by the hall mirror, vaguely amused to see that her hair is sticking up on one side in a faintly ridiculous way. She attempts to smooth it down, but it won't cooperate. Oh, well. The UPS man will have to deal.

She buttons the buttons on her shirt that have come undone and opens the door with a polite smile.

The man on the doorstep turns to her, with a quizzical expression, followed by a frown.

"Oh," he says. "I was expecting the housekeeper."

Meredith frowns back. There is something familiar about him. As her eyes scan his face, trying to place him, the smile slides off his as he looks at her.

"Do we know each other?" he says, squinting slightly as if scrolling through his memory banks to place her.

"I was just thinking the same thing," she says, and as she does, he breaks into a smile, pointing at her.

"Bookstore girl!" he exclaims with a laugh.

Meredith's hands fly to her hair. It's him! The cute man from the bookstore. But what on earth is he doing here? "What are you doing here?" she says, because she can't think of anything else.

"I could say the same thing to you, but I've just realized who you are. I've been looking at pictures of you, and your sisters, for days now. Sorry, I don't mean to sound creepy."

"Well, it is just a little bit creepy," Meredith admits as she shuts the door ever so slightly, taking a step back. But then she realizes she's being ridiculous. He doesn't feel threatening; he feels friendly and warm. "Who are you?" She peers at him. "And what *are* you doing here?"

"I'm so sorry!" He shakes his head as Meredith silently prays he not be creepy. He is far too cute to be creepy. "I'm Billy," he says. "I'm a journalist. Your mother didn't tell you? I'm a filmmaker too, and I've been talking to your mom about making a documentary about her, or maybe writing a piece. We arranged a meeting today?" Meredith looks blank. "She really didn't tell you?" He frowns, unsure of what to say next.

"No. But come in, please. She's upstairs, but I can go and talk to her."

"Thank you." Billy comes in, taking his messenger bag off and putting it down in the hallway. "I have plenty of time. Shall I wait in . . . the sunroom?"

Meredith is trying to subtly play with her hair and attempting to smooth it down, but smiles hugely and says, "Yes! Great idea. I'll go upstairs and see if my mom is ready. It may be a while. She's not moving so well. She told you about the neuropathy?"

"Yes. She wants it on film. Her illness. A . . . retrospective about her life . . ."

"Yes. She mentioned it, even though I didn't know you were coming. Please, go through. We'll both be down in a bit."

Billy walks down the hallway as Meredith races upstairs to her room, groaning with horror as she stops to look at her reflection. "Fuck," she whispers, mortified that the cute man from the bookstore is now in her house, and this is the impression she made.

She tears the elastic band off her ponytail and wets her hands under the faucet, dampening her hair before blow-drying it straight and smooth. She kicks off her pajama bottoms and squeezes into jeans that are only about one size too small. I look voluptuous, she tells herself. At least I have a smallish waist. If Beyoncé and Nicki Minaj can celebrate big butts and thighs, I can too. She slips her feet into wedges, then back out. They look ridiculous, as if she is making far too much of an effort. The flip-flops go on, then the tiniest bit of makeup, so little it is almost imperceptible, just enough to enhance her natural features. Mascara to elongate her lashes, shimmery highlighter to give her the appearance of cheekbones, a touch of pale pink lip gloss on her full lips. She steps back, examining her reflection. Her hair was cut in a bob last year, at Derek's suggestion. He likes it perfectly coiffed, as it is now, which is not how Meredith likes it.

She opens a drawer in her vanity table and pulls out a curling iron she hasn't looked at in over a decade. She works quickly, curling her hair just enough for a sexy, tousled beach look, tipping her head upside down and shaking her hair out, this time smiling for real when she looks in the mirror.

She goes into her mother's bedroom and sits on the bed.

"You look nice." Her mother doesn't miss a beat. "He's handsome, that Billy. That was him at the door, wasn't it?"

"Is he handsome? I hadn't noticed," lies Meredith smoothly. "Which wig shall we put on today?"

thirty

Nell gives Greta the whistle-stop tour of Westport by truck. She comes off the Merritt Parkway and drives her up Partrick Road, down Old Hill, pointing out the historic homes and pretty old stacked stone walls.

On through town, where they stop at Neat and grab a coffee, sitting on a bench overlooking the Saugatuck River, Nell telling stories about Westport, not realizing she is also telling stories about her life.

They get back in the truck and drive down Riverside, turning into the sweeping driveway of the rowing club. "It wasn't like this when I was young," Nell says, telling Greta about Lewis Calder, about the original rowing club, Coach Mangan, what it felt like to be on the water.

"You didn't keep rowing?"

"I wish I had," Nell says, smiling. "But once I had River, and the farm, it was too much."

"Maybe you can start again now," Greta says. "I don't think it's ever

too late to pursue happiness. Especially when you already know what makes you happy."

"Maybe," says Nell, watching the launch on the river, a quad glide past, the oars moving as one. She is absolutely still as she watches them, remembering the magic and grace of being in a boat that moved like that. "Maybe." She turns to Greta. "What makes *you* happy?"

"My daughter," says Greta. "My friends. I like living in St. Louis, although I am ready for an adventure. I was a big traveler when I was young, and it has been a while since I've gone anywhere other than to California for the retreats. I would quite like to go somewhere else, now that Daisy is grown."

"Where do you have in mind?"

"I prefer life to unfold in the way that it is going to. I'm quite sure the universe will reveal itself in time."

"I'm not good at that," says Nell. "I like to know exactly what's going to happen. I don't like surprises."

"Really?" Greta tilts her head. "The best parts of my life have tended to be the most unexpected."

Nell thinks about asking what she means, but she doesn't. There is a part of her that is scared to ask, scared of what she might hear.

"Shall we go?" Nell says instead, as they continue their journey down memory lane. Nell takes her to Main Street, pointing out the places, now closed, that were important throughout her childhood. The Remarkable Book Shop, Klein's, Sally's, Bill's Smoke Shop, the farmers' market where Lizzy helped out. Il Villano, where a friend's older sister confessed, after two weeks of working there as a waitress, that they kept a gun in the warming drawer behind the line. Backstage, where they used to go drinking and dancing, when Lewis had a friend on the door who would let them in, even though they were underage. The Westport Country Playhouse, where their mother

appeared in countless plays and script readings, even sat on the board for a period of years. The arts center, where Meredith volunteered and where she submitted paintings for its member shows.

"Meredith paints?" Greta asks this a short while later, after their journey has taken them on to Southport. They parked outside the Spic and Span and ordered sandwiches to eat by the harbor, just as Lizzy suggested, with bottles of iced tea and a packet of chips.

"Sort of. Wow, this is lovely." They sit on a bench and watch the boats bob, and it is just as beautiful and serene as Lizzy promised. Not romantic, though. Painterly, perhaps.

"Meredith doesn't paint anymore," continues Nell, taking a bite and washing it down with a swig of iced tea. "Accounting appears to have scrubbed the artist from her soul."

"Was she any good?"

"Meredith would say she was terrible."

"Is that true?"

Nell shakes her head. "She is enormously talented. Her paintings weren't as good, but that was because she wasn't comfortable with oils; she never really knew how they worked and she was trying to accomplish too much. She would do these beautiful sketches, and took art classes in London for a while, doing lovely work. I always thought she hadn't really found her calling, that she would suddenly realize she was amazing at making jewelry, or design, but she chose accounting and doesn't do anything artistic anymore as far as I know."

"How sad. What made her choose accounting?"

"Our father. He had remarried and wasn't very present. I think Meredith thought if she chose something he approved of—law or business, or accounting—he might pay attention to her again."

"Did it work?"

"Does it ever?"

Greta shakes her head sadly. "What a terribly sad thing it is, when parents remarry and have second families that entirely displace the children of the first. Is that why you didn't ever marry? Because of River?"

Nell is startled. "No. Not consciously, at any rate, although perhaps there was some of that. I never met anyone after Lewis, or rather, no one who was . . . important enough to make me want to open my life and accept someone into it." She takes another bite. "What about you? I don't know anything about you, other than you aren't married to Daisy's father. Did you have a relationship that was difficult for Daisy?" She flushes slightly, unused to having this kind of conversation, to revealing the intimacies and intricacies of her life.

Greta pulls open the bag of chips. "Daisy was easy," she says. "And there were no more children for her to feel displaced. Her father and I have remained best friends."

"Lucky you. That seems so unusual."

"There was much that was unusual about our relationship. I shouldn't ever have married him, but I was trying to do the right thing, make my parents happy, follow the path expected of me, instead of the path I was too frightened to admit I wanted to follow."

Nell says nothing. She waits.

"I was attracted to women, although I wasn't fully aware of it at the time," says Greta, matter-of-factly, as Nell's heart starts to pound. "In my senior year things became physical between my best friend and I. We finally admitted that we both had feelings for each other. Her parents discovered us and were furious. They sent her off to school in Texas to split us up. My own parents didn't understand, so I tried very hard to make everyone happy by finding a nice young man when I went to college, and settling down with him, forcing myself to pretend that I was just like everyone else."

Nell says nothing, her heart still pounding, her cheeks flushed. Greta glances at her before carrying on.

"We were married for twelve years, and they were good years. Wonderful years, even though there was no physical side. We didn't have sex for ten of those years, and I probably could have kept pretending. I had completely shut down that side of the relationship, and I told myself it was normal, that all old married people felt like this."

"Even though you weren't old," says Nell.

"Exactly."

"So what happened? Why did you split up?"

"Because I fell in love with a woman at work. She was one of the facilitators at the retreat. I never thought I would be unfaithful, but . . ." She smiles at the memory and gives a simple shrug. "I fell in love."

"You had an affair with a woman?"

"Well. It wasn't quite as straightforward as that. We were together at retreats over a long period of time, during which I suppose we had an emotional affair. Nothing happened, at least nothing physical, not while I was married to Daisy's father. But it was clear to both of us that it would, that the only reason it hadn't was because we were both mustering all of our willpower. It was obvious to me that although I have been attracted to men, I am much more attracted to women." She looks at Nell, holds her gaze.

Nell feels as if she can't breathe. "How did your husband take it?"

"It wasn't a shock. I think we both knew it was only ever a matter of time. I could stay married to my best friend as long as I didn't meet a woman. And I had met a woman."

"So you left him and . . . ?"

Greta smiles. "I did leave him, and we remained friends, and Marsha and I lived together for ten years. We split up three years ago."

"I'm sorry," says Nell, who finds she isn't. What she is, amazingly, is alight, her whole body buzzing and tingling as Greta tells her story. She recognizes her story; she knows, instantly and with no doubt whatsoever, because she has lived it, without ever realizing it.

"Goodness, why?" says Greta, who puts down her sandwich and looks down at Nell's hand, resting on the bench between them.

Nell looks down too, Greta's hand just inches from her own, as her heart leaps into her mouth, her body aflame as her fingers involuntarily reach for Greta's.

She looks up and into Greta's eyes, confused. This is her story, she knows, with relief and fear and excitement, as everything in her life suddenly makes sense. As her fingers touch Greta's, she feels a jolt of something suspiciously like electricity, making her feel light-headed and dizzy. She looks at Greta, smiling with wonder, and relief, watching her hand entwine with Greta's, marveling at how this feels.

She looks at Greta's face then, at her hair blowing onto her cheek, her warm eyes, her searching gaze, and all Nell can think is that she wants to kiss her. She hasn't felt this way about anyone since Lewis Calder, since she was a teenager. And now she is thinking this about a woman. Though if she is honest, she has felt this before, with a woman, but she has never allowed that thought to come out; she felt shame and guilt, and pushed those thoughts deep, deep down, refusing to give them attention, refusing to acknowledge that they might have been real.

Nell opens her mouth to say something, but nothing comes out. She glances around, but there is no one there. Just the two of them, sitting on a bench, holding hands. When Greta leans forward and kisses her, her soft lips meeting hers for the briefest of kisses, Nell sighs with desire, as her whole body melts.

thirty-one

I miss you!" Lizzy croons through the camera to Connor, blinking back the tears. She had not realized how much she missed her son until she saw his small face looking at her on the phone, telling her about his day at school.

"Let me see the chickens," says Connor, taking his father's phone into the living room and crawling onto the sofa.

Lizzy walks around the yard to the chicken coop, showing off Nell's farm, giving Connor the guided tour. "Here they are," she says, holding the phone at arm's length. "See those big ones with the great big feathery tails? Those are roosters. Aren't they handsome?"

"Let me see," says Connor. "I want to be there. I want to see the roosters."

"I wish you were here," says Lizzy, surprised that it is true, surprised that she loves her son as much as she does, even though she is the first to admit she does not have a maternal bone in her body. James once told her, very early on, that her energy was masculine, and she

knew what he meant. It wasn't that she was butch, or looked like a man, but that she was driven and ambitious and didn't care what people thought of her. It never occurred to her to please anyone other than herself. Which was why James was in charge of child rearing. They both agreed he was the more compassionate parent, that he was, in many ways, the more maternal. It just seemed to make such good sense that Lizzy would be the earner while James stayed home to raise the kids.

Kid. It doesn't look like there are any more on the horizon, not given their sex life the last few years. Lizzy thought childbirth had killed her libido, her desire. Even when she felt loving toward her husband, she couldn't be bothered with sex. It was enough to have loving companionship, to climb into bed at night feeling safe next to his sleeping form. She was grateful she got home as late as she did, grateful that James was always asleep, that she didn't have to push his hands away or shrink from affection just in case it turned into something more. She had presumed that side of her life was over, like a switch that had been flicked to the off position. It was normal. Surely.

She would flirt innocently with Sean, which gave her enough of a buzz, never thinking about anything happening. They were both married. Both happily married. Until the night they found themselves alone after a supper club, and the flirting seemed a little more intense, a little different, and before she knew it, she was gasping at her body responding to someone touching her, in a way she had thought it never would again.

It was only sex, she told herself, racked with guilt the first few times it happened, telling Sean each time that this was the last time, this could never happen again. But then she found she could compartmentalize, and she barely saw James anyway, and neither of them were the slightest bit interested in the physical side of the relationship anymore, so maybe . . . maybe . . . it was not the worst thing in the world.

Maybe . . . maybe . . . if no one else knew, maybe they would get to have their cake and eat it too.

It was easy to keep the deception going, to find herself in a full-blown affair, given how little she saw her husband. By the time she got up in the morning, he was often out, dropping Connor at preschool, grocery shopping, doing errands. They might pass at lunchtime or in the afternoon, but with Lizzy's TV schedule what it was, they were seeing each other less and less. She was seeing Connor less and less.

And now it's still happening, and none of it feels good. She keeps trying to end it with Sean, but they can't seem to stay away from each other. She keeps trying to change her schedule, get someone else to take over the bulk of the cooking for the supper clubs. But it just keeps getting busier. Every time she has tried to bring someone else in, there is a problem, and they never prepare the food in quite the same way.

I need to be a better mother, she thinks, gazing at Connor on her iPhone screen as she blows him kisses and ends the call. I need to figure this thing out, because it's not fair to any of us. She walks back to the house, hands in her pockets, looking out around the countryside and marveling at how she now appreciates this bucolic view in a way she never did before.

What if she did move out here? For a second she allows herself to indulge in a fantasy she tries not to think about too often. What if Sean left his wife, as he sometimes talks about doing? He has the same marriage she has with James. He loves his wife, but he's not in love with her; they have become like brother and sister.

What if Sean left his wife, remaining great friends, naturally, and she left James, and they started again out here? What if they bought a small house, made new friends, shed their old lives entirely? What if they stopped the supper clubs and started a farm restaurant, like Dan Barber did with Blue Hill at Stone Barns? Why couldn't she do that in Connecticut? Sean would have his children every other

weekend, and maybe he'd go into the city a couple of nights a week to see them. She could bring Connor out here, but let him visit with James in the city. They could work it out. It would all be fine.

She stops. What is she thinking? She has never thought of her and Sean together. That was supposed to be just sex. Wasn't it? Why has she found herself fantasizing about a life she didn't even think she wanted?

Her phone buzzes again and she looks down. It's from Francine, one of their young waitresses.

I need to talk to you. It's urgent. Can you call now?

Lizzy frowns. These young women and their dramas. She tends not to get involved, likes to stay on the sidelines. She's the chef. Sean is the one who takes care of the business side of things, and staff problems, as far as Lizzy is concerned, fall under the business side of things.

Is Sean around? Can you talk to him?
I need to talk to YOU.

Lizzy sighs. I'm in CT with family. Can it wait?

No. I can drive out. I need to see you. Can I come today?

Lizzy resists the urge to throw the phone in the nearest bucket of water.

No, not tonight. Tomorrow morning then.

And she gives her the address, wishing that everyone would leave her alone. She looks up as Nell's truck approaches, and she walks over as her sister and Greta emerge.

"Hey, guys," Lizzy says, sighing. "What's the plan for tonight?"

"We're going to Mom's at six."

"Okay. Do I need to cook?"

"Meredith said she'd roast a chicken and make a big salad. Greta is going to make spiced chickpea fritters for us as a vegetarian option."

Lizzy turns to Greta. "You're going to join us for dinner?"

Greta shakes her head. "No. But I'll send the fritters with Nell. This is your family time."

"Thank you." As much as cooking is Lizzy's passion, there is nothing quite like someone else cooking for her. No one has invited her to their house for dinner in years, unless they have a superhot caterer cooking and can be sure Lizzy will be suitably impressed. What no one realizes is that it's the very act of being cooked for that is so special for Lizzy, regardless of the result. True, she wouldn't particularly want tough, chewy steak or overcooked broccoli, but most people can do what Meredith is proposing tonight: cover a chicken with olive oil, salt and pepper; stuff the cavity with a couple of cut lemons, some garlic cloves, and herbs; and roast it in the oven for an hour or so. Most people can empty a bag of arugula into a bowl, slice some avocado into it, maybe some cherry tomatoes, and drizzle it with olive oil and balsamic vinegar. All of which will taste better to Lizzy than anything she could make herself because her sister has made it for her. Spiced chickpea fritters is just an unexpectedly delightful bonus.

"Yeah, but Meredith says Mom isn't really eating. She's been having some choking issues so she's doing liquid."

"That sounds terrible. I really think we should speak to her doctors. It's insane that they don't know what's going on. I'll make her a smoothie. Can I help myself to spinach and kale in the garden?"

"Of course," Nell says, and she sees Lizzy squinting at her. "What?"

"What have you done?" Lizzy examines her face.

"What do you mean? I haven't done anything," Nell says quickly,

the memory of Greta kissing her flashing into her mind and making her flush with . . . what? Guilt? Shame? What does she have to feel guilty or ashamed about? She wouldn't want anyone to know, she thinks—before thinking: Why not? Who cares? Who would care?

"There's something different about you," Lizzy persists, in the way only Lizzy can. "Seriously, did you have, like, Botox or something?"

Nell barks with laughter as Greta grins. "Maybe your sister's happy," Greta says, as she and Nell walk up the stairs, leaving Lizzy watching them, a frown on her face as she tries to figure out what it is.

thirty-two

I had no idea you were this good a cook," Lizzy says, plucking a chunk of crispy skin off the chicken and taking a bite, then swooning. "Look at this! This is the perfect color! And gorgeously seasoned. Meri, you used the perfect amount of salt. I am so impressed."

Meri pulls a tray of crispy roast potatoes out of the oven and Lizzy starts to laugh. "You did not! How do you even know how to make roast potatoes like that? You live in England. The food is terrible there."

"You really need to not say that," Meredith says, with all seriousness. "Every time I hear anyone talk about terrible English food, it's basically showing their naiveté and parochial, unsophisticated palate."

"Um, hardly." Lizzy laughs. "Hello? This is me you're talking to. Celebrated chef, et cetera, et cetera. I think I know what I'm talking about."

"When was the last time you were in London eating in restaurants? Never?"

"Fifteen years ago. And the memories remain."

"Bollocks, as we say in England," Meredith says with a smug smile. "If you were as sophisticated as you think you are, you would not only have traveled to London, but you would have realized the food there is pretty much the best in the world."

"You have to say that, you live there. Anyway, I will come back, for your wedding to Derek."

Meredith says nothing. She isn't planning on telling them they aren't invited. She isn't planning on discussing Derek at all. "Also, this is Julia Child's recipe for chicken."

"Aha! So your amazing recipe for roast chicken isn't English but American, thus proving that we do have the best food here."

"It proves nothing other than Julia Child has a great roast chicken recipe, learned, I might add, in Paris. The roast potatoes that you are admiring—and yes, you may have one—are scuffed with a fork after they're blanched to crisp them up as soon as they hit the sizzling duck fat."

"Duck fat!" Lizzy marvels. "Where did you learn about duck fat for roast potatoes?"

"Not from an American. It was either Nigella or Delia. Either way, a Brit." She watches Lizzy chew on the potato. "Now, tell me that roast potato isn't the best you've ever had."

"I've gotta give it to you," Lizzy says reluctantly, chewing the potato and popping another into her mouth. "These are pretty fucking awesome." She leans closer, lowering her voice conspiratorially. "Have you seen Nell?"

"Not since this morning. Why?"

"There's something different about her. I can't figure it out."

"Different? Like what?"

"She looked . . . happy. Which is weird, don't you think? Nell never looks happy. She's always intensely frowning and serious. Why is she happy?"

"Lizzy!" Meredith berates her, even as she tries not to laugh. "How about, 'Yay, Nell, figuring out how to be happy.'"

"I do feel 'yay, Nell'! I just want to know what it is that's making her happy. Or who. Do you think she's met someone? My spidey senses are telling me she's met someone. Who do you think it is? Do you think it's someone we know?"

Meredith shakes her head. "I have no idea and, frankly, it's none of my business." The doorbell rings and Meredith smooths her hair back.

"That's the journalist?" asks Lizzy.

Meredith shrugs and says, "I'll get it." She leaves Lizzy in the kitchen to help herself to more potatoes as she walks to the door, trying to still the butterflies that have suddenly appeared.

"Hey." Billy walks in as Meredith steps back. Then he pauses, and Meredith awkwardly extends a hand, not sure how to greet him.

"I think we know each other well enough now to kiss hello," he says, leaning forward and kissing her on one cheek as she blushes. "You look so nice."

"You mean, I'm not in my pajamas with bedhead and puffy eyes," Meredith says, attempting to laugh off her appearance the previous time she opened the door to find him on the doorstep. He has no idea she went out shopping for new clothes today, bored of the careful, color-coordinated skirts and tops, the middle-aged dresses Derek likes to see her in. He has no idea she looked, with a feeling of nausea, at the midheel wedges Derek approves of and tossed them in the trash.

She went to Calypso, which was having a huge sale. She found the kinds of clothes she adored, the kinds of clothes that always made her pause when she saw them in the pages of a magazine, the kinds of clothes Derek abhorred. Floaty tunics embroidered and beaded, elegant loose linen pants, silky, feminine skirts. She tried on outfit after outfit, delighting in how feminine she felt, how pretty, how good it

was to be in the kind of clothes she would never wear in London. They were—oh, how flattering they were, showing off the best of her figure and hiding the worst, and she felt oh so wonderful in them. The tunics and loose pants hid her middle, the extra weight she was carrying, although she didn't feel dumpy, she realized. Over the last couple of days she had been feeling quite beautiful, and not once had she had her usual thought that if only she were fifteen pounds thinner, then everything would be perfect. And now tonight, in a simple kaftan dress with a beaded necklace, she feels confident in a way she never does at home, even though she still has no idea how to receive a compliment, particularly when it comes from a man like Billy.

"I thought you looked fantastic in pajamas with bedhead and puffy eyes," says Billy, who doesn't appear to be joking. "I'm just saying, all you women think you look better done up, but most men like the natural look."

"I'll take that as a compliment," says Meredith, leading him into the kitchen, wishing she hadn't put on quite so much makeup, wondering if she ought to excuse herself and wipe off some of the eyeshadow.

"Do," he says, walking in and introducing himself to Lizzy.

"The famous journalist arrives," says Lizzy, narrowing her eyes as she shakes his hand and looks him up and down. "I'm presuming I ought to be on my guard?"

"Not at all," he says, his smile easy and light. "You have my word that everything tonight is off the record. We're still in the early stages of figuring out what we're going to be doing. I've brought a video camera, so I might shoot some footage tonight, just of the family, but really I want to try and get to know you a little. I'll just hang out and maybe ask some questions, and fade into the background a bit."

"You don't look like the kind of man who fades into the background," Lizzy says.

"Trust me, I am."

She peers at him. "You look kind of familiar. Have you ever been to one of my supper clubs?"

"No! I can't get a ticket! If you're offering, I'd love to come. Everyone says they're ridiculous."

"You know flattery will get you everywhere."

"I'm a journalist. I do know," he says. "But I don't have to tell you how hot the tickets to your supper clubs are."

"We can figure something out. You're sure we haven't met?"

"I don't think so."

"What's your name again?"

"Billy Hart."

"Oh, my God. Weren't you married to Veronica?"

The color drains from his face. "How do you know Veronica?"

"I catered her wedding. Her . . . second wedding." She grimaces. "Is this where our budding friendship goes totally south?"

"That depends." Billy is shaken but refuses to show it. "What do you think of her?"

"She's gorgeous. And sweet. But the husband is a bit of a nightmare."

"We can be friends," says Billy, as the tension disappears, and the front door opens again, Nell, River, and Daisy walking in.

"Where's your mom?" Meredith asks Daisy. "She's not coming?"

"She said she didn't want to intrude on a family night," explains River. "Mom said it would be fine, but she wouldn't come."

"Oh," says Meredith, as Nell walks to the other side of the room.

Oh? thinks Lizzy, watching the flush fade from Nell's cheeks, before a thought snakes into her head. No, she thinks. Surely that can't be the explanation. Nell? Surely not.

River and Daisy go upstairs to see his grandmother, as Lizzy calls Nell back to the counter, where Billy is pulling down a bottle of tequila from the top shelf and dusting it off.

"Tequila?" Lizzy is impressed. "Now we're talking. Shots? Do we have limes and salt?"

"I wasn't planning on shots," says Billy, after introducing himself to Nell. "I'm allergic to wine, and vodka gives me headaches. Tequila is the only thing that I seem to be okay with."

"Now this is my kind of man!" Lizzy grins at Meredith, who gives her a hard glare.

Why is Lizzy flirting with Billy when she has a husband and child at home? A husband and child she seems barely to mention or even think about. "How is James?" Meredith says. "And Connor? Isn't it his birthday soon?"

Lizzy says, "My husband and son are both fine, thank you for asking. Ice, anyone?" She leans in to Meredith as she walks past her and whispers, low, so no one else can hear, "Don't worry, he's all yours," and walks on before Meredith has a chance to say she isn't interested in Billy.

She's *not* interested in Billy. How could she be interested in Billy when she's getting married to Derek? Also, Billy isn't interested in her. He's far too handsome to be interested in her. Granted, once upon a time someone like Billy might have been interested in someone like her, but that was over ten years ago, when she was gorgeous for about five minutes, when she looked, and felt, worthy. Not now that she is approaching forty with eye bags and extra poundage, not to mention a fiancé. How lucky she is to have Derek, she thinks.

She looks up to find Billy watching her, raising his glass to her, and smiling. She returns the smile and finds herself holding his gaze just a little longer than feels altogether necessary. What is this? she thinks. He can't be interested in her, surely not. She thinks of Derek, of how she finds him less handsome than . . . nice. Approachable. Easy. Of how grateful he is that she is with him, will be his wife.

Derek, she tells herself. My future happiness and peace lie with

Derek. This young man may be handsome, and he may be paying me attention, or pretending to pay me attention, but it means nothing. He probably just wants to get closer to my mother or get information out of me. I will not flirt with him. I will not be that gullible.

"Excuse me," she says, going upstairs to her bedroom and looking at all the makeup she applied earlier, which now looks slightly desperate and wholly ridiculous. Grabbing a cotton ball, she rubs the eyeshadow off, smudging it into a big mess that makes her appear to have two black eyes. With a sigh she scrapes her hair back with an elastic and scrubs her face with soap and water. There. No one could accuse her of flirting with Billy now.

There is a knock on the door, which Meredith opens to find Lizzy. "What's going on?" says Meredith as she pulls the hair band off.

"Mom's not so good," says Lizzy. "She can't get out of bed."

"I know. She couldn't this afternoon either. I keep thinking she doesn't want to, like that time she wouldn't get out of bed for the whole year."

Lizzy rolls her eyes. "Did anyone ever actually give her a diagnosis for that year?"

"I believe *Dr. Sunshine* diagnosed herself with mono, until she read about Lyme disease and suddenly it was Lyme."

"If memory serves correctly, it wasn't just Lyme disease, it was *chronic* Lyme," says Lizzy, as they both smile.

"Naturally," says Meredith. "But this time it's different. I'm beginning to think this is far beyond her old antics. It started dawning on me today that this is really bad. Like, I think she might be dying, bad. But that doesn't make sense, does it? We have known about every ache, pain, illness, fever, and it was always a near-death experience. I keep thinking there's no way she would be seriously ill and not make it all about her, but . . . this is different. Do you think it's . . . like, MS or something?"

"Yes. I do. I don't know what else it could be, with the tingling and weakness and all that stuff. I want to talk to her doctors. I want to know why the hell they aren't testing for that stuff."

"I totally agree," says Meredith. "Let's tell her we want to meet with her doctors. Let's see if we can go and see them tomorrow."

"Okay. Good. That makes me feel better. I can't in the morning, though. I have one of my waitresses coming up to talk to me about some crisis."

Meredith stares at her sister. "Does she know you're the least compassionate person in the world and a terrible person to come to in a crisis?"

"Clearly not. But she's about to find out." Lizzy gives a crooked grin. "God, these young girls. They need so much babysitting. By the way, I wasn't flirting with your boyfriend down there, and I'm sorry if that's how it seemed. I wouldn't ever do that."

Meredith blushes. "First of all, he's not my boyfriend. Secondly, it's fine for you to flirt with whoever you want, even though I think it's kind of weird, given that you are married and you do have a child, which, granted, is kind of hard to believe, given that you have barely mentioned them."

Lizzy stares at her. "You're right," she says eventually, sinking onto Meredith's bed. "I'm a shitty fucking mother and a terrible wife, and I am royally screwing up my life."

Meredith shuffles from foot to foot, astonished that Lizzy didn't attack her with insults. Worse than that, she's utterly disconcerted that Lizzy now has tears in her eyes.

"I don't know what I'm going to do," Lizzy says as she shakes her head. "I never thought I'd end up like this."

Meredith sits gingerly down next to her, laying an arm awkwardly around her sister's shoulders. "What's going on?"

"It's all so complicated. I'm not happy. James and I are barely speak-

ing, and I just don't know how to fix it. We've been in couples counseling, but honestly, my heart just isn't in it anymore. I feel like—" She
pauses and takes a deep breath. "I feel like my marriage is gasping its
last breaths, and maybe it's better for everyone if we just quit now,
admit it's not working, and figure out how to move forward in a way
that feels fair and loving to Connor." She looks at Meredith. "What do
you think?"

"You're asking *me*? I'm not exactly an expert on relationships," says
Meredith. "Anything but. I think you and James probably need to
decide what you want. No one can do that for you."

She pauses, looking at her sister, thinking of how envious she has
always been of her, the baby of the family who was handed everything
on a silver platter, who never seemed to struggle or find life difficult,
the way Meredith did. She was extroverted, gorgeous, and slim, and
everything was always easy for her. Or so Meredith thought.

"Is there someone else?" she asks, not thinking about the words
until they are out there.

Lizzy looks up. "No," she says quickly.

A little too quickly, perhaps, thinks Meredith, but before she has
a chance to ask anything else, Lizzy is standing.

"Come on," she says. "Better get back to the others."

thirty-three

Lizzy sidles up to Daisy in the kitchen.

"So, Daisy." Lizzy leans against the counter next to her. "You seem like a very normal person. What are you doing hanging out with our crazy family?"

River grins from across the room. "The family might be crazy, but I'm not. Thanks to my very stable mom, I'm a great boyfriend, wouldn't you say?"

"You're the best," says Daisy, toasting him with a bottle of beer.

"Didn't you say you're twenty?" Meredith eyes the bottle of beer. "I'm not sure you should be drinking that."

"Meredith!" say Nell and Lizzy at the same time.

"I'm twenty-one next month," says Daisy. "I think I'll be okay."

Lizzy turns her head so Meredith doesn't see and rolls her eyes surreptitiously at Nell, who suppresses a smile.

"So what's your story, Daisy?" Lizzy asks. "I like your mom. Tell us three interesting things about you that we don't know."

"Hm. Good question. I don't usually get asked stuff like that. Okay. I have tattoos."

"Interesting," says Lizzy. "Where and what? I'll show you mine if you show me yours."

Daisy pulls the shoulder of her T-shirt down to reveal a small "om" sign on one shoulder and a penguin on the other.

"The om I get, but what's the significance of the penguin?"

Daisy shrugs. "I just like them. What's yours?"

"Since when do you have a tattoo?" asks Meredith, frowning.

"Tattoos." Lizzy grins. "Plural." She pushes a sleeve up to reveal a carving knife, delicately drawn and finely shaded so it looks like a pen and ink sketch rather than a tattoo.

"Wow," breathes River, walking over. "That's very cool."

"And this . . ." She pulls the neck down and turns around to reveal a whisk on her shoulder blade. "And this . . ." She unbuttons her pants, pulls them down, and turns around to show a wooden spoon on her left butt cheek.

Meredith blushes, noting that Billy is in the room, even though he's politely not looking. "Lizzy! Don't pull your pants down."

"What? It's a tattoo. I have panties on, for God's sake."

"Barely," says Meredith, wondering how Lizzy stays so slim, how her body is so perfect, envious of how she has no qualms about dropping her pants in a room filled with people, two of whom are relative strangers. One of whom is a very cute man, who, much to her relief, still isn't looking. "A thong isn't exactly panties."

"For God's sake, Meri. Relax. Have another glass of wine," says Lizzy, buttoning her pants back up.

"Those are awesome," breathes Daisy.

"Thank you. Anyone else have a tattoo? Meredith?"

Meredith shakes her head.

"Nell?"

Nell shakes her head as Lizzy turns to see Billy at the counter, making notes.

"You're not writing down our conversation, are you?" Lizzy asks.

He looks up, startled. "I am, but I wouldn't ever write anything without your full approval. I'm mostly scribbling my own observations about the house, the family. I still haven't decided whether I'm going to film this, or write a piece. Or, in fact, whether there is even a piece to write."

"Can we have it in writing, that we have full approval?" says Lizzy, who is always suspicious of journalists.

"You already have it. I gave a letter to your mom. But I'm happy to do one for each of you. Does that work?"

"It does. What about tattoos? Anything? You look too clean-cut to have a tattoo."

Billy shrugs before standing up, lifting his T-shirt, and turning around as Meredith suppresses a gasp. The tattoo is small, on his shoulder, an old Corona typewriter. Everyone moves closer to admire the delicacy, what a cool tattoo it is.

"I got it when I got divorced," Billy says. "Something of a midlife crisis, perhaps, but I wanted to remind myself of the first great love of my life, which is writing. I wanted to remind myself never to get sidetracked again."

"Nice," says Lizzy approvingly.

Meredith feels like she can't breathe. He lifted his shirt, and just before he turned around she saw his abs, his stomach, the line of dark hair that stretched from his navel down under the waistline of his pants, and she is almost vibrating with lust, in a way so unfamiliar to her, she doesn't know what to do.

"Hey, Meri? You okay?" Lizzy notices. Of course Lizzy notices.

"I think I've had a bit too much wine," says Meredith, standing up abruptly. "I'm just going to the bathroom."

She leaves, as Daisy directs attention back to Lizzy. "When did you get your tattoos?"

"I got the one on my back just before I turned eighteen, but no one knew. My parents would have killed me. How about you? When did you get yours?"

"Also at eighteen. My mom came with me."

"I knew I liked her," says Lizzy. "That's very cool."

"She wanted to make sure it was a good tattoo. She had a friend who went to a tattoo parlor in New York when she was on vacation, and walked in off the street on impulse, and the guy was terrible. She has a terrible tattoo that she never would have picked. My mom wanted to make sure I got something delicate, and her ex-girlfriend had tattoos, so we got suggestions from her."

Lizzy perks up, as Nell takes a deep breath. She hadn't expected this topic to come up quite so soon, but now that it has, she knows her sister: there's no way she will let this one drop.

"When you say 'ex-girlfriend,'" Lizzy inquires, "do you mean ex-girlfriend as in, your mom is gay?"

Daisy bristles. "Why? Is that a problem?"

"Oh, my God, no!" says Lizzy. "The opposite! Are you kidding? I think that's amazing. I'm just surprised because your mom seems so . . . momlike. I don't mean that as an insult. I just wouldn't have guessed. Do you mind me asking about your dad? Was your mom always gay? What's the story?"

Daisy relaxes. "You should really ask her; she's happy to talk about it. I can tell you that she says now she always knew, but she wanted to be like everyone else. She thought if she got married and had a child—and she wanted kids, anyway—she would be 'normal.'" Daisy makes quotation signs with her fingers as she says the word.

"And?"

"I think as she got older it became harder to live a lie. And she met

someone. A woman. And . . . that was it. My dad and her are still really good friends, and she's so much happier now."

"Does she have a partner now?"

"No. She likes being in a relationship, but she's been on her own for a little while. She's happy. She's in a good place."

Lizzy sees Nell out of the corner of her eye, focused on her beer. "So what's her type?" she asks innocently, wondering if it might be a tall, rangy farm owner with long, straight blond hair always worn in a tight ponytail at the base of her neck. Wondering how it took her so long to figure this out. This, surely, is the difference she saw in Nell today, the light in her eyes. And all of it fits into place: Nell's reluctance to have a relationship, her disinterest in men. Lizzy has seen her around men, and even when they pay attention to her, she is oblivious.

Lizzy always thought this was a reaction against their mother, who turned into a sex kitten whenever a man walked into a room. Her mother would practically purr, whether it was a friend, a plumber, or her agent. She knew exactly what to do to wrap every man she met around her finger, so Lizzy spent her whole life presuming Nell was consciously doing the opposite, that it was precisely because of her mother that Nell was deliberately so sexless.

Lizzy knows herself to be a huge flirt, but it is charming, rather than sexual. She is tough at work, but can sweet-talk anyone into anything. Nell can't do that, not with men. Perhaps, perhaps, this might help explain why she has always been so shut down. God, could her sister find a way to be happy?

"She doesn't have a type," Daisy says, laughing. "Why? Do you know anyone?"

"Maybe," says Lizzy slowly as she lifts the bottle of beer to her lips and takes a swig. "Although my favorite lesbian just got married."

"To a woman?" clarifies Daisy.

"Yes. She was married to a man, and has kids, and then, like your

mom, realized it was a part of her that couldn't stay suppressed. I think it's awesome, by the way," says Lizzy. "Honestly? I don't think it matters who you love, just as long as you love. Who cares whether it's a man or a woman? Why does that have anything more to do with the person inside than the color of someone's skin? Personally, I'm pretty fucking disappointed that I seem to be one hundred percent heterosexual."

"I don't know," says Daisy. "I kind of think it's a continuum. I mean, most people say they're one hundred percent heterosexual, but they probably aren't. Some people might be more open, some less. Most people live somewhere on the continuum. Of course, when you're one hundred percent, you find it impossible to imagine there's a continuum, because you believe everyone must be the same as you."

River stares at her, nervous. "So what are you?"

"I would say probably around eighty-five percent straight, with a fifteen percent possibility of falling in love with a woman. I've never met a woman I've been attracted to, but as my mother's daughter, I have to say I can't rule out the possibility."

Lizzy peers at Meredith, who is just walking back into the room. "What about you, Meri? Have you ever had a fantasy about a woman?"

"Oh, my God, no!" says Meredith. "What on earth are you guys talking about?"

"I think we should go and see Mom," says Nell, hoping they don't know how her heart is pounding as she quickly changes the subject, knowing she's about to be asked next, knowing she's not ready for this, not ready to tell her sisters anything. Knowing she won't be able to hide it if asked. "Mom's upstairs on her own and we're supposed to be having dinner with her."

"You're right," says Lizzy. "I can't believe I'm actually going to say this, but I've been enjoying my time with my sisters so much, I had forgotten why we're here."

"Oh, ha, ha," says Meredith, used to her sister's sarcasm.

But Lizzy looks at her, wide-eyed. "I swear I wasn't being sarcastic," she says, earnestly. "I really don't remember the last time the three of us were together having fun. Billy?" She turns as he looks up. "Don't write this down." She turns back to Meredith and Nell. "This has been really nice. We've all drifted so far apart, and I have been totally okay with that. I get that we're all so different, but . . . I'm deeply appreciative of all of us being together now. You're my family." She looks at Nell, then Meredith. "Like it or not. It matters."

River walks over to them with a grin, his arms outstretched. "Is this when we hug it out?" he says, tilting his head at his mother, who gives him an imperceptible shake of her head. "Come on, Mom. We are family. Let's hug it out."

Lizzy steps in with a grin, as does Nell, with a reluctant smile.

"Come on, Aunt Meri," croons River, as Meredith shakes her head then finds herself stepping in, all of them with their arms around each other.

Nell is the first to break free, awkward with any kind of physical intimacy with her sisters, even if she's always loved her hugs with River. "Shall we just take food upstairs and eat it in Mom's bedroom?"

"Great idea," says Lizzy. "By the way"—she turns to Daisy, who is watching the family love-in with a large smile on her face—"don't think you've gotten away with it. I did ask you to tell us three things and I haven't forgotten about the other two. Just in case you were wondering."

"I think I've told you enough," Daisy says with a grin. "Maybe, if you're lucky, you'll get more out of me another time!"

thirty-four

Lizzy brings Ronni up a smoothie while the others take up their food on plates, pulling chairs up the stairs and placing them around Ronni's bed so they can all eat together.

"I wish you could eat," says Meredith, frowning as her mother pretends to sip at the smoothie when Meredith holds the glass to her lips.

"Don't worry, dear. I'm not hungry," says Ronni, looking at her family around her bed with a big smile. "That looks delicious. Lizzy, you're such a good girl, cooking for everyone."

"It wasn't me," Lizzy says quickly. "Meredith, it turns out, is quite the cook as well. I have no idea how you managed to raise the two of us, but it seems I'm not the only one who knows how to make delicious food."

Meredith flushes with pleasure at the compliment, but their mother ignores it. "The smoothie is delicious," she says to Lizzy, even though everyone can see she hasn't actually tasted it.

Meredith feels like she is going to cry. Once again, all these years

later, her mother has to put her down by ignoring her, bestowing the few compliments she chooses to give to Lizzy. Once again, all these years later, it still hurts.

"The chicken is better," says Lizzy pointedly. "Anyone can make a smoothie."

"Don't put yourself down, darling," says Ronni.

"Don't put your other daughter down," says Lizzy, staring at her mother in what would have been a confrontational way had Ronni not looked away.

"I'm sorry," Ronni says, looking at Meredith, who stares at her mother, not sure she has ever heard her apologize before. "I didn't mean that your chicken isn't delicious. I wish I could taste it, but I'm not good with solid foods these days."

"Think of the weight you'll lose," says River, who is sitting on the bed and seems to have not noticed, or decided to joke around, the fact that his grandmother is already half her normal body weight. "You could start a new diet! The Ronni Sunshine eat-nothing-and-drop-ten-pounds-a-week diet! You could become the next Dr. Atkins. The Sunshine diet!"

"You mean I could finally make my fortune?"

The girls all tilt their heads. This was the touchiest of subjects that they all always avoided. One would have thought that after Ronni Sunshine's career, their family would be loaded, millionaires. But their mother went to great pains to explain they had only ever been comfortable, and it was only because Ronni kept working. Ronni always kept working.

"I love having you all here," says Ronni, looking at each of her girls, her grandson, graciously avoiding the subject yet again. "And there is something important I have to tell you."

"It's MS, isn't it?" Lizzy says, jumping in.

"No. It's not MS."

"It's something like that, though?" Lizzy is the only one talking, though the other two are staring at their mother, waiting.

"It is amyotrophic lateral sclerosis."

"What is that?" whispers Meredith.

"Oh, fuck," says Lizzy, the color draining from her face. "It's ALS. Lou Gehrig's disease."

"You mean it's fatal?" says River, shocked. "You're going to die?"

Ronni looks at him. "Everyone's going to die, my darling. I'm just going to die a little sooner than I would have liked."

A hush falls upon the room. Forks are put down, and they each stare into space, letting the words settle on their shoulders, seep into their skin.

Meredith is silently leaking tears as her shoulders start shaking. She refuses to let the tears out, calmed only when she feels Billy's hand gently stroking her back. She concentrates on breathing in through her nose, and out through her mouth, until she calms down.

Nell is silent, as always, but she goes to put her hand on River's shoulder. He is looking at his grandmother with sorrow and concern.

"How soon?" says Lizzy, her face impassive.

"This week."

"What? How can you possibly know that? There's no way you're going to die this week—that's absurd." Her phone is already in hand, her fingers flying across the screen as she Googles. "I understand you don't feel like eating, but there are so many new treatments for everything now. There's no way you're going to die this week. Look at Stephen Hawking," she says. "It's exactly what he has and he's had it forever. This doesn't mean . . . We don't know what it means. People are working on research and cures all the time; they're finding new drugs all the time. Look at the new immunotherapy drugs for stage four melanoma. It used to be a death sentence and now people are finding themselves cancer free. It may not be terrible . . ."

"Lizzy." Their mother's voice is surprisingly strong. "Even if by some miracle my life was prolonged in the way Stephen Hawking's has been, do you think I would want to live like that? In a wheelchair, paralyzed, with a voice box and a feeding tube? I've lost the use of my legs, and it is spreading. Fast."

"How long have you known?" Meredith asks, her voice shaking.

"About two months. But apparently I've had it a long time. We just didn't know what the symptoms meant. And trust me, I have done all the research and I am out of options. There is nothing that can be done."

"The weakness," Nell says dully, trying to help her sisters walk through the reality of this news. "The dizziness."

"The fatigue," says Meredith, sick with guilt for not insisting their mother have more tests, get to the bottom of it when all the MRIs, EKGs, scans, and blood work showed nothing. Not that it would have made a difference.

"Are they quite sure?" says Lizzy. "Are they *sure* it's not something else?"

"They are sure," says Ronni. "And as time progresses I will lose everything—my ability to walk, to eat, to breathe. But my brain will be intact, so I will know exactly what's going on. I will be a prisoner in my own body."

"What do we do?" wails Meredith suddenly. "What can we do?"

Lizzy goes to put her arm around her sister as Ronni looks at each of her daughters, then takes a deep breath. "That's why you're here. I want three more days with my family, and then I want you all to help me take my own life."

There is silence.

"You're kidding, right?" says Lizzy, snorting before shaking her head. "You're not kidding?"

"I am sadly not kidding. The paralysis on my left side is spreading,

and soon I will be completely unable to move, then unable to breathe on my own. I will know exactly what's going on, but will not be able to speak or otherwise communicate. I have been living with this diagnosis for some time, and I have thought long and hard about what I want and do not want, and what I am going to do. And what I am going to do is to leave this world in the way I choose, on my terms, with my daughters by my side."

"You're asking us to help kill you?" Meredith is in shock.

"I was thinking of asking a right-to-die advocate to come and help me. I thought about having someone with me, but I don't want a stranger here. Other than you, Billy." She flashes him a smile. "I want my girls. I want to spend as much time as I can over the next three days with you, even though I still get very dizzy and tired." She paused. "What I want most is for you to not try and talk me out of it." She sighs and sinks back into the pillows. "I'm sorry. I'm tired already. I am glad you're all here, and I hope you can do this for me. I know I haven't been the best of mothers, but I have always loved you. So much." She closes her eyes.

"No fucking way." Lizzy stands up abruptly, making Meredith jump. "I don't accept this. I might be willing to consider assisted suicide, but only after we have exhausted every other option. Three days? I've never heard of anything so awful. You're granting us three days before having us *kill* you?" She starts pacing the room. "How are we expected to live with that on our conscience for the rest of our lives? You're right that you may not have been perfect, but you're our *mother* and there's no way we could live with ourselves knowing that we hadn't explored everything. There are new treatments for all kinds of diseases that were once fatal. Who knows what they're developing in Germany or, I don't know, the Philippines? I will not agree to this until we have explored everything. Three days? No fucking way."

Lizzy turns and runs out of the room, as Nell and Meredith exchange glances.

"I'll go after her," says Nell, who leaves but doesn't follow Lizzy down the stairs. Instead she leans against the wall outside her mother's bedroom, relieved she is no longer carrying the burden alone, and shocked. It is now becoming real. Tears trickle down her cheeks as she realizes that Lizzy is right. She may not have been perfect, but she is the only mother they have. She can hear Meredith sobbing from inside the bedroom, as her mother tries to reassure her. River comes out, choking back tears, and Nell takes him in her arms.

An hour later, when she has calmed down, Lizzy goes back into the bedroom, embarrassed that her first reaction was anger. Her first reaction is always anger, she is coming to realize. When she is scared or anxious or sad, the only way she knows to express it is through anger. And later, as always, she is sorry. Everyone left the room when Ronni became tired, but Lizzy waits.

Her mother is lying there in the semidarkness, her eyes closed. Lizzy feels her eyes fill with tears, and sits on the chair next to the bed. As she does so, her mother's eyes fly open and settle on her youngest daughter.

"I thought you were asleep," says Lizzy, her voice breaking. "I was just going to sit here for a bit. I've found places that are doing experimental stem cell treatment . . ."

"Shh," says Ronni. "Not now."

Lizzy stops talking, even though doing something—searching online, making phone calls—makes her feel less helpless. It might be the only way she can cope with such momentous news.

"Why aren't you asleep?" whispers Lizzy.

"I don't sleep well at night," says Ronni. "I'm exhausted all the time, but at night I get these terrible leg cramps, like the worst charley horses you can imagine."

"Can I bring you a painkiller?" says Lizzy.

"Yes, please. They're somewhere downstairs. Bring me four."

"Four? Why four? You're not going to kill yourself with four, are you?"

"No. That's what I need to help. I'll space them out throughout the night. One every four or five hours. Two if it gets really bad."

Lizzy goes downstairs to the corner of the kitchen where the pill bottle is kept. The label says one to two. She empties three into the palm of her hand and pours some water into a glass.

In the room, her mother motions for her to put it all on the nightstand. "It's a little better," she says. "I'll take them during the night when they wake me. If I can ever get to sleep," she adds.

Lizzy looks at her mother. "I have something that may make you sleep," she says slowly. "It's an e-cigarette."

"Darling, I haven't smoked in years," says Ronni. "I can't imagine I'm going to start now. Although it might be nice to spend the last three days doing all the vices I once gave up. Do you have any cocaine?"

"Mom!" says Lizzy, pausing and leaning closer. "Are you serious? Because I can get some . . ."

"No, I'm not serious," she murmurs, smiling at her joke.

"But I do have medical marijuana," says Lizzy. "That's what that e-cigarette is. And it will help you sleep like a baby."

"Really?" Ronni is skeptical. "Where did you get it?"

"From a friend. Apparently there's a dispensary somewhere around here so we can get you a card and get some closer to home."

Lizzy refuses to consider the thought that her mother might be serious about three more days. If she gives her enough options, surely she can change her mind. "This stuff"—she reaches into the back pocket of her pants and pulls out a slender black metal cigarette—"is the good stuff. This is sent to me by a friend in Colorado. Here. If I hold it to your mouth, sip on it. Don't take a huge draw, just take sips."

She reaches forward and holds it to her mother's lips, as her mother inhales.

"Sip, Mom. Sip."

Her mother coughs a little, and Lizzy holds a glass of water to her mouth, before her mother indicates she wants some more. Lizzy holds the e-cigarette up again, and her mother sips this time, then sinks back with a smile.

"I feel tingly," she says. "In a good way rather than bad."

"Nice, right?" says Lizzy, smiling.

"It's very good," says her mother, looking peaceful for the first time that night. "Tell me about you, Lizzy. What's the real stuff?"

Lizzy nods. She knows what her mother means. "I'm having an affair with my business partner, a married man, and James found out and made me promise to end it. I did, and agreed to do couples counseling and work on our marriage. But then it started again, and this time he doesn't know, and our marriage feels dead in the water. We feel like two people who have completely lost sight of why we are together, and we have grown so far apart, I don't honestly think there's any chance of us getting back together again. And then I have Connor, who I love so much, and I don't want to hurt him by making him a child of divorce, but I worry I'm hurting him more by staying in something that is a farce. And I worry that I'm a terrible mother, that I'm causing him permanent damage because I don't seem to have the mothering gene, and . . ." She stops and takes a deep breath, then a hit on the e-cigarette. "What do you think, Mom?" Lizzy is aware that she has never asked her mother's advice in her adult life. "What should I do?"

"I don't know." Ronni smiles, her eyes closing. "But I trust you to find the right answer."

Lizzy is at first stunned at her words. Certainly not the kind of thing her very judgmental mother ever said to her before.

"You were always my favorite, Lizzy," she adds. "You know that. Don't tell your sisters. You're my driven little firecracker, so talented, so ambitious, so gorgeous. I have no doubt life will unfold in the right way for you." She pauses for a minute, then whispers, "But, my God, I wish I had raised you differently."

Lizzy chuckles. "Been a better mother? Don't worry about it. I turned out pretty good."

"No," says her mother, turning her head to gaze at her daughter. "You didn't. I spoiled you, in every sense of the word. I love you, but you've grown up to be selfish, to step all over people, to never worry about consequences. You think you can get away with everything, and you hurt people. You have no idea how much you are hurting your husband."

Lizzy stares at her mother as guilt and anger combine. Did she know before today? How could she have known?

"What are you talking about?" Lizzy says slowly.

"James told me you were having an affair. He turned to me, of all people, to advise him. I don't judge you, Lizzy, and God knows I was no saint in my marriage, but I wish I had parented you better. I wish you had had consequences."

"Are you serious?" Lizzy's anger sparks. "You're basically seconds away from dying and this is what you have to tell me? Jesus Christ." She exhales loudly, standing up and pocketing the e-cigarette. "I'm not listening to this. I'll just assume this is the ALS taking over your brain." And, snorting with disdain, she walks out of the room.

Downstairs, Lizzy finds River, Daisy, and Nell on stools around the kitchen counter, drinking vodka.

"I'll go upstairs and see her," says Nell, until Lizzy tells her she's being a bitch.

"She is?" Nell looks surprised. "I'm surprised she has the energy."

"Oh, that veil is definitely fucking on," says Lizzy, pulling the e-cigarette back out of her pocket, because right now she needs it more than ever.

"What did she say?" asks Nell.

"That I was spoiled and selfish and never thought about anyone other than myself."

"She didn't!" River's eyes are wide.

Nell shrugs with a reluctant grimace. "It's not entirely untrue," she says quietly.

Lizzy shakes her head and inhales.

River leans forward, watching his aunt inhale, then reaches out and takes the e-cigarette.

"Niiice," he says. "Indica, right? May I?"

"No," says Nell, snatching it away. "You're not going to get high in front of your mother."

"You don't really get high. Just mellow and sleepy," says Lizzy. "Honestly, it's the same as having a drink, and you're all sitting here drinking vodka. I left her room feeling like I was going to kill someone and I feel better already. Seriously, I feel pretty mellow, all things considered."

"It's true," says River. "And this is better for you than drinking."

"Right. Whatever," says Nell, holding out her hand. "Mothers first." She takes a huge inhalation, sputtering and coughing when she's done.

"You're supposed to sip it," says River.

"Great. Now you tell me," she sputters, looking up at River when she has stopped coughing. "How on earth do you know so much about it anyway?"

"I was a college student," he says. "In Boulder, Colorado. How do you think I know?"

Lizzy's eyes light up. "I totally forgot you were in Boulder. You can send it to me now."

"No, he can't. My son isn't going to be your drug dealer."

"It's legal in Colorado."

"And when it's legal here you can get your own."

"Okay," grumbles Lizzy as the e-cigarette is passed around, everyone sitting in silence for a while. "Where's Meredith? And Billy?"

"They went for a walk," says Daisy. "They've been gone quite a while."

"Do you think she likes him?" Lizzy says, after a pause.

"I think, after tonight's news, it's totally irrelevant," says Nell.

"Really? Because I think we could do with something to distract ourselves from the horror of our mother having a terminal illness and wanting us to murder her in three days."

"I don't know that I see it as murder," says Nell, serious as ever. "River and Daisy were just showing me beautiful stories of people who have terminal diseases, and in a couple of cases ALS, who have these parties where they surround themselves with friends and family to say good-bye before taking their own lives."

"I'm all for it," says Lizzy, "in principle. But *three days' notice*? You can't summon us home because you're sick, then tell us you're dying, then tell us, whoops, actually, sorry I forgot to mention it, but that dying business is going to take place in *three days*. If we absolutely know there's no relief, no cure, no nothing, I would totally do that, have some amazing party, but not in three days."

"You're the one who said you were so busy you couldn't stay. But anyway, it's ALS," says Nell. "There is no cure."

"And as I said before, Stephen Hawking."

"Who appears to be an anomaly. Even if she were to live, you know our vain, glamorous mother wouldn't want to live like that."

"It's not the point. Who knows what stem cell treatments may be available around the corner? We need more than three days."

Nell stares at her sister. "Look, I don't entirely disagree with you. Part of me wants to respect her wishes, and the other part agrees that we need more time. She needs more time. But I don't think it's getting any better."

"We have three days. At least three days," says River. "And everything always seems worse at night. Maybe she'll feel differently in the morning. Maybe we'll all feel differently in the morning."

They turn as they hear the front door open. A moment later Meredith walks into the kitchen, looking tired. Behind her, disheveled, sweaty, grinning, with a large bag hitched over his shoulder, is Derek.

He drops the bag and puts his hands up with a smile and in a voice that is far too happy and far too loud, he exclaims, "Surprise!"

thirty-five

Meredith excused herself to take Derek upstairs. River snuck up and came back to report there were angry whispers coming from behind the closed door of their room.

Billy is sitting at the kitchen counter, taking notes.

"Tell me again . . ." he says, to no one in particular. Nell is at the sink washing up; River is drying; Daisy is at the kitchen table reading the paper. "When's the wedding?"

Lizzy drags a stool over. "We don't know. We don't think we've been invited because darling Derek disapproves of us. We're all trying to push it out of our minds because he's so awful."

Billy puts down his notebook and grimaces. "I am clearly supposed to be completely objective, but . . ." He pauses, deliberating whether or not to continue, before his words come out in a burst. "What the hell is she doing with him?"

"We don't know. I think she has such low self-esteem she thinks he's the best she can get. And you have to admit, he is good-looking."

Billy looks horrified.

"I know, I know, but that's the only explanation," says Lizzy.

"Why would she have low self-esteem? She's gorgeous and sweet and . . . I don't know, she just seems lovely." And he blushes as Lizzy shoves him in the arm.

"And if you'd kissed her on that walk maybe she'd see that she doesn't have to settle for the Dreadful Derek. Honestly, Billy, I know you're here to get a story, but now that you're here, you may as well make yourself part of the family for real. Couldn't you have kissed her?"

Billy shakes his head with an embarrassed laugh. "I may think she's lovely, but I barely know her. That's not my style."

"Know her, *schmo* her. So what? Urgh." Lizzy's shoulders sag. "I can't believe that in the middle of all this, he's here."

Nell turns from the sink, then comes to sit down with them. "I don't think she'll go through with it," she says.

"She won't if this one declares his undying lust," Lizzy says, gesturing to Billy and then raising her hands in the air, an innocent look on her face. "*What?* It's not like no one's noticed."

Billy suppresses a laugh. "I'm not going to kiss her on the night she just found out her mother is dying, much less when she is engaged to someone else, who just arrived from London."

Lizzy blanches, steadying herself on the counter, the smile dropping from her face. "Shit," she whispers. "I can't believe it. I keep going in and out of this reality. Our mother is dying." She turns to Nell. "How is that possible?"

"I know. I haven't been close to her for years, but . . . I didn't expect this to happen. Three days . . ."

"Nothing's going to happen in three days," snaps Lizzy. "That's the only thing I'm sure of."

Nell says nothing, thinking about her relationship with her mother, all the missed opportunities, the resentment she felt whenever her

mother phoned. She remembers talking to someone in the café once, who said she had had a terrible relationship with her mother. She had hated her mother her entire life, and when her mother, a difficult, vain, vicious woman, had unexpectedly died, the daughter had felt relief. Her eyes had clouded over slightly. "That was ten years ago," she said. "Now I just miss her."

I won't miss my mother, Nell thought.

Now, sitting in the kitchen, tuning out as Lizzy keeps talking, she's not sure she'll feel relief. All she knows is that her mother is dying, and not just dying but choosing to end her life soon, and she feels so much more than she expected.

Panic. Her mind is flooded with all the things she has never said. Fear. Her mother, who has always been so frightening in her invulnerability, is somehow more terrifying now that she is vulnerable, frail, old.

Nell has found something entirely unexpected happening since her mother told them. Sitting in her mother's kitchen, alongside the fear and the panic and the impending loss, perhaps for the first time in her life, she feels a deep sense of love.

Up until right this moment she never knew it was there.

thirty-six

The house is quiet, her mother asleep, everyone else gone home. Derek is waiting upstairs for her, in bed. She will be expected to make love and shudders at the thought, unaware that she grimaces.

She had been deep in conversation with Billy as they walked along the boardwalk at Compo Beach, Billy listening as she spoke about her mother, their relationship, her sisters, how surprised she was at the way they had come together, stopped bickering, were actually kind of connecting. He was being there as a friend, he'd said, not as a journalist, and he felt like a friend, or at least, like someone who cared, even though he was a man she didn't know.

Occasionally she would glance at his face, thinking how handsome he was, how much she wanted to reach out and touch his skin, if only to see how it felt. When they had stopped, she had looked at his lips and was shocked to find herself picturing what it might be like to kiss him. They had talked and talked, and when her voice started quaver-

ing and tears spilled down her cheeks, he had rubbed her back until it passed.

They were walking into the driveway when the town car pulled up. It must be a mistake, she thought; what would a town car be doing here this late at night? Surely they had the wrong address.

The driver jumped out and opened the rear door before Meredith had a chance to tell him of his mistake, and out stepped Derek, with his handsome grin, disheveled from the flight, his shirt slightly askew, his hair tousled, and—not for the first time, but perhaps it was the first time she had noticed herself doing it—she recoiled.

As Billy politely introduced himself, she stood back and looked at the two men, side by side. One was quiet, thoughtful, and seemed sincere. The other struck her in that moment as being not dissimilar to a Shakespearean fool.

I hate him, she thought, even as she allowed herself to be hugged. *I hate him.*

She allowed herself to be held, catching a whiff of his smell as her nose was buried into his neck, and although it was fair that he should be sweaty and tired, and smell slightly sour, it occurred to her that she hated his smell. She had always hated his smell.

"I'd better go," said Billy, later that night, after he had made notes in the kitchen, by which time Derek was resting upstairs. Billy said good-bye to the others, and Meredith walked him to the door, feeling an unexpected sense of loss that he was leaving.

"Are you okay?" he said, just before he left.

She shrugged. "I'm not great at surprises."

He looked at her. "All surprises, or just surprises you don't really want?"

And she felt a lump in her throat. "What am I going to do?" she whispered, hoping the desperation wasn't as obvious as it felt.

Billy stepped toward her. For a second, a terrifying, glorious, exciting second, she thought he might kiss her. He leaned toward her and said, an urgency in his voice, "Don't settle. Don't ever settle." After kissing her on the cheek, he turned and left.

Meredith stood on the doorstep and watched him climb into his car, watched him pull out of the driveway. What did that mean? she thought, even as she knew he was right. This wasn't about Billy. There was something there, some chemistry between them, but that was irrelevant. What mattered was what he had said: *Don't settle.* But all along she had been fighting everything in her that told her the same thing, had deliberately silenced the voice that screamed dissent. When she awoke in the middle of the night unable to breathe, feeling a terrifying weight on her chest, anxiety at what she was about to do filling her eyes, her ears, her nose, she would tell herself she was being stupid, would make list after list in her head of why Derek was right for her, why he was the sensible choice.

She *is* settling. Billy knows it, and she knows it. And now Derek is here, and what the hell is she supposed to do?

What she does is take a deep breath, turn off the rest of the downstairs lights, and go upstairs. When she is in their room with the door closed, she faces him down. In London, she is never able to face him down. She is always aware that he is her superior at work, a partner in their firm, someone who should be respected.

But now he is here, in her childhood home, without an invitation, and for the first time in their relationship, she does not feel the need to defer to him. For the first time in their relationship, he is not her superior. For the first time in their relationship, she is thinking about what *she* wants, and not about him.

"I'm really unhappy," she says, facing him, ignoring his outstretched arms. "I can't believe you just turned up here, in the midst of this family turmoil, without checking with me."

"Darling!" He steps toward her, but she steps back. "I know you're going through trauma with your family. You always go through trauma with your family, so I came here to support you. Frankly, I'm a little disappointed with your reaction. All I do is think about you and how to make you happy, and you're not the slightest bit grateful. If you want to know the truth, I think it's completely within my rights to be rather appalled by your behavior. I understand that being around your family is upsetting to you, but for you to take it out on me, to somehow blame me for doing something so thoughtful, is—"

"Stop it," she hisses. "You always do this. You always take my words and twist them so I end up looking like the one who's doing something wrong. I am trying to tell you that I did not want a surprise, that I'm not happy you didn't tell me you were coming." But even as she says the words, she feels herself weakening. This is what he does to her, forces her to express herself in a way that is palatable to him, rather than be honest about what she feels.

"I didn't tell you because I didn't want you to feel pressured," says Derek. "I suspected your sisters might have said I couldn't come if they had known. What?" He notices her shocked expression. "You think it's not obvious that they don't like me?" He snorts. "Look, I thought I was doing the right thing. Come here." He opens his arms as Meredith falters before stepping in.

What else can she do?

I don't have to settle, she tells herself, thinking of Billy. *I don't have to settle*. But nor does she know how to get out of the trap she has laid for herself.

Derek squeezes her tightly, then starts kissing her neck. Oh no, she thinks. I can't do this. She steps back, adopting an expression of what she hopes is disappointment and apology.

"I have my period," she says, knowing Derek won't touch her when she has her period. Her periods have miraculously gotten longer and

longer since she has been with Derek. Before, they were an average of four days. Now, she is able to stretch them out for almost two weeks, during which Derek will not lay a finger on her.

He frowns. "Didn't you have a super long one that ended just as you were leaving for America?"

Bugger. He wasn't supposed to remember that.

"I did." Meredith nods, her brain frantically whirring. "And I stopped for a few days, then started again yesterday, which is so bizarre. I'm a little worried there's something wrong."

Derek falls, hook, line, and sinker. "Poor darling. You must make an appointment with the gynecologist when you get home. Maybe there's someone here you can see."

"I don't have insurance here."

"Oh." He pouts like a little boy. "I'll just have to wait for my goodies until we get home. That's okay. I'm tired anyway. Let's just get into bed and cuddle."

He unbuttons his shirt as Meredith averts her eyes, trying not to compare him to Billy, although she can't help thinking of Billy in his T-shirt, how attractive he is.

She undresses herself, pulls on pajamas, and climbs into bed. She rolls on her side, facing away from him. She allows Derek to spoon against her back, because at least she doesn't have to smell him, doesn't have to look at him. She waits for him to start snoring before she unravels herself and steps quietly out of bed.

She can't do this tonight. The bed is too small, and her dislike of the man she is planning to marry too strong. She leaves and goes down the hall to the spare room and, slipping under the covers, she is soon fast asleep.

thirty-seven

Lizzy drives one car, Nell, River, and Daisy another, as they head back to the farm in silence, all of them looking out the window as they drive, each of them lost in thought.

"This was a rough night," Lizzy says when she finally pulls into the driveway next to Nell's truck and steps out, the still and quiet of the night air punctuated by the car doors slamming. She hasn't been able to stop thinking about what her mother said. It was so easy to dismiss it, but if it isn't true, why have the words been echoing around and around all evening?

"I feel drained," admits Nell, walking into the house.

Lizzy pauses by the door, then steps back. "I'm going to go for a walk," she says.

"A walk? It's pitch-black. You won't be able to see anything."

"I need to make a couple of phone calls. I'll just go and find somewhere quiet."

"Don't go beyond the hay barn or there won't be any service," says

Nell, before peering at her sister in the darkness. "It's very late. Who are you calling at this hour? James?"

"Yes," lies Lizzy, setting off down the yard, where she pulls the heavy wood door of the hay barn aside and climbs up the mountain of last year's hay bales until she reaches the top, before lying back and inhaling deeply.

This smells of childhood, of innocence, of a time when all she had to worry about was getting her homework in on time and whether or not she'd win the part in the school play. When she was a kid and Nell had a job here on the weekends, she would visit from time to time, and she and Jackie would climb up to the hay bales and hide, telling each other ghost stories for hours, talking about nothing, and everything, until Nell finished work and came looking for them, striding into the hay barn and yelling their names.

She sits up, leaning back against a hay bale, shifting to get comfortable, before checking her phone has service. It's 10:34 p.m. Too late for normal people to make, or take, phone calls, but the food business isn't a normal business. The pop-up supper club is tomorrow night, which means Sean will be busy organizing last-minute details. He sent her a long e-mail this morning, telling her exactly what the menu changes were, which staff members would be working the night, what bartender they were using.

But they haven't connected about anything other than the logistics of work since she got here, and tonight, above all other nights, she needs to hear his voice; she needs to talk about the real stuff. She punches his name on her speed dial as she smiles, wondering just when it was that Sean became her emotional go-to, for that is what he has become. When she is happy, sad, excited, disturbed, or stressed, or utterly disbelieving that her mother has ALS and is choosing to take her own life in three days, the person she now chooses to share it with is Sean.

The phone rings three times, before going to voice mail. Which

means the phone is turned on, that Sean is choosing not to answer it, but instead directing it to voice mail. She frowns and dials again. This time it goes straight to voice mail; this time he has switched it off.

As my business partner, she types furiously into the phone, you need to PICK UP THE FUCKING PHONE WHEN I CALL.

She calls again, but nothing, and a swell of rage overtakes her. "You fucker!" she shrieks, hurling her cell phone into a hay bale. "Fucking asshole!" she screams, knowing, from all those years gone by, that no one can hear her.

He's probably with his wife, she tells herself. He'll probably excuse himself and call me back. She retrieves the phone and looks hopefully at the screen, but there is nothing. No dots signifying a response. Nothing.

How can he abandon me on a night I really need him? she thinks, now almost close to tears. She looks at her phone, goes into Contacts, and presses James's name. Maybe he'll pick up. And if not, she'll keep going down her contact list until she finds someone who will.

James picks up on the fourth ring, his voice heavy with sleep.

"Are you asleep?" she snaps, when it is obvious he was.

"I'm awake now," he says, as she pictures him sitting up in bed, snapping on the lamp. She pictures their bedroom, the mussed-up teal and white bedspread, the bamboo blind that is broken, half raised in a permanent slant, the John Marshall cow print on the wall opposite the bed, a huge, gentle black and white cow against a hot pink background. She pictures the Louis *Somethingth* sofa at the end of their bed that they found on the street one Saturday afternoon, years ago, that they claimed by sitting on it, phoning friends until they found someone with a truck who could come and help them move it to their house. She reupholstered it in lavender velvet, which was now as faded as its original velour, thanks to beating sunlight and all manner of Connor's bodily fluids staining and weathering it to its original state.

She thinks of how she used to lie on the sofa when she was nursing

Connor, listening to music as the stripes of sunlight fell across the burp cloth, completely at peace, with an absolute assurance that this was what her body was designed for, that motherhood was the pinnacle of all she would ever achieve.

What happened? she thinks, listening to the rustle of James propping himself up with the pillows from her side of the bed. When did it all change?

"What's up?" he says. "What time is it?"

"Almost eleven, I think," she says. "Sorry for phoning so late. I needed to talk."

"That's okay. How's it going there with your family?"

"Not so good," she says, tears springing into her eyes. "Urgh. I can't believe I'm getting emotional. This is so stupid," she berates herself. "It's not like she was ever a great mother to begin with. But . . . she has ALS."

"Whoa." James sounds completely alert. "Oh, my God. I'm so sorry."

"I know. Thank you. And as if that doesn't completely suck, she wants us to help her take her own life. And as if that doesn't completely suck, she wants to do it in three days. Can you believe it? My mother wants to be dead in three days. My fucking nightmarish, selfish, disinterested, loving-conditionally mother is planning on dying, and I will never get a chance to make this better." Lizzy breaks into sobs, as James listens; she's sniffing and sniveling, talking through her tears. "I have hated her for so much of my life, and now she's dying, and I don't know what to do."

"Oh, Lizzy," James says simply when she has calmed down. "Can we come out? Connor and me? Can we come and be with you?"

"No," Lizzy wails. "I don't know. Maybe. I don't know what to do." She is now hiccuping her sorrow as she regresses to the frightened child she has never allowed herself to be. Not Lizzy. Lizzy is strong and fearless. Lizzy is charmed and invincible. Bad stuff does not happen to Lizzy because she does not allow it.

But this is out of her control, and she is unprepared for the flood of emotion that is overtaking her.

"We'll come out tomorrow." James is calm, and calming. Just like he was at the start. "We will get the train out. We'll figure out what to do when we get there. How does that sound?"

"Okay," sniffles Lizzy, her sobs and hiccups gradually subsiding. "Okay."

After they hang up, she climbs down from the hay bale, her head already pounding from the tears, wiping her eyes as she makes her way back to the house. She's not at all sure how James will help. What's he going to do? she thinks. Bring his virtual reality games and sit in Nell's living room playing them all day? But she catches herself in the cruelty of the thought and pushes it aside. The very fact that he answered the phone, that he is offering to bring Connor, is consolation enough.

thirty-eight

Nell is in bed, scribbling notes on the notepad she keeps on her night table, lists of what needs to be done on the farm tomorrow morning and who should do it. Usually she is organized enough that she puts these lists up in the barn the night before, so when the workers arrive they see the tasks and who is on which shift, but family has gotten in the way today. She will have to get up at the crack of dawn and put them up.

She keeps sighing, putting the pen down, and thinking about the events of the evening. Three days. She feels numb and disbelieving. Three days. What will it be like, she wonders, to be a motherless daughter? Will she, like the woman she once spoke to in the café that time, feel relief? Or will she feel regret?

Lizzy is right, of course, about three days being insane. But their mother seemed resolute. She had always been the sort of woman who changed her mind, who trilled that it was a woman's prerogative, and yet this didn't seem like something that would change.

Everything about this is different. There is no drama, Nell realizes. This isn't about seeking attention. There is a resigned quality to her mother that she hasn't seen before. Lizzy may not want to accept it, but Nell doesn't see how their mother will change her mind, not when she is so resolute.

There is a light knock on her door. "Come in," says Nell, unsurprised, relieved, and nervous to see Greta framed in the hallway light. This is the one thing she hasn't thought about, she realizes. The one thing that has been squashed by the events of the evening.

"May I?" Greta pads in and sits on the bed. She is wearing pajamas and an old, soft robe of Nell's that she left in the caretaker's cottage for her. It is a baby blue and suits her.

"The kids told me about your mother. I wanted to check in on you and see how you are."

"I'm okay." Nell shrugs, the memory of their kiss flashing into her head as she looks at Greta, flushing. Did it really happen? Did she imagine the chemistry they had, the kiss?

Greta just looks at her. "Do you want to talk?"

"I don't really know what to say." Nell looks at her, her face screwed up in a grimace of discomfort as Greta nods.

"I understand," she says. "You must be shocked."

Nell nods, an unfamiliar lump in her throat. "I'm sorry," she whispers. "I'm not quite sure where this is coming from."

"This is your mother," Greta says, and there is so much compassion in her voice, so much empathy, so much love, that Nell finds her shoulders heaving as she tries to swallow a sob.

Greta climbs on the bed then and takes Nell in her arms. Nell heaves sobs, crying quietly onto her shoulder as Greta holds her tightly and strokes her hair; and when, eventually, the sobs subside, Greta kisses her eyes, her cheeks, her mouth, and lays her gently back against the pillows.

"Would you like me to stay with you?" she asks.

Nell nods.

Greta takes off her robe and climbs under the covers. She puts an arm around Nell and pulls her close, murmuring gently. Nell's body slowly unclenches, and she relaxes.

And soon, the two of them are fast asleep.

thirty-nine

"I thought I'd bring you brea— Whoa! This is not what I expected."

Lizzy is standing in Nell's bedroom doorway with a large mug of tea in one hand and a plate on which sits a muffin, some butter, and jelly in the other. "Not that I didn't expect it, exactly, I just didn't expect it so soon. Actually"—she grins at Nell and Greta, who are only just rousing themselves from sleep—"I just have to say that I think it's perfect, and it all makes sense, and frankly, Nell, if I'd really thought about it I probably would have realized years ago. I'll just go and grab another cup of tea and a muffin for you, Greta." She backs out of the room, grinning from ear to ear. "And very sorry to disturb. Also"—she pops her head back around the doorway, with a big thumbs-up—"yay, lesbians. Big fan." Finally she disappears out of the room.

"Did she actually say 'yay, lesbians'?" says Greta, leaning back on the pillows and turning to Nell, watching the corners of Nell's mouth twitch.

"She did. That's my sister. She actually said that." Nell shakes her

head with a smile that turns into laughter, which becomes more and more hysterical, the two of them leaning on each other, heaving with helpless laughter.

"Oh, God," Greta says after a while, wiping the tears of mirth from her eyes. "How do we tell her that nothing happened?"

"Right," says Nell, feeling a swell of disappointment deep in her belly. Nothing happened. She fell asleep with Greta's arm wrapped around her, Greta's head resting on hers, and woke up, just now, in the same position, both of them moving apart only when Lizzy burst into the room. Now they are both leaning back against the headboard, Greta's head turned to Nell's.

"Although," Greta says, "if I recall correctly, I did kiss you yesterday."

"You did," agrees Nell, a flutter in her stomach as the room seems to still and she stares into Greta's eyes. "What do you think about kissing me today?" Nell finds herself saying, a lurch in her groin.

"I think," Greta says, moving closer, not taking her eyes off Nell's, "that's an excellent idea," and she softly moves her lips onto Nell's, taking her bottom lip between her own before their tongues meet, and Nell dissolves in a sigh of pleasure.

"Lock the door," whispers Greta when they pull apart, Nell trembling with desire. But Greta gets up to do it, then climbs back on the bed and dips her head to kiss Nell properly. This time, the kiss goes on and on and on.

Nell kisses like she can't get enough. She is ravenous, wanting to taste, to touch, to explore. Greta lifts her top, exposing her breasts, and Nell traces the curve of one breast, one nipple, with her fingers before taking it in her mouth.

It is so soft, thinks Nell, allowing herself to be transported, allowing herself to give in to the flickers of lust, to every fiber of her body feeling alive.

She is so soft. All curves and gentleness and deep, hidden space. Nell licks and smells and inhales and laughs . . . and—oh! This is what it feels like! So soft! So good! She is on fire, aquiver, weak, and—oh! This! And a bliss washes over her like she has never felt before.

Afterward, in Greta's arms, after they have shouted to Lizzy to go away and not disturb them, after they have giggled when she shouted that she was leaving the tea outside the door, afterward Nell cannot stop smiling.

"Was it that good?" Greta whispers with a smile as she traces Nell's lips with her finger, as Nell kisses her finger, kisses all her fingers, licks her palm, wanting to bury herself in this woman.

"I don't know if I have the words," Nell says softly, thinking there aren't enough words in the English language to describe what her body has just gone through, what she has just gone through. "It was . . . transformative. Earth-shattering. Cataclysmic."

"It *was* that good?" Greta smiles as she leans her head on Nell's shoulder and traces her fingers down her neck, down her chest, around her breast, stroking over her nipple, which rises to attention as Nell catches her breath.

"It was," Nell whispers, amazed at how her body feels, what this woman's touch is doing to her, what it is like to be able to slip her hand between her legs, how exciting it is to feel her there, her sacred space, the moistness that is for her, and her alone. "And it was something more," Nell whispers as it is Greta's turn to gasp. "It felt like coming home."

forty

"Do you really think we have to be with her?" says River, setting plates on the kitchen table. "I love Ronron, but I'm not sure I want to be there when she dies."

They are in the kitchen, Lizzy stirring scrambled eggs, yellow and creamy, flecked with fresh herbs. Nell, having placed croissants she grabbed from the coffee shop into a linen-lined basket, is dolloping homemade jam into a small ramekin, but a smile is playing on her lips as she relives, over and over, the way her body sang this morning, the joy of discovering something she never knew she was missing until today.

"It's just awful," says Lizzy, taking the pan off the stove but continuing to stir with a wooden spoon. "I keep forgetting, then remembering. Jesus. ALS. Why couldn't it have been something like cancer? At least there's a fucking chance."

"Fuck," says River, emboldened by his aunt's swearing. "I just . . .

Do you think she means she wants us there in the room? Because I don't know if I really want to be there in the room. I mean, do I get a say in it? It's awful. The whole thing is awful, and it sucks massively that she's really sick and she's going to die, but do I actually have to be in the room and watch her go? I mean, I think that's pretty gross. If that's okay to say. I'm sorry. Maybe I shouldn't be saying all of this."

Nell doesn't know how to respond, but Lizzy speaks up. "It's okay, honey." She reaches over and pats his back. "First of all, I don't think we should be worrying about this now. I think we have a little more time than we think. We need a little more time. Also, though: Yeah. I get it. I definitely don't want to see a dead body, especially my mother's."

"Lizzy," Nell says slowly, pushing thoughts of Greta out of her head, "if she says she wants three days, don't you think we should maybe respect her wishes? We have no idea what kind of pain she's in. If it's unbearable, is it really fair to ask her not to do something that will alleviate that pain?"

"Yeah, when it's death, yeah. I do think that's fair," Lizzy snaps, before taking a breath. "Look, I'm sorry. I know there are beautiful people who do beautiful ceremonies in states where it's legal. Trust me, I've been up pretty much all night reading about it. I know people throw parties, and make the decision when and how they're going to go. I'm not saying I don't think we should do that. I'm just saying we need more time. Don't call us home, announce you have ALS, and tell us that you're planning on being dead in three days."

"I know," says Nell. "I feel the same way. I just don't think we have any idea what she's going through. I feel so guilty that I barely see her. I'm right here. Every time she calls and asks for my help, I feel resentment and anger. And now all I feel is guilt and regret. I want longer too. I just don't know if that's fair."

"I don't know," says Lizzy. "Have you ever seen a dead body?"

Nell shakes her head as Daisy walks in. "No."

River turns to Daisy. "Have you?"

"Have I what?"

"Ever seen a dead body?"

"No, but my mom has."

"Your mom has what?" Greta walks into the room, her hair now pulled back in a ponytail much like Nell's, her face looking clean and scrubbed and smelling of coconut and almonds.

I liked her hair loose, thinks Nell. My God, she is beautiful. An image of Greta's head between her legs, her quick, clever tongue, slips into her head, and she shivers, a pang of lust that forces her to cross her legs.

Greta Whitstable, she thinks. Oh, Greta Whitstable. What have you done to me?

"Seen a dead body," says Daisy. "Didn't Ken ask you to check on him when he died, to make sure he was dead? He was paranoid about being buried alive so he had Mom agree to come and see him before they took him away."

"Ken?" Nell asks.

"A friend," says Greta, giving Nell a knowing look, a look that Nell interprets as "Don't worry. I am yours." "He had cancer," explains Greta. "It wasn't nearly as frightening as I thought it would be," she adds. "It wasn't Ken anymore. It was just . . . a husk. A shell. It was entirely clear to me that his spirit had gone elsewhere, and in some ways it was quite beautiful. It allowed me to have closure. To let go."

"That does sound beautiful, actually," says Lizzy. "Not scary. I wonder if we'll be able to let go."

"She says she wants three days. Imagine if those three days are filled with love, filled with happiness," says Greta. "Imagine if you were able to forgive whatever transgressions you might each think one

another has made. Imagine if you could hold her as she moves to the next world. That doesn't sound scary; it sounds quite beautiful."

"It does," says Lizzy. "But no way it's happening in three days. Three months, maybe." She looks at her watch. "Shit. Francine is probably here. I said I'd meet her in the coffee shop. I've got to run. I'll be back as soon as I can, and if you've already left for Mom's, I'll get an Uber and meet you there." Blowing kisses around the table, Lizzy disappears.

forty-one

Francine is sitting in a corner of the café, her head bowed over her phone. She has worked for Lizzy for over a year and is one of the best. She's hardworking, has no ego, and is gorgeous, in that particularly French way. Tiny, olive-skinned, she has thick brown hair, large brown eyes, and an ever-present smile. She is always calm on the job, has a great disposition with the clients. When things go wrong, and they always go wrong, Francine shrugs it off. There is no drama with her, Lizzy realizes.

Which is why it's so odd that something is going on that needed to be discussed in person. As she walks over, she realizes it could only be that Francine is leaving. Which is not good news.

Francine sees Lizzy. She puts her phone down and stands up to give Lizzy a hug, kissing her on one cheek, then the other.

"These are really good," she says, holding up a half-eaten croissant. "These might be the best croissants I've eaten outside of France. They're definitely the best croissants I've eaten in America."

"That's high praise," says Lizzy. "My sister has a . . . friend . . . staying, who, it turns out, is this extraordinary baker. She made these ridiculous muffins yesterday that were insane, and now it turns out she's incredible at croissants. I want to get her to bake for us." Lizzy is aware that Francine has not asked to meet to discuss croissants, but she doesn't want to hear the words that she might be leaving.

"Okay," Lizzy says, pulling out a chair and sitting down hard. "What's the story? You're leaving, aren't you?"

Francine's eyes fill with tears. "It's not as easy as that," she says, with a slight nod. "I think I do have to leave, because it's too painful to stay."

Lizzy reaches across the table and covers her hand, shocked. This isn't a side of Francine she has ever seen, vulnerable and fragile.

"What's going on?" she says, presuming it is a family matter. Her parents are still in France, she remembers. And a brother. A family illness?

Francine lifts heavy eyes to meet Lizzy's. "It's Sean," she says simply.

"Sean?" Lizzy sits back, not understanding. "What about Sean?"

"I . . . Oh, God. We have been so careful for no one to know, and he made me swear at the beginning that you must never know, but now things have gone too far and I don't know who else to turn to."

Lizzy's heart is pounding, her mouth dry, as her brain struggles to compute what Francine is saying.

"You and Sean. You're having an affair?" Lizzy can hardly breathe.

"It isn't just an affair. He was going to leave his wife for me," Francine says, unaware of Lizzy's churning emotions. "We had it all planned, and then I got pregnant, and"—the tears are back, this time spilling down her cheeks—"I miscarried last week, and he didn't come to see me, and wouldn't respond to my calls or texts, and now he has told me it is over." She looks pleadingly at Lizzy. "I can't stay. It's too

painful. I am so sorry. I know what you must think about me having an affair with a married man. I am not proud of myself. I thought this was not an affair. I thought this was the love of my life, and we would . . ." She shrugs, dismissing her own naiveté. "I thought I would live happily ever after. Stupid, huh? God." She shakes her head. "I have been so stupid."

"How long has this been going on?" It takes everything Lizzy has for her voice to emerge as normal.

"Nine months."

Nine months? thinks Lizzy, as a wave of rage starts to build. Nine months during which Sean was pulling her into pantries and bathrooms and behind barns. *Nine months* during which they would occasionally book a hotel, if the event was far away, and have the luxury of sharing a bed, of falling asleep in each other's arms, of waking up and having breakfast, just like every other normal couple.

Nine months during which Lizzy too thought it was more than an affair. Of her too thinking that he was going to leave his wife and children, if she left James. Nine months of falling for him, of living for those stolen moments together, of never being able to walk away, no matter how hard she tried.

And all the time, he was fucking Francine. Not just fucking, it would seem, but spinning the same bullshit, the same stories, the same lies. Lizzy thinks of how he makes love, the stroking, the murmuring, the way he insists on making her come before he enters her, how he says her pleasure makes him happy.

"What?" says Francine, alert.

"What?"

"You just said, 'Your pleasure makes me happy.' How do you know? How do you know he says that?"

Oh, shit, thinks Lizzy, who had no idea she had said that out loud. "You're not the only one," she says to Francine. "This isn't the first

time he has done this. I'm so sorry. He's a fucking sleaze, and a liar. I am sorry that you thought he was someone special, and I'm sorrier still that you have gone through a miscarriage. The only thing I'm absolutely sure of is that you're better off without him. You are so much better off without him."

Francine nods. "I know. Intellectually I know that; it's just hard. I feel so much emotion, and I still can't believe he just disappeared when I miscarried. Now I realize he was just pretending to be happy when I told him I was pregnant. He was obviously terrified." She looks back at Lizzy. "I love working for you, Lizzy. I think you are an amazing woman. You have always treated me so well. You treat all of us well, and you have good . . . boundaries."

"Yes, I do. Something that . . . *Sean* should have learned." Lizzy is almost foaming at the mouth, her fury red-hot, as she stops herself from using every curse word she has ever known. And with her anger comes disgust—at herself, at falling for it, at believing the same shit he was feeding Francine at the same time.

"But I have to leave," says Francine. "I can't work knowing he will be there. I am so sorry. I have been so happy and it is the best job I have had, but—" She shakes her head. "All good things come to an end."

"What if Sean wasn't there?" Lizzy finds herself saying, as the anger subsides enough for her brain to slowly click into gear.

"You would do that for me?" Francine is shocked.

"It's not just because of you. As I said, it isn't the first time. I think he's now too much of a liability."

"It's none of my business, but he's your partner. How do you even split from him? Other than falling pregnant by him and miscarrying." She snorts at her sad joke.

Lizzy doesn't crack a smile, her brain working too hard and too fast. "What if . . ." She speaks slowly, looking out the French doors of the café, beyond the gravel courtyard, to the cluster of barns in the

distance. "What if I tried something else? It's something I've been thinking of for a while, and I've been speaking to my sister about it. What if I started something out here? On this farm."

Francine looks around. "Here? In this coffee shop?"

"No. We can maybe do something in here, but I've been talking to my sister about taking over the large hay barn, and using this as a semipermanent base for the pop-ups. But as I think about it, maybe it makes more sense to do something permanent. We could call it something like The Farm Table: supper on the farm. What if I left the supper clubs in the city altogether and moved out here?"

She is thinking out loud, all the thoughts she has had over the past few days, the conversations she has had with Nell, cementing as she speaks. "Sean can keep the supper clubs. It won't work in the same way without me, anyway. That's not ego talking, but people come for me. He doesn't even have to buy me out. He can keep it. They'll come here because this is mine, and it will have nothing to do with Sean."

"Oh, my God. You are serious? You would actually do this?"

"I've been thinking about this for a while. You coming here and telling me what's been going on has just expedited what I was already planning. Jesus." She shakes her head again in disbelief. "What a sleaze. We are all better off without him."

"You know all the staff will follow you." Francine is smiling for the first time since Lizzy walked in. "If you want them to. Their loyalty is with you."

"That's great." Lizzy is distracted, her anger rising again. She forces her attention back to Francine. "Thank you for telling me, and I'm sorry you had to go through this. I'm sorry we all have to go through this. And you have no idea how grateful I am. Can we keep this between us?"

"You have my word."

"And you won't say anything to Sean?"

"Absolutely not. I've taken a week's vacation after the . . . Well. You know. I need the money, but I don't want to go back and see him."

"We'll figure it out," says Lizzy.

Her overwhelming urge is to get him on the phone and scream at him. Instead, she goes into the barn, climbs to the top of the hay, and howls in there.

"Lizzy?" Nell comes running in. "What's going on?"

"Fuck!" Lizzy shouts from the top. "I didn't know you were here. I thought you had left to go to Mom's house."

"I'm going soon. Why are you screaming in the hay barn? Is someone with you?"

"No. I'm furious. It's a long story." Lizzy peers at Nell, standing in the barn, looking up. "Want to come up?"

Nell walks over to the hay and starts to climb. Once she sits down next to her, Lizzy tells her everything. When she finishes, she says, "You're a good listener. I'd forgotten what a good listener you are."

Nell smiles. "It's because I don't talk much. I'm much more comfortable listening."

"But what do you think? Can you believe that fucking sleaze? Can you believe he was sleeping with me, and with my number one waitress, and, frankly, with God only knows who else? Thank God I used condoms. Who knows what I might have caught. What do I do? I want to just tear him a new asshole. I'm so goddamned angry."

"You don't speak to him," says Nell. "You retain a lawyer. I know someone great in Westport. You stay unemotional and calm. The lawyer will help you figure out the best way to move forward."

"And what about using Fieldstone Farm as a base for my new company?"

Nell looks at her sister. "Yes." She nods. "Let's do it."

"What?" Lizzy shrieks, her first smile in two hours, as she flings her arms around her sister. "You're serious?"

"I am. If it doesn't work, it doesn't work, but I need to do something else with the farm. We need to bring in more money." She laughs as Lizzy keeps squeezing her tightly, refusing to let her go.

"Oh, my God, oh, my God! I'm so excited!"

"Okay, okay." Nell disengages. "And your waitress? If you can't get rid of Sean immediately and want to find something else for her, I could do with someone else helping out here."

"That's a lovely offer. Thank you. I'll speak to her. It would be perfect, actually. And Greta could bake for us out here too! Wouldn't that be amazing? Keeping it in the family! How perfect is that?"

Nell shakes her head. "I don't know. Greta's going back to St. Louis in a week. At least, that's her plan."

"Plans can change," Lizzy says. "Especially when you've just met the woman who's going to change your life."

"I don't know that she's going to change my life," says Nell, even as she thinks that she already has.

"I wasn't talking about her. I was talking about you. You're going to change *her* life."

"I don't know about that," says Nell, embarrassed.

"Nell"—Lizzy grabs her sister's hand—"there's something special between you two. I was being facetious when I was saying 'yay, lesbians,' but truly, I think it's amazing that you have found whatever you have found together."

"We've only just met," says Nell, flustered.

"So what? I can see it. I bet you anything Greta doesn't leave. Or, if she leaves, she comes right back."

"You're such a romantic." Nell laughs.

"I am, and I'm also insightful. I know shit. How do you think I built the business I did? How do you think I know that we're going to

build something incredible here? You're never going to have to worry about money again."

"I hope you're right." She looks at her phone. "Meredith is texting, asking where we are."

"Oh, God," groans Lizzy. "Avoiding the Dreadful Derek."

"Come on," Nell says, smiling. "We'd better go."

forty-two

Derek has always been very good at errands. He likes being useful, and this morning, rather than have him underfoot in the house, Meredith sends him off to Trader Joe's to buy some wraps and salads for lunch.

He came into her room this morning, waking her by sitting on the bed and stroking her arm like a cat, hurt that she had left their bed and found somewhere else to sleep, hurt that he had woken up alone.

Meredith tried to reassure him, keeping her voice light as if it was no big deal, but it was a big deal. The thought of sleeping in the bed with him again tonight, the thought of feeling his large, sweaty body on top of hers as he covers her face with pecks, like an overeager, pompous sparrow, fills her with horror.

She finds herself thinking about Billy. He seems positively boyish, next to Derek. Simple, unpretentious, clever. He is down-to-earth and so relaxed. Not at all the sort of man she would expect to pay attention to her, but he seems to be paying attention to her.

What does it mean? Nothing, she realizes, given that she lives in London, that he is here to write about her mother, and more specifically, she now knows, her mother's illness and imminent death. Of course nothing is going to happen between them. Not now, certainly. And there is the small fact that she is engaged to another man who happens to now be here.

Derek. Her mother. Her sisters. It all feels overwhelming. Perhaps that's all Billy is, a distraction from thinking about, or dealing with, the things in her life that are so painful, that fill her with a sadness so great, it is easier to focus on what feels suspiciously like a schoolgirl crush.

He probably doesn't like me, she thinks. He couldn't possibly like me. Maybe he just feels sorry for me. But he was so sweet on their walk, so attentive, asking all the right questions, showing interest and no hint of judgment in how he spoke to her. She found herself opening up to him in a way that felt unfamiliar.

And then bloody Derek showed up, with his loud, awkward laugh and his hairy back, and the way he insists on telling Meredith what to do. Thank God she has gotten rid of him for an hour or so, and where on earth are her sisters?

On the way to taking laundry downstairs, she stops in her mother's bedroom.

"Shall I sit you up?" she asks, hiding her shock at her mother's appearance. Ronni's face is stripped of everything, gaunt and hollow, but she smiles as Meredith walks over to the bed.

Meredith props the pillows up behind her mother. "Mom, I'm wondering about maybe looking into getting you a wheelchair. Maybe we could get you one of those chair lifts for the stairs. As lovely as your bedroom is, don't you want to spend some time downstairs? Imagine if we made it really comfortable for you. Your friends could come around and sit with you."

"What friends?" says her mother, when she is propped up. "They've all disappeared."

Hm, thinks Meredith. That is surely more to do with how her mother treated her friendships, breezing in and out, disappearing for years at a time when she was busy touring or busy with other people or simply busy, jumping back into people's lives only when she needed something.

"How are you today?"

"Not great," she says. "I'm having these terrible nerve twitches. It's called fasciculations. Sometimes I can see them jumping under my skin. Can you bring me up my painkillers?"

"You know I can't bring you up the whole bottle," says Meredith, aware of the risk of her mother deciding to swallow them all in one fell swoop when no one is looking. "How many do you need?"

"Four would be good. I'll take two now and save two for later."

"Okay," Meredith agrees, going downstairs to get the pills. She comes back and walks into the room, setting everything on the nightstand as her mother watches her.

"Have you lost weight?" her mother says suddenly, looking Meredith up and down.

Meredith has noticed, as it happens, that the prewedding weight she recently gained seems to be melting away. She doesn't know how much, exactly, but she hasn't had an appetite, and this morning when she pulled on the new pants, they were looser and baggier than yesterday.

Derek saw her in the pants, and the beaded tunic, and frowned. "That's a bit bohemian, isn't it?" he said, disapproval written all over his face.

"Is it? I love this outfit," she said, and he sniffed and looked away, saying nothing more.

She had felt beautiful this morning, until Derek looked her up and down. Now, even though she has lost weight, her mother's words rile her, as they have always done, making her feel that her mother's love for her is conditional upon her being thin, being pretty, being good enough.

"I don't know," lies Meredith, trying not to let her discomfort be heard.

"You're perfect the way you are," says her mother, and when Meredith looks at her in surprise, her mother is smiling, as if she means it.

"So beautiful," says her mother, awkwardly patting the bed with the one hand that still, vaguely, works, grimacing slightly as she does so.

"Are you in pain?" asks Meredith, and her mother nods. "Do you want to take a painkiller now?"

"Not yet. Just sit with me for a bit. Your fiancé, is he here?"
Meredith nods.

"Yes. I thought I heard his distinctive voice this morning. Remind me, when is the wedding?"

"Early October."

"I know this is a sensitive subject, my darling, but I don't have much time. You can't storm out when I say this to you."

"Okay," Meredith says, numb at hearing her mother saying she doesn't have much time. Surely they can change her mind, can't they?

"Think very hard about the person you are marrying. It is not something to be taken lightly. I only know this because I was a horrible wife, and I have had many years to think about marriage, and what I did wrong, and what makes a good marriage. I wish I had stayed with your father. He was a very good man, and very good to me. He was loving and supportive, and wanted me to find success in whatever field I chose. What he didn't do was control me, or try to mold me into a little wife, some old-fashioned, muted version of who I was. I saw many

men do that to many women I knew. They would choose these vibrant, talented, beautiful women, and suck the life and passion and beauty out of them by bullying them into submission. I love you, Meredith, and you are so much more than you have ever allowed yourself to be. You don't need a man to be happy, and you don't need a man who won't allow you to be the real Meredith. Remember your art?"

Meredith nods, swallowing the lump in her throat.

"You were so talented," her mother says, smiling. "It is such a pity you didn't pursue that. Don't marry someone because you think you need a partner. And don't marry someone who tries to mold you into what he wants his wife to be. You're better than that. Marry, if you do at all, only someone who loves you just the way you are. Because you are precious. There. I've said my piece. Are you still talking to me?"

Meredith nods, stunned into silence.

"You are so beautiful, Meri. I know I have spent a lifetime criticizing you, making comments about your weight, and I am so sorry. I didn't know any better. I was corrupted by Hollywood, and convinced that being slim and beautiful was the key to happiness. I just wanted you to be happy. I realized far too late how irrelevant it is. You're beautiful, Meredith, exactly as you are."

Meredith stares at her, not believing her.

"You don't believe me." Her mother sighs. "I should have said this years ago. Not that it makes any difference what I think. But you are so special, too special to end up with a man who isn't your equal. Derek may be handsome, but that's really all he has going for him. You, on the other hand, are such a creative, clever, sweet girl. I always saw you as a painter, or a potter, some kind of artist. Remember those beautiful pots you threw on the wheel at school? You have such an open, kind heart. You were always my favorite," she says, as Meredith's heart threatens to burst.

She leans her head down on her mother's chest as her mother croons into her hair. "My favorite," she murmurs. "Don't tell your sisters."

Downstairs, Meredith finds Lizzy and Nell pulling into the driveway; when they come inside, Nell is carrying a brown paper bag filled with croissants.

"Greta the magnificent," explains Lizzy. "She's on a baking binge. I don't know. Maybe she's in love or something." She casts a sideways glance at Nell, who studiously avoids looking at her, even as she suppresses a small smile.

"You look nice." Lizzy reaches over and fingers the sleeve of Meredith's tunic. "I love that batik. Really nice, Meri. These flowy boho clothes suit you."

Meredith smiles. "Thank you."

"How's Mom?"

"Amazing," says Meredith. "She's . . . amazing."

"Like, up-and-walking amazing or not-being-a-bitch amazing?" says Lizzy, pausing, wondering if this all might have been a great act after all.

"No, don't be silly. Neither. Like . . . understanding, kind, and loving. She is completely different."

"What? How? She was mean as hell to me. What did she talk to you about?"

Meredith sighs deeply. "About me. About who she thought I would become when I was a child. And about marriage and what she wanted for me."

"I guess she was nicer to you than she was with me." Lizzy rolls her eyes. "She doesn't want Derek for you, does she?"

Meredith shrugs. "I knew she didn't, but she was able to express

why. She basically said she thinks he's controlling, that he's trying to squeeze me into some image he has of what his wife should be, and that I would completely lose myself if I married him. I don't know, she didn't use those words exactly, but that's essentially what she was saying." Meredith casts a nervous glance out the window, looking for Derek.

"Yeah? And?"

Nell walks over. "And is that news to you?"

"No. I just . . ." Meredith's shoulders slump as she sinks onto a kitchen chair. "It has been like playing a role. I was so flattered that a partner in my firm, someone like Derek, who's handsome, who everyone loves, even noticed me, I found myself drawn into this relationship and trying so hard to be someone I'm not."

"*Who* loves Derek?" says Lizzy in horror. "I don't love Derek. I think he's an unctuous little man."

"People at work love him."

"Oh. Accountants on his payroll. Right. So you've been trying to be the perfect wife while the real Meredith, the Meredith who is creative and fun, who loves dressing in bohemian"—she peers closer, asks, "Calypso?" and Meredith nods—"Calypso outfits is struggling to be seen, except she's worried Derek wouldn't like her."

"Yes," says Meredith. "Exactly."

Lizzy frowns. "Is it relevant that Billy has a crush on you?"

"He doesn't!" protests Meredith. Weakly. "I don't think he does."

"He does," says Lizzy, "although whether or not anything happens between you is kind of irrelevant. The point is that men like Billy, clever, fun, handsome, nonpompous men like Billy, *like* you. They are attracted to you. If you could do something about your low self-esteem, you'd find a world of possibility out there. That low self-esteem, by the way, that caused you to say yes rather than pee yourself

laughing when Derek first asked you out on a date. Derek is not the best you can get. Oh, my God. If that were true, why not just kill yourself now?"

"Lizzy!" Nell says, casting her eyes up to the ceiling where their mother lies.

"Sorry for the inappropriate turn of phrase. But there are hundreds of men like Billy who would be so lucky, so ridiculously, unbelievably lucky to have you. You have no idea. Derek must wake up every day thinking he's hit the jackpot, because he doesn't deserve you. You are worth a hundred Dereks."

Meredith stares at her sister. "Do you really mean that?"

"Yes," says Lizzy, turning to look at Nell.

"She does," says Nell. "And she's right."

"Speak of the devil," says Lizzy, turning to look out the window as their mother's Lexus pulls into the driveway, driven by Derek.

"I have no idea how to do this," whispers Meredith.

"Dump his sorry ass," says Lizzy, but Nell intervenes.

"You can do it kindly," says Nell.

All three of them watch as Derek gathers the shopping bags from the backseat of the car.

"You can just simply say your feelings have changed," Nell tells her. "You don't have to be cruel."

"Even though it's kind of more fun to be cruel," says Lizzy, thinking instantly of Sean. "Fucking sleaze," she says.

Meredith's head whips around, a frown on her face. "What?"

"Not Derek. I was thinking about someone else. Sorry."

"Hello, darling," Derek says as he walks into the kitchen, going up to Meredith and kissing her on the top of her head, as Lizzy makes a face at Nell across the room.

"Derek," Meredith says quietly, "we need to talk."

They go to the back porch and down the steps into the yard, Meredith's heart pounding with what she's about to say. But she is so full of what her mother said, what her sisters said. And unlike last time, when she stormed out of the Four Seasons restaurant vowing never to speak to them again, this time she felt their love. They were telling the truth, and they were doing it from a place of love.

Derek is frowning at her. "What's the matter?" He attempts to open her arms, as if hugging her will fix whatever she is about to say, but Meredith takes a step back.

"Derek, I have had a few days by myself, and I've come to realize a number of things that aren't working for me." She wants to kick herself. These aren't the words she wants to use. "I know we are supposed to be getting married in three months, but I am having second thoughts."

The color drains from Derek's face.

"I think we need to take a break," she says, wincing at causing someone else pain, instantly trying to make the pain less. "Just while I figure things out."

"Do you mean postpone the wedding?" Derek is confused. "For how long?"

"I don't really mean postpone," Meredith says, after a pause. "I don't think I want to get married."

Derek smiles with relief. "Oh! This is just last-minute wedding nerves, and it's completely normal. Darling, it would be more strange if you didn't feel like this. Trust me. You will be absolutely fine. Now come here." This time he opens his arms, but Meredith just stares at him, unmoving.

"Okay," she says, taking a step away from him, her decision to be kind, her nerves, her not wanting to hurt him, now squashed by irritation. "You're not listening. You never listen to me. You always tell

me how to feel and how to think, and I am not allowed to have any voice. You need to listen to me now." She slows down, speaking slowly and clearly. "I don't want to get married. I don't want to marry you. I don't want to continue our relationship. I didn't ask you to come here, and now I want you to leave."

"You are joking," says Derek, staring at her, unable to believe what he is hearing.

"Do I look like I'm joking?" says Meredith, a thousand other sentences going through her head, none of which must be said out loud.

I don't want to ever have sex with you again, she thinks. I don't want to sit across the table from you in a restaurant as you order for me. I don't want to feel your heavy arm reaching over to me in bed. I don't want to kiss you, or smell you, or taste you. I never want to feel your skin on mine again.

"What about our wedding? What about the hundreds of clients? What am I supposed to tell them? This is not acceptable," he sputters.

"I don't care what you tell them," says Meredith. "Tell them I'm having a midlife crisis if you want. I will be giving the company my written notice today," she says, although she is surprised to hear those words emerging. But as soon as they are said out loud, she feels a weight lifting. "I am sorry, Derek, but you and I are not meant to be together. We never were. And it is my fault that I couldn't see it earlier."

Derek hisses something under his breath, muttering words Meredith has no wish to hear. He spins on his heel and stomps toward the house, tripping on the first step up to the porch, cursing out loud before turning back to her.

"I'm the best thing that will ever happen to you," he says. "You will never find anyone to look after you like I would have done. I hope you find what you're looking for, even though it's unlikely, isn't it, at your age." Seemingly satisfied at having gotten a final dig in, he lurches up the porch and into the house.

A half hour later, he is gone. Meredith tried to say good-bye, to end things somehow on terms if not good, at least passable, but he wouldn't look at her, wouldn't speak to her. He just marched toward the car waiting for him at the end of the driveway, his jaw clenched, threw his bag in the backseat, climbed in behind it, and rode off.

Meredith, Lizzy, and Nell all watched from the dining room window, Lizzy snaking an arm around Meredith's waist and leaning her head on her shoulder.

"Is he actually gone?" whispers Meredith, when they can no longer hear the car.

"He is," says Nell as Meredith turns to her, disbelief and relief in her eyes. Nell gives her a high five, then spontaneously pulls her in for a brief hug. "Well done," she says. "That must have been hard for you."

Meredith shakes her head. "I can't believe it. I can't believe I did it." She turns to Lizzy. "Can you believe I did it?"

Lizzy whoops and grabs Meredith, waltzing her around the dining room, singing, "Fuck, yeah, Meri! You finally stood up for yourself!"

Meredith laughs, as she allows Lizzy to waltz her into the kitchen; there Lizzy stops and stands in front of her. "Here's the deal, Meredith. Life is whatever you choose to make it. You never have to let anyone control you, nor give up your power in order to make someone happy. The only way any of us finds happiness is to figure out what it is that we need, and go after it. You hated your fiancé and now—"

"I didn't hate him," grumbles Meredith.

"Yeah, you did. That's okay. He's hateable. And now he's gone. You hate your job. Oh, come on, don't even. You hate your job and you just told a partner you're handing in your written notice. The world is your oyster, Meredith. Now you just have to figure out what you want to do. How do you feel? Be honest. How does it feel to walk away from two giant parts of your life that were making you miserable?"

"Honestly?" Meredith grins. "As you would say, it feels fanfuck-ingtastic."

"I know." Lizzy looks at her watch. "I'd better text James. He's coming out to the farm, but I'll tell him to come here. Is Mom up?"

"She was watching that HGTV show she likes," Nell calls from the other room. "I'll go up and check on her."

"Okay." Meredith looks out the window to see Billy pulling up in his car. "I'm going to go for a walk. I'll see if Billy wants to come."

forty-three

Ronni Sunshine is propped up against the pillows, more alert than Nell has seen her these last few times. She turns her head from the TV and smiles as Nell walks in.

"I'm just checking up on you," says Nell. "Is there anything I can get you?"

"Where is everyone?"

"Downstairs. Lizzy's on the phone and Meredith just went for a walk with Billy."

"Billy? What about Derek?"

"Ah." Nell sits on the chair next to her mother's bed. "Meredith just did the unthinkable. She ended her engagement."

A wide smile spreads on Ronni's face. "Thank God," she says. "Thank heavens she saw the light. Is he gone?" Nell nods. "What a dreadful, pompous man he is."

"She is leaving her job as well. Who knows, maybe she'll move back home. Maybe . . ." Nell pauses as an idea strikes. "Maybe Meredith

can move in here and look after you? That would be a reason to keep going, wouldn't it, Mom? You haven't spent proper time with her in years, and if she were back here, she could be with you while we research treatments."

Ronni smiles, choosing not to respond. "Where is Lily?" she asks.

"We decided to give her a couple of days off," Nell says. "The poor woman is exhausted. We would have told you earlier, but you were asleep. Why are you looking so sad?"

"I won't see her." Her mother sighs.

"Mom," Nell says quietly, "it's not going to happen, you know that, right? We aren't going to help you take your own life. None of us are ready for that, and we don't believe you're ready. We need more time."

Her mother winces.

"What's the matter? Is it the spasms? Do you need painkillers?"

"Yes, please, darling," Ronni says. "Can you bring me four?"

"I'm not bringing you four," Nell says. "I checked the dosage the other day. It's one to two."

"Two doesn't do anything anymore," says Ronni. "Bring me four and I promise I won't take more than two at a time."

Nell stands up.

"Wait," says her mother. "Come here."

Nell moves to the bed and takes her mother's hand, resting it in her own, knowing her mother can no longer move it.

"Lovely Nell," Ronni says, smiling. "My firstborn. Do you know how you changed my life when you were born? I was obsessed with you. I couldn't tear myself away from you. When you were asleep I would go in and sit next to the crib and just watch you. My heart would swell with so much love for you, I don't know how it didn't burst. My quiet, strong observer. You have always watched, Nell, never plunging in the way Lizzy does, and you have a strength and self-possession Meredith does not. And River, child of your own, what a beautiful boy

child you have grown, all by yourself. Lewis Calder . . ." She gives a slight shake of her head. "What a waste of space he was, other than to give you River. How I wish you had found someone to make you happy. I know you don't think you need anyone, but love would soften you, Nell, allow you to let your guard down."

"Maybe," says Nell, thinking of Greta as a smile plays on her lips.

"Is there something I should know?" asks her mother, eyes widening in deliberate surprise, although Nell suspects her mother knows something already.

"Maybe." Nell blushes. "It's early days. Too early to say anything, really. It might be nothing."

"Is he lovely?"

Nell freezes. What does she say? How does she tell her? This isn't something her mother can handle, surely.

"Or is it a she?" asks her mother simply as Nell looks at her in shock.

"How did you . . . ?"

"It was a lucky guess. Whoever she is, she is lucky. Love is love, Nell, in whatever form or shape it comes, and those of us who have found it must not let anything get in the way. I never taught you how to love, and I am sorry I was so uninvolved with you. I neglected you. And I wish I had done things differently."

"I survived," Nell says flatly, attempting to shrug it off.

"But you haven't thrived. And that is my fault. I was raised by parents who told me that every single thing I did was charmed. They showered me with attention and praise, and I grew up hating them for it, blaming them for growing into an adult who needed ridiculous amounts of attention and praise in order to feel worthy. I thought I was doing you a favor by withholding it. I thought you would develop strength of character, self-possession, without needing shallow praise or attention to make your way in life."

"Looks like you did a pretty good job," says Nell. "I just can't seem to get to a place where I can thank you for it."

"I don't blame you for being angry. I'm angry. With myself. I only realize now that I could have done things differently. In life there's always a balance. My childhood was one extreme, and as a result, I raised you with the other extreme. Neither is right."

"Don't worry about it, Mom," says Nell, thinking how this is far too little, too late.

"I did the best I could, given how I was raised," her mother persists. "If I could go back and do it differently, I would."

Nell looks at her mother then and sees her eyes brimming with tears.

She has no more time, Nell realizes with shock. No more time to figure it out, to work through the differences, to heal the distance with her mother. This is it. And something in her softens as unexpected tears spring into her eyes.

"I forgive you," Nell says, finding as the words come out that she means it. "It has all worked out for me. At least I hope it might. I think I may finally have a glimpse of what happiness feels like."

"My lovely, strong Nell. You were always my favorite." She sighs, closing her eyes. "Don't tell your sisters."

Nell's heart swells as she leans over and gives her mother a kiss.

"Go get my pills," says her mother, smiling into her daughter's eyes. "I love you so much. I love all of you so much."

forty-four

"Mommy!" Connor rushes out of the car and races toward Lizzy, who picks him up, squeezes him tight, and bursts into tears.

James follows behind him, grabbing from the backseat the ubiquitous bag filled with toys, snacks, and baby wipes to clean up the mess he will inevitably make.

Lizzy croons into Connor's hair as he starts to wriggle, demanding to be put down, to run around this huge driveway! Climb those trees! Race in circles on the lawn!

She turns to James, wiping the tears off her cheeks and smiling. There he is, she thinks. Heartbreakingly familiar and stable and loyal. There he is, my husband, who is raising our son, who may play computer games too much but is such a good man, the man I should have been paying attention to all along.

It feels like it has been months since she saw him. She may not have been in Connecticut for long, but it's true, she hasn't really seen him in

months, all her attention sucked up by Sean, by the excitement and thrill of the affair she kept trying to give up. The affair that is over for good.

I never saw it, she thinks. I never saw how much I would be giving up. Stupid, stupid me. She walks toward James, uncomfortable, no idea how to greet him. The dynamic of their relationship had always been that James was the lover, and Lizzy the loved. He had loved her more, had pursued her, had poured affection and sweetness all over her. Until he didn't.

He stands, watching her.

"Hi," she says, a half smile on her face, wondering if she should hug him. Wondering how long it has been since she and her husband have even touched, let alone hugged.

"Hey," he says. "I'm sorry I'm a bit later than planned. We decided to drive rather than take the train, and then traffic on I-95 was hell."

"Traffic on I-95 is always hell," says Lizzy. "I don't know what happened. It always used to be an hour, and now it never seems to be less than two."

"Yup. So. How is everything here?"

"It's . . . sad. And uncertain. And also, there's exciting stuff. Lots of changes. We really need to talk."

"I know," says James. "I know."

"Meredith is out for a walk, but Nell's here. Maybe we could leave Connor with her for a bit and, I don't know, go for a coffee or something? Does that sound okay?"

"Sure," James says. "That sounds perfect."

Nell of course is more than happy to be with Connor, so Lizzy and James are soon at Neat, which is quiet, just a few people dotted around at tables, with one person at the counter.

"I remember coming here last year," says James, looking around. "And it was packed."

"Yeah. This time of year, the whole town is on Nantucket," says Lizzy.

"Really? Why would people leave? You have the beach right here."

"I know, but it's still home, you still have your usual shit to do. Tons of people in Westport head to Nantucket for the summer. I hear Iceland is pretty big this year too, and apparently Greece is particularly hot. Nice for us, though. It means we get a table. When were you here last year?" asks Lizzy. "What for?"

James colors. "Just a meeting."

"I know you talked to my mother," she says gently. "She told me you asked her for advice. Was that when you were here?"

He nods. "I guess you're mad that I went behind your back?"

"No. I'm sorry that we couldn't figure it out between the two of us. I totally understand why you turned to her."

James looks relieved.

They sit, order cappuccinos, and Lizzy takes a deep breath and starts to tell James about her plans. She tells him about the farm. Although he has visited, he can't picture the hay barn, so she describes it in detail. She tells him about setting up a permanent base, with plans for pop-up supper clubs in the orchard, although the details have yet to be worked out. She tells him that they could all move out there, to Easton or Redding or Ridgefield or Georgetown—somewhere where Connor could ride a bike and grow up learning where food comes from, not by visiting farmers' markets, but by growing it themselves.

"It would be a fresh start." Lizzy's excitement is bubbling up. "I know things have been really hard between us, but we could start fresh here. I have such a good feeling about this, James. I think this is what we need, this is what we've needed for so long. If we keep doing what we've been doing, we will get what we have always got, and that isn't enough. I want something different for my life. I want something different for Connor. And I want something different for us." She stops,

filled with anticipation, the expectation that James will see it, that he will jump on board.

James nods, thinking. "And what about Sean?" he says.

"I'm going to take on a lawyer to figure out how to disentangle our partnership. He can keep the supper clubs in the city. I plan on doing this by myself. I don't need a partner anymore. I'd love you to be more involved, which I think you can be once Connor starts kindergarten this year. We can do this, you and me." She grins.

"What about your affair with Sean?"

Lizzy's heart lurches. "That's over. You know that's over."

"I know you said it was over," James says quietly. "I know we went to couples counseling because you promised it was over and you would give our marriage a go. And I know it has been continuing ever since. So, I guess I'll ask again. What about Sean?"

"It really is over now," whispers Lizzy, stricken. She has no idea how he knows, and she cannot ask.

"I think our marriage is too," says James. "I'm sorry this is happening now, when your mother is going through what she is going through, but I can't do this anymore." He shakes his head, sadness all over his face. "The betrayal is too much. I'm excited for you that you have these ideas and I'm sure Nell's farm is the perfect spot. And honestly, I'm not averse to moving out here with Connor if you go through with this. As you pointed out, Connor will be starting kindergarten soon, and we could put him in public schools here, and I'll have more time. I can freelance from anywhere. I could find a place close to you so we can split our time with Connor." He stops, noticing that Lizzy is crying. "I'm sorry," he says.

"I get it," says Lizzy, thinking, oh, the irony, that here it is: the consequences her mother said she never dealt with. She rubs her eyes with the end of her sleeve. "I've been a fucking idiot and this is totally what I deserve. I'm sorry. I'm so, so sorry."

"Yeah," says James. "Me too."

forty-five

"W here's Billy?" says Nell, after Meredith has arrived back at the house on her own, thrilled to see Connor, who she has only met twice, and briefly at that.

"He left," says Meredith. "There isn't a story here. Not with Mom planning on assisted suicide, like, now."

"It's not going to be now," says Nell. "She's going to have to wait."

"I know that, and I said that to Billy, but as he pointed out, it's just going to be sadness. He wants to write something, but there's no documentary, and he feels like he's intruding by being here."

Nell frowns. "We like him being here. It isn't an intrusion. And Mom invited him."

"Yes, but he's gone. He says he'll drop by later and say good-bye to Mom, explain to her that he has what he needs to write a retrospective about her. You know he taped her, right? Talking about her life?"

"No. I didn't. Are you okay with him leaving?" Nell peers at her sister.

"I'm fine. Why?"

"You do like him, don't you?"

Meredith shrugs. "I just got rid of my fiancé this morning, and quit my job. I have absolutely no idea what my future holds. I don't know where I'm going to work, where I'm going to live, whether or not I'm going to stay in London."

"You might come back home?"

"I just don't know. I was so desperate to leave America when I was young. But I've really liked being back this time. I had forgotten how lovely Westport is, how easy it is to live here. My God, you can park anywhere! And the weather is glorious. And there's no traffic!"

"That's not actually true," says Nell. "The traffic is awful."

"When you've navigated Swiss Cottage in rush hour on a daily basis, trust me, you won't be saying that," says Meredith. "I've tried so hard to make London my home, and there's a part of me that feels it is. But I'm also realizing that this is home too, and maybe I need to come back and give it another chance. This isn't about Billy," she says quickly. "He has said that if I come back, he'd love to take me out for dinner, but who knows if that will happen. I might not come back; he might meet someone . . ."

"*You* might meet someone," says Nell, as Connor comes running in, naked.

"Auntie Nell, Auntie Nell, can you take me swimming?"

Nell and Meredith burst out laughing. "Give me five minutes," says Nell. "Go back and watch the end of the show and then I'll take you."

"'Kay," he says, disappearing into the family room.

"He's so cute," says Meredith, still grinning. "I'd like to get to know him properly. I'd like to spend more time with all of you."

"I would like that. You know, Lizzy and I have been talking about setting up some kind of supper club, and maybe a restaurant, at the farm."

"That sounds awesome!"

"Maybe you could be involved."

Meredith bursts out laughing. "Ha! I can cook a decent roast, but that's about it. Thank you, but I have no interest in working in the food business."

"Okay. But maybe there's something else. Maybe you could decorate. Or start painting again and sell the art in the restaurant. I don't know. Something that uses your artistic side."

"Yeah. Mom said the same thing. Not about the farm, but about using my creativity. I've been thinking about it a lot. Maybe I'll start classes again. I would love that."

"It would be nice for the three of us to be home," Nell says, surprised there is a tear welling in her eye. "I never thought I would say that, but it has been nice having you all here."

"I agree," says Meredith, realizing she has never seen Nell display emotion like this before. "It's been nice being with you and Lizzy. More than nice." She shrugs and wipes the tear as she and Nell smile at each other.

"It's home."

forty-six

M om?" Lizzy leans over her mom, frowning. There is something not right, but she isn't sure what it is, as if there is a fog in her brain preventing her from seeing clearly. "Mom? Wake up. Mom? Mom? Mom!" she screams as she shakes her mother, feels how warm she is, even though there is no breath coming from her mouth.

Meredith and Nell come running up the stairs, bursting into the bedroom as Lizzy turns to them in fury, grief, disbelief.

"She's gone!" she says. "I think she's dead. Someone gave her the pills. We said we wouldn't do it. Who did it? Who gave her the pills?"

"The pills are downstairs," Nell says dully, sinking onto the bed. "No one gave her the pills. I gave her four this morning, but that isn't enough to—"

"I gave her four this morning," says Meredith, shaky with shock and guilt, as the tears start to fall.

"Fuck!" Lizzy bursts out. "I gave them to her last night. She didn't

take them. She didn't take any of yours either, did she? Did you see her swallow them?"

Meredith is openly sobbing now, Nell wiping a tear from her cheek as they both shake their heads. Meredith leans over the bed and lays her cheek against her mother's and kisses her, her eyes closed as her shoulders heave.

"She's been stockpiling for days," says Lizzy, stricken as it dawns on her. "She knew we wouldn't let her go. She told us three days, and she knew we'd watch her like hawks. That's why she did it early. I can't believe it. She got all of us to bring her pills, and she hid them, knowing she would do this before she told us. Fuck. Crafty fucking buzzard." Lizzy wipes the tears from her eyes, sinking into a chair.

"What do we do?" asks Meredith, hiccuping. "Who do we call?"

"I don't know," says Lizzy. "Funeral home? I have no idea. Is she definitely dead?"

They turn to look at the body, and they still. It is just as Greta described: nothing more than a husk, the soul having left, a body at peace.

Moments pass, until Nell says quietly, "Do you think maybe we should say a few words now? Maybe share some memories or say something good."

"Yes." Lizzy nods and rises from the chair. "We need closure. Here." She reaches out both hands, as her sisters stand up and clasp them. "Nell, you're the oldest. You start."

"I have no idea what to say." Nell closes her eyes briefly. "Okay. She drove me more nuts than I ever thought possible. She dragged me to the theater, to musicals, when I was tiny, and then took me backstage, pretending that it was to make me happy, but actually it was so everyone could fawn all over her. The great Ronni Sunshine had come to see the show! I'd be given a lollipop and left by myself in the corner of the dressing room while she posed for picture after picture. I thought

she was the most glamorous mother in the whole world. When she came to school I felt so proud that you could feel a frisson of excitement throughout the school. All my friends wanted to come home and meet her, get her autograph, have some of her magic brush off on them."

Meredith and Lizzy both smile through their tears, both remembering exactly what that was like.

"She was dramatic and grand and demanding and exacting, and she could be loving, warm, and fun, the most exciting mother in the world. And I do think she loved me. Now, I think she loved me, although I wasn't always sure . . ." She trails off, wiping the tears, looking at Meredith.

"I remember all of that. And I remember feeling totally inadequate. I could never be as beautiful, as glamorous, as exciting, or as thin"—Meredith shrugs—"as her. Remember all those crazy diets she would do?" Her sisters nod, Nell laughing through her tears. "And she would always come to my bedroom and knock on my door and say she wanted me to do it with her because I was her special daughter and she needed us to be a team, but I knew she was only asking me because I was fat." Lizzy bursts out laughing. "I did feel special doing it with her, even though I cheated every day. She always wondered why I didn't lose weight, and I never told her it was because I had Twinkies and Ho Hos for lunch every day. I so wanted to please her. Whether it was by what I looked like or the choices I made. And then I realized I would never be able to, so I moved far away, where I wouldn't have to see the daily disappointment in her eyes." She looks at her sisters. "Maybe I was wrong. I never thought she loved and accepted me as I was, but maybe I was wrong. Maybe I shouldn't have gone."

"You did the right thing for you at the time," says Lizzy. "I think I got the best version of her. I know I'm the baby, and I was totally spoiled, and because I knew I could get away with everything, she

worked a little harder with me, I think. She loved showing me off. She would take me to her movie sets, where I'd charm the pants off everyone and be given amazing gifts all day."

"I remember those gifts," says Nell. "I remember you always coming home with gifts."

"There was one time she was away and I threw a party and basically trashed the house."

"I remember that," says Meredith. "I came home and found you."

"And remember her precious white shag carpet in the living room that was covered in red wine stains and cigarette burns? She said she had been wanting to replace it for months. Even though it was only six months old."

"You got away with murder," says Meredith. "Always."

"I know," says Lizzy. "I was the only one who wasn't scared. Remember when she had the veil on and she'd start screaming at all of us? I would just laugh, but you were so terrified, Meri."

"I would hide in my room shaking like a leaf," remembers Meredith.

"I would leave the house," Nell says, with a shrug. "I just removed myself from her rages."

"God, she was difficult," says Meredith. "Except for you, Lizzy."

"That's because I was her favorite," Lizzy says.

"Actually . . ." Meredith remembers sitting on her mother's bed, feeling, perhaps for the first time in her life, the warmth of her mother's unconditional love. "I think I was."

"No. She said it was me," Nell says. "She said . . ."

The others smile as it dawns on them too, as they say it as one: "Don't tell your sisters."

"I love you, Mom," whispers Nell, kissing her mother on the forehead and both cheeks.

"I love you, Mom," says Lizzy, holding her mother's hand, bringing

it up to her cheek and cradling it there before kissing it and laying it back down.

"I love you, Mom," says Meredith, wiping the tears and laying her head briefly on her mother's chest, before kissing her forehead and standing back, taking her sisters' hands as all three of them come together, their arms around one another, and they start to cry.

forty-seven

The coroner has gone, the men with him appropriately muted and respectful as they paid their condolences and carried the body outside and to the mortuary.

Lizzy sees them out and shuts the door behind them, leaning back against it as she lets out a big whoosh of air.

"Fuck," she says, shaking her head. "I can't believe it. She's dead, and the last fucking thing she said to me was that I was her biggest mistake."

Meredith moves over to her and lays a hand on her arm. She knows Lizzy is upset and that, much like their mother, Lizzy has never been able to express sadness, fear, or pain with anything other than anger. "She didn't mean it," says Meri. "You know she didn't mean it. She loved you so much."

"Turns out she fucking didn't," snaps Lizzy.

"That's not what she said." Nell walks into the hallway. "She said

she had regrets about spoiling you. And come on, Lizzy. You were spoiled."

"Maybe I was," Lizzy says, "but I never had any of her. Did you ever stop to think that maybe indulging me was in place of any actual attention? Because let's face it, by the time I was born, her career was in full swing and she was basically never, ever there. So yeah, I got away with stuff, but only because she was an absent mother. You both got her. She was there for you in a way she never was with me."

"You think she was better with us?" Nell's voice rises with indignation. "She wasn't this perfect mother who suddenly turned into a bitch when you were born. She was always hell. And I have no idea where you get this idea that she was present for me in any way, but it's laughable."

"She wasn't there for us either," says Meredith. "Maybe she was physically at home more, but the only memories I have are of having to tiptoe around on eggshells, always."

"You've spent your whole life tiptoeing on eggshells," says Lizzy, shaking her head.

"What is that supposed to mean? Jesus, Lizzy. I'm trying to support you, and showing sympathy, and you have to come out with some barbed comment? What's the matter with you?"

Lizzy whirls on her. "This is what's the matter with me. Our mother just died, and you and Nell both had these amazing kumbaya moments with her where she apologized for everything, and the two of you forgave her, and the last thing she said to me was that she had failed me as a parent, and that I was selfish and spoiled and treated people like shit. And I will never, ever get the chance to heal that, or make it different, and that will always be the last thing I remember about her. I will never have the chance to prove her wrong." As she speaks, her voice rises and, entirely uncharacteristically, cracks. Out of nowhere, Lizzy

is sobbing like a child, her shoulders heaving as sob after sob comes bursting out of her mouth.

Meredith rushes over and throws her arms around Lizzy, unsure as to whether or not she will be pushed away. But Lizzy collapses into Meredith, allows herself to be held and comforted and loved, as tears fall down both their cheeks.

Nell waits, watching. "It wasn't a big kumbaya moment," she says when the sobs have started to subside. "She did apologize, but I didn't forgive her, exactly. I just realized there's no point in still holding it against her. She did the best she could."

"She was a shitty mother to all of us," says Meredith, gently. "But I feel the same way as Nell. I'm tired of my constant sadness and disappointment that she wasn't better, or different. She was who she was. And even her saying what she said to you was kind of perfect, because it was so her: selfish. She never thought about anyone other than herself. It's like she didn't know how. But she was the only mother we had. And I did love her anyway."

Lizzy nods silently.

"And she did have some good points," points out Nell. "When she was good, she could be huge fun."

"She was very good at buying gifts," says Meri, and Lizzy and Nell both nod with the memory of all the gifts over all the years.

"It's weird, isn't it?" says Nell. "For all her crazy narcissism and self-absorption, she was a really thoughtful gift buyer. She always bought the exact thing you didn't know you wanted, but fell completely in love with."

"God, that's so true," says Meredith. "Maybe we have all been too hard on her. You can't do that unless you are thoughtful, surely? She never bought the obvious; she bought the thing you'd mentioned you loved six months earlier, in passing. How did she do that?"

"So she was good at gifts. If she actually *was* thoughtful," says

Lizzy, "she wouldn't have made the last conversation with me about me being a disaster."

"She probably didn't know that was going to be your last proper conversation. And that's not what she said," Nell points out, gently. "Right? Didn't she say you were spoiled and selfish? Maybe you are a little bit selfish. Maybe this is a wake-up call to do things differently. I don't know. Maybe she said what she said out of love for you, because she didn't want to see you make any more mistakes like the ones she had made."

Lizzy sighs and is quiet for a few moments. Then she says, "Normally this is when I'd be storming out. But . . ." She shakes her head. "This is it." She looks at each of her sisters. "Given that our deadbeat dad doesn't count, we only have each other. There isn't anyone else who's ever going to call us on our shit again."

"James might call you on your shit," says Meredith.

"Nah. He wouldn't dare." The ghost of a smile plays upon Lizzy's lips. "I can't believe she's gone." She holds her arms out to her sisters. "It feels totally surreal. Can we please never lose touch or fall out with each other again? Even if the truth hurts, can we please always fucking tell each other the truth? At least that way we'll be keeping Mom alive." She gives them a sad smile and keeps her arms out for her sisters to step in.

And they do. The three girls stand in the hallway, arms wrapped around each other, their foreheads touching as they breathe deeply, before looking into each other's eyes and nodding silently.

"Shall we go back to the farm?" Nell says eventually. "This house is beginning to feel like a morgue."

Greta places a tray filled with mugs of steaming tea on the table.

"We need milk and sugar," says Lizzy, getting up and going to the fridge.

"It's an English thing," says James, who accompanied them back to the farm. "What is it your mom used to call it? Builder's tea?"

Nell smiles at the memory. "Yes. Hot, sweet, and milky. It's the ultimate cure-all."

"I'm starving," says Meredith. "Do you have anything to eat?"

Greta disappears into the pantry, coming back with a plate of brownies, which everyone reaches for as soon as they hit the table.

"Big emotion always makes me want to eat," says Lizzy, taking the smallest of brownies for herself and another for Connor, who is sitting in the corner of the kitchen playing with Lego bricks from James's bag. "Christ. I can't believe she's dead. I keep going in and out, thinking about other stuff then circling back, always, to *my mom is dead*." She shakes her head with a sigh, taking a bite of brownie. She pauses to stare at the brownie. "These are great. Salted caramel and banana?"

Greta nods. "I love cooking for a chef. You always know what it is."

"No one cooks for me," says Lizzy. "Everyone's terrified. I don't even remember the last time anyone invited me for dinner."

"That's probably why my roast chicken tasted so good," says Meredith.

"No. Your roast chicken was that good, but everyone says they're too intimidated to cook for me." She looks at Greta. "I love that you're confident in your baking skills. As you should be. And I love that these were waiting for us today. Thank you, Greta."

"Thank you," echoes Meredith, noting that Nell bestows upon Greta a radiant smile, and when Greta sees it, she lights up in return, the two women holding each other's gazes for a tad longer than Meredith would expect.

"Can I get fresh eggs from the chickens?" Meredith says suddenly. "Lizzy, come with me?"

Lizzy frowns at her, but gets up and follows her out the door, bringing Connor along to see the chickens. "What? Salted caramel banana

brownies aren't enough for you?" she says. "You need an omelette as well? Connor, this way; we can go and see the goats after."

"No," Meredith whispers, looking back to check no one is following them, making sure Connor is a safe distance away so he won't overhear and repeat anything she says. "Am I going completely crazy or is there something going on between Nell and Greta?"

Lizzy stops and faces her. "What makes you say that?"

"The way they just looked at each other. It was . . . I don't know. I've never seen Nell look like that, and even though I don't know Greta, it seemed the feeling was pretty mutual."

"So what are you asking?"

"Do you think Nell is a lesbian?" breathes Meredith, eyes wide.

"I have no idea what Nell is, and I'm quite certain she doesn't either, but do I think she and Greta have the hots for each other. Yes. Okay, swear you won't say anything, but I walked in on them this morning. In bed. You know." She makes big eyes.

"Having sex?" Meredith is openmouthed.

"Yes! Well, they weren't actually in flagrante delicto, but it's pretty clear that's where they were heading."

"Wow. This is a lot to process. I had no idea. Do you think Nell has always known?"

Lizzy lets out a bark of laughter. "Nell, the most emotionally unevolved person on the planet? No. But I'm very happy she knows now. It's sweet. It's lovely that there's someone around who makes her happy. Who knows whether it's something that will last, but God knows right now we could all do with someone to support us."

"You've got James," says Meredith, feeling a pang of loss at Derek leaving, followed by the relief, once again, that she never has to kiss him again.

"It's great that he has offered to stay up here with us through this," says Lizzy. "But he wants to separate."

"Are you serious?"

"Yes. I deserve it. He knows about the affair."

"I thought the affair was over."

"It is."

"What about if you tried couples counseling?"

"Done that. James won't forgive me this time."

"You mean this isn't the first time?"

"It's complicated." Lizzy shakes her head and sighs. "He did say that if I moved out here he would move out too so we could coparent Connor."

"How do you feel about that?"

"Relieved. Sad. Shocked. Numb." She looks at Meredith helplessly. "Mom is dead. My marriage is over. My business is fucked. Okay, not fucked, but changing. Everything is changing. I have no idea how to feel about anything."

"I know." Meredith slips an arm around her sister's waist. "I feel the same way."

By the time they get back to the kitchen with a dozen fresh eggs deposited in various pockets, Meredith has decided she will stay on in their mother's house to help with the funeral arrangements, to be there with and for her sisters while they decide what to do with the house.

"Do you think she had a will?" asks Lizzy.

"Of course she had a will," says Nell. "She always held it over our heads as punishment. Remember all the times she threatened to cut us out of it?"

"She never said that to me," says Lizzy innocently, and Meredith punches her in the arm.

"She did," Meredith says. "I heard her."

"Oh. Well, then I never believed her," says Lizzy. "Do you think she actually did have a will? And if she did, do you think she left me

that diamond and citrine pendant on that funky chain? Because if she didn't, I'm just telling you now, that necklace is mine." She looks at Nell. "You can have her Wellington boots."

"Thanks," says Nell. "That's very generous of you."

"My pleasure." Lizzy turns to Meredith. "And you can have that painting of her in the living room."

"You mean that garish nineteen-sixties thing that all of us have always laughed at?"

"That would be the one."

"Great. Thanks. But I guess we'll need to call her lawyer. I'll do it. I don't mind taking on that role."

"Also, can I have the vintage Mercedes? You can have the Lexus, Nell. And there's a bike in the garage that has your name all over it, Meri."

"It will all be sorted out in the will," says Meredith. "In the meantime, no, you can't have the Mercedes or the necklace, or anything else, until we sit down and find out what she wanted. Even though"— she shoots Lizzy a look—"she probably did leave everything special to you."

"I was her favorite." Lizzy grins.

"No. We all were," says Meredith, smiling back, before taking a deep breath as a wave of grief washes over her. "Fuck," she breathes in a whisper. "She's dead. I can't believe she's dead."

"It wasn't as bad as I thought it would be," says River, after a pause in which everyone wipes a tear from their eyes. "Seeing her. Greta was right, it didn't seem like her. It really was as if her soul had departed."

"I'm still trying to get over the fact that she had ALS," James says. "When I saw her last year she looked great. I wish I'd been a better son-in-law."

"We're not going to do that now," says Lizzy. "We're not going to do that ever—regret what we didn't do, didn't say, could have done

differently. God knows, there's much she could have done differently as well. In the end, she went out the way she wanted to. We didn't want to let her go, and she went anyway. I'm not going to allow myself to dwell in regret. And in the end"—she looks at her sisters—"wasn't it good, at the end? She let you both go with love, and even though my ending wasn't what I would have chosen, I know she was doing that out of love as well. What more could anyone ask?"

Meredith and Nell both nod, Meredith swallowing a lump. "You're right. I felt loved at the end. I do think she always loved us. She just didn't know how to show it."

Lizzy looks at Connor and calls him over, hauling him onto her lap and covering his head with kisses as he giggles and squirms.

I don't have to be the same, she thinks. I can do it differently. Whatever I may have done in the last few years, I can do things differently from today.

She looks up to find James watching her, sadness in his eyes.

Maybe I can learn how to be less selfish. Maybe I can start loving my family now.

epilogue

Lizzy is whirling around the makeshift kitchen, her hair scraped back in a messy bun, her apron already stained with grease and fat, her most comfortable clogs a pain in the ass as she trips over tree roots, trying to plate on the trestle tables outside the café.

Most of her team are working this supper club. She doesn't know if they'll stay, but that they are here for her first trial on the farm is both grounding and reassuring. To have the staff she knows, staff who understand the shorthand of what it takes to make these supper clubs run smoothly, who understand *her* shorthand, has gone a long way to still her nerves.

Why is she nervous? she wonders. She has done these a million times before. She knows what to cook, how to serve it, how to create a few hours of magic under a canopy of lights and a velvet autumn sky. The only difference tonight is that she no longer has Sean as a partner. Months of legal wrangling saw to that. She gave him the New York

business, and a settlement, much to her fury, although it was the most logical way of moving on.

It's only money, she told herself, grinding her teeth as she wrote the check. I will make it again.

And here she is, she thinks, making money again, in the first supper club since she moved out to Connecticut, the first of the fall.

She looks over to the bar, where James is working, as Connor helps to decant cherries into ramekins, popping one into his mouth every few minutes, after he's checked that no one is watching. Lizzy grins. She is watching. It had never occurred to her to involve James, or to allow Connor to come, but she was a bartender short as of yesterday, and James offered.

He looks up and grins at her, and she smiles back, grateful for him, for this new life, however it should pan out. The farmhouse she is renting down the road has a small guest cottage, and James has moved into that, so they can share Connor, who races from cottage to farmhouse and back again every night, not understanding that his parents are trying to lead separate lives.

Last week, Connor insisted Daddy join them for dinner. And one dinner turned into three. James seemed completely different, Lizzy thought, watching him over the table. He had been so distracted, and lazy, and . . . slothlike in their old life. That was what she used to think, when she got back to a filthy house in Brooklyn at the end of a grueling day.

Ever since he moved out here, he has seemed energized. He looks better, brighter, and more clear-eyed, and he is laughing more. The other night, Connor said something ridiculous and she and James laughed until tears ran down their cheeks. She couldn't remember the last time she had laughed with James. It felt good. They aren't talking divorce. Not yet. Maybe they won't have to.

The orchard looks beautiful. The leaves are turning red and gold,

a carpet falling to the floor of grass as they strung the lights earlier that day. The workers looked mortified and started to pick up the leaves, but Lizzy stopped them. "It's perfect," she said. "Leave them."

The tables are covered in crisp white tablecloths with burlap runners and hollowed-out pumpkins filled with draping goldenrod and burnt russet helenium. The candles lining the tables are a dark orange, and hay bales have been put together for a seating area off to one side, sofas and coffee tables created out of hay, covered in burlap with russet pillows.

Nell is walking around, hands clasped behind her back, sniffing the air and looking around. Does she like it? wonders Lizzy. Nell is the source of her nerves; Nell is the reason tonight matters so much. She wants Nell to understand, and not regret inviting Lizzy out here. She wants Nell to fall in love with the supper club concept at Fieldstone Farm, understand the what, the why, and the how.

For Nell doesn't need the money now. Their mother's will made it clear they would all be fine financially. Apparently, Ronni Sunshine had been wealthy all along after all. They speculated about why she had never let them know, never indulged them in an opulent lifestyle as children. In the past, they might have accused her of being cheap and selfish with her money. Now, they wondered if she wanted them to have a normal childhood, wanted the money to take care of each of them so they wouldn't have to worry in old age. Now, they feel like they know her better, and that might indeed have been the case.

After she died, Billy came to see them with the video he had filmed on the day he met Ronni. He had shot her in the sunroom, asking her questions about her daughters, and all of them were astonished to hear their mother acknowledge her mistakes on camera, how she had unwittingly and unknowingly alienated her daughters, pushed them far apart not just from her, but from each other. She talked about each of them, why she loved them, how she could have done things differently,

what she hoped for their future and their lives. Her daughters watched, holding each other's hands, tears streaming down their faces.

And then they found out how much money was left. Lizzy expected Nell to rescind her offer to partner for the supper club, but she didn't. She said she still wanted to give it a go, that it would be fun.

Lizzy watches as Greta appears, calling Nell over and saying something to her that makes Nell smile. She watches as Greta leans in to Nell, who strokes her back and gives her an absentminded kiss on the top of her head, the two of them smiling into each other's eyes before continuing their walk, together.

Lucky Nell, she thinks. Greta never left. Temporarily, to wrap things up in St. Louis, but then she was back, cooking in the mornings, working in the café, mothering, nurturing, and loving everyone who crosses her path. How lucky Nell is. How lucky all of them are. Look at Nell, beaming, finally at peace in her skin. All these years of bottling everything up, and now with this woman in her life, she is blossoming, a flower that stayed in the dark for too long.

Lizzy is called back to the kitchen and turns, unaware there's a smile on her face. Meredith is waiting for her, with a glass of champagne.

"I thought Billy was coming with you tonight," says Lizzy, noting his absence.

"He was, but he got called away on a story." Meredith smiles, thinking of how he kissed her good-bye yesterday morning, how she pulled him back into bed, unable to get enough of him, his smell, his taste, his everything.

"And you're serious about moving in together?" asks Lizzy. "You don't think it's a little soon?"

Meredith shrugs. "It might be. If it all goes horribly wrong, I guess it will have been a little soon."

"Wow. This is all so . . . adventurous of you." Lizzy grins.

"I know. I am loving this relationship, which is mostly about sex, and it is fantastic."

"The sex or the relationship?"

"Both!" Meredith says. "Who knows if it has substance behind it? I do know I don't want to get married, or engaged, possibly ever. I'm very happy with things the way they are."

Nell walks over with Greta. "Where's our champagne?" she says, and Meredith runs over to the bar and grabs a couple more glasses.

"Cheers." She raises her glass, chinking with Nell, Lizzy, and Greta.

"Here's to new beginnings," says Lizzy, surveying the orchard as they all turn to take in the beauty as a fiery sun starts to sink behind the trees.

"New beginnings," echoes Nell, looking at Greta. "And new loves."

"And family," says Greta, looking at Lizzy, Meredith, and finally holding Nell's gaze. "I may not share the same blood, but I've come home. To the Sunshine girls."

"The Sunshine girls," echoes Lizzy. "I've got all my sisters and me."

the Sunshine Sisters

JANE GREEN

....
....

questions for discussion

1. In her youth, Ronni makes choices to further her career, often at the expense of her family, but we also see moments of doubt and, later in her life, regret. Do you think her choices are entirely selfish? Do you empathize with any of her conflicts? What would you have done differently in her shoes?

2. It seems as though in her own way, Ronni has her daughters' best interests at heart, even if this sometimes hurts them. For instance, she constantly criticizes Meredith's weight but also worries about her daughter's engagement. In what way is Ronni's relationship with her daughters like or unlike many parent-child relationships? How do you think parents can strike a balance between communicating parental wisdom and allowing their children to make their own decisions? Does Ronni ultimately succeed in doing so?

3. Nell often remarks that Ronni is a much better grandmother than she was a mother. Why do you think this is?

4. Do you think Ronni's last attempt to bring her daughters together makes up for her wrongdoings as a mother?

5. Do you empathize with Ronni's wish to die on her own terms? If you were in her daughters' place, would you comply with her wishes? Why or why not?

6. It's often difficult to change old habits, but the Sunshine sisters discover that they must in order to truly connect as a family. Do you find that you revert back to certain habits or roles around your family members? Do you think it's possible to change these habits and, consequently, your familial relationships?

7. Throughout the book, we see that Ronni and her daughters have difficulty opening up to one another and communicating their true feelings. Oftentimes, it leads to conflict, such as Nell and Lizzy's argument over using the farm for the pop-up supper club, or the family's disapproval of Meredith's fiancé. Why do you think it is so difficult for them to be truly vulnerable and open around one another? Do you find you have the same difficulties with your family members?

8. In many ways, the sisters refuse to confront their own problems but are remarkably perceptive at parsing one another's issues and even predicting romance. Do you sometimes experience the same disparity

in perception in your own life? Have you ever had a similar situation with a family member or close friend?

9. In the present day, the Sunshine sisters are not truly content with their lives and choices. Why do you think this is? Do you think it has anything to do with their familial relationships?

10. While talking about relationships with Nell, Meredith says, "There's a large part of me that thinks it's better to have stability, and kindness, and friendship. Those are the things that make a relationship last, I think. Not chemistry." Do you agree? How important were each of these factors in the sisters' relationships? Do you think they would agree with Meredith's statement in the end?

11. How is Greta the perfect match for Nell despite being a completely unexpected romantic partner?

12. Are you satisfied with the way things end for the Sunshine sisters?

READ ON FOR AN EXCERPT FROM JANE GREEN'S NOVEL

Falling

I t's lovely," she lies, in her most gracious of voices, looking around at the tired wood paneling lining the walls of the living room, floor to ceiling. As she looks down, her gaze lands on well-worn salmon-pink shag carpeting and she quickly conceals her horror.

Emma wonders if this house might not be beyond even her capabilities to transform. Perhaps the landlord would let her paint it? Surely he would let her paint it—who wouldn't want to lighten up this room, so dark it feels more like a cave? She would paint it for free, *and* pull up that carpet. Maybe she would be lucky and find a hardwood floor underneath; even if it was merely concrete, surely it wouldn't cost too much to stick down some inexpensive sisal.

This room could be transformed, she determines. Lipstick on a pig is her specialty.

Her landlord, or potential landlord, smiles. "Hey, I know it's not everyone's taste today," he says. "Why do people want everything to be gray and modern?"

Emma is surprised by his comment, surprised frankly by his interest in making small talk. "I hate that look," Emma offers. It happens that she does agree, quite passionately, in fact. "None of those decorated houses feel like real homes."

"Exactly!" he says in delight. "This is a home."

Struck by his words, by the obvious sincerity with which they are spoken, she turns to look at her potential landlord for the first time. She can't help but feel struck by the sight of him. He is not too tall, only a few inches taller than her, with skin tanned by the sun and an easy smile that seems to put her at ease. It isn't so much that she finds him attractive, but that there is something familiar about him, a recognition, a sense of having somehow met him before.

Perhaps because she has remained silent, he goes on to add, "At least, it was a home. My grandparents lived here for forty years."

Yes, thinks Emma, *it looks like it. It smells like it, too.* The air is fusty. Of course old people had lived here. That explains the wood paneling and the floral wallpaper in the family room; it also explains the salmon-pink carpet and avocado-green bathroom suite with matching tile.

"How would you feel about me putting . . ." Emma pauses, wondering how to say this diplomatically. She doesn't want to jump in and tell him she'd like to tear everything out and start again. He probably doesn't want to change anything; his voice had softened when he mentioned his grandparents. She has an odd reluctance to offend him, and senses she'll need to take this slowly if she wants this house. ". . . a woman's touch on the house?"

"A woman's touch!" The landlord smiles and nods approvingly. "That's exactly what I've been saying this house needs for years. A woman's touch."

She follows him into the kitchen at the back of the house and her heart sinks slightly. It hasn't been touched since the fifties, rough wood cabinets bumpy with layers of white paint, although pretty black

iron hardware. Formica countertops with large cracks, and linoleum floors. A stove that is so ancient as to be fashionable again, and, surprisingly, a large modern stainless-steel fridge.

Emma looks at the fridge and raises an eyebrow as she looks over at the landlord.

Damn, she thinks. *What was his name again? Donald? Derek? Something like that.*

"The old fridge gave up last year," he explains. "The tenants picked out this one. And I paid for it," he adds quickly, as if to reassure her that he is a good landlord, on top of everything, ready to jump in and deal with problems.

"Great," says Emma, wandering over to the back door and peering out through the glass onto a fenced-in garden, or what could be a garden if the weeds were cleared. "Can I go outside?" she asks, already out the door.

He follows her out, apologizing for the weeds. They both stand there as Emma looks around, her imagination already firing. There are two filthy peeling rattan chairs stacked off to the side, surrounded by boxes and baskets: in other words, trash.

The landlord turns to look and immediately apologizes. "I haven't been out here," he explains. "Obviously all of that will be gone. I can replace those chairs with new ones."

Emma is again struck by him. His eagerness to please doesn't seem solely mercenary. He wants her to know that he cares about the house and yard. "Do I get to choose what kinds of chairs the new ones are? Like the fridge?" Emma says.

"As long as they're not too expensive."

"I am the expert at renovating on a shoestring." She smiles.

"You're my kind of woman." He laughs, as Emma flushes slightly and turns away. A flirtatious landlord is the last thing she wants right now. "Sorry." He apologizes immediately, realizing his mistake. "I was

kidding. But I'm happy for you to choose things as long as they're within the budget."

Emma looks up at the sky, noting the sun, looking at the shadows to try to figure out which way the garden faces. "Southwest," she guesses, and he turns to her with a smile.

"You're a sun worshipper?"

"With this pale English skin?" She laughs and shakes her head. "I turn into one giant freckle in the sun. But I am a gardener. At least, a frustrated one. For years and years, I lived in flats in London dreaming of having a garden of my own. Then for the last five years I've been on the top of a high-rise in Battery Park." Good lord. Why is she suddenly giving him her life story?

"Ah, so you're a city girl."

"Not by choice."

"You're ready to be out here?"

"Ready to be steps from the beach, in a gorgeous town where the pace of life is relaxed and the pressure is off? No. Definitely not."

He laughs. "I've lived here my whole life, and wouldn't move anywhere else. How did you find Westport?"

"I have a friend who lives here, who I used to work with. She moved out three years ago after she had a baby, and she loves it. I've been out to visit her quite a few times, and something about this place feels right. I never thought I'd be able to move out here permanently, but . . . I needed to make some big changes in my life. Moving somewhere like this, with a quieter pace of life, seemed like a good first step."

"I saw on your application you're a banker. That's quite a commute."

"Actually," Emma says, "I took a package. I'm now officially unemployed, albeit with a very nice severance. I hope that won't be a problem?"

"As long as you pay your rent, nothing's a problem. What are you going to do here in town?"

Emma is struck again by the sincerity of his interest. He is not just making small talk, she is sure of it. He's looking at her, making her feel like he cares about what she'll say next. She shakes her head. "Thankfully, I have enough to have a little bit of breathing space. I don't really know. I've always had a dream about doing something with the home. Interior design, gardening, that sort of thing. I've been doing an online course to get the official qualification. Now all I need are clients."

"And a house to do up."

"And a garden to transform. Preferably one that faces southwest." She grins as she looks around the garden.

He grins, too. "Then you've found it. It seems that you and this house were meant to be. Although, you couldn't do anything major to it without consulting with me."

"Of course." Emma laughs politely. She couldn't move in *unless* she did something major with the house. As it is, it's completely awful, but stepping back to take it in, even with all its flaws, she thinks she could turn this into a charming beach cottage.

The landlord seems like a nice guy. He may be resistant to her changes at first, but she surmises that she could ask forgiveness rather than permission for most things. If he walked into this room and found the wood painted a lovely chalky white, the floors covered with sisal, the single lightbulb replaced with a pretty glass pendant light, surely he would be thrilled. Who *wouldn't* be thrilled at someone transforming their house for nothing? He would undoubtedly get more money for it next time he decides to rent it out.

The truth is that Emma Montague isn't looking for somewhere permanent just yet. She's just looking for a place to call home for the next year or so. A year to try to recover from the last five years of working in finance in New York. A year to try to figure out what kind of life she wants to live. For five years she has lived a life that wasn't

hers. Five years of utter exhaustion; five years of keeping her head down and working like the devil, putting away enough money to be able to afford to do what she is doing now, leaving the rat race and pursuing her dream. Her goal is to figure out what her dream is. Right now she only knows that the beginning step is to find a world and a life that feels like her own; a life in which she finally feels she belongs.

It starts with a house. She is itching to buy, but it is more sensible to rent, making sure this is where she wants to live. Still, the rentals down by the beach, here in Westport, Connecticut, are mostly prohibitive for a single girl with a budget, even an ex-banker. The last thing she wants to do is blow all her savings on rent.

This house, this dated, fusty house, is entirely within her budget, precisely because it *is* so dated and fusty. It is the perfect size—two bedrooms with a living room, kitchen, and family room that would make a perfect office.

And best of all there is a garden, or rather more than enough space for one. She can finally plant vegetables. She can put a gravel path down the middle, can grow tomatoes, cucumbers, and lettuce, plant roses and clematis over the fence at the back. She imagines a long, rustic table, a small group of friends sitting around, bottles of rosé and candles interspersed with galvanized steel pots of lavender running down the center. Laughter. Happy faces. Everyone lit by the glow of summer and love.

Emma shakes her head to bring herself back to earth. She knows only one person—her friend Sophie Munster—here in Westport. She has no other local friends she can invite to sit around the table, and since she's something of an introvert, it may take a little while to find them. But she will find them.

Although a bit of a loner, she is loyal, and fun, when she finds people with whom she is comfortable. She is thinking of taking up yoga, and maybe knitting. There are evening classes at the local yarn store,

Sophie says. They should both go. Sophie grew up here, although she went away to boarding school. She has friends from grade school, though, and seems to know almost everyone in town. Surely it's only a matter of time before Emma's fantasy of summer evenings comes true.

For as long as she can remember, Emma Montague has had a fascination with America. Growing up in her upper-crust family in Somerset, England, sent off to boarding school, then moving to London after university to enter the world of banking, she had the persistent belief that this was not supposed to be her life.

As a little girl, she had never quite felt she fitted in. She was loved and treasured, but her boisterous, overbearing mother and loving but somewhat beleaguered and introverted father didn't quite know how to connect with their quiet, studious child. The place she felt happiest, the place she found her solace and joy, was in the pages of books.

She read all the time. It was so much easier than dealing with the chaos of her playmates during recess. She was close to one or two of her classmates, but she only liked seeing them one at a time. Otherwise, she was happier with her books. She was the child with the flashlight under the duvet late into every night. She would breeze through a book in a day and a half, then read it six more times.

She fell in love with America through the pages of these books. Her dull, patrician life in Somerset felt very staid compared to the lives of Jo and her sisters in *Little Women*, and Katy in the What Katy Did series. She devoured the stories of Laura Ingalls Wilder and dreamed of having a farm out in the middle of nowhere, growing all her own vegetables, raising her own animals.

Life then got in the way, sweeping her up into the cutthroat world of London finance, not because she had a passion for finance, but

because it was what all the girls were doing at that time. First London, then New York. Finally, now that she has extricated herself, it looks like she has a shot at the kind of life she might actually want to live.

Westport, Connecticut, may not be Walton's Mountain, but there are enough trees for her to pretend, and the beauty of the beach on the doorstep is something she now realizes she has always wanted.

When she was living in Manhattan she would go running along the river every day before work. The sunlight glinting off the water brought a calm and peace to every morning. She hadn't known how much she wanted to be by the water until Sophie drove her to Compo Beach for a walk one weekend. That was the moment she knew this was where she wanted to be.

There had been a tremendous expectation for the life Emma was supposed to have led, at least from her parents. And she had tried to fit into the life they had designed for her. Namely, to work at a pretend job for a few years to enable her to meet the right kind of husband, before quickly getting pregnant, giving up work, and going on to raise three or four beautiful children in a lovely stone manse in Somerset. Preferably near her parents. Have a couple of dogs, Gordon setters or pointers, possibly golden retrievers; have lots of local women friends who come for coffee. Get involved in the village fair and perhaps, given her love of books, institute a reading mentoring program in the less well-off town twenty minutes away.

Emma knew the path well, as it was the path so many of her childhood friends had taken. At thirty-seven, she is the only one still unmarried, apart from Imogen Cutliffe, who is one of the leading lights of British screen and stage and about to star as the lead in a film starring Bradley Cooper. Emma is the only one who continued to work and rise up the corporate ladder, putting all her focus on making money. It wasn't that she cared about money for the sake of money, but that it was the only path out: making enough money to retire from

banking in her thirties, and the freedom to pursue her dream. If she could figure out what her dream was.

She hadn't known her life was going to turn out like this. For a long time she imagined she would indeed follow the path her parents expected of her. She dated Rufus Fairfax for years throughout her twenties, not because she loved him, but because her parents loved him and he seemed to check all the right boxes. He was a banker in the firm where she worked, he was handsome (although he had not an ounce of sex appeal, as far as she was concerned), and he was of the right stock. Clever, but not very funny; in fact, he was achingly dull. But they looked so good together! They seemed to fit so perfectly together that everyone assumed they would get married from the moment they started going out. And Emma had presumed everyone was right, that everyone knew something she did not, and she was the one who must have been wrong.

She determined to make it work. She and Rufus spent their weekdays in London, both of them burning the candle at both ends, and their weekends in the country, usually staying with friends in crumbling old piles that were impossibly drafty, with terrible food and lots of drink to distract from the fact that everyone was freezing cold and permanently starving.

Rufus had a huge group of friends from boarding school that Emma always found rather awful. They were shockingly loud, and arrogant, fueled by absurdly expensive bottles of wine that they ordered in restaurants to prove they could afford them. They shouted inside jokes from when they were all thirteen, their wives and girlfriends sitting with smiles plastered on their faces, pretending to be amused.

Emma started leaving these evenings early, claiming headaches and making her way up to bed during those country weekends, earplugs tucked into her overnight bag to help her sleep through the

inevitable banging and shouting in the early hours of the morning when the party eventually broke up.

None of this fazed Rufus, who proposed to her four times. The first time, he did so after a romantic dinner at Hakkasan, gazing at her over the course of the evening with a hopeful kind of love that Emma found slightly discomfiting. Each time, Emma said she just wasn't quite ready. Eventually, five years ago, Rufus issued an ultimatum: If she wouldn't marry him, he would find someone else who would, and with a great dramatic flounce, he packed up his things and left their Kensington flat. Emma knew he thought she would beg him to come back within a week or so, but from the minute he was gone, she felt nothing other than tremendous relief.

She had been playing the part of adoring girlfriend, probably—hopefully—soon-to-be wife, for so long that she had forgotten how liberating it was to simply be herself. She saw girlfriends from university she hadn't seen for ages because Rufus disapproved of their drinking ("Darling, there's nothing quite so ghastly as a woman publicly drunk"). She got into bed at seven thirty P.M. with hummus and chips for dinner, and spent hours watching terrible reality television that Rufus would never have condoned.

She was happy, and happier still when she was called in to her superior's office and asked if she would consider taking up a position with the bank in New York. They were starting a new private wealth management operation, specifically for English expatriates living on the East Coast of the United States, and they needed someone to head client relations.

They would put together a package, they said. All moving expenses would be paid. She would be set up in an apartment, and there would be a healthy relocation allowance. They offered all of this as if to sweeten the deal, as if Emma weren't using everything she had, sitting in her office in her oh-so-staid black Givenchy skirt and Manolo

Blahnik d'Orsay heels (the perfect combination of elegant and sexy), not to break out in a scream of joy and twirl around the room, punching the air and whooping in a mad happy dance.

It was the fresh start she had been longing for, and better yet, in New York! The place she had always imagined living! Well, perhaps not quite New York City. She preferred to see herself in rural Vermont, or Maine, but at least it was across the pond, and she would get a green card, and at some point surely, surely, she'd make it out of the city and into the farmhouse of her dreams.

This is not the farmhouse of her dreams. This isn't even the beach cottage of her dreams. But it could be. With just a little bit of work, if her oddly welcoming landlord acquiesced, she could transform this into something, if not quite magnificent, at least beachy, and airy, and filled with charm.

They walk back through the house, Emma trying to see through the wallpaper, the linoleum, the salmon-pink flat shag-pile carpet, as the landlord shows her out.

"It was great to meet you, Emma," he says, meeting her gaze with a friendly smile and shaking her hand with a grip so firm she crumples slightly before flexing her fingers.

"Ouch!" she says, laughing.

"I'm so sorry!" he says, clearly mortified.

"It's fine." She smiles. What a friendly man he is. "I wasn't expecting that, is all."

"I'm Italian," he says, by way of explanation, which makes no sense to Emma whatsoever. "My family is known for its handshakes."

"Really?" She peers at him.

"No. I'll work on it. Do you want to think about the house and let me know when you've made a decision?"

"That sounds great," she says, wishing she could remember his name.

"Dominic," he says, as if reading her mind.

"Dominic," she says confidently, as if she had remembered all the time. "Thank you so much. I'll be in touch."

"I can't believe you didn't invite me!" Sophie walks back into the kitchen, having put her soon-to-be two-year-old down for a nap. "I would have loved to see it. Which house is it again?"

"The gray one with the overgrown garden?" says Emma, scooping up a handful of Goldfish crackers from the bowl Sophie's son, Jackson, hadn't touched. "On Compo. About four in. Maybe six. I don't know. Close to the end of the road."

"But it was awful?"

"It wasn't *awful*. It's just that it wasn't great. But I've looked at everything online, and if I want something great it's going to cost me at least twice as much. It seems ridiculous to pay so much money on rent, especially since I don't know what I'm going to be doing or where I'm going to land. I'd much rather be frugal, or at least moderately frugal, and rent something I can turn into my own." She sighs. "If he doesn't let me change the inside I'll just do it and say I'm sorry afterwards. At least we've established that he's definitely fine with me putting a garden in. And I could put a gorgeous garden in."

"That won't help you much in winter."

"No, but it will give me something to look forward to. And can we not talk about winter yet? It's June, for heaven's sake. The last thing I want to think about is snow."

Sophie shakes her head. "I can't believe you're actually going to be moving out here!" She grins suddenly. "This is the most exciting thing that's ever happened to me."

"Apart from marrying Rob and having Jackson, you mean?"

"Well, yes. Apart from that. But it will be just like old times when we worked together. We can hang out every day. Imagine if we could get Hilary Trader to come and live here, too. God, we'd have fun. We're going to have fun anyway, even if it's just you and me. Do you need a second opinion about the house? Because I'm really happy to go see it if you need me to."

"Oh, you're sweet," says Emma, blanching in horror at the thought of her friend, in her immaculate, brand-new, pseudo-modern farmhouse, every wall horizontally planked with perfect high-gloss white wood, her kitchen a panorama of white marble and gray cabinets, every chandelier hanging from the ten-foot ceilings a perfect cluster of crystal globes dripping from polished nickel fixtures, walking into the grimy little cottage by the beach.

"You would hate it," Emma says. "You would think it the most disgusting house you have ever seen."

Sophie looks offended. "Why would you say that? Just because I live in a new house doesn't mean I can't appreciate older homes."

"Darling, this house isn't just old, it's dead. I have huge plans for it if I decide to take it, and I'm not even sure about that. But I honestly don't think even you, with your glorious taste, would be able to see through the brown flowery wallpaper and threadbare salmon carpet."

Sophie wrinkles her pretty little nose. "That sounds gross."

Emma laughs. "It is. But all that can be changed. I'm going to see a couple more rentals later this afternoon and, hopefully, by the end of the day, I will have made a decision."